ALONE WITH THE HORRORS

ALONE WITH THE HORRORS

The Great Short Fiction
of Ramsey Campbell, 1961–1991

Ramsey Campbell

TOR®

A TOM DOHERTY ASSOCIATES BOOK

NEW YORK

ALONE WITH THE HORRORS: THE GREAT SHORT FICTION OF
RAMSEY CAMPBELL, 1961–1991

This book is printed on acid-free paper.

A Tor Book
Published by Tom Doherty Associates, LLC
175 Fifth Avenue
New York, NY 10010

www.tor.com

Tor® is a registered trademark of Tom Doherty Associates, LLC.

Library of Congress Cataloging-in-Publication Data

Campbell, Ramsey, 1946–
    Alone with the horrors : the great short fiction of Ramsey Campbell, 1961–1991 /Ramsey
Campbell.—1st Tor ed.
        p. cm.
    "A Tom Doherty Associates book."
    ISBN 0-765-30767-7 (alk. paper)
    EAN 978-0765-30767-5
    1. Horror tales, English. I. Title.

PR6053.A4855A6 2004
823'.914—dc22

2003071149

First Tor Edition: May 2004

Printed in the United States of America

0 9 8 7 6 5 4 3 2 1

For T. E. D. Klein,

who helped launch me

and wrote tales for me

to aspire to

Contents

Introduction: So Far

Some horror stories are not ghost stories, and some ghost stories are not horror stories, but these terms have often been used interchangeably since long before I was born. I'm in favour of this. Many horror stories communicate awe as well as (sometimes instead of) shock, and it is surely inadequate to lump these stories together with fiction that seeks only to disgust, in a category regarded as the deplorable relative of the ghost story. Quite a few of the stories collected herein are ghost stories, and I hope that at least some of the others offer a little of the quality that has always appealed to me in the best horror fiction, a sense of something larger than is shown.

In 1991 I'd been in print for thirty years, and had these thirty-seven tales to show for them—at least, these are most of the ones my editor at Arkham House, the late Jim Turner, and I thought were representative. One of Jim's criteria was that the contents should be stuff only I could have written, a flattering notion that excluded such tales as "The Guide", which otherwise I would have put in. For the record, the book incorporates my British collection *Dark Feasts,* with the solitary exception of "The Whining", no significant loss.

I've made one substitution. Previous editions of *Alone with the Horrors* have led off with "The Room in the Castle", my earliest tale to be professionally published. The idea was to show how I began. Here instead is something rarer to perform the same service. It too dates from when I was doing my best to imitate Lovecraft, but "The Tower from Yuggoth" (1961) demonstrates how I fared before August Derleth took me under his editorial wing. It was published in *Goudy,* a fanzine edited by my friend Pat Kearney, who later wrote a greenbacked history of Olympia Press. It was illustrated by Eddie Jones, another old friend but sadly a late one. At the time it felt very much like the start of my career as a writer; now it looks more like a phase I needed Derleth to rescue me from. At least it's eldritch—it keeps saying as much—and it also offers cackling trees and curse-muttering streams. The reader may end up knowing how they felt, and my notion of how Massachusetts rustics spoke may also be productive of a shudder. Had I conjured him up from his essential salts for an opinion, Lovecraft would undoubtedly have pointed out these excesses and many other flaws. And watch out for those peculiar erections in the woods! I used the term in utter innocence, not then having experienced any of them while awake. No doubt a Christian Brotherly promise of hell if one encouraged such developments helped.

Substantially rewritten as "The Mine on Yuggoth", the story appeared in *The Inhabitant of the Lake,* my first published book. In 1964 I was several kinds of lucky to find a publisher, and one kind depended on my having written a Lovecraftian book for Arkham House, the only publisher likely even to have considered it and one of the very few then to be publishing horror. In those days one had time to read everything that was appearing in the field, even the bad stuff, of which there seems to have been proportionately less than now, but I'll rant about this situation later. Suffice it for the moment to say that much of even the best new work—Matheson, Aickman, Leiber, Kirk, as vastly different examples—was being published with less of a fanfare than it deserved.

I mentioned imitation. I've made this point elsewhere, and I do my best not to repeat myself, but this bears repeating: there is nothing wrong with learning your craft by imitation while you discover what you want to write about. In other fields imitation isn't, so far as I know, even an issue. It's common for painters to learn by creating studies of their predecessors' work. Beethoven's first symphony sounds like Haydn, Wagner's symphony sounds like Beethoven, Richard Strauss's first opera sounds remarkably Wagnerian, and there's an early symphonic poem by Bartók that sounds very much like Richard Strauss, but who could mistake the mature work of these composers for the music of anyone else? In my smaller way, once I'd filled a book with my attempts to be Lovecraft I was determined to sound like myself, and *Alone with the Horrors* may stand as a record of the first thirty years of that process.

In 1964 I took some faltering steps away from Lovecraft and kept fleeing back to him. Among the products of this was "The Successor", one of several tales I found so unsatisfactory that I rewrote them from scratch some years later. In this case the result was "Cold Print" (1966/67), whose protagonist was to some extent based on a Civil Service colleague who did indeed ask to borrow my exciting (Olympia Press) books but found Genet dull as ditchwater, in the old phrase. I had also just read the first edition of Robin Wood's great book on Hitchcock's films, hence the way the tale accuses the reader of wanting the coda, as though I hadn't wanted it myself.

Another 1964 first draft was "The Reshaping of Rossiter," a clumsy piece rewritten in 1967 as "The Scar." Looking back, I'm struck by how even at that age I was able to create a believable nuclear family from observation, though certainly not of my own domestic background. Perhaps I can also claim to have been writing about child abuse long before it became a fashionable theme in horror fiction. Certainly the vulnerability of children is one of my recurring themes.

I had my first go at "The Interloper" in 1963 and a fresh one in 1968. In the first version the boy tells his tale to a child psychiatrist who proves to be the creature of the title. My memory is that the psychiatrist was none too convincing a character, even though I was taken to see one at the age of seven or so, apparently because I rolled my eyes a lot and suffered from night terrors. By contrast, the final draft of the tale was a strange kind of revenge on the sort of schooling I'd had to suffer at the hands of Christian Brothers and their lay staff (not all of either, I should add—Ray Thomas, my last English teacher, had a genius for communicating his love of the language and literature); the incident involving the teacher and the poetry notebook actually happened, and the red-haired mathematics teacher was fully as much of a stool as I portray, though the book in question was the first draft of *The Inhabitant of the Lake*.

All this rewriting, and other examples too, had made me surer of myself. "The Guy" (1968) saw just one draft. It was an attempt to use the traditional British ghost story to address social themes. Geoff Ryman has suggested that M. R. James's ghosts were attempts to ignore the real terrors of life; whatever the truth of that, I saw increasingly less reason why my stories should (though it can be argued that my Lovecraft imitations did). My tales were becoming more autobiographical, and "The End of a Summer's Day" (1968) has its roots in a very similar bus trip I took to such a cave with my ex-fiancée of the previous year. I've heard quite a few interpretations of the story. For the record, I've always taken the man in the cave to be a projection of Maria's fears about her husband, which of course doesn't mean the encounter can be explained away.

The Chicago and San Francisco tales of Fritz Leiber were now my models in various ways. I wanted to achieve that sense of supernatural terror which derives from the everyday urban landscape rather than invading it, and I greatly admired—still do—how Fritz wrote thoroughly contemporary weird tales that were nevertheless rooted in the best traditions of the field and drew some of their strength from uniting British and American influences. One of mine in which I used an actual Liverpool location—"The Man in the

Underpass"—has a special significance for me: it was the first tale I wrote after having, encouraged by T. E. D. Klein's exegesis of *Demons by Daylight* and by my wife, Jenny, stepped into the abyss of full-time writing in July 1973. To begin with I wrote only on weekdays. Lord, did I need to learn.

"The Companion" dates from later that year, and is set in New Brighton, just along the coast from me as I write, in all but name. The town did indeed contain two fairgrounds, one derelict, for a while, but I fiddled with the geography a little for the purposes of the narrative. Of all my old stories—there are many—that I keep being tempted to tinker with, this may well be the most frustrating. The second half seems effective enough to make me wish I could purge the earlier section of clumsiness. Damon Knight looked at the story for *Orbit* and declared that he didn't know what was going on in it half the time. I admit it was one of those tales it seemed more important to write than to understand, but then ever since my first viewing of *Last Year in Marienbad* I've felt that an enigma can be more satisfying than any solution. Too many horror stories, films in particular, strike me as weighed down by explanation.

Admittedly there's nothing enigmatic about "Call First" or "Heading Home," both from early 1974. They're perhaps the best of a handful of pieces written for a Marvel comic that originally proposed to print terse tales of traditional terrors with a twist as text 'twixt the strips. By the time this proved not to be, I'd had fun writing stories in emulation of the EC horror comics of the fifties. I've long felt that a story that ends with a twist needs to be rewarding even if you foresee the end, and I hope that's true of this pair.

"In the Bag" (1974) is a ghost story I submitted to the *Times* ghost story competition, though it wasn't written with that in mind. I rather hoped it might appear in the anthology derived from the competition, but the judges (Kingsley Amis, Patricia Highsmith, and Christopher Lee) must have decided otherwise. However, it did gain me my first British Fantasy Award. As David Drake has pointed out, the punning title is inappropriately jokey—a lingering effect of writing the horror-comic tales, perhaps—but I try not to cheat my readers by changing titles once a story has been published.

"Baby" (1974) is set around Granby Street in Liverpool, later one of the locations for *The Doll Who Ate His Mother*. It owes its presence in this book to my good friend J. K. Potter, who designed and illustrated the Arkham House edition. He expressed amazement that Jim Turner and I had omitted the tale, and provided an image to justify his enthusiasm.

"The Chimney" (1975) is disguised autobiography—disguised from me at the time of writing, that is. Was it while reading it aloud at Jack Sullivan's apartment in New York that I became aware of its subtext? It was certainly under those circumstances that I discovered how funny a story it was, though the laughter died well before the end. Robert Aickman described it as the best tale of mine that he'd read, but his correspondence with Cherry Wilder betrays how little he meant by that. Still, it gained me my first World Fantasy Award, and Fritz Leiber told me this was announced to "great applause." Harlan Ellison (also present, I believe) had no time for it. "It was a terrible story," he wanted the readers of *Comics Journal* to know, "and should not have won the award."

"The Brood" (1976) had its origins in the view of streetlamps on Princes Avenue from the window of Jenny's and my first flat, which we later lent to the protagonists of *The Face That Must Die*. When my biographer, David Mathew, recently attempted to photograph me in front of the building, a tenant demanded to know what we were up to. This was one of the rare instances where I found myself assuaging someone's paranoia.

"The Gap" (1977) indulges my fondness for jigsaws. You'll find me playing cards and Monopoly too, not to mention Nim, at which only my daughter can beat me. Role-playing games (I leave aside the erotic variety) have never tempted me, however, though in my inadvertent way I generated a book of them (*Ramsey Campbell's Goatswood*) published by Chaosium. As for the tale, it depressed Charles L. Grant too much for him to publish, although he did anthologise some of the others herein.

"The Voice of the Beach" (1977) was my first concerted attempt to achieve a modicum of Lovecraft's cosmic terror by returning to the principles that led him to create his mythos. The setting is a hallucinated version of the coast of Freshfield, a nature reserve almost facing my workroom window across the Mersey. Recently I made a book-length attempt at the Lovecraftian in *The Darkest Part of the Woods*. I continue to believe that the finest modern Lovecraftian work of fiction—in its documentary approach, its use of hints and allusions to build up a sense of supernatural dread, and the psychological realism of its characters—is *The Blair Witch Project*.

"Out of Copyright" (1977) had no specific anthologist in mind, but Ray Bradbury thought it did, and enthused about it on that basis. "Above the World" (1977) derived much of its imagery and setting from my one wholly positive, not to mention visionary, LSD experience. The hotel is the very one where Jenny and I spent our belated honeymoon and some other holidays. In the early nineties, a short independent film, *Return to Love*, was based on the story, though without reading the final credits you mightn't realise; indeed, the title gives fair warning.

"Mackintosh Willy" (1977) was suggested by graffiti within a concrete shelter in the very park the story uses. When I approached I saw that the letters in fact spelled MACK TOSH WILLY. Close by was an area of new concrete, roped off but with the footprints of some scamp embedded in it, and these two elements gave birth to the tale. When J. K. and I were visiting Liverpool locations for the first edition of this book I took him to the shelter, but alas, the legend had been erased from it.

The entire location of "The Show Goes On" (1978)—the cinema, I mean—is no more. It was the Hippodrome in Liverpool, and I thought I'd failed to do it justice in an earlier tale, "The Dark Show". It was built as a music hall, and behind the screen was a maze of passages and dressing-rooms, as I discovered with increasing unease one night when I missed my way to a rear exit. Eventually I reached a pair of barred doors beyond which, as I tried to budge them, a dim illumination seemed to show me figures making for them. Homeless folk, very possibly—they didn't look at all well—but when, years later, I was able, as a film reviewer, to attend the last night of the cinema and explore its less public areas, I never managed to find those doors again.

Only global warming is likely to do away with the location of "The Ferries" (1978), though the spring tides drive small animals out of the grass onto the promenade—at least, we must hope they're small animals. "Midnight Hobo" (1978) also had a real setting, a bridge under a railway in Tuebrook in Liverpool. As for Roy and Derrick, they were suggested by a relationship between personnel at Radio Merseyside: Roy was my old producer Tony Wolfe, and Derrick—well, I really mustn't say. Roy's grisly interview with the starlet was based pretty closely on one I had to conduct with a member of the cast of a seventies British sex comedy. According to the Internet Movie Database, she made one more film.

Angela Carter has suggested that the horror story is a holiday from morality. It often is, especially when it uses the idea of supernatural evil as an alibi for horrors we are quite capable of perpetrating ourselves, but it needn't be, as I hope "The Depths" (1978) and others of my tales confirm. I've always thought of this one as a companion piece to my novel *The Nameless*. Jaume Balagueró's fine film demonstrates how much of that can be stripped away, but I think the central metaphor of giving up your name and with it your responsibility for your actions and your right to choose is more timely than ever—indeed, perhaps it's time I wrote about it again. "The Depths" is concerned with the process of demonisation, another way of finding someone else to blame. I'm sure I'm guilty of it myself; the worst writing in my field gives me any number of excuses.

"Down There" (1978) very nearly joined my other unfinished short stories. I tried to write it when our daughter was just a few weeks old. I felt compelled to write even under those circumstances, but my imagination couldn't grasp the material for several days. I was about to abandon the effort when the image of a fire escape viewed from above in the rain came alive, and so did the tale. The early pages of the first draft had to be taken apart and thoroughly reworked, but there's no harm in that—in fact, it has become increasingly my way. Alas, it wasn't when I wrote "The Companion".

With a little more sexual explicitness "The Fit" (1979) might have found a place in *Scared Stiff* (two stories from which have been deleted from the present book, but you can find them in the expanded Tor edition of my tales of sex and death). Whereas those stories explore what happens to the horror story if sexual themes become overt, "The Fit" may be said to squint at the effects of Freudian knowingness. Fanny Cave indeed! I'd originally written "The Depths" for my anthology *New Terrors,* but when Andrew J. Offutt sent in a story that seemed to share the theme, I wrote "The Fit" as a substitute for mine.

My memory suggests that "Hearing is Believing" (1979) was an attempt to write about a haunting by a single sense. "The Hands" (1980) came out of an encounter in the street with a lady bearing a clipboard. I'm reminded of the slogan on the British poster for *Devils of Monza*: "She was no ordinary nun." Indeed, the real lady wasn't one at all—I suppose some lingering Catholicism effected the transformation for the purposes of the tale. This seems as good a point as any to mention my forthcoming novel *Spanked by Nuns*.

"Again" (1980) appeared in the *Twilight Zone* magazine under T. E. D. Klein's editorship, although I gather Rod Serling's widow took some persuading. One British journal found the tale too disturbing to publish, while a British Sunday newspaper magazine dismissed it as "not horrid enough." Who would have expected Catherine Morland to take up editing? The story saw a powerful graphic adaptation by Michael Zulli in the adult comic *Taboo,* which was apparently one reason why the publication was and perhaps still is liable to be seized by British Customs.

Two novels occupied my time for the next three years, to the exclusion of any other fiction. While picnicking with the family in Delamere Forest to celebrate having finished *Incarnate* I thought of the basis for "Just Waiting" (1983), and the genesis of a new short story felt like a celebration too. My touch here and in "Seeing the World" (1983) is lighter than it used to be, or so I like to think. That doesn't mean what's lit up isn't still dark.

"Old Clothes" (1983) was an attempt to develop the notion of apports. I'm as loath as Lovecraft ever was to use stale occult ideas, but I think this one let me have some fun. In 1984 Alan Ryan asked me for a new Halloween story, and "Apples" was the result. It became the occasion of one of my more memorable encounters with a copy-editor, though only after the American edition had respected my text. The British paperback version of the tale proved to have suffered something like a hundred changes. The excellent Nick Webb, the managing director of Sphere, had the edition withdrawn and pulped. Had I not written "Out of Copyright" by then, I might well have turned it into a tale about a copy editor. Of course not all such folk are interfering bloody fools, but perhaps an example of what befell "Apples" is in order. Where I'd written

His dad and mum were like that, they were teachers and tried to make him friends at our school they taught at, boys who didn't like getting dirty and always had combs and handkerchiefs . . .

The copy editor thought I should have written

His mum and dad were like that. They were teachers and tried to make friends for him at our school, where they taught boys who didn't like getting dirty and always had combs and handkerchiefs . . .

I rest my case, and my head.

"The Other Side" (1985) was an attempt to equal the surrealism of J. K. Potter's picture on which it was based. The last thing I wanted to do was end the story with his image, since the combination would have had much the same effect as the infamous *Weird Tales* illustration that gave away one of Lovecraft's best endings. The image can be found on page 97 of J. K.'s superb Paper Tiger collection *Horripilations*, which also contains (among much else) his illustrations for the aborted limited edition of *The Influence*.

Kathryn Cramer asked me to write a story in which the building in which it took place would (I may be paraphrasing) itself figure as a character. She certainly didn't mean her letter to potential contributors to be disconcerting, but she pointed to several stories of mine as epitomising her theme, which made me feel expected to imitate myself and daunted by the task. I struggled to come up with an idea until circumstances gave me one, as happens often enough to let me believe in synchronicity. The Campbell family had just moved into the house in which I now write, but we hadn't yet sold the previous one, to which I daily walked. I forget how long it took me to notice that here was the germ of "Where the Heart Is" (1986).

"Boiled Alive" (1986)—a title I hoped folk would recognise was meant to be intemperate—was also conceived in response to an invitation, this time from David Pringle of *Interzone*. When I try to write science fiction my style generally stiffens up, and so I attempted to be ungenerically offbeat instead. That isn't to say I don't think it's a horror story: I think all the stories in this collection are. I'd certainly call "Another World" (1987) one, and it too was invited, by Paul Gamble ("Gamma") when he worked for Forbidden Planet in London. His idea was an anthology of tales on the theme of a forbidden planet, though when Roz Kaveney took over the editorship she chose stories simply on the basis that the author had signed at the bookshop. I had, but I cleaved to the theme as well.

As for "End of the Line" (1991), what can I say? It is, but may also have begun a lighter style of comedy in my stuff. Whatever the tone, though, it's still pretty dark in here. I hope the jokes are inextricable from the terror. However, it was less with laughter than with a sneer that a hypnotist who claimed to reawaken people's memories of their past lives once advised me to study his career for when I "started writing seriously," rather as if those responsible for *The Amityville Horror* had accused, say, Shirley Jackson of having her tongue in her cheek when she wrote *The Haunting of Hill House*. I see no reason why dealing with the fantastic requires one to write bullshit, and I submit this collection as evidence.

In the thirty years covered by this book I saw horror fiction become enormously more popular and luxuriant. I use the last word, as tends to be my way with words, for its ambiguity. There's certainly something to be said in favour of the growth of a field which has produced so many good new writers and so much good writing. One of its appeals to me, ever since I became aware of the tales of M. R. James, is the way the best work achieves its effects through the use of style, the selection of language. On the other hand, the field has sprouted writers whose fiction I can best describe as Janet and John primers of mutilation, where the length of the sentences, paragraphs, and chapters betrays the maximum attention span of either the audience or the writer or more probably both. There are also quite a bunch of writers with more pretensions whose basic drive appears to be to outdo one another in disgustingness. "It is very easy to be nauseating," M. R. James wrote more than sixty years ago, and the evidence is all around us. However, I hope that in time the genre will return to the mainstream, where it came from and where it belongs.

What to do? Nothing, really, except keep writing and wait for the verdict of history. The field is big enough for everyone, after all. I came into it because I wanted to repay some of the pleasure it had given me—particularly the work of those writers who, as David Aylward put it, "used to strive for awe"—and I stay in it because it allows me to talk about whatever themes I want to address and because I have by no means found its limits. Perhaps in the next thirty years, but I rather hope not. I like to think my best story is the one I haven't written yet, and that's why I continue to write.

RAMSEY CAMPBELL
Wallasey, Merseyside
1 December 2002

ALONE WITH THE HORRORS

The Tower from Yuggoth

I

Of late there has been a renewal of interest in cases of inexplicable happenings.
From this it seems inevitable that further interest be shown in the case
of Edward Wingate Armitage, who was consigned to St Mary's Hospital,
Arkham, in early 1929, later to be taken to an institution. His life had always
been, by choice, the life of an outcast and recluse; for the greater part of his
life outside the institution he had been interested in the occult and forbidden; and his supposed finding of incontrovertible evidence in his research
into certain legendary presences outside Arkham, which sent him into that
period of insanity from which he never recovered, might therefore have
been a seeming triviality, portentous only to his already slightly deranged
mind. Certainly there were, and still are, certain Cyclopean geological anom-
alies in the woods toward Dunwich; but no trace could be found of that
which Armitage shudderingly described as set at the highest point of those
strange slabs of rock, which admittedly did bear a certain resemblance to titan stair-treads. However, there undoubtedly was something more than the
vast steps that Armitage glimpsed, for he had known of their existence for
some time, and certain other things connected with the case lead an unbi-
ased outsider to believe that the case is not quite so simple as the doctors
would have it believed.

Edward Wingate Armitage was born in early 1879 of upper-class parents.
As an infant, nothing peculiar may be noted concerning him. He accompanied his parents to their weekly attendance at the Congregationalist church;
at home he played, ate, and slept with regularity, and in general acted as a
normal child would. However, the house's welfare was naturally attended by
servants, most of which, in the manner of servants, had a tendency to talk
more to children than the elder Armitages; and so it was that a three-year-
old was noted to show unaccountable interest in what fell out of space on the
Gardner farm in that year of 1882. The elder Armitages were forced to speak

more than once to the servants on the subject of what was fitting for discussion with Edward.

A few years later, after a period in which Edward declined to leave the house except for walks with his parents, a change was seen to occur. It was in the summer of 1886 that this became particularly noticeable. He would indeed leave the house, but could not be seen playing anywhere nearby, though servants often saw him leave with a book from the house library under his arm—that library which had been partially built up of books from the inherited property of a grandfather. Certain of these books were on subjects occult and morbid, and Edward had been warned not to touch them—his father often considering their destruction, for he was a definite Congregationalist, and disliked such books' being in the house; but never did he put this idea into practice. None of these books appeared to be missing while Edward was away, but the father was unsure quite how many there were; and the boy was never met returning, so that he might have returned whatever books he had taken. He invariably said that he had been "out walking"; but certain newspaper items, dealing with curious signs found scratched in the soil of graveyards, and certain peculiar erections, together with bodies of various wild creatures, found in the woods, gave the parents cause to wonder.

It was at this time, also, that the boy began to be avoided by all the children in the vicinity. This inexplicable avoidance began immediately after a young girl had accompanied Edward, or rather followed him, on one of his silent trips. She had seen him enter a grove of trees outside Arkham, where a peculiar arrangement of stones in the centre, somewhat resembling a monolith, caught her eye. Characteristic of the cold-bloodedness of children in those times, she did not cry out when he procured a small rat, tied helpless near the monolith, and slit its throat with a pocket-knife. As he began to read in some unknown and vaguely horrible language from the book, an eldritch shadow seemed to pass across the landscape. Then came a sinister muffled roaring sound; sinister because, the girl swore, the roaring followed the syllables shrieked by Edward Armitage, like some hideous antiphonal response. She fled, telling her friends later but not her parents. Both the parents of the various children and Edward's parents inquired into the resultant avoidance, but could elicit no information. Only tales handed down through various families now make this tale available, and it is doubtful how much of it can be believed.

As time passed, Edward's father contracted typhoid fever, further complications assured that it would be fatal, and in 1913 he was taken to St Mary's

Hospital (later to see another Armitage's consignment there) where, on the twelfth of May, he died.

After the funeral, Edward was left in the care of his mother. Bereaved of her husband, she had now only her son on whom to lavish affection. Edward's upbringing after this stage was much less strict: he was able to read and use whatever books in the library he wanted; his mother did not object to this, but she disliked his frequent trips at night, whose destination he refused to reveal. It was noticeable that after one of these nocturnal trips the morning paper would be missing; and Edward, who rose before anyone else in the house, denied that it ever arrived on these occasions. One maid who showed a tendency to speak of certain nocturnal atrocities reported in the missing papers, was dismissed after the boy had told his mother of certain thefts which could only have been committed by this maid.

It was in 1916 that Edward left home to enrol at Miskatonic University. For a short time he gave most of his leisure up to study mathematics; but it was not long before he gained access to the restricted section of the library. After this step, his former leisure studying was eclipsed by a feverish perusal of those books residing in the library and about which so much has been written and conjectured. The hellish *Necronomicon* engulfed his attention in particular; and the amount of time which he spent in taking notes and copying passages from this tome of terror was only cut short by the repeated adjurations of his tutors to devote more time to his mathematical work.

However, it is obvious that he still found time to peruse these monstrous volumes; and toward such evidence is the curiously hinting tale of his tutor. Calling at the student's study while he was away, the mathematics tutor was constrained to enter and examine a few notebooks scattered over the bed. One of these was taken up with notes on the orthodox studies Edward was following; the tutor glanced through this, noting the care with which the notes had been prepared. A second was composed of passages copied from various sources—a few in Latin, but most in other, alien languages, set off by certain monstrous diagrams and signs. But the notebook which startled the tutor more than the cabalistic signs and non-human inscriptions was that containing certain speculations and references to rites and sacrifices performed by students at Miskatonic. He took this to the principal, who decided not to act as yet, but, since there were numerous references to an "Aklo Sabaoth" to be performed the next night, to send a party of tutors to spy on these proceedings.

The next night certain students were observed to leave their rooms at different hours and not to return; several of these were followed by tutors asked by the principal to report on that night's proceedings. Most of the students made their way by devious routes to a large clearing in the otherwise almost impenetrable woods west of the Aylesbury Road. Edward was noted to be one of those who seemed to be presiding over the strange gathering. He and six others, all wearing strange and sinister objects around their necks, were standing on a huge, roughly circular slab in the centre of the clearing. As the first ray of the pallid crescent moon touched the slab, the seven standing upon it moved to stand on the ground beside it, and began to gibber and shriek strange half-coherent ritual invocations.

It is only believed by one or two of the watching professors that these invocations, in languages meant for no human tongue, elicited any response. Undoubtedly it was a disturbing sight, those seven students yelling sinister syllables at that slab of stone and moving further from it on each chorused reply from the encircling watchers. This being so, the impressions of the hidden tutors may be understood. Probably it was simply an atmospheric effect which made the vast slab appear to rise, slowly and painfully; and it must merely have been nervous tension which brought one savant to hint at a huge scaly claw which reached from beneath, and a pale bloated head which pushed up the slab. It must certainly have been the marks of something natural which were found by the next day's daylight party, for such marks would lead one to believe that the reaching claw had seven fingers. At a chorused shriek from all the participants, a cloud passed over the moon, and the clearing was plunged into abysmal darkness. When the place was again illuminated, it was totally empty; the slab again was in position; and the watchers stole away, disturbed and changed by this vague glimpse of nether spheres.

The following day saw a terrible interview with the principal, by Edward, among others. His mother, perplexed, was summoned across the city; and after she and Edward had visited the principal's office, when the door was locked, they left the university, never to return. Edward had to be escorted from the office by two of his former, non-decadent fellow-students, during which he screamed curses at the unmoved principal, and called down the vengeance of Yog-Sothoth on him.

The crosstown trip was utterly unpleasant to Mrs Armitage. Her son was continuously mumbling in strange accents and swearing that he would see the principal "visited." The disturbing interview at Miskatonic University had brought on a sickening faintness and weakness of her heart, and the pavement seemed to hump and roll under her feet while the houses appeared to close in on her and totter precariously. They reached their extensive house on High Street only barely before the woman collapsed in her reaction to that terrible interview. Edward, meanwhile, left her in the front room while he repaired to the study. He seemed to be bent on discovering a certain formula; and he returned in a rage when all the forbidden books in his library would not yield it.

For some days after Armitage, now eighteen years old, went about the house in a state of morbid introspection. From various hints dropped in what little conversation he had, it became obvious that he was mourning his loss of access to the blasphemous *Necronomicon*. His mother, who was fast succumbing to that heart weakness started by the unpleasant affair at the university, suggested that he should take up research into things a little nearer reality. Showing contempt at first for his mother's naïveté, he began to perceive possibilities, apparently, in this system, and told her that he might pursue research "a mite closer to home."

It was perhaps fortunate that, on November 17, Mrs Armitage was rushed to the hospital, taken with a bad fit of heart failure, the aftermath of Edward's dismissal. That night, without regaining consciousness, she died.

Freed from her restraining influence, unaffected by long university hours, and having no need to work because supported by the extensive estate he had inherited, Edward Wingate Armitage began that line of research which was to lead to the revelation of so many unsettling facts, and, finally, to his madness in 1929.

II

Christmas 1917 saw Edward Armitage's mourning period end. After the New Year holidays were ended, passers-by would notice him, now equipped with a small sports car—the only luxury he had bought with the recently inherited estate—driving in the direction of the countryside end of High Street. At such times he would start out in the early morning, and not be seen to return until late evening. When met out on the rough country roads outside Arkham, he was seen to drive at the highest speed he could drag out of the car. More than one person recollects that he turned off the road into an even more primitive driveway to a decrepit, ancient farmhouse. Those who were curious enough to inquire as to the owner of the archaic homestead were told that the old man was reputed to have an amazing amount of knowledge concerning forbidden practices in Massachusetts and was even reputed to have participated in certain of these practices.

From the notes in that capacious notebook which he always carried, Armitage's trip may be reconstructed. The drive through the brooding country, unchanged for incredible aeons before the advent of civilisation in New England, is recalled in detail in the first pages, as if Edward was afraid that something might prevent him from remembering the route. The exact position of the turning off the Innsmouth road is marked on a small sketch-map.

At this point, the biographer can only imagine Armitage's route. The walks up the muddy pathway to the farmhouse, between tottering, clawing, moss-covered trees, and the reaching of the leaning building on a slight rise, may be conjectured. One can but imagine Armitage's turning to stare back across the undulant fields, colourless under the glaring sun and first mist of morning. Far off could be seen the steeple of the Arkham Congregational church, towering over the glistening gambrel roofs of the busy town. In the other direction, unseen over the horizon, would lie Innsmouth, with its half-human inhabitants, avoided by normal Arkham folk. Armitage would look out across the lonely landscape, and finally turn to batter on the door of the farmhouse before him. After repeated summonses, the shuffling footsteps of Enoch Pierce, the half-deaf owner, would be heard down the oak floorboards of the passage.

The aspect of this man at their first meeting somehow startled the visitor. He had a long beard, a few straggling strands of hair falling over his forehead. He fumbled senilely as he spoke, but a certain fire in his eyes belied his appearance of senility. But the attribute which so startled Armitage was the curious air which hung about this primitive rustic, of great wisdom and unbelievable age. At first he tried to close Armitage out, until Armitage pronounced certain words in a pre-human language which seemed to satisfy Pierce. He ushered the visitor into the sparsely furnished living-room, and began to question him as to his reason for visiting. Armitage, making certain that the old man's sons were occupied out in the fields, turned his own questions on the old rustic. The man began to listen with growing interest, sometimes mixed with unease.

Armitage, it appeared, was desperately in need of a certain mineral, not to be found anywhere on earth except under the ice in certain sunken cities in the Arctic, but mined extensively on Yuggoth. This metal had various peculiar characteristics, and he felt that if he could discover where the crustacean beings of the black world had their outpost on earth, he could have traffic with them by virtue of the most potent incantation in R'lyehian, using the hideous and terrific name of Azathoth. Now that he had lost access to the Miskatonic copy of the *Necronomicon*, he would first be trying the surrounding country before visiting Harvard to attempt to peruse their copy. He had a feeling that perhaps the ancient rustic, with his reputed store of forbidden knowledge, might enlighten him, either as to the incantation or the location of the Massachusetts outpost of the race from Yuggoth. Could the man assist him?

The old man stared unseeingly at his visitor, as though his vision had suddenly opened on the abysmal, lightless vacuum of outer gulfs. He seemed to recollect something unpleasant from out of the far past. Finally he shuddered, and, now and then stretching forth a bony hand to grip his listener's lapel, he spoke.

"Listen, young Sir, 'tain't as if I haven't ben mixed up in turrible doin's. I had a friend onct as would go down to the Devil's Steps, an' he swore as he'd soon have them Yuggoth ones about him, ministerin' at every word he spoke. He thaought he had words as would overcome them that fly over the steps. But let me tell yew, he went too far. They faound him out in the woods, and 'twas so horrible a sight that three of them as carried him wasn't never the same since. Bust open, his chest and his throat was, and his face was all blue. Said as haow it was ungodly, them from Arkham did. But those as knew, they said those up the steps flew off with him into space where his lungs bust.

"Don't be hasty naow, young Sir. 'Tis too dangerous to go and seek up them Devil's Steps. But there's something out in the woods by the Aylesbury Road that could give you what you want, mebbe, and it ain't so much a hater of men as them from Yuggoth nohaow. You may've ben to it—it's under a slab of rock, and the Aklo Sabaoth brings it—but mebbe ye didn't think of asking for what ye need? It's easier to hold, anyhaow—ye don't even need Alhazred for the right words. An' it might get things from them from Yuggoth for ye. 'Tis worth a try, anyhaow—before ye gets mixed up in what might kill ye."

Armitage, dissatisfied, could gain no more information concerning the outpost at Devil's Steps, that vast geological anomaly beyond Arkham. He left the farmhouse in an uncertain frame of mind. A few nights later, he records, he visited the titan slab in the woods west of the Aylesbury Road. Seemingly the alien ritual had little effect, needing a larger number of participants; at any rate, he heard sounds below as of a vast body stirring, but nothing else.

The next recorded trip is that to Harvard University, where he searched the pages of their copy of Alhazred's massive hideous blasphemy. Either theirs was an incomplete edition, or he was mistaken in thinking that the volume contained the terrible words, for he came away enraged and convinced that he needed the *R'lyeh Text*, the only copy of which, he was aware, resided at Miskatonic University.

He returned the next day to Arkham, and proceeded to call at the Enoch Pierce homestead again. The old farmer listened uneasily to Armitage's tale of his lack of success, both in raising the daemon in the clearing and at Harvard. The recluse seemed to have had an even greater change of heart since his visitor had last seen him, for at first he even declined to aid the seeker in raising the thing in the wood. He doubted, so he said, that it would be able to supply Edward with the necessary incantations to subdue the crustaceans from Yuggoth; he also doubted that even two participants would be capable of stirring it from below its slab. Also, quite frankly, he was slightly disturbed by the whole proceedings. He disliked to be connected with anything concerning those Armitage ultimately wished to contact, even so indirectly as this would concern him. And, finally, he might be able to tell Armitage where to procure the incantation.

Armitage, however, was adamant. He meant to call up that below the slab off the Aylesbury Road, and he would try this before following any more of the venerable rustic's doubtful recommendations; and since it was unlikely that anyone else would accompany him to this ritual, it would be necessary to ask the aid of Pierce. When the man further demurred, Armitage spoke a few words, of which only the hideous name Yog-Sothoth was intelligible. But Pierce (so the other recorded in that invaluable notebook) paled, and said that he would consider the suggestions.

The Aklo Sabaoth only being useful for the invocation of daemons on nights of the first phase of the moon, the two had to await the crescent moon for almost a month. 1918 was a year of mist and storm over Arkham, so that even the full moon was only a whitish glow in the sky in that month of March. But Armitage only realised the necessity of deferring the ritual when the night of the first quarter arrived moonless, a definitely adverse condition.

These unfortunate meteorological conditions did not end, in fact, until early 1919, Armitage now being twenty years of age. Not many of the neighbours realised he was so young—the monstrous wisdom he had acquired from reading the forbidden books in his library and that at the Miskatonic— and those who knew about his real age somehow did not dare to speak what they knew. That was why nobody was able to stop him as he left the house at dusk, one night in April 1919.

The wind howled over the countryside as the sports car drew up at the end of the driveway to the Pierce farmhouse. The countryside, in the lurid light across the horizon with faint threads of mist rising from the marshy field, resembled some landscape out of hideous Leng in central Asia. A more sensitive person might have been uneasy at the brooding eldritch country; but Armitage would not be affected by this, for the sights he was to see that night were far more horrible, such as give threats to sanity and outlook. Muttering certain words at the not-yet-risen sliver of moon, he pounded on the oaken door.

The old man mumbled affrightedly at the sight of his visitor, and tried to turn him away with pleas of something to be done that night which was very pressing. But he had promised Armitage that he would accompany him, and his visitor held him to that promise though it had been made over a year before. He escorted Pierce out to the waiting sports car, in which they drove off across the grim, primeval landscape. All too soon they turned off to reach the Aylesbury Road. The drive down it was a nightmarish affair of close half-demolished lichenous brick walls, grassy verges with huge darkly-coloured pools, and stunted trees, twisted into grotesque shapes which creaked in the screaming wind and leaned terrifyingly toward the road. But however morbid the drive may have seemed, it could have been no consolation to Pierce when the car drew off the road near an especially dense belt of forest.

The trip down the pathway between the towering trees may only be imagined. But the walk through the fungoid-phosphorescent boles and path-blocking twisted roots soon widened out into a clearing—the clearing of that horrible survival from aeons before humanity occurred. Armitage waited impatiently as the moon's thin rays began to trickle across the boundary of the clearing. He had insisted that Pierce stand near the slab of vast mineral, and that person now shuddered as he watched the accursed sliver of moon creep up toward the zenith.

Finally, as the first beam of pallid light struck the circular stone, the searcher began to shriek those mercifully forbidden words in the Aklo language, the terrified farmer joining in the responses. At first, no sound could be heard except certain movements far off among the trees; but as the moonbeams progressed across the pitted grey expanse both Armitage and his disturbed companion began to hear a sound far below in the earth, as of some Cyclopean body crawling from unremembered abysses. The thing scrabbled monstrously in some black pit under the earth, and so greatly was the sound muffled that it was not until the slab began to creak upward hideously that the watchers realised the nearness of the alien horror. Enoch Pierce turned as if to flee, but Armitage screamed that he should hold his ground, and he turned back to face whatever monstrosity might rise from the pit.

First of all came the claws and arms, and when Pierce saw the number of arms he almost screamed outright. Then, as these dug into the soil around that hole into nether deeps, the thing raised itself almost out of the hole, and its head came into sight, pressing up the impossibly heavy slab of unknown material. That bloated, scaly head, with its obscenely wide mouth and one staring orb, was in view for but an instant; for then the arm of the hideousness shot out into the moonlight, swept up the hapless Pierce, and whipped back into the blackness. The stone slab crashed back into place, and a ghastly shriek from the victim yelled out beneath the stone, to be cut off horribly a second later.

Then, however, Armitage, shaken by the horror he had seen but still mindful of his mission, pronounced the final invocation of the Sabaoth. A terrible croaking rang out in the clearing, seeming to come across incredible gulfs of space. It spoke in no human tongue, but the hearer understood only too perfectly. He added a potent list of the powers which he had called out of space and time, and began to explain the mission on which he had sought the abomination's aid.

It is at this point in the notes of Edward Wingate Armitage that an air of puzzlement is remarked by all commentators. He recounts, with a growing air of disbelief and definite unease, that he explained to the lurker below the slab that he wished to learn the long invocation of the powers of Azathoth. On the mention of that monstrous and alien name, the shambler in the concealed pit began to stir as if disturbed, and chanted hideously in cosmic rhythms, as if to ward off some danger or malefic power. Armitage, startled at the demonstration of the potency of that terrific name, continued that his reason for wishing to learn this chant was to protect himself in traffic with the crustacean beings from black Yuggoth on the rim. But at the reference to these rumoured entities, a positive shriek of terror rang out from below the earth, and a vast scrabbling and slithering, fast dying away, became apparent. Then there was silence in the clearing, except for the flapping and crying of an inexplicable flock of whippoorwills, passing overhead at that moment.

III

One can learn little more about the ways of Edward Wingate Armitage for the next few years. There are notes concerning a passage to Asia in 1922; the seeker apparently visited an ancient castle, much avoided by the neighbouring peasantry, for the seemingly deserted stronghold was reputed to be on the edge of a certain abnormal Central Asian plateau. He speaks of a certain tower room in which something had been prisoned, and of an awakening of that which still sat in a curiously carved throne facing the door. To this certain commentators link references to something carried on the homeward passage in a stout tightly-sealed box, the odour of which was so repulsive that it had to be kept in the owner's cabin at the request of other passengers. But nothing could be gleaned from whatever he brought home in the box, and it can only be conjectured what was done with the box and its contents; though there may be some connection with what a party of men from Miskatonic, summoned by an uneasy surgeon at St Mary's, found in Armitage's house and transported out to a lonely spot beyond Arkham, after which they poured kerosene over it and made certain that nothing remained afterward.

In early 1923 Armitage journeyed to Australia, there being certain legends of survivals there that he wished to verify. The notes are few at this point, but it seems likely that he discovered nothing beyond legends of a shunned desert stretch where a buried alien city was said to lie. Upon making a journey to the avoided terrain, he remarked that frequent spirals of dust arose in the place for no visible reason, and often twisted into very peculiar and vaguely disturbing shapes. Often, also, a singular ululation—a fluted whistling which seemed almost coherent—resounded out of empty space; but no amount of invocation would make anything appear beyond the eldritchly twining clouds of dust.

In the summer of 1924 Armitage removed from the High Street residence to an extensive place at the less-inhabited end of the Aylesbury Road. Perhaps he had grown to hate the pressing crowds in the city; more likely, however, he wished to follow certain pursuits that must not be seen by anyone. Frequent trips to that abnormality beneath the stone in the woods are recorded; but presumably the lack of participants made the ritual useless, for no response could be elicited. Once or twice there is a rise of defiance, noticeable in the tenor of the notes, but before he actually visited the Devil's Steps and its monstrous secrets, he would always repent his foolhardiness. Even so, he was becoming desperate with the lack of that unearthly mineral that he needed. It is better not to think of what his actions and fate might have been, had he not finally discovered a route to learning that long-sought and forbidden incantation.

But it was soon after, in March of the memorable year 1925, that Armitage recollected words of Enoch Pierce before that last horrible April night in the haunted clearing. Perhaps he had been rereading his notes; at any rate, he remembered Pierce's plea that he might be able to tell him where to procure the incantation, one day in 1918. At the time he had believed that this was merely a lie to defer the awful moonlight ritual; but now he wondered if it might not have had some foundation in reality, for the rustic had known a number of people possessing rare occult knowledge. One of these might conceivably know that incantation.

The next day he drove to the homestead, which was even more decayed and tottering than he remembered. Pierce's wife was dead, and the two sons now lived there alone, eking out a meagre income from the pitiful herd of cattle and few poultry. They were extremely displeased to see him, suspecting that their father's inexplicable disappearance had been effected by something which Armitage had "called aout of space"; but their fear overcame their hatred, so that they invited him into the parlour, albeit with unintelligible whisperings to each other. One, the younger, excused himself to tend the herd; the other listened uneasily to the visitor's questions. Who were the friends of his father who might have been connected with witchcraft, black magic and the like? Which, if any, were alive today? Where did they live? And, most important, which would be likely to know more than had Enoch Pierce?

The son's slow response resembled that of his vanished father. Most of the men who had aided Pierce in his forbidden searching were all gone now. He had had one who had only come after his father made certain actions and spoke alien words, and it had once been let drop that he had been hung in that all-embracing purgation at Salem in 1692. The great majority of the rest had also vanished inexplicably after the father had not returned, and his son seemed to consider that these were of the same kind as the fugitive from Salem. One who had come up from Portsmouth, however, kept house just outside Dunwich, or had used to. But he thought that even he might have died, and only been present in the house at Dunwich when called by the vanished Pierce to aid him with the volumes there.

Excitement now began to take hold of Armitage. A man who had come from Portsmouth probably would have been driven to his new home by witchcraft frenzy in 1692, if this peculiar reference to his death before Pierce met him was to be taken literally. Pierce had had a startling amount of knowledge, but if this eldritch being had been called to his aid, it might conceivably be much more wise. And the references to the many tomes in the house outside Dunwich—why, this private library might even include the *R'lyeh Text* of nameless wisdom! So great was his excitement at the possible long-forgotten vistas that might be opening before him, that Armitage even stopped to thank the plainly hostile being before him as he hurried out to his waiting car.

But disappointment awaited him at the end of his frenzied drive to Dunwich. The house of the Portsmouth refugee was found easily enough, on the crest of a hill—or, rather, what was left of the house. Only three nights before it had caught fire. A party of men, in the vicinity for no particular reason, somehow neglected to call the fire brigade; and the ancient house, with all its rumoured contents, was destroyed except for one or two incombustibles— such as a skeleton, human only as to the skull, but otherwise so unearthly that only voluminous clothing could allow its living counterpart to pass for a human being.

Bitterly disappointed and desperate, Armitage returned to his house off the Aylesbury Road. He began to search, it would appear, for a parallel formula in the books of the library. But even this could not be found; and he began to slip into a lassitude and depression born of desperation.

It is pointed out by those commentators wishing to see a sane and wholesome explanation for that last occurrence in the woods between Dunwich and Arkham that in early 1928 Armitage began to take drugs. Previously he had been without hope of any road to the ritual he wanted; now, with the foolhardiness of his sudden addiction, came a resolve to carry out a quickly-conceived plan to enter Miskatonic University and carry off their copy of the volume he sought. He would need a dark night, and even the March of that year had phenomenally light nights. He was forced to wait impatiently until October, when a series of heavy rainstorms all over the region forced him to procrastinate still further. It was not until December that the series of deluges ended; and on the day before he was to carry out his individual assault on the university, he happened to buy a copy of the *Arkham Advertiser*, and in so doing he became aware of the first of a series of events which were to lead to that frightful outcome.

The piece which caught his eye was in the inside pages of the paper, for the editor believed that it was so choked with hellish speculation as to be of little portent. It dealt with a hill in the Dunwich country already known for a disaster in 1925. The lower regions of the hill had been inundated in the phenomenal floods in that region, and when the hill had been revealed fully again by the sinking of the water, a tunnel into inner depths was seen. It led to a door in the rock below the soil, securely sealed, so that the water had not passed it. The inhabitants of the neighbourhood seemed to be afraid of approaching the place; and the reporter said humorously that it was unlikely that anyone from Arkham would be interested in investigating, so that it might remain an unsolved mystery. A rather ironic pronouncement, for Armitage, as soon as he realised what might be in that room, returned home and drove as fast as possible to the hill beyond Dunwich.

He drew up in a side road, which would have led past the hill of the revealed secret but for the lower part of the road's being covered in water. Leaving the car in the higher section of the road, Armitage began to approach the newly-found room, walking on raised ground at the side of the route, dry but slightly yielding. Soon reaching the passage into the hill, he began to walk down the twilit tunnel, which was now completely free from moisture. The door at its end swung open at a touch—for although it was so completely sealed, the portal was balanced, in reality, in a manner once very well known in various pre-human civilisations.

The place was unlit, and the searcher was forced to switch on a torch which he had carried with him. The place revealed was a small room with walls of bare rock, bookcases around three of the walls, that facing the door being piled high with large and peculiarly-shaped boxes, covered with moss, charred earth and other less describable materials. In the higher shelf of the left-hand set were a large number of papers and envelopes. But Armitage's eye did not linger on this, for below were various hide-covered volumes, and in the centre of the shelf was a copy of the aeons-old *R'lyeh Text*. He took this down, noting that it seemed as complete as that up at Miskatonic, and made to carry it out to the car. As an afterthought, he decided to include the bundles of letters and papers on the top shelf, for the private documents of such a person of wisdom might yield much of interest to such a delver into fearful knowledge. He was not seen by anyone as he entered the car and drove off—not even that party of men who arrived with dynamite a few minutes after and caused the destruction later reported in a slightly satirical half-column in the *Advertiser*.

Upon reaching the Aylesbury Road residence, he entered the library and began to examine his acquisitions. First he turned through the *Text* in an attempt to find the incantation he had sought for so many years. He discovered it easily—it had been underlined, and the former owner had written beside it in the margin: "for traffick with Yuggoth". It was indeed the right chant, and the reader could not hold back a shudder at the hideous cadences and rhythms which it recalled to his mental ear.

He turned to the documents. The man's name, he discovered, had been Simon Frye, and at once it became apparent that the nameless suspicions of the time of death of Frye must have been correct. For the date of that first letter, with its archaic spelling and handwriting, was 1688; and none in the pile bore a later date than 1735. One—addressed, it would seem, to England, but never sent—was dated 1723, and so much had it impressed the reader that he had put a large star in red ink at the top of the yellowed missive. It may not be amiss to quote it in full.

Brother in Azathoth,

Your letter was receiv'd by me some Days ago, and so great has been my Excitement that I could not send you a letter to tell you of my good fortune. I have, as you well must know, a great yearning for ye Text. My half-human Compatriot in Asia has now sent me a Copy of ye Volume of Terror, and if it had been in my possession when Cotton Mather had tried to destroy ye Coven, he would have had some Thing call'd down on him! But I wish to go to ye Steps of ye Devil beyond Dunwich and call those from Yuggoth. So I thank you for ye Vial of Powder of Ibn Ghazi which was enclos'd in yr Letter, and send my Hope that ye Box which I enclos'd some time ago will help you to invoke Yogge-Sothothe, and no Thing give your Occupation away.

Azathoth ph'nafn Ogthrod
S. Frye.

A second missive was clipped to this by Armitage, and it can be conjectured that the second gave him a different outlook on his forthcoming traffic than did the first. The latter was dated 1723, a few months after the first, and since it came from Asia, it is presumable that the writer was Frye's "half-human Compatriot".

Brother in Azathoth,

I write this as a warning, and hope that I do not send too late. You know that my Father was one of those from ye black world which you seek, and you must know how many Foulnesses have come down to this Earth from Yuggoth. But for exceeding Horror and Malevolence, those of ye shell-bodies are ye greatest. Tho' my Father indeed was one of those that was call'd long ago, and my Mother liv'd too near to ye terrible Plateau of Leng, I have always avoid'd ye Things which come down from that Globe on ye Rim. I have walk'd with Abominations which come up out of ye Darkness below ye Pyramid, and have had Traffick with those that came down from ye Stars with great Cthulhut, but ye Monsters from Yuggoth are all Horrours of all ye Cosmos, and even Cthulhut did not come from so near ye Rim at first. I would have

let them take you off into ye Gulf, because of my Father; but no Man
should ever have Traffick with such, and I warn you not to go to y^e
Steps, or anywhere else which is known to be an Outpost of Yuggoth.
Azathoth mgwi'nglui cf'ayak
James M.

But later documents of Frye show that he did indeed visit the Devil's Steps, though inexplicably not until 1735, after which no more is heard of him. Pierce's references to a friend who "would go down to the Devil's Steps" may be recalled. The description of his fate also returns to mind in hideous detail.

An imaginative person may imagine Armitage as he stared out of the window into the sunset over far-off Arkham's gambrel roofs, making it resemble some fabulous city seen far off in the red dusk of a crystal dream. For a minute, perhaps, he almost wished to be back among the quaint New England scenery and mellow architecture which he used to see from his window on busy High Street. Transiently, he may have felt a hate and repulsion for the frightful things in which he had dabbled, and the abnormalities he had called out of space and earth. But the dreadful *R'lyeh Text* lay open before him, and he thought of the legendary powers of the stone which he would gain from traffic with the trans-spatial entities. The warnings of "James M." had had no effect almost two centuries ago; and his warning was unsuccessful on this modern sorcerer.

IV

It was on a day of wailing winds and lurid skies that Edward Wingate Armitage left his house on Aylesbury Road to drive out to the Devil's Steps beyond Dunwich. The Yuletide and New Year holidays did not suit his purpose, for too many people might conceivably take it into their heads to drive in the lonely Dunwich region, and question his drive into the most secluded and shunned part of the woods. For this reason the trip was postponed until a day in early January 1929.

The hitherto invaluable information in Armitage's notebook now gives out, for he was in no condition to note down events when he returned from that frightful experience on that last cataclysmic day which led to his insanity and entrance to an institution. One must now rely on the seeming insane ravings of a madman if one is to learn anything about the journey and its aftermath. When, finally, he was discovered, after passers-by had heard strange sounds from the house on the Aylesbury Road, he had succeeded in destroying most of the volumes in his library, including the fabulous *R'lyeh Text*. Only a few books of hexerei and other unimportant tomes were left, together with the documents of Simon Frye and, of course, Armitage's notebook. The man babbled of a monstrous focal point of outer-dimensional activity, and screamed that he knew how the abominations from that black sphere on the rim moved between the earth and their terrible home. Under sedatives he calmed somewhat, and began to tell his tale with a little more coherency. He was, it became obvious, hopelessly insane; and little can be believed of what he hints and recounts in his delirium.

Concerning the actual journey he is fairly coherent, and one would not think that anything abnormal had happened. He speaks of the nearing of Dunwich, where the trees rattled and cackled hideously, and pitchy streams flowed by the road and disappeared into unseen and unspeakable gulfs. The wind that dropped into a brooding silence seemed to affect him with unease, and the shrieking flocks of whippoorwills that were disturbingly silent near his destination, those horrendous Devil's Steps, made him vaguely disquieted. But this was no more than the usual disturbance of the mind of travellers in that witchcraft-haunted region.

When he came to the crossroads near Dunwich, where certain persons had been buried with stakes through their hearts, he left the car and began to follow a curse-muttering stream which flowed through the overgrown forest. On one side was a rough path, leading off into archways of vine-entangled trees; on the other great cliffs towered up to unbelievable heights, with strange signs cut into the rock here and there. He narrowly escaped falling into the hellishly-coloured stream once or twice, and it seemed an aeon before the waters plunged into a curiously artificial-looking tunnel, the path widened out into marshy ground, and he saw the fabled Devil's Steps leading up into mist and seeming to touch the dismal, overhanging sky.

As he crossed the marshy tract of land before his destination, he noticed certain eldritch marks in the soft earth. If they were footprints, they must have been of beings of which it is better not to think. They led back and forth, but they often seemed to disappear into the pit of the stream, and most of them ended at the shunned Steps. But Armitage, determined now to find whatever lay at the top of that Cyclopean stairway of rock and overcome it with his abominable incantation, did not hesitate more than a moment. He reached the first of the strata of unknown mineral and began to climb with the aid of a pickaxe.

Only a painful memory remains in his diseased mind of that interminable climb up into space, where the only sounds were the noise of his axe and that unhealthy trickle of water far below. His mind must have been full of conjectures as to what might be seen when he reached the top of the hidden plateau. Possibly some alien onyx temple would come into view, or perhaps a whole windowless city of that trans-spatial race. Possibly a lake might lie in the centre of a horizonless expanse, hiding some ghastly aquatic deity, or conceivably a gathering of the entities might swim into view. How long he struggled upward and occupied himself with speculations born of something like terror can never be known. But it is certain that what he did see was nothing resembling what he imagined, for he recounts that when his head came over the edge of the last step he gasped in amazement —and perhaps a little in loathing. At any rate, it is one of the last things he can recall with complete coherency.

In the centre of a lichen-grown plain stood three closely-set windowless stone towers. All about the rest of the plain grew a fortunately unknown species of vegetation, which resembled nothing which ever spawned on the face of earth elsewhere, with its grey fungoid stem and long twining decayed leaves, which leaned and flapped in Armitage's direction as he clambered over the edge of the plateau.

The half-nauseated searcher reeled between the fungi and leaned over the edge of one of a few pits, gouged so deep into the rock that their lowest point was lost in tenebrous blackness. These, he presumed, must be the mines on earth of the crustaceans from Yuggoth. No sign of movement could be seen, though there were metallic sounds somewhere far down in the dark. There was no evidence beyond this in any of the other pits, either, and he realised that he must seek elsewhere—in other words, in those forbidding black towers in the centre of the plain.

He began to pick his way through the fungi, doing his best to avoid passing near them, for it seemed very repugnant to him that one of those blindly reaching grey members should touch him. Armitage was thankful when the last of the hateful nodding things was out of reach, for there was an extensive cleared space around each tower. The seeker decided to enter the central steeple; they seemed alike, each being about thirty feet high, without windows, as on the lightless planet of their origin, with a peculiarly angled doorway revealing stairs climbing up into total blackness. Armitage, however, had carried a torch with him, and, shining it up the alien passage, he forced himself to enter the somehow terrible building, reminding himself of the incantation.

Armitage's steps rang hollowly on the carven stairs, seeming to resound through illimitable gulfs of space. The darkness which barred the way ahead and soon closed in behind seemed to have an almost tangible quality, and the seeker disliked the way the blackness seemed to move and twist beyond the radius of his torch-beam. He knew that the tower was windowless only because the buildings had no windows on lightless Yuggoth, but his mind would persist in conjecturing what blasphemous abnormalities the lack of windows might hide in the tower. One could never be sure what might be standing around the bend in the dizzyingly spiralling steps, and those hieroglyphics and crude drawings of fabulous spheres beyond were not comforting to the thoughts of the climber in the dark.

He had been ascending the lightless stairs for some time when he became aware of a strange feeling, as if he was about to suffer some terrible psychic displacement. There was no apparent reason why he should imagine such eldritch ideas, but it seemed as though he was about to be dragged forth from his body, or fall into some bottomless charnel pit. Those strange hieroglyphic characters all seemed to be indicating something unseen around that ever-present bend in the passageway. Was it simply a trick of light or vision that there appeared to be no steps above a certain point, and nothing except a totally dark expanse which even his torch's light would not penetrate? He drew back in affright, but once again curiosity overcame disquiet, and he continued to ascend the stairs. Upon reaching that anomalous wall of blackness, he closed his eyes involuntarily and rose one more step into the unseen section of the passage beyond the barrier.

Armitage cried out as he fell on the steps at the other side. It was as if his body had been momentarily torn apart into atoms and recombined in an infinitesimal instant. The agony he had suffered had never registered on his brain, but there was a memory of unspeakable psychic torture, resembling a memory from another life. He now lay on stairs seemingly a continuation of the steps on the other side of the barrier, but different in several essential respects. For one thing, the others had been bare and worn away; these, however, were covered with mineral dust. The walls, too, were grown with small glistening fungi, obviously of a type not seen in sane places of the world, instead of the curious, sometimes disturbingly alien hieroglyphics.

When he had recovered from that indescribable sensation, Armitage continued up the stairs. Though he felt as if he had been changed physically in some non-visible way, he noticed that the torch, to which he had clung through all that unendurable instant, still lit when he pressed the stud. He held the torch out in front of him, the beam stretching out some five feet from the ground. He rounded the inevitable bend in the stairs, and shone the ray into a face.

What that face was like, and of what body it was the face, he does not dare to tell. There are certain things which are better known by no sane man. If the whole truth about certain cosmic relationships, and the implication of the beings which exist in certain spheres, were known by the world, the whole of the human race would be shrieking in terror and gibbering for oblivion. And the thing which Armitage saw at last—one of those hideous crustacean beings which had come through space from the rim-world—was one such cosmically terrible being. But even though his mind shrivelled up inside his skull at the unspeakable sight which leered and hopped before him in the light of the torch, Armitage had enough composure left to scream that painfully-sought incantation at the monstrosity. It seemed to cringe—though it was difficult to correlate the motions of something so grotesquely proportioned and abnormally shaped—and clattered off down the steps. As it reached that black barrier across the stairs, it seemed to grow infinitely huge and become something even more monstrous, before it shrank to an infinitesimal point on the ebony curtain and disappeared altogether, as the clattering claws became silent.

Reeling against the lichenous wall, Armitage attempted to forget that fungoid abomination which had burst on him around that corner. As his mind returned to equilibrium from that seething void of suspicion, he began to climb again, not thinking of what might yet lurk in the upper regions of the tower. The darkness now seemed even more material, as if at any moment it might close in on the hapless Armitage.

It was about the time that Armitage began to realise that he had been climbing the darkened stairway far longer than he should have in a thirty-foot tower, that he saw the ceiling of the tower. The nitrous, dripping rock seemed to meet the stairs with no means of exit, but almost immediately he saw the curiously-angled trapdoor where steps and ceiling met. Now came the time of ultimate hesitation. Why would a trapdoor open out onto a circular roof, thirty feet above the ground, of small diameter? What nameless terror might await the opening of the trapdoor? But, having come this far, he did not wish to pass through that barrier of agony without having glimpsed what might lie above. So he pushed the door open with his shoulders and stepped out on the roof.

Even in his lunacy, Armitage does not pretend to have a plausible explanation for certain aspects of his fantastic tale. He insists that the barrier across the passageway was not as meaningless as sanity would have it appear, and thinks it was in reality a barrier between points that should have been millions of miles apart, had it not been for some awful tampering with the structure of the cosmos. He seems to conjecture that the barrier changed him bodily—otherwise, according to his story, the circumstances in which he found himself would have led to asphyxiation and burst lungs with the first breath he took on that other side of the barrier. He explains that the abominations of the plateau did not capture him because he shrieked the incantation incessantly as he plunged down the tower's stairway and climbed back feverishly down the Devil's Steps. None of this may be disproved—and as for those disturbing hints concerning "bodily changes," X-ray examinations show certain modifications of the lungs and other organs for which the doctors cannot easily account.

As he clambered on the roof, Armitage wondered if the sight of that stunted horror on the stairs had already unhinged his mind. How could he not have noticed these towers which his torch's beams picked out on every side as far as its light would reach? And how could it now be black night, when he had reached the Devil's Steps well before midday? His torch, shining down the side of his vantage tower, showed black streets where abominable blasphemies moved among hideous gardens of those greyish nodding fungi and vast black windowless towers.

Confused and terrified, he stared out at the ebony void of space which stretched infinitely away from him, and of the crystalline, distorted stars which shimmered in the gulf. Then he stared again in growing, horrible realisation at those far-off constellations—and their positions. For the positions of the constellations were never seen thus on Earth; and Edward Wingate Armitage knew in that cataclysmic instant that this place of fungoid gardens and streets of windowless stone towers, whither he had come through that barrier between dimensions, was none other than Yuggoth.

Cold Print

*. . . for even the minions of Cthulhu dare not speak of Y'golonac;
yet the time will come when Y'golonac strides forth from the loneliness of aeons to walk once more among men. . . .*

—REVELATIONS OF GLAAKI,

VOLUME 12

Sam Strutt licked his fingers and wiped them on his handkerchief; his fingertips were grey with snow from the pole on the bus platform. Then he coaxed
his book out of the polythene bag on the seat beside him, withdrew the bus-
ticket from between the pages, held it against the cover to protect the latter
from his fingers, and began to read. As often happened the conductor
assumed that the ticket authorised Strutt's present journey; Strutt did not
enlighten him. Outside, the snow whirled down the side streets and slipped
beneath the wheels of cautious cars.

The slush splashed into his boots as he stepped down outside Brichester
Central and, snuggling the bag beneath his coat for extra safety, pushed his
way towards the bookstall, treading on the settling snowflakes. The glass
panels of the stall were not quite closed; snow had filtered through and
dulled the glossy paperbacks. "Look at that!" Strutt complained to a young
man who stood next to him and anxiously surveyed the crowd, drawing his
neck down inside his collar like a tortoise. "Isn't that disgusting? These
people just don't care!" The young man, still searching the wet faces,
agreed abstractedly. Strutt strode to the other counter of the stall, where
the assistant was handing out newspapers. "I say!" called Strutt. The assistant, sorting change for a customer, gestured him to wait. Over the paperbacks, through the steaming glass, Strutt watched the young man rush
forward and embrace a girl, then gently dry her face with a handkerchief.
Strutt glanced at the newspaper held by the man awaiting change. BRUTAL
MURDER IN RUINED CHURCH, he read; the previous night a body had been
found inside the roofless walls of a church in Lower Brichester; when the

snow had been cleared from this marble image, frightful mutilations had been revealed covering the corpse, oval mutilations which resembled— The man took the paper and his change away into the station. The assistant turned to Strutt with a smile: "Sorry to keep you waiting." "Yes," said Strutt. "Do you realise those books are getting snowed on? People may want to buy them, you know." "Do *you*?" the assistant replied. Strutt tightened his lips and turned back into the snow-filled gusts. Behind him he heard the ring of glass pane meeting pane.

GOOD BOOKS ON THE HIGHWAY provided shelter; he closed out the lashing sleet and stood taking stock. On the shelves the current titles showed their faces while the others turned their backs. Girls were giggling over comic Christmas cards; an unshaven man was swept in on a flake-edged blast and halted, staring around uneasily. Strutt clucked his tongue; tramps shouldn't be allowed in bookshops to soil the books. Glancing sideways to observe whether the man would bend back the covers or break the spines, Strutt moved among the shelves, but could not find what he sought. Chatting with the cashier, however, was an assistant who had praised *Last Exit to Brooklyn* to him when he had bought it last week, and had listened patiently to a list of Strutt's recent reading, though he had not seemed to recognise the titles. Strutt approached him and enquired "Hello—any more exciting books this week?"

The man faced him, puzzled. "Any more—?"

"You know, books like this?" Strutt held up his polythene bag to show the grey Ultimate Press cover of *The Caning-Master* by Hector Q.

"Ah, no. I don't think we have." He tapped his lip. "Except—Jean Genet?"

"Who? Oh, you mean *Jennet*. No, thanks, he's dull as ditch-water."

"Well, I'm sorry, sir, I'm afraid I can't help you."

"Oh." Strutt felt rebuffed. The man seemed not to recognise him, or perhaps he was pretending. Strutt had met his kind before and had them mutely patronise his reading. He scanned the shelves again, but no cover caught his eye. At the door he furtively unbuttoned his shirt to protect his book still further, and a hand fell on his arm. Lined with grime, the hand slid down to his and touched his bag. Strutt shook it off angrily and confronted the tramp.

"Wait a minute!" the man hissed. "Are you after more books like that? I know where we can get some."

This approach offended Strutt's self-righteous sense of reading books which had no right to be suppressed. He snatched the bag out of the fingers closing on it. "So you like them too, do you?"

"Oh, yes, I've got lots."

Strutt sprang his trap. "Such as?"

"Oh, *Adam and Evan, Take Me How You Like*, all the Harrison adventures, you know, there's lots."

Strutt grudgingly admitted that the man's offer seemed genuine. The assistant at the cash-desk was eyeing them; Strutt stared back. "All right," he said. "Where's this place you're talking about?"

The other took his arm and pulled him eagerly into the slanting snow. Clutching shut their collars, pedestrians were slipping between the cars as they waited for a skidded bus ahead to be removed; flakes were crushed into the corners of the windscreens by the wipers. The man dragged Strutt amid the horns which brayed and honked, then between two store windows from which girls watched smugly as they dressed headless figures, and down an alley. Strutt recognised the area as one which he vainly combed for back-street bookshops; disappointing alcoves of men's magazines, occasional hot pungent breaths from kitchens, cars fitted with caps of snow, loud pubs warm against the weather. Strutt's guide dodged into the doorway of a public bar to shake his coat; the white glaze cracked and fell from him. Strutt joined the man and adjusted the book in its bag, snuggled beneath his shirt. He stamped the crust loose from his boots, stopping when the other followed suit; he did not wish to be connected with the man even by such a trivial action. He looked with distaste at his companion, at his swollen nose through which he was now snorting back snot, at the stubble shifting on the cheeks as they inflated and the man blew on his trembling hands. Strutt had a horror of touching anyone who was not fastidious. Beyond the doorway flakes were already obscuring their footprints, and the man said "I get terrible thirsty walking fast like this."

"So that's the game, is it?" But the bookshop lay ahead. Strutt led the way into the bar and bought two pints from a colossal barmaid, her bosom bristling with ruffles, who billowed back and forth with glasses and worked the pumps with gusto. Old men sucked at pipes in vague alcoves, a radio blared marches, men clutching tankards aimed with jovial inaccuracy at dartboard or spittoon. Strutt flapped his overcoat and hung it next to him; the other retained his and stared into his beer. Determined not to talk, Strutt surveyed the murky mirrors which reflected gesticulating parties around littered tables not directly visible. But he was gradually surprised by the taciturnity of his table-mate; surely these people (he thought) were remarkably loquacious, in fact virtually impossible to silence? This was intolerable; sitting idly in an airless back-street bar when he could be on the move or reading—something must be done. He gulped down his beer and thumped the glass upon its mat.

The other started. Then, visibly abashed, he began to sip, seeming oddly nervous. At last it was obvious that he was dawdling over the froth, and he set down his glass and stared at it. "It looks as if it's time to go," said Strutt.

The man looked up; fear widened his eyes. "Christ, I'm wet," he muttered. "I'll take you again when the snow goes off."

"That's the game, is it?" Strutt shouted. In the mirrors, eyes sought him. "You don't get that drink out of me for nothing! I haven't come this far—!!"

The man swung round and back, trapped. "All right, all right, only maybe I won't find it in this weather."

Strutt found this remark too inane to comment. He rose and, buttoning his coat strode into the arcs of snow, glaring behind to ensure he was followed.

The last few shop-fronts, behind them pyramids of tins marked with misspelt placards, were cast out by lines of furtively curtained windows set in unrelieved vistas of red brick; behind the panes Christmas decorations hung like wreaths. Across the road, framed in a bedroom window, a middle-aged woman drew the curtains and hid the teenage boy at her shoulder. "Hel-*lo*, there they go," Strutt did not say; he felt he could control the figure ahead without speaking to him, and indeed had no desire to speak to the man as he halted trembling, no doubt from the cold, and hurried onward as Strutt, an inch taller than his five-and-a-half feet and better built, loomed behind him. For an instant, as a body of snow drove towards him down the street, flakes overexposing the landscape and cutting his cheeks like transitory razors of ice, Strutt yearned to speak, to tell of nights when he lay awake in his room, hearing the landlady's daughter being beaten by her father in the attic bedroom above, straining to catch muffled sounds through the creak of bedsprings, perhaps from the couple below. But the moment passed, swept away by the snow; the end of the street had opened, split by a traffic-island into two roads thickly draped with snow, one curling away to hide between the houses, the other short, attached to a roundabout. Now Strutt knew where he was. From a bus earlier in the week he had noticed the KEEP LEFT sign lying helpless on its back on the traffic-island, its face kicked in.

They crossed the roundabout, negotiated the crumbling lips of ruts full of deceptively glazed pools collecting behind the bulldozer treads of a redevelopment scheme, and onward through the whirling white to a patch of waste ground where a lone fireplace drank the snow. Strutt's guide scuttled into an alley and Strutt followed, intent on keeping close to the other as he knocked powdered snow from dustbin lids and flinched from backyard doors at which dogs clawed and snarled. The man dodged left, then right, between the close labyrinthine walls, among houses whose cruel edges of jagged windowpanes and thrusting askew doors even the snow, kinder to buildings than to their occupants, could not soften. A last turning, and the man slithered onto a pavement beside the remnants of a store, its front gaping emptily to frame wine-bottles abandoned beneath a HEIN 57 VARIET poster. A dollop of snow fell from the awning's skeleton to be swallowed by the drift below. The man shook, but as Strutt confronted him, pointed fearfully to the opposite pavement. "That's it, I've brought you here."

The tracks of slush splashed up Strutt's trouser legs as he ran across, checking mentally that while the man had tried to disorient him he had deduced which main road lay some five hundred yards away, then read the inscription over the shop: AMERICAN BOOKS BOUGHT AND SOLD. He touched a railing which protected an opaque window below street level, wet rust gritting beneath his nails, and surveyed the display in the window facing him: *History of the Rod*—a book he had found monotonous—thrusting out its shoulders among science-fiction novels by Aldiss, Tubb, and Harrison, which hid shamefacedly behind lurid covers; *Le Sadisme au Cinéma;* Robbe-Grillet's *Voyeur* looking lost; *The Naked Lunch*—nothing worth his journey there, Strutt thought. "All right, it's about time we went in," he urged the man inside, and with a glance up the eroded red brick at the first-floor window, the back of a dressing-table mirror shoved against it to replace one pane, entered also. The other had halted again, and for an unpleasant second Strutt's fingers brushed the man's musty overcoat. "Come on, where's the books?" he demanded, shoving past into the shop.

The yellow daylight was made murkier by the window display and the pin-up magazines hanging on the inside of the glass-panelled door; dust hung lazily in the stray beams. Strutt stopped to read the covers of paperbacks stuffed into cardboard boxes on one table, but the boxes contained only Westerns, fantasies, and American erotica, selling at half price. Grimacing at the books which stretched wide their corners like flowering petals, Strutt bypassed the hardcovers and squinted behind the counter, slightly preoccupied; as he had closed the door beneath its tongueless bell, he had imagined he had heard a cry somewhere near, quickly cut off. No doubt round here you hear that sort of thing all the time, he thought, and turned on the other. "Well, I don't see what I came for. Doesn't anybody work in this place?"

Wide-eyed, the man gazed past Strutt's shoulder; Strutt looked back and saw the frosted-glass panel of a door, one corner of the glass repaired with cardboard, black against a dim yellow light which filtered through the panel. The bookseller's office, presumably—had he heard Strutt's remark? Strutt confronted the door, ready to face impertinence. Then the man pushed by him, searching distractedly behind the counter, fumbling open a glass-fronted bookcase full of volumes in brown paper jackets and finally extracting a parcel in grey paper from its hiding-place in one corner of a shelf. He thrust it at Strutt, muttering "This is one, this is one," and watched, the skin beneath his eyes twitching, as Strutt tore off the paper.

The Secret Life of Wackford Squeers— "Ah, that's fine," Strutt approved, forgetting himself momentarily, and reached for his wallet; but greasy fingers clawed at his wrist. "Pay next time," the man pleaded. Strutt hesitated; could he get away with the book without paying? At that moment, a shadow rippled across the frosted glass: a headless man dragging something heavy. Decapitated by the frosted glass and by his hunched position, Strutt decided, then realised that the shopkeeper must be in contact with Ultimate Press; he must not prejudice this contact by stealing a book. He knocked away the frantic fingers and counted out two pounds; but the other backed away, stretching out his fingers in stark fear, and crouched against the office door from whose pane the silhouette had disappeared, before flinching almost into Strutt's arms. Strutt pushed him back and laid the notes in the space left on the shelf by *Wackford Squeers,* then turned on him. "Don't you intend to wrap it up? No, on second thoughts I'll do it myself."

The roller on the counter rumbled forth a streamer of brown paper; Strutt sought an undiscoloured stretch. As he parcelled the book, disentangling his feet from the rejected coil, something crashed to the floor. The other had retreated towards the street door until one dangling cuff-button had hooked the corner of a carton full of paperbacks; he froze above the scattered books, mouth and hands gaping wide, one foot atop an open novel like a broken moth, and around him motes floated into beams of light mottled by the sifting snow. Somewhere a lock clicked. Strutt breathed hard, taped the package and, circling the man in distaste, opened the door. The cold attacked his legs. He began to mount the steps and the other flurried in pursuit. The man's foot was on the doorstep when a heavy tread approached across the boards. The man spun about, and below Strutt the door slammed. Strutt waited; then it occurred to him that he could hurry and shake off his guide. He reached the street and a powdered breeze pecked at his cheeks, cleaning away the stale dust of the shop. He turned away his face and, kicking the rind of snow from the headline of a sodden newspaper, made for the main road which he knew to pass close by.

Strutt woke shivering. The neon sign outside the window of his flat, a cliché but relentless as toothache, was garishly defined against the night every five seconds, and by this and the shafts of cold Strutt knew that it was early morning. He closed his eyes again, but though his lids were hot and heavy his mind would not be lulled. Beyond the limits of his memory lurked the dream which had awoken him; he moved uneasily. For some reason he thought of a passage from the previous evening's reading: "As Adam reached the door he felt Evan's hand grip his, twisting his arm behind his back, forcing him to the floor—" His eyes opened and sought the bookcase as if for reassurance; yes, there was the book, secure within its covers, carefully aligned with its fellows. He recalled returning home one evening to find *Miss Whippe, Old-Style Governess,* thrust inside *Prefects and Fags,* straddled by *Prefects and Fags;* the landlady had explained that she must have replaced them wrongly after dusting, but Strutt knew that she had damaged them vindictively. He had bought a case that locked, and when she asked him for the key had replied "Thanks, I think I can do them justice." You couldn't make friends nowadays. He closed his eyes again; the room and bookcase, created in five seconds by the neon and destroyed with equal regularity, filled him with their emptiness, reminding him that weeks lay ahead before the beginning of next term, when he would confront the first class of the morning and add "You know me by now" to his usual introduction, "You play fair with me and I'll play fair with you," a warning which some boy would be sure to test, and Strutt would have him; he saw the expanse of white gym-short seat stretched tight down on which he would bring a gym-shoe with satisfying force—Strutt relaxed; soothed by an overwhelming echo of the pounding feet on the wooden gymnasium floor, the fevered shaking of the wall-bars as the boys swarmed ceilingwards and he stared up from below, he slept.

Panting, he drove himself through his morning exercises, then tossed off the fruit juice which was always his first call on the tray brought up by the landlady's daughter. Viciously he banged the glass back on the tray; the glass splintered (he'd say it was an accident; he paid enough rent to cover, he might as well get a little satisfaction for his money). "Bet you have a fab Christmas," the girl had said, surveying the room. He'd made to grab her round the waist and curb her pert femininity—but she'd already gone, her skirt's pleats whirling, leaving his stomach hotly knotted in anticipation.

Later he trudged to the supermarket. From several front gardens came the teeth-grinding scrape of spades clearing snow; these faded and were answered by the crushed squeak of snow engulfing boots. When he emerged from the supermarket clutching an armful of cans, a snowball whipped by his face to thud against the window, a translucent beard spreading down the pane like the fluid from the noses of those boys who felt Strutt's wrath most often, for he was determined to beat this ugliness, this revoltingness, out of them. Strutt glared about him for the marksman—a seven-year-old, boarding his tricycle for a quick retreat. Strutt moved involuntarily as if to pull the boy across his knee. But the street was not deserted; even now the child's mother, in slacks and curlers peeking from beneath a headscarf, was slapping her son's hand. "I've told you, *don't* do that. —Sorry," she called to Strutt. "Yes, I'm sure," he snarled, and tramped back to his flat. His heart pumped uncontrollably. He wished fervently that he could talk to someone as he had talked to the bookseller on the edge of Goatswood who had shared his urges; when the man had died earlier that year Strutt had felt abandoned in a tacitly conspiring, hostile world. Perhaps the new shop's owner might prove similarly sympathetic? Strutt hoped that the man who had conducted him there yesterday would not be in attendance, but if he was, surely he could be got rid of—a bookseller dealing with Ultimate Press must be a man after Strutt's own heart, who would be as opposed as he to that other's presence while they were talking frankly. As well as this discussion, Strutt needed books to read over Christmas, and *Squeers* would not last him long; the shop would scarcely be closed on Christmas Eve. Thus reassured, he unloaded the cans on the kitchen table and ran downstairs.

Strutt stepped from the bus in silence; the engine's throb was quickly muffled among the laden houses. The piled snow waited for some sound. He splashed through the tracks of cars to the pavement, its dull coat depressed by countless overlapping footprints. The road twisted slyly; as soon as the main road was out of sight the side street revealed its real character. The snow laid over the house-fronts became threadbare; rusty protrusions poked through. One or two windows showed Christmas trees, their ageing needles falling out, their branches tipped with luridly sputtering lights. Strutt, however, had no eye for this but kept his gaze on the pavement, seeking to avoid stains circled by dogs' pawmarks. Once he met the gaze of an old woman staring down at a point below her window which was perhaps the extent of her outside world. Momentarily chilled, he hurried on, pursued by a woman who, on the evidence within her pram, had given birth to a litter of newspapers, and halted before the shop.

Though the orange sky could scarcely have illuminated the interior, no electric gleam was visible through the magazines, and the torn notice hanging behind the grime might read CLOSED. Slowly Strutt descended the steps. The pram squealed by, the latest flakes spreading across the newspapers. Strutt stared at its inquisitive proprietor, turned and almost fell into sudden darkness. The door had opened and a figure blocked the doorway.

"You're not shut, surely?" Strutt's tongue tangled.

"Perhaps not. Can I help you?"

"I was here yesterday. Ultimate Press book," Strutt replied to the face level with his own and uncomfortably close.

"Of course you were, yes, I recall." The other swayed incessantly like an athlete limbering up, and his voice wavered constantly from bass to falsetto, dismaying Strutt. "Well, come in before the snow gets to you," the other said and slammed the door behind them, evoking a note from the ghost of the bell's tongue.

The bookseller—this was he, Strutt presumed—loomed behind him, a head taller; down in the half-light, among the vague vindictive corners of the tables, Strutt felt an obscure compulsion to assert himself somehow, and remarked "I hope you found the money for the book. Your man didn't seem to want me to pay. Some people would have taken him at his word."

"He's not with us today." The bookseller switched on the light inside his office. As his lined pouched face was lit up it seemed to grow; the eyes were sunk in sagging stars of wrinkles; the cheeks and forehead bulged from furrows; the head floated like a half-inflated balloon above the stuffed tweed suit. Beneath the unshaded bulb the walls pressed close, surrounding a battered desk from which overflowed fingerprinted copies of *The Bookseller* thrust aside by a black typewriter clogged with dirt, beside which lay a stub of sealing-wax and an open box of matches. Two chairs faced each other across the desk, and behind it was a closed door. Strutt seated himself before the desk, brushing dust to the floor. The bookseller paced round him and suddenly, as if struck by the question, demanded "Tell me, why d'you read these books?"

This was a question often aimed at Strutt by the English master in the staffroom until he had ceased to read his novels in the breaks. Its sudden reappearance caught him off guard, and he could only call on his old riposte. "How d'you mean, why? Why not?"

"I wasn't being critical," the other hurried on, moving restlessly around the desk. "I'm genuinely interested. I was going to make the point that don't you want what you read about to happen, in a sense?"

"Well, maybe." Strutt was suspicious of the trend of this discussion, and wished that he could dominate; his words seemed to plunge into the snow-cloaked silence inside the dusty walls to vanish immediately, leaving no impression.

"I mean this: when you read a book don't you make it happen before you, in your mind? Particularly if you consciously attempt to visualise, but that's not essential. You might cast the book away from you, of course. I knew a bookseller who worked on this theory; you don't get much time to be yourself in this sort of area, but when he could he worked on it, though he never quite formulated— Wait a minute, I'll show you something."

He leapt away from the desk and into the shop. Strutt wondered what was beyond the door behind the desk. He half rose but, peering back, saw the bookseller already returning through the drifting shadows with a volume extracted from among the Lovecrafts and Derleths.

"This ties in with your Ultimate Press books, really," the other said, banging the office door to as he entered. "They're publishing a book by Johannes Henricus Pott next year, so we hear, and that's concerned with forbidden lore as well, like this one; you'll no doubt be amazed to hear that they think they may have to leave some of Pott in the original Latin. This here should interest you, though; the only copy. You probably won't know the *Revelations of Glaaki*; it's a sort of Bible written under supernatural guidance. There were only eleven volumes—but this is the twelfth, written by a man at the top of Mercy Hill guided through his dreams." His voice grew unsteadier as he continued. "I don't know how it got out; I suppose the man's family may have found it in some attic after his death and thought it worth a few coppers, who knows? My bookseller—well, he knew of the *Revelations,* and he realised this was priceless; but he didn't want the seller to realise he had a find and perhaps take it to the library or the University, so he took it off his hands as part of a job lot and said he might use it for scribbling. When he read it— Well, there was one passage that for testing his theory looked like a godsend. Look."

The bookseller circled Strutt again and placed the book in his lap, his arms resting on Strutt's shoulders. Strutt compressed his lips and glanced up at the other's face; but some strength weakened, refusing to support his disapproval, and he opened the book. It was an old ledger, its hinges cracking, its yellowed pages covered by irregular lines of scrawny handwriting. Throughout the introductory monologue Strutt had been baffled; now the book was before him, it vaguely recalled those bundles of duplicated typewritten sheets which had been passed around the toilets in his adolescence. "Revelations" suggested the forbidden. Thus intrigued, he read at random. Up here in Lower Brichester the bare bulb defined each scrap of flaking paint on the door opposite, and hands moved on his shoulders, but somewhere down below he would be pursued through darkness by vast soft footsteps; when he turned to look, a swollen glowing figure was upon him— What was all this about? A hand gripped his left shoulder and the right hand turned pages; finally one finger underlined a phrase:

Beyond a gulf in the subterranean night a passage leads to a wall of massive bricks, and beyond the wall rises Y'golonac to be served by the tattered eyeless figures of the dark. Long has he slept beyond the wall, and those which crawl over the bricks scuttle across his body never knowing it to be Y'golonac; but when his name is spoken or read he comes forth to be worshipped or to feed and take on the shape and soul of those he feeds upon. For those who read of evil and search for its form within their minds call forth evil, and so may Y'golonac return to walk among men and await that time when the earth is cleared off and Cthulhu rises from his tomb among the weeds, Glaaki thrusts open the crystal trapdoor, the brood of Eihort are born into daylight, Shub-Niggurath strides forth to smash the moon-lens, Byatis bursts forth from his prison, Daoloth tears away illusion to expose the reality concealed behind.

The hands on his shoulders shifted constantly, slackening and tightening. The voice fluctuated. "What did you think of that?"

Strutt thought it was rubbish, but somewhere his courage had slipped; he replied unevenly "Well, it's—not the sort of thing you see on sale."

"You found it interesting?" The voice was deepening; now it was an overwhelming bass. The other swung round behind the desk; he seemed taller— his head struck the bulb, setting shadows peering from the corners and withdrawing, and peering again. "You're interested?" His expression was intense, as far as it could be made out; for the light moved darkness in the hollows of his face, as if the bone structure were melting visibly.

In the murk in Strutt's mind appeared a suspicion; had he not heard from his dear dead friend the Goatswood bookseller that a black magic cult existed in Brichester, a circle of young men dominated by somebody Franklin or Franklyn? Was he being interviewed for this? "I wouldn't say that," he countered.

"Listen. There was a bookseller who read this, and I told him you may be the high priest of Y'golonac. You will call down the shapes of night to worship him at the times of year; you will prostrate yourself before him and in return you will survive when the earth is cleared off for the Great Old Ones; you will go beyond the rim to what stirs out of the light. . . ."

Before he could consider Strutt blurted "Are you talking about me?" He had realised he was alone in a room with a madman.

"No, no, I meant the bookseller. But the offer now is for you."

"Well, I'm sorry, I've got other things to do." Strutt prepared to stand up.

"He refused also." The timbre of the voice grated in Strutt's ears. "I had to kill him."

Strutt froze. How did one treat the insane? Pacify them. "Now, now, hold on a minute. . . ."

"How can it benefit you to doubt? I have more proof at my disposal than you could bear. You will be my high priest, or you will never leave this room."

For the first time in his life, as the shadows between the harsh oppressive walls moved slower as if anticipating, Strutt battled to control an emotion; he subdued his mingled fear and ire with calm. "If you don't mind, I've got to meet somebody."

"Not when your fulfilment lies here between these walls." The voice was thickening. "You know I killed the bookseller—it was in your papers. He fled into the ruined church, but I caught him with my hands. . . . Then I left the book in the shop to be read, but the only one who picked it up by mistake was the man who brought you here. . . . Fool! He went mad and cowered in the corner when he saw the mouths! I kept him because I thought he might bring some of his friends who wallow in physical taboos and lose the true experiences, those places forbidden to the spirit. But he only contacted you and brought you here while I was feeding. There is food occasionally; young boys who come here for books in secret; they make sure nobody knows what they read!—and can be persuaded to look at the *Revelations*. Imbecile! He can no longer betray me with his fumbling—but I knew you would return. Now you will be mine."

Strutt's teeth ground together silently until he thought his jaws would break; he stood up, nodding, and handed the volume of the *Revelations* towards the figure; he was poised, and when the hand closed on the ledger he would dart for the office door.

"You can't get out, you know; it's locked." The bookseller rocked on his feet, but did not start towards him; the shadows now were mercilessly clear and dust hung in the silence. "You're not afraid—you look too calculating. Is it possible that you still do not believe? All right"—he laid his hands on the doorknob behind the desk—"do you want to see what is left of my food?"

A door opened in Strutt's mind, and he recoiled from what might lie beyond. "No! No!" he shrieked. Fury followed his involuntary display of fear; he wished he had a cane to subjugate the figure taunting him. Judging by the face, he thought, the bulges filling the tweed suit must be of fat; if they should struggle, Strutt would win. "Let's get this clear," he shouted, "we've played games long enough! You'll let me out of here or I—" but he found himself glaring about for a weapon. Suddenly he thought of the book still in his hand. He snatched the matchbox from the desk, behind which the figure watched, ominously impassive. Strutt struck a match, then pinched the boards between finger and thumb and shook out the pages. "I'll burn this book!" he threatened.

The figure tensed, and Strutt went cold with fear of his next move. He touched the flame to paper, and the pages curled and were consumed so swiftly that Strutt had only the impression of bright fire and shadows growing unsteadily massive on the walls before he was shaking ashes to the floor. For a moment they faced each other, immobile. After the flames a darkness had rushed into Strutt's eyes. Through it he saw the tweed tear loudly as the figure expanded.

Strutt threw himself against the office door, which resisted. He drew back his fist, and watched with an odd timeless detachment as it shattered the frosted glass; the act seemed to isolate him, as if suspending all action outside himself. Through the knives of glass, on which gleamed drops of blood, he saw the snowflakes settle through the amber light, infinitely far; too far to call for help. A horror filled him of being overpowered from behind. From the back of the office came a sound; Strutt spun and as he did so closed his eyes, terrified to face the source of such a sound—but when he opened them he saw why the shadow on the frosted pane yesterday had been headless, and he screamed. As the desk was thrust aside by the towering naked figure, on whose surface still hung rags of the tweed suit, Strutt's last thought was an unbelieving conviction that this was happening because he had read the *Revelations;* somewhere, someone had *wanted* this to happen to him. It wasn't playing fair, he hadn't done anything to deserve this—but before he could scream out his protest his breath was cut off, as the hands descended on his face and the wet red mouths opened in their palms.

The Scar

"It was most odd on the bus today," Lindsay Rice said.

Jack Rossiter threw his cigarette into the fire and lit another. His wife Harriet glanced at him uneasily; she could see he was in no mood for her brother's circumlocutions.

"Most odd," said Lindsay. "Rather upsetting, in fact. It reminded me, the Germans—now was it the Germans? Yes, I think it was the Germans—used to have this thing about doppelgängers, the idea being that if you saw your double it meant you were going to die. But of course you didn't see him. That's right, of course, I should explain."

Jack moved in his armchair. "I'm sorry, Lindsay," he interrupted, "I just don't see where you're tending. I'm sorry."

"It's all right, Lindsay," Harriet said. "Jack's been a bit tired lately. Go on."

But at that moment the children tumbled into the room like pierrots, their striped pyjamas bold against the pastel lines of wallpaper. "Douglas tried to throw me into the bath, and he hasn't brushed his teeth!" Elaine shouted triumphantly.

"There'll be spankings for two in a minute," Jack threatened, but he smiled. "Good night, darling. Good night, darling. No, you've had a hard day, darling, I'll put them to bed."

"Not so hard as you," Harriet said, standing up. "You stay and talk to Lindsay."

Jack grimaced inwardly; he had wanted Harriet to rest, but somehow it now appeared as if he'd been trying to escape Lindsay. "Sorry, Lindsay, you were saying?" he prompted as the thumping on the staircase ceased.

"Oh, yes, on the bus. Well, it was this morning, I saw someone who looked like you. I was going to speak to him until I realised." Rice glanced around the room; although his weekly invitation was of some years' standing, he could never remember exactly where everything was. Not that it mattered: the whole was solid. Armchairs, television, bookcase full of Penguins and book-club editions and Shorrock's *Valuer's Manual*—there it was, on top of the bookcase, the wedding photograph which Jack had carefully framed for Harriet. "Yes, he was as thin as you've been getting, but he had a scar from here to here." Rice encompassed his left temple and jawbone with finger and thumb like dividers.

"So he wasn't really my double. My time hasn't run out after all."

"Well, I hope not!" Rice laughed a little too long; Jack felt his mouth stretching as he forced it to be sociable. "We've been slackening off at the office," Rice said. "How are things at the jeweller's? Nothing stolen yet, I hope?"

"No, everything's under control," Jack replied. Feet ran across the floor above. "Hang on, Lindsay," he said, "sounds like Harriet's having trouble."

Harriet had quelled the rebellion when he arrived; she closed the door of the children's room and regarded him. "Christ, the man's tact!" he exploded.

"Shh, Jack, he'll hear you." She put her arms around him. "Don't be cruel to Lindsay," she pleaded. "You know I always had the best of everything and Lindsay never did—unhappy at school, always being put down by my father, never daring to open his mouth—darling, you know he finds it difficult to talk to people. Now I've got you. Surely we can spare him kindness at least."

"Of course we can." He stroked her hair. "It's just that—damn it, not only does he say I'm losing weight as though I'm being underfed or something, but he asks me if the shop's been broken into yet!"

"Poor darling, don't worry. I'm sure the police will catch them before they raid the shop. And if not, there's always insurance."

"Yes, there's insurance, but it won't rebuild my display! Can't you understand I take as much pride in my shop as you take in the house? Probably some jumped-up little skinheads who throw the loot away once their tarty little teenyboppers have played with it!"

"That doesn't sound like you at all, Jack," Harriet said.

"I'm sorry, love. You know I'm really here. Come on, I'd better fix up tomorrow night with Lindsay."

"If you feel like a rest we could have him round here."

"No, he opens out a bit when he's in a pub. Besides, I like the walk to Lower Brichester."

"Just so long as you come back in one piece, my love."

Rice heard them on the stairs. He hurried back to his chair from the bookcase where he had been inspecting the titles. One of these days he must offer to lend them some books—anything to make them like him more. He knew he'd driven Jack upstairs. Why couldn't he be direct instead of circling the point like a wobbling whirligig? But every time he tried to grasp an intention or a statement it slid out of reach. Even if he hung a sign on his bedroom wall—he'd once thought of one: "I shall act directly"—he would forget it before he left the flat. Even as he forgot his musings when Jack and Harriet entered the room.

"I'd better be off," he said. "You never can tell with the last bus round here."

"I'll see you tomorrow night, then," Jack told him, patting his shoulder. "I'll call round and pick you up."

But he never had the courage to invite them to his flat, Lindsay thought; he knew it wasn't good enough for them. Not that they would show it— rather would they do everything to hide their feelings out of kindness, which would be worse. Tomorrow night as usual he would be downstairs early to wait for Jack in the doorway. He waved to them as they stood linked in their bright frame, then struck off down the empty road. The fields were grey and silent, and above the semidetached roofs the moon was set in a plush ring of cold November mist. At the bus-stop he thought: I wish I could do something for them so they'd be grateful to me.

Harriet was bending over the cooker; she heard no footsteps—she had no chance to turn before the newspaper was over her face.

"I see the old Jack's back with us," she said, fighting off the *Brichester Herald*.

"You haven't seen it?" He guided her hand to the headline: YOUTHS ARRESTED—ADMIT TO JEWEL THEFTS. He was beaming; he read the report again with Harriet, the three boys who'd hoped to stockpile jewellery but had been unable to market it without attracting the police. "Maybe now we can all get some sleep," he said. "Maybe I can give up smoking."

"Don't give it up for me, Jack, I know you need it. But if you *did* give it up I'd be very happy."

Douglas and Elaine appeared, pummelling towards their tea. "Now just you sit down and wait," Jack said, "or we'll eat it for you."

After tea he lit a cigarette, then glanced at Harriet. "Don't worry, darling," she advised. "Take things easy for a while. Come on, monsters, you can help clear up." She knew the signs—spilled sugar, dropped knife; Jack would turn hypertense with relief if he didn't rest.

But ten minutes later he was in the kitchen. "Must go," he said. "Give myself time for a stroll before I meet Lindsay. Anyway, the news ought to give the conversation a lift."

"Come back whole, darling," Harriet said, not knowing.

Yes, he liked to walk through Lower Brichester. He'd made the walk, with variations, for almost two years; ever since his night out drinking with Rice had settled into habit. It had been his suggestion, primarily to please Harriet, for he knew she liked to think he and Lindsay were friends; but by now he met Lindsay out of a sense of duty, which was rarely proof against annoyance as the evening wore on. Never mind, there was the walk. If he felt insecure, as he often did when walking—the night, Harriet elsewhere—he gained a paradoxical sense of security from Lower Brichester; the bleared fish-and-chip shop windows, the crowds outside pubs, a drunk punching someone's face with a soft moist sound—it reassured him to think that here was a level to which he could never be reduced.

Headlights blazed down a side street, billowing with mist and motorcycle fumes. They spotlighted a broken wall across the street from Rossiter; a group of girls huddled on the shattered bricks, laughing forth fog as the motorcycle gang fondled them roughly with words. Rossiter gazed at them; no doubt the jewel thieves had been of the same mould. He felt a little guilty as he watched the girls, embracing themselves to keep out the cold; but he had his answer ready—nothing would change them, they were fixed; if he had money, it was because he could use it properly. He turned onward; he would have to use the alley on the right if he were not to keep Rice waiting.

Suddenly the shrieks of laughter behind the roaring engines were cut off. A headlight was feeling its way along the walls, finding one house protruding part of a ruined frontage like a piece of jigsaw, the next dismally curtained, its neighbour shuttered with corrugated tin, its makeshift door torn down like an infuriating lid. For a moment the beam followed a figure: a man in a long black coat swaying along the pavement, a grey woollen sock pulled down over his face. The girls huddled closer, silently. Jack shuddered; the exploratory progress of the figure seemed unformed, undirected. Then the light was gone; the girls giggled in the darkness, and beyond a streetlamp the figure fumbled into the tin-shuttered house. Jack turned up his coat collar and hurried into the alley. The engines roared louder.

He was halfway up the alley when he heard the footsteps. The walls were narrow; there was barely room for the other, who seemed in a hurry, to pass. Jack pressed against the wall; it was cold and rough beneath his hand. Behind him the footsteps stopped.

He looked back. The entrance to the alley whirled with fumes, against which a figure moved towards him, vaguely outlined. It held something in its hand. Jack felt automatically for his lighter. Then the figure spoke.

"You're Jack Rossiter." The voice was soft and anonymous yet somehow penetrated the crescendi of the motorcycles. "I'll be visiting your shop soon."

For a moment Jack thought he must know the man, though his face was merely a black egg in the shadows; but something in the figure's slow approach warned him. Suddenly he knew what that remark implied. Cold rushed into his stomach, and metal glinted in the figure's hand. Jack retreated along the wall, his fingers searching frantically for a door. His foot tangled with an abandoned tin; he kicked it towards the figure and ran.

The fog boiled round him; metal clattered; a foot hooked his ankle and tripped him. The engines were screaming; as Jack raised his head a car's beam thrust into his eyes. He scrabbled at potato peelings and sardine tins, and struggled to his knees. A foot between his shoulders ground him down. The car's light dimmed and vanished. He struggled onto his back, cold peel sticking to his cheek, and the foot pressed on his heart. The metal closed in the figure's palm. Above him hands displayed the tin which he had kicked. The insidious voice said something. When the words reached him, Rossiter began to tear at the leg in horror and fury. The black egg bent nearer. The foot pressed harder, and the rusty lid of the tin came down towards Jack's face.

Though the bandage was off he could still feel the cut, blazing now and then from his temple to his jawbone. He forced himself to forget; he stuffed fuel into the living-room fire and opened his book. But it failed to soothe him. Don't brood, he told himself savagely, worse is probably happening in Lower Brichester at this moment. If only Harriet hadn't seen him unbandaged at the hospital! He could feel her pain more keenly than his own since he'd come home. He kept thinking of her letting the kettle scream so that he wouldn't hear her sobbing in the kitchen. Then she'd brought him coffee, her face still wet beneath her hair from water to wash away the tears. Why had he told her at the hospital "It's not what he did to me, it's what he said he'd do to Douglas and Elaine"? He cursed himself for spreading more suffering than he himself had had to stand. Even Rice had seemed to feel himself obscurely to blame, although Jack had insisted that it was his own fault for walking through that area.

"Go and say good-night to Daddy," Harriet called.

The children padded in. "Daddy's face is getting better," Elaine said.

He saw the black egg bearing down on them. God, he swore, if he should lay one finger—! "Daddy's surviving his accident," he told them. "Good night, children."

Presently he heard Harriet slowly descending the stairs, each step a thought. Suddenly she rushed into the room and hid her face on his chest. "Oh please, please, darling, what did he say about the children?" she cried.

"I won't have you disturbed, my love," he said, holding her as she trembled. "I can worry enough for both of us. And as long as you take them there and back to school, it doesn't matter what the sod said."

"And what about your shop?" she asked through her tears.

"Never mind the shop!" He tried not to think of his dream of the smashed window, of the foul disorder he might find one morning. "The police will find him, don't worry."

"But you couldn't even describe—" The doorbell rang. "Oh God, it's Lindsay," she said. "Could you go, darling? I can't let him see me like this."

"Oh, that's good—I mean I'm glad you've got the bandage off," said Lindsay. Behind him the fog swallowed the bedraggled trees and blotted out the fields. He stared at Jack, then muttered "Sorry, better let you close the door."

"Come in and get some fire," Jack said. "Harriet will have the coffee ready in a minute."

Rice plodded round the room, then sat down opposite Jack. He stared at the wedding photograph. He rubbed his hands and gazed at them. He looked up at the ceiling. At last he turned to Jack: "What"—he glanced around wildly—"what's that you're reading?"

"*The Heart of the Matter.* Second time, in fact. You should try it sometime."

Harriet looked in, dabbing at one eye. "Think I rubbed in some soap," she explained. "Hello, Lindsay. If we're talking about books, Jack, you said you'd read *The Lord of the Rings.*"

"Well, I can't now, darling, since I'm working tomorrow. Back to work at last, Lindsay. Heaven knows what sort of a state the shop will be in with Phillips in charge."

"You always said you could rely on him in an emergency," Harriet protested.

"Well, this is the test. Yes, white as usual for me, please, darling."

Harriet withdrew to the kitchen. "I read a book this week," Rice caught at the conversation, "about a man—what's his name, no, I forget—whose friend is in danger from someone, he finds out—and he finally pulls this someone off a cliff and gets killed himself." He was about to add "At least he did something with himself. I don't like books about people failing," but Jack took the cue:

"A little unrealistic for me," he said, "after what happened."

"Oh, I never asked," Rice's hands gripped each other, "where did it?"

"Just off the street parallel to yours, the next but two. In the alley."

"But that's where"—he lost something again—"where there's all sorts of violence."

"You shouldn't live so near it, Lindsay," Harriet said above a tray. "Make the effort. Move soon."

"Depressing night," Jack remarked as he helped Rice don his coat. "Drop that book in sometime, Lindsay. I'd like to read it."

Of course he wouldn't, Rice thought as he breathed in the curling fog and met the trees forming from the murk; he'd been trying to be kind. Rice had failed again. Why had he been unable to speak, to tell Jack that he had seen his double leave the bus and enter an abandoned house opposite that alley? The night of the mutilation Rice had waited in his doorway, feeling forsaken, sure that Jack had decided not to come; ashamed now, he blamed himself— Jack would be whole now if Rice hadn't made him feel it was his duty to meet him. Something was going to happen; he sensed it looming. If he could only warn them, prevent it—but prevent what? He saw the figures falling from the cliff-top against the azure sky, the seagulls screaming around him— but the mist hung about him miserably, stifling his intentions. He began to hurry to the bus-stop.

The week unfolded wearily. It was as formless in Rice's mind as the obscured fields when he walked up the Rossiters' street again, his book collecting droplets in his hand. He rang the bell and waited, shivering; the windows were blurred by mist.

"Oh, Lindsay," said Harriet. She had run to the door; it was clear she had been crying. "I don't know whether—"

Jack appeared in the hall, one hand possessively gripping the living-room door-frame, the cigarette upon his lip flaking down his shirt. "Is it your night already?" he demanded of Rice. "I thought it'd be early to bed for us. Come in, for God's sake, don't freeze us to death."

Harriet threw Lindsay a pleading look which he could not interpret. "Sorry," he said. "I didn't know you were tired."

"Who said tired? Come on, man, start thinking! God, I give up." Jack threw up his hands and whirled into the living-room.

"Lindsay, Jack's been having a terrible time. The shop was broken into last night."

"What's all that whispering?" a voice shouted. "Aren't I one of the family anymore?"

"Jack, don't be illogical. Surely Lindsay and I can talk." But she motioned Lindsay into the living-room.

"Treating me like a stranger in my own house!"

Lindsay dropped the book. Suddenly he realised what he'd seen: Jack's face was paler, thinner than last week; the scar looked older than seemed possible. He bent for the book. No, what he was thinking was absurd; Harriet would have noticed. Jack was simply worried. It must be worry.

"Brought me a book, have you? Let's see it, then. Oh, for God's sake, Lindsay, I can't waste my time with this sort of thing!"

"Jack!" cried Harriet. "Lindsay brought it specially."

"Don't pity Lindsay, he won't thank you for it. You think we're patronising you, don't you, Lindsay? Inviting you up the posh end of town?"

This couldn't be, Rice thought; not in this pastel living-room, not with the wedding photograph fixed forever; their lives were solid, not ephemeral like his own. "I—don't know what you mean," he faltered.

"Jack, I won't have you speaking to Lindsay like that," Harriet said. "Lindsay, would you help me make the coffee?"

"Siding with your brother now," Jack accused. "I don't need him at a time like this, I need you. You've forgotten the shop already, but I haven't. I suppose I needn't expect any comfort tonight."

"Oh, Jack, try and get a grip on yourself," but now her voice was softer. Don't! Lindsay warned her frantically. That's exactly what he wants!

"Take your book, Lindsay," Jack said through his fingers, "and make sure you're invited in future." Harriet glanced at him in anguish and hurried Lindsay out.

"I'm sorry you've been hurt, Lindsay," she said. "Of course you're always welcome here. You know we love you. Jack didn't mean it. I knew something would happen when I heard about the shop. Jack just ran out of it and didn't come back for hours. But I didn't know it would be like this—" Her voice broke. "Maybe you'd better not come again until Jack's more stable. I'll tell you when it's over. You do understand, don't you?"

"Of course, it doesn't matter," Lindsay said, trembling with formless thoughts. On the hall table a newspaper had been crumpled furiously; he saw the headline—JEWELLER'S RAIDED—DISPLAYS DESTROYED. "Can I have the paper?" he asked.

"Take it, please. I'll get in touch with you, I promise. Don't lose heart."

As the door closed Rice heard Jack call "Harriet!" in what sounded like despair. Above, the children were silhouetted on their bedroom window; as Rice trudged away the fog engulfed them. At the bus-stop he read the report; a window broken, destruction everywhere. He gazed ahead blindly. Shafts of bilious yellow pierced the fog, then the grey returned. "Start thinking," was it? Oh yes, he could think—think how easy it would be to fake a raid, knowing the insurance would rebuild what had been destroyed—but he didn't want the implications; the idea was insane, anyway. Who would destroy simply in order to have an excuse for appearing emaciated, unstable? But his thoughts returned to Harriet; he avoided thinking what might be happening in that house. You're jealous! he tried to tell himself. He's her husband! He has the right! Rice became aware that he was holding the book which he had brought for Jack. He stared at the tangled figures falling through blue drops of condensation, then thrust the book into the litter-bin between empty tins and a sherry bottle. He stood waiting in the fog.

The fog trickled through Rice's kitchen window. He leaned his weight on the sash, but again it refused to shut. He shrugged helplessly and tipped the beans into the saucepan. The tap dripped once; he gripped it and screwed it down. Below the window someone came out coughing and shattered something in the dustbin. The tap dripped. He moved towards it, and the bell rang.

It was Harriet in a headscarf. "Oh, don't come in," he said. "It's not fit, I mean—"

"Don't be silly, Lindsay," she told him edgily. "Let me in." Her eyes gathered details: the twiglike crack in one corner of the ceiling, the alarm clock whose hand had been amputated, the cobweb supporting the lamp-flex from the ceiling like a bracket. "But this is so depressing," she said. "Don't stay here, Lindsay. You must move."

"It's just the bed's not made," he tried to explain, but he could see her despairing. He had to turn the subject. "Jack all right?" he asked, then remembered, but too late.

She pulled off her headscarf. "Lindsay, he hasn't been himself since they wrecked the shop," she said with determined calm. "Rows all the time, breaking things—he broke our photograph. He goes out and gets drunk half the evenings. I've never seen him so irrational." Her voice faded. "And there are other things—that I can't tell you about—"

"That's awful. That's terrible." He couldn't bear to see Harriet like this; she was the only one he had ever loved. "Couldn't you get him to see someone, I mean—"

"We've already had a row about that. That was when he broke our photograph."

"How about the children? How's he been to them?" Instantly two pieces fitted together; he waited, chill with horror, for her answer.

"He tells them off for playing, but I can protect them."

How could she be so blind? "Suppose he should do something to them," he said. "You'll have to get out."

"That's one thing I won't do. He's my husband, Lindsay. It's up to me to look after him."

She can't believe that! Lindsay cried. He tottered on the edge of revelation, and fought with his tongue. "Don't you think he's acting as if he was a different person?" He could not be more explicit.

"After what happened that's not so surprising." She drew her headscarf through her fingers and pulled it back, drew and pulled, drew and pulled; Lindsay looked away. "He's left all the displays in Phillips' hands. He's breaking down, Lindsay. I've got to nurse him back. He'll survive, I know he will."

Survive! Lindsay thought with bitterness and horror. And suddenly he remembered that Harriet had been upstairs when he'd described his encounter on the bus; she would never realise, and his tongue would never allow him to tell her. Behind her compassion he sensed a terrible devotion to Jack which he could not break. She was as trapped as he was in this flat. Yet if he could not speak, he must act. The plan against him was clear: he'd been banished from the Rossiters' home, he was unable to protest, Harriet would be alone. There was only one false assumption in the plan, and it concerned himself. It must be false. He could help. He gazed at Harriet; she would never understand, but perhaps she needn't suspect.

The beans sputtered and smouldered in the pan. "Oh, Lindsay, I'm awfully sorry," Harriet said. "You must have your tea. I've got to get back before he comes home. I only called to tell you not to come round for a while. Please don't, I'll be all right."

"I'll stay away until you tell me," Lindsay lied. As she reached the hall he called out; he felt bound to make what would happen as easy as he could for her. "If anything should happen"—he fumbled— "you know, while Jack's— disturbed—I can always help to look after the children."

Rice could hear the children screaming from the end of the street. He began to walk towards the cries. He hadn't meant to go near the house; if his plan was to succeed, Harriet must not see him. Harriet—why wasn't she protecting the children? It couldn't be the Rossiters' house, he argued desperately; sounds like that couldn't reach the length of the street. But the cries continued, piercing with terror and pain; they dragged his footsteps nearer. He reached the house and could no longer doubt. The bedrooms were curtained, the house was impossibly impassive, reflecting no part of the horror within; the fog clung greyly to the grass like scum on reeds. He could hear Elaine sobbing something and then screaming. Rice wanted to break in, to stop the sounds, to discover what was holding Harriet back; but if he went in his plan would be destroyed. His palms prickled; he wavered miserably, and the silver pavement slithered beneath him.

The front door of the next house opened and a man—portly, red-faced, bespectacled, grey hair, black overcoat, valise clenched in his hand like a weapon—strode down the path, grinning at the screams. He passed Rice and turned at his aghast expression: "What's the matter, friend," he asked with amusement in his voice, "never have your behind tanned when you were a kid?"

"But listen to them!" Rice said unevenly. "They're *screaming!*"

"And I should damn well think so, too," the other retorted. "You know Jack Rossiter? Decent chap. About as much of a sadist as I am, and his kids ran in just now when we were having breakfast with some nonsense about their father doing something dreadful to them. I grabbed them by the scruff of their necks and dragged them back. One thing wrong with Rossiter—he was too soft with those kids, and I'm glad he seems to have learned some sense. Listen, you know who taught kids to tell tales on their parents? The bloody Nazis, that's who. There'll be no kids turning into bloody Nazis in this country if *I* can help it!"

He moved away, glancing back at Rice as if suspicious of him. The cries had faded; perhaps a door had closed. Stunned, Rice realised that he had been seen near the house; his plan was in danger. "Well, I mustn't waste any more time," he called, trying to sound casual, and hurried after the man. "I've got to catch my bus."

At the bus-stop, next to the man who was scanning the headlines and swearing, Rice watched the street for the figure he awaited, shivering with cold and indecision, his nostrils smarting with the faint stench of wet smoke. A bus arrived; his companion boarded. Rice stamped his feet and stared into the distance as if awaiting another; an inner critic told him he was overacting. When the bus had darkened and merged with fog, he retraced his steps. At the corner of the street he saw the fog solidify into a striding shape. The mist pulled back like web from the scarred face.

"Oh, Jack, can you spare a few minutes?" he said.

"Why, it's the prodigal brother-in-law!" came in a mist steaming from the mouth beside the scar. "I thought Harriet had warned you off? I'm in a hurry."

Again Rice was caught by a compulsion to rush into the house, to discover what had happened to Harriet. But there were the children to protect; he must make sure they would never scream again. "I thought I saw you—I mean, I did see you in Lower Brichester a few weeks ago," he said, feeling the fog obscuring security. "You were going into a ruined house."

"Who, me? It must have been my—" But the voice stopped; breath hung before his face.

Rice let his hatred drive out the words. "Your double? But then where did he go? Come on, I'll show you the house."

For a moment Rice doubted; perhaps the figure would laugh and stride into the mist. Ice sliced through his toes; he tottered and then plunged. "How did you make sure there was nobody about?" he forced through swollen lips. "When you got rid of him?"

The eyes flickered; the scar shifted. "Who, Phillips? God, man, I never did know what you meant half the time. He'll be wondering where I am—I'll have to think up a story to satisfy him."

"I think you'll be able to do that." Cold with fear as he was, Rice was still warmed by fulfilment as he sensed that he had the upper hand, that he was able to taunt as had the man on the cliff-top before the plunge. He plunged into the fog, knowing that now he would be followed.

The grey fields were abruptly blocked by a more solid anonymity, the streets of Lower Brichester, suffocating individuality, erasing it through generations. Whenever he'd walked through these streets with Jack on the short route to the pub each glance of Jack's had reminded him that he was part of this anonymity, this inertia. But no longer, he told himself. Signs of life were sparse: a postman cycled creaking by; beyond a window a radio announcer laughed; a cat curled among milk-bottles. The door was rolled down on a pinball arcade, and a girl in a cheap fur coat was leaping about in the doorway of a boutique to keep herself warm until the keys arrived. Rice felt eyes finger the girl, then revert to him; they had watched him since the beginning of the journey, although the figure seemed to face always forward. Rice glanced at the other; he was gazing in the direction of his stride, and a block of ice grew in Rice's stomach while the glazing of the pavement cracked beneath his feet.

They passed a square foundation enshrining a rusty pram; here a bomb had blown a house asunder. The next street, Rice realised, and dug his nails into the rubber of the torch in his pocket. The blitz had almost bypassed Brichester; here and there one passed from curtained windows to a gaping house, eventually rebuilt if in the town, neglected in Lower Brichester. Was this the key? Had someone been driven underground by blitz conditions, or had something been released by bombing? In either case, what form of camouflage would they have had to adopt to live? Rice thought he knew, but he didn't want to think it through; he wanted to put an end to it. And round a corner the abandoned house focused into view.

A car purred somewhere; the pavement was faintly numbered for hopscotch. Rice gazed about covertly; there must be nobody in sight. And at his side the figure did the same. Terrified, Rice yet had to repress a nervous giggle. "There's the house," he said. "I suppose you'll want to go in."

"If you've got something to show me." The scar wrinkled again.

Bricks were heaped in what had been the garden; ice glistened in their pores. Rice could see nothing through the windows, which were shuttered with tin. A grey corrugated sheet had been peeled back from the doorway; it scraped at Rice's ankle as he entered.

The light was dim; he gripped his torch. Above him a shattered skylight illuminated a staircase full of holes through which moist dust fell. To his right a door, one panel gouged out, still hung from a hinge. He hurried into the room, kicking a stray brick.

The fireplace gaped, half curtained by a hanging strip of wallpaper. Otherwise the room was bare, deserted probably for years. Of course the people of the neighbourhood didn't have to know exactly what was here to avoid it. In the hall tin rasped.

Rice ran into the kitchen, ahead on the left. Fog had penetrated a broken window; it filled his mouth as he panted. Opposite the cloven sink he saw a door. He wrenched it open, and in the other room the brick clattered.

Rice's hands were gloved in frozen iron; his nails were shards of ice thrust into the fingertips, melting into his blood. One hand clutched towards the back door. He tottered forward and heard the children scream, thought once of Harriet, saw the figures on the cliff. I'm not a hero! he mouthed. How in God's name did I get here? And the answer came: because he'd never really believed what he'd suspected. But the torch was shining, and he swung it down the steps beyond the open door.

They led into a cellar; bricks were scattered on the floor, bent knives and forks, soiled plates leading the torch-beam to tattered blankets huddled against the walls, hints of others in the shadows. And in one corner lay a man, surrounded by tins and a strip of corrugated metal.

The body glistened. Trembling, his mouth gaping at the stench which thickened the air, Rice descended, and the torch's circle shrank. The man in the corner was dressed in red. Rice moved nearer. With a shock he realised that the man was naked, shining with red paint which also marked the tins and strip of metal. Suddenly he wrenched away and retched.

For a moment he was engulfed by nausea; then he heard footsteps in the kitchen. His fingers burned like wax and blushed at their clumsiness, but he caught up a brick. "You've found what you expected, have you?" the voice called.

Rice reached the steps, and a figure loomed above him, blotting out the light. With studied calm it felt about in the kitchen and produced a strip of corrugated tin. "Fancy," it said, "I thought I'd have to bring you here to see Harriet. Now it'll have to be the other way round." Rice had no time to think; focusing his horror, fear and disgust with his lifetime of inaction, he threw the brick.

Rice was shaking by the time he had finished. He picked up the torch from the bottom step and as if compelled turned its beam on the two corpses. Yes, they were of the same stature—they would have been identical, except that the face of the first was an abstract crimson oval. Rice shuddered away from his fascination. He must see Harriet—it didn't matter what excuse he gave, illness or anything, so long as he saw her. He shone the beam towards the steps to light his way, and the torch was wrested from his hand.

He didn't think; he threw himself up the steps and into the kitchen. The bolts and lock on the back door had been rusted shut for years. Footsteps padded up the steps. He fell into the other room. Outside an ambulance howled its way to hospital. Almost tripping on the brick, he reached the hall. The ambulance's blue light flashed in the doorway and passed, and a figure with a grey sock covering its face blocked the doorway.

Rice backed away. No, he thought in despair, he couldn't fail now; the fall from the cliff had ended the menace. But already he knew. He backed into something soft, and a hand closed over his mouth. The figure plodded towards him; the grey wool sucked in and out. The figure was his height, his build. He heard himself saying "I can always help to look after the children." And as the figure grasped a brick he knew what face waited beneath the wool.

The Interloper

When Scott entered the classroom it was as if a vacuum-jar had been clamped over the class. Thirteen conversations were truncated; thirty boys stood, thirty folding seats slammed back; a geometry set crashed, scattered; John Norris coughed nervously, falsely, wondering if Scott had heard him saying seconds before to Dave Pierce "The Catacombs at lunchtime, then?" Scott's gaze froze about him. "All right, sit down," said Scott. "I don't want this period wasted." He sat. The congregation sat. Homework books were flurried open. John sensed Scott's haste, and pin-cushions grew in his palms; he thought of the solution on which everyone else agreed; he lived for the arrival of the Inspector in the afternoon, when Scott surely couldn't take it out of him.

"Answer to the first one. Robbins?" On the bus that morning, during breaks in the dawn game of musical window-seats, they'd compared solutions. ("What'd you get, Norris?" "34.5." "You sure? I had 17.31." "So did I." "Yes, I did too.") The pins stung. "Correct, x = 2.03 or −3.7. Anybody not get that? Any questions?" But nobody dared stand unless so ordered. "Next. Thomas?" Thomas stood, adjusted his homework, gave vent to a spurious sigh of desperate concentration. Scott drummed a stick of chalk, swept down in dusty robes on Thomas. "Come on, lad, you can't dither in an exam. 27.5 is the answer, isn't it?" Thomas beamed. "That's right, sir, of course." "No, it isn't, you blockhead!" Scott strode behind Thomas to peer at his homework, drove his knuckles into Thomas's kidney with an accuracy born of years of practice. "Wake your ideas up, lad! Fuller, can you show Thomas how to think?"

The exam in six months, possessing Scott with terrifying force. The Inspector's visit, driving Scott to fury at being subdued in the afternoon. Oh, God, John prayed, don't let him ask me question five. "That's it, Fuller. Go on, sit down, Thomas, we don't need you as class figurehead. Hawks, what have you got for the next one?" The class next door roared with laughter, Foghorn Ford must be taking them, the English master, John's favourite, who let him write poetry in class sometimes when he'd turned in particularly good homework. Silence. Laughter. John was jealous. Scott was behind him somewhere, pacing closer: "Come on, come *on*, Hawks!" Further down the corridor cracked the flat sound of a strap. Some of the masters you could come to terms with, like the art master; you had only to emulate the skunk to get rid of him. But Strutt, the gym master—he'd have your gym-shoe off for that. And you couldn't do much about Collins's geography class—"Spit" they called him, because sitting on his front row was like standing on a stormy promenade. Yet no class was so suffocated by fear as Scott's. One lunch-hour when John had been writing poetry Thomas had snatched his notebook and Scott had come in and confiscated it; when John had protested Scott had slapped his face. Dave Pierce had told John to protest to Foghorn Ford, but he hadn't had the courage. Next door Ford's class laughed. Further off the strap came down: *Whap!* Silence. Laughter. *Whap! Whap! WHAP!* John felt Dave's eyes on him, deploring. He turned to nod and Scott said "Norris!"

He stood. More moist pins stabbed. On the still air hung chalk and Scott's aftershave. "Yes, sir," he stammered.

"Yes, sir. The first time I repeat myself it has to be to you. Question five, Norris, question five!"

The Inspector. The Catacombs at lunchtime. Foghorn Ford always called him "Mr Norris." None of these could comfort him; fear twinged up from his bowels like wind. "34.5, sir?" he pleaded.

"Norris—Thomas I can understand, because he's an idiot, but you—I showed you how to do this one on the board yesterday. Don't tell me you weren't here."

"I was here, sir. I didn't understand, sir."

"You didn't understand, sir. You didn't ask, sir, did you? You were writing poetry about it, were you? Come out here." Scott cast his robes back; chalk whirled into the air.

John wanted to shut his eyes, but that wasn't permitted; the class was watching, willing him to represent them in the ritual without shaming them. Scott pulled John's left hand straight, adjusted it to correct height with the strap. He aimed. John's thumb closed inadvertently. Scott flicked it aside with the strap. The crowd was hushed, tense. The strap came down. John's hand swelled with hectic blood.

"Now, Pierce," said Scott. "I'm sure you can enlighten your friend."

A bell shrilled. Ford's class pelted to the playground, flattening against the wall to file as Scott approached. "Time for a drink, Ford?" he called. John averted his face as he passed, swollen with fear and hatred. "Scott's not too bad really," Dave Pierce said. "Better than that swine Ford, anyway, keeping me in last week."

Disloyal to his throbbing puffed-up palm, thought John bitterly. "Glad you think so," he muttered.

"Never mind, John. Did you hear this one? Two men go to a doctor, see—"

John could guess the sort of thing: he didn't like to hear it, couldn't join in the secret snigger at "Edgar Allan *Poe*," "oui-oui," and so on. "We'd better hurry," he interrupted. "You get past the gate and I'll be under the wall."

He strolled past the playground; boys walking, talking, shivering in the pale February light which might have been shed by the gnawed slice of moon on the horizon; a group in one corner huddled round photographs, another conferring over homework for the afternoon; beyond, on the misty playing-field, a few of Strutt's favourites running in gym-suits. On the bus that morning a man cradling a briefcase had offered to help John with his homework, but he was obscurely scared of strange men. He stood against the wall beyond the playground. When Dave's lunch pass flew over, he caught it and made for the gate.

A prefect leaned against the railings; he straightened himself, frowning, as befitted his position—one day a week for the school spirit, he'd rather be at the pub. Above his head words were scratched on the KING GEORGE V GRAMMAR sign through the caretaker's third coat of paint, in defiance of the headmaster's regular threats. John flashed the pass from his good hand and escaped.

Down the road Dave was waiting by fragments of a new school: a lone shining coffee-urn on a counter, pyramids of chairs, skulls drawn in white-wash on the one plate-glass pane; a plane had left a fading slash of white-wash on the sky. "How do we get to The Catacombs?" Dave asked.

"I don't know," John answered, feeling comfort drain, emptying the hour. "I thought you did."

Heels clicked by in unison. "Let's follow these girls, then. They're a bit of all right," Dave said. "They may be going."

John drew into himself; if they turned they'd laugh at his school blazer. Their pink coats swung, luring Dave; their perfume trailed behind them— The Catacombs would be thick with that and smoke. He followed Dave. The girls leapt across the road, running as if to jettison their legs, and were lost in a pillared pub between a shuttered betting-shop and the Co-operative Social Club. Dave was set to follow, but John heard drumming somewhere beneath the side street to their left. "It's up here," he said. "Come on, we've lost ten minutes already."

Cars on the main road swept past almost silently; in the side street they could hear beneath their feet a pounding drum, a blurred electric guitar. Somewhere down there were The Catacombs—but the walls betrayed no entrance to this converted cellar, reclaimed by the city in its blind subterranean search for space. Menace throbbed into the drum from the rhythm of John's hot hand. Spiders shifted somnolently in a white web wall within a crevice. A figure approached down the alley, a newspaper-seller with an armful of *Brichester Heralds,* his coat furred and patched as the walls. John drew back. The man passed in silence, one hand on the bricks. As he leaned on the wall opposite the boys it gave slightly; a door disguised as uneven stone swung inwards from its socket. The man levered himself onward.

"That must be it," Dave said, stepping forward.

"I'm not so sure." The man had reached the main road and was croaking *"Brichester Herald!"* John glanced back and saw the pub door open. Scott appeared and strode towards him.

"No," John said. He thrust Dave through the opening; his last glimpse was of Scott buying a *Brichester Herald.* "That was your friend Scott," he snarled at Dave.

"Well, it's not my fault." Dave pointed ahead, down a stone corridor leading to a faint blue light around a turn. "That must be The Catacombs."

"Are you sure?" John asked, walking. "The music's getting fainter. In fact, I can't hear it anymore."

"I couldn't really hear it anymore when we came in," Dave admitted. "Come on, it's got to be here." They rounded a turn.

A wan blue glow narrowed away into dimness. Slowly a perspective formed; a long stone passage, faintly glistening, too narrow to admit them abreast, perhaps turning in the distance—somehow lit by its own stones, luminously blue. It lured curiosity, yet John grasped Dave's arm. "This can't be it," he said. "We'd better not go on."

"I am, anyway. I want to see where it leads."

"Wait a minute," John said. "I just want to go back and see—" But he couldn't pronounce his inner turmoil. He was already frightened; they might get lost and not be back for Scott's class this afternoon. If Dave wanted to go on, let him. He was going back.

He turned the corner of the stagnant blue light and plunged into darkness. The moistness of the air hinted of lightless underground pools; the only sound was the sliding of his heels on slimy stone. He reached the wall ahead, the door. There was no door.

One fingernail, exploring, broke. He bit it off. His left hand, still sore, flinched from the wet unbroken stone. Suddenly alone and threatened, John fled back into the blue twilight, slipping in his own tracks. Dave was not waiting.

"Oh, God," John moaned. His eyes adjusted. Far down the perspective he made out a vague shape vanishing, its shadows suppressed by the unwavering light. He hurled himself into the corridor, arms scraping the stone, the archway hurling by above him, a turquoise spider plummeting on an azure thread, winding itself back. Globules beaded the brick; still plunging headlong, John brushed his forehead with his hand. Ahead the figure halted, waiting. "The door's shut. We can't get out," John panted, sobbing for breath.

"Then you'll have to come with me," Dave said. "There must be another way out of this place, whatever it is."

"But we're going downwards," John discovered.

"I know that. So we'll have to go up again somewhere. Maybe— Look!"

They were still walking; they had turned another bend. The passage twisted onward, glowing. John tried not to look at Dave; the light had drained his face of blood, and doubt glinted faintly in his eyes. On the stone floor wisps of cobweb, tinted blue, led to another turn. And in the left-hand wall Dave had seen an opening, foreshortened. He ran to it; John followed, robbed of The Catacombs, seeking a way back to Scott's next class, to the Inspector. Dave faced the opening, and the doubt in his eyes brightened.

It was an opening, but a dead end: an archway six feet high, a foot deep, empty except for filaments of cobweb which their breath sucked out to float and fall back. Dave peered in, and a spider as large as a thumb ran from a matted corner. He threw himself aside; but the spider was empty, rattling on the stone.

John had pressed past to the next bend. Another downward twist; another alcove. He waited for Dave to join him. The second alcove was thick with cobwebs; they filled it, shining dully, shifting as Dave again took the lead. The boys were running; the light congealed about them, the ceiling descended, threads of cobweb drifted down. A turn, an alcove, webs. Another. Glancing sideways, John was chilled by a formless horror; the cobwebs in the alcove suggested a shape which he should be able to distinguish. But another fear burned this away like acid: returning late for Scott's class. "Look, it's widening!" Dave shouted. Before John could see beyond him, they had toppled out into an open space.

It was a circular vaulted chamber; above their heads a dome shone blue through webs like clouds. In the walls gaped other archways, radiating from the circular pool in the centre of the chamber. The pool was still. Its surface was a beaded mat of cobwebs like a rotting jewelled veil. "I don't get it," Dave whispered; his voice settled through the air, disturbing shining airborne wisps. John said nothing. Then Dave touched his arm and pointed.

Beyond the pool, between two archways, stood a rack of clothes: hats, caps, a black overcoat, a tweed suit, a pinstripe with an incongruous orange handkerchief like a flag, a grey. They filled John with nightmare horror. "It must be a tramp," he said desperately.

"With all these things? I'm going to have a closer look." Dave moved round the pool.

"No, Dave, wait!" John skidded round the pool in pursuit; one foot slipped on the pool's rim. He looked down, and his reflection was caught by cobwebs, jewelled with droplets, swallowed up. His voice vanished into corridors. "It's past one now! You try one passage and I'll try another. One of them must lead out." Immediately he realised that he would be alone in his corridor among the matted alcoves; but at least he'd diverted Dave from the suits.

"That's the best idea, yes. Just wait till I have a look at these. It won't take a minute."

"You do that if you want to!" cried John. "I'm getting back!" He fell into the passage next to that through which they had entered; the first alcove was less than a minute ahead. He looked back miserably. Dave was peering at the suits. John forced himself over the harsh blue stone. Then Dave screamed.

John knew he had to run—but to Dave or away? He was too old for blind heroism, too young for conscious selflessness. His legs trembled; he felt sick. He turned.

Dave hadn't moved, but one suit lay crumpled at his feet. He was staring at what it had hung upon, too far for John to see in the blue haze. John's hand pulsed and perspired. He stretched out his fingers towards Dave as if to draw him forward; Dave's hands were warding off whatever was before him. John tore his feet free of the urge to flee. As he began to trudge forward, a figure moved between him and Dave. Cobwebs held to its shape like an aura. John recognised the profile and the patched coat. It was the newspaper-seller.

John struggled to shriek a warning to Dave—but of what? His lips were gummed shut as if by cobwebs. His legs were tied to the stone. The man moved round the pool, beyond John's vision. John's lips worked, and Dave turned. His mouth opened, but this time no scream came. He backed around the pool, past the suits. And something appeared, hopping towards him inside the patched overcoat: long arms with claws reaching far beyond the sleeves, a head protruding far above the collar, and from what must have been a mouth a pouring stream of white which drifted into the air and sank towards Dave's face as he fell, finally screaming. John clapped his hands over his ears as he ran towards the outside world, but Dave's screams had already been muffled.

As he fled past the first alcove, the web moaned feebly and opened a glazed eye. No more, he prayed, no more. Each turning was the last; each stretch was cruelly telescoped by the unrelenting light. His lungs were burning; each sucked breath drew a wisp of cobweb into his throat. In one alcove a girl's eyes pleaded; her hand stretched a wedding-ring towards him. He screamed to blot out her stifled cries. In answer came a sound of something hopping round a bend behind him, of something wet slapping the walls. A web-wisp brushed his cheek. He blundered onward. Another bend. He heaved around it hoarsely, and saw daylight.

The door was propped with an empty milk-bottle; someone had found and blocked it, perhaps meaning to return. He staggered out onto a patch of waste ground: a broken bed, a disembowelled car, a baby's rattle encrusted with mud. Reaching behind him, he wrenched out the bottle. The door became one with the earth. Then he fell face downwards on the bed.

Dave! He was down there in an alcove! John jerked to his feet, shivering. Through the slight drizzle he saw people passing, eyeing him oddly. He couldn't tell them; they might be from the pool. Someone had to know. Dave was in The Catacombs—no, in the catacombs. Someone. Where was he? He sidled to the pavement, watching them all, ready to scream if one came near. Up the road from the school, in the opposite direction to that they'd taken so long ago. Even further from home than he'd thought. Ford. He'd tell Ford that Dave was in The Catacombs. He made for the school; the tangled lines of rain on the pavement looked like something he'd forgotten.

Scott was waiting at the gate. He folded his arms as John appeared. John's terror kicked him in the stomach. Scott's lips opened, waiting; then his gaze slipped from John to someone behind him, and his expression altered. "All right, Norris, you'd better get to class," he said.

It was the Inspector! John thought as he hurried up the stairs to the familiar faces. He didn't know where Ford was—perhaps he could tell the Inspector that Dave was in The Catacombs. If Scott would let him. He'd have to—he was scared of the Inspector. "He's scared of the Inspector," he said to Dave. "What?" said Hawks behind him.

Scott and the Inspector entered; Scott held the door politely. The class stood, raising chalk-dust and a cobweb from John's blazer, which was grey with wisps, he saw. But then so was the Inspector's pinstripe suit: even the orange handkerchief in his top pocket. "Dave, sir—Mr. Ford—" cried John, and vomited into his open desk. "My God!" shouted Scott. "Please, Mr. Scott," said the Inspector in a voice light yet clinging as cobwebs, "the boy's ill. He looks frightened. I'll take him downstairs and arrange something for him."

"Shall I wait?" hissed Scott.

"Better start your class, Mr. Scott. I'll have time to find out all I want to know about them."

Bare corridors. Leaping tiles smelling of polish. A strap cracking. Somewhere, laughter. A headlong latecomer who gaped at John and the figure leading him by the wrist. The tuning of the school orchestra. The dining-room, bare tables, metal plates. The cloakroom, racks of coats stirring in a draught. "I don't think we can entrust you to anyone else's care," said the Inspector.

The gates, deserted. They turned towards the pillared pub, the side street. There was still time. The fingers on his wrist were no longer fingers. The eyes were veiled as the pool. Two women with wheel-baskets were approaching. But his mouth was already choked closed by fear. They passed on towards the side street. Yet his ears were clear, and he heard the comment one woman made.

"Did you see that? I'll wager another case of 'unwillingly to school'!"

The Guy

You can't hide from Guy Fawkes Night. This year as usual I played Beethoven's Fifth to blot out sound and memory, turned it loud and tried to read, fought back faces from the past as they appeared. In September and October the echoes of lone fireworks, the protests of distant startled dogs, the flopping faceless figures propped at bus-stops or wheeled in prams by children, had jarred into focus scenes I'd thought I had erased. Finally, as always, I stood up and succumbed. Walking, I saw memories, fading like the exploding molten claws upon the sky. On waste ground at the edge of Lower Brichester a gutted bonfire smouldered. Children stood about it, shaking sparklers as a dog shakes a rat. Then wood spat fire and flared; a man dragged off his boy to bed. Defined by flame, the child's face fell in upon itself like a pumpkin wizening from last week's Hallowe'en. He sobbed and gasped, but no words came. And I remembered.

A papier-mâché hand, a burning fuse, a scream that never came— But the memory was framed by the day's events; the houses of the past, my own and Joe Turner's, were overlaid by the picture I'd built up from behind my desk that morning, the imagined home of the boy who'd stood before me accused of setting fireworks in a car's exhaust pipe: drunken father, weak wife, back-garden lavatory, all the trimmings—I could see it clearly without having seen it. My parents hadn't liked my change of ambition from banker to probation officer; faced with the choice, I'd left them. "Don't you know they all carry razors these days?" my father had protested round his pipe. "Get yourself a little security. Then you can help them if you must. Look at your mother—don't you think the clothes she gives away mean anything?" Referred to, my mother had joined in. "If you deal with such people all day, Denis, you'll become like them." The same prejudices at which I'd squirmed when I was at school: when the Turners moved into our road.

Joe Turner was in the class next door to me; he'd started there that term when the Turners had come up from Lower Brichester. Sometimes, walking past their house, I'd heard arguments, the crash of china, a man's voice shouting "Just because we've moved in with the toffs, don't go turning my house into Buckingham Palace!" That was Mr Turner. One night I'd seen him staggering home, leaning on our gate and swearing; my father had been ready to go out to him, but my mother had restrained him. "Stay in, don't lower yourself." She was disgusted because Mr Turner was drunk; I'd realised that but couldn't see how this was different from the parties at our house, the Martini bottles, the man who'd fallen into my bedroom one night and apologised, then been loudly sick on the landing. I was sorry for Mr Turner because my parents had instantly disliked him. "I don't object to them as people. I don't know them, not that I want to," my father had said. "It's simply that they'll bring down the property values for the entire street if they're not watched." "Have you seen their back garden?" my mother responded. "Already they've dumped an old dresser out there." "Perhaps they're getting ready for a bonfire," I suggested. "Well, remember you've to stay away," my mother warned. "You're not to mix with such people." I was fourteen, ready to resent such prohibitions. And of course I was to have no bonfire; it might dull the house's paint or raze the garden. Instead, a Beethoven symphony for the collection I didn't then appreciate. "Why not?" I complained. "I go to school with him." "You may," my father agreed, "but just because the school sees fit to lower its standards doesn't mean we have to fall in with the crowd." "I don't see what's wrong with Joe," I said. A look spoke between my parents. "Someday," said my mother, "when you're older—"

There was always something about Joe they wouldn't specify. I thought I knew what they found objectionable; the acts schoolboys admire are usually deplored by their parents. Joe Turner's exploits had taken on the stature of legend for us. For example, the day he'd sworn at a teacher who'd caned him, paying interest on his words. "Some night I'll get him," Joe told me walking home, spitting further than I ever could. Or the magazines he showed us, stolen from his father as he said: he told terrifying stories of his father's buckled belt. "I Kept the U.S. Army Going," by a Fräulein; my vocabulary grew enormously in two months, until the only time my father ever hit me. I felt enriched by Joe; soon it was him and me against the teachers, running from the lavatories, hiding sticks of chalk. Joe knew things; the tales of Lower Brichester he told me as we walked home were real, not like the jokes the others told, sniggering in corners; Joe didn't have to creep into a corner to talk. In the two months since he'd run after me and parodied my suburban accent until we'd fought and become inseparable, he showed me sides of life I never knew existed. All of which helped me to understand the people who appear before my desk. Even the seat behind my desk belongs to Joe as much as to me; it was Joe who showed me injustice.

It was late October, two weeks before the bonfire, that fragments of the picture began to fit together. From my window, writing homework, I'd watched early rockets spit a last star and fall far off; once I'd found a cardboard cylinder trodden into the pavement. That was magic: not the Beethoven. So that when Joe said "I bet you won't be coming to my bonfire," I flared up readily. "Why shouldn't I?" I attacked him, throwing a stone into someone's garden.

"Because your parents don't like us." He threw a stone and cracked mine open.

"*We're* us," I said loyally. "I'll be coming. What's the matter, don't you like it up here in Brichester?"

"It's all right. My father didn't want to move. I couldn't care less, really. It was my mother. She was scared."

I imagined I knew what he meant: stones through the front windows, boys backing girls into alleys, knives and bottles outside the pubs; I'd probably have been as scared. But he continued "She didn't want to live where my brother was."

We ran from a stretched rain and stood beneath an inscribed bus-shelter; two housewives disapproved of us and brought umbrellas down like shields. "Where's your brother now? In the Army?" In those days that was my idea of heroism.

"He was younger than me. He's dead." The umbrellas lifted a little, then determinedly came down.

"Hell." I wasn't equipped to deal with such things. "What happened?" I asked, curiosity intermixed with sympathy.

"Of course only ill-brought-up boys try to impress with made-up stories," came from beneath the umbrellas.

Joe made a sign at them in which I hurriedly joined. We went out into the thinning lines of drizzle. I didn't like to ask again; I waited for Joe to take me into his trust. But he was silent until he reached our road, suburban villas pronged with TV aerials, curtains drawn back to display front-room riches. "You won't really come to my bonfire," he repeated suddenly: his eyes gleamed like the murderer's in the film we'd surreptitiously seen last Saturday, luring the girl towards his camera with its built-in spike.

"See if I don't."

"Well, I'd better say good-bye now. You won't want to be seen near your house with me."

"You watch this!" I shouted angrily, and strode with him arm in arm to his door. Joe beat on the knocker, which hung by a screw. "You're not coming in, are you?" he asked.

"If you've no objection." The door opened and Joe's mother appeared, patched jumper, encircled eyes and curlers: she saw me and frowned. "I'm Joe's friend," I tried to ingratiate myself.

"I didn't know he had any up this end." But she closed the door behind us. "Your father's not feeling well," she told Joe.

"Who's that?" a man's voice roared beyond the hall, the ancient coatstand where an overcoat hung by a ragged tag, the banister wrenched dangerously by some unsteady passage. "Is that Joe just come in? Have you been spilling paraffin round the house, you little bastard?"

Joe's mother glanced at him and winced, then hurried with Joe towards the voice. Left alone, I followed. Vests hung in the kitchen; Mr Turner sat in vest and braces at the table with his feet up, spitting into the sink, a Guinness at his side. "Of course he hasn't, Fred," she intervened unevenly.

"Then it's you," her husband shouted at her. "You've got that trunk hidden somewhere. I'll find it and fix it for good, my girl, don't you worry. I heard them moving round in there last night."

"Oh, my God," Mrs Turner muttered. "Shut up, will you, shut up, shut up. . . ."

Her husband snarled at her, tried to stand up, raised a foot and thumped it on the table. "You watch out, my girl," he threatened. Then he noticed me in the doorway. "Who the bloody hell's that?" he yelled.

"A friend of Joe's. I'll make some tea," she told me, trying to ignore her husband's mumbling.

"I'll do it," Joe said; he seemed anxious to please.

"No, it's all right. You go and talk to your friend."

"I'll help you carry it in."

"Don't bother. I can manage." She looked at Joe strangely, I couldn't tell why: I know now she was scared.

"How much bloody tea do you think we've got in this house?" Mr Turner bawled. "Every little bastard Joe brings home gets a free meal, is that what you think?" I'd become the victim and I didn't like it; I looked at Joe and his mother in turn, attempting to convey my regret for having been a witness, for my incomprehension, for fleeing, for everything. Then I escaped from the misshapen house.

In the next week our walks home were jagged with silence, the unspoken. I said no more about Joe's brother; nor did he. The bonfire approached, and

I waited to be invited again; I felt that my experience in Joe's house had rendered our friendship unstable. Meanwhile, each night as I worked in my bedroom, hissing trails of sparks explored the sky; distant shots resounded like warfare. One night, a week before Guy Fawkes, I abandoned my history homework in the middle of a sentence, stared round my room, at my father's inherited *Children's Encyclopaedia* beneath my Army posters, and stood up to gaze from the window. Three gardens from mine I could see the Turners'; during the day they had built their bonfire. The moon was up; it gleamed in a greenhouse like eyes. On top of the bonfire, above a toilet seat and piled planks like a gutted roof, stood the guy. Its arms were crucified across its wooden body; it swayed in a breeze. Its head turned back and forth beneath the moon; its paper face lifted to me. There was something horrible about that featureless grey expanse, as if eyes which should have been watching me were not. I drew back from the window and opened my door, for downstairs I'd heard my father say "—paraffin."

"To have a bonfire after that," my mother said; a glass clinked. "It's unfeeling. They're like animals."

"Hold on now, it wasn't ever proved," said my father. "You can't condemn someone without a fair trial."

"I know. You've only got to look at him. I know."

"Well, we'll agree to differ. Remind me tomorrow, I must buy that Beethoven."

Nothing about a trunk. In a far garden a ball of fire leapt up screaming. I picked up my history sentence, and next day, drop-kicking a can to Joe, I said "What was your brother called?"

"Frankie." Savagely he kicked the can against a bus-stop. I wanted to trust him. "You never did tell me what happened," I prompted.

His eyes fastened on the can; they glazed with fear, distrust, the look I've seen before my desk when I've enquired into family backgrounds. He strode exaggeratedly to the can and crumpled it beneath his heel. Suddenly he muttered "We had a bonfire. It was going out. My father got a can of paraffin and we threw it on the fire. It spilled on Frankie. We called an ambulance, but they didn't come in time."

I was silent; it hadn't helped my trust. "I bet they all think we're cruel round here, having a bonfire this year," Joe said.

"They don't know anything about it. Anyway, you're not," I told him. I couldn't repeat what my parents had said: I wasn't ready to oppose them.

"It was my mother's idea to have one this year. I think she wants to make me forget." Or somehow to prove to herself that she was wrong to suspect:

not that I made this connection then. "I don't want to have a bonfire all by myself," Joe continued.

"You won't. I'll be there," I said. Some part of me trusted him.

At dinner on Guy Fawkes Night, after my usual taste of table wine, I told my parents "They've let us off homework tonight," which was true. "I'm going to see *The Bridge on the River Kwai* with some friends from school," which wasn't.

"I don't see why not," my mother said. "Joe Turner won't be there, will he?"

"No, he won't." He wouldn't.

"You won't have time to listen to this, then," my father said, reaching beneath *The Times* on the coffee table to produce Beethoven's Seventh. For a moment I was ashamed: they trusted me, they bought me presents, and I betrayed them. But they condemned Joe without ever having met him. I knew Joe; I'd seen how withdrawn his parents were from him; tonight he'd be alone if I didn't keep my word. "Thanks very much," I said, and took the record to my room.

Night had fallen; curtains glowed and shadows moved. I glanced back, but my parents weren't watching. Again I felt a twinge of shame. In the sky around me it had started; green stars sparkled blue and fell; the twinkling blue star of an ambulance swept past. I stood before the Turners' door. Mr Turner swearing, drinking; I didn't want to face that. Once more I was ashamed; if Joe could stand him, it was up to me to do so for Joe's sake. I knocked.

Mr Turner pulled the door from my grasp. "Oh, it's you," he said, falling against the door-frame, hooking his braces over his shoulder. I half expected him to close me out, but he seemed triumphant about something. "I'm not the bloody butler," he said. "Come in or don't, it's all the same to me."

I heard voices in the front room; I entered. Joe was on the floor, counting out fireworks: volcanoes, worms, wheels, stiff-tailed rockets. Around him stood boys I'd never seen before; one had a headscarved girl on his arm and was fondling her. I knew they were from Lower Brichester. I looked at Joe, waiting to be greeted. "There you are," he said, glancing up. "These are some of my friends from where I used to live."

I felt out of place, no longer important, in a sense betrayed; I'd thought it would be Joe and me. But it was his home; it wasn't my place to judge—already I'd determined not to harden prejudice as my parents had. I tried to smile at the girl. She stared back; I suppressed my suburban accent. Ill at ease, I stood near the door, peering into the hall as Mrs Turner came downstairs. Her eyes were red; she'd been crying. She confronted her husband in the kitchen, out of sight. "Well, now you've built your bonfire, aren't you going out to watch?" she demanded.

"It was your idea, not mine, my girl. I'm not getting dressed to go out and play with all his little bastards. I've done my bit for the bonfire," he laughed.

"You're scared," she taunted. "Scared that you might see something."

"Not me, my girl. Not anymore. I'm not going to hear them moving about anymore."

"What are you saying?" she cried, suddenly audibly afraid—and Joe said "Wake up, everyone, time to start." We carried fireworks through the kitchen; Mr Turner's feet were on the table, he lay back with his eyes closed, smiling; his wife turned from him to us with a kind of desperation. A vest dripped on me.

The gravel path was strewn with twigs; what had been a flower-bed was now waste, heaped with wood. The girl tacked Catherine wheels to the fence; the boys staked out the soil with Guinness bottles, thrusting a rocket into each mouth. I glanced up at the bonfire against the arcs of fire among the stars, remembering the wooden figure like a witch's skeleton at the stake. "Where's the guy?" I asked Joe.

"Come on, you lot, who's got the guy?" Joe called. But everyone protested ignorance. We went back into the kitchen. "Has anyone seen our guy?" Joe asked.

"Someone must have stolen it," his mother said uneasily. "You'd think up this way they'd know better."

"After I dressed it up, too," his father mumbled, and turned quickly to his Guinness.

We searched upstairs, though I couldn't see why. Nothing beneath a rumpled double bed but curlers. Joe's room featured a battle of wooden model aeroplanes and a sharp smell of glue like paraffin. One room was an attic: dusty mirrors, footballs, boots, fractured chair-leg. Behind two mirrors I found a trunk whose lock had been forced. I opened it without thinking, but it was empty. "The hell with it," Joe said finally. "It's the fireworks they've all come for, anyway."

The girl had set one wheel whirling, spurting sparks. They lit up Mrs Turner's face staring from the kitchen window before she moved away; her husband's eyes were closed, his mouth open and wheezing. Joe took a match and bent to the bonfire; fire raced up a privet twig. Above us hands of fire dulled against the night. One of the boys sent a rocket whooping into space; its falling sparks left dents of darkness on my eyes. I had no matches; I approached the boy and asked for one. He passed me a handful. Beyond the fire, now angled with planes of flame, the girl was giggling with her escort. I struck a match on my sole and counted: "Ten, nine, eight, seven, six—" when the rocket leapt. I'd forgotten to muffle my accent, but nobody cared. I was happy.

The girl came back with her escort from a region where chimneys were limned on fans of white electric fire. "The bonfire's going out," said Joe. I gave him some of my matches. Red-hot flecks spun through the smoke and vanished; the smoke clogged our nostrils—it would be catarrh in the morning.

Over the houses rose a red star. It hung steady, dazzling, eternal. Our gasps and cheers were silenced. The white house-walls turned red, like cardboard in a fire about to flame. As suddenly, the star sank and was extinguished; in another garden someone clapped. Everything was dimmed; Joe felt his way to the bonfire and struck matches.

Someone stood up from the corner of the house and moved behind me. I looked round, but the face was grey and formless after the star. A hand touched my arm; it seemed light as paper. The figure moved towards Joe. My sleeve was wet. I lifted it to my nose and sniffed; it was stained with paraffin. I might have called out if Joe's mother hadn't screamed.

Everyone but Joe turned startled to the kitchen. Mr Turner stirred and stared at her. "You must be bloody off your nut," he snarled, "waking me like that."

"Frankie's clothes!" she cried, trying to claw at his face. "What have you done with them?"

"I told you I'd find your trunk, my girl," he laughed, beating her off. "I thought I'd do something for the bonfire, like dressing up the guy."

She sat down at the table and sobbed. Everyone was watching aghast, embarrassed. Our eyes were readjusting; we could see each other's red-hot faces. Suddenly, terrified, I looked towards Joe. He was kneeling by the bonfire, thrusting matches deep. My eyes searched the shadows. Near the hedge stood a Guinness bottle which should have held a rocket. Desperately, I searched beyond. A figure was creeping along the hedge towards Joe. As I discovered it, it leapt.

Joe twisted round, still kneeling, as it reached him. The fire caught; fear flared from Joe's face. His mouth gaped; so did mine as I struggled to call the others, still watching the kitchen. The figure wore trousers and a blazer, but its hands— My tongue trembled in my mouth. I caught at one boy's arm, but he pulled away. Joe's head went back; he overbalanced, clawing at the earth. The rocket plunged into his mouth; the figure's other hand fell on the bonfire. Flames blazed through its arms, down to the rocket's fuse.

The brick dug into my face; I'd clapped my hands over my ears and pressed my head against the wall. The girl ran screaming into the house. I couldn't leave the wall until I understood. Which is why each pebble is embedded in my forehead: I never left that wall. Perhaps subconsciously Joe had meant to spill the paraffin; who knows? But why had his father given it to him? Perhaps Joe had wanted it to happen, but what justice demanded that revenge? I reject it, still searching for the truth in each face before my desk while I work to release them from backgrounds like my own and Joe Turner's. The office tomorrow, thank God.

When the strongest of us went unwillingly towards what lay by the bonfire, away from the screams and shouting in the kitchen and the smoking Guinness bottles, we found a papier-mâché hand.

The End of a Summer's Day

"Don't sit there, missus," the guide shouted, *"you'll get your knickers wet!"*

Maria leapt from the stone at the entrance to the cave. She felt degraded; she saw the others laugh at her and follow the guide—the boisterous couple whose laughter she'd heard the length of the bus, the weak pale spinster led by the bearded woman who'd scoffed at the faltering Chinese in front, the others anonymous as the murmur bouncing from the bus roof like bees. She wouldn't follow; she'd preserve her dignity, hold herself apart from them. Then Tony gripped her hand, strengthening her. She glanced back once at the sunlight on the vast hillside tufted with trees, the birds cast down like leaves by the wind above the hamburger stall, and let him lead her.

Into blindness. The guide's torch was cut off around a corner. Below the railed walk they could sense the river rushing from the sunlight. Tony pulled her blouse aside and kissed her shoulder. Maria Thornton, she whispered as an invocation, Maria Thornton. Good-bye, Maria West, good-bye forever. The river thrust into blind tunnels.

They hurried towards the echoing laughter. In a dark niche between two ridged stalactites they saw a couple: the girl's head was back, gulping as at water, their heads rotated on the axis of their mouths like planets in the darkness. For a moment Maria was chilled; it took her back to the coach—the pane through which she'd sometimes stared had been bleared by hair-cream from some past kiss. She touched what for a long time she couldn't bring herself to name: they'd finally decided on Tony's "manhood." On the bus she'd caressed him for reassurance, as the bearded woman's taunts and the Chinese gropings grew in her ears; nobody had noticed. "Tony Thornton," she intoned as a charm.

A light fanned out from the tunnel ahead; the tallow stalactites gleamed. "Come on, missus," the guide called, "slap him down!"

The party had gathered in a vault; someone lit a cigarette and threw the match into the river, where it hissed and died among hamburger-papers. "I am come here to holiday," the Chinese told anyone who'd listen.

"Isn't it marvellous?" the bearded woman chortled, ignoring the spinster pulling at her hand. "Listen, Chinky, you've come here *on* holiday, right? *On* holiday. You'd think English wasn't good enough for him," she shouted.

"Oh, Tony, I hate this," Maria whispered, hanging back.

"No need to, darling. She's compensating for fear of ridicule and he's temporarily rootless. He'll be back home soon," he said, squeezing her hand, strong as stone but not hard or cold.

"Come on, you lot," the guide urged them on, holding his torch high. "I don't want to lose you all. I brought up last week's party only yesterday."

"Oh, God! Oh, hoo hoo hoo!" shrieked the boisterous couple, spilling mirth. "Hey, mate, don't leave me alone with him!" screamed the wife.

The party was drawn forward by a shifting ring of light, torn by stalactites like tusks. Behind her Maria heard the couple from the niche whisper and embrace. She kissed Tony hungrily. One night they'd eaten in a dingy café: dog-eared tablecloths, congealed ketchup, waitresses wiping plates on serviettes. At another table she'd watched a couple eat, legs touching. "She's probably his mistress," Tony had said in her ear; gently he showed her such things, which previously she'd wanted to ignore. "Do you want me to be your mistress, Tony?" she'd said, half-laughing, half-yearning, instantly ashamed—but his face had opened. "No, Maria, I want you to be my wife."

Deep in shade a blind face with drooping lips of tallow mouthed. Peering upwards, Maria saw them everywhere: the cave walls were like those childhood puzzle-pictures which once had frightened her, forests from whose trees faces formed like dryads. She clung to Tony's arm. When they were engaged she'd agreed to holiday with him; they'd settled for coach-trips, memories to which they had returned for their honeymoon. One day, nine months ago, they'd left the coach and found a tower above the sea; they'd run through the hot sand and climbed. At the top they'd gazed out on the sea on which gulls floated like leaves, and Tony had said "I like the perfume." "It's lavender-water," she'd replied, and suddenly burst into tears. "Oh, Tony, lavender-water, like a spinster! I can't cook, I take ages to get ready, I'll be no good in bed—I'm meant to be a spinster!" But he'd raised her face and met her eyes; above them pigeons were shaken out from the tower like handkerchiefs. "Let me prove you're not a spinster," he said.

The guide carried his torch across a subterranean bridge; beneath in the black water, he strode like an inverted Christ. The faces of the party peered from the river and were swept glittering away. "Now, all of you just listen for a moment," the guide said, on the other side. "I don't advise anyone to come down here without me. If it rains this river rises as far as that roof." He pointed. But now, when he should be grave, his voice still grinned. "I don't like him," Maria whispered. "You couldn't rely on him if anything happened. I'm glad you're here, Tony." His hand closed on hers. "It can't last forever," he told her. She knew he was thinking of the hotel, and laid her head against his shoulder.

"So long as the roof doesn't *cave in!*" yelled the boisterous man.

"Cave in!" the guide shouted, resonating from the walls; the faces above gave no sign that they'd heard. "Ha, ha, very good! Must remember that one." He poured his torch-beam into a low tunnel and ushered them onward. Behind her on the bridge Maria heard the couple from the niche. She lifted her head from Tony's shoulder. Thinking of the hotel—the first pain had faded, but in the darkness of their bedroom Tony seemed to leave her; the weight on her body, the thrust inside her, the hands exploring blindly, were no longer Tony. Yet she wasn't ready to leave the light on. Even afterwards, as they lay quiet, bodies touching trustingly, she never felt that peace which releases the tongue, enabling her to tell him what she felt. Often she dreamed of the tower above the sea; one day they'd return there and she'd be wholly his at last.

The vault was vast. The walls curved up like ribs, fanged with dislocated teeth about to salivate and close. Behind her, emerging from the tunnel, the other couple gasped. Stalactites thrust from the roof like inverted Oriental turrets or hung like giant candles ready to drip. The walls held back from the torch-beam; Maria sensed the faces. In the depths dripped laughter. The party clustered like moths around the exploring torch. "Come on, lovebirds, come closer," the guide echoed. "I've brought thirty of you down and I don't want to have to fiddle my inventory." Maria thrust her fingers between Tony's and moved forward, staying at the edge of light.

"Now before we go on I want to warn you all," the guide said sinisterly. "Was anybody here in the blackout? Not you, missus, I don't believe it! That's your father you're with, isn't it, not your husband!" The boisterous woman spluttered. "Even if you were," the guide continued, "you've never seen complete darkness. There's no such thing on God's earth. Of course that doesn't apply down here. You see?" He switched off the torch.

Darkness caved in on them. Maria lost Tony's hand and, groping found it. "Oh, God! Where was Moses!" yelled the boisterous couple. The young girl from the niche giggled. Somewhere, it seemed across a universe, a cigarette glowed. Whispers settled through the blackness. Maria's hand clenched on Tony's; she was back in the bedroom, blind, yearning for the tower above the sea.

"I hope we haven't lost anyone," the guide's face said, lit from below like a waxwork. "That's it for today. I hope someone knows the way out, that's all." He waved the torch to draw the procession. Laughing silhouettes made for the tunnel. Maria still felt afraid of the figure in the dark; she pulled Tony towards the torch. Suddenly she was ashamed, and turned to kiss him. The man whose hand she was holding was not Tony.

Maria fell back. As the light's edge drew away, the face went out. "Tony!" she cried, and ran towards the tunnel.

"Wait," the man called. "Don't leave me. I can't see."

The guide returned; figures crawled from the tunnel like insects, drawn by the light. "Don't be too long, lovebirds," he complained. "I've got another party in an hour."

"My husband," Maria said unevenly. "I've lost him. Please find him for me."

"Don't tell me he's run out on you!" Behind the guide the party had re-formed within the vault; Maria searched the faces shaken by the roving torch-beam, but none of them was Tony's. "There he is, missus!" the guide said, pointing. "Were you going to leave him behind?"

Maria turned joyfully; he was pointing at the man behind her. The man was moving back and forth in shadow, arms outstretched. The torch-beam touched his face, and she saw why. He was blind.

"That's not my husband," Maria said, holding her voice in check.

"Looks like him to me, love. That your wife, mate?" Then he saw the man's eyes. His voice hardened. "Come on," he told Maria, "you'd better look after him."

"Is husband?" the Chinese said. "Is not husband? No."

"What's that, mate?" asked the guide—but the bearded woman shouted "Don't listen to the Chink, he can't even speak our language! You saw them together, didn't you?" she prompted, gripping her companion's arm.

"I can't say I did," the spinster said.

"Of course you did! They were sitting right behind us!"

"Well, maybe I did," the spinster admitted.

"Just fancy," the boisterous woman said, "bringing a blind man on a trip like this! Cruel, I call it."

Maria was surrounded by stone faces, mouthing words which her blood swept from her ears. She turned desperately to the vault, the man stumbling in a circle, the darkness beyond which anything might lie. "Please," she pleaded, "someone must have seen my husband? My Tony?" Faces gaped from the walls and ceiling, lines leading off into the depths. "You were behind us," she cried to the girl from the niche. "Didn't you see?"

"I don't know," the girl mused. "He doesn't look the right build to me."

"You know he isn't!" Maria cried, her hands grasping darkness. "His clothes are wrong! Please help me look for Tony!"

"Don't get involved," the girl's escort hissed. "You can see how she is."

"I think we've all had enough," the guide said. "Are you going to take care of him or not?"

"Just let me have your torch for a minute," Maria sobbed.

"Now I couldn't do that, could I? Suppose you dropped it?"

Maria stretched her hand towards the torch, still torn by hope, and a hand fumbled into hers. It was the blind man. "I don't like all this noise," he said. "Whoever you are, please help me."

"There you are," the guide rebuked, "now you've upset him. Show's over. Everybody out." And he lit up the gaping tunnel.

"Wonder what she'd have done with the torch?" "The blind leading the blind, if you ask me," voices chattered in the passage. The guide helped the blind man through the mouth. Maria, left inside the vault, began to walk into the darkness, arms outstretched to Tony, but immediately the dark was rent and the guide had caught her arm. "Now then, none of that," he threatened. "Listen, I brought thirty down and thirty's what I've got. Be a good girl and think about that."

He shoved her out of the tunnel. The blind man was surrounded. "Here she is," said someone. "Now you'll be all right." Maria shuddered. "I'll take him if you don't feel well," the guide said, suddenly solicitous. But they'd led the blind man forward and closed his hand on hers. The guide moved to the head of the party; the tunnel mouth darkened, was swallowed. "Tony!" Maria screamed, hearing only her own echo. "Don't," the blind man pleaded piteously.

She heard the river sweep beneath the bridge, choked with darkness, erasing Tony Thornton. For a moment she could have thrust the blind man into the gulf and run back to the vault. But his hand gripped hers with the ruthlessness of need. Around her faces laughed and melted as the torch passed. They'd conspired, she told herself, to make away with Tony and to bring this other forth. She must fall in with them; they could leave her dead in some side tunnel. She looked down into the river and saw the sightless eyes beside her, unaware of her.

The guide's torch failed. Daylight flooded down the hillside just beyond. Anonymous figures chewed and waited at the hamburger-stall. "All right, let's make sure everybody's here," the guide said. "I don't like the look of that sky." He counted; faces turned to her; the guide's gaze passed over her and hurried onward. At her back the cave opened inviting, protective. "Where are we?" the blind man asked feebly. "It feels like summer."

Maria thought of the coach-trip ahead; the Chinese and the girl unsure but unwilling to speak, the bearded woman looking back to disapprove of her, the boisterous couple discussing her audibly—and deep in the caves Tony, perhaps unconscious, perhaps crawling over stone, calling out to her in darkness. She thought she heard him cry her name; it might have been a bird on the hill. The guide was waiting; the party shuffled, impatient. Suddenly she pushed the blind man forward; he stumbled out into the summer day. The others muttered protests; the guide called out—but she was running headlong into darkness, the last glint of sunlight broken by her tears like the sea beneath the tower, the river rushing by beneath. As the light vanished, she heard the first faint patter of the rain.

The Man in the Underpass

I'm Lynn. I'm nearly eleven. I was born in Liverpool, in Tuebrook.
I go to Tuebrook County Primary School. This year I've been taking my
little brother Jim to the Infants. Every morning we walk to school. It's only
six hundred yards away. I know that because our class had to find out for
Mrs Chandler for a project. We cross one street and then walk up Buckingham Road. At the end we go down the underpass under West Derby Road.
My little brother calls it underpants. And then just at the other end, there's
the school.

The underpass is what my story's all about.

It isn't very high, my best friend June's big sister can touch the roof without jumping. In the roof there are long lights like ice chopped up. That's
what Mrs Chandler means when she says something is a nice image. Usually
some of the lights are broken, and there are plugs hanging down like buds.
When you walk through you can hear the traffic overhead, it feels as if your
ears are shaking when buses drive over. When we were little we used to stand
in the middle so the buses would make our ears tickle. And we used to shout
and make ghosty noises because then it sounded like a cave.

Then the skinheads started to wait for the little kids in the underpass, so
they got a lollipop man to cross us over and we weren't supposed to go
down. Sometimes we did, because some of the traffic wouldn't stop for the
lollipop man and we wanted to watch our programmes on TV. Then the lady
in the greengrocer's would tell on us and we got spanked. I think we're too
old to be spanked. June would cry when she was spanked, because she's a bit
of a little kid sometimes. So we stopped going down until the skinheads went
somewhere else. June's big sister says they're all taking LSD now.

When we could go down again it wasn't like the same place. They'd been
spraying paint all over the walls. The walls used to be white, but now they
were like the advertisements you see at the films, when the colours keep
changing and dazzling you. They were green and gold and pink like lipstick
and white and grey and blood-red. They were words we wouldn't say at

home, like tits, and all the things skinheads say. Like "TUEBROOK SKINS RULE OK," only they'd painted it over twice, so it was as if something was wrong with your eyes.

June and I were reading everything on the way to school when Tonia came down. She lives in the next street from me, with her father. She used to go to St John the Evangelist, but now she goes to Tuebrook County Primary with us. June doesn't like her because she says Tonia thinks she's better than us and knows more. She never comes round to play with me, but I think she's lonely and her mother doesn't live with them, only a lady who stays with them sometimes. I heard that in the sweetshop before the sweetshop lady started nodding to tell them I was there. Anyway, Tonia started acting shocked at the things they'd painted on the walls. "I don't think you should let your little brother see these things. They aren't good for him." Jim's seen our mother and father with no clothes on, but June said "Oh, come on, Lynn. We weren't looking anyway, only playing," and she pretended to pee at Tonia, and we ran off.

Tonia was nearly late for assembly. She'd been looking at the man painted on the wall where the underpass dips in the middle. Mrs Chandler smiled at her but didn't say anything. If it had been us she'd have pretended to be cross, but she wouldn't really mind if we laughed, because she likes us laughing. I suppose Tonia must have been looking at the man on the wall because she hadn't seen anything like him before, she was flushed and biting her lip and smiling at the same time. My story's about him too, in a funny way, at least I think it is. He was as tall as the roof, and his spout was sticking up almost as far as his chin. Someone had painted him in white—really they'd just drawn round him, but then someone else had written on the wall, so he was full of colours. He'd got one foot on each side of the drain in the middle of the underpass, that the gutter runs down to. Jim said the man was going to pee, so I had to tell him he wouldn't be going to pee when his spout's like that.

Anyway, that was the day Mrs Chandler told us the theatre group was coming to do a play for us. June said "Are they going to make us laugh?" and Mrs Chandler said "Oh yes, they'll shout at you if you don't laugh." Then we had to write about our parents. I like writing about people, but June likes writing about football and music best. Tonia suddenly started crying and tore up her paper, so Mrs Chandler had to put her arms round her and talk to her, but we couldn't hear what she was saying. June got jealous and kept asking Mrs Chandler things, so Mrs Chandler put her in charge of the mice's cage all week.

When we got home Tonia stayed behind in the playground. I saw her go into the underpass, but the last time I looked she hadn't come out. My mother was still at Bingo, and Jim was crying so I smacked him, then I had to make him a fried egg so he'd stop. When my father came in he said "Should have made me one as well. You're a lot better housewife than," and he stopped. But my mother had won and gave him half, so he didn't shout at her.

After tea I went to the wine shop to get them some crisps. Jim sat on the railings at the top of the underpass and was seeing how far he could lean back holding on with his heels, so I had to run out and smack him. I broke my arm when I was little, doing that on the railings. Then I saw Tonia coming out of the underpass. "Haven't you had your tea yet?" I said. She must have been in a mood, because she got all red and said "I've had my dinner, if that's what you mean. We have it exactly the same time every day, if you must know. You don't think I've been down there all this time, do you?" I do try to make friends with her, but it's hard.

The next afternoon we had the play. There were five people in it, three men and two women. It was very good, and everyone laughed. I liked the part best when one of the men has to be the moon, so he has a torch and tries to get into it to be the man in the moon. They borrowed Mrs Chandler's guitar, that she brings when we have singing, and they all sang at the end and we pretended to throw money, then they threw sweets for us. I told Mrs Chandler I liked it, and she said it was from *A Midsummer Night's Dream* because it was nearly midsummer. I said I'd like to read it, so she said to ask for it at the library.

Then it was time to go home, and June asked one of the actors to cross her over the road. She told him he'd got a lovely face. Well, he had, but it's just like June to say something like that. She's bold sometimes. She said "Oh, and this is Lynn. She's my best friend, so you can talk to her too." I think she wanted him to come on his own, but he called the others to look at the colours in the underpass. So we all went down there instead. I saw Tonia watching us, and she looked as if she was going to cry, as if we'd found her special hiding-place or something, then she ran after us.

They all started shouting and gasping like little kids watching fireworks. "Look at the figure in the middle. It's almost a work of art," one of the women said. "Ebsolutely Eztec," a man said. I don't think he really talked like that, he was just trying to be funny. Tonia pulled at the one with the lovely face and said, "What does he mean?" "He means Aztec, love," he said. "I'm not your love," Tonia said. The man looked upset, because he was only being friendly, but he spelt Aztec for her. "Just the place for a midsummer sacrifice," one of the men said. "I don't think the Aztecs were bothered about seasons. They cut hearts out all the year round," another one said. Then they all walked us home and said we should try to start a youth theatre with Mrs Chandler. But Tonia stayed in the underpass.

The next day I went to the library after school. It's a nice place, except they chase you if you mess even a little bit. The librarian has a red face and shouts at the little kids if they don't understand what he means, and doesn't like showing you where the books are. But the girls are nice, and they'll talk to you and look for books for you. I got *A Midsummer Night's Dream* out. I didn't really understand it, except for the funny parts we saw at school. I'd like Mrs Chandler to help me with it, but I think she'd be too busy. I can read it again when I'm older.

I saw Tonia's father when I was there. He was getting a book about Aztecs for her. He said it was for a project. She must have told him that. It's stupid, because she could have told the truth. The librarian got him a book out of the men's library. "This will probably be a bit advanced for her," he said. Tonia's father started shouting. "Don't talk about what you don't know. She's an extremely intelligent child. I've had more than enough of that sort of comment at home." The librarian was getting redder and redder, and he saw me looking, so I ran out.

Next morning Tonia brought the book to school. "I've got something to show you," she told June and me. Then she heard Mrs Chandler coming, so she hid the book in her desk. She could have shown her, Mrs Chandler would have been interested. At playtime she brought it out with her. We all had to crowd round her so the teachers wouldn't see. There were pictures of Aztec statues that looked like the floors you see in really old buildings. And there were some drawings, like the ones little kids do, funny but you aren't supposed to laugh. Some of them had no clothes on. "Don't let everyone see," Tonia said. "I don't know what you're worried about. They don't worry us," I said, because the way she was showing us made the pictures seem dirty, though they weren't really. It was like a picture of Jesus we used to giggle at when we were little, because he was only wearing a cloth. I suppose she never used to play doctors and nurses, so she couldn't have seen anything, like the man in the underpass.

When we went out to play at dinnertime she brought the book again. She started reading bits out of it, about the Aztecs using pee for dyeing clothes, and eating dogs and burning people and cutting their hearts out and eating them. She said one part meant that when they made a sacrifice their gods would appear. "No it doesn't," June said. "They were just men dressed up."

"Well, it does," Tonia said. "The gods came and walked among them." "You're the best reader, Lynn. You say what it says," June said. Actually June was right, but Tonia was biting her lip and I didn't want to be mean, so I said she was right. June wouldn't speak to me when we walked home.

But the next day I had to be specially nice to June, because Mrs Chandler said so, so we were friends again. June was upset all day, that was why Mrs Chandler said to be nice to her. Someone had left the mice's cage unlocked and they'd escaped. June was crying, because she liked to watch them and she loves animals, only she hadn't any since when her kitten tried to get up under the railway bridge where you can hear pigeons, and fell off and got killed. Mrs Chandler said for everyone to be nice to June, so we were. Except Tonia, who avoided us all day and didn't talk to anyone. I thought then she was sad for June.

On Saturday we went to the baths by the library. The baths are like a big toilet with tiled walls and slippery floors. We said we'd teach Tonia to swim, but her father wouldn't let her come in case she got her asthma and drowned. We had to stop some boys pushing Jim and the other little kids in. There must be something wrong with them to do that. I think they ought to go and see a doctor, like Tonia with her asthma. Only June's big sister says it isn't the ordinary doctor Tonia needs to go and see.

Then we went home to watch Doctor Who. It was good, only Jim got all excited watching the giant maggots chasing Doctor Who and nearly had to go to bed. My mother had bought some lovely curtains with her Bingo money, all red and purple, and she was putting them up in the front room so our maisonette would look different from the others. There wasn't any football on TV, so my father went out for a drink and gave us money for lemonade. June had to go home because her auntie was coming, so I took Jim to get the lemonade.

On the way we met Tonia. She didn't speak to us. She was running and she looked as if she'd been sick. I wasn't sure, because it had got all dark as if someone had poured dirty dishwater into the sky. Anyway, I went to the wine shop and when I'd bought the lemonade I looked for Jim but he wasn't there. I didn't hear him go out, because I'd told him to stay in the shop but they'd left the door open to let air in. He'd run down the underpass. Little kids are like moths when they see a light sometimes. So I went to get him and I nearly slipped, because someone had just been throwing red paint all over the place. It was even on the lights, and someone had tried to paint the man on the wall with it. Jim said it was blood and I told him not to be soft. But it did look nasty. I didn't even want my supper.

It rained all Sunday, so nothing happened. Except June brought the *Liverpool Echo* round because one of my poems was in it. I'd sent it in so long ago that I'd forgotten. They only put your first name and your age, as if you didn't want anyone to know it was you. I think it's stupid.

Next day when we were coming home we saw the man who empties the bins on West Derby Road talking to the ladies from the wine shop. There's a concrete bin on top of the underpass, with a band going round it saying LITTER LITTER LITTER. He'd found four mice cut up in the bin. June started crying when we got to our road. She cries a lot sometimes and I have to put my arm round her, like my father when he heard Labour hadn't won the election. She thought they were the mice from our classroom. I said they couldn't be, because nobody could have caught them.

The next night June and I took Jim home, then we went to the library. We left him playing with the little girls from up the street. When we got back he wasn't there. My mother got all worried but we said we'd look for him. We looked under the railway bridge, because he likes to go in the workshop there to listen to the noise, that sounds like the squeak they put on the TV to remind you to switch it off. But he wasn't there, so we looked on the waste ground by the railway line, because he likes playing with the bricks there more than the building blocks he got for Christmas. He was sitting there waiting to see a train. He said a girl had taken the little girls to see a man who showed them nice things.

Some policemen came to school one day to tell us not to go with men like that, because they were ill, so we thought we'd better tell our parents. But just as we were coming home we saw Tonia with the little girls. She looked as if she wanted to run away when she saw us, then June shouted "What've you been doing with those kids?" "It wasn't anything, only a drawing on the wall," one of the little girls said. "You wouldn't even let Jim look at him the other day," I said. "Well, he wouldn't have wanted to come," Tonia said. "You just let them play next time. Jim was having fun," I said.

The next day a puppy came into the playground and we all played with it. It rolled on its back to make us tickle it, then it peed on the caretaker's bike and he chased it away. Tonia played with it most and when it came back to the playground, she threw sweets out of the window for it until Mrs Chandler said not to. We were painting, and Tonia did a lovely one with lots of colours, instead of the ones she usually does which are all dark. Mrs Chandler said it was very good, and you could tell she was really pleased. But she asked Tonia why the man was standing with his back to us, and Tonia blushed and said she couldn't paint faces very well, though she can when she wants to. I painted a puppy eating a bone and Mrs Chandler liked that too.

When it was time to go home Tonia stayed behind to ask Mrs Chandler about painting faces, as if she didn't know how. We thought she wanted to walk along with Mrs Chandler, but instead she ran out of the school when everyone had gone and went down the underpass with the puppy. We saw her because I had to get some apples from the greengrocer's. That's a funny shop, because the boards have got all dirty with potatoes, and sometimes the ladies talk to people and forget we're there. So we were in there a long time and Tonia and the puppy hadn't come up. "Let's see what she's doing," June said. Just as we went down the ramp the puppy ran out with Tonia chasing it. She had a penknife. "I was only pretending. I wouldn't kill it really," she said. "You shouldn't have a knife at all," I said. Then she went off because we wouldn't help her find the puppy.

After tea Jim and the little girls were climbing on a lorry, so I had to tell them the man would shout when he came back. They all ran up the street and started shouting "Pop a cat a petal, pop a cat a petal." Little kids are funny sometimes. I asked them what it meant and one of the little girls said "That's what that girl said we had to say to the man on the wall." I told her not to play with Tonia, because Tonia could do things they shouldn't.

Next day I asked Mrs Chandler what it meant. She had to look it up, then she said it was a volcano in Mexico. At dinnertime I asked Tonia why she'd told the little girls to say it. Tonia went red and said it was her secret. "Then you shouldn't have told them. Anyway, it's only a volcano," June said, because she'd heard Mrs Chandler tell me. "No, it isn't," Tonia said. "It's his name. It's a god's name." "It's a volcano in Mexico," I said. "Lynn should know. She's the best reader, and she had a poem in the paper," June said. "I didn't see it," Tonia said. "Well, I did. It said Lynn," June said. "That could be anyone," Tonia said. "You're making it up." "No she isn't," June said. "She'll have you a fight." So we went behind the school and had a fight, and I won.

Tonia was crying and said she'd tell Mrs Chandler, but she didn't. She was quiet all afternoon, and she waited for us when we were going home. "I don't care if you did have a poem in the paper," she said. "I've seen something you haven't." "What is it?" I said. "If you meet me tonight I'll show you," she said. "Just you. She can't come." "June's my best friend. She's got to come too or I won't," I said. "All right, but you've got to promise not to tell anyone," Tonia said. "Wait till it's nearly dark and meet me at the end of my road."

So I had to say I was going to hear a record at June's, and she had to say she was coming to ours. We met Tonia at nine o'clock. She was very quiet and wouldn't say anything, just started walking and didn't look to see if we

were coming. Sometimes I don't like the dark, because the cars look like animals asleep, and everything seems bigger. It makes me feel like a little kid. We
could see all the people in the houses watching TV with the lights out, and I
wished I was back at home. Anyway, we followed Tonia, and she stopped at
the top of the underpass.

"Oh, it's only that stupid thing on the wall," June said. "No, it isn't," Tonia
said. "There's a real man down there if you look." "Well, I don't want to see
him," June said. "What's so special about him?" I said. "He's a god," Tonia
said. "He's not. He's just a man playing with his thing," June said. "He probably wouldn't want you to see him anyway," Tonia said. "I'm going down.
You go home." "We'll come with you to make sure you're all right," I said, but
really I was excited without knowing why.

We went down the ramp where nobody would see us and Tonia said we
had to take our knickers off and say "Pop a cat a petal," only whisper it so
people wouldn't hear us. "You're just like a little kid," June said. "I'm not taking my knickers off." "Well, pull your dress up then," Tonia said. "No, you do
it first," I said. "I don't need to," Tonia said. "You've got to go first," I said. So
she did, and we all started whispering "Pop a cat a petal," and when we were
behind her we pulled our dresses down again. Then Tonia was in the underpass and we were still round the corner of the ramp. We dared each other to
go first, then I said "Let's go in together."

So June pushed me in and I pulled her in, and we started saying "Pop a cat
a petal" again, only we weren't saying it very well because we couldn't stop
giggling. But then I got dizzy. All the lights in the underpass were flickering
like a fire when it's going out, and the colours were swaying, and all the passage was like it was glittering slowly, and Tonia was standing in the middle
swaying as if she was dancing with the light. Then June screamed and I think
I did, because I thought I saw a man.

It must have been our eyes, because the light was so funny. But we thought
we saw a giant standing behind Tonia. He was covered with paint, and he was
as tall as the roof. He hadn't any clothes on, so he couldn't have been there
really, but it looked as if his spout was swaying like an elephant's trunk
reaching up. But it must have been just the light, because he hadn't got a
face, only paint, and he looked like those cut-out photographs they put in
shop windows. Anyway, when we screamed Tonia looked round and saw we
were nowhere near her. She looked as if she could have hit us. And when we
looked again there wasn't any giant, only the man back on the wall.

"He wanted you," Tonia said. "You should have gone to him." "No thank
you," June said. "And if we get into trouble at home I'll batter you." Then we

ran home, but they didn't ask me anything, because they'd heard my father had to be on strike again.

Next day Tonia wouldn't speak to us. We heard her telling someone else that she knew something they didn't, so we told them that she only wanted you to take your knickers down. Then she wanted to walk home with us. "He's angry because you ran away," she said. "He wanted a sacrifice." June wouldn't let her, but I said "You can walk on the other side of the road if you want, but we won't talk to you." So she did, and she was crying and I felt a bit mean, but June wouldn't let me go over.

Saturday was horrible, because my parents had a row about the strike, and Jim started crying and they both shouted at him and had another row, and he was sick all down the stairs, so I cleaned it up. Then there wasn't any disinfectant, and my mother said my father never bought anything we needed, and he said I wasn't the maid to do all the dirty jobs. So I went upstairs and had a cry, then I played with Jim in our room, and it was just getting dark when I saw June coming down our road with her mother.

I thought they might have found out where we'd been last night, but it wasn't that. June's mother wanted her to stay with us, because her big sister had been attacked in the underpass and she didn't want June upset. So Jim slept with my parents and they had to be friends again, and June and I talked in bed until we fell asleep. June's big sister had just been walking through the underpass when a man grabbed her from behind. "Did he rape her?" I said. "He must have. Do you think it hurts?" June said. "It can't hurt much or people wouldn't do it," I said.

On Sunday June went home again, because her big sister had gone to hospital. I heard my parents talking about it when I was in the kitchen. "It's most peculiar," my mother said. "The doctor said she hadn't been touched." "I wouldn't have thought people needed to imagine that sort of thing these days at her age," my father said. I don't know what he meant.

On Monday Mrs Chandler said we weren't to go in the underpass again until she said. Tonia said we couldn't get hurt in the daytime, with the police station just up the road. But Mrs Chandler said she'd spank us herself if she heard we'd been down, and you could tell she wasn't joking.

At dinnertime there were policemen in the underpass. We went to the top to listen. The traffic was noisy, so we couldn't hear everything they said, but we heard one shout "Bring me an envelope. There's something caught on the drain." And another one said "Drugs, by the look of it." Then Tonia started coughing and we all had to run away before they caught us. I think she did it on purpose.

When I went home I had to go to the greengrocer's. So I pretended I was waiting for someone by the underpass, because I saw a policeman going down. He must have gone to tell the one who was watching, because I heard him say "You won't believe this. They weren't drugs at all. They were hearts." "Hearts?" said the other one. "Yes, of some kind of small animal," he said. "Two of them. I'm wondering how they tie in with those mice in the bin up there. They'd been mutilated, if you remember. But there ought to be two more hearts. They couldn't have gone down the drain because it's been clogged for weeks." "I'll tell you something else," the other one said. "I don't think that's red paint on this light." I didn't want to hear anymore, so I turned round to go, and I saw Tonia listening at the other end. Then she saw me and ran away.

So I know who took the mice out of the classroom, and I think I know why she looked as if she'd been sick that night, but I don't want to speak to her to find out. I wish I could tell Mrs Chandler about it, but we promised not to tell about the underpass, and June would be terribly upset if she knew about the mice. Her big sister is home again now, but she won't go out at night, and she keeps shivering. I suppose Tonia might leave it alone now, because it's nearly the holidays. Only I heard her talking the other day in the playground. She might just have been boasting, because she looked all proud of herself, and she looked at the policeman at the top of the underpass as if she wished he'd go away, and she said "Pop a cat a petal did it to me too."

The Companion

When Stone reached the fairground, having been misdirected twice, he thought it looked more like a gigantic amusement arcade. A couple of paper cups tumbled and rattled on the shore beneath the promenade, and the cold insinuating October wind scooped the Mersey across the slabs of red rock that formed the beach, across the broken bottles and abandoned tyres. Beneath the stubby white mock turrets of the long fairground façade, the shops displayed souvenirs and fish and chips. Among them, in the fairground entrances, scraps of paper whirled.

Stone almost walked away. This wasn't his best holiday. One fairground in Wales had been closed, and this one certainly wasn't what he'd expected. The guidebook had made it sound like a genuine fairground, sideshows you must stride among not looking in case their barkers lured you in, the sudden shock of waterfalls cascading down what looked like painted cardboard, the shots and bells and wooden concussions of target galleries, the girls' shrieks overhead, the slippery armour and juicy crunch of toffee-apples, the illuminations springing alight against a darkening sky. But at least, he thought, he had chosen his time well. If he went in now he might have the fairground almost to himself.

As he reached an entrance, he saw his mother eating fish and chips from a paper tray. What nonsense! She would never have eaten standing up in public—"like a horse," as she'd used to say. But he watched as she hurried out of the shop, face averted from him and the wind. Of course, it had been the way she ate, with little snatching motions of her fork and mouth. He pushed the incident to the side of his mind in the hope that it would fall away, and hurried through the entrance, into the clamour of colour and noise.

The high roof with its bare iron girders reminded him at once of a railway station, but the place was noisier still. The uproar—the echoing sirens and jets and dangerous groaning of metal—was trapped, and was deafening. It was so overwhelming that he had to remind himself he could see, even if he couldn't hear.

But there wasn't much to see. The machines looked faded and dusty. Cars like huge armchairs were lurching and spinning helplessly along a switchback, a canvas canopy was closing over an endless parade of seats, a great disc tasselled with seats was lifting towards the roof, dangling a lone couple over its gears. With so few people in sight it seemed almost that the machines, frustrated by inaction, were operating themselves. For a moment Stone had the impression of being shut in a dusty room where the toys, as in childhood tales, had come to life.

He shrugged vaguely and turned to leave. Perhaps he could drive to the fairground at Southport, though it was a good few miles across the Mersey. His holiday was dwindling rapidly. He wondered how they were managing at the tax office in his absence. Slower as usual, no doubt.

Then he saw the roundabout. It was like a toy forgotten by another child and left here, or handed down the generations. Beneath its ornate scrolled canopy the horses rode on poles towards their reflections in a ring of mirrors. The horses were white wood or wood painted white, their bodies dappled with purple, red, and green, and some of their sketched faces too. On the hub, above a notice MADE IN AMSTERDAM, an organ piped to itself. Around it Stone saw carved fish, mermen, zephyrs, a head and shoulders smoking a pipe in a frame, a landscape of hills and lake and unfurling perched hawk. "Oh yes," Stone said.

As he clambered onto the platform he felt a hint of embarrassment, but nobody seemed to be watching. "Can you pay me," said the head in the frame. "My boy's gone for a minute."

The man's hair was the colour of the smoke from his pipe. His lips puckered on the stem and smiled. "It's a good roundabout," Stone said.

"You know about them, do you?"

"Well, a little." The man looked disappointed, and Stone hurried on. "I know a lot of fairgrounds. They're my holiday, you see, every year. Each year I cover a different area. I may write a book." The idea had occasionally tempted him—but he hadn't taken notes, and he still had ten years to retirement, for which the book had suggested itself as an activity.

"You go alone every year?"

"It has its merits. Less expensive, for one thing. Helps me save. Before I retire I mean to see Disneyland and Vienna." He thought of the Big Wheel, Harry Lime, the earth falling away beneath. "I'll get on," he said.

He patted the unyielding shoulders of the horse, and remembered a childhood friend who'd had a rocking horse in his bedroom. Stone had ridden it a few times, more and more wildly when it was nearly time to go home; his friend's bedroom was brighter than his, and as he clung to the wooden shoulders he was clutching the friendly room too. Funny thinking of that now, he thought. Because I haven't been on a roundabout for years, I suppose.

The roundabout stirred; the horse lifted him, let him sink. As they moved forward, slowly gathering momentum, Stone saw a crowd surging through one of the entrances and spreading through the funfair. He grimaced: it had been his fairground for a little while, they needn't have arrived just as he was enjoying his roundabout.

The crowd swung away. A jangle of pinball machines sailed by. Amid the Dodgems a giant with a barrel body was spinning, flapping its limp arms, a red electric cigar thrust in its blank grin and throbbing in time with its slow thick laughter. A tinny voice read Bingo numbers, buzzing indistinctly. Perhaps it was because he hadn't eaten for a while, saving himself for the toffee-apples, but he was growing dizzy—it felt like the whirling blurred shot of the fair in *Saturday Night and Sunday Morning*, a fair he hadn't liked because it was too grim. Give him *Strangers on a Train, Some Came Running, The Third Man*, even the fairground murder in *Horrors of the Black Museum*. He shook his head to try to control his pouring thoughts.

But the fair was spinning faster. The Ghost Train's station raced by, howling and screaming. People strolling past the roundabout looked jerky as drawings in a thaumatrope. Here came the Ghost Train once more, and Stone glimpsed the queue beneath the beckoning green corpse. They were staring at him. No, he realised next time round, they were staring at the roundabout. He was just something that kept appearing as they watched. At the end of the queue, staring and poking around inside his nostrils, stood Stone's father.

Stone gripped the horse's neck as he began to fall. The man was already wandering away towards the Dodgems. Why was his mind so traitorous today? It wouldn't be so bad if the comparisons it made weren't so repulsive. Why, he'd never met a man or woman to compare with his parents. Admired people, yes, but not in the same way. Not since the two polished boxes had been lowered into holes and hidden. Noise and colour spun about him and inside him. Why wasn't he allowing himself to think about his parents' death? He knew why he was blocking, and that should be his salvation: at the age of ten he'd suffered death and hell every night.

He clung to the wood in the whirlpool and remembered. His father had denied him a nightlight and his mother had nodded, saying "Yes, I think it's time." He'd lain in bed, terrified to move in case he betrayed his presence to the darkness, mouthing "Please God don't let it" over and over. He lay so that he could see the faint grey vertical line of the window between the curtains in the far distance, but even that light seemed to be receding. He knew that death and hell would be like this. Sometimes, as he began to blur with sleep and the room grew larger and the shapes dark against the darkness awoke, he couldn't tell that he hadn't already died.

He sat back as the horse slowed and he began to slip forward across its neck. What then? Eventually he'd seen through the self-perpetuating trap of religious guilt, of hell, of not daring not to believe in it because then it would get you. For a while he'd been vaguely uneasy in dark places, but not sufficiently so to track down the feeling and conquer it. After a while it had dissipated, along with his parents' overt disapproval of his atheism. Yes, he thought as his memories and the roundabout slowed, I was happiest then, lying in bed hearing and feeling them and the house around me. Then, when he was thirty, a telephone call had summoned him to the hole in the road, to the sight of the car like a dead black beetle protruding from the hole. There had been a moment of sheer vertiginous terror, and then it was over. His parents had gone into darkness. That was enough. It was the one almost religious observance he imposed on himself: think no more.

And there was no reason to do so now. He staggered away from the roundabout, towards the pinball arcade that occupied most of one side of the funfair. He remembered how, when he lay mouthing soundless pleas in bed, he would sometimes stop and think of what he'd read about dreams: that they might last for hours but in reality occupied only a split second. Was the same true of thoughts? And prayers, when you had nothing but darkness by which to tell the time? Besides defending him, his prayers were counting off the moments before dawn. Perhaps he had used up only a minute, only a second of darkness. Death and hell—what strange ideas I used to have, he thought. Especially for a ten-year-old. I wonder where they went. Away with short trousers and pimples and everything else I grew out of, of course.

Three boys of about twelve were crowded around a pinball machine. As they moved apart momentarily he saw that they were trying to start it with a coin on a piece of wire. He took a stride towards them and opened his mouth—but suppose they turned on him? If they set about him, pulled him down and kicked him, his shouts would never be heard for the uproar.

There was no sign of an attendant. Stone hurried back to the roundabout, where several little girls were mounting horses. "Those boys are up to no good," he complained to the man in the frame.

"You! Yes, you! I've seen you before. Don't let me see you again," the man shouted. They dispersed, swaggering.

"Things didn't use to be like this," Stone said, breathing hard with relief. "I suppose your roundabout is all that's left of the old fairground."

"The old one? No, this didn't come from there."

"I thought the old one must have been taken over."

"No, it's still there, what's left of it," the man said. "I don't know what you'd find there now. Through that exit is the quickest way. You'll come to the side entrance in five minutes, if it's still open."

The moon had risen. It glided along the rooftops as Stone emerged from the back of the funfair and hurried along the terraced street. Its light lingered on the tips of chimneys and the peaks of roofs. Inside the houses, above slivers of earth or stone that passed for front gardens, Stone saw faces silvered by television.

At the end of the terrace, beyond a wider road, he saw an identical street paralleled by an alley. Just keep going. The moon cleared the roofs as he crossed the intersection, and left a whitish patch on his vision. He was trying to blink it away as he reached the street, and so he wasn't certain if he glimpsed a group of boys emerging from the street he'd just left and running into the alley.

Anxiety hurried him onward while he wondered if he should turn back. His car was on the promenade; he could reach it in five minutes. They must be the boys he had seen in the pinball arcade, out for revenge. Quite possibly they had knives or broken bottles; no doubt they knew how to use them from the television. His heels clacked in the silence. Dark exits from the alley gaped between the houses. He tried to set his feet down gently as he ran. The boys were making no sound at all, at least none that reached him. If they managed to overbalance him they could smash his bones while he struggled to rise. At his age that could be worse than dangerous. Another exit lurked between the houses, which looked threatening in their weight and impassivity. He must stay on his feet whatever happened. If the boys got hold of his arms he could only shout for help. The houses fell back as the street curved, their opposite numbers loomed closer. In front of him, beyond a wall of corrugated tin, lay the old fairground.

He halted panting, trying to quell his breath before it blotted out any sounds in the alley. Where he had hoped to find a well-lit road to the promenade, both sides of the street ended as if lopped, and the way was blocked by the wall of tin. In the middle, however, the tin had been prised back like a lid, and a jagged entrance yawned among the sharp shadows and moonlit inscriptions. The fairground was closed and deserted.

As he realised that the last exit was back beyond the curve of the street,

Stone stepped through the gap in the tin. He stared down the street, which was empty but for scattered fragments of brick and glass. It occurred to him that they might not have been the same boys after all. He pulled the tin to behind him and looked around.

The circular booths, the long target galleries, the low roller coaster, the ark and the crazy house, draped shadow over each other and merged with the dimness of the paths between. Even the roundabout was hooded by darkness hanging from its canopy. Such wood as he could see in the moonlight looked ragged, the paint patchy. But between the silent machines and stalls one ride was faintly illuminated: the Ghost Train.

He walked towards it. Its front was emitting a pale green glow which at first sight looked like moonlight, but which was brighter than the white tinge the moon imparted to the adjoining rides. Stone could see one car on the rails, close to the entrance to the ride. As he approached, he glimpsed from the corner of his eye a group of men, stallholders presumably, talking and gesticulating in the shadows between two stalls. So the fairground wasn't entirely deserted. They might be about to close, but perhaps they would allow him one ride, seeing that the Ghost Train was still lit. He hoped they hadn't seen him using the vandals' entrance.

As he reached the ride and realised that the glow came from a coat of luminous paint, liberally applied but now rather dull and threadbare, he heard a loud clang from the tin wall. It might have been someone throwing a brick, or someone reopening the torn door; the stalls obstructed his view. He glanced quickly about for another exit, but found none. He might run into a dead end. It was best to stay where he was. He couldn't trust the stallholders; they might live nearby, they might know the boys or even be their parents. As a child he'd once run to someone who had proved to be his attacker's unhelpful father. He climbed into the Ghost Train car.

Nothing happened. Nobody was attending the ride. Stone strained his ears. Neither the boys, if they were there, nor the attendant seemed to be approaching. If he called out the boys would hear him. Instead, frustrated and furious, he began to kick the metal inside the nose of the car.

Immediately the car trundled forward over the lip of an incline in the track and plunged through the Ghost Train doors into darkness.

As he swung round an unseen clattering curve, surrounded by noise and the dark, Stone felt as if he had suddenly become the victim of delirium. He remembered his storm-racked childhood bed and the teeming darkness pouring into him. Why on earth had he come on this ride? He'd never liked the ghost trains as a child, and as he grew up he had instinctively avoided them. He'd allowed his panic to trap him. The boys might be waiting when he emerged. Well, in that case he would appeal to whoever was operating the ride. He sat back, gripping the wooden seat beneath him with both hands, and gave himself up to the straining of metal, the abrupt swoops of the car, and the darkness.

Then, as his anxiety about the outcome of the ride diminished, another impression began to trickle back. As the car had swung around the first curve he'd glimpsed an illuminated shape, two illuminated shapes, withdrawn so swiftly that he'd had no time to glance up at them. He had the impression that they had been the faces of a man and a woman, gazing down at him. At once they had vanished into the darkness or been swept away by it. It seemed to him for some reason very important to remember their expressions.

Before he could pursue this, he saw a greyish glow ahead of him. He felt an unreasoning hope that it would be a window, which might give him an idea of the extent of the darkness. But already he could see that its shape was too irregular. A little closer and he could make it out. It was a large stuffed grey rabbit with huge glass or plastic eyes, squatting upright in an alcove with its front paws extended before it. Not a dead rabbit, of course: a toy. Beneath him the car was clattering and shaking, yet he had the odd notion that this was a deliberate effect, that in fact the car had halted and the rabbit was approaching or growing. Rubbish, he thought. It was a pretty feeble ghost, anyway. Childish. His hands pulled at splinters on the wooden seat beneath him. The rabbit rushed towards him as the track descended a slight slope. One of its eyes was loose, and whitish stuffing hung down its cheek from the hole. The rabbit was at least four feet tall. As the car almost collided with it before whipping away around a curve, the rabbit toppled towards him and the light which illuminated it went out.

Stone gasped and clutched his chest. He'd twisted round to look behind him at the darkness where he judged the rabbit to have been, until a spasm wrenched him frontwards again. Light tickling drifted over his face. He shuddered, then relaxed. Of course they always had threads hanging down for cobwebs, his friends had told him that. But no wonder the fairground was deserted, if this was the best they could do. Giant toys lit up, indeed. Not only cheap but liable to give children nightmares.

The car coursed up a slight incline and down again before shaking itself in a frenzy around several curves. Trying to soften you up before the next shock, Stone thought. Not me, thank you very much. He lay back in his seat and sighed loudly with boredom. The sound hung on his ears like muffs. Why did I do that? he wondered. It's not as if the operator can hear me. Then who can?

Having spent its energy on the curves, the car was slowing. Stone peered ahead, trying to anticipate. Obviously he was meant to relax before the car startled him with a sudden jerk. As he peered, he found his eyes were adjusting to the darkness. At least he could make out a few feet ahead, at the side of the track, a squat and bulky grey shape. He squinted as the car coasted towards it. It was a large armchair.

The car came abreast of it and halted. Stone peered at the chair. In the dim hectic flecked light, which seemed to attract and outline all the restless discs on his eyes, the chair somehow looked larger than he. Perhaps it was further away than he'd thought. Some clothes thrown over the back of the chair looked diminished by it, but they could be a child's clothes. If nothing else, Stone thought, it's instructive to watch my mind working. Now let's get on.

Then he noticed that the almost invisible light was flickering. Either that, which was possible although he couldn't determine the source of the light, or the clothes were shifting; very gradually but nonetheless definitely, as if something hidden by them were lifting them to peer out, perhaps preparatory to emerging. Stone leaned towards the chair. Let's see what it is, let's get it over with. But the light was far too dim, the chair too distant. Probably he would be unable to see it even when it emerged, the way the light had been allowed to run down, unless he left the car and went closer.

He had one hand on the side of the car when he realised that if the car moved off while he was out of it he would be left to grope his way through the darkness. He slumped back, and as he did so he glimpsed a violent movement among the clothes near the seat of the chair. He glanced towards it. Before his eyes could focus, the dim grey light was extinguished.

Stone sat for a moment, all of him concentrating on the silence, the blind darkness. Then he began to kick frantically at the nose of the car. The car shook a little with his attack, but stayed where it was. By the time it decided to move foward, the pressure of his blood seemed to be turning the darkness red.

When the car nosed its way around the next curve, slowing as if sniffing the track ahead, Stone heard a mute thud and creak of wood above the noise of the wheels. It came from in front of him. The sort of thing you hear in a house at night, he thought. Soon be out now.

Without warning a face came rushing towards him out of the darkness a few feet ahead. It jerked forward as he did. Of course it would, he thought with a grimace, sinking back and watching his face sink briefly into the mirror. Now he could see that he and the car were surrounded by a faint light which extended as far as the wooden frame of the mirror. Must be the end of the ride. They can't get any more obvious than that. Effective in its way, I suppose.

He watched himself in the mirror as the car followed the curve past. His silhouette loomed on the greyish light, which had fallen behind. Suddenly he frowned. His silhouette was moving independent of the movement of the car. It was beginning to swing out of the limits of the mirror. Then he remembered the wardrobe that had stood at the foot of his childhood bed, and realised what was happening. The mirror was set in a door, which was opening.

Stone pressed himself against the opposite side of the car, which had slowed almost to a halt. No, no, he thought, it mustn't. Don't. He heard a grinding of gears behind him; unmeshed metal shrieked. He threw his body forward, against the nose of the car. In the darkness to his left he heard the creak of the door and a soft thud. The car moved a little, then caught the gears and ground forward.

As the light went out behind him, Stone felt a weight fall beside him on the seat.

He cried out. Or tried to, for as he gulped in air it seemed to draw darkness into his lungs, darkness that swelled and poured into his heart and brain. There was a moment in which he knew nothing, as if he'd become darkness and silence and the memory of suffering. Then the car was rattling on, the darkness was sweeping over him and by, and the nose of the car banged open the doors and plunged out into the night.

As the car swung onto the length of track outside the Ghost Train, Stone caught sight of the gap between the stalls where he had thought he'd seen the stallholders. A welling moonlight showed him that between the stalls stood a pile of sacks, nodding and gesticulating in the wind. Then the seat beside him emerged from the shadow, and he looked down.

Next to him on the seat was a shrunken hooded figure. It wore a faded jacket and trousers striped and patched in various colours, indistinguishable in the receding moonlight. The head almost reached his shoulder. Its arms hung slack at its sides, and its feet drummed laxly on the metal beneath the seat. Shrinking away, Stone reached for the front of the car to pull himself to his feet, and the figure's head fell back.

Stone closed his eyes. When he opened them he saw within the hood an oval of white cloth upon which—black crosses for eyes, a barred crescent for a mouth—a grinning face was stitched.

As he had suddenly realised that the car hadn't halted nor even slowed before plunging down the incline back into the Ghost Train, Stone did not immediately notice that the figure had taken his hand.

Call First

It was the other porters who made Ned determined to know who answered the phone in the old man's house.

Not that he hadn't wanted to know before. He'd felt it was his right almost as soon as the whole thing had begun, months ago. He'd been sitting behind his desk in the library entrance, waiting for someone to try to take a bag into the library so he could shout after them that they couldn't, when the reference librarian ushered the old man up to Ned's desk and said "Let this gentleman use your phone." Maybe he hadn't meant every time the old man came to the library, but then he should have said so. The old man used to talk to the librarian and tell him things about books even he didn't know, which was why he let him phone. All Ned could do was feel resentful. People weren't supposed to use his phone, and even he wasn't allowed to phone outside the building. And it wasn't as if the old man's calls were interesting. Ned wouldn't have minded if they'd been worth hearing.

"I'm coming home now." That was all he ever said; then he'd put down the receiver and hurry away. It was the way he said it that made Ned wonder. There was no feeling behind the words, they sounded as if he were saying them only because he had to, perhaps wishing he needn't. Ned knew people talked like that: his parents did in church and most of the time at home. He wondered if the old man was calling his wife, because he wore a ring on his wedding-finger, although in the claw where a stone should be was what looked like a piece of yellow fingernail. But Ned didn't think it could be his wife; each day the old man came he left the library at the same time, so why would he bother to phone?

Then there was the way the old man looked at Ned when he phoned: as if he didn't matter and couldn't understand, the way most of the porters looked at him. That was the look that swelled up inside Ned one day and made him persuade one of the other porters to take charge of his desk while Ned waited to listen in on the old man's call. The girl who always smiled at Ned was on the switchboard, and they listened together. They heard the phone in the house ringing then lifted, and the old man's call and his receiver going down: nothing else, not even breathing apart from the old man's. "Who do you think it is?" the girl said, but Ned thought she'd laugh if he said he didn't know. He shrugged extravagantly and left.

Now he was determined. The next time the old man came to the library Ned phoned his house, having read what the old man dialled. When the ringing began its pulse sounded deliberately slow, and Ned felt the pumping of his blood rushing ahead. Seven trills and the phone in the house opened with a violent click. Ned held his breath, but all he could hear was his blood thumping in his ears. "Hello," he said and after a silence, clearing his throat, "Hello!" Perhaps it was one of those answering machines people in films used in the office. He felt foolish and uneasy greeting the wide silent metal ear, and put down the receiver. He was in bed and falling asleep before he wondered why the old man should tell an answering machine that he was coming home.

The following day, in the bar where all the porters went at lunchtime, Ned told them about the silently listening phone. "He's weird, that old man," he said, but now the others had finished joking with him they no longer seemed interested, and he had to make a grab for the conversation. "He reads weird books," he said. "All about witches and magic. Real ones, not stories."

"Now tell us something we didn't know," someone said, and the conversation turned its back on Ned. His attention began to wander, he lost his hold on what was being said, he had to smile and nod as usual when they looked at him, and he was thinking: they're looking at me like the old man does. I'll show them. I'll go in his house and see who's there. Maybe I'll take something that'll show I've been there. Then they'll have to listen.

But next day at lunchtime, when he arrived at the address he'd seen on the old man's library card, Ned felt more like knocking at the front door and running away. The house was menacingly big, the end house of a street whose other windows were brightly bricked up. Exposed foundations like broken teeth protruded from the mud that surrounded the street, while the mud was walled in by a five-storey crescent of flats that looked as if it had been designed in sections to be fitted together by a two-year-old. Ned tried to keep the house between him and the flats, even though they were hundreds of yards away, as he peered in the windows.

All he could see through the grimy front window was bare floorboards; when he coaxed himself to look through the side window, the same. He dreaded being caught by the old man, even though he'd seen him sitting behind a pile of books ten minutes ago. It had taken Ned that long to walk here;

the old man couldn't walk so fast, and there wasn't a bus he could catch. At last he dodged round the back and peered into the kitchen: a few plates in the sink, some tins of food, an old cooker. Nobody to be seen. He returned to the front, wondering what to do. Maybe he'd knock after all. He took hold of the bar of the knocker, trying to think what he'd say, and the door opened.

The hall leading back to the kitchen was long and dim. Ned stood shuffling indecisively on the step. He would have to decide soon, for his lunch-hour was dwindling. It was like one of the empty houses he'd used to play in with the other children, daring each other to go up the tottering stairs. Even the things in the kitchen didn't make it seem lived in. He'd show them all. He went in. Acknowledging a vague idea that the old man's companion was out, he closed the door to hear if they returned.

On his right was the front room; on his left, past the stairs and the phone, another of the bare rooms he'd seen. He tiptoed upstairs. The stairs creaked and swayed a little, perhaps unused to anyone of Ned's weight. He reached the landing, breathing heavily, feeling dust chafe his throat. Stairs led up to a closed attic door, but he looked in the rooms off the landing.

Two of the doors which he opened stealthily showed him nothing but boards and flurries of floating dust. The landing in front of the third looked cleaner, as if the door were often opened. He pulled it towards him, holding it up all the way so it didn't scrape the floor, and went in.

Most of it didn't seem to make sense. There was a single bed with faded sheets. Against the walls were tables and piles of old books. Even some of the books looked disused. There were black candles and racks of small cardboard boxes. On one of the tables lay a single book. Ned padded across the fragments of carpet and opened the book in a thin path of sunlight through the shutters.

Inside the sagging covers was a page which Ned slowly realised had been ripped from the Bible. It was the story of Lazarus. Scribbles that might be letters filled the margins, and at the bottom of the page: "p. 491." Suddenly inspired, Ned turned to that page in the book. It showed a drawing of a corpse sitting up in his coffin, but the book was all in the language they sometimes used in church: Latin. He thought of asking one of the librarians what it meant. Then he remembered that he needed proof he'd been in the house. He stuffed the page from the Bible into his pocket.

As he crept swiftly downstairs, something was troubling him. He reached the hall and thought he knew what it was. He still didn't know who lived in the house with the old man. If they lived in the back perhaps there would be signs in the kitchen. Though if it was his wife, Ned thought as he hurried down the hall, she couldn't be like Ned's mother, who would never have left torn strips of wallpaper hanging at shoulder height from both walls. He'd reached the kitchen door when he realised what had been bothering him. When he'd emerged from the bedroom, the attic door had been open.

He looked back involuntarily, and saw a woman walking away from him down the hall.

He was behind the closed kitchen door before he had time to feel fear. That came only when he saw that the back door was nailed rustily shut. Then he controlled himself. She was only a woman, she couldn't do much if she found him. He opened the door minutely. The hall was empty.

Halfway down the hall he had to slip into the side room, heart punching his chest, for she'd appeared again from between the stairs and the front door. He felt the beginnings of anger and recklessness, and they grew faster when he opened the door and had to flinch back as he saw her hand passing. The fingers looked famished, the colour of old lard, with long yellow cracked nails. There was no nail on her wedding-finger, which wore a plain ring. She was returning from the direction of the kitchen, which was why Ned hadn't expected her.

Through the opening of the door he heard her padding upstairs. She sounded barefoot. He waited until he couldn't hear her, then edged out into the hall. The door began to swing open behind him with a faint creak, and he drew it stealthily closed. He paced towards the front door. If he hadn't seen her shadow creeping down the stairs he would have come face to face with her.

He'd retreated to the kitchen, and was near to panic, when he realised she knew he was in the house. She was playing a game with him. At once he was furious. She was only an old woman, her body beneath the long white dress was sure to be as thin as her hands, she could only shout when she saw him, she couldn't stop him leaving. In a minute he'd be late for work. He threw open the kitchen door and swaggered down the hall.

The sight of her lifting the phone receiver broke his stride for a moment. Perhaps she was phoning the police. He hadn't done anything, she could have her Bible page back. But she laid the receiver beside the phone. Why? Was she making sure the old man couldn't ring?

As she unbent from stooping to the phone she grasped two uprights of the banisters to support herself. They gave a loud splintering creak and bent together. Ned halted, confused. He was still struggling to react when she turned towards him, and he saw her face. Part of it was still on the bone.

He didn't back away until she began to advance on him, her nails tearing new strips from both walls. All he could see was her eyes, unsupported by flesh. His mind was backing away faster than he was, but it had come up against a terrible insight. He even knew why she'd made sure the old man couldn't interrupt until she'd finished. His calls weren't like speaking to an answering machine at all. They were exactly like switching off a burglar alarm.

Heading Home

Somewhere above you can hear your wife and the young man talking. You strain yourself upwards, your muscles trembling like water, and manage to shift your unsteady balance onto the next stair.

They must think he finished you. They haven't even bothered to close the cellar door, and it's the trickle of flickering light through the crack that you're striving towards. Anyone else but you would be dead. He must have dragged you from the laboratory and thrown you down the stairs into the cellar, where you regained consciousness on the dusty stone. Your left cheek still feels like a rigid plate slipped into your flesh where it struck the floor. You rest on the stair you've reached and listen.

They're silent now. It must be night, since they've lit the hall lamp whose flame is peeking into the cellar. They can't intend to leave the house until tomorrow, if at all. You can only guess what they're doing now, alone in the house. Your numb lips crack again as you grin. Let them enjoy themselves while they can.

He didn't leave you many muscles you can use; it was a thorough job. No wonder they feel safe. Now you have to concentrate yourself in those muscles that still function. Swaying, you manage to raise yourself momentarily to a position where you can grip the next higher stair. You clench on your advantage. Then, pushing with muscles you'd almost forgotten you had, you manage to lever yourself one step higher.

You manoeuvre yourself until you're sitting upright. There's less risk that way of losing your balance for a moment and rolling all the way down to the cellar floor, where you began climbing hours ago. Then you rest. Only six more stairs.

You wonder again how they met. Of course you should have known that it was going on, but your work was your wife and you couldn't spare the time to watch over the woman you'd married. You should have realised that when she went to the village she would meet people and mightn't be as silent as at home. But her room might have been as far from yours as the village is from the house: you gave little thought to the people in either.

Not that you blame yourself. When you met her—in the town where you attended the University—you'd thought she understood how important your work was. It wasn't as if you'd intended to trick her. It was only when she tried to seduce you from your work, both for her own gratification and because she was afraid of it, that you barred her from your companionship by silence.

You can hear the voices again. They're on the upper floor. You don't know whether they're celebrating or comforting each other as guilt settles on them. It doesn't matter. So long as he didn't close the laboratory door when he returned from the cellar. If it's closed you'll never be able to open it. And if you can't get into the laboratory he's killed you after all. You raise yourself, your muscles shuddering with the effort, your cheeks chafing against the wooden stair. You won't relax until you can see the laboratory door.

You're reaching for the top stair when you slip. Your chin comes down on it and slides back. You grip the stair with your jaws, feeling splinters lodge between your teeth. Your neck scrapes the lower stair, but it has lost all feeling save an ache fading slowly into dullness. Only your jaws are preventing you from falling back where you started, and they're throbbing as if nails are being driven into the hinges with measured strokes. You close them tighter, pounding with pain, then you overbalance yourself onto the top stair. You teeter for a moment, then you're secure.

But you don't rest yet. You edge yourself forward and sit up so that you can peer out of the cellar. The outline of the laboratory door billows slightly as the lamp flickers. It occurs to you that they've lit the lamp because she's terrified of you, lying dead beyond the main staircase as she thinks. You laugh silently. You can afford to. When the flame steadies you can see darkness gaping for inches around the laboratory door.

You listen to their voices upstairs, and rest. You know he's a butcher, because he once helped one of the servants to carry the meat from the village. In any case, you could have told his profession from what he has done to you. You're still astonished that she should have taken up with him. From the little you knew of the village people you were delighted that they avoided your house.

You remember the day the new priest came to see you. You could tell he'd heard all the wildest village tales about your experiments. You were surprised he didn't try to ward you off with a cross. When he found you could argue his theology into a corner he left, a twitch pulling his smile awry. He'd tried to persuade you both to attend church, but your wife sat silent throughout. It had been then that you decided to trust her to go to the village. As you paid off the servants you told yourself she would be less likely to talk. You grin fiercely. If you'd been as accurate in your experiments you would be dead.

Upstairs they're still talking. You rock forward and try to wedge yourself between the cellar door and its frame. With your limited control it's difficult, and you find yourself leaning in the crack without any purchase on the wood. Your weight hasn't moved the door, which is heavier than you have ever before had cause to realise. Eventually you manage to wedge yourself in the crack, gripping the frame with all your strength. The door rests on you, and you nudge your weight clumsily against it.

It creaks away from you a little, then swings back, crushing you. It has always hung unevenly and persisted in standing ajar; it never troubled you before. Now the strength he left you, even focused like light through a burning-glass, seems unequal to shifting the door. Trapped in the crack, you relax for a moment. Then, as if to take it unawares, you close your grip on the frame and shove against the door, pushing yourself forward as it swings away.

It comes back, answering the force of your shove, and you aren't clear. But you're still falling into the hall, and as the door chops into the frame you fall on your back, beyond the sweep of the door. You're free of the cellar, but on your back you're helpless. The slowing door can move more than you can. All the muscles you've been using can only work aimlessly and loll in the air. You're laid out on the hall floor like a laboratory subject, beneath the steadying flame.

Then you hear the butcher call to your wife "I'll see" and start downstairs.

You begin to twitch all the muscles on your right side frantically. You roll a little towards that side, then your wild twitching rocks you back. The flame shakes above you, making your shadow play the cruel trick of achieving the movement you're struggling for. He's at the halfway landing now. You work your right side again and hold your muscles still as you begin to turn that way. Suddenly you've swung over your point of equilibrium and are lying on your right side. You strain your aching muscles to inch you forward, but the laboratory is several feet away, and you're by no means moving in a straight line. His footsteps resound. Then you hear your wife's terrified voice, entreating him back. There's a long pondering silence. Then he hurries back upstairs.

You don't let yourself rest until you're inside the laboratory, although by then your ache feels like a cold stiff surface within your flesh and your mouth tastes like a dusty hole in stone. Once beyond the door you sit still, gazing about. Moonlight is spread from the window to the door. Your gaze seeks the bench where you were working when he found you. He hasn't cleared up any of the material which your convulsions threw to the floor. Glinting on the floor you can see a needle, and nearby the surgical thread which you never had occasion to use. You relax to prepare for your last concerted effort, and remember.

You recall the day you perfected the solution. As soon as you'd quaffed it you felt your brain achieve a piercing alertness, become precisely and continually aware of the messages of each nerve and preside over them, making minute adjustments at the first hint of danger. You knew this was what you'd worked for, but you couldn't prove it to yourself until the day you felt the stirrings of cancer. Then your brain seemed to condense into a keen strand of energy that stretched down and seared the cancer out. That was proof. You were immortal.

Not that some of the research you'd had to carry out wasn't unpleasant. It had taken you a great deal of furtive expenditure at the mortuaries to discover that some of the extracts you needed for the solution had to be taken from the living brain. The villagers thought the children had drowned, for their clothes were found on the river-bank. Medical progress, you told yourself, has always involved suffering.

Perhaps your wife suspected something of this stage of your work, or perhaps she and the butcher had simply decided to rid themselves of you. In any case, you were working at your bench, trying to synthesise your discovery, when you heard him enter. He must have rushed at you, for before you could turn you felt a blazing slash gape in the back of your neck. Then you awoke on the cellar floor.

You edge yourself forward across the laboratory. Your greatest exertion is past, but this is the most exacting part. When you're nearly touching your prone body you have to turn round. You move yourself with your jaws and steer with your tongue. It's difficult, but less so than tonguing yourself upright on your neck to rest on the stairs. Then you fit yourself to your shoulders, groping with your mind to feel the nerves linking again.

Now you'll have to hold yourself unflinching or you'll roll apart. With your mind you can do it. Gingerly, so as not to part yourself, you stretch out your arm for the surgical needle and thread.

In the Bag

The boy's face struggled within the plastic bag. The bag laboured like a dying heart as the boy panted frantically, as if suffocated by the thickening mist of his own breath. His eyes were grey blank holes, full of fog beneath the plastic. As his mouth gaped desperately the bag closed on his face, tight and moist, giving him the appearance of a wrapped fish, not quite dead.

It wasn't his son's face. Clarke shook his head violently to clear it of the notion as he hurried towards the assembly hall. It might have been, but Peter had had enough sense and strength to rip the bag with a stone before trying to pull it off. He'd had more strength than. . . . Clarke shook his head hurriedly and strode into the hall. He didn't propose to let himself be distracted. Peter had survived, but that was no thanks to the culprit.

The assembled school clattered to its feet and hushed. Clarke strode down the side aisle to the sound of belated clatters from the folding seats, like the last drops of rain after a downpour. Somewhere amid the muted chorus of nervous coughs, someone was rustling plastic. They wouldn't dare breathe when he'd finished with them. Five strides took him onto the stage. He nodded curtly to the teaching staff and faced the school.

"Someone put a plastic bag over a boy's head today," he said. "I had thought all of you understood that you come here to learn to be men. I had thought that even those of you who do not shine academically had learned to distinguish right from wrong. Apparently I was mistaken. Very well. If you behave like children, you must expect to be treated like children."

The school stirred; the sound included the crackling of plastic. Behind him Clarke heard some of the teachers sit forward, growing tense. Let them protest if they liked. So long as this was his school its discipline would be his.

"You will all stand in silence until the culprit owns up."

Tiers of heads stretched before him, growing taller as they receded, on the ground of their green uniforms. Towards the middle he could see Peter's head. He'd forgotten to excuse the boy from assembly, but it was too late now. In any case, the boy looked less annoyed by the oversight than embarrassed by his father's behaviour. Did he think Clarke was treating the school thus simply because Peter was his son? Not at all; three years ago Clarke had used the same method when someone had dropped a firework in a boy's duffel hood. Though the culprit had not come forward, Clarke had had the satisfaction of knowing he had been punished among the rest.

The heads were billiard balls, arranged on baize. Here and there one swayed uneasily then hurriedly steadied as Clarke's gaze seized it. A whole row shifted restlessly, one after another. Plastic crackled softly, jarring Clarke from his thoughts.

"It seems that the culprit is not a man but a coward," he said. "Very well. Someone must have seen what he did and who he is. No man will protect a coward from his just deserts. Don't worry that your fellows may look down on you for betraying him. If they do not admire you for behaving like a man, they are not men."

The ranks of heads swayed gently, hypnotically. One of them must have seen what had happened to Peter: someone running softly behind him as he crossed the playing-field, dragging the bag over his head, twisting it tight about his neck, and stretching it into a knot at the back. . . . Plastic rustled secretly, deep in the hall, somewhere near Peter. Was the culprit taunting Clarke? He grew cold with fury. He scrutinised the faces, searching for the unease which those closest to the sound must feel; but all the faces were defiantly bland, including Peter's. So they refused to help him even so meagrely. Very well.

"No doubt some of you think this is an easy way to avoid your lessons," he said. "I think so, too. Instead, from tomorrow you will all assemble here when school is over and stand in silence for an hour. This will continue until the culprit is found. Please be sure to tell your parents tonight. You are dismissed."

He strode to his office without a backward glance; his demeanour commanded his staff to carry on his discipline. But he had not reached his office when he began to feel dissatisfied. He was grasping the door handle when he realised what was wrong. Peter must still feel himself doubly a victim.

A class came trooping along the corridor, protesting loudly, hastily silent. "Henry Clegg," he said. "Go to IIIA and tell Peter Clarke to come to my office immediately."

He searched the faces of the passing boys for furtiveness. Then he noticed that although he'd turned the handle and was pushing, the door refused to move. Within, he heard a flurried crackling rustle. He threw his weight against the door, and it fell open. Paper rose from his desk and sank back limply. He closed the window, which he'd left ajar; mist was inching towards it, across the playing-field. He must have heard a draught fumbling with his papers.

A few minutes later Peter knocked and entered. He stood before Clarke's desk, clearly unsure how to address his father. Really, Clarke thought, the boy should call him sir at school; there was no reason why Peter should show him less respect than any other pupil.

"You understand I didn't mean that you should stay after school, Peter," he said. "I hope that won't cause embarrassment between you and your friends. But you must realise that I cannot make an exception of them, too."

For an unguarded moment he felt as though he were justifying himself to his own son. "Very well," Peter said. "Father."

Clarke nodded for him to return to his lesson, but the boy stood struggling to speak. "What is it?" Clarke said. "You can speak freely to me."

"One of the other boys . . . asked Mr Elland if you were . . . right to give the detention, and Mr Elland said he didn't think you were."

"Thank you, Peter. I shall speak to Mr Elland later. But for now, you had better return to his class."

He gazed at the boy, and then at the closed door. He would have liked to see Peter proud of his action, but the boy looked self-conscious and rather disturbed. Perhaps he would discuss the matter with him at home, though that broke his own rule that school affairs should be raised with Peter only in school. He had enough self-discipline not to break his own rules without excellent reason.

Self-discipline must be discussed with Elland later. Clarke sat at his desk to draft a letter to the parents. Laxity in the wearing of school uniform. A fitting sense of pride. The school as a community. Loyalty, a virtue we must foster at all costs. The present decline in standards.

But the rustle of paper distracted him. He'd righted the wrong he had done Peter, he would deal with Elland later; yet he was dissatisfied. With what? The paper prompted him, rustling. There was no use pretending. He must remember what the sound reminded him of.

It reminded him of the sound the plastic bag had made once he'd put it over Derek's head.

His mind writhed aside, distracting him with memories that were more worthy of his attention. They were difficult enough to remember—painful indeed. Sometimes it had seemed that his whole life had been contrived to force him to remember.

Whenever he had sat an examination someone had constantly rustled paper behind him. Nobody else had heard it; after one examination, when he'd tackled the boy who had been sitting behind him, the others had defended the accused. Realising that the sound was in himself, in the effect of stress on his senses, Clarke had gone to examinations prepared to hear it; he'd battled to ignore it, and had passed. He'd known he must; that was only justice.

Then there had been the school play; that had been the worst incident, the most embarrassing. He had produced the play from his own pared-down script, determined to make an impression in his first teaching post. But Macbeth had stalked onto the heath to a sound from the wings as of someone's straining to blow up a balloon, wheezing and panting faintly. Clarke had pursued the sound through the wings, finding only a timidly bewildered boy with a thunder-sheet. Nevertheless, the headmaster had applauded rapidly and lengthily at the curtain. Eventually, since he himself hadn't been blamed, Clarke ceased cross-examining his pupils.

Since then his career had done him more than justice. Sitting at his desk now, he relaxed; he couldn't remember when he'd felt so much at ease with his memories. Of course there had been later disturbing incidents. One spring evening he had been sitting on a park bench with Edna, courting her, and had glanced away from the calm green sunset to see an inflated plastic bag caught among branches. The bag had seemed to pant violently in its struggles with the breeze; then it had begun to nod sluggishly. He'd run across the lawn in panic, but before he reached the bag, it had been snatched away, to retreat nodding into the darkness between the trees. For a moment, vaguely amid his panic, it had made him think of the unidentified boy who had appeared beside him in a class photograph, face blurred into a grey blob. Edna had asked him no questions, and he'd been grateful to forget the incident. But the panic still lay in his memory, now he looked.

It was like the panic he'd felt while awaiting Peter's birth. That had been late in the marriage; there might have been complications. Clarke had waited, trying to slow his breath, holding himself back; panic had been waiting just ahead. If there were any justice, Edna at least would survive. He'd heard someone approaching swiftly beyond the bend in the hospital corridor: a purposeful crackling rustle—a nurse. He had felt pinned down by panic; he'd known that the sound was bearing death towards him. But the nurse must have turned aside beyond the bend. Instead, a doctor had appeared to call him in to see his wife and son. For the only time in his life, Clarke had rushed away to be sick with relief.

As if he had vomited out what haunted him, the panic had never seized him again. But Derek remained deep in his mind, waiting. Each time his thoughts brushed the memory they shrank away; each time it seemed more shameful and horrible. He had never been able to look at it directly.

But why not? He had looked at all these memories without flinching. He had dealt with Peter, later he would deal with Elland. He felt unassailably right, incapable of wrong. He would not be doing himself justice if he did not take his chance.

He sat forward, as if to interview his memory. He coaxed his mind towards it, trying to relax, reassuring himself. There was nothing to fear, he was wholly secure. He must trust his sense of innate rightness; not to remember would be to betray it. He braced himself, closing his eyes. At the age of ten, he had killed another boy.

He and Derek had been playing at the end of the street, near the disused railway line. They weren't supposed to be there, but their parents rarely checked. The summer sun had been trying to shake off trails of soot that rose from the factory chimneys. The boys had been playing at spacemen, inspired by the cover of a magazine crumpled among the rubble. They'd found a plastic bag.

Clarke had worn it first. It had hung against his ears like blankets when he breathed; his ears had been full of his breathing, the bag had grown stuffily hot and misty at once, clinging to his face. Then Derek had snatched it for himself.

Clarke hadn't liked him really, hadn't counted him as much of a friend. Derek was sly, he grabbed other people's toys, he played vindictive tricks on others then whined if they turned on him. When he did wrong he tried to pass the blame to someone else—but that day Clarke had had nobody else to play with. They'd wanted to play spacemen chasing Martians over the waste ground of the moon, but Derek's helmet had kept flying off. Clarke had pulled it tight at the back of Derek's neck, to tie a careful knot.

They ran until Derek fell down. He'd lain kicking on the rubble, pulling at the bag, at his neck. The bag had ballooned, then had fastened on his face like grey skin, again and again. His fingernails had squeaked faintly on the plastic; he'd sounded as though he were trying to cough. When Clarke had stooped to help him he'd kicked out blindly and viciously. Dismayed by the sight, infuriated by the rebuff, Clarke had run away. Realising that he didn't know where he was running to he'd panicked and had hidden in the outside toilet for hours, long after the woman's screams had gone by, and the ambulance.

Though nobody had known he and Derek had been together—since Derek's sister and her boyfriend were supposed to have kept the boy with them in the park—Clarke had waited, on the edge of panic, for Derek's father to knock at the front door. But the next day his mother had told him Derek had had an accident; he'd been warned never to play with plastic bags, and that was all. It wasn't enough, he'd decided years later, while watching a fight; too many of his classmates' parents weren't enough for their children; he'd known then what his career was to be. By then he had been able to relax, except for the depths of his mind.

He'd allowed himself to forget; yet today he was hounding a boy for a lesser crime.

No. It wasn't the same. Whoever had played that trick on Peter must have known what he was doing. But Clarke, at ten years old, hadn't known what he was doing to Derek. He had never needed to feel guilt at all.

Secure in that knowledge, he remembered at last why he had. He'd sat on the outside toilet, hearing the screams. Very gradually, a sly grin had spread across his mouth. It served Derek right. Someone had played a trick on him, for a change. He wouldn't be able to pass it back. Clarke had hugged himself, rocking on the seat, giggling silently, starting guiltily when a soft unidentified thumping at the door had threatened him.

He gazed at the memory. It no longer made him writhe; after all, he had been only a child. He would be able to tell Edna at last. That was what had disturbed him most that evening in the park; it hadn't seemed right that he couldn't tell her. That injustice had lurked deep within their marriage. He smiled broadly. "I didn't know what I was doing," he told himself again, aloud.

"But you know now," said a muffled voice behind him.

He sprang to his feet. He had been dozing. Behind him, of course, there was only the window and the unhurried mist. He glanced at his watch. He was to talk to his sixth-form class about ethics: he felt he would enjoy the subject even more than usual. As he closed his door he glimpsed something moving in the indistinct depths of the trees beyond the playing-field, like a fading trace of a memory: a tree, no doubt.

When the class had sat down again he waited for a moment, hoping they might question the ethics of the detention he'd ordered. They should be men enough to ask him. But they only gazed, and he began to discuss the relationship between laws and morality. A Christian country. The individual's debt to society. Our common duty to help the law. The administration of justice. Justice.

He'd waxed passionate, striding the aisles, when he happened to look out of the window. A man dressed in drab shapeless clothes was standing at the edge of the trees. In the almost burnt-out sunlight his face shone dully, featurelessly. Shadows or mist made the grey mass of his face seem to flutter.

The janitor was skulking distantly in the bottom corner of the pane, like a detail squeezed in by a painter. He was pretending to weed the flower-beds. "Who is that man?" Clarke called angrily. "He has no right to be here." But there was nobody except the janitor in sight.

Clarke groped for his interrupted theme. The age of culpability: one of the class must have asked about that—he remembered having heard a voice. The age of legal responsibility. Must not be used as an excuse. Conscience cannot be silenced forever. The law cannot absolve. One does not feel guilt without being guilty. Someone was standing outside the window.

As Clarke whirled to look, something, perhaps the tic that was plucking at his eye, made the man's face seem the colour of mist, and quaking. But when he looked there was nothing but the field and the mist and the twilight, running together darkly like a drowned painting.

"Who was that?" Clarke demanded. "Did anyone see?"

"A man," said Paul Hammond, a sensitive boy. "He looked as if he was going to have a fit." Nobody else had seen anything.

"Do your job properly," Clarke shouted at the janitor. "Keep your eyes open. He's gone round there, round the corner." The afternoon had crept surreptitiously by; he had almost reached the end of school. He searched for a phrase to sum up the lesson. "Remember, you cannot call yourself a man unless you face your conscience." On the last words he had to outshout the bell.

He strode to Elland's classroom, his gown rising and sailing behind him. The man was chatting to a group of boys. "Will you come to my office when you've finished, please," Clarke said, leaning in.

Waiting in his office, he felt calm as the plane of mist before him. It reminded him of a still pool; a pool whose opaque stillness hid its depths; an unnaturally still and opaque pool; a pool from whose depths a figure was rising, about to shatter the surface. It must be the janitor, searching behind the mist. Clarke shook himself angrily and turned as Elland came in.

"Have you been questioning my authority in front of your class?"

"Not exactly, no. I answered a question."

"Don't quibble. You are perfectly aware of what I mean. I will not have the discipline of my school undermined in this way."

"Boys of that age can see straight through hypocrisy, you know," the teacher said, interrupting the opening remarks of Clarke's lecture. "I was asked what I thought. I'm not a convincing liar, and I shouldn't have thought you'd want me to be. I'm sure they would have found my lying more disturbing than the truth. And that wouldn't have helped the discipline, now would it?"

"Don't interrogate me. Don't you realise what you said in front of my son? Does that mean nothing to you?"

"It was your son who asked me what I thought."

Clarke stared at him, hoping for signs of a lie. But at last he had to dismiss him. "I'll speak to you more tomorrow," he said vaguely. The man had been telling the truth; he had clearly been surprised even to have to tell it. But that meant that Peter had lied to his father.

Clarke threw the draft of the letter into his briefcase. There was no time to be lost. He must follow Peter home immediately and set the boy back on the right path. A boy who was capable of one lie was capable of many.

Far down the corridor the boys shouted, the wooden echoes of their footsteps fading. At the door to the mist Clarke hesitated. Perhaps Peter found it difficult to talk to him at school. He would ask him about the incident again at home, to give him a last chance. Perhaps it was partly Clarke's fault, for not making it clear how the boy should address him at school. He must make sure Edna didn't intervene, gently, anxiously. He would insist that she leave them alone.

The fog pretended to defer to him as he strode. It was fog now: trees developed from it, black and glistening, then dissolved again. One tree rustled as he passed. But surely it had no leaves? He hadn't time to go back and look. The sound must have been the rattling of the tree's wire cage, muffled and distorted by the fog.

Home was half a mile away, along three main roads. Peter would already have arrived there, with a group of friends; Clarke hoped he hadn't invited them in. No matter; they would certainly leave when they saw their headmaster.

Buses groped along the dual carriageway, their engines subdued and hoarse. The sketch of a lamppost bobbed up from the fog, filling out and darkening; another, another. On the central reservation beyond the fog, a faint persistent rustling seemed to be pacing Clarke. This was always an untidy street. But there was no wind to stir the litter, no wind to cause the sound that was creeping patiently and purposefully along just behind him, coming abreast of him as he halted, growing louder. He flinched from the dark shape that swam up beside him, but it was a car. And of course it must have been disturbing the litter on the road. He let the car pass, and the rustling faded ahead.

As he neared the second road the white flare of mercury-vapour lamps was gradually mixed with the warmer orange of sodium, contradicted by the chill of the fog. Cars passed like stealthy hearses. The fog sopped up the sodium glow; the orange fog hung thickly around him, like a billowing sack. He felt suffocated. Of course he did, for heaven's sake. The fog was clogging his lungs. He would soon be home.

He strode into the third road, where home was. The orange sack glided with him, over the whitening pavement. The fog seemed too thick, almost a liquid from which lampposts sailed up slowly, trailing orange streaks. Striding through the suppressed quiet, he realised he had encountered nobody on the roads. All at once he was glad: he could see a figure surfacing darkly before him, fog streaming from it, its blank face looming forward to meet him. He could see nothing of the kind. He was home.

As he fumbled for his keys, the nearby streetlamp blazed through a passing rift in the fog. The lamp was dazzling; its light penetrated the thickset curtains Edna had hung in the front rooms; and it showed a man standing at its foot. He was dressed like a tramp, in ancient clothes, and his face gleamed dully in the orange light, like bronze. As Clarke glanced away to help his hands find his elusive keys he realised that the man seemed to have no face, only the gleaming almost immobile surface. He glared back at the pavement, but there was nobody. The fog, which must have obscured the man's face, closed again.

One room was lighted: the kitchen, at the far end of the hall. Edna and Peter must be in there. Since the house was silent, the boy could not have invited in his friends. Clarke closed the front door, glad to see the last of the fog, and hurried down the hall. He had taken three steps when something slithered beneath his feet. He peered at it, on the faint edge of light from the kitchen. It was a plastic bag.

In a moment, during which his head seemed to clench and grow lightless as he hastily straightened up, he realised that it was one of the bags Edna used to protect food. Several were scattered along the hall. She must have dropped them out of the packet, she mustn't have noticed. He ran along the hall, towards the light, towards the silent kitchen. The kitchen was empty.

He began to call to Edna and to Peter as he ran back through the house, slipping on the scattered bags, bruising his shoulder against the wall. He pulled open the dining-room door, but although the china was chiming from his footsteps, there was nobody within. He ran on, skidding, and wrenched open the door of the living-room. The faintest of orange glows had managed to gather in the room. He was groping distractedly for the light-switch when he made out Edna and Peter, sitting waiting for him in the dark. Their heads gleamed faintly.

After a very long time he switched on the light.

He switched it off at once. He had seen enough; he had seen their gaping mouths stuffed full of sucked-in plastic. His mind had refused to let him see their eyes. He stood in the orange dark, gazing at the still figures. When he made a sound, it resounded through the house.

At last he stumbled into the hall. He had nowhere else to go. He knew the moment was right. The blur in the lighted kitchen doorway was a figure: a man, vague as fog and very thin. Its stiff arms rose jerkily, perhaps hampered by pain, perhaps savouring the moment. Grey blotches peered from its face. He heard the rustling as it uncovered its head.

Baby

When the old woman reached the shops Dutton began to lag further behind. Though his hands were as deep in his pockets as they could go, they were shaking. It's all right, he told himself, stay behind. The last thing you want is for her to notice you now. But he knew he'd fallen behind because he was losing his nerve.

The November wind blundered out of the side streets and shook him. As he hurried across each intersection, head trembling deep in his collar, he couldn't help searching the doorways for Tommy, Maud, even old Frank, anyone with a bottle. But nobody sat against the dull paint of the doors, beneath the bricked-up windows; nothing moved except tangles of sodden paper and leaves. No, he thought, trying to seize his mind before it began to shake like his body. He hadn't stayed sober for so long to lapse now, when he was so close to what he'd stayed sober for.

She'd drawn ahead; he was four blocks behind now. Not far enough behind. He'd better dodge into the next side street before she looked back and saw him. But then one of the shopkeepers might see him hiding and call the police. Or she might turn somewhere while he was hiding, and he would lose her. The stubble on his cheeks crawled with sweat, which clung to the whole of his body; he couldn't tell if it was boiling or frozen. For a couple of steps he limped rapidly to catch up with the old woman, then he held himself back. She was about to look at him.

Fear flashed through him as if his sweat were charged. He made himself gaze at the shops, at the stalls outside: water chestnuts, capsicums, aubergines, dhal—the little notices on sticks said so, but they were alien to him; they didn't help him hold on to his mind. Their price-flags fluttered, tiny and nerve-racking as the prickling of his cheeks.

Then he heard the pram. Its sound was deep in the blustering of the wind, but it was unmistakable. He'd heard it too often, coming towards the house, fading into the room below his. It sounded like the start of a rusty metal yawn, abruptly interrupted by a brief squeal, over and over. It was the sound of his goal, of the reason why he'd stayed sober all night. He brought the pockets of his coat together, propping the iron bar more securely against his chest inside the coat.

She had reached the maze of marshy ground and broken houses beyond the shops. At last, Dutton thought, and began to run. The bar thumped his chest until it bruised. His trousers chafed his thighs like sandpaper, his calves throbbed, but he ran stumbling past the morose shoppers, the defiantly cheerful shopkeepers, the continuing almost ghostly trade of the street. As soon as she was out of sight of the shops, near one of the dilapidated houses, he would have her. At once he halted, drenched in sweat. He couldn't do it.

He stood laughing mirthlessly at himself as newspapers swooped at him. He was going to kill the old woman, was he? Him, who hadn't been able to keep a job for more than a week for years? Him, who had known he wasn't going to keep a job before he started working at it, until the social security had reluctantly agreed with him? Him, who could boast of nothing but the book he cashed weekly at the post office? He was going to kill her?

His mind sounded like his mother. Too much so to dishearten him entirely: it wasn't him, he could answer back. He remembered when he'd started drinking seriously. He'd felt then that if the social security took an interest in him he would be able to hold down a job; but they hadn't bothered to conceal their indifference, and soon after that they'd given him his book. But now it was different. He didn't need anyone's encouragement. He'd proved that by not touching a drink since yesterday afternoon. If he could do that, he could do anything.

He shoved past a woman wheeling a pramful of groceries, and ran faster to outdistance the trembling that spread through his body. His shoes crackled faintly with the plastic bags in which his feet were wrapped. He was going to kill her, because of the contemptuous way she'd looked at him in the hall, exactly as his mother had used to; because while he was suffering poverty, she had chosen worse and flaunted her happiness; because although her coat had acquired a thick hem of mud from trailing, though the coat gaped like frayed lips between her shoulders, she was always smiling secretly, unassailably. He let the thoughts seep through his mind, gathering darkly and heavily in the depths. He *was* going to kill her—because she looked too old for life, too ugly and wizened to live; because she walked as if to do so were a punishment; because her smile must be a paralysed grimace of pain, after all; because her tuneless crooning often kept him awake half the night, though he stamped on her ceiling; because he needed her secret wealth. She had turned and was coming back towards him, past the shops.

His face huddled into his collar as he stumbled away, across the road. That was enough. He'd tried, he couldn't do more. If circumstances hadn't saved him he would have failed. He would have been arrested, and for nothing. He shifted the bar uneasily within his coat, anxious to be rid of it. He gazed at the burst husk of a premature firework, lying trampled on the pavement. It reminded him of himself. He turned hastily as the old woman came opposite him, and stared in a toy-shop window.

An orange baby with fat wrinkled dusty joints stared back at him. Beside it, reflected in a dark gap among the early Christmas toys and fireworks for tomorrow night, he saw the old woman. She had pushed her pram alongside a greengrocer's stall; now she let it go. Dutton peered closer, frowning.

He was sure she hadn't pushed the pram before letting go. Yet it had sped away, past the greengrocer's stall, then halted suddenly. He was still peering when she wheeled it out of the reflection, into the depths full of toys. He began to follow her at once, hardly shaking. Even if he hadn't needed her wealth to give him a chance in life, he had to know what was in that pram.

What wealth? How did he know about it? He struggled to remember. Betty, no, Maud had told him, the day she hadn't drunk too much to recall. She'd read about the old woman in the paper, years ago: about how she'd been swindled by a man whom nobody could trace. She'd given the man her money, her jewels, her house, and her relatives had set the police on him. But then she had been in the paper herself, saying she hadn't been swindled at all, that it was none of their business what she'd gained from the trade; and Maud supposed they'd believed her, because that was the last she had seen of the woman in the paper.

But soon after that Maud had seen her in town, wheeling her pram and smiling to herself. She'd often seen her in the crowds, and then the old woman had moved into the room beneath Dutton, older and wearier now but still smiling. "That shows she got something out of it," Maud said. "What else has she got to smile about? But where she keeps it, that's the thing." She'd shown Dutton a bit she had kept of the paper, and it did look like the old woman, smiling up from a blot of fluff and sweat.

The old woman had nearly reached home now. Dutton stumbled over a paving-stone that had cracked and collapsed like ice on a pool. The iron bar nudged his chest impatiently, tearing his skin. Nearly there now. He had to remember why he was doing this. If he could hold all that in his mind he would be able to kill her. He muttered; his furred tongue crawled in his mouth like a dying caterpillar. He must remember.

He'd gone into her room one day. A month ago, two? Never mind! he thought viciously. He'd been drunk enough to take the risk, not too drunk to make sense of what he'd found. He'd staggered into the house and straight into her room. Since he knew she didn't lock the door, he'd expected to find nothing; yet he was astonished to find so little. In the strained light through the encrusted window, stained patches of wallpaper slumped and bulged. The bed knelt at one corner, for a leg had given way; the dirty sheets had slipped down to conceal the damage. Otherwise the room was bare, no sign even of the pram. The pram. Of course.

He had tried to glimpse what was in the pram. He'd pressed his cheek against his window whenever he heard her approaching, but each time the pram's hood was in the way. Once he'd run downstairs and peered into the pram as she opened her door, but she had pulled the pram away like a chair in a practical joke, and gazed at him with amazement, amusement, profound contempt.

And last week, in the street, he'd been so drunk he had reeled at her and wrenched the pram's handle from her grasp. He'd staggered around to look beneath the hood—but she had already kicked the pram, sending it sailing down a canted side road, and had flown screaming at him, her nails aimed straight for his eyes. When he'd fallen in the gutter she had turned away, laughing with the crowd. As he had pushed himself unsteadily to his feet, his hand deep in sodden litter, he was sure he'd glimpsed the pram halting inches short of crashing into a wall, apparently by itself.

He had decided then, as his hand slithered in the pulp. In his mind she'd joined the people who were laughing inwardly at him: the social security, the clerks in the post office. Only she was laughing aloud, encouraging the crowd to laugh. He would kill her for that. He'd persuaded himself for days that he would. She'd soon have no reason to laugh at his poverty, at the book he hid crumpled in his hand as he waited in the post office. And last night, writhing on his bed amid the darkly crawling walls, listening to her incessant contented wailing, he'd known that he would kill her.

He would kill her. Now.

He was running, his hands gloved in his pockets and swinging together before him at the end of the metal bar, running past a shop whose windows were boarded up with dislocated doors, past the faintly whistling waste ground and, beneath his window in the side of the house, a dormant restlessly creaking bonfire taller than himself. She must have reached her room by now.

The street was deserted. Bricks lay in the roadway, unmoved by the tugging of the wind. He wavered on the front step, listening for sounds in the house. The baby wasn't crying in the cellar, which meant those people must be out; nobody was in the kitchen; even if the old man in the room opposite Dutton's were home, he was deaf. Dutton floundered into the hall, then halted as if at the end of a chain.

He couldn't do it here. He stared at the smudged and faded whorls of the wallpaper, the patterns of numbers scribbled above the patch where the telephone had used to be, the way the stairs turned sharply in the gloom just below the landing. The bar hung half out of his coat. He could have killed her beyond the shops, but this was too familiar. He couldn't imagine a killing here, where everything suffocated even the thought of change—everything, even the creaking of the floorboards.

The floorboards were creaking. She would hear them. All at once he felt he was drowning in sweat. She would come out and see the iron bar, and know what he'd meant to do. She would call the police. He pulled out the bar, tearing a button-hole, and blundered into her room.

The old woman was at the far end of the room, her back to him. She was turning away from the pram, stooped over as if holding an object against her belly. From her mouth came the sound that had kept him awake so often, a contented lulling sound. For the first time he could hear what she was saying. "Baby," she was crooning, "baby." She might have been speaking to a lover or a child.

In a moment she would see him. He limped swiftly forward, his padding footsteps puffing up dust to discolour the dim light more, and swung the iron bar at her head.

He'd forgotten how heavy the bar was. It pulled him down towards her, by his weakened arms. He felt her head give, and heard a muffled crackling beneath her hair. Momentarily, as he clung to the bar as it rested in her head against the wall, he was face to face with her, with her eyes and mouth as they worked spasmodically and went slack.

He recoiled, most of all because there was the beginning of a wry smile in her eyes until they faded. Then she fell with a great flat thud, shockingly heavy and loud. Dust rolled out from beneath her, rising about Dutton's face as he fought a sneeze, settling on the dark patch that was spreading over the old woman's colourless hair.

Dutton closed his eyes and gripped the bar, propping it against the wall, resting his forehead on the lukewarm metal. His stomach writhed, worse than in the mornings, sending convulsions through his whole body. At last he managed to open his eyes and look down again. She lay with one cheek in the dust, her hair darkening, her arms sprawled on either side of her. They had been holding nothing to her belly. In the dim light she looked like a

sleeping drunk, a sack, almost nothing at all. Dutton remembered the crackling of her head and found himself giggling hysterically, uncontrollably.

He had to be quick. Someone might hear him. Stepping over her, he unbuttoned the pram's apron and pulled it back.

At first he couldn't make out what the pram contained. He had to crane
himself over, holding his body back from obscuring the light. The pram was
full of groceries—cabbage, sprouts, potatoes. Dutton shook his head, bewildered, suspecting his eyes of practical joking. He pulled the pram over to the
window, remembering only just in time to disguise his hand in the rag he
kept as a handkerchief.

The windowpanes looked like the back of a fireplace. Dutton rubbed
them with his handkerchief but succeeded only in smudging the grime. He
peered into the pram again. It was still almost packed with groceries; only,
near the head of the pram, there was a clear space about a foot in diameter. It
was empty.

He began to throw out the vegetables. Potatoes trundled thundering over
the floorboards, a rolling cabbage scooped up dust in its leaves. The vegetables were fresh, yet she had entered none of the shops, and he was sure he
hadn't seen her filching. He was trying to recall what in fact he had seen
when his wrapped hand touched something at the bottom of the pram: something hard, round, several round objects, a corner beneath one, a surface that
struck cold through his handkerchief—glass. He lifted the corner and the
framed photograph came up out of the darkness, its round transparent cargo
rolling. They almost rolled off before he laid the photograph on the corner
of the pram, for his grip had slackened as the globes rolled apart to let the
old woman stare up at him.

She was decades younger, and there was no doubt she was the woman
Maud had shown him. And here were her treasures, delivered to him on her
photograph as if on a tray. He grinned wildly and stooped to admire them.
He froze in that position, hunched over in disbelief.

There were four of the globes. They were transparent, full of floating
specks of light that gradually settled. He stared numbly at them. Close to his
eyes threads of sunlight through the window selected sparkling motes of
dust, then let them go. Surely he must be wrong. Surely this wasn't what he'd
suffered all night for. But he could see no other explanation. The old woman
had been wholly mad. The treasures that had kept her smiling, the treasures
she had fought him for, were nothing but four fake snowstorm globes of the
kind he'd seen in dozens of toy shops.

He convulsed as if seized by nausea. With his wrapped hand he swept all four globes off the photograph, snarling.

They took a long time to fall. They took long enough for him to notice, and to stare at them. They seemed to be sinking through the air as slowly as dust, turning enormously like worlds, filling the whole of his attention. In each of them a faint image was appearing: in one a landscape, in another a calm and luminous face.

It must be the angle at which you held them to the light. They were falling so slowly he could catch them yet, could catch the face and the landscape which he could almost see, the other images which trembled at the very edge of recognition, images like a sweet and piercing song, approaching from inaudibility. They were falling slowly—yet he was only making to move towards them when the globes smashed on the floor, their fragments parting like petals. He heard no sound at all.

He stood shaking in the dimness. He had had enough. He felt his trembling hands wrap the stained bar in his handkerchief. The rag was large enough; it had always made a companionable bulge in his pocket. He sniffed, and wondered if the old woman's pockets were empty. It was only when he stooped to search that he saw the enormous bulge in her coat, over her belly.

Part of his mind was warning him, but his fingers wrenched eagerly at her buttons. He threw her coat open, in the dust. Then he recoiled, gasping. Beneath the faded flowers of her dress she was heavily pregnant.

She couldn't be. Who would have touched her? Her coat hadn't bulged like that in the street, he was sure. But there was no mistaking the swelling of her belly. He pushed himself away from her, his hands against the damp wall. The light was so dim and thick he felt he was struggling in mud. He gazed at the swollen lifeless body, then he turned and ran.

Still there was nobody in the street. He stumbled to the waste ground and thrust the wrapped bar deep in the bonfire. Tomorrow night the blood would be burned away. As he limped through the broken streets, the old woman's room hung about him. At last, in a doorway two streets distant, he found Tommy.

He collapsed on the doorstep and seized the bottle Tommy offered him. The cloying wine poured down his throat; bile rose to meet it, but he choked them down. As the wind blustered at his chest it seemed to kindle the wine in him. There was no pregnant corpse in the settling dust, no room thick with dim light, no crackling head. He tilted his head back, gulping.

Tommy was trying to wrest the bottle from him. The neck tapped viciously against Dutton's teeth, but he held it between his lips and thrust his tongue up to hurry the last drops; then he hurled the bottle into the gutter, where it smashed, echoing between the blank houses. As he threw it, a police car entered the road.

Dutton sat inert while the policemen strolled towards him. Tommy was levering himself away rapidly, crutch thumping. Dutton knew one of the policemen: Constable Wayne. "We can't pretend we didn't see that, Billy," Wayne told him. "Be a good boy and you'll be out in the morning."

The wine smudged the world around Dutton for a while. The cell wall was a screen on which he could put pictures to the sounds of the police station: footsteps, shouts, telephones, spoons rattling in mugs. His eyes were coaxing the graffiti from beneath the new paint when, distant but clear, he heard a voice say "What about Billy Dutton?"

"Him knock an old woman's head in?" Wayne's voice said. "I don't reckon he could do that, even sober. Besides, I brought him in around the time of death. He wasn't capable of handling a bottle, let alone a murder."

Later a young policeman brought Dutton a mug of tea and some ageing cheese sandwiches wrapped in greaseproof paper, then stood frowning with mingled disapproval and embarrassment while Dutton was sick. Yet though Dutton lay rocking with nausea for most of the night, though frequently he stood up and roamed unsteadily about the cell and felt as if his nausea was sinking deep within him like dregs, always he could hear Wayne's words. The words freed him of guilt. He had risked, and lost, and that was all. When he left the cell he could return to his old life. He would buy a bottle and celebrate with Tommy, Maud, even old Frank.

He could hear an odd sound far out in the night, separate from the musings of the city, the barking dogs, the foghorns on the Mersey. He propped himself on one elbow to listen. Now that it was coming closer he could make it out: a sound like an interrupted metal yawn. It was groaning towards him; it was beside him. He awoke shouting and saw Wayne opening his cell. It must have been the hinges of the door.

"It's about time you saw someone who can help you," Wayne said.

Perhaps he was threatening to give Dutton's address to a social worker or someone like that. Let him, Dutton thought. They couldn't force their way into his room so long as he didn't do wrong. He was sure that was true, it must be.

Three doors away from the police station was a pub, a Wine Lodge. They must have let him sleep while he could; the Wine Lodge was already open. Dutton bought a bottle and crossed to the opposite pavement, which was the edge of the derelict area towards which he'd pursued the old woman.

The dull sunlight seemed to seep out of the ruined walls. Dutton trudged over the orange mud, past stagnant puddles in the shape of footprints; water welled up around his shoes, the mud sucked them loudly. As soon as there were walls between him and the police station he unstoppered the bottle and drank. He felt like a flower opening to the sun. Still walking, he hadn't lowered the bottle when he caught sight of old Frank sitting on the step of a derelict house.

"Here's Billy," Frank shouted, and the others appeared in the empty window. At the edge of the waste land a police car was roving; that must be why they had taken refuge.

They came forward as best they could to welcome him. "You won't be wanting to go home tonight," Maud said.

"Why not?" In fact there was no reason why he shouldn't know—he could have told them what he'd overheard Wayne discussing—but he wouldn't take the risk. They were ready to suspect anyone, these people; you couldn't trust them.

"Someone did for that old woman," Frank said. "The one in the room below you. Bashed her head in and took her pram."

Dutton's throat closed involuntarily; wine welled up from his lips, around the neck of the bottle. "Took her pram?" he coughed, weeping. "Are you sure?"

"Sure as I was standing outside when they carried her out. The police knew her, you know, her and her pram. They used to look in to make sure she was all right. She wouldn't have left her pram anywhere, they said. Someone took it."

"So you won't be wanting to go home tonight. You can warm my bed if you like," Maud said toothlessly, lips wrinkling.

"What would anyone want to kill her for?" Betty said, dragging her grey hair over the scarred side of her face. "She hadn't got anything."

"She had once. She was rich. She bought something with all that," Maud said.

"Don't care. She didn't have anything worth killing her for. Did she, Billy?"

"No," Dutton said, and stumbled hurriedly on: "There wasn't anything in that pram. I know. I looked in it once when she was going in her room. She was poorer than us."

"Unless she was a witch," Maud said.

Dutton shook the bottle to quicken the liquor. In a moment it would take hold of him completely, he'd be floating on it, Maud's words would drift by like flotsam on a warm sea. "What?" he said.

"Unless she was a witch. Then she could have given everything she owned, and her soul as well, to that man they never found, and still have had something for it that nobody could see, or wouldn't understand if they did see." She panted, having managed her speech, and drank.

"That woman was a witch right enough," Tommy said, challenging the splintered floor with his crutch. "I used to go by there at night and hear her singing to herself. There was something not right there."

"I sing," Frank said, standing up menacingly, and did so: "Rock of Ages." "Am I a witch, eh? Am I a witch?"

"They weren't hymns she was singing, I'll be bound. If I hadn't seen her in the street I'd have said she was a darkey. Jungle music, it was. Mumbo-jumbo."

"She was singing to her baby," Dutton said loosely.

"She didn't have a baby, Billy," Maud said. "Only a pram."

"She was going to have one."

"You're the man who should know, are you?" Frank demanded. "She could have fooled me. She was flat as a pancake when they carried her out. Flat as a pancake."

Dutton stared at Frank for as long as he could, before he had to look away from the deformed strawberry of the man's nose. He seemed to be telling the truth. Two memories were circling Dutton, trying to perch on his thoughts: a little girl who'd been peering in the old woman's window one day, suddenly running away and calling back—inappropriately, it had seemed at the time—"Fat cow"; the corpse on the dusty floor, indisputably pregnant even in the dim light. "Flat as a pancake," Frank repeated.

Dutton was still struggling to understand when Maud said "What's that?"

Dutton could hear nothing but the rushing of his blood. "Sounds like a car," Betty said.

"Too small for a car. Needs oiling, whatever it is."

What were they talking about? Why were they talking about things he couldn't understand, that he couldn't even hear, that disturbed him? "What?" Dutton yelled.

They all stared at him, focusing elaborately, and Tommy thumped his crutch angrily. "It's gone now," Maud said at last.

There was a silence until Betty said sleepily "If she was a witch where was her familiar?"

"Her what?" Dutton said, as the bottle blurred and dissolved above his eyes. She didn't know what she was talking about. Nor did he, he shouted at himself. Nor did he.

"Her familiar. A kind of, you know, creature that would do things for her.

Bring her food, that kind of thing. A cat, or something. She hadn't anything like that. She wouldn't have been able to hide it."

Nowhere to hide it, Dutton thought. In her pram—but her pram had been empty. The top of his head was rising, floating away; it didn't matter. Betty's hand wobbled at the edge of his vision, spilling wine towards him. He grabbed the bottle as her eyes closed. He tried to drink but couldn't find his mouth. Somehow he managed to stopper the bottle with his finger, and a moment later was asleep.

When he awoke he was alone in the dark.

Among the bricks that were bruising his chest was the bottle, still glued to his finger. He clambered to his feet, deafened by the clattering of bricks, and dug the bottle into his pocket for safety, finger and all. He groped his way out of the house, sniffing, searching vainly for his handkerchief. A wall reeled back from him and he fell, scraping his shoulder. Eventually he reached the doorway.

Night had fallen. Amid the mutter of the city, fireworks were already sputtering; distant chimneys sprang up momentarily against a spray of white fire. Far ahead, between the tipsily shifting walls, the lights of the shops blinked faintly at Dutton. He took a draught to fend off the icy plucking of the wind, then he stuffed the bottle in his pocket and made for the lights.

The mud was lying in wait for him. It swallowed his feet with an approving sound. It poured into his shoes, seeping into the plastic bags. It squeezed out from beneath unsteady paving-stones, where there were any. He snarled at it and stamped, sending it over his trouser cuffs. It stretched glistening faintly before him as far as he could see.

Cars were taking a short cut from the main road, past the shops. Dutton stood and waited for their lights to sweep over the mud, lighting up his way. He emptied the bottle into himself. Headlights swung towards him, blazing abruptly in puddles, pinching up silver edges of ruts from the darkness, touching a small still dark object between the walls to Dutton's left.

He glared towards that, through the pale fading firework display on his eyeballs. It had been low and squat, he was sure; part of it had been raised, like a hood. Suddenly he recoiled from the restless darkness and began to run wildly. He fell with a flat splash and heaved himself up, his hands gloved in grit and mud. He stumbled towards the swaying lights and glared about whenever headlights flashed between the walls. Around him the walls seemed as unstable as the ground.

He was close enough to the shops for the individual sounds of the street to have separated themselves from the muted anonymous roar of the city, when he fell again. He fell into darkness behind walls, and scrabbled in the mud, slithering grittily. When he regained his feet he peered desperately about, trying to hold things still. The lights of the street, sinking, leaping back into place and sinking, sinking; the walls around him, wavering and drooping; a dwarfish fragment of wall close to him, on his left. Headlights slipped past him and corrected him. It wasn't a fragment of wall. It was a pram.

In that moment of frozen clarity he could see the twin clawmarks its wheels had scored in the mud, reaching back into darkness. Then the darkness rushed at him as his ankles tangled and he lost his footing. He was reeling helplessly towards the pram.

A second before he reached it he lashed out blindly with one foot. He tottered in a socket of mud, but he felt his foot strike metal, and heard the pram fall. He whirled about, running towards the whirling lights, changing his direction when they steadied. The next time headlights passed him he twisted about to look. The force of his movement spun him back again and on, towards the lights. But he was sure he'd seen the pram upturned in the mud, and shaking like a turtle trying to right itself.

Once among the shops he felt safe. This was his territory. People were hurrying home from work, children were running errands; cars laden with packages butted their way towards the suburbs, honking. He'd stay here, where there were people; he wouldn't go home to his room.

He began to stroll, rolling unsteadily. He gazed in the shop windows, whose contents sank like a loose television image. When he reached a launderette he halted, frowning, and couldn't understand why. Was it something he'd heard? Yes, there was a sound somewhere amid the impatient clamour of the traffic: a yawn of metal cut short by a high squeal. It was something like that, not entirely, not the sound he remembered, only the sound of a car. Within the launderette things whirled, whirled; so did the launderette; so did the pavement. Dutton forced himself onward, cursing as he almost fell over a child. He shoved the child aside and collided with a pram.

Bulging out from beneath its hood was a swollen faceless head of blue plastic. Folds of its wrinkled wormlike body squeezed over the side of the pram; within the blue transparent body he could see white coils and rolls of washing, like tripe. Dutton thrust it away, choking. The woman wheeling it aimed a blow at him and pushed the pram into the launderette.

He ran helplessly forward, trying to retrieve his balance. Mud trickled through the burst plastic in his shoes and grated between his toes. He fell, slapping the pavement with himself. When someone tried to help him up he snarled and rolled out of their reach.

He was cold and wet. His coat had soaked up all the water his falls had squeezed out of the mud. He couldn't go home, couldn't warm himself in bed; he had to stay here, out on the street. His mouth tasted like an abandoned bottle. He glared about, roaring at anyone who came near. Then, over the jerking segments of the line of car roofs, he saw Maud hurrying down a side street, carrying a bottle wrapped in newspaper.

That was what he needed. A ball of fire sprang up spinning and whooping above the roofs. Dutton surged towards the pedestrian crossing, whose two green stick-figures were squeaking at each other across the path through the cars. He was almost there when a pram rushed at him from an alley.

He grappled with it, hurling it from him. It was only a pram, never mind, he must catch up with Maud. But a white featureless head nodded towards him on a scrawny neck, craning out from beneath the hood; a head that slipped awry, rolling loose on its neck, as the strings that tied it came unknotted. It was only a guy begging pennies for cut-price fireworks. Before he realised that, Dutton had overbalanced away from it into the road, in front of a released car.

There was a howl of brakes, another, a tinkle of glass. Dutton found himself staring up from beneath a front bumper. Wheels blocked his vision on either side, like huge oppressive earmuffs. People were shouting at each other, someone was shouting at him, the crowd was chattering, laughing. When someone tried to help him to his feet he kicked out and clung to the bumper. Nothing could touch him now, he was safe, they wouldn't dare to. Eventually someone took hold of his arm and wouldn't let go until he stood up. It was Constable Wayne.

"Come on, Billy," Wayne said. "That's enough for today. Go home."

"I won't go home!" Dutton cried in panic.

"Do you mean to tell me you're sending him home and that's all?" a woman shouted above the clamour of her jacketed Pekinese. "What about my headlight?"

"I'll deal with him," Wayne said. "My colleague will take your statements. Don't give me any trouble, Billy," he said, taking a firmer hold on Dutton's arm.

Dutton found himself being marched along the street, towards his room. "I'm not going home," he shouted.

"You are, and I'll see that you do." A fire engine was elbowing its way through the traffic, braying. In the middle of a side street, between walls that quaked with the light of a huge bonfire, children were stoning firemen.

"I won't," Dutton said, pleading. "If you make me I'll get out again. I've drunk too much. I'll do something bad, I'll hurt someone."

"You aren't one of those. Go home now and sleep it off. You know we've no room for you on Saturday nights. And tonight of all nights we don't want to be bothered with you."

They had almost reached the house. Wayne gazed up at the dormant bonfire on the waste ground. "We'll have to see about that," he said. But Dutton hardly heard him. As the house swayed towards him, a rocket exploded low and snatched the house forward for a moment from the darkness. In the old woman's room, at the bottom of the windowpane, he saw a metal bar: the handle of a pram.

Dutton began to struggle again. "I'm not going in there!" he shouted, searching his mind wildly for anything. "I killed that old woman! I knocked her head in, it was me!"

"That's enough of that, now," Wayne said, dragging him up the steps. "You're lucky I can see you're drunk."

Dutton clenched the front door-frame with both hands. "There's something in there!" he screamed. "In her room!"

"There's nothing at all," Wayne said. "Come here and I'll show you." He propelled Dutton into the hall and, switching on his torch, pushed open the old woman's door with his foot. "Now, what's in here?" he demanded. "Nothing."

Dutton looked in, ready to flinch. The torch-beam swept impatiently about the room, revealing nothing but dust. The bed had been pushed beneath the window during the police search. Its headrail was visible through the pane: a metal bar.

Dutton sagged with relief. Only Wayne's grip kept him from falling. He turned as Wayne hurried him towards the stairs, and saw the mouth of darkness just below the landing. It was waiting for him, its lips working. He tried to pull back, but Wayne was becoming more impatient. "See me upstairs," Dutton pleaded.

"Oh, it's the horrors, is it? Come on now, quickly." Wayne stayed where he was, but shone his torch into the mouth, which paled. Dutton stumbled upstairs as far as the lips, which flickered tentatively towards him. He heard the constable clatter up behind him, and the darkness fell back further. Before him, sharp and bright amid the darkness, was his door.

"Switch on your light, be quick," Wayne said.

The room was exactly as Dutton had left it. And why not? he thought, confident all at once. He never locked it, there was nothing to steal, but now the familiarity of everything seemed welcoming: the rumpled bed; the wardrobe, rusted open and plainly empty; the washbasin; the grimy coinmeter. "All right," he called down to Wayne, and bolted the door.

He stood for a long time against the door while his head swam slowly back to him. The wind reached for him through the wide-open window. He couldn't remember having opened it so wide, but it didn't matter. Once he was steady he would close it, then he'd go to bed. The blankets were raised like a cowl at the pillow, waiting for him. He heard Constable Wayne walk away. Eventually he heard the children light the bonfire.

When blackening tatters of fire began to flutter towards the house he limped to close the window. The bonfire was roaring; the heat collided with him. He remembered with a shock of pleasure that the iron bar was deep in the blaze. He sniffed and groped vainly for his handkerchief as the smoke stung his nostrils. Never mind. He squinted at the black object at the peak of the bonfire, which the flames had just reached. Then he fell back involuntarily. It was the pram.

He slammed the window. Bright orange faces glanced up at him, then turned away. There was no mistaking the pram, for he saw the photograph within the hood strain with the heat, and shatter. He tested his feelings gingerly and realised he could release the thoughts he'd held back, at last. The pursuit was over. It had given up. And suddenly he knew why.

It had been the old woman's familiar. He'd known that as soon as Betty had mentioned the idea, but he hadn't dared think in case it heard him thinking; devils could do that. The old woman had taken it out in her pram, and it had stolen food for her. But it hadn't lived in the pram. It had lived inside the old woman. That was what he'd seen in her room, only it had got out before the police had found the body.

He switched off the light. The room stayed almost as bright, from the blaze. He fumbled with his buttons and removed his outer clothes. The walls shook; his mouth was beginning to taste like dregs again. It didn't matter. If he couldn't sleep he could go out and buy a bottle. Tomorrow he could cash his book. He needn't be afraid to go out now.

It must have thrown itself on the bonfire because devils lived in fire. It must have realised at last that he wasn't like the old woman, that it couldn't live inside him. He stumbled towards the bed. A shadow was moving on the pillow. He baulked, then he saw it was the shadow of the blanket's cowl. He pulled the blanket back.

He had just realised how like the hood of a pram the shape of the blanket had been when the long spidery arms unfolded from the bed, and the powerful claws reached eagerly to part him.

The Chimney

Maybe most of it was only fear. But not the last thing, not that. To blame my fear for that would be worst of all.

I was twelve years old and beginning to conquer my fears. I even went upstairs to do my homework, and managed to ignore the chimney. I had to be brave, because of my parents—because of my mother.

She had always been afraid for me. The very first day I had gone to school I'd seen her watching. Her expression had reminded me of the face of a girl I'd glimpsed on television, watching men lock her husband behind bars; I was frightened all that first day. And when children had hysterics or began to bully me, or the teacher lost her temper, these things only confirmed my fears—and my mother's, when I told her what had happened each day.

Now I was at grammar school. I had been there for much of a year. I'd felt awkward in my new uniform and old shoes; the building seemed enormous, crowded with too many strange children and teachers. I'd felt I was an outsider; friendly approaches made me nervous and sullen, when people laughed and I didn't know why I was sure they were laughing at me. After a while the other boys treated me as I seemed to want to be treated: the lads from the poorer districts mocked my suburban accent, the suburban boys sneered at my shoes.

Often I'd sat praying that the teacher wouldn't ask me a question I couldn't answer, sat paralysed by my dread of having to stand up in the waiting watchful silence. If a teacher shouted at someone my heart jumped painfully; once I'd felt the stain of my shock creeping insidiously down my thigh. Yet I did well in the end-of-term examinations, because I was terrified of failing; for nights afterwards they were another reason why I couldn't sleep.

My mother read the signs of all this on my face. More and more, once I'd told her what was wrong, I had to persuade her there was nothing worse that I'd kept back. Some mornings as I lay in bed, trying to hold back half past seven, I'd be sick; I would grope miserably downstairs, white-faced, and my mother would keep me home. Once or twice, when my fear wasn't quite enough, I made myself sick. "Look at him. You can't expect him to go like that"—but my father would only shake his head and grunt, dismissing us both.

I knew my father found me embarrassing. This year he'd had less time for me than usual; his shop—The Anything Shop, nearby in the suburbanised village—was failing to compete with the new supermarket. But before that trouble I'd often seen him staring up at my mother and me: both of us taller than him, his eyes said, yet both scared of our own shadows. At those times I glimpsed his despair.

So my parents weren't reassuring. Yet at night I tried to stay with them as long as I could—for my worst fears were upstairs, in my room.

It was a large room, two rooms knocked into one by the previous owner. It overlooked the small back gardens. The smaller of the fireplaces had been bricked up; in winter, the larger held a fire, which my mother always feared would set fire to the room—but she let it alone, for I'd screamed when I thought she was going to take that light away: even though the firelight only added to the terrors of the room.

The shadows moved things. The mesh of the fireguard fluttered enlarged on the wall; sometimes, at the edge of sleep, it became a swaying web, and its spinner came sidling down from a corner of the ceiling. Everything was unstable; walls shifted, my clothes crawled on the back of the chair. Once, when I'd left my jacket slumped over the chair, the collar's dark upturned lack of a face began to nod forward stealthily; the holes at the ends of the sleeves worked like mouths, and I didn't dare get up to hang the jacket properly. The room grew in the dark: sounds outside, footsteps and laughter, dogs encouraging each other to bark, only emphasised the size of my trap of darkness, how distant everything else was. And there was a dimmer room, in the mirror of the wardrobe beyond the foot of the bed. There was a bed in that room, and beside it a dim nightlight in a plastic lantern. Once I'd wakened to see a face staring dimly at me from the mirror; a figure had sat up when I had, and I'd almost cried out. Often I'd stared at the dim staring face, until I'd had to hide beneath the sheets.

Of course this couldn't go on for the rest of my life. On my twelfth birthday I set about the conquest of my room.

I was happy amid my presents. I had a jigsaw, a box of coloured pencils, a book of space stories. They had come from my father's shop, but they were mine now. Because I was relaxed, no doubt because she wished I could always be so, my mother said "Would you be happier if you went to another school?"

It was Saturday; I wanted to forget Monday. Besides, I imagined all schools were as frightening. "No, I'm all right," I said.

"Are you happy at school now?" she said incredulously.

"Yes, it's all right."

"Are you sure?"

"Yes, really, it's all right. I mean, I'm happy now."

The snap of the letter-slot saved me from further lying. Three birthday cards: two from neighbours who talked to me when I served them in the shop—an old lady who always carried a poodle, our next-door neighbour Dr Flynn—and a card from my parents. I'd seen all three cards in the shop, which spoilt them somehow.

As I stood in the hall I heard my father. "You've got to control yourself," he was saying. "You only upset the child. If you didn't go on at him he wouldn't be half so bad."

It infuriated me to be called a child. "But I worry so," my mother said brokenly. "He can't look after himself."

"You don't let him try. You'll have him afraid to go up to bed next."

But I already was. Was that my mother's fault? I remembered her putting the nightlight by my bed when I was very young, checking the flex and the bulb each night—I'd taken to lying awake, dreading that one or the other would fail. Standing in the hall, I saw dimly that my mother and I encouraged each other's fears. One of us had to stop. I had to stop. Even when I was frightened, I mustn't let her see. It wouldn't be the first time I'd hidden my feelings from her. In the living-room I said "I'm going upstairs to play."

Sometimes in the summer I didn't mind playing there—but this was March, and a dark day. Still, I could switch the light on. And my room contained the only table I could have to myself and my jigsaw.

I spilled the jigsaw onto the table. The chair sat with its back to the dark yawn of the fireplace; I moved it hastily to the foot of the bed, facing the door. I spread the jigsaw. There was a piece of the edge, another. By lunchtime I'd assembled the edge. "You look pleased with yourself," my father said.

I didn't notice the approach of night. I was fitting together my own blue sky, above fragmented cottages. After dinner I hurried to put in the pieces I'd placed mentally while eating. I hesitated outside my room. I should have to reach into the dark for the light-switch. When I did, the wallpaper filled with bright multiplied aeroplanes and engines. I wished we could afford to redecorate my room, it seemed childish now.

The fireplace gaped. I retrieved the fireguard from the cupboard under the stairs, where my father had stored it now the nights were a little warmer.

It covered the soot-encrusted yawn. The room felt comfortable now. I'd never seen before how much space it gave me for play.

I even felt safe in bed. I switched out the nightlight—but that was too much; I grabbed the light. I didn't mind its glow on its own, without the jagged lurid jig of the shadows. And the fireguard was comforting. It made me feel that nothing could emerge from the chimney.

On Monday I took my space stories to school. People asked to look at them; eventually they lent me books. In the following weeks some of my fears began to fade. Questions darting from desk to desk still made me uneasy, but if I had to stand up without the answer at least I knew the other boys weren't sneering at me, not all of them; I was beginning to have friends. I started to sympathise with their own ignorant silences. In the July examinations I was more relaxed, and scored more marks. I was even sorry to leave my friends for the summer; I invited some of them home.

I felt triumphant. I'd calmed my mother and my room all by myself, just by realising what had to be done. I suppose that sense of triumph helped me. It must have given me a little strength with which to face the real terror.

It was early August, the week before our holiday. My mother was worrying over the luggage, my father was trying to calculate his accounts; they were beginning to chafe against each other. I went to my room, to stay out of their way.

I was halfway through a jigsaw, which one of my friends had swapped for mine. People sat in back gardens, letting the evening settle on them; between the houses the sky was pale yellow. I inserted pieces easily, relaxed by the nearness of our holiday. I listened to the slowing of the city, a radio fluttering along a street, something moving behind the fireguard, in the chimney.

No. It was my mother in the next room, moving luggage. It was someone dragging, dragging something, anything, outside. But I couldn't deceive my ears. In the chimney something large had moved.

It might have been a bird, stunned or dying, struggling feebly—except that a bird would have sounded wilder. It could have been a mouse, even a rat, if such things are found in chimneys. But it sounded like a large body, groping stealthily in the dark: something large that didn't want me to hear it. It sounded like the worst terror of my infancy.

I'd almost forgotten that. When I was three years old my mother had let me watch television; it was bad for my eyes, but just this once, near Christmas. . . . I'd seen two children asleep in bed, an enormous crimson man emerging from the fireplace, creeping towards them. They weren't going to wake up! "Burglar! Burglar!" I'd screamed, beginning to cry. "No, dear, it's

Father Christmas," my mother said, hastily switching off the television. "He always comes out of the chimney."

Perhaps if she'd said "down" rather than "out of". . . . For months after that, and in the weeks before several Christmases, I lay awake listening fearfully for movement in the chimney: I was sure a fat grinning figure would creep upon me if I slept. My mother had told me the presents that appeared at the end of my bed were left by Father Christmas, but now the mysterious visitor had a face and a huge body, squeezed into the dark chimney among the soot. When I heard the wind breathing in the chimney I had to trap my screams between my lips.

Of course at last I began to suspect there was no Father Christmas: how did he manage to steal into my father's shop for my presents? He was a childish idea, I was almost sure—but I was too embarrassed to ask my parents or my friends. But I wanted not to believe in him, that silent lurker in the chimney; and now I didn't, not really. Except that something large was moving softly behind the fireguard.

It had stopped. I stared at the wire mesh, half expecting a fat pale face to stare out of the grate. There was nothing but the fenced dark. Cats were moaning in a garden, an ice-cream van wandered brightly. After a while I forced myself to pull the fireguard away.

I was taller than the fireplace now. But I had to stoop to peer up the dark soot-ridged throat, and then it loomed over me, darkness full of menace, of the threat of a huge figure bursting out at me, its red mouth crammed with sparkling teeth. As I peered up, trembling a little, and tried to persuade myself that what I'd heard had flown away or scurried back into its hole, soot came trickling down from the dark—and I heard the sound of a huge body squeezed into the sooty passage, settling itself carefully, more comfortably in its burrow.

I slammed the guard into place, and fled. I had to gulp to breathe. I ran onto the landing, trying to catch my breath so as to cry for help. Downstairs my mother was nervously asking whether she should pack another of my father's shirts. "Yes, if you like," he said irritably.

No, I mustn't cry out. I'd vowed not to upset her. But how could I go back into my room? Suddenly I had a thought that seemed to help. At school we'd learned how sweeps had used to send small boys up chimneys. There had hardly been room for the boys to climb. How could a large man fit in there?

He couldn't. Gradually I managed to persuade myself. At last I opened the door of my room. The chimney was silent; there was no wind. I tried not to think that he was holding himself still, waiting to squeeze out stealthily, waiting for the dark. Later, lying in the steady glow from my plastic lantern, I tried to hold on to the silence, tried to believe there was nothing near me to shatter it. There was nothing except, eventually, sleep.

Perhaps if I'd cried out on the landing I would have been saved from my fear. But I was happy with my rationality. Only once, nearly asleep, I wished the fire were lit, because it would burn anything that might be hiding in the chimney; that had never occurred to me before. But it didn't matter, for the next day we went on holiday.

My parents liked to sleep in the sunlight, beneath newspaper masks; in the evenings they liked to stroll along the wide sandy streets. I didn't, and befriended Nigel, the son of another family who were staying in the boarding-house. My mother encouraged the friendship: such a nice boy, two years older than me; he'd look after me. He had money, and the hope of a moustache shadowing his pimply upper lip. One evening he took me to the fairground, where we met two girls; he and the older girl went to buy ice creams while her young friend and I stared at each other timidly. I couldn't believe the young girl didn't like jigsaws. Later, while I was contradicting her, Nigel and his companion disappeared behind the Ghost Train—but Nigel reappeared almost at once, red-faced, his left cheek redder. "Where's Rose?" I asked, bewildered.

"She had to go." He seemed furious that I'd asked.

"Isn't she coming back?"

"No." He was glancing irritably about for a change of subject. "What a super bike," he said, pointing as it glided between the stalls. "Have you got a bike?"

"No," I said. "I keep asking Father Christmas, but—" I wished that hadn't got past me, for he was staring at me, winking at the young girl.

"Do you still believe in him?" he demanded scornfully.

"No, of course I don't. I was only kidding." Did he believe me? He was edging towards the young girl now, putting his arm around her; soon she excused herself, and didn't come back—I never knew her name. I was annoyed he'd made her run away. "Where did Rose go?" I said persistently.

He didn't tell me. But perhaps he resented my insistence, for as the family left the boarding-house I heard him say loudly to his mother "He still believes in Father Christmas." My mother heard that too, and glanced anxiously at me.

Well, I didn't. There was nobody in the chimney, waiting for me to come home. I didn't care that we were going home the next day. That night I pulled away the fireguard and saw a fat pale face hanging down into the fireplace, like an underbelly, upside-down and smiling. But I managed to wake, and eventually the sea lulled me back to sleep.

As soon as we reached home I ran upstairs. I uncovered the fireplace and stood staring, to discover what I felt. Gradually I filled with the scorn Nigel would have felt, had he known of my fear. How could I have been so childish? The chimney was only a passage for smoke, a hole into which the wind wandered sometimes. That night, exhausted by the journey home, I slept at once.

The nights darkened into October; the darkness behind the mesh grew thicker. I'd used to feel, as summer waned, that the chimney was insinuating its darkness into my room. Now the sight only reminded me I'd have a fire soon. The fire would be comforting.

It was October when my father's Christmas cards arrived, on a Saturday; I was working in the shop. It annoyed him to have to anticipate Christmas so much, to compete with the supermarket. I hardly noticed the cards: my head felt muffled, my body cold—perhaps it was the weather's sudden hint of winter.

My mother came into the shop that afternoon. I watched her pretend not to have seen the cards. When I looked away she began to pick them up timidly, as if they were unfaithful letters, glancing anxiously at me. I didn't know what was in her mind. My head was throbbing. I wasn't going home sick. I earned pocket money in the shop. Besides, I didn't want my father to think I was still weak.

Nor did I want my mother to worry. That night I lay slumped in a chair, pretending to read. Words trickled down the page; I felt like dirty clothes someone had thrown on the chair. My father was at the shop taking stock. My mother sat gazing at me. I pretended harder; the words waltzed slowly. At last she said "Are you listening?"

I was now, though I didn't look up. "Yes," I said hoarsely, unplugging my throat with a roar.

"Do you remember when you were a baby? There was a film you saw, of Father Christmas coming out of the chimney." Her voice sounded bravely careless, falsely light, as if she were determined to make some awful revelation. I couldn't look up. "Yes," I said.

Her silence made me glance up. She looked as she had on my first day at school: full of loss, of despair. Perhaps she was realising I had to grow up, but to my throbbing head her look suggested only terror—as if she were about to deliver me up as a sacrifice. "I couldn't tell you the truth then," she said. "You were too young."

The truth was terror; her expression promised that. "Father Christmas isn't really like that," she said.

My illness must have shown by then. She gazed at me; her lips trembled. "I can't," she said, turning her face away. "Your father must tell you."

But that left me poised on the edge of terror. I felt unnerved, rustily tense. I wanted very much to lie down. "I'm going to my room," I said. I stumbled upstairs, hardly aware of doing so. As much as anything I was fleeing her unease. The stairs swayed a little, they felt unnaturally soft underfoot. I hurried dully into my room. I slapped the light-switch and missed. I was walking uncontrollably forward into blinding dark. A figure came to meet me, soft and huge in the dark of my room.

I cried out. I managed to stagger back onto the landing, grabbing the light-switch as I went. The lighted room was empty. My mother came running upstairs, almost falling. "What is it, what is it?" she cried.

I mustn't say. "I'm ill. I feel sick." I did, and a minute later I was. She patted my back as I knelt by the toilet. When she'd put me to bed she made to go next door, for the doctor. "Don't leave me," I pleaded. The walls of the room swayed as if tugged by firelight, the fireplace was huge and very dark. As soon as my father opened the door she ran downstairs, crying "He's ill, he's ill! Go for the doctor!"

The doctor came and prescribed for my fever. My mother sat up beside me. Eventually my father came to suggest it was time she went to bed. They were going to leave me alone in my room. "Make a fire," I pleaded.

My mother touched my forehead. "But you're burning," she said.

"No, I'm cold! I want a fire! Please!" So she made one, tired as she was. I saw my father's disgust as he watched me use her worry against her to get what I wanted, his disgust with her for letting herself be used.

I didn't care. My mother's halting words had overgrown my mind. What had she been unable to tell me? Had it to do with the sounds I'd heard in the chimney? The room lolled around me; nothing was sure. But the fire would make sure for me. Nothing in the chimney could survive it.

I made my mother stay until the fire was blazing. Suppose a huge shape burst forth from the hearth, dripping fire? When at last I let go I lay lapped by the firelight and meshy shadows, which seemed lulling now, in my warm room.

I felt feverish, but not unpleasantly. I was content to voyage on my rocking bed; the ceiling swayed past above me. While I slept the fire went out. My fever kept me warm; I slid out of bed and, pulling away the fireguard, reached up the chimney. At the length of my arms I touched something heavy, hanging down in the dark; it yielded, then soft fat fingers groped down and closed on my wrist. My mother was holding my wrist as she washed my hands. "You mustn't get out of bed," she said when she realised I was awake.

I stared stupidly at her. "You'd got out of bed. You were sleepwalking," she explained. "You had your hands right up the chimney." I saw now that she was washing caked soot from my hands; tracks of ash led towards the bed.

It had been only a dream. One moment the fat hand had been gripping my wrist, the next it was my mother's cool slim fingers. My mother played word games and timid chess with me while I stayed in bed, that day and the next.

The third night I felt better. The fire fluttered gently; I felt comfortably warm. Tomorrow I'd get up. I should have to go back to school soon, but I didn't mind that unduly. I lay and listened to the breathing of the wind in the chimney.

When I awoke the fire had gone out. The room was full of darkness. The wind still breathed, but it seemed somehow closer. It was above me. Someone was standing over me. It couldn't be either of my parents, not in the sightless darkness.

I lay rigid. Most of all I wished that I hadn't let Nigel's imagined contempt persuade me to do without a nightlight. The breathing was slow, irregular; it sounded clogged and feeble. As I tried to inch silently towards the far side of the bed, the source of the breathing stooped towards me. I felt its breath waver on my face, and the breath sprinkled me with something like dry rain.

When I had lain paralysed for what felt like blind hours, the breathing went away. It was in the chimney, dislodging soot; it might be the wind. But I knew it had come out to let me know that whatever the fire had done to it, it hadn't been killed. It had emerged to tell me it would come for me on Christmas Eve. I began to scream.

I wouldn't tell my mother why. She washed my face, which was freckled with soot. "You've been sleepwalking again," she tried to reassure me, but I wouldn't let her leave me until daylight. When she'd gone I saw the ashy tracks leading from the chimney to the bed.

Perhaps I had been sleepwalking and dreaming. I searched vainly for my nightlight. I would have been ashamed to ask for a new one, and that helped me to feel I could do without. At dinner I felt secure enough to say I didn't know why I had screamed.

"But you must remember. You sounded so frightened. You upset me."

My father was folding the evening paper into a thick wad the size of a pocketbook, which he could read beside his plate. "Leave the boy alone," he said. "You imagine all sorts of things when you're feverish. I did when I was his age."

It was the first time he'd admitted anything like weakness to me. If he'd managed to survive his nightmares, why should mine disturb me more? Tired out by the demands of my fever, I slept soundly that night. The chimney was silent except for the flapping of flames.

But my father didn't help me again. One November afternoon I was standing behind the counter, hoping for customers. My father pottered, grumpily fingering packets of nylons, tins of pet food, Dinky toys, babies' rattles, cards, searching for signs of theft. Suddenly he snatched a Christmas card and strode to the counter. "Sit down," he said grimly.

He was waving the card at me, like evidence. I sat down on a shelf, but then a lady came into the shop; the bell thumped. I stood up to sell her nylons. When she'd gone I gazed at my father, anxious to hear the worst. "Just sit down," he said.

He couldn't stand my being taller than he was. His size embarrassed him, but he wouldn't let me see that; he pretended I had to sit down out of respect. "Your mother says she tried to tell you about Father Christmas," he said.

She must have told him that weeks earlier. He'd put off talking to me—because we'd never been close, and now we were growing further apart. "I don't know why she couldn't tell you," he said.

But he wasn't telling me either. He was looking at me as if I were a stranger he had to chat to. I felt uneasy, unsure now that I wanted to hear what he had to say. A man was approaching the shop. I stood up, hoping he'd interrupt.

He did, and I served him. Then, to delay my father's revelation, I adjusted stacks of tins. My father stared at me in disgust. "If you don't watch out you'll be as bad as your mother."

I found the idea of being like my mother strange, indefinably disturbing. But he wouldn't let me be like him, wouldn't let me near. All right, I'd be brave, I'd listen to what he had to say. But he said "Oh, it's not worth me trying to tell you. You'll find out."

He meant I must find out for myself that Father Christmas was a childish fantasy. He didn't mean he wanted the thing from the chimney to come for me, the disgust in his eyes didn't mean that, it didn't. He meant that I had to behave like a man.

And I could. I'd show him. The chimney was silent. I needn't worry until Christmas Eve. Nor then. There was nothing to come out.

One evening as I walked home I saw Dr Flynn in his front room. He was standing before a mirror, gazing at his red fur-trimmed hooded suit; he stooped to pick up his beard. My mother told me that he was going to act Father Christmas at the children's hospital. She seemed on the whole glad that I'd seen. So was I: it proved the pretence was only for children.

Except that the glimpse reminded me how near Christmas was. As the nights closed on the days, and the days rushed by—the end-of-term party, the turkey, decorations in the house—I grew tense, trying to prepare myself. For what? For nothing, nothing at all. Well, I would know soon—for suddenly it was Christmas Eve.

I was busy all day. I washed up as my mother prepared Christmas dinner. I brought her ingredients, and hurried to buy some she'd used up. I stuck the day's cards to tapes above the mantelpiece. I carried home a tinsel tree which nobody had bought. But being busy only made the day move faster. Before I knew it the windows were full of night.

Christmas Eve. Well, it didn't worry me. I was too old for that sort of thing. The tinsel tree rustled when anyone passed it, light rolled in tinsel globes, streamers flinched back when doors opened. Whenever I glanced at the wall above the mantelpiece I saw half a dozen red-cheeked smiling bearded faces swinging restlessly on tapes.

The night piled against the windows. I chattered to my mother about her shouting father, her elder sisters, the time her sisters had locked her in a cellar. My father grunted occasionally—even when I'd run out of subjects to discuss with my mother, and tried to talk to him about the shop. At least he hadn't noticed how late I was staying up. But he had. "It's about time everyone was in bed," he said with a kind of suppressed fury.

"Can I have some more coal?" My mother would never let me have a coal-scuttle in the bedroom—she didn't want me going near the fire. "To put on now," I said. Surely she must say yes. "It'll be cold in the morning," I said.

"Yes, you take some. You don't want to be cold when you're looking at what Father—at your presents."

I hurried upstairs with the scuttle. Over its clatter I heard my father say "Are you still at that? Can't you let him grow up?"

I almost emptied the scuttle into the fire, which rose roaring and crackling. My father's voice was an angry mumble, seeping through the floor. When I carried the scuttle down my mother's eyes were red, my father looked furiously determined. I'd always found their arguments frightening; I was glad to hurry to my room.

It seemed welcoming. The fire was bright within the mesh. I heard my mother come upstairs. That was comforting too: she was nearer now. I heard my father go next door—to wish the doctor Happy Christmas, I supposed. I didn't mind the reminder. There was nothing of Christmas Eve in my room, except the pillowcase on the floor at the foot of the bed. I pushed it aside with one foot, the better to ignore it.

I slid into bed. My father came upstairs; I heard further mumblings of argument through the bedroom wall. At last they stopped, and I tried to relax. I lay, glad of the silence.

A wind was rushing the house. It puffed down the chimney; smoke trickled through the fireguard. Now the wind was breathing brokenly. It was only the wind. It didn't bother me.

Perhaps I'd put too much coal on the fire. The room was hot; I was sweating. I felt almost feverish. The huge mesh flicked over the wall repeatedly, nervously, like a rapid net. Within the mirror the dimmer room danced.

Suddenly I was a little afraid. Not that something would come out of the chimney, that was stupid: afraid that my feeling of fever would make me delirious again. It seemed years since I'd been disturbed by the sight of the room in the mirror, but I was disturbed now. There was something wrong with that dim jerking room.

The wind breathed. Only the wind, I couldn't hear it changing. A fat billow of smoke squeezed through the mesh. The room seemed more oppressive now, and smelled of smoke. It didn't smell entirely like coal smoke, but I couldn't tell what else was burning. I didn't want to get up to find out.

I must lie still. Otherwise I'd be writhing about trying to clutch at sleep, as I had the second night of my fever, and sometimes in summer. I must sleep before the room grew too hot. I must keep my eyes shut. I mustn't be distracted by the faint trickling of soot, nor the panting of the wind, nor the shadows and orange light that snatched at my eyes through my eyelids.

I woke in darkness. The fire had gone out. No, it was still there when I opened my eyes: subdued orange crawled on embers, a few weak flames leapt repetitively. The room was moving more slowly now. The dim room in the mirror, the face peering out at me, jerked faintly, as if almost dead.

I couldn't look at that. I slid further down the bed, dragging the pillow into my nest. I was too hot, but at least beneath the sheets I felt safe. I began to relax. Then I realised what I'd seen. The light had been dim, but I was almost sure the fireguard was standing away from the hearth.

I must have mistaken that, in the dim light. I wasn't feverish, I couldn't have sleepwalked again. There was no need for me to look, I was comfortable. But I was beginning to admit that I had better look when I heard the slithering in the chimney.

Something large was coming down. A fall of soot: I could hear the scattering pats of soot in the grate, thrown down by the harsh halting wind. But the wind was emerging from the fireplace, into the room. It was above me, panting through its obstructed throat.

I lay staring up at the mask of my sheets. I trembled from holding myself immobile. My held breath filled me painfully as lumps of rock. I had only to lie there until whatever was above me went away. It couldn't touch me.

The clogged breath bent nearer; I could hear its dry rattling. Then something began to fumble at the sheets over my face. It plucked feebly at them, trying to grasp them, as if it had hardly anything to grasp with. My own hands clutched at the sheets from within, but couldn't hold them down entirely. The sheets were being tugged from me, a fraction at a time. Soon I would be face to face with my visitor.

I was lying there with my eyes squeezed tight when it let go of the sheets and went away. My throbbing lungs had forced me to take shallow breaths; now I breathed silently open-mouthed, though that filled my mouth with fluff. The tolling of my ears subsided, and I realised the thing had not returned to the chimney. It was still in the room.

I couldn't hear its breathing; it couldn't be near me. Only that thought allowed me to look—that, and the desperate hope that I might escape, since it moved so slowly. I peeled the sheets down from my face slowly, stealthily, until my eyes were bare. My heartbeats shook me. In the sluggishly shifting light I saw a figure at the foot of the bed.

Its red costume was thickly furred with soot. It had its back to me; its breathing was muffled by the hood. What shocked me most was its size. It occurred to me, somewhere amid my engulfing terror, that burning shrivels things. The figure stood in the mirror as well, in the dim twitching room. A face peered out of the hood in the mirror, like a charred turnip carved with a rigid grin.

The stunted figure was still moving painfully. It edged round the foot of the bed and stooped to my pillowcase. I saw it draw the pillowcase up over itself and sink down. As it sank its hood fell back, and I saw the charred turnip roll about in the hood, as if there were almost nothing left to support it.

I should have had to pass the pillowcase to reach the door. I couldn't move. The room seemed enormous, and was growing darker; my parents were far away. At last I managed to drag the sheets over my face, and pulled the pillow, like muffs, around my ears.

I had lain sleeplessly for hours when I heard a movement at the foot of the bed. The thing had got out of its sack again. It was coming towards me. It was tugging at the sheets, more strongly now. Before I could catch hold of the sheets I glimpsed a red fur-trimmed sleeve, and was screaming.

"Let go, will you," my father said irritably. "Good God, it's only me."

He was wearing Dr Flynn's disguise, which flapped about him—the jacket, at least; his pyjama cuffs peeked beneath it. I stopped screaming and began to giggle hysterically. I think he would have struck me, but my mother ran in. "It's all right. All right," she reassured me, and explained to him "It's the shock."

He was making angrily for the door when she said "Oh, don't go yet, Albert. Stay while he opens his presents," and, lifting the bulging pillowcase from the floor, dumped it beside me.

I couldn't push it away, I couldn't let her see my terror. I made myself pull out my presents into the daylight, books, sweets, ballpoints; as I groped deeper I wondered whether the charred face would crumble when I touched it. Sweat pricked my hands; they shook with horror—they could, because my mother couldn't see them.

The pillowcase contained nothing but presents and a pinch of soot. When I was sure it was empty I slumped against the headboard, panting. "He's tired," my mother said, in defence of my ingratitude. "He was up very late last night."

Later I managed an accident, dropping the pillowcase on the fire downstairs. I managed to eat Christmas dinner, and to go to bed that night. I lay awake, even though I was sure nothing would come out of the chimney now. Later I realised why my father had come to my room in the morning dressed like that; he'd intended me to catch him, to cure me of the pretence. But it was many years before I enjoyed Christmas very much.

When I left school I went to work in libraries. Ten years later I married. My wife and I crossed town weekly to visit my parents. My mother chattered, my father was taciturn. I don't think he ever quite forgave me for laughing at him.

One winter night our telephone rang. I answered it, hoping it wasn't the police. My library was then suffering from robberies. All I wanted was to sit before the fire and imagine the glittering cold outside. But it was Dr Flynn.

"Your parents' house is on fire," he told me. "Your father's trapped in there. Your mother needs you."

They'd had a friend to stay. My mother had lit the fire in the guest-room, my old bedroom. A spark had eluded the fireguard; the carpet had caught fire. Impatient for the fire engine, my father had run back into the house to put the fire out, but had been overcome. All this I learned later. Now I drove coldly across town, towards the glow in the sky.

The glow was doused by the time I arrived. Smoke scrolled over the roof. But my mother had found a coal sack and was struggling still to run into the house, to beat the fire; her friend and Dr Flynn held her back. She dropped the sack and ran to me. "Oh, it's your father. It's Albert," she repeated through her weeping.

The firemen withdrew their hose. The ambulance stood winking. I saw the front door open, and a stretcher carried out. The path was wet and frosty. One stretcher-bearer slipped, and the contents of the stretcher spilled over the path.

I saw Dr Flynn glance at my mother. Only the fear that she might turn caused him to act. He grabbed the sack and, running to the path, scooped up what lay scattered there. I saw the charred head roll on the lip of the sack before it dropped within. I had seen that already, years ago.

My mother came to live with us, but we could see she was pining; my parents must have loved each other, in their way. She died a year later. Perhaps I killed them both. I know that what emerged from the chimney was in some sense my father. But surely that was a premonition. Surely my fear could never have reached out to make him die that way.

The Brood

He'd had an almost unbearable day. As he walked home his self-control still oppressed him, like rusty armour. Climbing the stairs, he tore open his mail: a glossy pamphlet from a binoculars firm, a humbler folder from the Wild Life Preservation Society. Irritably he threw them on the bed and sat by the window, to relax.

It was autumn. Night had begun to cramp the days. Beneath golden trees, a procession of cars advanced along Princes Avenue, as though to a funeral; crowds hurried home. The incessant anonymous parade, dwarfed by three storeys, depressed him. Faces like these vague twilit miniatures—selfishly ingrown, convinced that nothing was their fault—brought their pets to his office.

But where were all the local characters? He enjoyed watching them, they fascinated him. Where was the man who ran about the avenue, chasing butterflies of litter and stuffing them into his satchel? Or the man who strode violently, head down in no gale, shouting at the air? Or the Rainbow Man, who appeared on the hottest days obese with sweaters, each of a different garish colour? Blackband hadn't seen any of these people for weeks.

The crowds thinned; cars straggled. Groups of streetlamps lit, tinting leaves sodium, unnaturally gold. Often that lighting had meant—Why, there she was, emerging from the side street almost on cue: the Lady of the Lamp.

Her gait was elderly. Her face was withered as an old blanched apple; the rest of her head was wrapped in a tattered grey scarf. Her voluminous ankle-length coat, patched with remnants of colour, swayed as she walked. She reached the central reservation of the avenue, and stood beneath a lamp.

Though there was a pedestrian crossing beside her, people deliberately crossed elsewhere. They would, Blackband thought sourly: just as they ignored the packs of stray dogs that were always someone else's responsibility—ignored them, or hoped someone would put them to sleep. Perhaps they felt the human strays should be put to sleep, perhaps that was where the Rainbow Man and the rest had gone!

The woman was pacing restlessly. She circled the lamp, as though the blurred disc of light at its foot were a stage. Her shadow resembled the elaborate hand of a clock.

Surely she was too old to be a prostitute. Might she have been one, who was now compelled to enact her memories? His binoculars drew her face closer: intent as a sleepwalker's, introverted as a foetus. Her head bobbed against gravel, foreshortened by the false perspective of the lenses. She moved offscreen.

Three months ago, when he'd moved to this flat, there had been two old women. One night he had seen them, circling adjacent lamps. The other woman had been slower, more sleepy. At last the Lady of the Lamp had led her home; they'd moved slowly as exhausted sleepers. For days he'd thought of the two women in their long faded coats, trudging around the lamps in the deserted avenue, as though afraid to go home in the growing dark.

The sight of the lone woman still unnerved him, a little. Darkness was crowding his flat. He drew the curtains, which the lamps stained orange. Watching had relaxed him somewhat. Time to make a salad.

The kitchen overlooked the old women's house. See the World from the Attics of Princes Avenue. All Human Life Is Here. Backyards penned in rubble and crumbling toilet sheds; on the far side of the back street, houses were lidless boxes of smoke. The house directly beneath his window was dark, as always. How could the two women—if both were still alive—survive in there? But at least they could look after themselves, or call for aid; they were human, after all. It was their pets that bothered him.

He had never seen the torpid woman again. Since she had vanished, her companion had begun to take animals home; he'd seen her coaxing them towards the house. No doubt they were company for her friend; but what life could animals enjoy in the lightless probably condemnable house? And why so many? Did they escape to their homes, or stray again? He shook his head: the women's loneliness was no excuse. They cared as little for their pets as did those owners who came, whining like their dogs, to his office.

Perhaps the woman was waiting beneath the lamps for cats to drop from the trees, like fruit. He meant the thought as a joke. But when he'd finished preparing dinner, the idea troubled him sufficiently that he switched off the light in the main room and peered through the curtains.

The bright gravel was bare. Parting the curtains, he saw the woman hurrying unsteadily towards her street. She was carrying a kitten: her head bowed over the fur cradled in her arms; her whole body seemed to enfold it.

As he emerged from the kitchen again, carrying plates, he heard her door creak open and shut. Another one, he thought uneasily.

By the end of the week she'd taken in a stray dog, and Blackband was wondering what should be done.

The women would have to move eventually. The houses adjoining theirs were empty, the windows shattered targets. But how could they take their menagerie with them? They'd set them loose to roam or, weeping, take them to be put to sleep.

Something ought to be done, but not by him. He came home to rest. He was used to removing chicken bones from throats; it was suffering the excuses that exhausted him—Fido always had his bit of chicken, it had never happened before, they couldn't understand. He would nod curtly, with a slight pained smile. "Oh yes?" he would repeat tonelessly. "Oh yes?"

Not that that would work with the Lady of the Lamp. But then, he didn't intend to confront her: what on earth could he have said? That he'd take all the animals off her hands? Hardly. Besides, the thought of confronting her made him uncomfortable.

She was growing more eccentric. Each day she appeared a little earlier. Often she would move away into the dark, then hurry back into the flat bright pool. It was as though light were her drug.

People stared at her, and fled. They disliked her because she was odd. All she had to do to please them, Blackband thought, was be normal: overfeed her pets until their stomachs scraped the ground, lock them in cars to suffocate in the heat, leave them alone in the house all day then beat them for chewing. Compared to most of the owners he met, she was Saint Francis.

He watched television. Insects were courting and mating. Their ritual dances engrossed and moved him: the play of colours, the elaborate racial patterns of the life-force which they instinctively decoded and enacted. Microphotography presented them to him. If only people were as beautiful and fascinating!

Even his fascination with the Lady of the Lamp was no longer unalloyed; he resented that. Was she falling ill? She walked painfully slowly, stooped over, and looked shrunken. Nevertheless, each night she kept her vigil, wandering sluggishly in the pools of light like a sleepwalker.

How could she cope with her animals now? How might she be treating them? Surely there were social workers in some of the cars nosing home, someone must notice how much she needed help. Once he made for the door to the stairs, but already his throat was parched of words. The thought of speaking to her wound him tight inside. It wasn't his job, he had enough to confront. The spring in his guts coiled tighter, until he moved away from the door.

One night an early policeman appeared. Usually the police emerged near midnight, disarming people of knives and broken glass, forcing them into the vans. Blackband watched eagerly. Surely the man must escort her home, see what the house hid. Blackband glanced back to the splash of light beneath the lamp. It was deserted.

How could she have moved so fast? He stared, baffled. A dim shape lurked at the corner of his eyes. Glancing nervously, he saw the woman standing on the bright disc several lamps away, considerably further from the policeman than he'd thought. Why should he have been so mistaken?

Before he could ponder, a sound distracted him: a loud fluttering, as though a bird were trapped and frantic in the kitchen. But the room was empty. Any bird must have escaped through the open window. Was that a flicker of movement below, in the dark house? Perhaps the bird had flown in there.

The policeman had moved on. The woman was trudging her island of light; her coat's hem dragged over the gravel. For a while Blackband watched, musing uneasily, trying to think what the fluttering had resembled more than the sound of a bird's wings.

Perhaps that was why, in the early hours, he saw a man stumbling through the derelict back streets. Jagged hurdles of rubble blocked the way; the man clambered, panting dryly, gulping dust as well as breath. He seemed only exhausted and uneasy, but Blackband could see what was pursuing him: a great wide shadow-coloured stain, creeping vaguely over the rooftops. The stain was alive, for its face mouthed—though at first, from its colour and texture, he thought the head was the moon. Its eyes gleamed hungrily. As the fluttering made the man turn and scream, the face sailed down on its stain towards him.

Next day was unusually trying: a dog with a broken leg and a suffering owner, you'll hurt his leg, can't you be more gentle, oh come here, baby, what did the nasty man do to you; a senile cat and its protector, isn't the usual vet here today, he never used to do that, are you sure you know what you're doing. But later, as he watched the woman's obsessive trudging, the dream of the stain returned to him. Suddenly he realised he had never seen her during daylight.

So that was it! he thought, sniggering. She'd been a vampire all the time! A difficult job to keep when you hadn't a tooth in your head. He reeled in her face with the focusing-screw. Yes, she was toothless. Perhaps she used false fangs, or sucked through her gums. But he couldn't sustain his joke for long. Her faced peered out of the frame of her grey scarf, as though from a web. As she circled she was muttering incessantly. Her tongue worked as though her mouth were too small for it. Her eyes were fixed as the heads of grey nails impaling her skull.

He laid the binoculars aside, and was glad that she'd become more distant. But even the sight of her trudging in miniature troubled him. In her eyes he had seen that she didn't want to do what she was doing.

She was crossing the roadway, advancing towards his gate. For a moment, unreasonably and with a sour uprush of dread, he was sure she intended to come in. But she was staring at the hedge. Her hands fluttered, warding off a fear; her eyes and her mouth were stretched wide. She stood quivering, then she stumbled towards her street, almost running.

He made himself go down. Each leaf of the hedge held an orange sodium glow, like wet paint. But there was nothing among the leaves, and nothing could have struggled out, for the twigs were intricately bound by spiderwebs, gleaming like gold wire.

The next day was Sunday. He rode a train beneath the Mersey and went tramping the Wirral Way nature trail. Red-faced men, and women who had paralysed their hair with spray, stared as though he'd invaded their garden. A few butterflies perched on flowers; their wings settled together delicately, then they flickered away above the banks of the abandoned railway cutting. They were too quick for him to enjoy, even with his binoculars; he kept remembering how near death their species were. His moping had slowed him, he felt barred from his surroundings by his inability to confront the old woman. He couldn't speak to her, there were no words he could use, but meanwhile her animals might be suffering. He dreaded going home to another night of helpless watching.

Could he look into the house while she was wandering? She might leave the door unlocked. At some time he had become intuitively sure that her companion was dead. Twilight gained on him, urging him back to Liverpool.

He gazed nervously down at the lamps. Anything was preferable to his impotence. But his feelings had trapped him into committing himself before he was ready. Could he really go down when she emerged? Suppose the other woman was still alive, and screamed? Good God, he needn't go in if he didn't want to. On the gravel, light lay bare as a row of plates on a shelf. He found himself thinking, with a secret eagerness, that she might already have had her wander.

As he made dinner, he kept hurrying irritably to the front window. Television failed to engross him; he watched the avenue instead. Discs of light dwindled away, impaled by their lamps. Below the kitchen window stood a block of night and silence. Eventually he went to bed, but heard fluttering—flights of litter in the derelict streets, no doubt. His dreams gave the litter a human face.

Throughout Monday he was on edge, anxious to hurry home and be done; he was distracted. Oh, poor Chubbles, is the man hurting you! He managed to leave early. Day was trailing down the sky as he reached the avenue. Swiftly he brewed coffee and sat sipping, watching.

The caravan of cars faltered, interrupted by gaps. The last homecomers hurried away, clearing the stage. But the woman failed to take her cue. His cooking of dinner was fragmented; he hurried repeatedly back to the window. Where was the bloody woman, was she on strike? Not until the following night, when she had still not appeared, did he begin to suspect he'd seen the last of her.

His intense relief was short-lived. If she had died of whatever had been shrinking her, what would happen to her animals? Should he find out what was wrong? But there was no reason to think she'd died. Probably she, and her friend before her, had gone to stay with relatives. No doubt the animals had escaped long before—he'd never seen or heard any of them since she had taken them in. Darkness stood hushed and bulky beneath his kitchen window.

For several days the back streets were quiet, except for the flapping of litter or birds. It became easier to glance at the dark house. Soon they'd demolish it; already children had shattered all the windows. Now, when he lay awaiting sleep, the thought of the vague house soothed him, weighed his mind down gently.

That night he awoke twice. He'd left the kitchen window ajar, hoping to lose some of the unseasonable heat. Drifting through the window came a man's low moaning. Was he trying to form words? His voice was muffled, blurred as a dying radio. He must be drunk; perhaps he had fallen, for there was a faint scrape of rubble. Blackband hid within his eyelids, courting sleep. At last the shapeless moaning faded. There was silence, except for the feeble stony scraping. Blackband lay and grumbled, until sleep led him to a face that crept over heaps of rubble.

Some hours later he woke again. The lifelessness of four o'clock surrounded him, the dim air seemed sluggish and ponderous. Had he dreamed the new sound? It returned, and made him flinch: a chorus of thin piteous wailing, reaching weakly upwards towards the kitchen. For a moment, on the edge of dream, it sounded like babies. How could babies be crying in an abandoned house? The voices were too thin. They were kittens.

He lay in the heavy dark, hemmed in by shapes that the night deformed. He willed the sounds to cease, and eventually they did. When he awoke again, belatedly, he had time only to hurry to work.

In the evening the house was silent as a draped cage. Someone must have rescued the kittens. But in the early hours the crying woke him: fretful, bewildered, famished. He couldn't go down now, he had no light. The crying was muffled, as though beneath stone. Again it kept him awake, again he was late for work.

His loss of sleep nagged him. His smile sagged impatiently, his nods were contemptuous twitches. "Yes," he agreed with a woman who said she'd been careless to slam her dog's paw in a door, and when she raised her eyebrows haughtily "Yes, I can see that." He could see her deciding to find another vet. Let her, let someone else suffer her. He had problems of his own.

He borrowed the office flashlight, to placate his anxiety. Surely he wouldn't need to enter the house, surely someone else—He walked home, towards the darker sky. Night thickened like soot on the buildings.

He prepared dinner quickly. No need to dawdle in the kitchen, no point in staring down. He was hurrying; he dropped a spoon, which reverberated shrilly in his mind, nerve-racking. Slow down, slow down. A breeze piped incessantly outside, in the rubble. No, not a breeze. When he made himself raise the sash he heard the crying, thin as wind in crevices.

It seemed weaker now, dismal and desperate: intolerable. Could nobody else hear it, did nobody care? He gripped the windowsill; a breeze tried feebly to tug at his fingers. Suddenly, compelled by vague anger, he grabbed the flashlight and trudged reluctantly downstairs.

A pigeon hobbled on the avenue, dangling the stump of one leg, twitching clogged wings; cars brisked by. The back street was scattered with debris, as though a herd had moved on, leaving its refuse to manure the pavingstones. His flashlight groped over the heaped pavement, trying to determine which house had been troubling him.

Only by standing back to align his own window with the house could he decide, and even then he was unsure. How could the old woman have clambered over the jagged pile that blocked the doorway? The front door sprawled splintered in the hall, on a heap of the fallen ceiling, amid peelings of wallpaper. He must be mistaken. But as his flashlight dodged about the hall, picking up debris then letting it drop back into the dark, he heard the crying, faint and muffled. It was somewhere within.

He ventured forward, treading carefully. He had to drag the door into the street before he could proceed. Beyond the door the floorboards were cobbled with rubble. Plaster swayed about him, glistening. His light wobbled ahead of him, then led him towards a gaping doorway on the right. The light spread into the room, dimming.

A door lay on its back. Boards poked like exposed ribs through the plaster of the ceiling; torn paper dangled. There was no carton full of starving kittens; in fact, the room was bare. Moist stains engulfed the walls.

He groped along the hall, to the kitchen. The stove was fat with grime. The wallpaper had collapsed entirely, draping indistinguishable shapes that stirred as the flashlight glanced at them. Through the furred window, he made out the light in his own kitchen, orange-shaded, blurred. How could two women have survived here?

At once he regretted that thought. The old woman's face loomed behind him: eyes still as metal, skin the colour of pale bone. He turned nervously; the light capered. Of course there was only the quivering mouth of the hall. But the face was present now, peering from behind the draped shapes around him.

He was about to give up—he was already full of the gasp of relief he would give when he reached the avenue—when he heard the crying. It was almost breathless, as though close to death: a shrill feeble wheezing. He couldn't bear it. He hurried into the hall.

Might the creatures be upstairs? His light showed splintered holes in most of the stairs; through them he glimpsed a huge symmetrical stain on the wall. Surely the woman could never have climbed up there—but that left only the cellar.

The door was beside him. The flashlight, followed by his hand, groped for the knob. The face was near him in the shadows; its fixed eyes gleamed. He dreaded finding her fallen on the cellar steps. But the crying pleaded. He dragged the door open; it scraped over rubble. He thrust the flashlight into the dank opening. He stood gaping, bewildered.

Beneath him lay a low stone room. Its walls glistened darkly. The place was full of debris: bricks, planks, broken lengths of wood. Draping the debris, or tangled beneath it, were numerous old clothes. Threads of a white substance were tethered to everything, and drifted feebly now the door was opened.

In one corner loomed a large pale bulk. His light twitched towards it. It was a white bag of some material, not cloth. It had been torn open; except for a sifting of rubble, and a tangle of what might have been fragments of dully painted cardboard, it was empty.

The crying wailed, somewhere beneath the planks. Several sweeps of the light showed that the cellar was otherwise deserted. Though the face mouthed behind him, he ventured down. For God's sake, get it over with; he knew he would never dare return. A swath had been cleared through the dust on the steps, as though something had dragged itself out of the cellar, or had been dragged in.

His movements disturbed the tethered threads; they rose like feelers, fluttering delicately. The white bag stirred, its torn mouth worked. Without knowing why, he stayed as far from that corner as he could.

The crying had come from the far end of the cellar. As he picked his way hurriedly over the rubble he caught sight of a group of clothes. They were violently coloured sweaters, which the Rainbow Man had worn. They slumped over planks; they nestled inside one another, as though the man had withered or had been sucked out.

Staring uneasily about, Blackband saw that all the clothes were stained. There was blood on all of them, though not a great deal on any. The ceiling hung close to him, oppressive and vague. Darkness had blotted out the steps and the door. He caught at them with the light, and stumbled towards them.

The crying made him falter. Surely there were fewer voices, and they seemed to sob. He was nearer the voices than the steps. If he could find the creatures at once, snatch them up and flee—He clambered over the treacherous debris, towards a gap in the rubble. The bag mouthed emptily; threads plucked at him, almost impalpably. As he thrust the flashlight's beam into the gap, darkness rushed to surround him.

Beneath the debris a pit had been dug. Parts of its earth walls had collapsed, but protruding from the fallen soil he could see bones. They looked too large for an animal's. In the centre of the pit, sprinkled with earth, lay a cat. Little of it remained, except for its skin and bones; its skin was covered with deep pockmarks. But its eyes seemed to move feebly.

Appalled, he stooped. He had no idea what to do. He never knew, for the walls of the pit were shifting. Soil trickled scattering as a face the size of his fist emerged. There were several; their limbless bodies squirmed from the earth all around the pit. From toothless mouths, their sharp tongues flickered out towards the cat. As he fled they began wailing dreadfully.

He chased the light towards the steps. He fell, cutting his knees. He thought the face with its gleaming eyes would meet him in the hall. He ran from the cellar, flailing his flashlight at the air. As he stumbled down the street he could still see the faces that had crawled from the soil: rudimentary beneath translucent skin, but beginning to be human.

He leaned against his gatepost in the lamplight, retching. Images and memories tumbled disordered through his mind. The face crawling over the roofs. Only seen at night. Vampire. The fluttering at the window. Her terror at the hedge full of spiders. *Calyptra*, what was it, *Calyptra eustrigata*. Vampire moth.

Vague though they were, the implications terrified him. He fled into his building, but halted fearfully on the stairs. The things must be destroyed: to delay would be insane. Suppose their hunger brought them crawling out of the cellar tonight, towards his flat—Absurd though it must be, he couldn't forget that they might have seen his face.

He stood giggling, dismayed. Whom did you call in these circumstances? The police, an exterminator? Nothing would relieve his horror until he saw the brood destroyed, and the only way to see that was to do the job himself. Burn. Petrol. He dawdled on the stairs, delaying, thinking he knew none of the other tenants from whom to borrow the fuel.

He ran to the nearby garage. "Have you got any petrol?"

The man glared at him, suspecting a joke. "You'd be surprised. How much do you want?"

How much indeed! He restrained his giggling. Perhaps he should ask the man's advice! Excuse me, how much petrol do you need for—"A gallon," he stammered.

As soon as he reached the back street he switched on his flashlight. Crowds of rubble lined the pavements. Far above the dark house he saw his orange light. He stepped over the debris into the hall. The swaying light brought the face forward to meet him. Of course the hall was empty.

He forced himself forward. Plucked by the flashlight, the cellar door flapped soundlessly. Couldn't he just set fire to the house? But that might leave the brood untouched. Don't think, go down quickly. Above the stairs the stain loomed.

In the cellar nothing had changed. The bag gaped, the clothes lay emptied. Struggling to unscrew the cap of the petrol can, he almost dropped the flashlight. He kicked wood into the pit and began to pour the petrol. At once he heard the wailing beneath him. "Shut up!" he screamed, to drown out the sound. "Shut up! Shut up!"

The can took its time in gulping itself empty; the petrol seemed thick as oil. He hurled the can clattering away, and ran to the steps. He fumbled with matches, gripping the flashlight between his knees. As he threw them, the lit matches went out. Not until he ventured back to the pit, clutching a ball of paper from his pocket, did he succeed in making a flame that reached his goal. There was a whoof of fire, and a chorus of interminable feeble shrieking.

As he clambered sickened towards the hall, he heard a fluttering above him. Wallpaper, stirring in a wind: it sounded moist. But there was no wind, for the air clung clammily to him. He slithered over the rubble into the hall, darting his light about. Something white bulked at the top of the stairs.

It was another torn bag. He hadn't been able to see it before. It slumped emptily. Beside it the stain spread over the wall. That stain was too symmetrical; it resembled an inverted coat. Momentarily he thought the paper was drooping, tugged perhaps by his unsteady light, for the stain had begun to creep down towards him. Eyes glared at him from its dangling face. Though the face was upside-down he knew it at once. From its gargoyle mouth a tongue reached for him.

He whirled to flee. But the darkness that filled the front door was more than night, for it was advancing audibly. He stumbled, panicking, and rubble slipped from beneath his feet. He fell from the cellar steps, onto piled stone. Though he felt almost no pain, he heard his spine break.

His mind writhed helplessly. His body refused to heed it in any way, and lay on the rubble, trapping him. He could hear cars on the avenue, radio sets and the sounds of cutlery in flats, distant and indifferent. The cries were petering out now. He tried to scream, but only his eyes could move. As they struggled, he glimpsed through a slit in the cellar wall the orange light in his kitchen.

His flashlight lay on the steps, dimmed by its fall. Before long a rustling darkness came slowly down the steps, blotting out the light. He heard sounds in the dark, and something that was not flesh nestled against him. His throat managed a choked shriek that was almost inaudible, even to him. Eventually the face crawled away towards the hall, and the light returned. From the corner of his eye he could see what surrounded him. They were round, still, practically featureless: as yet, hardly even alive.

The Gap

Tate was fitting a bird into the sky when he heard the car. He hurried to the window. Sunlit cars blazed, a double-stranded necklace on the distant main road; clouds transformed above the hills, assembling the sky. Yes, it was the Dewhursts: he could see them, packed into the front seat of their Fiat as it ventured into the drive. On his table, scraps of cloud were scattered around the jigsaw. The Dewhursts weren't due for an hour. He glanced at the displaced fragments and then, resigned, went to the stairs.

By the time he'd strolled downstairs and opened the front door, they were just emerging from the car. David's coat buttons displayed various colours of thread. Next came his wife Dottie: her real name was Carla, but they felt that Dave and Dottie looked a more attractive combination on book covers—a notion with which millions of readers seemed to agree. She looked like a cartoonist's American tourist: trousers bulging like sausages, carefully silvered hair. Sometimes Tate wished that his writer's eye could be less oppressively alert to telling details.

Dewhurst gestured at his car like a conjuror unveiling an astonishment. "And here are our friends that we promised you."

Had it been a promise? It had seemed more a side effect of inviting the Dewhursts. And when had their friend turned plural? Still, Tate was unable to feel much resentment; he was too full of having completed his witchcraft novel.

The young man's aggressive bony face was topped with hair short as turf; the girl's face was almost the colour and texture of chalk. "This is Don Skelton," Dewhurst said. "Don, Lionel Tate. You two should have plenty to talk about, you're in the same field. And this is Don's friend, er—" Skelton stared at the large old villa as if he couldn't believe he was meant to be impressed.

He let the girl drag his case upstairs; she refused to yield it to Tate when he protested. "This is your room," he told Skelton, and felt like a disapproving landlady. "I had no idea you wouldn't be alone."

"Don't worry, there'll be room for her."

If the girl had been more attractive, if her tangled hair had been less inert and her face less hungry, mightn't he have envied Skelton? "There'll be cocktails before dinner, if that's your scene," he said to the closed door.

The jigsaw helped him relax. Evening eased into the house, shadows deepened within the large windows. The table glowed darkly through the last gap, then he snapped the piece home. Was that an echo of the snap behind him? He turned, but nobody was watching him.

As he shaved in one of the bathrooms he heard someone go downstairs. Good Lord, he wasn't a very efficient host. He hurried down, achieving the bow of his tie just as he reached the lounge, but idling within were only Skelton and the girl. At least she now wore something like an evening dress; the top of her pale chest was spattered with freckles. "We generally change before going out to dinner," Tate said.

Skelton shrugged his crumpled shoulders. "Go ahead."

Alcohol made Skelton more talkative. "I'll have somewhere like this," he said, glancing at the Victorian carved mahogany suite. After a calculated pause he added "But better."

Tate made a last effort to reach him. "I'm afraid I haven't read anything of yours."

"There won't be many people who'll be able to say that." It sounded oddly threatening. He reached in his briefcase for a book. "I'll give you something to keep."

Tate glimpsed carved boxes, a camera, a small round gleam that twinged him with indefinable apprehension before the case snapped shut. Silver letters shone on the paperback, which was glossy as coal: *The Black Road.*

A virgin was being mutilated, gloated over by the elegant prose. Tate searched for a question that wouldn't sound insulting. At last he managed "What are your themes?"

"Autobiography." Perhaps Skelton was one of those writers of the macabre who needed to joke defensively about their work, for the Dewhursts were laughing.

Dinner at the inn was nerve-racking. Candlelight made food hop restlessly on plates, waiters loomed beneath the low beams and flung their vague shadows over the tables. The Dewhursts grew merry, but couldn't draw the girl into the conversation. When a waiter gave Skelton's clothes a withering glance he demanded of Tate "Do you believe in witchcraft?"

"Well, I had to do a lot of research for my book. Some of the things I read made me think."

"No," Skelton said impatiently. "Do you *believe* in it—as a way of life?"

"Good heavens no. Certainly not."

"Then why waste your time writing about it?" He was still watching the disapproving waiter. Was it the candlelight that twitched his lips? "He's going to drop that," he said.

The waiter's shadow seemed to lose its balance before he did. His trayful of food crashed onto a table. Candles broke, flaring; light swayed the oak beams. Flaming wax spilled over the waiter's jacket, hot food leapt into his face.

"You're a writer," Skelton said, ignoring the commotion, "yet you've no idea of the power of words. There aren't many of us left who have." He smiled as waiters guided the injured man away. "Mind you, words are only part of it. Science hasn't robbed us of power, it's given us more tools. Telephones, cameras—so many ways to announce power."

Obviously he was drunk. The Dewhursts gazed at him as if he were a favourite, if somewhat irrepressible, child. Tate was glad to head home. Lights shone through his windows, charms against burglary; the girl hurried towards them, ahead of the rest of the party. Skelton dawdled, happy with the dark.

After his guests had gone to bed, Tate carried Skelton's book upstairs with him. Skelton's contempt had fastened on the doubts he always felt on having completed a new book. He'd see what sort of performance Skelton had to offer, since he thought so much of himself.

Less than halfway through he flung the book across the room. The narrator had sought perversions, taken all the drugs available, sampled most crimes in pursuit of his power; his favourite pastime was theft. Most of the scenes were pornographic. So this was autobiography, was it? Certainly drugs would explain the state of the speechless girl.

Tate's eyes were raw with nights of revision and typing. As he read *The Black Road,* the walls had seemed to waver and advance; the furniture had flexed its legs. He needed sleep, not Skelton's trash.

Dawn woke him. Oh God, he knew what he'd seen gleaming in Skelton's case—an eye. Surely that was a dream, born of a particularly disgusting image in the book. He tried to turn his back on the image, but he couldn't sleep. Unpleasant glimpses jerked him awake: his own novel with an oily black cover, friends snubbing him, his incredulous disgust on rereading his own book. Could his book be accused of Skelton's sins? Never before had he been so unsure about his work.

There was only one way to reassure himself, or otherwise. Tying himself into his dressing-gown, he tiptoed past the closed doors to his study. Could he reread his entire novel before breakfast? Long morning shadows drew imperceptibly into themselves. A woman's protruded from his open study.

Why was his housekeeper early? In a moment he saw that he had been as absurdly trusting as the Dewhursts. The silent girl stood just within the doorway. As a guard she was a failure, for Tate had time to glimpse Skelton at his desk, gathering pages from the typescript of his novel.

The girl began to shriek, an uneven wailing sound that seemed not to need to catch breath. Though it was distracting as a police car's siren, he kept his gaze on Skelton. "Get out," he said.

A suspicion seized him. "No, on second thoughts—stay where you are." Skelton stood, looking pained like the victim of an inefficient store detective, while Tate made sure that all the pages were still on his desk. Those which Skelton had selected were the best researched. In an intolerable way it was a tribute.

The Dewhursts appeared, blinking as they wrapped themselves in dressing-gowns. "What on earth's the matter?" Carla demanded.

"Your friend is a thief."

"Oh, dear me," Dewhurst protested. "Just because of what he said about his book? Don't believe everything he says."

"I'd advise you to choose your friends more carefully."

"I think we're perfectly good judges of people. What else do you think could have made our books so successful?"

Tate was too angry to restrain himself. "Technical competence, fourth-form wit, naïve faith in people, and a promise of life after death. You sell your readers what they want—anything but the truth."

He watched them trudge out. The girl was still making a sound, somewhere between panting and wailing, as she bumped the case downstairs. He didn't help her. As they squeezed into the car, only Skelton glanced back at him. His smile seemed almost warm, certainly content. Tate found it insufferable, and looked away.

When they'd gone, petrol fumes and all, he read through his novel. It seemed intelligent and unsensational—up to his standard. He hoped his publishers thought so. How would it read in print? Nothing of his ever satisfied him—but he was his least important reader.

Should he have called the police? It seemed trivial now. Pity about the Dewhursts—but if they were so stupid, he was well rid of them. The police would catch up with Skelton if he did much of what his book boasted.

After lunch Tate strolled towards the hills. Slopes blazed green; countless flames of grass swayed gently. The horizon was dusty with clouds. He lay enjoying the pace of the sky. At twilight the large emptiness of the house was soothing. He strolled back from the inn after a meal, refusing to glance at the nodding shapes that creaked and rustled beside him.

He slept well. Why should that surprise him when he woke? The mail waited at the end of his bed, placed there quietly by his housekeeper. The envelope with the blue-and-red fringe was from his New York agent—a new American paperback sale, hurrah. What else? A bill peering through its cellophane window, yet another circular, and a rattling carton wrapped in brown paper.

His address was anonymously typed on the carton; there was no return address. The contents shifted dryly, waves of shards. At last he stripped off the wrapping. When he opened the blank carton, its contents spilled out at him and were what he'd thought they must be: a jigsaw.

Was it a peace offering from the Dewhursts? Perhaps they'd chosen one without a cover picture because they thought he might enjoy the difficulty. And so he would. He broke up the sky and woodland on the table, and scooped them into their box. Beyond the window, trees and clouds wavered.

He began to sort out the edge of the jigsaw. Ah, there was the fourth corner. A warm breeze fluttered in the curtains. Behind him the door inched open on the emptiness of the house.

Noon had withdrawn most shadows from the room by the time he had assembled the edge. Most of the jumbled fragments were glossily brown, like furniture; but there was a human figure—no, two. He assembled them partially—one dressed in a suit, one in denim—then went downstairs to the salad his housekeeper had left him.

The jigsaw had freed his mind to compose. A story of rivalry between authors—a murder story? Two collaborators, one of whom became resentful, jealous, determined to achieve fame by himself? But he couldn't imagine anyone collaborating with Skelton. He consigned the idea to the bin at the back of his mind.

He strolled upstairs. What was his housekeeper doing? Had she knocked the jigsaw off the table? No, of course not; she had gone home hours ago—it was only the shadow of a tree fumbling about the floor.

The incomplete figures waited. The eye of a fragment gazed up at him. He shouldn't do all the easy sections first. Surely there must be points at which he could build inwards from the edge. Yes, there was one: the leg of an item of furniture. At once he saw three more pieces. It was an Empire cabinet. The shadow of a cloud groped towards him.

Connections grew clear. He'd reached the stage where his subconscious directed his attention to the appropriate pieces. The room was fitting together: a walnut canterbury, a mahogany table, a whatnot. When the shape leaned towards him he started, scattering fragments, but it must have been a tree outside the window. It didn't take much to make him nervous now. He had recognised the room in the jigsaw.

Should he break it up unfinished? That would be admitting that it had disturbed him: absurd. He fitted the suited figure into place at the assembled table. Before he had put together the face, with its single eye in profile, he could see that the figure was himself.

He stood finishing a jigsaw, and was turning to glance behind him. When had the photograph been taken? When had the figure in denim crept behind him, unheard? Irritably resisting an urge to glance over his shoulder, he thumped the figure into place and snapped home the last pieces.

Perhaps it was Skelton: its denims were frayed and stained enough. But all the pieces which would have composed the face were missing. Reflected sunlight on the table within the gap gave the figure a flat pale gleam for a face.

"Damned nonsense!" He whirled, but there was only the unsteady door edging its shadow over the carpet. Skelton must have superimposed the figure; no doubt he had enjoyed making it look menacing—stepping eagerly forward, its hands outstretched. Had he meant there to be a hole where its face should be, to obscure its intentions?

Tate held the box like a waste-bin, and swept in the disintegrating jigsaw. The sound behind him was nothing but an echo of its fall; he refused to turn. He left the box on the table. Should he show it to the Dewhursts? No doubt they would shrug it off as a joke—and really, it was ridiculous to take it even so seriously.

He strode to the inn. He must have his housekeeper prepare dinner more often. He was early—because he was hungry, that was all; why should he want to be home before dark? On the path, part of an insect writhed.

The inn was serving a large party. He had to wait, at a table hardly bigger than a stool. Waiters and diners, their faces obscured, surrounded him. He found himself glancing compulsively each time candlelight leapt onto a face. When eventually he hurried home, his mind was muttering at the restless shapes on both sides of the path: go away, go away.

A distant car blinked and was gone. His house's were the only lights to be seen. They seemed less heartening than lost in the night. No, his housekeeper hadn't let herself in. He was damned if he'd search all the rooms to make sure. The presence he sensed was only the heat, squatting in the house. When he tired of trying to read, the heat went to bed with him.

Eventually it woke him. Dawn made the room into a charcoal drawing. He sat up in panic. Nothing was watching him over the foot of the bed, which was somehow the trouble: beyond the bed, an absence hovered in the air. When it rose, he saw that it was perched on shoulders. The dim figure groped rapidly around the bed. As it bore down on him its hands lifted, alert and eager as a dowser's.

He screamed, and the light was dashed from his eyes. He lay trembling in absolute darkness. Was he still asleep? Had he been seized by his worst nightmare, of blindness? Very gradually a sketch of the room gathered about him, as though developing from fog. Only then did he dare switch on the light. He waited for the dawn before he slept again.

When he heard footsteps downstairs, he rose. It was idiotic that he'd lain brooding for hours over a dream. Before he did anything else he would throw away the obnoxious jigsaw. He hurried to its room, and faltered. Flat sunlight occupied the table.

He called his housekeeper. "Have you moved a box from here?"

"No, Mr Tate." When he frowned, dissatisfied, she said haughtily "Certainly not."

She seemed nervous—because of his distrust, or because she was lying? She must have thrown away the box by mistake and was afraid to own up. Questioning her further would only cause unpleasantness.

He avoided her throughout the morning, though her sounds in other rooms disturbed him, as did occasional glimpses of her shadow. Why was he tempted to ask her to stay? It was absurd. When she'd left, he was glad to be able to listen to the emptiness of the house.

Gradually his pleasure faded. The warmly sunlit house seemed too bright, expectantly so, like a stage awaiting a first act. He was still listening, but less to absorb the silence than to penetrate it: in search of what? He wandered desultorily. His compulsion to glance about infuriated him. He had never realised how many shadows each room contained.

After lunch he struggled to begin to organise his ideas for his next book, at least roughly. It was too soon after the last one. His mind felt empty as the house. In which of them was there a sense of intrusion, of patient distant lurking? No, of course his housekeeper hadn't returned. Sunlight drained from the house, leaving a congealed residue of heat. Shadows crept imperceptibly.

He needed an engrossing film—the Bergman at the Academy. He'd go now, and eat in London. Impulsively he stuffed *The Black Road* into his pocket, to get the thing out of the house. The slam of the front door echoed through the deserted rooms. From trees and walls and bushes, shadows spread; their outlines were restless with grass. A bird dodged about to pull struggling entrails out of the ground.

Was the railway station unattended? Eventually a shuffling, hollow with wood, responded to his knocks at the ticket window. As he paid, Tate realised that he'd let himself be driven from his house by nothing more than doubts. There were drawbacks to writing fantastic fiction, it seemed.

His realisation made him feel vulnerable. He paced the short platform. Flowers in a bed spelt the station's name; lampposts thrust forward their dull heads. He was alone but for a man seated in the waiting-room on the opposite platform. The window was dusty, and bright reflected clouds were caught in the glass; he couldn't distinguish the man's face. Why should he want to?

The train came dawdling. It carried few passengers, like the last exhibits of a run-down waxworks. Stations passed, displaying empty platforms. Fields stretched away towards the sinking light.

At each station the train halted, hoping for passengers but always disappointed—until, just before London, Tate saw a man striding in pursuit. On which platform? He could see only the man's reflection: bluish clothes, blurred face. The empty carriage creaked around him; metal scuttled beneath his feet. Though the train was gathering speed, the man kept pace with it. Still he was only striding; he seemed to feel no need to run. Good Lord, how long were his legs? A sudden explosion of foliage filled the window. When it fell away, the strider had gone.

Charing Cross Station was still busy. A giant's voice blundered among its rafters. As Tate hurried out, avoiding a miniature train of trolleys, silver gleamed at him from the bookstall. *The Black Road,* and there again, at another spot on the display: *The Black Road.* If someone stole them, that would be a fair irony. Of the people around him, several wore denim.

He ate curry in the Wampo Egg on the Charing Cross Road. He knew better restaurants nearby, but they were on side streets; he preferred to stay on the main road—never mind why. Denimed figures peered at the menu in the window. The menu obscured his view of their faces.

He bypassed Leicester Square Underground. He didn't care to go down into that dark, where trains burrowed, clanking. Besides, he had time to stroll; it was a pleasant evening. The colours of the bookshops cooled.

He glimpsed books of his in a couple of shops, which was heartening. But Skelton's title glared from Booksmith's window. Was that a gap beside it in the display? No, it was a reflected alley, for here came a figure striding down it. Tate turned and located the alley, but the figure must have stepped aside.

He made for Oxford Street. Skelton's book was there too, in Claude Gill's. Beyond it, on the ghost of the opposite pavement, a denimed figure watched. Tate whirled, but a bus idled past, blocking his view. Certainly there were a good many strollers wearing denim.

When he reached the Academy Cinema he had glimpsed a figure several times, both walking through window displays and, most frustratingly, pacing him on the opposite pavement, at the edge of his vision. He walked past the cinema, thinking how many faces he would be unable to see in its dark.

Instinctively drawn towards the brightest lights, he headed down Poland Street. Twilight had reached the narrow streets of Soho, awakening the neon. SEX SHOP, SEX AIDS, SCANDINAVIAN FILMS. The shops cramped one another, a shoulder-to-shoulder row of touts. In one window framed by livery neon, between *Spanking Letters* and *Rubber News,* he saw Skelton's book.

Pedestrians and cars crowded the streets. Whenever Tate glanced across, he glimpsed a figure in denim on the other pavement. Of course it needn't be the same one each time—it was impossible to tell, for he could never catch sight of the face. He had never realised how many faces you couldn't see in crowds. He'd made for these streets precisely in order to be among people.

Really, this was absurd. He'd allowed himself to be driven among the seedy bookshops in search of company, like a fugitive from Edgar Allan Poe—and by what? An idiotic conversation, an equally asinine jigsaw, a few stray glimpses? It proved that curses could work on the imagination—but good heavens, that was no reason for him to feel apprehensive. Yet he did, for behind the walkers painted with neon a figure was moving like a hunter, close to the wall. Tate's fear tasted of curry.

Very well, his pursuer existed. That could be readily explained: it was Skelton, skulking. How snugly those two words fitted together! Skelton must have seen him gazing at *The Black Road* in the window. It would be just like Skelton to stroll about admiring his own work in displays. He must have decided to chase Tate, to unnerve him.

He must glimpse Skelton's face, then pounce. Abruptly he crossed the street, through a break in the sequence of cars. Neon, entangled with neon afterimages, danced on his eyelids. Where was the skulker? Had he dodged into a shop? In a moment Tate saw him, on the pavement he'd just vacated. By the time Tate's vision struggled clear of afterimages, the face was obscured by the crowd.

Tate dashed across the street again, with the same result. So Skelton was going to play at manoeuvring, was he? Well, Tate could play too. He dodged into a shop. Amplified panting pounded rhythmically beyond an inner doorway. "Hardcore film now showing, sir," said the Indian behind the counter. Men, some wearing denim, stood at racks of magazines. All kept their faces averted from Tate.

He was behaving ridiculously—which frightened him: he'd let his defences be penetrated. How long did he mean to indulge in this absurd chase? How was he to put a stop to it?

He peered out of the shop. Passers-by glanced at him as though he was touting. Pavements twitched, restless with neon. The battle of lights jerked the shadows of the crowd. Faces shone green, burned red.

If he could just spot Skelton. . . . What would he do? Next to Tate's doorway was an alley, empty save for darkness. At the far end, another street glared. He could dodge through the alley and lose his pursuer. Perhaps he would find a policeman; that would teach Skelton—he'd had enough of this poor excuse for a joke.

There was Skelton, lurking in a dark doorway almost opposite. Tate made as if to chase him, and at once the figure sneaked away behind a group of strollers. Tate darted into the alley.

His footsteps clanged back from the walls. Beyond the scrawny exit, figures passed like a peepshow. A wall grazed his shoulder; a burden knocked repetitively against his thigh. It was *The Black Road,* still crumpled in his pocket. He flung it away. It caught at his feet in the dark until he trampled on it; he heard its spine break. Good riddance.

He was halfway down the alley, where its darkness was strongest. He looked back to confirm that nobody had followed him. Stumbling a little, he faced forward again, and the hands of the figure before him grabbed his shoulders.

He recoiled gasping. The wall struck his shoulder-blades. Darkness stood in front of him, but he felt the body clasp him close, so as to thrust its unseen face into his. His face felt seized by ice; he couldn't distinguish the shape of what touched it. Then the clasp had gone, and there was silence.

He stood shivering. His hands groped at his sides, as though afraid to move. He understood why he could see nothing—there was no light so deep in the alley—but why couldn't he hear? Even the taste of curry had vanished. His head felt anesthetised, and somehow insubstantial. He found that he didn't dare turn to look at either lighted street. Slowly, reluctantly, his hands groped upwards towards his face.

The Voice of the Beach

I

I met Neal at the station.

Of course I can describe it, I have only to go up the road and look, but there is no need. That isn't what I have to get out of me. It isn't me, it's out there, it can be described. I need all my energy for that, all my concentration, but perhaps it will help if I can remember before that, when everything looked manageable, expressible, familiar enough—when I could bear to look out of the window.

Neal was standing alone on the small platform, and now I see that I dare not go up the road after all, or out of the house. It doesn't matter, my memories are clear, they will help me hold on. Neal must have rebuffed the station-master, who was happy to chat to anyone. He was gazing at the bare tracks, sharpened by June light, as they cut their way through the forest—gazing at them as a suicide might gaze at a razor. He saw me and swept his hair back from his face, over his shoulders. Suffering had pared his face down, stretched the skin tighter and paler over the skull. I can remember exactly how he looked before

"I thought I'd missed the station," he said, though surely the station's name was visible enough, despite the flowers that scaled the board. If only he had! "I had to make so many changes. Never mind. Christ, it's good to see you. You look marvellous. I expect you can thank the sea for that." His eyes had brightened, and he sounded so full of life that it was spilling out of him in a tumble of words, but his handshake felt like cold bone.

I hurried him along the road that led home and to the   He was beginning to screw up his eyes at the sunlight, and I thought I should get him inside; presumably headaches were among his symptoms. At first the road is gravel, fragments of which always succeed in working their way into your shoes. Where the trees fade out as though stifled by sand, a concrete path turns aside. Sand sifts over the gravel; you can hear the gritty conflict under-foot, and the musing of the sea. Beyond the path stands this crescent of bun-galows. Surely all this is still true. But I remember now that the bungalows looked unreal against the burning blue sky and the dunes like embryo hills; they looked like a dream set down in the piercing light of June.

"You must be doing well to afford this." Neal sounded listless, envious only because he felt it was expected. If only he had stayed that way! But once inside the bungalow he seemed pleased by everything—the view, my books on show in the living-room bookcase, my typewriter displaying a token page that bore a token phrase, the Breughel prints that used to remind me of hu-manity. Abruptly, with a moody eagerness that I hardly remarked at the time, he said "Shall we have a look at the beach?"

There, I've written the word. I can describe the beach, I must describe it, it is all that's in my head. I have my notebook which I took with me that day. Neal led the way along the gravel path. Beyond the concrete turn-off to the bungalows the gravel was engulfed almost at once by sand, despite the thick ranks of low bushes that had been planted to keep back the sand. We squeezed between the bushes, which were determined to close their ranks across the gravel.

Once through, we felt the breeze whose waves passed through the mar-ram grass that spiked the dunes. Neal's hair streamed back, pale as the grass. The trudged dunes were slowing him down, eager as he was. We slithered down to the beach, and the sound of the unfurling sea leapt closer, as though we'd awakened it from dreaming. The wind fluttered trapped in my ears, leafed through my notebook as I scribbled the image of wakening and thought with an appalling innocence: perhaps I can use that image. Now we were walled off from the rest of the world by the dunes, faceless mounds with unkempt green wigs, mounds almost as white as the sun.

Even then I felt that the beach was somehow separate from its surround-ings: introverted, I remember thinking. I put it down to the shifting haze which hovered above the sea, the haze which I could never focus, whose dis-tance I could never quite judge. From the self-contained stage of the beach the bungalows looked absurdly intrusive, anachronisms rejected by the geo-morphological time of sand and sea. Even the skeletal car and the other de-bris, half engulfed by the beach near the coast road, looked less alien. These are my memories, the most stable things left to me, and I must go on. I found today that I cannot go back any further.

Neal was staring, eyes narrowed against the glare, along the waste of beach that stretched in the opposite direction from the coast road and curved out of sight. "Doesn't anyone come down here? There's no pollution, is there?"

"It depends on who you believe." Often the beach seemed to give me a headache, even when there was no glare—and then there was the way the beach looked at night. "Still, I think most folk go up the coast to the resorts. That's the only reason I can think of."

We were walking. Beside us the edge of the glittering sea moved in several directions simultaneously. Moist sand, sleek as satin, displayed shells which appeared to flash patterns, faster than my mind could grasp. Pinpoint mirrors of sand gleamed, rapid as Morse. My notes say this is how it seemed.

"Don't your neighbours ever come down?"

Neal's voice made me start. I had been engrossed in the designs of shell and sand. Momentarily I was unable to judge the width of the beach: a few paces or miles? I grasped my sense of perspective, but a headache was starting, a dull impalpable grip that encircled my cranium. Now I know what all this meant, but I want to remember how I felt before I knew.

"Very seldom," I said. "Some of them think there's quicksand." One old lady, sitting in her garden to glare at the dunes like Canute versus sand, had told me that warning notices kept sinking. I'd never encountered quicksand, but I always brought my stick to help me trudge.

"So I'll have the beach to myself."

I took that to be a hint. At least he would leave me alone if I wanted to work. "The bungalow people are mostly retired," I said. "Those who aren't in wheelchairs go driving. I imagine they've had enough of sand, even if they aren't past walking on it." Once, further up the beach, I'd encountered nudists censoring themselves with towels or straw hats as they ventured down to the sea, but Neal could find out about them for himself. I wonder now if I ever saw them at all, or simply felt that I should.

Was he listening? His head was cocked, but not towards me. He'd slowed, and was staring at the ridges and furrows of the beach, at which the sea was lapping. All at once the ridges reminded me of convolutions of the brain, and I took out my notebook as the grip on my skull tightened. The beach as a subconscious, my notes say: the horizon as the imagination—sunlight set a ship ablaze on the edge of the world, an image that impressed me as vividly yet indefinably symbolic—the debris as memories, half-buried, half-comprehensible. But then what were the bungalows, perched above the dunes like boxes carved of dazzling bone?

I glanced up. A cloud had leaned towards me. No, it had been more as though the cloud were rushing at the beach from the horizon, dauntingly fast. Had it been a cloud? It had seemed more massive than a ship. The sky was empty now, and I told myself that it had been an effect of the haze—the magnified shadow of a gull, perhaps.

My start had enlivened Neal, who began to chatter like a television wakened by a kick. "It'll be good for me to be alone here, to get used to being alone. Mary and the children found themselves another home, you see. He earns more money than I'll ever see, if that's what they want. He's the head-of-the-house type, if that's what they want. I couldn't be that now if I tried, not with the way my nerves are now." I can still hear everything he said, and I suppose that I knew what had been wrong with him. Now they are just words.

"That's why I'm talking so much," he said, and picked up a spiral shell, I thought to quiet himself.

"That's much too small. You'll never hear anything in that."

Minutes passed before he took it away from his ear and handed it to me. "No?" he said.

I put it to my ear and wasn't sure what I was hearing. No, I didn't throw the shell away, I didn't crush it underfoot; in any case, how could I have done that to the rest of the beach? I was straining to hear, straining to make out how the sound differed from the usual whisper of a shell. Was it that it seemed to have a rhythm I couldn't define, or that it sounded shrunken by distance rather than cramped by the shell? I felt expectant, entranced— precisely the feeling I'd tried so often to communicate in my fiction, I believe. Something stooped towards me from the horizon. I jerked, and dropped the shell.

There was nothing but the dazzle of sunlight that leapt at me from the waves. The haze above the sea had darkened, staining the light, and I told myself that was what I'd seen. But when Neal picked up another shell I felt uneasy. The grip on my skull was very tight now. As I regarded the vistas of empty sea and sky and beach my expectancy grew oppressive, too imminent, no longer enjoyable.

"I think I'll head back now. Maybe you should as well," I said, rummaging for an uncontrived reason, "just in case there is quicksand."

"All right. It's in all of them," he said, displaying an even smaller shell to which he'd just listened. I remember thinking that his observation was so self-evident as to be meaningless.

As I turned towards the bungalows the glitter of the sea clung to my eyes.

Afterimages crowded among the debris. They were moving; I strained to make out their shape. What did they resemble? Symbols—hieroglyphs? Limbs writhing rapidly, as if in a ritual dance? They made the debris appear to shift, to crumble. The herd of faceless dunes seemed to edge forward; an image leaned towards me out of the sky. I closed my eyes, to calm their antics, and wondered if I should take the warnings of pollution more seriously.

We walked towards the confusion of footprints that climbed the dunes. Neal glanced about at the sparkling sand. Never before had the beach so impressed me as a complex of patterns, and perhaps that means it was already too late. Spotlighted by the sun, it looked so artificial that I came close to doubting how it felt underfoot.

The bungalows looked unconvincing too. Still, when we'd slumped in our chairs for a while, letting the relative dimness soothe our eyes while our bodies guzzled every hint of coolness, I forgot about the beach. We shared two litres of wine and talked about my work, about his lack of any since graduating.

Later I prepared melon, salads, water ices. Neal watched, obviously embarrassed that he couldn't help. He seemed lost without Mary. One more reason not to marry, I thought, congratulating myself.

As we ate he kept staring out at the beach. A ship was caught in the amber sunset: a dream of escape. I felt the image less deeply than I'd experienced the metaphors of the beach; it was less oppressive. The band around my head had faded.

When it grew dark Neal pressed close to the pane. "What's that?" he demanded.

I switched out the light so that he could see. Beyond the dim humps of the dunes the beach was glowing, a dull pallor like moonlight stifled by fog. Do all beaches glow at night? "That's what makes people say there's pollution," I said.

"Not the light," he said impatiently. "The other things. What's moving?"

I squinted through the pane. For minutes I could see nothing but the muffled glow. At last, when my eyes were smarting, I began to see forms thin and stiff as scarecrows jerking into various contorted poses. Gazing for so long was bound to produce something of the kind, and I took them to be afterimages of the tangle, barely visible, of bushes.

"I think I'll go and see."

"I shouldn't go down there at night," I said, having realised that I'd never gone to the beach at night and that I felt a definite, though irrational, aversion to doing so.

Eventually he went to bed. Despite all his travelling, he'd needed to drink to make himself sleepy. I heard him open his bedroom window, which overlooked the beach. There is so much still to write, so much to struggle through, and what good can it do me now?

II

I had taken the bungalow, one of the few entries in my diary says, to give myself the chance to write without being distracted by city life—the cries of the telephone, the tolling of the doorbell, the omnipresent clamour—only to discover, once I'd left it behind, that city life was my theme. But I was a compulsive writer: if I failed to write for more than a few days I became depressed. Writing was the way I overcame the depression of not writing. Now writing seems to be my only way of hanging on to what remains of myself, of delaying the end.

The day after Neal arrived, I typed a few lines of a sample chapter. It wasn't a technique I enjoyed—tearing a chapter out of the context of a novel that didn't yet exist. In any case, I was distracted by the beach, compelled to scribble notes about it, trying to define the images it suggested. I hoped these notes might build into a story. I was picking at the notes in search of their story when Neal said "Maybe I can lose myself for a bit in the countryside."

"Mm," I said curtly, not looking up.

"Didn't you say there was a deserted village?"

By the time I directed him I would have lost the thread of my thoughts. The thread had been frayed and tangled, anyway. As long as I was compelled to think about the beach I might just as well be down there. I can still write as if I don't know the end, it helps me not to think of   "I'll come with you," I said.

The weather was nervous. Archipelagos of cloud floated low on the hazy sky, above the sea; great Rorschach blots rose from behind the slate hills, like dissolved stone. As we squeezed through the bushes, a shadow came hunching over the dunes to meet us. When my foot touched the beach a moist shadowy chill seized me, as though the sand disguised a lurking marsh. Then sunlight spilled over the beach, which leapt into clarity.

I strode, though Neal appeared to want to dawdle. I wasn't anxious to linger: after all, I told myself, it might rain. Glinting mosaics of grains of sand changed restlessly around me, never quite achieving a pattern. Patches of sand, flat shapeless elongated ghosts, glided over the beach and faltered, waiting for another breeze. Neal kept peering at them as though to make out their shapes.

Half a mile along the beach the dunes began to sag, to level out. The slate hills were closing in. Were they the source of the insidious chill? Perhaps I was feeling the damp; a penumbra of moisture welled up around each of my footprints. The large wet shapes seemed quite unrelated to my prints, an effect which I found unnerving. When I glanced back, it looked as though something enormous was imitating my walk.

The humidity was almost suffocating. My head felt clamped by tension. Wind blundered booming in my ears, even when I could feel no breeze. Its jerky rhythm was distracting because indefinable. Grey cloud had flooded the sky; together with the hills and the thickening haze above the sea, it caged the beach. At the edge of my eye the convolutions of the beach seemed to writhe, to struggle to form patterns. The insistent sparkling nagged at my mind.

I'd begun to wonder whether I had been blaming imagined pollution for the effects of heat and humidity—I was debating whether to turn back before I grew dizzy or nauseous—when Neal said "Is that it?"

I peered ahead, trying to squint the dazzle of waves from my eyes. A quarter of a mile away the hills ousted the dunes completely. Beneath the spiky slate a few uprights of rock protruded from the beach like standing stones. They glowed sullenly as copper through the haze; they were encrusted with sand. Surely that wasn't the village.

"Yes, that's it," Neal said, and strode forward.

I followed him, because the village must be further on. The veil of haze drew back, the vertical rocks gleamed unobscured, and I halted bewildered. The rocks weren't encrusted at all; they were slate, grey as the table of rock on which they stood above the beach. Though the slate was jagged, some of its gaps were regular: windows, doorways. Here and there walls still formed corners. How could the haze have distorted my view so spectacularly?

Neal was climbing rough steps carved out of the slate table. Without warning, as I stood confused by my misperception, I felt utterly alone. A bowl of dull haze trapped me on the bare sand. Slate, or something more massive and vague, loomed over me. The kaleidoscope of shells was about to shift; the beach was ready to squirm, to reveal its pattern, shake off its artificiality. The massive looming would reach down, and

My start felt like a convulsive awakening. The table was deserted except for the fragments of buildings. I could hear only the wind, baying as though its mouth was vast and uncontrollable. "Neal," I called. Dismayed by the smallness of my voice, I shouted "Neal."

I heard what sounded like scales of armour chafing together—slate, of course. The grey walls shone lifelessly, cavitied as skulls; gaping windows displayed an absence of faces, of rooms. Then Neal's head poked out of half a wall. "Yes, come on," he said. "It's strange."

As I climbed the steps, sand gritted underfoot like sugar. Low drifts of sand were piled against the walls; patches glinted on the small plateau. Could that sand have made the whole place look encrusted and half-buried? I told myself that it had been an effect of the heat.

Broken walls surrounded me. They glared like storm clouds in lightning. They formed a maze whose centre was desertion. That image stirred another, too deep in my mind to be definable. The place was—not a maze, but a puzzle whose solution would clarify a pattern, a larger mystery. I realised that then; why couldn't I have fled?

I suppose I was held by the enigma of the village. I knew there were quarries in the hills above, but I'd never learned why the village had been abandoned. Perhaps its meagreness had killed it—I saw traces of less than a dozen buildings. It seemed further dwarfed by the beach; the sole visible trace of humanity, it dwindled beneath the gnawing of sand and the elements. I found it enervating, its lifelessness infectious. Should I stay with Neal, or risk leaving him there? Before I could decide, I heard him say amid a rattle of slate "This is interesting."

In what way? He was clambering about an exposed cellar, among shards of slate. Whatever the building had been, it had stood furthest from the sea. "I don't mean the cellar," Neal said. "I mean that."

Reluctantly I peered where he was pointing. In the cellar wall furthest from the beach, a rough alcove had been chipped out of the slate. It was perhaps a yard deep, but barely high enough to accommodate a huddled man. Neal was already crawling in. I heard slate crack beneath him; his feet protruded from the darkness. Of course they weren't about to jerk convulsively— but my nervousness made me back away when his muffled voice said "What's this?"

He backed out like a terrier with his prize. It was an old notebook, its pages stuck together in a moist wad. "Someone covered it up with slate," he said, as though that should tempt my interest.

Before I could prevent him he was sitting at the edge of the beach and peeling the pages gingerly apart. Not that I was worried that he might be destroying a fragment of history—I simply wasn't sure that I wanted to read whatever had been hidden in the cellar. Why couldn't I have followed my instincts?

He disengaged the first page carefully, then frowned. "This begins in the middle of something. There must be another book."

Handing me the notebook, he stalked away to scrabble in the cellar. I sat on the edge of the slate table and glanced at the page. It is before me now on my desk. The pages have crumbled since then—the yellowing paper looks more and more like sand—but the large writing is still legible, unsteady capitals in a hand that might once have been literate before it grew senile. No punctuation separates the words, though blotches sometimes do. Beneath the relentless light at the deserted village, the faded ink looked real, scarcely present at all.

FROM THE BEACH EVERYONES GONE NOW BUT ME ITS NOT SO BAD IN DAYTIME EXCEPT I CANT GO BUT AT NIGHT I CAN HEAR IT REACHING FOR [a blot of fungus had consumed a word here] AND THE VOICES ITS VOICE AND THE GLOWING AT LEAST IT HELPS ME SEE DOWN HERE WHEN IT COMES

I left it at that; my suddenly unsteady fingers might have torn the page. I wish to God they had. I was on edge with the struggle between humidity and the chill of slate and beach; I felt feverish. As I stared at the words they touched impressions, half-memories. If I looked up, would the beach have changed?

I heard Neal slithering on slate, turning over fragments. In my experience stones were best not turned over. Eventually he returned. I was dully fascinated by the shimmering of the beach; my fingers pinched the notebook shut.

"I can't find anything," he said. "I'll have to come back." He took the notebook from me and began to read, muttering "What? Jesus!" Gently he separated the next page from the wad. "This gets stranger," he murmured. "What kind of guy was this? Imagine what it must have been like to live inside his head."

How did he know it had been a man? I stared at the pages to prevent Neal from reading them aloud. At least it saved me from having to watch the antics of the beach, which moved like slow flames, but the introverted meandering words made me nervous.

IT CANT REACH DOWN HERE NOT YET BUT OUTSIDE IS CHANGING OUTSIDES PART OF THE PATTERN I READ THE PATTERN THATS WHY I CANT GO SAW THEM DANCING THE PATTERN WANTS ME

TO DANCE ITS ALIVE BUT ITS ONLY THE IMAGE BEING PUT TO-
GETHER

Neal was wide-eyed, fascinated. Feverish disorientation gripped my skull;
I felt too unwell to move. The heat-haze must be closing in; at the edge of my
vision, everything was shifting.

WHEN THE PATTERNS DONE IT CAN COME BACK AND GROW ITS
HUNGRY TO BE EVERYTHING I KNOW HOW IT WORKS THE SAND
MOVES AT NIGHT AND SUCKS YOU DOWN OR MAKES YOU GO
WHERE IT WANTS TO MAKE [a blotch had eaten several words] WHEN
THEY BUILT LEWIS THERE WERE OLD STONES THAT THEY MOVED
MAYBE THE STONES KEPT IT SMALL NOW ITS THE BEACH AT LEAST

On the next page the letters are much larger and more wavery. Had the
light begun to fail, or had the writer been retreating from the light—from
the entrance to the cellar? I didn't know which alternative I disliked more.

GOT TO WRITE HANDS SHAKY FROM CHIPPING TUNNEL AND NO
FOOD THEYRE SINGING NOW HELPING IT REACH CHANTING
WITH NO MOUTHS THEY SING AND DANCE THE PATTERN FOR IT
TO REACH THROUGH

Now there are very few words to the page. The letters are jagged, as
though the writer's hand kept twitching violently.

GLOW COMING ITS OUT THERE NOW ITS LOOKING IN AT ME IT
CANT GET HOLD IF I KEEP WRITING THEY WANT ME TO DANCE SO
ITLL GROW WANT ME TO BE

There it ends. "Ah, the influence of Joyce," I commented sourly. The remaining pages are blank except for fungus. I managed to stand up; my head
felt like a balloon pumped full of gas. "I'd like to go back now. I think I've a
touch of sunstroke."

A hundred yards away, I glanced back at the remnants of the village—
Lewis, I assumed it had been called. The stone remains wavered as though
striving to achieve a new shape; the haze made them look coppery, fat with a
crust of sand. I was desperate to get out of the heat.

Closer to the sea I felt slightly less oppressed—but the whispering of sand, the liquid murmur of waves, the bumbling of the wind, all chanted together insistently. Everywhere on the beach were patterns, demanding to be read.

Neal clutched the notebook under his arm. "What do you make of it?" he said eagerly.

His indifference to my health annoyed me, and hence so did the question. "He was mad," I said. "Living here—is it any wonder? Maybe he moved there after the place was abandoned. The beach must glow there too. That must have finished him. You saw how he tried to dig himself a refuge. That's all there is to it."

"Do you think so? I wonder," Neal said, and picked up a shell.

As he held the shell to his ear, his expression became so withdrawn and unreadable that I felt a pang of dismay. Was I seeing a symptom of his nervous trouble? He stood like a fragment of the village—as though the shell was holding him, rather than the reverse.

Eventually he mumbled "That's it, that's what he meant. Chanting with no mouths."

I took the shell only very reluctantly; my head was pounding. I pressed the shell to my ear, though I was deafened by the storm of my blood. If the shell was muttering, I couldn't bear the jaggedness of its rhythm. I seemed less to hear it than to feel it deep in my skull.

"Nothing like it," I said, almost snarling, and thrust the shell at him.

Now that I'd had to strain to hear it, I couldn't rid myself of the muttering; it seemed to underlie the sounds of wind and sea. I trudged onward, eyes half-shut. Moisture sprang up around my feet; the glistening shapes around my prints looked larger and more definite. I had to cling to my sense of my own size and shape.

When we neared home I couldn't see the bungalows. There appeared to be only the beach, grown huge and blinding. At last Neal heard a car leaving the crescent, and led me up the path of collapsed footprints.

In the bungalow I lay willing the lights and patterns to fade from my closed eyes. Neal's presence didn't soothe me, even though he was only poring over the notebook. He'd brought a handful of shells indoors. Occasionally he held one to his ear, muttering "It's still there, you know. It does sound like chanting." At least, I thought peevishly, I knew when something was a symptom of illness—but the trouble was that in my delirium I was tempted to agree with him. I felt I had almost heard what the sound was trying to be.

III

Next day Neal returned to the deserted village. He was gone for so long that even amid the clamour of my disordered senses, I grew anxious. I couldn't watch for him; whenever I tried, the white-hot beach began to judder, to quake, and set me shivering.

At last he returned, having failed to find another notebook. I hoped that would be the end of it, but his failure had simply frustrated him. His irritability chafed against mine. He managed to prepare a bedraggled salad, of which I ate little. As the tide of twilight rolled in from the horizon he sat by the window, gazing alternately at the beach and at the notebook.

Without warning he said "I'm going for a stroll. Can I borrow your stick?"

I guessed that he meant to go to the beach. Should he be trapped by darkness and sea, I was in no condition to go to his aid. "I'd rather you didn't," I said feebly.

"Don't worry, I won't lose it."

My lassitude suffocated my arguments. I lolled in my chair and through the open window heard him padding away, his footsteps muffled by sand. Soon there was only the vague slack rumble of the sea, blundering back and forth, and the faint hiss of sand in the bushes.

After half an hour I made myself stand up, though the ache in my head surged and surged, and gaze out at the whitish beach. The whole expanse appeared to flicker like hints of lightning. I strained my eyes. The beach looked crowded with debris, all of which danced to the flickering. I had to peer at every movement, but there was no sign of Neal.

I went out and stood between the bushes. The closer I approached the beach, the more crowded with obscure activity it seemed to be—but I suspected that much, if not all, of this could be blamed on my condition, for within five minutes my head felt so tight and unbalanced that I had to retreat indoors, away from the heat.

Though I'd meant to stay awake, I was dozing when Neal returned. I woke to find him gazing from the window. As I opened my eyes the beach lurched forward, shining. It didn't look crowded now, presumably because my eyes had had a rest. What could Neal see to preoccupy him so? "Enjoy your stroll?" I said sleepily.

He turned, and I felt a twinge of disquiet. His face looked stiff with doubt; his eyes were uneasy, a frown dug its ruts in his forehead. "It doesn't glow," he said.

Assuming I knew what he was talking about, I could only wonder how badly his nerves were affecting his perceptions. If anything, the beach looked brighter. "How do you mean?"

"The beach down by the village—it doesn't glow. Not anymore."

"Oh, I see."

He looked offended, almost contemptuous, though I couldn't understand why he'd expected me to be less indifferent. He withdrew into a scrutiny of the notebook. He might have been trying to solve an urgent problem.

Perhaps if I hadn't been ill I would have been able to divert Neal from his obsession, but I could hardly venture outside without growing dizzy; I could only wait in the bungalow for my state to improve. Neither Neal nor I had had sunstroke before, but he seemed to know how to treat it. "Keep drinking water. Cover yourself if you start shivering." He didn't mind my staying in— he seemed almost too eager to go out alone. Did that matter? Next day he was bound only for the library.

My state was crippling my thoughts, yet even if I'd been healthy I couldn't have imagined how he would look when he returned: excited, conspiratorial, smug. "I've got a story for you," he said at once.

Most such offers proved to be prolonged and dull. "Oh yes?" I said warily.

He sat forward as though to infect me with suspense. "That village we went to—it isn't called Lewis. It's called Strand."

Was he pausing to give me a chance to gasp or applaud? "Oh yes," I said without enthusiasm.

"Lewis was another village, further up the coast. It's deserted too."

That seemed to be his punch line. The antics of patterns within my eyelids had made me irritable. "It doesn't seem much of a story," I complained.

"Well, that's only the beginning." When his pause had forced me to open my eyes, he said "I read a book about your local unexplained mysteries."

"Why?"

"Look, if you don't want to hear—"

"Go on, go on, now you've started." Not to know might be even more nerve-racking.

"There wasn't much about Lewis," he said eventually, perhaps to give himself more time to improvise.

"Was there much at all?"

"Yes, certainly. It may not sound like much. Nobody knows why Lewis was abandoned, but then nobody knows that about Strand either." My impatience must have showed, for he added hastily "What I mean is, the people who left Strand wouldn't say why."

"Someone asked them?"

"The woman who wrote the book. She managed to track some of them down. They'd moved as far inland as they could, that was one thing she noticed. And they always had some kind of nervous disorder. Talking about Strand always made them more nervous, as though they felt that talking might make something happen, or something might hear."

"That's what the author said."

"Right."

"What was her name?"

Could he hear my suspicion? "Jesus *Christ*," he snarled, "I don't know. What does it matter?"

In fact it didn't, not to me. His story had made me feel worse. The noose had tightened round my skull, the twilit beach was swarming and vibrating. I closed my eyes. Shut up, I roared at him. Go away.

"There was one thing," he persisted. "One man said that kids kept going on the beach at night. Their parents tried all ways to stop them. Some of them questioned their kids, but it was as though the kids couldn't stop themselves. Why was that, do you think?" When I refused to answer he said irrelevantly "All this was in the 1930s."

I couldn't stand hearing children called kids. The recurring word had made me squirm: drips of slang, like water torture. And I'd never heard such a feeble punch line. His clumsiness as a storyteller enraged me; he couldn't even organise his material. I was sure he hadn't read any such book.

After a while I peered out from beneath my eyelids, hoping he'd decide that I was asleep. He was poring over the notebook again, and looked rapt. I only wished that people and reviewers would read my books as carefully. He kept rubbing his forehead, as though to enliven his brain.

I dozed. When I opened my eyes he was waiting for me. He shoved the notebook at me to demonstrate something. "Look, I'm sorry," I said without much effort to sound so. "I'm not in the mood."

He stalked into his room, emerging without the book but with my stick. "I'm going for a walk," he announced sulkily, like a spouse after a quarrel.

I dozed gratefully, for I felt more delirious; my head felt packed with grains of sand that gritted together. In fact, the whole of me was made of sand. Of course it was true that I was composed of particles, and I thought my delirium had found a metaphor for that. But the grains that floated through my inner vision were neither sand nor atoms. A member, dark and vague, was reaching for them. I struggled to awaken; I didn't want to distinguish its shape, and still less did I want to learn what it meant to do with the grains—for as the member sucked them into itself, engulfing them in a way that I refused to perceive, I saw that the grains were worlds and stars.

I woke shivering. My body felt uncontrollable and unfamiliar. I let it shake itself to rest—not that I had a choice, but I was concentrating on the problem of why I'd woken head raised, like a watchdog. What had I heard?

Perhaps only wind and sea: both seemed louder, more intense. My thoughts became entangled in their rhythm. I felt there had been another sound. The bushes threshed, sounding parched with sand. Had I heard Neal returning? I stumbled into his room. It was empty.

As I stood by his open window, straining my ears, I thought I heard his voice, blurred by the dull tumult of waves. I peered out. Beyond the low heads of the bushes, the glow of the beach shuddered towards me. I had to close my eyes, for I couldn't tell whether the restless scrawny shapes were crowding my eyeballs or the beach; it felt, somehow, like both. When I looked again, I seemed to see Neal.

Or was it Neal? The unsteady stifled glow aggravated the distortions of my vision. Was the object just a new piece of debris? I found its shape bewildering; my mind kept apprehending it as a symbol printed on the whitish expanse. The luminosity made it seem to shift, tentatively and jerkily, as though it were learning to pose. The light, or my eyes, surrounded it with dancing.

Had my sense of perspective left me? I was misjudging size, either of the beach or of the figure. Yes, it was a figure, however large it seemed. It was moving its arms like a limp puppet. And it was half-buried in the sand.

I staggered outside, shouting to Neal, and then I recoiled. The sky must be thick with a storm cloud; it felt suffocatingly massive, solid as rock, and close enough to crush me. I forced myself towards the bushes, though my head was pounding, squeezed into a lump of pain.

Almost at once I heard plodding on the dunes. My blood half deafened me; the footsteps sounded vague and immense. I peered along the dim path. At the edge of my vision the beach flickered repetitively. Immense darkness hovered over me. Unnervingly close to me, swollen by the glow, a head rose into view. For a moment my tension seemed likely to crack my skull. Then Neal spoke. His words were incomprehensible amid the wind, but it was his voice.

As we trudged back towards the lights the threat of a storm seemed to withdraw, and I blamed it on my tension. "Of course I'm all right," he muttered irritably. "I fell and that made me shout, that's all." Once we were inside I saw the evidence of his fall; his trousers were covered with sand up to the knees.

IV

Next day he hardly spoke to me. He went down early to the beach, and stayed there. I didn't know if he was obsessed or displaying pique. Perhaps he couldn't bear to be near me; invalids can find each other unbearable.

Often I glimpsed him, wandering beyond the dunes. He walked as though in an elaborate maze and scrutinised the beach. Was he searching for the key to the notebook? Was he looking for pollution? By the time he found it, I thought sourly, it would have infected him.

I felt too enervated to intervene. As I watched, Neal appeared to vanish intermittently; if I looked away, I couldn't locate him again for minutes. The beach blazed like bone, and was never still. I couldn't blame the aberrations of my vision solely on heat and haze.

When Neal returned, late that afternoon, I asked him to phone for a doctor. He looked taken aback, but eventually said "There's a box by the station, isn't there?"

"One of the neighbours would let you phone."

"No, I'll walk down. They're probably all wondering why you've let some long-haired freak squat in your house, as it is."

He went out, rubbing his forehead gingerly. He often did that now. That, and his preoccupation with the demented notebook, were additional reasons why I wanted a doctor: I felt Neal needed examining too.

By the time he returned, it was dusk. On the horizon, embers dulled in the sea. The glow of the beach was already stirring; it seemed to have intensified during the last few days. I told myself I had grown hypersensitive.

"Dr Lewis. He's coming tomorrow." Neal hesitated, then went on: "I think I'll just have a stroll on the beach. Want to come?"

"Good God no. I'm ill, can't you see?"

"I know that." His impatience was barely controlled. "A stroll might do you good. There isn't any sunlight now."

"I'll stay in until I've seen the doctor."

He looked disposed to argue, but his restlessness overcame him. As he left, his bearing seemed to curse me. Was his illness making him intolerant of mine, or did he feel that I'd rebuffed a gesture of reconciliation?

I felt too ill to watch him from the window. When I looked I could seldom distinguish him or make out which movements were his. He appeared to be walking slowly, poking at the beach with my stick. I wondered if he'd found quicksand. Again his path made me think of a maze.

I dozed, far longer than I'd intended. The doctor loomed over me. Peering into my eyes, he reached down. I began to struggle, as best I could: I'd glimpsed the depths of his eye-sockets, empty and dry as interstellar space. I didn't need his treatment, I would be fine if he left me alone, just let me go. But he had reached deep into me. As though I was a bladder that had burst, I felt myself flood into him; I felt vast emptiness absorb my substance and my self. Dimly I understood that it was nothing like emptiness—that my mind refused to perceive what it was, so alien and frightful was its teeming.

It was dawn. The muffled light teemed. The beach glowed fitfully. I gasped: someone was down on the beach, so huddled that he looked shapeless. He rose, levering himself up with my stick, and began to pace haphazardly. I knew at once that he'd spent the night on the beach.

After that I stayed awake. I couldn't imagine the state of his mind, and I was a little afraid of being asleep when he returned. But when, hours later, he came in to raid the kitchen for a piece of cheese, he seemed hardly to see me. He was muttering repetitively under his breath. His eyes looked dazzled by the beach, sunk in his obsession.

"When did the doctor say he was coming?"

"Later," he mumbled, and hurried down to the beach.

I hoped he would stay there until the doctor came. Occasionally I glimpsed him at his intricate pacing. Ripples of heat deformed him; his blurred flesh looked unstable. Whenever I glanced at the beach it leapt forward, dauntingly vivid. Cracks of light appeared in the sea. Clumps of grass seemed to rise twitching, as though the dunes were craning to watch Neal. Five minutes' vigil at the window was as much as I could bear.

The afternoon consumed time. It felt as lethargic and enervating as four in the morning. There was no sign of the doctor. I kept gazing from the front door. Nothing moved on the crescent except wind-borne hints of the beach.

Eventually I tried to phone. Though I could feel the heat of the pavement through the soles of my shoes, the day seemed bearable; only threats of pain plucked at my skull. But nobody was at home. The bungalows stood smugly in the evening light. When I attempted to walk to the phone box, the noose closed on my skull at once.

In my hall I halted startled, for Neal had thrown open the living-room door as I entered the house. He looked flushed and angry. "Where were you?" he demanded.

"I'm not a hospital case yet, you know. I was trying to phone the doctor."

Unfathomably, he looked relieved. "I'll go down now and call him."

While he was away I watched the beach sink into twilight. At the moment, this seemed to be the only time of day I could endure watching—the time at which shapes become obscure, most capable of metamorphosis. Perhaps this made the antics of the shore acceptable, more apparently natural. Now the beach resembled clouds in front of the moon; it drifted slowly and variously. If I gazed for long it looked nervous with lightning. The immense bulk of the night edged up from the horizon.

I didn't hear Neal return; I must have been fascinated by the view. I turned to find him watching me. Again he looked relieved—because I was still here? "He's coming soon," he said.

"Tonight, do you mean?"

"Yes, tonight. Why not?"

I didn't know many doctors who would come out at night to treat what was, however unpleasant for me, a relatively minor illness. Perhaps attitudes were different here in the country. Neal was heading for the back door, for the beach. "Do you think you could wait until he comes?" I said, groping for an excuse to detain him. "Just in case I feel worse."

"Yes, you're right." His gaze was opaque. "I'd better stay with you."

We waited. The dark mass closed over beach and bungalows. The nocturnal glow fluttered at the edge of my vision. When I glanced at the beach, the dim shapes were hectic. I seemed to be paying for my earlier fascination, for now the walls of the room looked active with faint patterns.

Where was the doctor? Neal seemed impatient too. The only sounds were the repetitive ticking of his footsteps and the irregular chant of the sea. He kept staring at me as if he wanted to speak; occasionally his mouth twitched. He resembled a child both eager to confess and afraid to do so.

Though he made me uneasy I tried to look encouraging, interested in whatever he might have to say. His pacing took him closer and closer to the beach door. Yes, I nodded, tell me, talk to me.

His eyes narrowed. Behind his eyelids he was pondering. Abruptly he sat opposite me. A kind of smile, tweaked awry, plucked at his lips. "I've got another story for you," he said.

"Really?" I sounded as intrigued as I could.

He picked up the notebook. "I worked it out from this."

So we'd returned to his obsession. As he twitched pages over, his face shifted constantly. His lips moved as though whispering the text. I heard the vast mumbling of the sea.

"Suppose this," he said all at once. "I only said suppose, mind you. This guy was living all alone in Strand. It must have affected his mind, you said that yourself—having to watch the beach every night. But just suppose it didn't send him mad? Suppose it affected his mind so that he saw things more clearly?"

I hid my impatience. "What things?"

"The beach." His tone reminded me of something—a particular kind of simplicity I couldn't quite place. "Of course we're only supposing. But from things you've read, don't you feel there are places that are closer to another sort of reality, another plane or dimension or whatever?"

"You mean the beach at Strand was like that?" I suggested, to encourage him.

"That's right. Did you feel it too?"

His eagerness startled me. "I felt ill, that's all. I still do."

"Sure. Yes, of course. I mean, we were only supposing. But look at what he says." He seemed glad to retreat into the notebook. "It started at Lewis where the old stones were, then it moved on up the coast to Strand. Doesn't that prove that what he was talking about is unlike anything we know?"

His mouth hung open, awaiting my agreement; it looked empty, robbed of sense. I glanced away, distracted by the fluttering glow beyond him. "I don't know what you mean."

"That's because you haven't read this properly." His impatience had turned harsh. "Look here," he demanded, poking his finger at a group of words as if they were a Bible's oracle.

WHEN THE PATTERNS READY IT CAN COME BACK. "So what is that supposed to mean?"

"I'll tell you what I think it means—what he meant." His low voice seemed to stumble among the rhythms of the beach. "You see how he keeps mentioning patterns. Suppose this other reality was once all there was? Then ours came into being and occupied some of its space. We didn't destroy it— it can't be destroyed. Maybe it withdrew a little, to bide its time. But it left a kind of imprint of itself, a kind of coded image of itself in our reality. And yet that image is itself in embryo, growing. You see, he says it's alive but it's only the image being put together. Things become part of its image, and that's how it grows. I'm sure that's what he meant."

I felt mentally exhausted and dismayed by all this. How much in need of a doctor was he? I couldn't help sounding a little derisive. "I don't see how you could have put all that together from that book."

"Who says I did?"

His vehemence was shocking. I had to break the tension, for the glare in his eyes looked as unnatural and nervous as the glow of the beach. I went to gaze from the front window, but there was no sign of the doctor. "Don't worry," Neal said. "He's coming."

I stood staring out at the lightless road until he said fretfully "Don't you want to hear the rest?"

He waited until I sat down. His tension was oppressive as the hovering sky. He gazed at me for what seemed minutes; the noose dug into my skull. At last he said "Does this beach feel like anywhere else to you?"

"It feels like a beach."

He shrugged that aside. "You see, he worked out that whatever came from the old stones kept moving towards the inhabited areas. That's how it added to itself. That's why it moved on from Lewis and then Strand."

"All nonsense, of course. Ravings."

"No. It isn't." There was no mistaking the fury that lurked, barely restrained, beneath his low voice. That fury seemed loose in the roaring night, in the wind and violent sea and looming sky. The beach trembled wakefully. "The next place it would move to would be here," he muttered. "It has to be."

"If you accepted the idea in the first place."

A hint of a grimace twitched his cheek; my comment might have been an annoying fly—certainly as trivial. "You can read the pattern out there if you try," he mumbled. "It takes all day. You begin to get a sense of what might be there. It's alive, though nothing like life as we recognise it."

I could only say whatever came into my head, to detain him until the doctor arrived. "Then how do you?"

He avoided the question, but only to betray the depths of his obsession. "Would an insect recognise us as a kind of life?"

Suddenly I realised that he intoned "the beach" as a priest might name his god. We must get away from the beach. Never mind the doctor now. "Look, Neal, I think we'd better—"

He interrupted me, eyes glaring spasmodically. "It's strongest at night. I think it soaks up energy during the day. Remember, he said that the quicksands only come out at night. They move, you know—they make you follow the pattern. And the sea is different at night. Things come out of it. They're like symbols and yet they're alive. I think the sea creates them. They help make the pattern live."

Appalled, I could only return to the front window and search for the lights of the doctor's car—for any lights at all.

"Yes, yes," Neal said, sounding less impatient than soothing. "He's coming." But as he spoke I glimpsed, reflected in the window, his secret triumphant grin.

Eventually I managed to say to his reflection "You didn't call a doctor, did you?"

"No." A smile made his lips tremble like quicksand. "But he's coming."

My stomach had begun to churn slowly; so had my head, and the room. Now I was afraid to stand with my back to Neal, but when I turned I was more afraid to ask the question. "Who?"

For a moment I thought he disdained to answer; he turned his back on me and gazed towards the beach—but I can't write any longer as if I have doubts, as if I don't know the end. The beach was his answer, its awesome transformation was, even if I wasn't sure what I was seeing. Was the beach swollen, puffed up as if by the irregular gasping of the sea? Was it swarming with indistinct shapes, parasites that scuttled dancing over it, sank into it, floated writhing to its surface? Did it quiver along the whole of its length like luminous gelatin? I tried to believe that all this was an effect of the brooding dark—but the dark had closed down so thickly that there might have been no light in the world outside except the fitful glow.

He craned his head back over his shoulder. The gleam in his eyes looked very like the glimmering outside. A web of saliva stretched between his bared teeth. He grinned with a frightful generosity; he'd decided to answer my question more directly. His lips moved as they had when he was reading. At last I heard what I'd tried not to suspect. He was making the sound that I'd tried not to hear in the shells.

Was it meant to be an invocation, or the name I'd asked for? I knew only that the sound, so liquid and inhuman that I could almost think it was shapeless, nauseated me, so much so that I couldn't separate it from the huge loose voices of wind and sea. It seemed to fill the room. The pounding of my skull tried to imitate its rhythm, which I found impossible to grasp, unbearable. I began to sidle along the wall towards the front door.

His body turned jerkily, as if dangling from his neck. His head laughed, if a sound like struggles in mud is laughter. "You're not going to try to get away?" he cried. "It was getting hold of you before I came, he was. You haven't a chance now, not since we brought him into the house," and he picked up a shell.

As he levelled the mouth of the shell at me my dizziness flooded my skull, hurling me forward. The walls seemed to glare and shake and break out in swarms; I thought that a dark bulk loomed at the window, filling it. Neal's mouth was working, but the nauseating sound might have been roaring deep in a cavern, or a shell. It sounded distant and huge, but coming closer and growing more definite—the voice of something vast and liquid that was gradually taking shape. Perhaps that was because I was listening, but I had no choice.

All at once Neal's free hand clamped his forehead. It looked like a pincer desperate to tear something out of his skull. "It's growing," he cried, somewhere between sobbing and ecstasy. As he spoke, the liquid chant seemed to abate not at all. Before I knew what he meant to do, he'd wrenched open the back door and was gone. In a nightmarish way, his nervous elaborate movements resembled dancing.

As the door crashed open, the roar of the night rushed in. Its leap in volume sounded eager, voracious. I stood paralysed, listening, and couldn't tell how like his chant it sounded. I heard his footsteps, soft and loose, running unevenly over the dunes. Minutes later I thought I heard a faint cry, which sounded immediately engulfed.

I slumped against a chair. I felt relieved, drained, uncaring. The sounds had returned to the beach, where they ought to be; the room looked stable now. Then I grew disgusted with myself. Suppose Neal was injured, or caught in quicksand? I'd allowed his hysteria to gain a temporary hold on my sick perceptions, I told myself—was I going to use that as an excuse not to try to save him?

At last I forced myself outside. All the bungalows were dark. The beach was glimmering, but not violently. I could see nothing wrong with the sky. Only my dizziness, and the throbbing of my head, threatened to distort my perceptions.

I made myself edge between the bushes, which hissed like snakes, mouths full of sand. The tangle of footprints made me stumble frequently. Sand rattled the spikes of marram grass. At the edge of the dunes, the path felt ready to slide me down to the beach.

The beach was crowded. I had to squint at many of the vague pieces of debris. My eyes grew used to the dimness, but I could see no sign of Neal. Then I peered closer. Was that a pair of sandals, half-buried? Before my giddiness could hurl me to the beach, I slithered down.

Yes, they were Neal's, and a path of bare footprints led away towards the crowd of debris. I poked gingerly at the sandals, and wished I had my stick to test for quicksand—but the sand in which they were partially engulfed was quite solid. Why had he tried to bury them?

I followed his prints, my eyes still adjusting. I refused to imitate his path, for it looped back on itself in intricate patterns which made me dizzy and wouldn't fade from my mind. His paces were irregular, a cripple's dance. He must be a puppet of his nerves, I thought. I was a little afraid to confront him, but I felt a duty to try.

His twistings led me among the debris. Low obscure shapes surrounded me: a jagged stump bristling with metal tendrils that groped in the air as I came near; half a car so rusty and misshapen that it looked like a child's fuzzy sketch; the hood of a pram within which glimmered a bald lump of sand. I was glad to emerge from that maze, for the dim objects seemed to shift; I'd even thought the bald lump was opening a crumbling mouth.

But on the open beach there were other distractions. The ripples and patterns of sand were clearer, and appeared to vibrate restlessly. I kept glancing towards the sea, not because its chant was troubling me—though, with its insistent loose rhythm, it was—but because I had a persistent impression that the waves were slowing, sluggish as treacle.

I stumbled, and had to turn back to see what had tripped me. The glow of the beach showed me Neal's shirt, the little of it that was left unburied. There was no mistaking it; I recognised its pattern. The glow made the nylon seem luminous, lit from within.

His prints danced back among the debris. Even then, God help me, I wondered if he was playing a sick joke—if he was waiting somewhere to leap out, to scare me into admitting I'd been impressed. I trudged angrily into the midst of the debris, and wished at once that I hadn't. All the objects were luminous, without shadows.

There was no question now: the glow of the beach was increasing. It made Neal's tracks look larger; their outlines shifted as I squinted at them. I stumbled hastily towards the deserted stretch of beach, and brushed against the half-engulfed car.

That was the moment at which the nightmare became real. I might have told myself that rust had eaten away the car until it was thin as a shell, but I was past deluding myself. All at once I knew that nothing on this beach was as it seemed, for as my hand collided with the car roof, which should have been painfully solid, I felt the roof crumble—and the entire structure flopped on the sand, from which it was at once indistinguishable.

I fled towards the open beach. But there was no relief, for the entire beach was glowing luridly, like mud struggling to suffocate a moon. Among the debris I glimpsed the rest of Neal's clothes, half absorbed by the beach. As I staggered into the open, I saw his tracks ahead—saw how they appeared to grow, to alter until they became unrecognisable, and then to peter out at a large dark shapeless patch on the sand.

I glared about, terrified. I couldn't see the bungalows. After minutes I succeeded in glimpsing the path, the mess of footprints cluttering the dune. I began to pace towards it, very slowly and quietly, so as not to be noticed by the beach and the looming sky.

But the dunes were receding. I think I began to scream then, scream almost in a whisper, for the faster I hurried, the further the dunes withdrew. The nightmare had overtaken perspective. Now I was running wildly, though I felt I was standing still. I'd run only a few steps when I had to recoil from sand that seized my feet so eagerly I almost heard it smack its lips. Minutes ago there had been no quicksand, for I could see my earlier prints embedded in that patch. I stood trapped, shivering uncontrollably, as the glow intensified and the lightless sky seemed to descend—and I felt the beach change.

Simultaneously I experienced something which, in a sense, was worse: I felt myself change. My dizziness whirled out of me. I felt light-headed but stable. At last I realised that I had never had sunstroke. Perhaps it had been my inner conflict—being forced to stay yet at the same time not daring to venture onto the beach, because of what my subconscious knew would happen.

And now it was happening. The beach had won. Perhaps Neal had given it the strength. Though I dared not look, I knew that the sea had stopped. Stranded objects, elaborate symbols composed of something like flesh, writhed on its paralysed margin. The clamour which surrounded me, chanting and gurgling, was not that of the sea: it was far too articulate, however repetitive. It was underfoot too—the voice of the beach, a whisper pronounced by so many sources that it was deafening.

I felt ridges of sand squirm beneath me. They were firm enough to bear my weight, but they felt nothing like sand. They were forcing me to shift my balance. In a moment I would have to dance, to imitate the jerking shapes that had ceased to pretend they were only debris, to join in the ritual of the objects that swarmed up from the congealed sea. Everything glistened in the quivering glow. I thought my flesh had begun to glow too.

Then, with a lurch of vertigo worse than any I'd experienced, I found myself momentarily detached from the nightmare. I seemed to be observing myself, a figure tiny and trivial as an insect, making a timid hysterical attempt to join in the dance of the teeming beach. The moment was brief, yet felt like eternity. Then I was back in my clumsy flesh, struggling to prance on the beach.

At once I was cold with terror. I shook like a victim of electricity, for I knew what viewpoint I'd shared. It was still watching me, indifferent as outer space—and it filled the sky. If I looked up I would see its eyes, or eye, if it had anything that I would recognise as such. My neck shivered as I held my head down. But I would have to look up in a moment, for I could feel the face, or whatever was up there, leaning closer—reaching down for me.

If I hadn't broken through my suffocating panic I would have been crushed to nothing. But my teeth tore my lip, and allowed me to scream. Released, I ran desperately, heedless of quicksand. The dunes crept back from me, the squirming beach glowed, the light flickered in the rhythm of the chanting. I was spared being engulfed—but when at last I reached the dunes, or was allowed to reach them, the dark massive presence still hovered overhead.

I clambered scrabbling up the path. My sobbing gasps filled my mouth with sand. My wild flight was from nothing that I'd seen. I was fleeing the knowledge, deep-rooted and undeniable, that what I perceived blotting out the sky was nothing but an acceptable metaphor. Appalling though the presence was, it was only my mind's version of what was there—a way of letting me glimpse it without going mad at once.

V

I have not seen Neal since—at least, not in a form that anyone else would recognise.

Next day, after a night during which I drank all the liquor I could find to douse my appalled thoughts and insights, I discovered that I couldn't leave. I pretended to myself that I was going to the beach to search for Neal. But the movements began at once; the patterns stirred. As I gazed, dully entranced, I felt something grow less dormant in my head, as though my skull had turned into a shell.

Perhaps I stood engrossed by the beach for hours. Movement distracted me: the skimming of a windblown patch of sand. As I glanced at it I saw that it resembled a giant mask, its features ragged and crumbling. Though its eyes and mouth couldn't keep their shape, it kept trying to resemble Neal's face. As it slithered whispering towards me I fled towards the path, moaning.

That night he came into the bungalow. I hadn't dared go to bed; I dozed in a chair, and frequently woke trembling. Was I awake when I saw his huge face squirming and transforming as it crawled out of the wall? Certainly I could hear his words, though his voice was the inhuman chorus I'd experienced on the beach. Worse, when I opened my eyes to glimpse what might have been only a shadow, not a large unstable form fading back into the substance of the wall, for a few seconds I could still hear that voice.

Each night, once the face had sunk back into the wall as into quicksand, the voice remained longer—and each night, struggling to break loose from the prison of my chair, I understood more of its revelations. I tried to believe all this was my imagination, and so, in a sense, it was. The glimpses of Neal were nothing more than acceptable metaphors for what Neal had become, and what I was becoming. My mind refused to perceive the truth more directly, yet I was possessed by a temptation, vertiginous and sickening, to learn what that truth might be.

For a while I struggled. I couldn't leave, but perhaps I could write. When I found that however bitterly I fought I could think of nothing but the beach, I wrote this. I hoped that writing about it might release me, but of course the more one thinks of the beach, the stronger its hold becomes.

Now I spend most of my time on the beach. It has taken me months to write this. Sometimes I see people staring at me from the bungalows. Do they wonder what I'm doing? They will find out when their time comes—everyone will. Neal must have satisfied it for a while; for the moment it is slower. But that means little. Its time is not like ours.

Each day the pattern is clearer. My pacing helps. Once you have glimpsed the pattern you must go back to read it, over and over. I can feel it growing in my mind. The sense of expectancy is overwhelming. Of course that sense was never mine. It was the hunger of the beach.

My time is near. The large moist prints that surround mine are more pronounced—the prints of what I am becoming. Its substance is everywhere, stealthy and insidious. Today, as I looked at the bungalows, I saw them change; they grew like fossils of themselves. They looked like dreams of the beach, and that is what they will become.

The voice is always with me now. Sometimes the congealing haze seems to mouth at me. At twilight the dunes edge forward to guard the beach. When the beach is dimmest I see other figures pacing out the pattern. Only those whom the beach has touched would see them; their outlines are unstable—some look more like coral than flesh. The quicksands make us trace the pattern, and he stoops from the depths beyond the sky to watch. The sea feeds me.

Often now I have what may be a dream. I glimpse what Neal has become, and how that is merely a fragment of the imprint which it will use to return to our world. Each time I come closer to recalling the insight when I wake. As my mind changes, it tries to prepare me for the end. Soon I shall be what Neal is. I tremble uncontrollably, I feel deathly sick, my mind struggles desperately not to know. Yet in a way I am resigned. After all, even if I managed to flee the beach, I could never escape the growth. I have understood enough to know that it would absorb me in time, when it becomes the world.

Out of Copyright

The widow gazed wistfully at the pile of books. "*I thought they might be* worth something."

"Oh, some are," Tharne said. "That one, for instance, will fetch a few pence. But I'm afraid that your husband collected books indiscriminately. Much of this stuff isn't worth the paper it's printed on. Look, I'll tell you what I'll do—I'll take the whole lot off your hands and give you the best price I can."

When he'd counted out the notes, the wad over his heart was scarcely reduced. He carried the bulging cartons of books to his van, down three gloomy flights of stairs, along the stone path which hid beneath lolling grass, between gateposts whose stone globes grew continents of moss. By the third descent he was panting. Nevertheless he grinned as he kicked grass aside; the visit had been worthwhile, certainly.

He drove out of the cracked and overgrown streets, past rusty cars laid open for surgery, old men propped on front steps to wither in the sun, prams left outside houses as though in the hope that a thief might adopt the baby. Sunlight leaping from windows and broken glass lanced his eyes. Heat made the streets and his perceptions waver. Glimpsed in the mirror or sensed looming at his back, the cartons resembled someone crouching behind him. They smelled more dusty than the streets.

Soon he reached the crescent. The tall Georgian houses shone white. Beneath them the van looked cheap, a tin toy littering the street. Still, it wasn't advisable to seem too wealthy when buying books.

He dumped the cartons in his hall, beside the elegant curve of the staircase. His secretary came to the door of her office. "Any luck?"

"Yes indeed. Some first editions and a lot of rare material. The man knew what he was collecting."

"Your mail came," she said in a tone which might have announced the police. This annoyed him: he prided himself on his legal knowledge, he observed the law scrupulously. "Well, well," he demanded, "who's saying what?"

"It's that American agent again. He says you have a moral obligation to pay Lewis's widow for those three stories. Otherwise, he says—let's see—'I shall have to seriously consider recommending my clients to boycott your anthologies.'"

"He says that, does he? The bastard. They'd be better off boycotting him." Tharne's face grew hot and swollen; he could hardly control his grin. "He's better at splitting infinitives than he is at looking after his people's affairs. He never renewed the copyright on those stories. We don't owe anyone a penny. And by God, you show me an author who needs the money. Rolling in it, all of them. Living off their royalties." A final injustice struck him; he smote his forehead. "Anyway, what the devil's it got to do with the widow? She didn't write the stories."

To burn up some of his rage, he struggled down to the cellar with the cartons. His blood drummed wildly. As he unpacked the cartons, dust smoked up to the light-bulbs. The cellar, already dim with its crowd of bookshelves, grew dimmer.

He piled the books neatly, sometimes shifting a book from one pile to another, as though playing Patience. When he reached the ace, he stopped. *Tales Beyond Life*, by Damien Damon. It was practically a legend; the book had never been reprinted in its entirety. The find could hardly have been more opportune. The book contained "The Dunning of Diavolo"—exactly what he needed to complete the new Tharne anthology, *Justice From Beyond the Grave*. He knocked lumps of dust from the top of the book, and turned to the story.

Even in death he would be recompensed. Might the resurrectionists have his corpse for a toy? Of a certainty—but only once those organs had been removed which his spirit would need, and the Rituals performed. This stipulation he had willed on his deathbed to his son. Unless his corpse was pacified, his curse would rise.

Undeed, had the father's estate been more readily available to clear the son's debts, this might have been an edifying tale of filial piety. Still, on a night when the moon gleamed like a sepulture, the father was plucked tuber-pallid from the earth.

Rather than sow superstitious scruples in the resurrectionists, the son had told them naught. Even so, the burrowers felt that they had mined an uncommon seam. Voiceless it might be, but the corpse had its forms of protest. Only by seizing its wrists could the corpse-miners elude the cold touch of its hands. Could they have closed its stiff lids, they might have borne its grin. On the contrary, neither would touch the gelatinous pebbles which bulged from its face. . . .

Tharne knew how the tale continued: Diavolo, the father, was dissected, but his limbs went snaking round the town in search of those who had betrayed him, and crawled down the throats of the victims to drag out the twins of those organs of which the corpse had been robbed. All good Gothic stuff—gory and satisfying, but not to be taken too seriously. They couldn't write like that nowadays; they'd lost the knack of proper Gothic writing. And yet they whined that they weren't paid enough!

Only one thing about the tale annoyed him: the misprint "undeed" for "indeed." Amusingly, it resembled "undead"—but that was no excuse for perpetrating it. The one reprint of the tale, in the 'twenties, had swarmed with literals. Well, this time the text would be perfect. Nothing appeared in a Tharne anthology until it satisfied him.

He checked the remaining text, then gave it to his secretary to retype. His timing was exact: a minute later the doorbell announced the book collector, who was as punctual as Tharne. They spent a mutually beneficial half-hour. "These I bought only this morning," Tharne said proudly. "They're yours for twenty pounds apiece."

The day seemed satisfactory until the phone rang. He heard the girl's startled squeak. She rang through to his office, sounding flustered. "Ronald Main wants to speak to you."

"Oh God. Tell him to write, if he still knows how. I've no time to waste in chatting, even if he has." But her cry had disturbed him; it sounded like a threat of inefficiency. Let Main see that someone round here wasn't to be shaken! "No, wait—put him on."

Main's orotund voice came rolling down the wire. "It has come to my notice that you have anthologised a story of mine without informing me."

Trust a writer to use as many words as he could! "There was no need to get in touch with you," Tharne said. "The story's out of copyright."

"That is hardly the issue. Aside from the matter of payment, which we shall certainly discuss, I want to take up with you the question of the text itself. Are you aware that whole sentences have been rewritten?"

"Yes, of course. That's part of my job. I am the editor, you know." Irritably Tharne restrained a sneeze; the smell of dust was very strong. "After all, it's an early story of yours. Objectively, don't you think I've improved it?" He oughtn't to sound as if he was weakening. "Anyway, I'm afraid that legally you've no rights."

Did that render Main speechless, or was he preparing a stronger attack? It scarcely mattered, for Tharne put down the phone. Then he strode down the hall to check his secretary's work. Was her typing as flustered as her voice had been?

Her office was hazy with floating dust. No wonder she was peering closely at the book—though she looked engrossed, almost entranced. As his shadow fell on the page she started; the typewriter carriage sprang to its limit, ringing. She demanded "Was that you before?"

"What do you mean?"

"Oh, nothing. Don't let it bother you." She seemed nervously annoyed—whether with him or with herself he couldn't tell.

At least her typing was accurate, though he could see where letters had had to be retyped. He might as well write the introduction to the story. He went down to fetch *Who's Who in Horror and Fantasy Fiction*. Dust teemed around the cellar lights and chafed his throat.

Here was Damien Damon, real name Sidney Drew: b. Chelsea, 30 April 1876; d.? 1911? "His life was even more bizarre and outrageous than his fiction. Some critics say that that is the only reason for his fame. . . ."

A small dry sound made Tharne glance up. Somewhere among the shelved books, a face peered at him through a gap. Of course it could be nothing of the sort, but it took him a while to locate a cover which had fallen open in a gap, and which must have resembled a face.

Upstairs he wrote the introduction. ". . . Without the help of an agent, and with no desire to make money from his writing, Damon became one of the most discussed in whispers writers of his day. Critics claim that it was scandals that he practised magic which gained him fame. But his posthumously published *Tales Beyond Life* shows that he was probably the last really first class writer in the tradition of Poe. . . ." Glancing up, Tharne caught sight of himself, pen in hand, at the desk in the mirror. So much for any nonsense that he didn't understand writers' problems! Why, he was a writer himself!

Only when he'd finished writing did he notice how quiet the house had become. It had the strained unnatural silence of a library. As he padded down the hall to deliver the text to his secretary his sounds felt muffled, detached from him.

His secretary was poring over the typescript of Damon's tale. She looked less efficient than anxious—searching for something she would rather not find? Dust hung about her in the amber light, and made her resemble a waxwork or a faded painting. Her arms dangled, forgotten. Her gaze was fixed on the page.

Before he could speak, the phone rang. That startled her so badly that he thought his presence might dismay her more. He retreated into the hall, and a dark shape stepped back behind him—his shadow, of course. He entered her office once more, making sure he was audible.

"It's Mr Main again," she said, almost wailing.

"Tell him to put it in writing."

"Mr Tharne says would you please send him a letter." Her training allowed her to regain control, yet she seemed unable to put down the phone until instructed. Tharne enjoyed the abrupt cessation of the outraged squeaking. "Now I think you'd better go home and get some rest," he said.

When she'd left he sat at her desk and read the typescripts. Yes, she had corrected the original; "undeed" was righted. The text seemed perfect, ready for the printer. Why then did he feel that something was wrong? Had she omitted a passage or otherwise changed the wording?

He'd compare the texts in his office, where he was more comfortable. As he rose, he noticed a few faint dusty marks on the carpet. They approached behind his secretary's chair, then veered away. He must have tracked dust from the cellar, which clearly needed sweeping. What did his housekeeper think she was paid for?

Again his footsteps sounded muted. Perhaps his ears were clogged with dust; there was certainly enough of it about. He had never noticed how strongly the house smelled of old books, nor how unpleasant the smell could be. His skin felt dry, itchy.

In his office he poured himself a large Scotch. It was late enough, he needn't feel guilty—indeed, twilight seemed unusually swift tonight, unless it was an effect of the swarms of dust. He didn't spend all day drinking, unlike some writers he could name.

He knocked clumps of dust from the book; it seemed almost to grow there, like grey fungus. Airborne dust whirled away from him and drifted back. He compared the texts, line by line. Surely they were identical, except for her single correction. Yet he felt there was some aspect of the typescript which he needed urgently to decipher. This frustration, and its irrationality, unnerved him.

He was still frowning at the pages, having refilled his glass to loosen up his thoughts, when the phone rang once. He grabbed it irritably, but the earpiece was as hushed as the house. Or was there, amid the electric hissing vague as a cascade of dust, a whisper? It was beyond the grasp of his hearing, except for a syllable or two which sounded like Latin—if it was there at all.

He jerked to his feet and hurried down the hall. Now that he thought about it, perhaps he'd heard his secretary's extension lifted as his phone had rung. Yes, her receiver was off the hook. It must have fallen off. As he replaced it, dust sifted out of the mouthpiece.

Was a piece of paper rustling in the hall? No, the hall was bare. Perhaps it was the typescript, stirred on his desk by a draught. He closed the door behind him, to exclude any draught—as well as the odour of something very old and dusty.

But the smell was stronger in his room. He sniffed gingerly at *Tales Beyond Life*. Why, there it was: the book reeked of dust. He shoved open the French windows, then he sat and stared at the typescript. He was beginning to regard it with positive dislike. He felt as though he had been given a code to crack; it was nerve-racking as an examination. Why was it only the typescript that bothered him, and not the original?

He flapped the typed pages, for they looked thinly coated with grey. Perhaps it was only the twilight, which seemed composed of dust. Even his Scotch tasted clogged. Just let him see what was wrong with this damned story, then he'd leave the room to its dust—and have a few well-chosen words for his housekeeper tomorrow.

There was only one difference between the texts: the capital *I*. Or had he missed another letter? Compulsively and irritably, refusing to glance at the grey lump which hovered at the edge of his vision, he checked the first few capitals. *E, M, O, R, T* . . . Suddenly he stopped, parched mouth open. Seizing his pen, he began to transcribe the capitals alone.

> *E mortuis revoco.*
> *From the dead I summon thee.*

Oh, it must be a joke, a mistake, a coincidence. But the next few capitals dashed his doubts. *From the dead I summon thee, from the dust I recreate thee.* . . . The entire story concealed a Latin invocation. It had been Damien Damon's last story and also, apparently, his last attempt at magic.

And it was Tharne's discovery. He must rewrite his introduction. Publicised correctly, the secret of the tale could help the book's sales a great deal. Why then was he unwilling to look up? Why was he tense as a trapped animal, ears straining painfully? Because of the thick smell of dust, the stealthy dry noises that his choked ears were unable to locate, the grey mass that hovered in front of him?

When at last he managed to look up, the jerk of his head twinged his neck. But his gasp was of relief. The grey blotch was only a chunk of dust, clinging to the mirror. Admittedly it was unpleasant; it resembled a face masked with dust, which also spilled from the face's dismayingly numerous openings. Really, he could live without it, much as he resented having to do his housekeeper's job for her.

When he rose, it took him a moment to realise that his reflection had partly blotted out the grey mass. In the further moment before he understood, two more reflected grey lumps rose beside it, behind him. Were they hands or wads of dust? Perhaps they were composed of both. It was impossible to tell, even when they closed over his face.

Above the World

Nobody was at Reception when Knox came downstairs. The dinner-gong hung mute in its frame; napkin pyramids guarded dining-tables; in the lounge, chairs sat emptily. Nothing moved, except fish in the aquarium, fluorescent gleams amid water that bubbled like lemonade. The visitors' book lay open on the counter. He riffled the pages idly, seeking his previous visit. A Manchester address caught his attention: but the name wasn't his—not any longer. The names were those of his wife and the man.

It took him a moment to realise. They must have been married by then. So the man's name had been Tooley, had it? Knox hadn't cared to know. He was pleased to find that he felt nothing but curiosity. Why had she returned here—for a kind of second honeymoon, to exorcise her memories of him?

When he emerged, it was raining. That ought to wash the fells clean of all but the dedicated walkers; he might be alone up there—no perambulatory radios, no families marking their path with trailing children. Above the hotel mist wandered among the pines, which grew pale and blurred, a spiky frieze of grey, then solidified, regaining their green. High on the scree slope, the Bishop of Barf protruded like a single deformed tooth.

The sight seemed to halt time, to turn it back. He had never left the Swan Hotel. In a moment Wendy would run out, having had to go back for her camera or her rucksack or something. "I wasn't long, was I? The bus hasn't gone, has it? Oh dear, I'm sorry." Of course these impressions were nonsense: he'd moved on, developed since his marriage, defined himself more clearly—but it cheered him that his memories were cool, disinterested. Life advanced relentlessly, powered by change. The Bishop shone white only because climbers painted the pinnacle each year, climbing the steep scree with buckets of whitewash from the Swan.

Here came the bus. It would be stuffed with wet campers slow as turtles, their backs burdened with tubular scaffolding and enormous rucksacks. Only once had he suffered such a ride. Had nothing changed? Not the Swan, the local food, the unobtrusive service, the long white seventeenth-century building which had so charmed Wendy. He had a table to himself; if you wanted to be left alone, nobody would bother you. Tonight there would be venison, which he hadn't tasted since his honeymoon. He'd returned determined to enjoy the Swan and the walks, determined not to let memories deny him those pleasures—and he'd found his qualms were groundless.

He strode down the Keswick road. Rain rushed over Bassenthwaite Lake and tapped on the hood of his cagoule. Why did the stone wall ahead seem significant? Had Wendy halted there once, because the wall was singing? "Oh look, aren't they beautiful." As he stooped towards the crevice, a cluster of hungry beaks had sprung out of the darkness, gaping. The glimpse had unnerved him: the inexorable growth of life, sprouting everywhere, even in stone. Moss choked the silent crevice now.

Somehow that image set him wondering where Wendy and the man had died. Mist had caught them, high on one or other of the fells; they'd died of exposure. That much he had heard from a friend of Wendy's, who had grown aloof from him and who had seemed to blame him for entrusting Wendy to an inexperienced climber—as if Knox should have taken care of her even after the marriage! He hadn't asked for details. He'd felt relieved when Wendy had announced that she'd found someone else. Habit, familiarity, and introversion had screened them from each other well before they'd separated.

He was passing a camp in a field. He hadn't slept in a tent since early in his marriage, and then only under protest. Rain slithered down bright canvas. The muffled voices of a man and a woman paced him from tent to tent. Irrationally, he peered between the tents to glimpse them—but it must be a radio programme. Though the voices sounded intensely engrossed in discussion, he could distinguish not a word. The camp looked deserted. Everyone must be under canvas, or walking.

By the time he reached Braithwaite village, the rain had stopped. Clouds paraded the sky; infrequent gaps let out June sunlight, which touched the heights of the surrounding fells. He made for the café at the foot of the Whinlatter Pass—not because Wendy had loved the little house, its homemade cakes and its shelves of books, but for something to read: he would let chance choose his reading. But the shop was closed. Beside it Coledale Beck pursued its wordless watery monologue.

Should he climb Grisedale Pike? He remembered the view from the summit, of Braithwaite and Keswick the colours of pigeons, white and grey amid the palette of fields. But climbers were toiling upwards towards the intermittent sun. Sometimes the spectacle of plodding walkers, fell boots creaking, sticks shoving at the ground, red faces puffing like trains in distress, made his climb seem a mechanical compulsion, absurd and mindless. Suppose the height was occupied by a class of children, heading like lemmings for the edge?

He'd go back to Barf: that would be lonely—unless one had Mr. Wainwright's guidebook, Barf appeared unclimbable. Returning through the village, he passed Braithwaite post office. That had delighted Wendy—a house just like the other small white houses in the row, except for the counter and grille in the front hall, beside the stairs. A postcard came fluttering down the garden path. Was that a stamp on its corner, or a patch of moss? Momentarily he thought he recognised the handwriting—but whose did it resemble? A breeze turned the card like a page. Where a picture might have been there was a covering of moss, which looked vaguely like a blurred view of two figures huddled together. The card slid by him, into the gutter, and lodged trembling in a grid, brandishing its message. Impulsively he made a grab for it—but before he could read the writing, the card fell between the bars.

He returned to the road to Thornthwaite. A sheen of sunlight clung to the macadam brows; hedges dripped dazzling silver. The voices still wandered about the deserted campsite, though now they sounded distant and echoing. Though their words remained inaudible, they seemed to be calling a name through the tents.

At Thornthwaite, only the hotel outshone the Bishop. As Knox glanced towards the coaching inn, Wendy appeared in his bedroom window. Of course it was a chambermaid—but the shock reverberated through him, for all at once he realised that he was staying in the room which he had shared with Wendy. Surely the proprietress of the Swan couldn't have intended this; it must be coincidence. Memories surged, disconcertingly vivid—collapsing happily on the bed after a day's walking, making love, not having to wake alone in the early hours. Just now, trudging along the road, he'd thought of going upstairs to rest. Abruptly he decided to spend the afternoon in walking.

Neither the hard road nor the soggy margin of Bassenthwaite Lake tempted him. He'd climb Barf, as he had intended. He didn't need Mr. Wainwright's book; he knew the way. Wendy had loved those handwritten guidebooks; she'd loved searching through them for the self-portrait of Mr Wainwright which was always hidden among the hand-drawn views—there he was, in Harris tweed, overlooking Lanthwaite Wood. No, Knox didn't need those books today.

The beginning of the path through Beckstones larch plantation was easy.

Soon he was climbing beside Beckstones Gill, his ears full of its intricate liquid clamour as the stream tumbled helplessly downhill, confined in its rocky groove. But the path grew steep. Surely it must have been elsewhere that Wendy had run ahead, mocking his slowness, while he puffed and cursed. By now most of his memories resembled anecdotes he'd overheard or had been told—blurred, lacking important details, sometimes contradictory.

He rested. Around him larches swayed numerous limbs, engrossed in their tethered dance. His breath eased; he ceased to be uncomfortably aware of his pulse. He stumped upwards, over the path of scattered slate. On both sides of him, ferns protruded from decay. Their highest leaves were wound into a ball, like green caterpillars on stalks.

A small rock-face blocked the path. He had to scramble across to the continuation. Lichen made the roots of trees indistinguishable from the rock. His foot slipped; he slithered, banging his elbow, clutching for handholds. Good Lord, the slope was short, at worst he would turn his ankle, he could still grab hold of rock, in any case someone was coming, he could hear voices vague as the stream's rush that obscured them. At last he was sure he was safe, though at the cost of a bruised hip. He sat and cursed his pounding heart. He didn't care who heard him—but perhaps nobody did, for the owners of the voices never appeared.

He struggled upwards. The larches gave way to spruce firs. Fallen trunks, splintered like bone, hindered his progress. How far had he still to climb? He must have laboured half a mile by now; it felt like more. The forest had grown oppressive. Elaborate lichens swelled brittle branches; everywhere he looked, life burgeoned parasitically, consuming the earth and the forest, a constant and ruthless renewal. He was sweating, and the clammy chill of the place failed to cool him.

Silence seized him. He could hear only the restless creaking of trees. For a long time he had been unable to glimpse the Swan; the sky was invisible, too, except in fragments caged by branches. All at once, as he climbed between close banks of mossy earth and rock, he yearned to reach the open. He felt suffocated, as though the omnipresent lichen were thick fog. He forced himself onward, panting harshly.

Pain halted him—pain that transfixed his heart and paralysed his limbs with shock. His head felt swollen, burning, deafened by blood. Beyond that uproar, were there voices? Could he cry for help? But he felt that he might never draw another breath.

As suddenly as it had attacked him, the pain was gone, though he felt as if it had burned a hollow where his heart had been. He slumped against rock.

His ears rang as though metal had been clapped over them. Oh God, the doctor had been right; he must take things easy. But if he had to forgo rambling, he would have nothing left that was worthwhile. At last he groped upwards out of the dank trough of earth, though he was still light-headed and unsure of his footing. The path felt distant and vague.

He reached the edge of the forest without further mishap. Beyond it, Beckstones Gill rushed over broken stones. The sky was layered with grey clouds. Across the stream, on the rise to the summit, bracken shone amid heather.

He crossed the stream and climbed the path. Below him the heathery slope plunged towards the small valley. A few crumbs of boats floated on Bassenthwaite. A constant quivering ran downhill through the heather; the wind dragged at his cagoule, whose fluttering deafened him. He felt unnervingly vulnerable, at the mercy of the gusts. His face had turned cold as bone. Sheep dodged away from him. Their swiftness made his battle with the air seem ridiculous, frustrating. He had lost all sense of time before he reached the summit—where he halted, entranced. At last his toil had meaning.

The world seemed laid out for him. Light and shadow drifted stately over the fells, which reached towards clouds no vaster than they. Across Bassenthwaite, fells higher than his own were only steps on the ascent to Skiddaw, on whose deceptively gentle outline gleamed patches of snow. A few dots, too distant to have limbs, crept along that ridge. The fells glowed with all the colours of foliage, grass, heather, bracken, except where vast tracts of rock broke through. Drifts of shadow half absorbed the colours; occasional sunlight renewed them.

The landscape was melting; he had to blink. Was he weeping, or had the wind stung his eyes? He couldn't tell; the vastness had charmed away his sense of himself. He felt calm, absolutely unselfconscious. He watched light advancing through Beckstones Plantation, possessing each successive rank of foliage. When he gazed across the lake again, that sight had transfigured the landscape.

Which lake was that on the horizon? He had never before noticed it. It lay like a fragment of slate, framed by two fells dark as storms—but above it, clouds were opening. Blue sky shone through the tangle of grey; veils of light descended from the ragged gap. The lake began to glow from within, intensely calm. Beyond it fields and trees grew clear, minute and luminous. Yes, he was weeping.

After a while he sat on a rock. Its coldness was indistinguishable from his own stony chill. He must go down shortly. He gazed out for a last view. The fells looked smooth, alluringly gentle; valleys were trickles of rock. He held up his finger for a red bug to crawl along. Closer to him, red dots were scurrying: ladybirds, condemned to explore the maze of grass-blades, to change course at each intersection. Their mindless urgency dismayed him.

They drew his gaze to the heather. He gazed deep into a tangled clump, at the breathtaking variety of colours, the intricacies of growth. As many must be hidden in each patch of heather: depths empty of meaning, and intended for no eye. All around him plants reproduced shapes endlessly: striving for perfection, or compelled to repeat themselves without end? If his gaze had been microscopic, he would have seen the repetitions of atomic particles, mindlessly clinging and building, possessed by the compulsion of matter to form patterns.

Suddenly it frightened him—he couldn't tell why. He felt unsafe. Perhaps it was the mass of cloud which had closed overhead like a stone lid. The colours of the summit had turned lurid, threatening. He headed back towards the wood. The faces of sheep gleamed like bone—he had never noticed before how they resembled munching skulls. A group of heads, chewing mechanically, glared white against the sky and kept their gaze on him.

He was glad to cross the stream, though he couldn't feel the water. He must hurry down before he grew colder. The hush of the woods embraced him. Had a sheep followed him? No, it was only the cry of a decaying trunk. He slipped quickly down the path, which his feet seemed hardly to touch.

The movement of silver-green lattices caged him. Branches and shadows swayed everywhere, entangled. The tips of some of the firs were luminously new. Winds stalked the depths of the forest, great vague forms on creaking stilts. Scents of growth and decay accompanied him. When he grabbed a branch to make sure of his footing, it broke, scattering flakes of lichen.

Again the forest grew too vivid; the trees seemed victims of the processes of growth, sucked dry by the lichen which at the same time lent them an elaborate patina of life. Wherever he looked, the forest seemed unbearably intricate. How, among all that, could he glimpse initials? Somehow they had seized his attention before he knew what they were. They were carved on a cracked and wrinkled tree: Wendy's initials, and the man's.

Or were they? Perhaps they were only cracks in the bark. Of course she and the man might well have climbed up here—but the more Knox squinted, the less clear the letters seemed. He couldn't recapture the angle of vision at which they had looked unmistakable.

He was still pacing back and forth before the trunk, as though trapped in a ritual, when stealthy movement made him turn. Was it the shifting of grey trees beneath the lowering largely unseen sky? No—it was a cloud or mist, descending swiftly from the summit, through the woods.

He glanced ahead for the path—and, with a shock that seemed to leave him hollow, realised that it was not there. Nor was it visible behind him as far back as the wall of mist. His reluctant fascination with the forest had lured him astray.

He strode back towards the mist, hushing his doubts. Surely the path couldn't be far. But the mist felt thick as icy water, and blinded him. He found himself slithering on decay towards a fall which, though invisible, threatened to be steep. A grab at a crumbling trunk saved him; but when he'd struggled onto safer ground, he could only retreat towards the tree which he had thought was inscribed.

He must press on, outdistancing the mist, and try to head downwards. Wasn't there a forest road below, quite close? But whenever he found an easy slope, it would become abruptly dangerous, often blocked by treacherous splintered logs. He was approaching panic. As much as anything, the hollow at the centre of himself dismayed him. He had tended to welcome it when it had grown there, in his marriage and afterwards; it had seemed safe, invulnerable. Now he found he had few inner resources with which to sustain himself.

The mist was only yards away. It had swallowed all the faint sounds of the wood. If he could only hear the stream, or better still a human voice, a vehicle on the forest road—if only he had gone back to the hotel for his whistle and compass— But there was a sound. Something was blundering towards him. Why was he indefinably distressed, rather than heartened?

Perhaps because the mist obscured it as it scuttled down the slope towards him; perhaps because it sounded too small for an adult human being, too swift, too lopsided. He thought of a child stumbling blindly down the decayed slope. But what child would be so voiceless? As it tumbled limping through the mist, Knox suppressed an urge to flee. He saw the object stagger against a misty root, and collapse there. Before he had ventured forward he saw that it was only a rucksack.

Yet he couldn't quite feel relieved. The rucksack was old, discoloured and patched with decay; mist drained it of colour. Where had it come from? Who had abandoned it, and why? It still moved feebly, as though inhabited. Of course there was a wind: the mist was billowing. Nevertheless he preferred not to go closer. The blurred tentative movements of the overgrown sack were unpleasant, somehow.

Still, perhaps the incident was opportune. It had made him glance upwards for an explanation. He found none—but he caught sight of a summit against the clouds. It wasn't Barf, for between the confusion of trees he could just distinguish two cairns, set close together. If he could reach them, he ought to be able to see his way more clearly. Was he hearing muffled voices up there? He hoped so, but hadn't time to listen.

He wasn't safe yet. The mist had slowed, but was still pursuing him. The slope above him was too steep to climb. He retreated between the trees, avoiding slippery roots which glistened dull silver, glancing upwards constantly for signs of the path. For a while he lost sight of the unknown summit. Only a glimpse of the cairns against the darkening sky mitigated his panic. Were they cairns, or figures sitting together? No, they were the wrong colour for people.

Above him the slope grew steeper. Worse, twilight was settling like mist into the woods. He glared downhill, but the fall was dim and precipitous; there was no sign of a road, only the grey web of innumerable branches. He groped onward, careless of his footing, desperate to glimpse a way. Surely a path must lead to the cairns. But would he reach it before dark? Could he heave himself up the slope now, using trees for handholds? Wait: wasn't that a path ahead, trailing down between the firs? He stumbled forward, afraid to run in case he slipped. He reached out to grab a tree, to lever himself past its trap of roots. But his fingers recoiled—the encrusted glimmering bark looked unnervingly like a face.

He refused to be reminded of anyone. He clung to the hollow within himself and fought off memories. Yet, as he passed close to the next tree, he seemed to glimpse the hint of a face composed of cracks in the bark, and of twilight. His imagination was conspiring with the dimness, that was all—but why, as he grasped a trunk to thrust himself onward, did each patch of lichen seem to suggest a face? The more closely he peered, enraged by his fears, the smaller and more numerous the swarming faces seemed. Were there many different faces, or many versions of a couple? Their expressions, though vague, seemed numerous and disturbing.

For a moment he was sure that he couldn't back away—that he must watch until the light was entirely gone, must glimpse faces yet smaller and clearer and more numerous. Panic hurled him away from the lichen, and sent him scrabbling upwards. His fingers dug into decay; ferns writhed and snapped when he grabbed them; the surrounding dimness teemed with faces. He kicked himself footholds, gouged the earth with his heels. He clutched at roots, which flaked, moist and chill. More than once he slithered back into the massing darkness. But his panic refused to be defeated. At last, as twilight merged the forest into an indistinguishable crowd of dimness, he scrambled up a slope that had commenced to be gentle, to the edge of the trees.

As soon as he had done so, his triumph collapsed beneath dismay. Even if he glimpsed a path from the summit, night would engulf it before he could make his way down. The sky was blackening. Against it loomed two hunched forms, heads turned to him. Suddenly joy seized him. He could hear voices— surely the sound was more than the muttering of wind. The two forms were human. They must know their way down, and he could join them.

He scrambled upwards. Beyond the trees, the slope grew steep again; but the heather provided easy holds, though his clambering felt almost vertical. The voices had ceased; perhaps they had heard him. But when he glanced up, the figures hadn't moved. A foot higher, and he saw that the faces turned to him were patches of moss; the figures were cairns, after all. It didn't matter: companionship waited at the summit; he'd heard voices, he was sure that he'd heard them, please let him have done so. And indeed, as he struggled up the last yards of the slope, the two grey figures rose with a squeaking and rattling of slate, and advanced heavily towards him.

Mackintosh Willy

To start with, he wasn't called Mackintosh Willy. I never knew who gave him that name. Was it one of those nicknames that seem to proceed from a group subconscious, names recognised by every member of the group yet apparently originated by none? One has to call one's fears something, if only to gain the illusion of control. Still, sometimes I wonder how much of his monstrousness we created. Wondering helps me not to ponder my responsibility for what happened at the end.

When I was ten I thought his name was written inside the shelter in the park. I saw it only from a distance; I wasn't one of those who made a game of braving the shelter. At ten I wasn't afraid to be timid—that came later, with adolescence.

Yet if you had walked past Newsham Park you might have wondered what there was to fear: why were children advancing, bold but wary, on the red-brick shelter by the twilit pool? Surely there could be no danger in the shallow shed, which might have held a couple of dozen bicycles. By now the fishermen and the model boats would have left the pool alone and still; lamps on the park road would have begun to dangle luminous tails in the water. The only sounds would be the whispering of children, the murmur of trees around the pool, perhaps a savage incomprehensible muttering whose source you would be unable to locate. Only a game, you might reassure yourself.

And of course it was: a game to conquer fear. If you had waited long enough you might have heard shapeless movement in the shelter, and a snarling. You might have glimpsed him as he came scuttling lopsidedly out of the shelter, like an injured spider from its lair. In the gathering darkness, how much of your glimpse would you believe? The unnerving swiftness of the obese limping shape? The head which seemed to belong to another, far smaller, body, and which was almost invisible within a grey Balaclava cap, except for the small eyes which glared through the loose hole?

All of that made us hate him. We were too young for tolerance—and besides, he was intolerant of us. Ever since we could remember he had been there, guarding his territory and his bottle of red biddy. If anyone ventured too close he would start muttering. Sometimes you could hear some of the words: "Damn bastard prying interfering snooper . . . thieving bastard layabout . . . think you're clever, eh? . . . I'll give you something clever. . . ."

We never saw him until it was growing dark: that was what made him into a monster. Perhaps during the day he joined his cronies elsewhere—on the steps of ruined churches in the centre of Liverpool, or lying on the grass in St John's Gardens, or crowding the benches opposite Edge Hill Public Library, whose stopped clock no doubt helped their draining of time. But if anything of this occurred to us, we dismissed it as irrelevant. He was a creature of the dark.

Shouldn't this have meant that the first time I saw him in daylight was the end? In fact, it was only the beginning.

It was a blazing day at the height of summer, my tenth. It was too hot to think of games to while away my school holidays. All I could do was walk errands for my parents, grumbling a little.

They owned a small newsagent's on West Derby Road. That day they were expecting promised copies of the *Tuebrook Bugle.* Even when he disagreed with them, my father always supported the independent papers—the *Bugle,* the *Liverpool Free Press:* at least they hadn't been swallowed or destroyed by a monopoly. The lateness of the *Bugle* worried him; had the paper given in? He sent me to find out.

I ran across West Derby Road just as the traffic lights at the top of the hill released a flood of cars. Only girls used the pedestrian subway so far as I was concerned; besides, it was flooded again. I strolled past the concrete police station into the park, to take the long way round. It was too hot to go anywhere quickly or even directly.

The park was crowded with games of football, parked prams, sunbathers draped over the greens. Patients sat outside the hospital on Orphan Drive beside the park. Around the lake, fishermen sat by transistor radios and whipped the air with hooks. Beyond the lake, model boats snarled across the shallow circular pool. I stopped to watch their patterns on the water, and caught sight of an object in the shelter.

At first I thought it was an old grey sack that someone had dumped on the bench. Perhaps it held rubbish—sticks which gave parts of it an angular look. Then I saw that the sack was an indeterminate stained garment, which might have been a mackintosh or raincoat of some kind. What I had vaguely assumed to be an ancient shopping bag, resting next to the sack, displayed a ragged patch of flesh and the dull gleam of an eye.

Exposed to daylight, he looked even more dismaying: so huge and still, less stupefied than dormant. The presence of the boatmen with their remote-control boxes reassured me. I ambled past the allotments to Pringle Street, where a terraced house was the editorial office of the *Bugle*.

Our copies were on the way, said Chrissie Maher the editor, and insisted on making me a cup of tea. She seemed a little upset when, having gulped the tea, I hurried out into the rain. Perhaps it was rude of me not to wait until the rain had stopped—but on this parched day I wanted to make the most of it, to bathe my face and my bare arms in the onslaught, gasping almost hysterically.

By the time I had passed the allotments, where cabbages rattled like toy machine-guns, the downpour was too heavy even for me. The park provided little cover; the trees let fall their own belated storms, miniature but drenching. The nearest shelter was by the pool, which had been abandoned to its web of ripples. I ran down the slippery tarmac hill, splashing through puddles, trying to blink away rain, hoping there would be room in the shelter.

There was plenty of room, both because the rain reached easily into the depths of the brick shed and because the shelter was not entirely empty. He lay as I had seen him, face upturned within the sodden Balaclava. Had the boatmen avoided looking closely at him? Raindrops struck his unblinking eyes and trickled over the patch of flesh.

I hadn't seen death before. I stood shivering and fascinated in the rain. I needn't be scared of him now. He'd stuffed himself into the grey coat until it split in several places; through the rents I glimpsed what might have been dark cloth or discoloured hairy flesh. Above him, on the shelter, were graffiti which at last I saw were not his name at all, but the names of three boys: MACK TOSH WILLY. They were partly erased, which no doubt was why one's mind tended to fill the gap.

I had to keep glancing at him. He grew more and more difficult to ignore; his presence was intensifying. His shapelessness, the rents in his coat, made me think of an old bag of washing, decayed and mouldy. His hand lurked in his sleeve; beside it, amid a scattering of Coca-Cola caps, lay fragments of the bottle whose contents had perhaps killed him. Rain roared on the dull green roof of the shelter; his staring eyes glistened and dripped. Suddenly I was frightened. I ran blindly home.

"There's someone dead in the park," I gasped. "The man who chases everyone."

"Look at you!" my mother cried. "Do you want pneumonia? Just you get out of those wet things this instant!"

Eventually I had a chance to repeat my news. By this time the rain had stopped. "Well, don't be telling us," my father said. "Tell the police. They're just across the road."

Did he think I had exaggerated a drunk into a corpse? He looked surprised when I hurried to the police station. But I couldn't miss the chance to venture in there—I believed that elder brothers of some of my schoolmates had been taken into the station and hadn't come out for years.

Beside a window which might have belonged to a ticket office was a bell which you rang to make the window's partition slide back and display a policeman. He frowned down at me. What was my name? What had I been doing in the park? Who had I been with? When a second head appeared beside him he said reluctantly "He thinks someone's passed out in the park."

A blue-and-white Mini called for me at the police station, like a taxi; on the roof a red sign said POLICE. People glanced in at me as though I were on my way to prison. Perhaps I was: suppose Mackintosh Willy had woken up and gone? How long a sentence did you get for lying? False diamonds sparkled on the grass and in the trees. I wished I'd persuaded my father to tell the police.

As the car halted, I saw the grey bulk in the shelter. The driver strode, stiff with dignity, to peer at it. "My God," I heard him say in disgust.

Did he know Mackintosh Willy? Perhaps, but that wasn't the point. "Look at this," he said to his colleague. "Ever see a corpse with pennies on the eyes? Just look at this, then. See what someone thought was a joke."

He looked shocked, sickened. He was blocking my view as he demanded "Did you do this?"

His white-faced anger, and my incomprehension, made me speechless. But his colleague said "It wouldn't be him. He wouldn't come and tell us afterwards, would he?"

As I tried to peer past them he said "Go on home, now. Go on." His gentleness seemed threatening. Suddenly frightened, I ran home through the park.

For a while I avoided the shelter. I had no reason to go near, except on the way home from school. Sometimes I'd used to see schoolmates tormenting Mackintosh Willy; sometimes, at a distance, I had joined them. Now the shelter yawned emptily, baring its dim bench. The dark pool stirred, disturbing the green beards of the stone margin. My main reason for avoiding the park was that there was nobody with whom to go.

Living on the main road was the trouble. I belonged to none of the side streets, where they played football among parked cars or chased through the back alleys. I was never invited to street parties. I felt like an outsider, particularly when I had to pass the groups of teenagers who sat on the railing above the pedestrian subway, lazily swinging their legs, waiting to pounce. I stayed at home, in the flat above the newsagent's, when I could, and read everything in the shop. But I grew frustrated: I did enough reading at school. All this was why I welcomed Mark. He could save me from my isolation.

Not that we became friends immediately. He was my parents' latest paperboy. For several days we examined each other warily. He was taller than me, which was intimidating, but seemed unsure how to arrange his lankiness. Eventually he said "What're you reading?"

He sounded as though reading was a waste of time. "A book," I retorted.

At last, when I'd let him see that it was Mickey Spillane, he said "Can I read it after you?"

"It isn't mine. It's the shop's."

"All right, so I'll buy it." He did so at once, paying my father. He was certainly wealthier than me. When my resentment of his gesture had cooled somewhat, I realised that he was letting me finish what was now his book. I dawdled over it to make him complain, but he never did. Perhaps he might be worth knowing.

My instinct was accurate: he proved to be generous—not only with money, though his father made plenty of that in home improvements, but also in introducing me to his friends. Quite soon I had my place in the tribe at the top of the pedestrian subway, though secretly I was glad that we never exchanged more than ritual insults with the other gangs. Perhaps the police station, looming in the background, restrained hostilities.

Mark was generous too with his ideas. Although Ben, a burly lad, was nominal leader of the gang, it was Mark who suggested most of our activities. Had he taken to delivering papers to save himself from boredom—or, as I wondered afterwards, to distract himself from his thoughts? It was Mark who brought his skates so that we could brave the slope of the pedestrian subway, who let us ride his bicycle around the side streets, who found ways into derelict houses, who brought his transistor radio so that we could hear the first Beatles records as the traffic passed unheeding on West Derby Road. But was all this a means of distracting us from the park?

No doubt it was inevitable that Ben resented his supremacy. Perhaps he deduced, in his slow and stolid way, that Mark disliked the park. Certainly he hit upon the ideal method to challenge him.

It was a hot summer evening. By then I was thirteen. Dust and fumes drifted in the wakes of cars; wagons clattered repetitively across the railway bridge. We lolled about the pavement, kicking Coca-Cola caps. Suddenly Ben said "I know something we can do."

We trooped after him, dodging an aggressive gang of taxis, towards the police station. He might have meant us to play some trick there; when he swaggered past, I'm sure everyone was relieved—everyone except Mark, for Ben was leading us onto Orphan Drive.

Heat shivered above the tarmac. Beside us in the park, twilight gathered beneath the trees, which stirred stealthily. The island in the lake creaked with ducks; swollen litter drifted sluggishly, or tried to climb the bank. I could sense Mark's nervousness. He had turned his radio louder; a misshapen Elvis Presley blundered out of the static, then sank back into incoherence as a neighbourhood waveband seeped into his voice. Why was Mark on edge? I could see only the dimming sky, trees on the far side of the lake diluted by haze, the gleam of bottle caps like eyes atop a floating mound of litter, the glittering of broken bottles in the lawns.

We passed the locked ice-cream kiosk. Ben was heading for the circular pool, whose margin was surrounded by a fluorescent orange tape tied between iron poles, a makeshift fence. I felt Mark's hesitation, as though he were a scared dog dragged by a lead. The lead was pride: he couldn't show fear, especially when none of us knew Ben's plan.

A new concrete path had been laid around the pool. "We'll write our names in that," Ben said.

The dark pool swayed, as though trying to douse reflected lights. Black clouds spread over the sky and loomed in the pool; the threat of a storm lurked behind us. The brick shelter was very dim, and looked cavernous. I strode to the orange fence, not wanting to be last, and poked the concrete with my toe. "We can't," I said; for some reason, I felt relieved. "It's set."

Someone had been there before us, before the concrete had hardened. Footprints led from the dark shelter towards us. As they advanced, they faded, no doubt because the concrete had been setting. They looked as though the man had suffered from a limp.

When I pointed them out, Mark flinched, for we heard the radio swing wide of comprehensibility. "What's up with you?" Ben demanded.

"Nothing."

"It's getting dark," I said, not as an answer but to coax everyone back towards the main road. But my remark inspired Ben; contempt grew in his eyes. "I know what it is," he said, gesturing at Mark. "This is where he used to be scared."

"Who was scared? I wasn't bloody scared."

"Not much you weren't. You didn't look it," Ben scoffed, and told us "Old Willy used to chase him all round the pool. He used to hate him, did old Willy. Mark used to run away from him. I never. *I* wasn't scared."

"You watch who you're calling scared. If you'd seen what I did to that old bastard—"

Perhaps the movements around us silenced him. Our surroundings were crowded with dark shifting: the sky unfurled darkness, muddy shapes rushed at us in the pool, a shadow huddled restlessly in one corner of the shelter. But Ben wasn't impressed by the drooping boast. "Go on," he sneered. "You're scared now. Bet you wouldn't dare go in his shelter."

"Who wouldn't? You watch it, you!"

"Go on, then. Let's see you do it."

We must all have been aware of Mark's fear. His whole body was stiff as a puppet's. I was ready to intervene—to say, lying, that the police were near—when he gave a shrug of despair and stepped forward. Climbing gingerly over the tape as though it were electrified, he advanced onto the concrete.

He strode towards the shelter. He had turned the radio full on; I could hear nothing else, only watch the shifting of dim shapes deep in the reflected sky, watch Mark stepping in the footprints for bravado. They swallowed his feet. He was nearly at the shelter when I saw him glance at the radio.

The song had slipped awry again; another waveband seeped in, a blurred muttering. I thought it must be Mark's infectious nervousness which made me hear it forming into words. "Come on, son. Let's have a look at you." But why shouldn't the words have been real, fragments of a radio play?

Mark was still walking, his gaze held by the radio. He seemed almost hypnotised; otherwise he would surely have flinched back from the huddled shadow which surged forward from the corner by the bench, even though it must have been the shadow of a cloud.

As his foot touched the shelter I called nervously "Come on, Mark. Let's go and skate." I felt as though I'd saved him. But when he came hurrying back, he refused to look at me or at anyone else.

For the next few days he hardly spoke to me. Perhaps he thought of avoiding my parents' shop. Certainly he stayed away from the gang—which turned out to be all to the good, for Ben, robbed of Mark's ideas, could think only of shoplifting. They were soon caught, for they weren't very skilful. After that my father had doubts about Mark, but Mark had always been scrupulously honest in deliveries; after some reflection, my father kept him on. Eventually Mark began to talk to me again, though not about the park.

That was frustrating: I wanted to tell him how the shelter looked now. I still passed it on my way home, though from a different school. Someone had been scrawling on the shelter. That was hardly unusual—graffiti filled the pedestrian subway, and even claimed the ends of streets—but the words were odd, to say the least: like scribbles on the walls of a psychotic's cell, or the gibberish of an invocation. DO THE BASTARD. BOTTLE UP HIS EYES. HOOK THEM OUT. PUSH HIS HEAD IN. Tangled amid them, like chewed bones, gleamed the eroded slashes of MACK TOSH WILLY.

I wasn't as frustrated by the conversational taboo as I might have been, for I'd met my first girlfriend. Kim was her name; she lived in a flat on my block, and because of her parents' trade, seemed always to smell of fish and chips. She obviously looked up to me—for one thing, I'd begun to read for pleasure again, which few of her friends could be bothered attempting. She told me her secrets, which was a new experience for me, strange and rather exciting—as was being seen on West Derby Road with a girl on my arm, any girl. I was happy to ignore the jeers of Ben and cronies.

She loved the park. Often we strolled through, scattering charitable crumbs to ducks. Most of all she loved to watch the model yachts, when the snarling model motorboats left them alone to glide over the pool. I enjoyed watching too, while holding her warm, if rather clammy, hand. The breeze carried away her culinary scent. But I couldn't help noticing that the shelter now displayed screaming faces with red bursts for eyes. I have never seen drawings of violence on walls elsewhere.

My relationship with Kim was short-lived. Like most such teenage experiences, our parting was not romantic and poignant, if partings ever are, but harsh and hysterical. It happened one evening as we made our way to the fair which visited Newsham Park each summer.

Across the lake we could hear shrieks that mingled panic and delight as cars on metal poles swung girls into the air, and the blurred roaring of an ancient pop song, like the voice of an enormous radio. On the Ferris wheel, coloured lights sailed up, painting airborne faces. The twilight shone like a Christmas tree; the lights swam in the pool. That was why Kim said "Let's sit and look first."

The only bench was in the shelter. Tangles of letters dripped tails of dried paint, like blood; mutilated faces shrieked soundlessly. Still, I thought I could bear the shelter. Sitting with Kim gave me the chance to touch her breasts, such as they were, through the collapsing deceptively large cups of her bra. Tonight she smelled of newspapers, as though she had been wrapped in them for me to take out; she must have been serving at the counter. Nevertheless

I kissed her, and ignored the fact that one corner of the shelter was dark as a spider's crevice.

But she had noticed; I felt her shrink away from the corner. Had she noticed more than I? Or was it her infectious wariness which made the dark beside us look more solid, about to shuffle towards us along the bench? I was uneasy, but the din and the lights of the fairground were reassuring. I determined to make the most of Kim's need for protection, but she pushed my hand away. "Don't," she said irritably, and made to stand up.

At that moment I heard a blurred voice. "Popeye," it muttered as if to itself; it sounded gleeful. "Popeye." Was it part of the fair? It might have been a stallholder's voice, distorted by the uproar, for it said "I've got something for you."

The struggles of Kim's hand in mine excited me. "Let me go," she was wailing. Because I managed not to be afraid, I was more pleased than dismayed by her fear—and I was eager to let my imagination flourish, for it was better than reading a ghost story. I peered into the dark corner to see what horrors I could imagine.

Then Kim wrenched herself free and ran around the pool. Disappointed and angry, I pursued her. "Go away," she cried. "You're horrible. I never want to speak to you again." For a while I chased her along the dim paths, but once I began to plead I grew furious with myself. She wasn't worth the embarrassment. I let her go, and returned to the fair, to wander desultorily for a while. When I'd stayed long enough to prevent my parents from wondering why I was home early, I walked home.

I meant to sit in the shelter for a while, to see if anything happened, but someone was already there. I couldn't make out much about him, and didn't like to go closer. He must have been wearing spectacles, for his eyes seemed perfectly circular and gleamed like metal, not like eyes at all.

I quickly forgot that glimpse, for I discovered Kim hadn't been exaggerating: she refused to speak to me. I stalked off to buy fish and chips elsewhere, and decided that I hadn't liked her anyway. My one lingering disappointment, I found glumly, was that I had nobody with whom to go to the fairground. Eventually, when the fair and the school holidays were approaching their end, I said to Mark "Shall we go to the fair tonight?"

He hesitated, but didn't seem especially wary. "All right," he said with the indifference we were beginning to affect about everything.

At sunset the horizon looked like a furnace, and that was how the park felt. Couples rambled sluggishly along the paths; panting dogs splashed in the lake. Between the trees the lights of the fairground shimmered and twinkled, cheap multicoloured stars. As we passed the pool, I noticed that the air was quivering above the footprints in the concrete, and looked darkened, perhaps by dust. Impulsively I said "What did you do to old Willy?"

"Shut up." I'd never heard Mark so savage or withdrawn. "I wish I hadn't done it."

I might have retorted to his rudeness, but instead I let myself be captured by the fairground, by the glade of light amid the balding rutted green. Couples and gangs roamed, harangued a shade half-heartedly by stallholders. Young children hid their faces in pink candy floss. A siren thin as a Christmas party hooter set the Dodgems running. Mark and I rode a tilting bucket above the fuzzy clamour of music, the splashes of glaring light, the cramped crowd. Secretly I felt a little sick, but the ride seemed to help Mark regain his confidence. Shortly, as we were playing a pinball machine with senile flippers, he said "Look, there's Lorna and what's-her-name."

It took me a while to be sure where he was pointing: at a tall bosomy girl, who probably looked several years older than she was, and a girl of about my height and age, her small bright face sketched with makeup. By this time I was following him eagerly.

The tall girl was Lorna; her friend's name was Carol. We strolled for a while, picking our way over power cables, and Carol and I began to like each other; her scent was sweet, if rather overpowering. As the fair began to close, Mark easily won trinkets at a shooting gallery and presented them to the girls, which helped us to persuade them to meet us on Saturday night. By now Mark never looked towards the shelter—I think not from wariness but because it had ceased to worry him, at least for the moment. I glanced across, and could just distinguish someone pacing unevenly round the pool, as if impatient for a delayed meeting.

If Mark had noticed, would it have made any difference? Not in the long run, I try to believe. But however I rationalise, I know that some of the blame was mine.

We were to meet Lorna and Carol on our side of the park in order to take them to the Carlton cinema, nearby. We arrived late, having taken our time over sprucing ourselves; we didn't want to seem too eager to meet them. Beside the police station, at the entrance to the park, a triangular island of pavement, large enough to contain a spinney of trees, divided the road. The girls were meant to be waiting at the nearest point of the triangle. But the island was deserted except for the caged darkness beneath the trees.

We waited. Shop windows on West Derby Road glared fluorescent green. Behind us trees whispered, creaking. We kept glancing into the park, but the only figure we could see on the dark paths was alone. Eventually, for something to do, we strolled desultorily around the island.

It was I who saw the message first, large letters scrawled on the corner nearest the park. Was it Lorna's or Carol's handwriting? It rather shocked me, for it looked semiliterate. But she must have had to use a stone as a pencil, which couldn't have helped; indeed, some letters had had to be dug out of the moss which coated stretches of the pavement. MARK SEE YOU AT THE SHELTER, the message said.

I felt him withdraw a little. "Which shelter?" he muttered.

"I expect they mean the one near the kiosk," I said, to reassure him.

We hurried along Orphan Drive. Above the lamps, patches of foliage shone harshly. Before we reached the pool we crossed the bridge, from which in daylight manna rained down to the ducks, and entered the park. The fair had gone into hibernation; the paths, and the mazes of tree trunks, were silent and very dark. Occasional dim movements made me think that we were passing the girls, but the figure that was wandering a nearby path looked far too bulky.

The shelter was at the edge of the main green, near the football pitch. Beyond the green, tower blocks loomed in glaring auras. Each of the four sides of the shelter was an alcove housing a bench. As we peered into each, jeers or curses challenged us.

"I know where they'll be," Mark said. "In the one by the bowling green. That's near where they live."

But we were closer to the shelter by the pool. Nevertheless I followed him onto the park road. As we turned towards the bowling green I glanced towards the pool, but the streetlamps dazzled me. I followed him along a narrow path between hedges to the green, and almost tripped over his ankles as he stopped short. The shelter was empty, alone with its view of the decaying Georgian houses on the far side of the bowling green.

To my surprise and annoyance, he still didn't head for the pool. Instead, we made for the disused bandstand hidden in a ring of bushes. Its only tune now was the clink of broken bricks. I was sure the girls wouldn't have called it a shelter, and of course it was deserted. Obese dim bushes hemmed us in. "Come on," I said, "or we'll miss them. They must be by the pool."

"They won't be there," he said—stupidly, I thought.

Did I realise how nervous he suddenly was? Perhaps, but it only annoyed me. After all, how else could I meet Carol again? I didn't know her address. "Oh, all right," I scoffed, "if you want us to miss them."

I saw him stiffen. Perhaps my contempt hurt him more than Ben's had;

for one thing, he was older. Before I knew what he intended he was striding towards the pool, so rapidly that I would have had to run to keep up with him—which, given the hostility that had flared between us, I refused to do. I strolled after him rather disdainfully. That was how I came to glimpse movement in one of the islands of dimness between the lamps of the park road. I glanced towards it and saw, several hundred yards away, the girls.

After a pause they responded to my waving—somewhat timidly, I thought. "There they are," I called to Mark. He must have been at the pool by now, but I had difficulty in glimpsing him beyond the glare of the lamps. I was beckoning the girls to hurry when I heard his radio blur into speech.

At first I was reminded of a sailor's parrot. "Aye aye," it was croaking. The distorted voice sounded cracked, uneven, almost too old to speak. "You know what I mean, son?" it grated triumphantly. "Aye aye." I was growing uneasy, for my mind had begun to interpret the words as "Eye eye" —when suddenly, dreadfully, I realised Mark hadn't brought his radio.

There might be someone in the shelter with a radio. But I was terrified, I wasn't sure why. I ran towards the pool calling "Come on, Mark, they're here!" The lamps dazzled me; everything swayed with my running—which was why I couldn't be sure what I saw.

I know I saw Mark at the shelter. He stood just within, confronting darkness. Before I could discern whether anyone else was there, Mark staggered out blindly, hands covering his face, and collapsed into the pool.

Did he drag something with him? Certainly by the time I reached the margin of the light he appeared to be tangled in something, and to be struggling feebly. He was drifting, or being dragged, towards the centre of the pool by a half-submerged heap of litter. At the end of the heap nearest Mark's face was a pale ragged patch in which gleamed two round objects— bottle caps? I could see all this because I was standing helpless, screaming at the girls "Quick, for Christ's sake! He's drowning!" He was drowning, and I couldn't swim.

"Don't be stupid," I heard Lorna say. That enraged me so much that I turned from the pool. "What do you mean?" I cried. "What do you mean, you stupid bitch?"

"Oh, be like that," she said haughtily, and refused to say more. But Carol took pity on my hysteria, and explained "It's only three feet deep. He'll never drown in there."

I wasn't sure that she knew what she was talking about, but that was no excuse for me not to try to rescue him. When I turned to the pool I gasped miserably, for he had vanished—sunk. I could only wade into the muddy water, which engulfed my legs and closed around my waist like ice, ponderously hindering me.

The floor of the pool was fattened with slimy litter. I slithered, terrified of losing my balance. Intuition urged me to head for the centre of the pool. And it was there I found him, as my sluggish kick collided with his ribs.

When I tried to raise him, I discovered that he was pinned down. I had to grope blindly over him in the chill water, feeling how still he was. Something like a swollen cloth bag, very large, lay over his face. I couldn't bear to touch it again, for its contents felt soft and fat. Instead I seized Mark's ankles and managed at last to drag him free. Then I struggled towards the edge of the pool, heaving him by his shoulders, lifting his head above water. His weight was dismaying. Eventually the girls waded out to help me.

But we were too late. When we dumped him on the concrete, his face stayed agape with horror; water lay stagnant in his mouth. I could see nothing wrong with his eyes. Carol grew hysterical, and it was Lorna who ran to the hospital, perhaps in order to get away from the sight of him. I only made Carol worse by demanding why they hadn't waited for us at the shelter; I wanted to feel they were to blame. But she denied they had written the message, and grew more hysterical when I asked why they hadn't waited at the island. The question, or the memory, seemed to frighten her.

I never saw her again. The few newspapers that bothered to report Mark's death gave the verdict "by misadventure." The police took a dislike to me after I insisted that there might be somebody else in the pool, for the draining revealed nobody. At least, I thought, whatever was there had gone away. Perhaps I could take some credit for that at least.

But perhaps I was too eager for reassurance. The last time I ventured near the shelter was years ago, one winter night on the way home from school. I had caught sight of a gleam in the depths of the shelter. As I went close, nervously watching both the shelter and the pool, I saw two discs glaring at me from the darkness beside the bench. They were Coca-Cola caps, not eyes at all, and it must have been the wind that set the pool slopping and sent the caps scuttling towards me. What frightened me most as I fled through the dark was that I wouldn't be able to see where I was running if, as I desperately wanted to, I put up my hands to protect my eyes.

The Show Goes On

The nails were worse than rusty; they had snapped. Under cover of several coats of paint, both the door and its frame had rotted. As Lee tugged at the door it collapsed towards him with a sound like that of an old cork leaving a bottle.

He hadn't used the storeroom since his father had nailed the door shut to keep the rats out of the shop. Both the shelves and the few items which had been left in the room—an open tin of paint, a broken-necked brush— looked merged into a single mass composed of grime and dust.

He was turning away, having vaguely noticed a dark patch that covered much of the dim wall at the back of the room, when he saw that it wasn't dampness. Beyond it he could just make out rows of regular outlines like teeth in a gaping mouth: seats in the old cinema.

He hadn't thought of the cinema for years. Old resurrected films on television, shrunken and packaged and robbed of flavour, never reminded him. It wasn't only that Cagney and Bogart and the rest had been larger than life, huge hovering faces like ancient idols; the cinema itself had had a personality—the screen framed by twin theatre boxes from the days of the music-hall, the faint smell and muttering of gaslights on the walls, the man-ager's wife and daughter serving in the auditorium and singing along with the musicals. In the years after the war you could get in for an armful of lemonade bottles, or a bag of vegetables if you owned one of the nearby al-lotments; there had been a greengrocer's old weighing machine inside the paybox. These days you had to watch films in concrete warrens, if you could afford to go at all.

Still, there was no point in reminiscing, for the old cinema was now a back entry for thieves. He was sure that was how they had robbed other shops on the block. At times he'd thought he heard them in the cinema; they sounded too large for rats. And now, by the look of the wall, they'd made themselves a secret entrance to his shop.

Mrs Entwistle was waiting at the counter. These days she shopped here less from need than from loyalty, remembering when his mother had used to bake bread at home to sell in the shop. "Just a sliced loaf," she said apologetically.

"Will you be going past Frank's yard?" Within its slippery wrapping the loaf felt ready to deflate, not like his mother's bread at all. "Could you tell him that my wall needs repairing urgently? I can't leave the shop."

Buses were carrying stragglers to work or to school. Ninety minutes later—he could tell the time by the passengers, which meant he needn't have his watch repaired—the buses were ferrying shoppers down to Liverpool city centre, and Frank still hadn't come. Grumbling to himself, Lee closed the shop for ten minutes.

The February wind came slashing up the hill from the Mersey, trailing smoke like ghosts of the factory chimneys. Down the slope a yellow machine clawed at the remains of houses. The Liver Buildings looked like a monument in a graveyard of concrete and stone.

Beyond Kiddiegear and The Wholefood Shop, Frank's yard was a maze of new timber. Frank was feeding the edge of a door to a shrieking circular blade. He gazed at Lee as though nobody had told him anything. When Lee kept his temper and explained, Frank said "No problem. Just give a moan when you're ready."

"I'm ready now."

"Ah, well. As soon as I've finished this job I'll whiz round." Lee had reached the exit when Frank said "I'll tell you something that'll amuse you. . . ."

Fifteen minutes later Lee arrived back, panting, at his shop. It was intact. He hurried around the outside of the cinema, but all the doors seemed immovable, and he couldn't find a secret entrance. Nevertheless he was sure that the thieves—children, probably—were sneaking in somehow.

The buses were full of old people now, sitting stiffly as china. The lunchtime trade trickled into the shop: men who couldn't buy their brand of cigarettes in the pub across the road, children sent on errands while their lunches went cold on tables or dried in ovens. An empty bus raced along the deserted street, and a scrawny youth in a leather jacket came into the shop, while his companion loitered in the doorway. Would Lee have a chance to defend himself, or at least to shout for help? But they weren't planning theft, only making sure they didn't miss a bus. Lee's heart felt both violent and fragile. Since the robberies had begun he'd felt that way too often.

The shop was still worth it. "Don't keep it up if you don't want to," his father had said, but it would have been admitting defeat to do anything else. Besides, he and his parents had been even closer here than at home. Since their death, he'd had to base his stock on items people wanted in a hurry or after the other shops had closed: flashlights, canned food, light-bulbs, cigarettes. Lee's Home-Baked Bread was a thing of the past, but it was still Lee's shop.

Packs of buses climbed the hill, carrying home the rush-hour crowds. When the newspaper van dumped a stack of the evening's *Liverpool Echo* on the doorstep, he knew Frank wasn't coming. He stormed round to the yard, but it was locked and deserted.

Well then, he would stay in the shop overnight; he'd nobody to go home for. Why, he had even made the thieves' job easier by helping the door to collapse. The sight of him in the lighted shop ought to deter thieves—it better had, for their sakes.

He bought two pork pies and some bottles of beer from the pub. Empty buses moved off from the stop like a series of cars on a fairground ride. He drank from his mother's Coronation mug, which always stood by the electric kettle.

He might as well have closed the shop at eight o'clock; apart from an old lady who didn't like his stock of cat food, nobody came. Eventually he locked the door and sat reading the paper, which seemed almost to be written in a new language: HEAD RAPS SHOCK AXE, said a headline about the sudden closing of a school.

Should he prop the storeroom door in place, lest he fall asleep? No, he ought to stay visible from the cinema, in the hope of scaring off the thieves. In his childhood they would hardly have dared sneak into the cinema, let alone steal—not in the last days of the cinema, when the old man had been roaming the aisles.

Everyone, perhaps even the manager, had been scared of him. Nobody Lee knew had ever seen his face. You would see him fumbling at the dim gaslights to turn them lower, then he'd begin to make sounds in the dark as though he was both muttering to himself and chewing something soft. He would creep up on talkative children and shine his flashlight into their eyes. As he hissed at them, a pale substance would spill from his mouth.

But they were scared of nothing these days, short of Lee's sitting in the shop all night, like a dummy. Already he felt irritable, frustrated. How much worse would he feel after a night of doing nothing except waste electricity on the lights and the fire?

He wasn't thinking straight. He might be able to do a great deal. He emptied the mug of beer, then he switched off the light and arranged himself on the chair as comfortably as possible. He might have to sit still for hours.

He only hoped they would venture close enough for him to see their faces. A flashlight lay ready beside him. Surely they were cowards who would run when they saw he wasn't scared of them. Perhaps he could chase them and find their secret entrance.

For a long time he heard nothing. Buses passed downhill, growing emptier and fewer. Through their growling he heard faint voices, but they were fading away from the pub, which was closing. Now the streets were deserted, except for the run-down grumble of the city. Wind shivered the window. The edge of the glow of the last few buses trailed vaguely over the storeroom entrance, making the outlines of cinema seats appear to stir. Between their sounds he strained his ears. Soon the last bus had gone.

He could just make out the outlines of the seats. If he gazed at them for long they seemed to waver, as did the storeroom doorway. Whenever he closed his eyes to rest them he heard faint tentative sounds: creaking, rattling. Perhaps the shop always sounded like that when there was nothing else to hear.

His head jerked up. No, he was sure he hadn't dozed: there had been a sound like a whisper, quickly suppressed. He hunched himself forward, ears ringing with strain. The backs of the cinema seats, vague forms like charcoal sketches on a charcoal background, appeared to nod towards him.

Was he visible by the glow of the electric fire? He switched it off stealthily, and sat listening, eyes squeezed shut. The sudden chill held him back from dozing.

Yes, there were stealthy movements in a large enclosed place. Were they creeping closer? His eyes sprang open to take them unawares, and he thought he glimpsed movement, dodging out of sight beyond the gap in the wall.

He sat absolutely still, though the cold was beginning to insinuate cramp into his right leg. He had no way of measuring the time that passed before he glimpsed movement again. Though it was so vague that he couldn't judge its speed, he had a nagging impression that someone had peered at him from the dark auditorium. He thought he heard floorboards creaking.

Were the thieves mocking him? They must think it was fun to play games with him, to watch him gazing stupidly through the wall they'd wrecked. Rage sprang him to his feet. Grabbing the flashlight, he strode through the doorway. He had to slow down in the storeroom, for he didn't want to touch the shelves fattened by grime. As soon as he reached the wall he flashed the light into the cinema.

The light just managed to reach the walls, however dimly. There was nobody in sight. On either side of the screen, which looked like a rectangle of fog, the theatre boxes were cups of darkness. It was hard to distinguish shadows from dim objects, which perhaps was why the rows of seats looked swollen.

The thieves must have retreated into one of the corridors, towards their secret entrance; he could hear distant muffled sounds. No doubt they were waiting for him to give up—but he would surprise them.

He stepped over a pile of rubble just beyond the wall. They mustn't have had time to clear it away when they had made the gap. The flashlight was heavy, reassuring; they'd better not come too near. As soon as he reached the near end of a row of seats and saw that they were folded back out of his way, he switched off the light.

Halfway down the row he touched a folding seat, which felt moist and puffy—fatter than it had looked. He didn't switch on the light, for he oughtn't to betray his presence more than was absolutely necessary. Besides, there was a faint sketchy glow from the road, through the shop. At least he would be able to find his way back easily—and he'd be damned if anyone else got there first.

When he reached the central aisle he risked another blink of light, to make sure the way was clear. Shadows sat up in all the nearest seats. A few springs had broken; seats lolled, spilling their innards. Underfoot the carpet felt like perished rubber; occasionally it squelched.

At the end of the aisle he halted, breathing inaudibly. After a while he heard movement resounding down a corridor to his left. All at once—good Lord, he'd forgotten that—he was glad the sounds weren't coming from his right, where the Gents' had been and still was, presumably. Surely even thieves would prefer to avoid the yard beyond that window, especially at night.

Blinking the light at the floor, he moved to his left. The darkness hovering overhead seemed enormous, dwarfing his furtive sounds. He had an odd impression that the screen was almost visible, as an imperceptible lightening of the dark above him. He was reminded of the last days of the cinema, in particular one night when the projectionist must have been drunk or asleep: the film had slowed and dimmed very gradually, flickering; the huge almost invisible figures had twitched and mouthed silently, unable to stop—it had seemed that the cinema was senile but refusing to die, or incapable of dying.

Another blink of light showed him the exit, a dark arch a head taller than he. A few scraps of linoleum clung to the stone floor of a low corridor. He remembered the way: a few yards ahead the corridor branched; one short branch led to a pair of exit doors, while the other turned behind the screen, towards a warren of old dressing-rooms.

When he reached the pair of doors he tested them, this time from within the building. Dim light drew a blurred sketch of their edges. The bars which ought to snap apart and release the doors felt like a single pole encrusted with harsh flakes. His rusty fingers scraped as he rubbed them together. Wind flung itself at the doors, as unable to move them as he was.

He paced back to the junction of the corridors, feeling his way with the toes of his shoes. There was a faint sound far down the other branch. Perhaps the thieves were skulking near their secret entrance, ready to flee. One blink of the light showed him that the floor was clear.

The corridor smelt dank and musty. He could tell when he strayed near the walls, for the chill intensified. The dark seemed to soak up those of his sounds that couldn't help being audible—the scrape of fallen plaster underfoot, the flap of a loose patch of linoleum which almost tripped him and which set his heart palpitating. It seemed a very long time before he reached the bend, which he coped with by feeling his way along the damp crumbling plaster of the wall. Then there was nothing but musty darkness for an even longer stretch, until something taller than he was loomed up in front of him.

It was another pair of double doors. Though they were ajar, and their bars looked rusted in the open position, he was reluctant to step through. The nervous flare of his light had shown him a shovel leaning against the wall; perhaps it had once been used to clear away fallen plaster. Thrusting the shovel between the doors, he squeezed through the gap, trying to make no noise.

He couldn't quite make himself switch off the flashlight. There seemed to be no need. In the right-hand wall were several doorways; he was sure one led to the secret entrance. If the thieves fled, he'd be able to hear which doorway they were using.

He crept along the passage. Shadows of dangling plaster moved with him. The first room was bare, and the colour of dust. It would have been built as a dressing-room, and perhaps the shapeless object, further blurred by wads of dust, which huddled in a corner had once been a costume. In the second deserted room another slumped, arms folded bonelessly. He had a hallucinatory impression that they were sleeping vagrants, stirring wakefully as his light touched them.

There was only one movement worth his attention: the stealthy restless movement he could hear somewhere ahead. Yes, it was beyond the last of the doorways, from which—he switched off the flashlight to be sure—a faint glow was emerging. That must come from the secret entrance.

He paused just ahead of the doorway. Might they be lying in wait for him? When the sound came again—a leathery sound, like the shifting of nervous feet in shoes—he could tell that it was at least as distant as the far side of the room. Creeping forward, he risked a glance within.

Though the room was dimmer than fog, he could see that it was empty: not even a dusty remnant of clothing or anything else on the floor. The meagre glow came from a window barred by a grille, beyond which he heard movement, fainter now. Were they waiting outside to open the grille as soon as he went away? Flashlight at the ready, he approached.

When he peered through the window, he thought at first there was nothing to see except a cramped empty yard: grey walls which looked furred by the dimness, grey flagstones, and—a little less dim—the sky. Another grille covered a window in an adjoining wall.

Then a memory clenched on his guts. He had recognised the yard.

Once, as a child, he had been meant to sneak into the Gents' and open the window so that his friends could get in without paying. He'd had to stand on the toilet seat in order to reach the window. Beyond a grille whose gaps were thin as matchsticks, he had just been able to make out a small dismal space enclosed by walls which looked coated with darkness or dirt. Even if he had been able to shift the grille he wouldn't have dared to do so, for something had been staring at him from a corner of the yard.

Of course it couldn't really have been staring. Perhaps it had been a half-deflated football; it looked leathery. It must have been there for a long time, for the two socketlike dents near its top were full of cobwebs. He'd fled, not caring what his friends might do to him—but in fact they hadn't been able to find their way to the yard. For years he hadn't wanted to look out of that window, especially when he'd dreamed—or had seemed to remember—that something had moved, gleaming, behind the cobwebs. When he'd been old enough to look out of the window without climbing up, the object was still there, growing dustier. Now there had been a gap low down in it, widening as years passed. It had resembled a grin stuffed with dirt.

Again he heard movement beyond the grille. He couldn't quite make out that corner of the yard, and retreated, trying to make no noise, before he could. Nearly at the corridor, he saw that a door lay open against the wall. He dragged the door shut as he emerged—to trap the thieves, that was all; if they were in the yard that might teach them a lesson. He would certainly have been uneasy if he had still been a child.

Then he halted, wondering what else he'd heard.

The scrape of the door on bare stone had almost covered up another sound from the direction of the cinema. Had the thieves outwitted him? Had they closed the double doors? When he switched on the flashlight, having fumbled and almost dropped it lens-first, he couldn't tell: perhaps the doors were ajar, but perhaps his nervousness was making the shadow between them appear wider than it was.

As he ran, careless now of whether he was heard, shadows of dead gas-lights splashed along the walls, swelling. Their pipes reminded him obscurely of breathing-tubes, clogged with dust. In the bare rooms, slumped dusty forms shifted with his passing.

The doors were still ajar, and looked untouched. When he stepped between them, the ceiling rocked with shadows; until he glanced up he felt that it was closing down. He'd done what he could in here, he ought to get back to the shop—but if he went forward, he would have to think. If the doors hadn't moved, then the sound he had almost heard must have come from somewhere else: perhaps the unlit cinema.

Before he could help it, he was remembering. The last weeks of the cinema had been best forgotten: half the audience had seemed to be there because there was nowhere else to go, old men trying to warm themselves against the grudging radiators; sometimes there would be the thud of an empty bottle or a fallen walking-stick. The tattered films had jerked from scene to scene like dreams. On the last night Lee had been there, the gaslights had gone out halfway through the film, and hadn't been lit at the end. He'd heard an old man falling and crying out as though he thought the darkness had come for him, a little girl screaming as if unable to wake from a nightmare, convinced perhaps that only the light had held the cinema in shape, prevented it from growing deformed. Then Lee had heard something else: a muttering mixed with soft chewing. It had sounded entirely at home in the dark.

But if someone was in the cinema now, it must be the thieves. He ought to hurry, before they reached his shop. He was hurrying, towards the other branch of the corridor, which led to the exit doors. Might he head off the thieves that way? He would be out of the building more quickly, that was the main thing—it didn't matter why.

The doors wouldn't budge. Though he wrenched at them until his palms smarted with rust, the bars didn't even quiver. Wind whined outside like a dog, and emphasised the stuffy mustiness of the corridor.

Suddenly he realised how much noise he was making. He desisted at once, for it would only make it more difficult for him to venture back into the cinema. Nor could he any longer avoid realising why.

Once before he'd sneaked out to this exit, to let in his friends who hadn't been able to find their way into the yard. Someone had told the usherette, who had come prowling down the central aisle, poking at people with her flashlight beam. As the light crept closer, he had been unable to move; the seat had seemed to box him in, his mouth and throat had felt choked with dust. Yet the panic he'd experienced then had been feeble compared to what he felt now—for if the cinema was still guarded against intruders, it was not by the manager's daughter.

He found he was trembling, and clawed at the wall. A large piece of plaster came away, crunching in his hand. The act of violence, mild though it was, went some way towards calming him. He wasn't a child, he was a shopkeeper who had managed to survive against the odds; he had no right to panic as the little girl had, in the dark. Was the knot that was twisting harder, harder, in his guts renewed panic, or disgust with himself? Hoping that it was the latter, he made himself hurry towards the auditorium.

When he saw what he had already noticed but managed to ignore, he faltered. A faint glow had crept into the corridor from the auditorium. Couldn't that mean that his eyes were adjusting? No, the glow was more than that. Gripping the edge of the archway so hard that his fingers twitched painfully, he peered into the cinema.

The gaslights were burning.

At least, blurred ovals hovered on the walls above their jets. Their light had always fallen short of the central aisle; now the glow left a swathe of dimness, half as wide as the auditorium which it divided. If the screen was faintly lit—if huge vague flattened forms were jerking there, rather than merely stains on the canvas—it failed to illuminate the cinema. He had no time to glance at the screen, for he could see that not all the seats were empty.

Perhaps they were only a few heaps of rubbish which were propped there—heaps which he hadn't been able to distinguish on first entering. He had begun to convince himself that this was true, and that in any case it didn't matter, when he noticed that the dimness was not altogether still. Part of it was moving.

No, it was not dimness. It was a glow, which was crawling jerkily over the rows of seats, towards the first of the objects propped up in them. Was the glow being carried along the central aisle? Thank God, he couldn't quite distinguish its source. Perhaps that source was making a faint sound, a moist somewhat rhythmic muttering that sounded worse than senile, or perhaps that was only the wind.

Lee began to creep along the front of the cinema, just beneath the screen. Surely his legs wouldn't let him down, though they felt flimsy, almost boneless. Once he reached the side aisle he would be safe and able to hurry, the gaslights would show him the way to the gap in his wall. Wouldn't they also make him more visible? That ought not to matter, for—his mind tried to flinch away from thinking—if anything was prowling in the central aisle, surely it couldn't outrun him.

He had just reached the wall when he thought he heard movement in the theatre box above him. It sounded dry as an insect, but much larger. Was it peering over the edge at him? He couldn't look up, only clatter along the bare floorboards beneath the gaslights, on which he could see no flames at all.

He still had yards to go before he reached the gap when the roving glow touched one of the heaps in the seats.

If he could have turned and run blindly, nothing would have stopped him; but a sickness that was panic weighed down his guts, and he couldn't move until he saw. Perhaps there wasn't much to see except an old coat full of lumps of dust or rubble, which was lolling in the seat; nothing to make the flashlight shudder in his hand and rap against the wall. But sunken in the gap between the lapels of the coat was what might have been an old Hallowe'en mask overgrown with dust. Surely it was dust that moved in the empty eyes—yet as the flashlight rapped more loudly against the wall, the mask turned slowly and unsteadily towards him.

Panic blinded him. He didn't know who he was nor where he was going. He knew only that he was very small and at bay in the vast dimness, through which a shape was directing a glow towards him. Behind the glow he could almost see a face from which something pale dangled. It wasn't a beard, for it was rooted in the gaping mouth.

He was thumping the wall with the flashlight as though to remind himself that one or the other was there. Yes, there was a wall, and he was backing along it: backing where? Towards the shop, his shop now, where he wouldn't need to use the flashlight, mustn't use the flashlight to illuminate whatever was pursuing him, mustn't see, for then he would never be able to move. Not far to go now, he wouldn't have to bear the dark much longer, must be nearly at the gap in the wall, for a glow was streaming from behind him. He was there now, all he had to do was turn his back on the cinema, turn quickly, just turn—

He had managed to turn halfway, trying to be blind without closing his eyes, when his free hand touched the object which was lolling in the nearest seat. Both the overcoat and its contents felt lumpy, patched with damp and dust. Nevertheless the arm stirred; the object at the end of it, which felt like a bundle of sticks wrapped in torn leather, tried to close on his hand.

Choking, he pulled himself free. Some of the sticks came loose and plumped on the rotten carpet. The flashlight fell beside them, and he heard glass breaking. It didn't matter, he was at the gap, he could hear movement in the shop, cars and buses beyond. He had no time to wonder who was in there before he turned.

The first thing he saw was that the light wasn't that of streetlamps; it was daylight. At once he saw why he had made the mistake: the gap was no longer there. Except for a single brick, the wall had been repaired.

He was yelling desperately at the man beyond the wall, and thumping the new bricks with his fists—he had begun to wonder why his voice was so faint and his blows so feeble—when the man's face appeared beyond the brick-sized gap. Lee staggered back as though he was fainting. Except that he had to stare up at the man's face, he might have been looking in a mirror.

He hadn't time to think. Crying out, he stumbled forward and tried to wrench the new bricks loose. Perhaps his adult self beyond the wall was aware of him in some way, for his face peered through the gap, looking triumphantly contemptuous of whoever was in the dark. Then the brick fitted snugly into place, cutting off the light.

Almost worse was the fact that it wasn't quite dark. As he began to claw at the bricks and mortar, he could see them far too clearly. Soon he might see what was holding the light, and that would be worst of all.

The Ferries

When Berry reached Parkgate promenade he heard the waves. He couldn't recall having heard them during his stroll down the winding road from Neston village, between banks whispering with grass, past the netted lights of windows. Beneath clouds diluted by moonlight, the movement of the waves looked indefinably strange. They sounded faint, not quite like water.

The promenade was scarcely two cars wide. Thin lanterns stood on concrete stalks above the sea wall, which was overlooked by an assortment of early Victorian buildings: antique shops, cafés that in the afternoons must be full of ladies taking tea and cakes, a nursing home, a private school that looked as though it had been built for something else. In the faltering moonlight all of them looked black and white. Some were Tudor-striped.

As he strolled—the June night was mild, he might as well enjoy himself as best he could now he was here—he passed the Marie Celeste Hotel. That must have appealed to his uncle. He was still grinning wryly when he reached his uncle's address.

Just then the moon emerged from the clouds, and he saw what was wrong with the waves. There was no water beyond the sea wall, only an expanse of swaying grass that stretched as far as he could see. The sight of the grass, overlooked by the promenade buildings as though it was still the River Dee, made him feel vaguely but intensely expectant, as though about to glimpse something on the pale parched waves.

Perhaps his uncle felt this too, for he was sitting at the black bow window on the first floor of the white house, gazing out beyond the sea wall. His eyes looked colourless as moonlight. It took three rings of the bell to move him.

Berry shouldn't feel resentful. After all, he was probably his uncle's only living relative. Nevertheless there were decisions to be made in London, at the publishers: books to be bought or rejected—several were likely to be auctioned. He'd come a long way hurriedly, by several trains; his uncle's call had sounded urgent enough for that, as urgent as the pips that had cut him off. Berry only wished he knew why he was here.

When at last his uncle opened the door, he looked unexpectedly old. Perhaps living ashore had aged him. He had always been small, but now he looked dwindled, though still tanned and leathery. In his spotless black blazer with its shining silvery buttons, and his tiny gleaming shoes, he resembled a doll of himself.

"Here we are again." Though he sounded gruff, his handshake was firm, and felt grateful for company. When he'd toiled upstairs, using the banisters as a series of walking-sticks, he growled "Sit you down."

There was no sense of the sea in the flat, not even maritime prints to enliven the timidly patterned wallpaper. Apart from a couple of large old trunks, the flat seemed to have nothing to do with his uncle. It felt like a waiting-room.

"Get that down you, James." His uncle's heartiness seemed faded; even the rum was a brand you could buy in the supermarkets, not one of the prizes he'd used to bring back from voyages. He sat gazing beyond the promenade, sipping the rum as though it was as good as any other.

"How are you, Uncle? It's good to see you." They hadn't seen each other for ten years, and Berry felt inhibited; besides, his uncle detested effusiveness. When he'd finished his rum he said "You sounded urgent on the phone."

"Aye." The years had made him even more taciturn. He seemed to resent being reminded of his call.

"I wouldn't have expected you to live so far from everything," Berry said, trying a different approach.

"It went away." Apparently he was talking about the sea, for he continued "There used to be thirteen hotels and a pier. All the best people came here to bathe. They said the streets were as elegant as Bath. The private school you passed, that was the old Assembly Rooms."

Though he was gazing across the sea wall, he didn't sound nostalgic. He sat absolutely still, as though relishing the stability of the room. He'd used to pace restlessly when talking, impatient to return to the sea.

"Then the Dee silted up," he was saying. "It doesn't reach here now, except at spring tides and in storms. That's when the rats and voles flee onto the promenade—hordes of them, they say. I haven't seen it, and I don't mean to."

"You're thinking of moving?"

"Aye." Frowning at his clenched fists, he muttered "Will you take me back with you tomorrow and let me stay until I find somewhere? I'll have my boxes sent on."

He mustn't want to make the journey alone in case he was taken ill. Still,

Berry couldn't help sounding a little impatient. "I don't live near the sea, you know."

"I know that." Reluctantly he added "I wish I lived further away."

Perhaps now that he'd had to leave the sea, his first love, he wanted to forget about it quickly. Berry could tell he'd been embarrassed to ask for help— a captain needing help from a nephew who was seasick on hovercraft! But he was a little old man now, and his tan was only a patina; all at once Berry saw how frail he was. "All right, Uncle," he said gently. "It won't be any trouble."

His uncle was nodding, not looking at him, but Berry could see he was moved. Perhaps now was the time to broach the idea Berry had had on the train. "On my way here," he said carefully, "I was remembering some of the tales you used to tell."

"You remember them, do you?" The old man didn't sound as though he wanted to. He drained a mouthful of rum in order to refill his glass. Had the salt smell that was wafting across the grass reminded him too vividly?

Berry had meant to suggest the idea of a book of his uncle's yarns, for quite a few had haunted him: the pigmies who could carry ten times their own weight, the flocks of birds that buried in guano any ships that ventured into their territory, the light whose source was neither sun nor moon but that outlined an island on the horizon, which receded if ships made for it. Would it be a children's book, or a book that tried to trace the sources? Perhaps this wasn't the time to discuss it, for the smell that was drifting through the window was stagnant, very old.

"There was one story I never told you."

Berry's head jerked up; he had been nodding off. Even his uncle had never begun stories as abruptly—as reluctantly—as this.

"Some of the men used to say it didn't matter if you saw it so long as you protected yourself." Was the old man talking to himself, to take his mind off the desiccated river, the stagnant smell? "One night we all saw it. One minute the sea was empty, the next that thing was there, close enough to swim to. Some of the men would almost have done that, to get it over with." He gulped a mouthful of rum and stared sharply out across the pale dry waves. "Only they could see the faces watching. None of us forgot that, ever. As soon as we got ashore all of us bought ourselves protection. Even I did," he said bitterly, "when I'd used to say civilised men kept pictures on walls."

Having struggled out of his blazer, which he'd unbuttoned carefully and tediously, he displayed his left forearm. Blinking sleepily, Berry made out a tattoo, a graceful sailing ship surrounded by a burst of light. Its masts resembled almost recognisable symbols.

"The younger fellows thought that was all we needed. We all wanted to believe that would keep us safe. I wonder how they feel now they're older." The old man turned quickly towards the window; he seemed angry that he'd been distracted. Something had changed his attitude drastically, for he had hated tattoos. It occurred to Berry, too late to prevent him from dozing, that his uncle had called him because he was afraid to be alone.

Berry's sleep was dark and profound. Half-submerged images floated by, so changed as to be unrecognisable. Sounds reached him rather as noise from the surface might try to reach the depths of the sea. It was impossible to tell how many times his uncle had cried out before the calls woke him.

"James . . ." The voice was receding, but at first Berry failed to notice this; he was too aware of the smell that filled the room. Something that smelled drowned in stagnant water was near him, so near that he could hear its creaking. At once he was awake, and so afraid that he thought he was about to be sick.

"James . . ." Both the creaking and the voice were fading. Eventually he managed to persuade himself that despite the stench, he was alone in the room. Forcing his eyes open, he stumbled to the window. Though it was hard to focus his eyes and see what was out there, his heart was already jolting.

The promenade was deserted; the buildings gleamed like bone. Above the sea wall the lanterns glowed thinly. The wide dry river was flooded with grass, which swayed in the moonlight, rustling and glinting. Over the silted river, leaving a wake of grass that looked whiter than the rest, a ship was receding.

It seemed to be the colour and the texture of the moon. Its sails looked stained patchily by mould. It was full of holes, all of which were misshapen by glistening vegetation. Were its decks crowded with figures? If so, he was grateful that he couldn't see their faces, for their movements made him think of drowned things lolling underwater, dragged back and forth by currents.

Sweat streamed into his eyes. When he'd blinked them clear, the moon was darkening. Now the ship looked more like a mound from which a few trees sprouted, and perhaps the crowd was only swaying bushes. Clouds closed over the moon, but he thought he could see a pale mass sailing away, over-topped by lurid sketches that might be masts. Was that his uncle's voice, its desperation overwhelmed by despair? When moonlight flooded the land-scape a few moments later, there was nothing but the waves of grass, from which a whiter swathe was fading.

He came to himself when he began shivering. An unseasonably chill wind was clearing away the stench of stagnant water. He gazed in dismay at his uncle's blazer, draped neatly over the empty chair.

There wasn't much that he could tell the police. He had been visiting his uncle, whom he hadn't seen for years. They had both had a good deal to drink, and his uncle, who had seemed prematurely aged, had begun talking incoherently and incomprehensibly. He'd woken to find that his uncle had wandered away, leaving his blazer, though it had been a cold night.

Did they believe him? They were slow and thorough, these policemen; their thoughts were as invisible as he meant his to be. Surely his guilt must be apparent, the shame of hiding the truth about his uncle, of virtually blackening his character. In one sense, though, that seemed hardly to matter: he was sure they wouldn't find his uncle alive. Eventually, since Berry could prove that he was needed in London, they let him go.

He trudged along the sweltering promenade. Children were scrambling up and down the sea wall, old people on sticks were being promenaded by relatives. In the hazy sunshine, most of the buildings were still black and white. Everywhere signs said FRESH SHRIMPS. In a shop that offered "Gifts and Bygones," ships were stiff in bottles. Waves of yellowing grass advanced, but never very far.

He ought to leave, and be grateful that he lived inland. If what he'd seen last night had been real, the threat was far larger than he was. There was nothing he could do.

But suppose he had only heard his uncle's voice on the silted river, and had hallucinated the rest? He'd been overtired, and confused by his uncle's ramblings; how soon had he wakened fully? He wanted to believe that the old man had wandered out beyond the promenade and had collapsed, or even that he was alive out there, still wandering.

There was only one way to find out. He would be in sight of the crowded promenade. Holding his briefcase above his head as though he was submerging, he clambered down the sea wall.

The grass was tougher than it looked. Large patches had to be struggled through. After five hundred yards he was sweating, yet he seemed to be no closer to the far bank, nor to anything else. Ahead through the haze he could just distinguish the colours of fields in their frames of trees and hedges. Factory chimneys resembled grey pencils. All this appeared to be receding.

He struggled onward. Grass snagged him, birds flew up on shrill wings, complaining. He could see no evidence of the wake he'd seen last night; nothing but the interminable grass, the screeching birds, the haze. Behind him the thick heat had blurred the promenade, the crowds were pale shadows. Their sounds had been swallowed by the hissing of grass.

He'd been tempted several times to turn back, and was on the point of doing so, when he saw a gleam in the dense grass ahead. It was near the place where he'd last glimpsed the ship, if he had done so. The gleaming object looked like a small shoe.

He had to persuade himself to go forward. He remembered the swaying figures on the decks, whose faces he'd dreaded to see. Nevertheless he advanced furiously, tearing a path through the grass with his briefcase. He was almost there before he saw that the object wasn't a shoe. It was a bottle.

When inertia carried him forward, he realised that the bottle wasn't empty. For an unpleasant moment he thought it contained the skeleton of a small animal. Peering through the grime that coated the glass, he made out a whitish model ship with tattered sails. Tiny overgrown holes gaped in it. Though its decks were empty, he had seen it before.

He stood up too quickly, and almost fell. The heat seemed to flood his skull. The ground underfoot felt unstable; a buzzing of insects attacked him; there was a hint of a stagnant smell. He was ready to run, dizzy as he was, to prevent himself from thinking.

Then he remembered his uncle's despairing cry: "James, James . . ." Even then, if he had been able to run, he might have done nothing—but his dizziness both hindered him and gave him time to feel ashamed. If there was a chance of helping his uncle, however impossible it seemed—He snatched up the bottle and threw it into his briefcase. Then, trying to forget about it, he stumbled back towards the crowds.

His uncle was calling him. He woke to the sound of a shriek. Faces were sailing past him, close enough to touch if he could have reached through the glass. It was only a train on the opposite line, rushing away from London. Nevertheless he couldn't sleep after that. He finished reading the typescript he'd brought with him, though he knew by now he didn't want to buy the book.

The state of his desk was worse than he'd feared. His secretary had answered most of his letters, but several books had piled up, demanding to be read. He was stuffing two of them into his briefcase, to be read on the bus and, if he wasn't too tired, at home, when he found he was holding the grimy bottle. At once he locked it in a drawer. Though he wasn't prepared to throw it away until he understood its purpose, he was equally reluctant to take it home.

That night he could neither sleep nor read. He tried strolling in Holland Park, but while that tired him further, it failed to calm him. The moonlit clouds that were streaming headlong across the sky made everything beneath them look unstable. Though he knew that the lit houses beyond the swaying trees were absolutely still, he kept feeling that the houses were rocking slyly, at anchor.

He lay trying to relax. Beyond the windows of his flat, Kensington High Street seemed louder than ever. Nervous speculation kept him awake. He felt he'd been meant to find the bottle, but for what purpose? Surely it couldn't harm him; after all, he had only once been to sea. How could he help his uncle? His idea of a book of stories was nagging him; perhaps he could write it himself, as a kind of monument to his uncle—except that the stories seemed to be drifting away into the dark, beyond his reach, just like the old man. When eventually he dozed, he thought he heard the old man calling.

In the morning his desk looked even worse; the pile of books had almost doubled. He managed to sort out a few that could be trusted to readers for reports. Of course, a drain must have overflowed outside the publishers; that was why only a patch of pavement had been wet this morning—he knew it hadn't rained. He consulted his diary for distractions.

Sales conference 11 A.M.: he succeeded in being coherent, and even in suggesting ideas, but his thoughts were elsewhere. The sky resembled sluggish smoke, as though the oppressive day was smouldering. His mind felt packed in grey stuffing. The sound of cars outside seemed unnaturally rhythmic, almost like waves.

Back at his desk he sat trying to think. Lack of sleep had isolated him in a no-man's-land of consciousness, close to hallucination. He felt cut off from whatever he was supposed to be doing. Though his hand kept reaching out impulsively, he left the drawer locked. There was no point in brooding over the model ship until he'd decided what to do.

Beyond the window his uncle cried out. No, someone was shouting to guide a lorry; the word wasn't "James" at all. But he still didn't know how to help his uncle, assuming that he could, assuming that it wasn't too late. Would removing the ship from the bottle achieve something? In any case, could one remove the ship at all? Perhaps he could consult an expert in such matters. "I know exactly whom you want," his secretary said, and arranged for them to meet tomorrow.

Dave Peeples lunch 12:30: ordinarily he would have enjoyed the game, especially since Peeples liked to discuss books in pubs, where he tended to drink himself into an agreeable state. Today's prize was attractive: a best-selling series that Peeples wanted to take to a new publisher. But today he found Peeples irritating—not only his satyr's expressions and postures, which were belied by his paunch, but also the faint smirk with which he constantly approved of himself. Still, if Berry managed to acquire the books, the strain would have been worthwhile.

They ate in the pub just around the corner from the publishers. Before long Berry grew frustrated; he was too enervated by lack of sleep to risk drinking much. Nor could he eat much, for the food tasted unpleasantly salty. Peeples seemed to notice nothing, and ate most of Berry's helping before he leaned back, patting his paunch.

"Well now," he said when Berry raised the subject of the books. "What about another drink?" Berry was glad to stand up, to feel the floor stable underfoot, for the drinkers at the edge of his vision had seemed to be swaying extravagantly.

"I'm not happy with the way my mob are promoting the books," Peeples admitted. "They seem to be letting them just lie there." Berry's response might have been more forceful if he hadn't been distracted by the chair that someone was rocking back and forth with a steady rhythmic creaking.

When Berry had finished making offers Peeples said "That doesn't sound bad. Still, I ought to tell you that several other people are interested." Berry wondered angrily whether he was simply touring publishers in search of free meals. The pub felt damp, the dimness appeared to be glistening. No doubt it was very humid.

Though the street was crowded, he was glad to emerge. "I'll be in touch," Peeples promised grudgingly, but at that moment Berry didn't care, for on the opposite pavement the old man's voice was crying "James!" It was only a newspaper-seller naming his wares, which didn't sound much like James. Surely a drain must have overflowed where the wet patch had been, for there was a stagnant smell.

Editors meeting 3 P.M.: he scarcely had time to gulp a mug of coffee beforehand, almost scalding his throat. Why did they have to schedule two meetings in one day? When there were silences in which people expected him to speak, he managed to say things that sounded positive and convincing. Nevertheless he heard little except for the waves of traffic, advancing and withdrawing, and the desperate cries in the street. What was that crossing the intersection, a long pale shape bearing objects like poles? It had gone before he could jerk his head round, and his colleagues were staring only at him.

It didn't matter. If any of these glimpses weren't hallucinations, surely they couldn't harm him. Otherwise, why hadn't he been harmed that night in Parkgate? It was rather a question of what he could do to the glimpses. "Yes, that's right," he said to a silence. "Of course it is."

Once he'd slept he would be better able to cope with everything. Tomorrow he would consult the expert. After the meeting he slumped at the desk, trying to find the energy to gather books together and head for home.

His secretary woke him. "Okay," he mumbled, "you go on." He'd follow her in a moment, when he was more awake. It occurred to him that if he hadn't dozed off in Parkgate, his uncle might have been safe. That was another reason to try to do something. He'd get up in a few moments. It wasn't dark yet.

When he woke again, it was.

He had to struggle to raise his head. His elbows had shoved piles of books to the edge of the desk. Outside, the street was quiet except for the whisper of an occasional car. Sodium lamps craned their necks towards his window. Beyond the frosted glass of his office cubicle, the maze of the open-plan office looked even more crowded with darkness than the space around his desk. When he switched on his desk-lamp, it showed him a blurred reflection of himself trapped in a small pool of brightness. Hurriedly he switched on the cubicle's main light.

Though he was by no means awake, he didn't intend to wait. He wanted to be out of the building, away from the locked drawer. Insomnia had left him feeling vulnerable, on edge. He swept a handful of books into the briefcase—God, they were becoming a bad joke—and emerged from his cubicle.

He felt uncomfortably isolated. The long angular room was lifeless; none of the desks seemed to retain any sense of the person who sat there. The desertion must be swallowing his sounds, which seemed not only dwarfed but robbed of resonance, as though surrounded by an emptiness that was very large.

His perceptions must be playing tricks. Underfoot the floor felt less stable than it ought to. At the edge of his vision the shadows of desks and cabinets appeared to be swaying, and he couldn't convince himself that the lights were still. He mustn't let any of this distract him. Time enough to think when he was home.

It took him far too long to cross the office, for he kept teetering against desks. Perhaps he should have taken time to waken fully, after all. When eventually he reached the lifts, he couldn't bring himself to use one; at least the stairs were open, though they were very dark. He groped, swaying, for the light-switch. Before he'd found it, he recoiled. The wall he had touched felt as though it were streaming with water.

A stagnant stench welled up out of the dark. When he grabbed the banister for support, that felt wet too. He mustn't panic: a door or window was open somewhere in the building, that was all he could hear creaking; its draught was making things feel cold—not wet—and was swinging the lights back and forth. Yes, he could feel the draught blustering at him, and smell what must be a drain.

He forced himself to step onto the stairs. Even the darkness was preferable to groping for the light-switch, when he no longer knew what he might touch. Nevertheless, by the time he reached the half-landing he was wishing for light. His vertigo seemed to have worsened, for he was reeling from side to side of the staircase. Was the creaking closer? He mustn't pause, plenty of time to feel ill once he was outside in a taxi; he ought to be able to hold off panic so long as he didn't glimpse the ship again—

He halted so abruptly that he almost fell. Without warning he'd remembered his uncle's monologue. Berry had been as dopey then as he was now, but one point was all at once terribly clear. Your first glimpse of the ship meant only that you would see it again. The second time, it came for you.

He hadn't seen it again. Surely he still had a chance. There were two exits from the building; the creaking and the growing stench would tell him which exit to avoid. He was stumbling downstairs because that was the alternative to falling. His mind was a grey void that hardly even registered the wetness of the banisters. The foyer was in sight now at the foot of the stairs, its linoleum gleaming; less than a flight of stairs now, less than a minute's stumbling—

But it was no linoleum. The floorboards were bare, when there ought not even to be boards, only concrete. Shadows swayed on them, cast by objects that, though out of sight for the moment, seemed to have bloated limbs. Water sloshed from side to side of the boards, which were the planks of a deck.

He almost let himself fall, in despair. Then he began to drag himself frantically up the stairs, which perhaps were swaying, after all. Through the windows he thought he saw the cityscape rising and falling. There seemed to be no refuge upstairs, for the stagnant stench was everywhere—but refuge was not what he was seeking.

He reeled across the office, which he'd darkened when leaving, into his cubicle. Perhaps papers were falling from desks only because he had staggered against them. His key felt ready to snap in half before the drawer opened.

He snatched out the bottle, in which something rattled insectlike, and stumbled to the window. Yes, he had been meant to find the bottle—but by whom, or by what? Wrenching open the lock of the window, he flung the bottle into the night.

He heard it smash a moment later. Whatever was inside it must certainly have smashed too. At once everything felt stable, so abruptly that he grew dizzier. He felt as though he'd just stepped onto land after a stormy voyage.

There was silence except for the murmur of the city, which sounded quite normal—or perhaps there was another sound, faint and receding fast. It might have been a gust of wind, but he thought it resembled a chorus of cries of relief so profound it was appalling. Was one of them his uncle's voice?

Berry slumped against the window, which felt like ice against his forehead. There was no reason to flee now, nor did he think he would be capable of moving for some time. Perhaps they would find him here in the morning. It hardly mattered, if he could get some sleep.

All at once he tried to hold himself absolutely still, in order to listen. Surely he needn't be nervous any longer, just because the ship in the bottle had been deserted, surely that didn't mean—But his legs were trembling, and infected the rest of his body until he couldn't even strain his ears. By then, however, he could hear far better than he would have liked.

Perhaps he had destroyed the ship, and set free its captives; but if it had had a captain, what else might Berry have set loose? The smell had grown worse than stagnant—and up the stairs, and now across the dark office, irregular but purposeful footsteps were sloshing.

Early next morning several people reported glimpses of a light, supposedly moving out from the Thames into the open sea. Some claimed the light had been accompanied by sounds like singing. One old man tried to insist that the light had contained the outline of a ship. The reports seemed little different from tales of objects in the skies, and were quickly dismissed, for London had a more spectacular mystery to solve: how a publisher's editor could be found in a first-floor office, not merely dead but drowned.

Midnight Hobo

As he reached home, Roy saw the old man who lived down the road chasing children from under the railway bridge. "Go on, out with you," he was crying as though they were cats in his flower-beds. He was brandishing his string-bags, which were always full of books.

Perhaps the children had been climbing up beneath the arch; that was where he kept glancing. Roy wasn't interested, for his co-presenter on the radio show was getting on his nerves. At least Don Derrick was only temporary, until the regular man came out of hospital. As a train ticked away its carriages over the bridge, Roy stormed into his house in search of a soothing drink.

The following night he remembered to glance under the arch. It did not seem likely that anyone could climb up there, nor that anyone would want to. Even in daylight you couldn't tell how much of the mass that clogged the corners was soot. Now the arch was a hovering block of darkness, relieved only by faint greyish sketches of girders. Roy heard the birds fluttering.

Today Derrick had been almost tolerable, but he made up for that the next day. Halfway through "Our Town Tonight" Roy had to interview the female lead from *The Man on Top,* a limp British sex comedy about a young man trying to seduce his way to fame. Most of the film's scrawny budget must have been spent on hiring a few guest comedians. Heaven only knew how the producers had been able to afford to send the girl touring to promote the film.

Though as an actress she was embarrassingly inexperienced, as an interviewee she was far worse. She sat like a girl even younger than she was, over-awed by staying up so late. A man from the film distributors watched over her like a nanny.

Whatever Roy asked her, her answers were never more than five words long. Over by the studio turntables, Derrick was fiddling impatiently with the control panel, making everyone nervous. In future Roy wouldn't let him near the controls.

Ah, here was a question that ought to inspire her. "How did you find the experience of working with so many veterans of comedy?"

"Oh, it really helped." He smiled desperate encouragement. "It really really did," she said miserably, her eyes pleading with him.

"What do you remember best about working with them?" When she looked close to panic he could only say "Are there any stories you can tell?"

"Oh—" At last she seemed nervously ready to speak, when Derrick interrupted "Well, I'm sure you've lots more interesting things to tell us. We'll come back to them in a few minutes, but first here's some music."

When the record was over he broke into the interview. "What sort of music do you like? What are your favourite things?" He might have been chatting to a girl in one of the discotheques where he worked. There wasn't much that Roy could do to prevent him, since the programme was being broadcast live: half-dead, more like.

Afterwards he cornered Derrick, who was laden with old 78s, a plastic layer cake of adolescent memories. "I told you at the outset that was going to be my interview. We don't cut into each other's interviews unless invited."

"Well, I didn't know." Derrick's doughy face was growing pinkly mottled, burning from within. If you poked him, would the mark remain, as though in putty? He must look his best in the dim light of discos. "You know now," Roy said.

"I thought you needed some help," Derrick said with a kind of timid defiance; he looked ready to flinch. "You didn't seem to be doing very well."

"I wasn't, once you interfered. Next time, please remember who's running the show."

Half an hour later Roy was still fuming. As he strode beneath the bridge he felt on edge; his echoes seemed unpleasantly shrill, the fluttering among the girders sounded more like restless scuttling. Perhaps he could open a bottle of wine with dinner.

He had nearly finished dinner when he wondered when the brood would hatch. Last week he'd seen the male bird carrying food to his mate in the hidden nest. When he'd washed up, he strolled under the bridge but could see only the girders gathering darkness. The old man with the string-bags was standing between his regimented flower-beds, watching Roy or the bridge. Emerging, Roy glanced back. In the May twilight the archway resembled a block of mud set into the sullen bricks.

Was there something he ought to have noticed? Next morning, on waking, he thought so—but he didn't have much time to think that day, for Derrick was sulking. He hardly spoke to Roy except when they were on the air, and even then his face belied his synthetic cheerfulness. They were like an estranged couple who were putting on a show for visitors.

Roy had done nothing to apologise for. If Derrick let his animosity show while he was broadcasting, it would be Derrick who'd have to explain. That made Roy feel almost at ease, which was why he noticed belatedly that he hadn't heard the birds singing under the bridge for days.

Nor had he seen them for almost a week; all he had heard was fluttering, as though they were unable to call. Perhaps a cat had caught them, perhaps that was what the fluttering had been. If anything was moving up there now, it sounded larger than a bird—but perhaps that was only his echoes, which seemed very distorted.

He had a casserole waiting in the oven. After dinner he browsed among the wavelengths of his stereo radio, and found a Mozart quartet on an East European frequency. As the calm deft phrases intertwined, he watched twilight smoothing the pebble-dashed houses, the tidy windows and flower-beds. A train crossed the bridge, providing a few bars of percussion, and prompted him to imagine how far the music was travelling.

In a pause between movements he heard the cat.

At first even when he turned the radio down, he couldn't make out what was wrong. The cat was hissing and snarling, but what had happened to its voice? Of course—it was distorted by echoes. No doubt it was among the girders beneath the bridge. He was about to turn up the music when the cat screamed.

He ran to the window, appalled. He'd heard cats fighting, but never a sound like that. Above the bridge two houses distant, a chain-gang of tele-graph poles looked embedded in the glassy sky. He could see nothing under-neath except a rhomb of dimness, rounded at the top. Reluctantly he ventured onto the deserted street.

It was not quite deserted. A dozen houses further from the bridge, the old man was glaring dismayed at the arch. As soon as Roy glanced at him, he dodged back into his house.

Roy couldn't see anything framed by the arch. Grass and weeds, which looked pale as growths found under stones, glimmered in the spaces be-tween bricks. Some of the bricks resembled moist fossilised sponges, ce-mented by glistening mud. Up among the girders, an irregular pale shape must be a larger patch of weeds. As he peered at it, it grew less clear, seemed to withdraw into the dark—but at least he couldn't see the cat.

He was walking slowly, peering up in an attempt to reassure himself, when he trod on the object. Though it felt soft, it snapped audibly. The walls, which were padded with dimness, seemed to swallow its echo. It took him a while to glance down.

At first he was reminded of one of the strings of dust that appeared in the spare room when, too often, he couldn't be bothered to clean. But when he stooped reluctantly, he saw fur and claws. It looked as it had felt: like a cat's foreleg.

He couldn't look up as he fled. Echoes sissified his footsteps. Was a large pale shape following him beneath the girders? Could he hear its scuttling, or was that himself? He didn't dare speculate until he'd slammed his door behind him.

Half an hour later a gang of girls wandered, yelling and shrieking, through the bridge. Wouldn't they have noticed the leg, or was there insufficient light? He slept badly and woke early, but could find no trace in the road under the bridge. Perhaps the evidence had been dragged away by a car. The unlucky cat might have been run over on the railway line—but in that case, why hadn't he heard a train? He couldn't make out any patch of vegetation among the girders, where it was impenetrably dark; there appeared to be nothing pale up there at all.

All things considered, he was glad to go to work, at least to begin with. Derrick stayed out of his way, except to mention that he'd invited a rock group to talk on tonight's show. "All right," Roy said, though he'd never heard of the group. "Ian's the producer. Arrange it with him."

"I've already done that," Derrick said smugly.

Perhaps his taste of power would make him less intolerable. Roy had no time to argue, for he had to interview an antipornography campaigner. Her glasses slithered down her nose, her face grew redder and redder, but her pharisaic expression never wavered. Not for the first time, he wished he were working for television.

That night he wished it even more, when Derrick led into the studio four figures who walked like a march of the condemned and who looked like inexpert caricatures of bands of the past five years. Roy had started a record and was sitting forward to chat with them, when Derrick said "I want to ask the questions. This is *my* interview."

Roy would have found this too pathetic even to notice, except that Derrick's guests were grinning to themselves; they were clearly in on the secret. When Roy had suffered Derrick's questions and their grudging answers for ten minutes—"Which singers do you like? Have you written any songs? Are you going to?"—he cut them off and wished the band success, which they certainly still needed.

When they'd gone, and a record was playing, Derrick turned on him. "I hadn't finished," he said petulantly. "I was still talking."

"You've every right to do so, but not on my programme."

"It's my programme too. You weren't the one who invited me. I'm going to tell Hugh Ward about you."

Roy hoped he would. The station manager would certainly have been listening to the banal interview. Roy was still cursing Derrick as he reached the bridge, where he baulked momentarily. No, he'd had enough stupidity for one day; he wasn't about to let the bridge bother him.

Yet it did. The weeds looked even paler, and drained; if he touched them—which he had no intention of doing—they might snap. The walls glistened with a liquid that looked slower and thicker than water: mixed with grime, presumably. Overhead, among the encrusted girders, something large was following him.

He was sure of that now. Though it stopped when he did, it wasn't his echoes. When he fled beyond the mouth of the bridge, it scuttled to the edge of the dark arch. As he stood still he heard it again, roaming back and forth restlessly, high in the dark. It was too large for a bird or a cat. For a moment he was sure that it was about to scuttle down the drooling wall at him.

Despite the heat, he locked all the windows. He'd grown used to the sounds of trains, so much so that they often helped him sleep, yet now he wished he lived further away. Though the nights were growing lighter, the arch looked oppressively ominous, a lair. That night every train on the bridge jarred him awake.

In the morning he was in no mood to tolerate Derrick. He'd get the better of him one way or the other—to start with, by speaking to Ward. But Derrick had already seen the station manager, and now Ward wasn't especially sympathetic to Roy; perhaps he felt that his judgement in hiring Derrick was being questioned. "He says his interview went badly because you inhibited him," he said, and when Roy protested "In any case, surely you can put up with him for a couple of weeks. After all, learning to get on with people is part of the job. We must be flexible."

Derrick was that all right, Roy thought furiously: flexible as putty, and as lacking in personality. During the whole of "Our Town Tonight" he and Derrick glared at or ignored each other. When they spoke on the air, it wasn't to each other. Derrick, Roy kept thinking: a tower over a bore—and the name contained "dreck," which seemed entirely appropriate. Most of all he resented being reduced to petulance himself. Thank God it was nearly the weekend— except that meant he would have to go home.

When he left the bus he walked home the long way, avoiding the bridge. From his gate he glanced at the arch, whose walls were already mossed with dimness, then looked quickly away. If he ignored it, put it out of his mind completely, perhaps nothing would happen. What could happen, for heaven's sake? Later, when an unlit train clanked over the bridge like the dragging of a giant chain in the dark, he realised why the trains had kept him awake: what might their vibrations disturb under the bridge?

Though the night made him uneasy, Saturday was worse. Children kept running through the bridge, screaming to wake the echoes. He watched anxiously until they emerged; the sunlight on the far side of the arch seemed a refuge.

He was growing obsessive, checking and rechecking the locks on all the windows, especially those nearest the bridge. That night he visited friends, and drank too much, and talked about everything that came into his head, except the bridge. It was waiting for him, mouth open, when he staggered home. Perhaps the racket of his clumsy footsteps had reached the arch, and was echoing faintly.

On Sunday his mouth was parched and rusty, his skull felt like a lump of lead that was being hammered out of shape. He could only sit at the bedroom window and be grateful that the sunlight was dull. Children were shrieking under the bridge. If anything happened there, he had no idea what he would do.

Eventually the street was quiet. The phrases of church bells drifted, interweaving, on the wind. Here came the old man, apparently taking his stringbags to church. No: he halted at the bridge and peered up for a while; then, looking dissatisfied but unwilling to linger, he turned away.

Roy had to know. He ran downstairs, though his brain felt as though it were slopping from side to side. "Excuse me—" (damn, he didn't know the old man's name) "er, could I ask what you were looking for?"

"You've been watching me, have you?"

"I've been watching the bridge. I mean, I think something's up there too. I just don't know what it is."

The old man frowned at him, perhaps deciding whether to trust him. Eventually he said "When you hear trains at night, do you ever wonder where they've been? They stop in all sorts of places miles from anywhere in the middle of the night. Suppose something decided to take a ride? Maybe it would get off again if it found somewhere like the place it came from. Sometimes trains stop on the bridge."

"But what is it?" He didn't realise he had raised his voice until he heard a faint echo. "Have you seen it? What does it want?"

"No, I haven't seen it." The old man seemed to resent the question, as though it was absurd or vindictive. "Maybe I've heard it, and that's too much as it is. I just hope it takes another ride. What does it want? Maybe it ran out of—" Surely his next word must have been "food," but it sounded more like "forms."

Without warning he seemed to remember Roy's job. "If you read a bit more you wouldn't need me to tell you," he said angrily, slapping his bagfuls of books. "You want to read instead of serving things up to people and taking them away from books."

Roy couldn't afford to appear resentful. "But since I haven't read them, can't you tell me—" He must be raising his voice, for the echo was growing clearer—and that must have been what made the old man flee. Roy was left gaping after him and wondering how his voice had managed to echo; when a train racketed over the bridge a few minutes later, it seemed to produce no echo at all.

The old man had been worse than useless. Suppose there was something under the bridge: it must be entrapped in the arch. Otherwise, why hadn't it been able to follow Roy beyond the mouth? He stood at his bedroom window, daring a shape to appear. The thing was a coward, and stupid—almost as stupid as he was for believing that anything was there. He must lie down, for his thoughts were cracking apart, floating away. The lullaby of bells for evening mass made him feel relatively safe.

Sleep took him back to the bridge. In the dark he could just make out a halted goods-train. Perhaps all the trucks were empty, except for the one from which something bloated and pale was rising. It clambered down, lolling from scrawny legs, and vanished under the bridge, where a bird was nesting. There was a sound less like the cry of a bird than the shriek of air being squeezed out of a body. Now something that looked almost like a bird sat in the nest—but its head was too large, its beak was lopsided, and it had no voice. Nevertheless the bird's returning mate ventured close enough to be seized. After a jump in the continuity, for which Roy was profoundly grateful, he glimpsed a shape that seemed to have lost the power to look like a bird, crawling into the darkest corners of the arch, among cobwebs laden with soot. Now a cat was caught beneath the arch, and screaming; but the shape that clung to the girder afterwards didn't look much like a cat, even before it scuttled back into its corner. Perhaps it needed more substantial food. Roy needn't be afraid, he was awake now and watching the featureless dark of the arch from his bedroom window. Yet he was dreadfully afraid, for he knew that his fear was a beacon that would allow something to reach for him. All at once the walls of his room were bare brick, the corners were masses of sooty cobweb, and out of the darkest corner a top-heavy shape was scuttling.

When he managed to wake, he was intensely grateful to find that it wasn't dark. Though he had the impression that he'd slept for hours, it was still twilight. He wasn't at all refreshed: his body felt odd—feverish, unfamiliar, exhausted as though by a struggle he couldn't recall. No doubt the nightmare, which had grown out of the old man's ramblings, was to blame.

He switched on the radio to try to rouse himself. What was wrong? They'd mixed up the signature tunes, this ought to be—He stood and gaped, unable to believe what he was hearing. It was Monday, not Sunday at all.

No wonder he felt so odd. He had no time to brood over that, for he was on the air in less than an hour. He was glad to be leaving. The twilight made it appear that the dark of the bridge was seeping towards the house. His perceptions must be disordered, for his movements seemed to echo in the rooms. Even the sound of a bird's claw on the roof-tiles made him nervous.

Despite his lateness, he took the long way to the main road. From the top of the bus he watched furry ropes of cloud, orange and red, being drawn past the ends of side streets. Branches clawing at the roof made him start. A small branch must have snapped off, for even when the trees had passed, a restless scraping continued for a while above him.

He'd rarely seen the city streets so deserted. Night was climbing the walls. He was neurotically aware of sounds in the empty streets. Birds fluttered sleepily on pediments, though he couldn't always see them. His footsteps sounded effeminate, panicky, thinned by the emptiness. The builder's scaffolding that clung to the outside of the radio station seemed to turn his echoes even more shrill.

The third-floor studio seemed to be crowded with people, all waiting for him. Ian the producer looked harassed, perhaps imagining an entire show with Derrick alone. Derrick was smirking, bragging his punctuality. Tonight's interviewees—a woman who wrote novels about doctors and nurses in love, the leader of a group of striking undertakers—clearly sensed something was wrong. Well, now nothing was.

Roy was almost glad to see Derrick. Trivial chat might be just what he needed to stabilise his mind; certainly it was all he could manage. Still, the novelist proved to be easy: every question produced an anecdote—her

Glasgow childhood, the novel she'd thrown out of the window because it was too like real life, the woman who wrote to her asking to be introduced to the men on whom she based her characters. Roy was happy to listen, happy not to talk, for his voice through the microphone seemed to be echoing.

"—and Mugsy Moore, and Poo-Poo, and Trixie the Oomph." Reading the dedications, Derrick sounded unnervingly serious. "And here's a letter from one of our listeners," he said to Roy without warning, "who wants to know if we aren't speaking to each other."

Had Derrick invented that in a bid for sympathy? "Yes, of course we are," Roy said impatiently. As soon as he'd started the record—his hands on the controls felt unfamiliar and clumsy, he must try to be less irritable—he complained "Something's wrong with the microphone. I'm getting an echo."

"I can't hear anything," Ian said.

"It isn't there now, only when I'm on the air."

Ian and one of the engineers stared through the glass at Roy for a while, then shook their heads. "There's nothing," Ian said through the headphones, though Roy could hear the echo growing worse, trapping his voice amid distortions of itself. When he removed the headphones, the echo was still audible. "If you people listening at home are wondering what's wrong with my voice"—he was growing coldly furious, for Derrick was shaking his head too, looking smug—"we're working on it."

Ian ushered the striking undertaker into the studio. Maybe he would take Roy's mind off the technical problems. And maybe not, for as soon as Roy introduced him, something began to rattle the scaffolding outside the window and squeak its claws or its beak on the glass. "After this next record we'll be talking to him," he said as quickly as he could find his way through echoes.

"What's wrong now?" Ian demanded.

"That." But the tubular framework was still, and the window was otherwise empty. It must have been a bird. No reason for them all to stare at him.

As soon as he came back on the air the sounds began again. Didn't Ian care that the listeners must be wondering what they were? Halfway through introducing the undertaker, Roy turned sharply. Though there wasn't time for anything to dodge out of sight, the window was blank.

That threw him. His words were stumbling among echoes, and he'd forgotten what he meant to say. Hadn't he said it already, before playing the record?

Suddenly, like an understudy seizing his great chance on the night when the star falls ill, Derrick took over. "Some listeners may wonder why we're digging this up, but other people may think that this strike is a grave under-taking. . . ." Roy was too distracted to be appalled, even when Derrick pounced with an anecdote about an old lady whose husband was still await-ing burial. Why, the man was a human vacuum: no personality to be de-pended on at all.

For the rest of the show, Roy said as little as possible. Short answers echoed less. He suppressed some of the monosyllables he was tempted to use. At last the signature tune was reached. Mopping his forehead theatri-cally, Derrick opened the window.

Good God, he would let it in! The problems of the show had distracted Roy from thinking, but there was nothing to muffle his panic now. Ian caught his arm. "Roy, if there's anything—" Even if he wanted to help, he was keeping Roy near the open window. Shrugging him off, Roy ran towards the lift.

As he waited, he saw Ian and the engineer stalking away down the corri-dor, murmuring about him. If he'd offended Ian, that couldn't be helped; he needed to be alone, to think, perhaps to argue himself out of his panic. He dodged into the lift, which resembled a grey windowless telephone box, fea-tureless except for the dogged subtraction of lit numbers. He felt walled in by grey. Never mind, in a minute he would be out in the open, better able to think—

But was he fleeing towards the thing he meant to elude?

The lift gaped at the ground floor. Should he ride it back to the third? Ian and the engineer would have gone down to the car park by now; there would only be Derrick and the open window. The cramped lift made him feel trapped, and he stepped quickly into the deserted foyer.

Beyond the glass doors he could see a section of pavement, which looked oily with sodium light. Around it the tubes of the scaffolding blazed like or-ange neon. As far as he could judge, the framework was totally still—but what might be waiting silently for him to step beneath? Suddenly the pave-ment seemed a trap which needed only a footfall to trigger it. He couldn't go out that way.

He was about to press the button to call the lift when he saw that the lit numbers were already counting down. For a moment—he didn't know why—he might have fled out of the building, had he been able. He was trapped between the lurid stage of pavement and the inexorable descent of the lift. By the time the lift doors squeaked open, his palms were stinging with sweat. But the figure that stumbled out of the lift, hindered a little by his ill-fitting clothes, was Derrick.

Roy could never have expected to be so glad to see him. Hastily, before he could lose his nerve, he pulled open the glass doors, only to find that he was still unable to step beneath the scaffolding. Derrick went first, his footsteps echoing in the deserted street. When nothing happened, Roy managed to follow. The glass doors snapped locked behind him.

Though the sodium glare was painfully bright, at least it showed that the scaffolding was empty. He could hear nothing overhead. Even his footsteps sounded less panicky now; it was Derrick's that were distorted, thinned and hasty. Never mind, Derrick's hurry was all to the good, whatever its cause; it would take them to the less deserted streets all the more quickly.

Shadows counted their paces. Five paces beyond each lamp their shadows drew ahead of them and grew as dark as they could, then pivoted around their feet and paled before the next lamp. He was still nervous, for he kept peering at the shadows—but how could he expect them not to be distorted? If the shadows were bothering him, he'd have some relief from them before long, for ahead there was a stretch of road where several lamps weren't working. He wished he were less alone with his fears. He wished Derrick would speak.

Perhaps that thought halted him where the shadows were clearest, to gaze at them in dismay.

His shadow wasn't unreasonably distorted. That was exactly the trouble. Without warning he was back in his nightmare, with no chance of awakening. He remembered that the thing in the nightmare had had no voice. No, Roy's shadow wasn't especially distorted—but beside it, produced by the same lamp, Derrick's shadow was.

Above all he mustn't panic; his nightmare had told him so. Perhaps he had a chance, for he'd halted several lamps short of the darkness. If he could just retreat towards the studio without breaking into a run, perhaps he would be safe. If he could bang on the glass doors without losing control, mightn't the caretaker be in time?

The worst thing he could do was glance aside. He mustn't see what was casting the shadow, which showed how the scrawny limbs beneath the bloated stomach were struggling free of the ill-fitting clothes. Though his whole body was trembling—for the face of the shadow had puckered and was reaching sideways towards him, off the head—he began, slower than a nightmare, to turn away.

The Depths

As Miles emerged, a woman and a pink-eyed dog stumped by. She glanced at the house; then, humming tunelessly, she aimed the same contemptuous look at Miles. As if the lead was a remote control, the dog began to growl. They thought Miles was the same as the house.

He almost wished that were true; at least it would have been a kind of contact. He strolled through West Derby village and groped in his mind for ideas. Pastels drained from the evening sky. Wood pigeons paraded in a tree-lined close. A mother was crying "Don't you dare go out of this garden again." A woman was brushing her driveway and singing that she was glad she was Bugs Bunny. Beyond a brace of cars, in a living-room that displayed a bar complete with beer-pumps, a couple listened to *Beethoven's Greatest Hits*.

Miles sat drinking beer at a table behind the Crown, at the edge of the bowling green. Apart from the click of bowls the summer evening seemed as blank as his mind. Yet the idea had promised to be exactly what he and his publisher needed: no more days of drinking tea until his head swam, of glaring at the sheet of paper in the typewriter while it glared an unanswerable challenge back at him. He hadn't realised until now how untrustworthy inspirations were.

Perhaps he ought to have foreseen the problem. The owners had told him that there was nothing wrong with the house—nothing except the aloofness and silent disgust of their neighbours. If they had known what had happened there they would never have bought the house; why should they be treated as though by living there they had taken on the guilt?

Still, that was no more unreasonable than the crime itself. The previous owner had been a bank manager, as relaxed as a man could be in his job; his wife had owned a small boutique. They'd seemed entirely at peace with each other. Nobody who had known them could believe what he had done to her. Everyone Miles approached had refused to discuss it, as though by keeping quiet about it they might prevent it from having taken place at all.

The deserted green was smudged with darkness. "We're closing now," the barmaid said, surprised that anyone was still outside. Miles lifted the faint sketch of a tankard and gulped a throatful of beer, grimacing. The more he researched the book, the weaker it seemed to be.

To make things worse, he'd told the television interviewer that it was near completion. At least the programme wouldn't be broadcast for months, by which time he might be well into a book about the locations of murder—but it wasn't the book he had promised his publisher, and he wasn't sure that it would have the same appeal.

Long dark houses slumbered beyond an archway between cottages, lit windows hovered in the arch. A signboard reserved a weedy patch of ground for a library. A grey figure was caged by the pillars of the village cross. On the roof of a pub extension gargoyles began barking, for they were dogs. A cottage claimed to be a sawmill, but the smell seemed to be of manure. Though his brain was taking notes, it wouldn't stop nagging.

He gazed across Lord Sefton's estate towards the tower blocks of Cantril Farm. Their windows were broken ranks of small bright perforations in the night. For a moment, as his mind wobbled on the edge of exhaustion, the unstable patterns of light seemed a code which he needed to break to solve his problems. But how could they have anything to do with it? Such a murder in Cantril Farm, in the concrete barracks among which Liverpool communities had been scattered, he might have understood; here in West Derby it didn't make sense.

As he entered the deserted close, he heard movements beneath eaves. It must be nesting birds, but it was as though the sedate house had secret thoughts. He was grinning as he pushed open his gate, until his hand recoiled. The white gate was stickily red.

It was paint. Someone had written SADIST in an ungainly dripping scrawl. The neighbours could erase that—he wouldn't be here much longer. He let himself into the house.

For a moment he hesitated, listening to the dark. Nothing fled as he switched on the lights. The hall was just a hall, surmounted by a concertina of stairs; the metal and vinyl of the kitchen gleamed like an Ideal Home display; the corduroy suite sat plump and smug on the dark green pelt of the living-room. He felt as though he was lodging in a show house, without even the company of a shelf of his books.

Yet it was here, from the kitchen to the living-room, that everything had happened—here that the bank manager had systematically rendered his wife unrecognisable as a human being. Miles stood in the empty room and tried to imagine the scene. Had her mind collapsed, or had she been unable to withdraw from what was being done to her? Had her husband known what he was doing, right up to the moment when he'd dug the carving-knife into his throat and run headlong at the wall?

It was no good: here at the scene of the crime, Miles found the whole thing literally unimaginable. For an uneasy moment he suspected that might have been true of the killer and his victim. As Miles went upstairs, he was planning the compromise to offer his publisher: *Murderers' Houses? Dark Places of the World?* Perhaps it mightn't be such a bad book after all.

When he switched off the lights, darkness came upstairs from the hall. He lay in bed and watched the shadows of the curtains furling and unfurling above him. He was touching the gate, which felt like flesh; it split open, and his hand plunged in. Though the image was unpleasant it seemed remote, drawing him down into sleep.

The room appeared to have grown much darker when he woke in the grip of utter panic.

He didn't dare move, not until he knew what was wrong. The shadows were frozen above him, the curtains hung like sheets of lead. His mouth tasted metallic, and made him think of blood. He was sure that he wasn't alone in the dark. The worst of it was that there was something he mustn't do—but he had no idea what it was.

He'd begun to search his mind desperately when he realised that was exactly what he ought not to have done. The thought which welled up was so atrocious that his head began to shudder. He was trying to shake out the thought, to deny that it was his. He grabbed the light-cord, to scare it back into the dark.

Was the light failing? The room looked steeped in dimness, a grimy fluid whose sediment clung to his eyes. If anything the light had made him worse, for another thought came welling up like bile, and another. They were worse than the atrocities which the house had seen. He had to get out of the house.

He slammed his suitcase—thank God he'd lived out of it, rather than use the wardrobe—and dragged it onto the landing. He was halfway down, and the thuds of the case on the stairs were making his scalp crawl, when he realised that he'd left a notebook in the living-room.

He faltered in the hallway. He mustn't be fully awake: the carpet felt moist underfoot. His skull felt soft and porous, no protection at all for his mind. He had to have the notebook. Shouldering the door aside, he strode blindly into the room.

The light which dangled spiderlike from the central plaster flower showed him the notebook on a fat armchair. Had the chairs soaked up all that had been done here? If he touched them, what might well up? But there was worse in his head, which was seething. He grabbed the notebook and ran into the hall, gasping for air.

His car sounded harsh as a saw among the sleeping houses. He felt as though the neat hygienic façades had cast him out. At least he had to concentrate on his driving, and was deaf to the rest of his mind. The road through Liverpool was unnaturally bright as a playing-field. When the Mersey Tunnel closed overhead he felt that an insubstantial but suffocating burden had settled on his scalp. At last he emerged, only to plunge into darkness.

Though his sleep was free of nightmares, they were waiting whenever he jerked awake. It was as if he kept struggling out of a dark pit, having repeatedly forgotten what was at the top. Sunlight blazed through the curtains as though they were tissue paper, but couldn't reach inside his head. Eventually, when he couldn't bear another such awakening, he stumbled to the bathroom.

When he'd washed and shaved he still felt grimy. It must be the lack of sleep. He sat gazing over his desk. The pebble-dashed houses of Neston blazed like the cloudless sky; their outlines were knife-edged. Next door's drain sounded like someone bubbling the last of a drink through a straw. All this was less vivid than his thoughts—but wasn't that as it should be?

An hour later he still hadn't written a word. The nightmares were crowding everything else out of his mind. Even to think required an effort that made his skin feel infested, swarming.

A random insight saved him. Mightn't it solve both his problems if he wrote the nightmares down? Since he'd had them in the house in West Derby—since he felt they had somehow been produced by the house—couldn't he discuss them in his book?

He scribbled them out until his tired eyes closed. When he reread what he'd written he grew feverishly ashamed. How could he imagine such things? If anything was obscene, they were. Nothing could have made him write down the idea which he'd left until last. Though he was tempted to tear up the notebook, he stuffed it out of sight at the back of a drawer and hurried out to forget.

He sat on the edge of the promenade and gazed across the Dee marshes. Heat-haze made the Welsh hills look like piles of smoke. Families strolled as though this were still a watering-place; children played carefully, inhibited by parents. The children seemed wary of Miles; perhaps they sensed his tension, saw how his fingers were digging into his thighs. He must write the book soon, to prove that he could.

Ranks of pebble-dashed houses, street after street of identical Siamese twins, marched him home. They reminded him of cells in a single organism. He wouldn't starve if he didn't write—not for a while, at any rate—but he felt uneasy whenever he had to dip into his savings; their unobtrusive growth was reassuring, a talisman of success. He missed his street and had to walk back. Even then he had to peer twice at the street name before he was sure it was his.

He sat in the living-room, too exhausted to make himself dinner. Van Gogh landscapes, frozen in the instant before they became unbearably intense, throbbed on the walls. Shelves of Miles's novels reminded him of how he'd lost momentum. The last nightmare was still demanding to be written, until he forced it into the depths of his mind. He would rather have no ideas than that.

When he woke, the nightmare had left him. He felt enervated but clean. He lit up his watch and found he'd slept for hours. It was time for the book programme. He'd switched on the television and was turning on the light when he heard his voice at the far end of the room, in the dark.

He was on television, but that was hardly reassuring; his one television interview wasn't due to be broadcast for months. It was as though he'd slept that time away. His face floated up from the grey of the screen as he sat down, cursing. By the time his book was published, nobody would remember this interview.

The linkman and the editing had invoked another writer now. Good God, was that all they were using of Miles? He remembered the cameras following him into the West Derby house, the neighbours glaring, shaking their heads. It was as though they'd managed to censor him, after all.

No, here he was again. "Jonathan Miles is a crime novelist who feels he can no longer rely on his imagination. Desperate for new ideas, he lived for several weeks in a house where, last year, a murder was committed." Miles was already losing his temper, but there was worse to come: they'd used none of his observations about the creative process, only the sequence in which he ushered the camera about the house like Hitchcock in the *Psycho* trailer. "Viewers who find this distasteful," the linkman said unctuously, "may be reassured to hear that the murder in question is not so topical or popular as Mr Miles seems to think."

Miles glared at the screen while the programme came to an end, while an announcer explained that "Where Do You Get Your Ideas?" had been broadcast ahead of schedule because of an industrial dispute. And now here was the news, all of it as bad as Miles felt. A child had been murdered, said a headline; a Chief Constable had described it as the worst case of his career. Miles felt guiltily resentful; no doubt it would help distract people from his book.

Then he sat forward, gaping. Surely he must have misheard; perhaps his insomnia was talking. The newsreader looked unreal as a talking bust, but his voice went on, measured, concerned, inexorable. "The baby was found in a microwave oven. Neighbours broke into the house on hearing the cries, but were unable to locate it in time." Even worse than the scene he was describing was the fact that it was the last of Miles's nightmares, the one he had refused to write down.

Couldn't it have been a coincidence? Coincidence, coincidence, the train chattered, and seemed likely to do so all the way to London. If he had somehow been able to predict what was going to happen, he didn't want to know—especially not now, when he could sense new nightmares forming.

He suppressed them before they grew clear. He needed to keep his mind uncluttered for the meeting with his publisher; he gazed out of the window, to relax. Trees turned as they passed, unravelling beneath foliage. On a platform a chorus line of commuters bent to their luggage, one by one. The train drew the sun after it through clouds, like a balloon.

Once out of Euston Station and its random patterns of swarming, he strolled to the publishers. Buildings glared like blocks of salt, which seemed to have drained all moisture from the air. He felt hot and grimy, anxious both to face the worst and to delay. Hugo Burgess had been ominously casual. "If you happen to be in London soon we might have a chat about things. . . ."

A receptionist on a dais that overlooked the foyer kept Miles waiting until he began to sweat. Eventually a lift produced Hugo, smiling apologetically. Was he apologising in advance for what he had to say? "I suppose you saw yourself on television," he said when they reached his office.

"Yes, I'm afraid so."

"I shouldn't give it another thought. The telly people are envious buggers. They begrudge every second they give to discussing books. Sometimes I think they resent the competition and get their own back by being patronising." He was pawing through the heaps of books and papers on his desk, apparently in search of the phone. "It did occur to me that it would be nice to publish fairly soon," he murmured.

Miles hadn't realised that sweat could break out in so ma
once. "I've run into some problems."

Burgess was peering at items he had rediscovered in the heap
said without looking up.

Miles summarised his new idea clumsily. Should he have ᵥ   ... ᴛᴏ
Burgess in advance? "I found there simply wasn't enough material in the
West Derby case," he pleaded.

"Well, we certainly don't want padding." When Burgess eventually glanced
up he looked encouraging. "The more facts we can offer the better. I think
the public is outgrowing fantasy, now that we're well and truly in the scien-
tific age. People want to feel informed. Writing needs to be as accurate as any
other science, don't you think?" He hauled a glossy pamphlet out of one of
the piles. "Yes, here it is. I'd call this the last gasp of fantasy."

It was a painting, lovingly detailed and photographically realistic, of a girl
who was being simultaneously mutilated and raped. It proved to be the
cover of a new magazine, *Ghastly*. Within the pamphlet the editor promised
"a quarterly that will wipe out the old horror pulps—everything they didn't
dare to be."

"It won't last," Burgess said. "Most people are embarrassed to admit to
reading fantasy now, and that will only make them more so. The book you're
planning is more what they want—something they know is true. That way
they don't feel they're indulging themselves." He disinterred the phone at
last. "Just let me call a car and we'll go into the West End for lunch."

Afterwards they continued drinking in Hugo's club. Miles thought Hugo
was trying to midwife the book. Later he dined alone, then lingered for a
while in the hotel bar; his spotlessly impersonal room had made him feel
isolated. Over the incessant trickle of muzak he kept hearing Burgess. "I
wonder how soon you'll be able to let me have sample chapters. . . ."

Next morning he was surprised how refreshed he felt, especially once
he'd taken a shower. Over lunch he unburdened himself to his agent. "I just
don't know when I'll be able to deliver the book. I don't know how much research may be involved."

"Now look, you mustn't worry about Hugo. I'll speak to him. I know he
won't mind waiting if he knows it's for the good of the book." Susie Barker
patted his hand; her bangles sounded like silver castanets. "Now here's an
idea for you. Why don't you do up a sample chapter or two on the West
Derby case? That way we'll keep Hugo happy, and I'll do my best to sell it as
an article."

When they'd kissed good-bye Miles strolled along the Charing Cross

..oad, composing the chapter in his head and looking for himself in book-shop displays. Miles, Miles, books said in a window stacked with crime novels. NIGHT OF ATROCITIES, headlines cried on an adjacent newspaper-stand.

He dodged into Foyle's. That was better: he occupied half a shelf, though his earliest titles looked faded and dusty. When he emerged he was content to drift with the rush-hour crowds—until a news-vendor's placard stopped him. BRITAIN'S NIGHT OF HORROR, it said.

It didn't matter, it had nothing to do with him. In that case, why couldn't he find out what had happened? He didn't need to buy a paper, he could read the report as the news-vendor snatched the top copy to reveal the same beneath. "Last night was Britain's worst night of murders in living memory. . . ."

Before he'd read halfway down the column the noise of the crowd seemed to close in, to grow incomprehensible and menacing. The newsprint was snatched away again and again like a macabre card trick. He sidled away from the newsstand as though from the scene of a crime, but already he'd recognised every detail. If he hadn't repressed them on the way to London he could have written the reports himself. He even knew what the newspaper had omitted to report: that one of the victims had been forced to eat parts of herself.

Weeks later the newspapers were still in an uproar. Though the moderates pointed out that the murders had been unrelated and unmotivated, committed by people with no previous history of violence or of any kind of crime, for most of the papers that only made it worse. They used the most unpleasant photographs of the criminals that they could find, and presented the crimes as evidence of the impotence of the law, of a total collapse of standards. Opinion polls declared that the majority was in favour of an immediate return of the death penalty. "MEN LIKE THESE MUST NOT GO UN-PUNISHED," a headline said, pretending it was quoting. Miles grew hot with frustration and guilt—for he felt he could have prevented the crimes.

All too soon after he'd come back from London, the nightmares had returned. His mind had already felt raw from brooding, and he had been unable to resist; he'd known only that he must get rid of them somehow. They were worse than the others: more urgent, more appalling.

He'd scribbled them out as though he was inspired, then he'd glared blindly at the blackened page. It hadn't been enough. The seething in his head, the crawling of his scalp, had not been relieved even slightly. This time he had to develop the ideas, imagine them fully, or they would cling and fester in his mind.

He'd spent the day and half the night writing, drinking tea until he hardly knew what he was doing. He'd invented character after character, building them like Frankenstein out of fragments of people, only to subject them to gloatingly prolonged atrocities, both the victims and the perpetrators.

When he'd finished, his head felt like an empty rusty can. He might have vomited if he had been able to stand. His gaze had fallen on a paragraph he'd written, and he'd swept the pages onto the floor, snarling with disgust. "Next morning he couldn't remember what he'd done—but when he reached in his pocket and touched the soft object his hand came out covered with blood. . . ."

He'd stumbled across the landing to his bedroom, desperate to forget his ravings. When he'd woken next morning he had been astonished to find that he'd fallen asleep as soon as he had gone to bed. As he'd lain there, feeling purged, an insight so powerful it was impossible to doubt had seized him. If he hadn't written out these things they would have happened in reality.

But he had written them out: they were no longer part of him. In fact they had never been so, however they had felt. That made him feel cleaner, absolved him of responsibility. He stuffed the sloganeering newspapers into the wastebasket and arranged his desk for work.

By God, there was nothing so enjoyable as feeling ready to write. While a pot of tea brewed he strolled about the house and revelled in the sunlight, his release from the nightmares, his surge of energy. Next door a man with a beard of shaving foam dodged out of sight, like a timid Santa Claus.

Miles had composed the first paragraph before he sat down to write, a trick that always helped him write more fluently—but a week later he was still struggling to get the chapter into publishable shape. All that he found crucial about his research—the idea that by staying in the West Derby house he had tapped a source of utter madness, which had probably caused the original murder—he'd had to suppress. Why, if he said any of that in print they would think he was mad himself. Indeed, once he'd thought of writing it, it no longer seemed convincing.

When he could no longer bear the sight of the article, he typed a fresh copy and sent it to Susie. She called the following day, which seemed encouragingly quick. Had he been so aware of what he was failing to write that he hadn't noticed what he'd achieved?

"Well, Jonathan, I have to say this," she said as soon as she'd greeted him. "It isn't up to your standard. Frankly, I think you ought to scrap it and start again."

"Oh." After a considerable pause he could think of nothing to say except "All right."

"You sound exhausted. Perhaps that's the trouble." When he didn't answer she said "You listen to your Auntie Susie. Forget the whole thing for a fort-night and go away on holiday. You've been driving yourself too hard—you looked tired the last time I saw you. I'll explain to Hugo, and I'll see if I can't talk up the article you're going to write when you come back."

She chatted reassuringly for a while, then left him staring at the phone. He was realising how much he'd counted on selling the article. Apart from royalties, which never amounted to as much as he expected, when had he last had the reassurance of a cheque? He couldn't go on holiday, for he would feel he hadn't earned it; if he spent the time worrying about the extrava-gance, that would be no holiday at all.

But wasn't he being unfair to himself? Weren't there stories he could sell?

He turned the idea over gingerly in his mind, as though something might crawl out from beneath—but really, he could see no arguments against it. Writing out the nightmares had drained them of power; they were just sto-ries now. As he dialled Hugo's number, to ask him for the address of the magazine, he was already thinking up a pseudonym for himself.

For a fortnight he walked around Anglesey. Everything was hallucinatorily intense: beyond cracks in the island's grassy coastline, the sea glittered as though crystallising and shattering; across the sea, Welsh hills and mist ap-peared to be creating each other. Beaches were composed of rocks like brown crusty loaves decorated with shells. Anemones unfurled deep in glassy pools. When night fell he lay on a slab of rock and watched the stars begin to swarm.

As he strolled he was improving the chapters in his mind, now that the first version had clarified his themes. He wrote the article in three days, and was sure it was publishable. Not only was it the fullest description yet of the murder, but he'd managed to explain the way the neighbours had behaved: they'd needed to dramatise their repudiation of all that had been done in the house, they'd used him as a scapegoat to cast out, to proclaim that it had nothing to do with them.

When he'd sent the manuscript to Susie he felt pleasantly tired. The houses of Neston grew silver in the evening, the horizon was turning to ash. Once the room was so dark that he couldn't read, he went to bed. As he drifted towards sleep he heard next door's drain bubbling to itself.

But what was causing bubbles to form in the greyish substance that re-sembled fluid less than flesh? They were slower and thicker than tar, and took longer to form. Their source was rushing upwards to confront him face to face. The surface was quivering, ready to erupt, when he awoke.

He felt hot and grimy, and somehow ashamed. The dream had been a distortion of the last thing he'd heard, that was all; surely it wouldn't prevent him from sleeping. A moment later he was clinging to it desperately; its dreaminess was comforting, and it was preferable by far to the ideas that were crowding into his mind. He knew now why he felt grimy.

He couldn't lose himself in sleep; the nightmares were embedded there, minute, precise, and appalling. When he switched on the light it seemed to isolate him. Night had bricked up all the windows. He couldn't bear to be alone with the nightmares—but there was only one way to be rid of them.

The following night he woke having fallen asleep at his desk. His last line met his eyes: "Hours later he sat back on his haunches, still chewing doggedly. . . ." When he gulped the lukewarm tea it tasted rusty as blood. His surroundings seemed remote, and he could regain them only by purging his mind. His task wasn't even half-finished. His eyes felt like dusty pebbles. The pen jerked in his hand, spattering the page.

Next morning Susie rang, wrenching him awake at his desk. "Your article is tremendous. I'm sure we'll do well with it. Now I wonder if you can let me have a chapter breakdown of the rest of the book to show Hugo?"

Miles was fully awake now, and appalled by what had happened in his mind while he had been sleeping. "No," he muttered.

"Are there any problems you'd like to tell me about?"

If only he could! But he couldn't tell her that while he had been asleep, having nearly discharged his task, a new crowd of nightmares had gathered in his mind and were clamouring to be written. Perhaps now they would never end.

"Come and see me if it would help," Susie said.

How could he, when his mind was screaming to be purged? But if he didn't force himself to leave his desk, perhaps he never would. "All right," he said dully. "I'll come down tomorrow."

When tomorrow came it meant only that he could switch off his desk-lamp; he was nowhere near finishing. He barely managed to find a seat on the train, which was crowded with football fans. Opened beer cans spat; the air grew rusty with the smell of beer. The train emerged roaring from a tunnel, but Miles was still in his own, which was far darker and more oppressive. Around him they were chanting football songs, which sounded distant as a waveband buried in static. He wrote under cover of his briefcase, so that nobody would glimpse what he was writing.

Though he still hadn't finished when he reached London, he no longer cared. The chatter of the wheels, the incessant chanting, the pounding of blood and nightmares in his skull, had numbed him. He sat for a while in Euston. The white tiles glared like ice, a huge voice loomed above him.

As soon as she saw him Susie demanded "Have you seen a doctor?"

Even a psychiatrist couldn't help him. "I'll be all right," he said, hiding behind a bright false smile.

"I've thought of some possibilities for your book," she said over lunch. "What about that house in Edinburgh where almost the same murder was committed twice, fifty years apart? The man who did the second always said he hadn't known about the first. . . ."

She obviously hoped to revive him with ideas—but the nightmare which was replaying itself, endless as a loop of film, would let nothing else into his skull. The victim had managed to tear one hand free and was trying to protect herself.

"And isn't there the lady in Sutton who collected bricks from the scenes of crimes? She was meaning to use them to build a miniature Black Museum. She ought to be worth tracing," Susie said as the man seized the flailing hand by its wrist. "And then if you want to extend the scope of the book there's the mother of the Meathook Murder victims, who still gets letters pretending to be from her children."

The man had captured the wrist now. Slowly and deliberately, with a grin that looked pale as a crack in clay, he—Miles was barely able to swallow; his head, and every sound in the restaurant, was pounding. "They sound like good ideas," he mumbled, to shut Susie up.

Back at her office, a royalty fee had arrived. She wrote him a cheque at once, as though that might cure him. As he slipped it into his briefcase, she caught sight of the notebooks in which he'd written on the train. "Are they something I can look at?" she said.

His surge of guilt was so intense that it was panic. "No, it's nothing, it's just something, no," he stammered.

Hours later he was walking. Men loitered behind boys playing pinball; the machines flashed like fireworks, splashing the men's masks. Addicts were gathering outside the all-night chemist's on Piccadilly; in the subterranean Gents', a starved youth washed blood from a syringe. Off Regent Street, Soho glared like an amusement arcade. On Oxford Street figures in expensive dresses, their bald heads gleaming, gestured broken-wristed in windows.

He had no idea why he was walking. Was he hoping the crowds would distract him? Was that why he peered at their faces, more and more desperately? Nobody looked at all reassuring. Women were perfect as corpses, men seemed to glow with concealed aggression; some were dragons, their mouths full of smoke.

He'd walked past the girl before he reacted. Gasping, he struggled through a knot of people on the corner of Dean Street and dashed across, against the lights. In the moments before she realised that he'd dodged ahead of her and was staring, he saw her bright quick eyes, the delicate web of veins beneath them, the freckles that peppered the bridge of her nose, the pulsing of blood in her neck. She was so intensely present to him that it was appalling.

Then she stepped aside, annoyed by him, whatever he was. He reached out, but couldn't quite seize her arm. He had to stop her somehow. "Don't," he cried.

At that, she fled. He'd started after her when two policemen blocked his path. Perhaps they hadn't noticed him, perhaps they wouldn't grab him— but it was too late; she was lost in the Oxford Street crowd. He turned and ran, fleeing back to his hotel.

As soon as he reached his room he began writing. His head felt stuffed with hot ash. He was scribbling so fast that he hardly knew what he was saying. How much time did he have? His hand was cramped and shaking, his writing was surrounded by a spittle of ink.

He was halfway through a sentence when, quite without warning, his mind went blank. His pen was clawing spasmodically at the page, but the urgency had gone; the nightmare had left him. He lay in the anonymous bed in the dark, hoping he was wrong.

In the morning he went down to the lobby as late as he could bear. The face of the girl he'd seen in Oxford Street stared up at him from a newspaper. In the photograph her eyes looked dull and reproachful, though perhaps they seemed so only to him. He fled upstairs without reading the report. He already knew more than the newspaper would have been able to tell.

Eventually he went home to Neston. It didn't matter where he went; the nightmares would find him. He was an outcast from surrounding reality. He was focused inwards on his raw wound of a mind, waiting for the next outbreak of horrors to infest him.

Next day he sat at his desk. The sunlit houses opposite glared back like empty pages. Even to think of writing made his skin prickle. He went walking, but it was no good: beyond the marshes, factories coughed into the sky; grass-blades whipped the air like razors; birds swooped, shrieking knives with wings. The sunlight seemed violent and pitiless, vampirising the landscape.

There seemed no reason why the nightmares should ever stop. Either he would be forced to write them out, to involve himself more and more deeply in them, or they would be acted out in reality. In any case he was at their mercy; there was nothing he could do.

But wasn't he avoiding the truth? It hadn't been coincidence that had given him the chance he'd missed in Oxford Street. Perhaps he had been capable of intervention all along, if he had only known. However dismaying the responsibility was, surely it was preferable to helplessness. His glimpse in Oxford Street had made all the victims unbearably human.

He sat waiting. Pale waves snaked across the surface of the grass; in the heat-haze they looked as though water was welling up from the marshes. His scalp felt shrunken, but that was only nervousness and the storm that was clotting overhead. When eventually the clouds moved on, unbroken, they left a sediment of twilight that clung to him as he trudged home.

No, it was more than that. His skin felt grimy, unclean. The nightmares were close. He hurried to let his car out of the garage, then he sat like a private detective in the driver's seat outside his house. His hands clenched on the steering wheel. His head began to crawl, to swarm.

He mustn't be trapped into self-disgust. He reminded himself that the nightmares weren't coming from him, and forced his mind to grasp them, to be guided by them. Shame made him feel coated in hot grease. When at last the car coasted forward, was it acting out his urge to flee? Should he follow that street sign, or that one?

Just as the signs grew meaningless because he'd stared too long, he knew which way to go. His instincts had been waiting to take hold, and they were urgent now. He drove through the lampless streets, where lit curtains cut rectangles from the night, and out into the larger dark.

He found he was heading for Chester. Trees beside the road were giant scarecrows, brandishing tattered foliage. Grey clouds crawled grublike across the sky; he could hardly distinguish them from the crawling in his skull. He was desperate to purge his mind.

Roman walls loomed between the timber buildings of Chester, which were black and white as the moon. A few couples were window-shopping along the enclosed rows above the streets. On the bridge that crossed the main street, a clock perched like a moon-faced bird. Miles remembered a day when he'd walked by the river, boats passing slowly as clouds, a brass band on a small bandstand playing "Blow the Wind Southerly." How could the nightmare take place here?

It could, for it was urging him deeper into the city. He was driving so fast through the spotless streets that he almost missed the police station. Its blue sign drew him aside. That was where he must go. Somehow he had to persuade them that he knew where a crime was taking place.

He was still yards away from the police station when his foot faltered on the accelerator. The car shuddered and tried to jerk forward, but that was no use. The nearer he came to the police station, the weaker his instinct became. Was it being suppressed by his nervousness? Whatever the reason, he could guide nobody except himself.

As soon as he turned the car the urgency seized him. It was agonising now. It rushed him out of the centre of Chester, into streets of small houses and shops that looked dusty as furniture shoved out of sight in an attic. They were deserted except for a man in an ankle-length overcoat, who limped by like a sack with a head.

Miles stamped on the brake as the car passed the mouth of an alley. Snatching the keys, he slammed the door and ran into the alley, between two shops whose posters looked ancient and faded as Victorian photographs. The walls of the alley were chunks of spiky darkness above which cramped windows peered, but he didn't need to see to know where he was going.

He was shocked to find how slowly he had to run, how out of condition he was. His lungs seemed to be filling with lumps of rust, his throat was scraped raw. He was less running than staggering forward. Amid the uproar of his senses, it took him a while to feel that he was too late.

He halted as best he could. His feet slithered on the uneven flagstones, his hands clawed at the walls. As soon as he began to listen he wished he had not. Ahead in the dark, there was a faint incessant shriek that seemed to be trying to emerge from more than one mouth. He knew there was only one victim.

Before long he made out a dark object further down the alley. In fact it was two objects, one of which lay on the flagstones while the other rose to its feet, a dull gleam in its hand. A moment later the figure with the gleam was fleeing, its footsteps flapping like wings between the close walls.

The shrieking had stopped. The dark object lay still. Miles forced himself forward, to see what he'd failed to prevent. As soon as he'd glimpsed it he staggered away, choking back a scream.

He'd achieved nothing except to delay writing out the rest of the horrors. They were breeding faster in his skull, which felt as though it was cracking. He drove home blindly. The hedgerows and the night had merged into a dark mass that spilled towards the road, smudging its edges. Perhaps he might crash—but he wasn't allowed that relief, for the nightmares were herding him back to his desk.

The scratching of his pen, and a low half-articulate moaning which he recognised sometimes as his voice, kept him company. Next day the snap of the letter-box made him drop his pen; otherwise he might not have been able to force himself away from the desk.

The package contained the first issue of *Ghastly*. "Hope you like it," the editor gushed. "It's already been banned in some areas, which has helped sales no end. You'll see we announce your stories as coming attractions, and we look forward to publishing them." On the cover the girl was still writhing, but the contents were far worse. Miles had read only a paragraph when he tore the glossy pages into shreds.

How could anyone enjoy reading that? The pebble-dashed houses of Neston gleamed innocently back at him. Who knew what his neighbours read behind their locked doors? Perhaps in time some of them would gloat over his pornographic horrors, reassuring themselves that this was only horror fiction, not pornography at all: just as he'd reassured himself that they were only stories now, nothing to do with reality—certainly nothing to do with him, the pseudonym said so—

The Neston houses gazed back at him, self-confident and bland: they looked as convinced of their innocence as he was trying to feel—and all at once he knew where the nightmares were coming from.

He couldn't see how that would help him. Before he'd begun to suffer from his writer's block, there had been occasions when a story had surged up from his unconscious and demanded to be written. Those stories had been products of his own mind, yet he couldn't shake them off except by writing—but now he was suffering nightmares on behalf of the world.

No wonder they were so terrible, or that they were growing worse. If material repressed into the unconscious was bound to erupt in some less manageable form, how much more powerful that must be when the unconscious was collective! Precisely because people were unable to come to terms with the crimes, repudiated them as utterly inhuman or simply unimaginable, the horrors would reappear in a worse form and possess whomever they pleased. He remembered thinking that the patterns of life in the tower blocks had something to do with the West Derby murder. They had, of course. Everything had.

And now the repressions were focused in him. There was no reason why they should ever leave him; on the contrary, they seemed likely to grow more numerous and more peremptory. Was he releasing them by writing them out, or was the writing another form of repudiation?

One was still left in his brain. It felt like a boil in his skull. Suddenly he knew that he wasn't equal to writing it out, whatever else might happen. Had his imagination burned out at last? He would be content never to write another word. It occurred to him that the book he'd discussed with Hugo was just another form of rejection: knowing you were reading about real people reassured you they were other than yourself.

He slumped at his desk. He was a burden of flesh that felt encrusted with grit. Nothing moved except the festering nightmare in his head. Unless he got rid of it somehow, it felt as though it would never go away. He'd failed twice to intervene in reality, but need he fail again? If he succeeded, was it possible that might change things for good?

He was at the front door when the phone rang. Was it Susie? If she knew what was filling his head, she would never want to speak to him again. He left the phone ringing in the dark house and fled to his car.

The pain in his skull urged him through the dimming fields and villages to Birkenhead, where it seemed to abandon him. Not that it had faded—his mind felt like an abscessed tooth—but it was no longer able to guide him. Was something anxious to prevent him from reaching his goal?

The bare streets of warehouses and factories and terraces went on for miles, brick-red slabs pierced far too seldom by windows. At the peak hour the town centre grew black with swarms of people, the Mersey Tunnel drew in endless sluggish segments of cars. He drove jerkily, staring at faces.

Eventually he left the car in Hamilton Square, overlooked by insurance offices caged by railings, and trudged towards the docks. Except for his footsteps, the streets were deserted. Perhaps the agony would be cured before he arrived wherever he was going. He was beyond caring what that implied.

It was dark now. At the end of rows of houses whose doors opened onto cracked pavements he saw docked ships, glaring metal mansions. Beneath the iron mesh of swing bridges, a scum of neon light floated on the oily water. Sunken rails snagged his feet. In pubs on street corners he heard tribes of dockers, a sullen wordless roar that sounded like a warning. Out here the moan of a ship on the Irish Sea was the only voice he heard.

When at last he halted, he had no idea where he was. The pavement on which he was walking was eaten away by rubbly ground; he could smell collapsed buildings. A roofless house stood like a rotten tooth, lit by a single streetlamp harsh as lightning. Streets still led from the opposite pavement, and despite the ache—which had aborted nearly all his thoughts—he knew that the street directly opposite was where he must go.

There was silence. Everything was yet to happen. The lull seemed to give him a brief chance to think. Suppose he managed to prevent it? Repressing the ideas of the crimes only made them erupt in a worse form—how much worse might it be to repress the crimes themselves?

Nevertheless he stepped forward. Something had to cure him of his agony. He stayed on the treacherous pavement of the side street, for the roadway was skinless, a mass of bricks and mud. Houses pressed close to him, almost forcing him into the road. Where their doors and windows ought to be were patches of new brick. The far end of the street was impenetrably dark.

When he reached it, he saw why. A wall at least ten feet high was built flush against the last houses. Peering upwards, he made out the glint of broken glass. He was closed in by the wall and the plugged houses, in the midst of desolation.

Without warning—quite irrelevantly, it seemed—he remembered something he'd read about years ago while researching a novel: the Mosaic ritual of the Day of Atonement. They'd driven out the scapegoat, burdened with all the sins of the people, into the wilderness. Another goat had been sacrificed. The images chafed together in his head; he couldn't grasp their meaning—and then he realised why there was so much room for them in his mind. The aching nightmare was fading.

At once he was unable to turn away from the wall, for he was atrociously afraid. He knew why this nightmare could not have been acted out without him. Along the bricked-up street he heard footsteps approaching.

When he risked a glance over his shoulder, he saw that there were two figures. Their faces were blacked out by the darkness, but the glints in their hands were sharp. He was trying to claw his way up the wall, though already his lungs were labouring. Everything was over—the sleepless nights, the poison in his brain, the nightmare of responsibility—but he knew that while he would soon not be able to scream, it would take him much longer to die.

Down There

"Hurry along there," Steve called as the girls trooped down the office. *"Last* one tonight. Mind the doors."

The girls smiled at Elaine as they passed her desk, but their smiles meant different things: just like you to make things more difficult for the rest of us, looks like you've been kept in after school, suppose you've nothing better to do, fancy having to put up with him by yourself. She didn't give a damn what they thought of her. No doubt they earned enough without working overtime, since all they did with their money was squander it on makeup and new clothes.

She only wished Steve wouldn't make a joke of everything: even the lifts, one of which had broken down entirely after sinking uncontrollably to the bottom of the shaft all day. She was glad that hadn't happened to her, even though she gathered the subbasement was no longer so disgusting. Still, the surviving lift had rid her of everyone now, including Mr Williams the union representative, who'd tried the longest to persuade her not to stay. He still hadn't forgiven the union for accepting a temporary move to this building; perhaps he was taking it out on her. Well, he'd gone now, into the November night and rain.

It had been raining all day. The warehouses outside the windows looked like melting chocolate; the river and the canals were opaque with tangled ripples. Cottages and terraces, some of them derelict, crowded up the steep hills towards the disused mines. Through the skeins of water on the glass their infrequent lights looked shaky as candle-flames.

She was safe from all that, in the long office above five untenanted floors and two basements. Ranks of filing cabinets stuffed with blue Inland Revenue files divided the office down the middle; smells of dust and old paper hung in the air. Beneath a fluttering fluorescent tube protruding files drowsed, jerked awake. Through the steamy window above an unquenchable radiator, she could just make out the frame where the top section of the fire-escape should be.

"Are you feeling exploited?" Steve said.

He'd heard Mr Williams's parting shot, calling her the employers' weapon against solidarity. "No, certainly not." She wished he would let her be quiet for a while. "I'm feeling hot," she said.

"Yes, it is a bit much." He stood up, mopping his forehead theatrically. "I'll go and sort out Mr Tuttle."

She doubted that he would find the caretaker, who was no doubt hidden somewhere with a bottle of cheap rum. At least he tried to hide his drinking, which was more than one could say for the obese half-chewed sandwiches he left on windowsills, in the room where tea was brewed, even once on someone's desk.

She turned idly to the window behind her chair and watched the indicator in the lobby counting down. Steve had reached the basement now. The letter *B* flickered, then brightened: he'd gone down to the subbasement, which had been meant to be kept secret from the indicator and from everyone except the holder of the key. Perhaps the finding of the cache down there had encouraged Mr Tuttle to be careless with food.

She couldn't help growing angry. If the man who had built these offices had had so much money, why hadn't he put it to better use? The offices had been merely a disguise for the subbasement, which was to have been his refuge. What had he feared? War, revolution, a nuclear disaster? All anyone knew was that he'd spent the months before he had been certified insane in smuggling food down there. He'd wasted all that food, left it there to rot, and he'd had no thought for the people who would have to work in the offices: no staircases, a fire-escape that fell apart when someone tried to paint it— but she was beginning to sound like Mr Williams, and there was no point in brooding.

The numbers were counting upwards, slow as a child's first sum. Eventually Steve appeared, the solution. "No sign of him," he said. "He's somewhere communing with alcohol, I expect. Most of the lights are off, which doesn't help."

That sounded like one of Mr Tuttle's ruses. "Did you go right down?" she said. "What's it like down there?"

"Huge. They say it's much bigger than any of the floors. You could play two football games at once in there." Was he exaggerating? His face was bland as a silent comedian's except for raised eyebrows. "They left the big doors open when they cleaned it up. If there were any lights I reckon you could see for miles. I'm only surprised it didn't cut into one of the sewers."

"I shouldn't think it could be any more smelly."

"It still reeks a bit, that's true. Do you want a look? Shall I take you down?" When he dodged towards her, as though to carry her away, she sat forward rigidly and held the arms of her chair against the desk. "No thank you," she said, though she'd felt a start of delicious apprehension.

"Did you ever hear what was supposed to have happened while they were cleaning up all the food? Tuttle told me, if you can believe him." She didn't want to hear; Mr Tuttle had annoyed her enough for one day. She leafed determinedly through a file, until Steve went up the office to his desk.

For a while she was able to concentrate. The sounds of the office merged into a background discreet as muzak: the rustle of papers, the rushes of the wind, the buzz of the defective fluorescent like an insect trying to bumble its way out of the tube. She manoeuvred files across her desk. This man was going to be happy, since they owed him money. This fellow wasn't, since he owed them some.

But the thought of the food had settled on her like the heat. Only this morning, in the room where the tea-urn stood, she'd found an ancient packet of Mr Tuttle's sandwiches in the waste-bin. No doubt the packet was still there, since the cleaners were refusing to work until the building was made safe. She seemed unable to rid herself of the memory.

No, it wasn't a memory she was smelling. As she glanced up, wrinkling her nostrils, she saw that Steve was doing so too. "Tuttle," he said, grimacing.

As though he'd given a cue, they heard movement on the floor below. Someone was dragging a wet cloth across linoleum. Was the caretaker doing the cleaners' job? More likely he'd spilled a bottle and was trying to wipe away the evidence. "I'll get him this time," Steve said, and ran towards the lobby.

Was he making too much noise? The soft moist dragging on the floor below had ceased. The air seemed thick with heat and dust and the stench of food; when she lit a cigarette, the smoke loomed reprovingly above her. She opened the thin louvres at the top of the nearest window, but that brought no relief. There was nothing else for it; she opened the window that gave onto the space where the fire-escape should be.

It was almost too much for her. A gust of rain dashed in, drenching her face while she clung to the handle. The window felt capable of smashing wide, of snatching her out into the storm. She managed to anchor the bar to the sill, and leaned out into the night to let the rain wash away the smell.

Nine feet below her she could see the fifth-floor platform of the fire-escape, its iron mesh slippery and streaming. The iron stairs that hung from it, poised to swing down to the next platform, seemed to dangle into a deep pit of rain whose sides were incessantly collapsing. The thought of having to jump to the platform made her flinch back; she could imagine herself losing her footing, slithering off into space.

She was about to close the window, for the flock of papers on her desk had begun to flap, when she glimpsed movement in the unlit warehouse opposite and just below her. She was reminded of a maggot, writhing in food. Of course, that was because she was glimpsing it through the warehouse windows, small dark holes. It was reflected from her building, which was why it looked so large and puffily vague. It must be Mr Tuttle, for as it moved, she heard a scuffling below her, retreating from the lifts.

She'd closed the window by the time Steve returned. "You didn't find him, did you? Never mind," she said, for he was frowning.

Did he feel she was spying on him? At once his face grew blank. Perhaps he resented her knowing, first that he'd gone down to the subbasement, now that he'd been outwitted. When he sat at his desk at the far end of the office, the emptiness between them felt like a rebuff. "Do you fancy some tea?" she said, to placate him.

"I'll make it. A special treat." He jumped up at once and strode to the lobby.

Why was he so eager? Five minutes later, as she leafed through someone's private life, she wondered if he meant to creep up on her, if that was the joke he had been planning behind his mask. Her father had used to pounce on her to make her shriek when she was little—when he had still been able to. She turned sharply, but Steve had pulled open the doors of the out-of-work lift-shaft and was peering down, apparently listening. Perhaps it was Mr Tuttle he meant to surprise, not her.

The tea was hot and fawn, but little else. Why did it seem to taste of the lingering stench? Of course, Steve hadn't closed the door of the room off the lobby, where Mr Tuttle's sandwiches must still be festering. She hurried out and slammed the door with the hand that wasn't covering her mouth.

On impulse she went to the doors of the lift-shaft where Steve had been listening. They opened easily as curtains; for a moment she was teetering on the edge. The shock blurred her vision, but she knew it wasn't Mr Tuttle who was climbing the lift-cord like a fat pale monkey on a stick. When she screwed up her eyes and peered into the dim well, of course there was nothing.

Steve was watching her when she returned to her desk. His face was absolutely noncommittal. Was he keeping something from her—a special joke, perhaps? Here it came; he was about to speak. "How's your father?" he said.

It sounded momentarily like a comedian's catch-phrase. "Oh, he's happier now," she blurted. "They've got a new stock of large-print books in the library."

"Is there someone who can sit with him?"

"Sometimes." The community spirit had faded once the mine owners had moved on, leaving the area honeycombed with mines, burdened with unemployment. People seemed locked into themselves, afraid of being robbed of the little they had left.

"I was wondering if he's all right on his own."

"He'll have to be, won't he." She was growing angry; he was as bad as Mr Williams, reminding her of things it was no use remembering.

"I was just thinking that if you want to slope off home, I won't tell anyone. You've already done more work than some of the rest of them would do in an evening."

She clenched her fists beneath the desk to hold on to her temper. He must want to leave early himself and so was trying to persuade her. No doubt he had problems of his own—perhaps they were the secret behind his face— but he mustn't try to make her act dishonestly. Or was he testing her? She knew so little about him. "He'll be perfectly safe," she said. "He can always knock on the wall if he needs anyone."

Though his face stayed blank his eyes, frustrated now, gave him away. Five minutes later he was craning out of the window over the fire-escape, while Elaine pinned flapping files down with both hands. Did he really expect his date, if that was his problem, to come out on a night like this? It would be just like a man to expect her to wait outside.

The worst of it was that Elaine felt disappointed, which was absurd and infuriating. She knew perfectly well that the only reason he was working tonight was that one of the seniors had to do so. Good God, what had she expected to come of an evening alone with him? They were both in their forties—they knew what they wanted by now, which in his case was bound to be someone younger than Elaine. She hoped he and his girlfriend would be very happy. Her hands on the files were tight fists.

When he slammed the window she saw that his face was glistening. Of course it wasn't sweat, only rain. He hurried away without looking at her, and vanished into the lift. Perhaps the girl was waiting in the doorway, unable to rouse Mr Tuttle to let her in. Elaine hoped Steve wouldn't bring her upstairs. She would be a distraction, that was why. Elaine was here to work.

And she wasn't about to be distracted by Steve and his attempts at jokes. She refused to turn when she heard the soft sounds by the lifts. No doubt he was peering through the lobby window at her, waiting for her to turn and jump. Or was it his girlfriend? As Elaine reached across her desk for a file she thought that the face was pale and very fat. Elaine was damned if she would give her the satisfaction of being noticed—but when she tried to work she couldn't concentrate. She turned angrily. The lobby was deserted.

In a minute she would lose her temper. She could see where he was hiding, or they were: the door of the room off the lobby was ajar. She turned away, determined to work, but the deserted office wouldn't let her; each alley between the filing cabinets was a hiding-place, the buzz of the defective light and the fusillade of rain could hide the sound of soft footsteps. It was no longer at all funny. He was going too far.

At last he came in from the lobby, with no attempt at stealth. Perhaps he had tired of the joke. He must have been to the street door: his forehead was wet, though it didn't look like rain. Would he go back to work now, and pretend that the urn's room was empty? No, he must have thought of a new ruse, for he began pacing from cabinet to cabinet, glancing at files, stuffing them back into place. Was he trying to make her as impatient as he appeared to be? His quick sharp footsteps seemed to grow louder and more nerve-racking, like the ticking of the clock when she was lying awake, afraid to doze off in case her father needed her. "Steve, for heaven's sake, what's wrong?"

He stopped in the act of pulling a file from its cabinet. He looked abashed, at a loss for words, like a schoolboy caught stealing. She couldn't help taking pity on him; her resentment had been presumptuous. "You didn't go down to find Mr Tuttle just now, did you?" she said, to make it easier for him.

But he looked even less at ease. "No, I didn't. I don't think he's here at all. I think he left hours ago."

Why must he lie? They had both heard the caretaker on the floor below. Steve seemed determined to go on. "As a matter of fact," he said, "I'm beginning to suspect that he sneaks off home as soon as he can once the building's empty."

He was speaking low, which annoyed her: didn't he want his girlfriend to hear? "But there's someone else in the building," he said.

"Oh yes," she retorted. "I'm sure there is." Why did he have to dawdle instead of coming out with the truth? He was worse than her father when he groped among his memories.

He frowned, obviously not sure how much she knew. "Whoever it is, they're up to no good. I'll tell you the rest once we're out of the building. We mustn't waste any more time."

His struggles to avoid the truth amused and irritated her. The moisture on his forehead wasn't rain at all. "If they're up to no good," she said innocently, "we ought to wait until the police arrive."

"No, we'll call the police once we're out." He seemed to be saying anything that came into his head. How much longer could he keep his face blank? "Listen," he said, his fist crumpling the file, "I'll tell you why Tuttle doesn't stay here at night. The cleaners too, I think he told them. When the men were cleaning out the subbasement, some of the food disappeared overnight. You understand what that means? Someone stole a hundredweight of rotten food. The men couldn't have cared less, they treated it as a joke, and there was no sign how anyone could have got in. But as he says, that could mean that whatever it was was clever enough to conceal the way in. Of course I thought he was drunk or joking, but now. . . ."

His words hung like dust in the air. She didn't trust herself to speak. How dare he expect her to swallow such rubbish, as if she were too stupid to know what was going on? Her reaction must have shown on her face; she had never heard him speak coldly before. "We must go immediately," he said.

Her face was blazing. "Is that an order?"

"Yes, it is. I'll make sure you don't lose by it." His voice grew authoritative. "I'll call the lift while you fetch your coat."

Blind with anger, she marched to the cloakroom at the far end of the office from the lobby. As she grabbed her coat the hangers clashed together, a shrill violent sound which went some way towards expressing her feelings. Since Steve had no coat, he would be soaked. Though that gave her no pleasure, she couldn't help smiling.

The windows were shaking with rain. In the deserted office her footsteps sounded high-pitched, nervous. No, she wasn't on edge, only furious. She didn't mind passing the alleys between the cabinets, she wouldn't deign to look, not even at the alley where a vague shadow was lurching forward; it was only the shadow of a cabinet, jerked by the defective light. She didn't falter until she came in sight of the lobby, where there was no sign of Steve.

Had he gone without her? Was he smuggling out his girlfriend? They weren't in the room off the lobby, which was open and empty; the overturned waste-bin seemed to demonstrate their haste. The doors of the disused lift-shaft were open too. They must have opened when Steve had called the other lift. Everything could be explained; there was no reason for her to feel that something was wrong.

But something was. Between the two lift-shafts, the call-button was glowing. That could mean only one thing: the working lift hadn't yet answered the call. There was no other exit from the lobby—but there was no sign of Steve.

When she made herself go to the disused lift-shaft, it was only in order to confirm that her thought was absurd. Clinging to the edges of the doorway, she leaned out. The lift was stranded in the subbasement, where it was very dim. At first all she could distinguish was that the trapdoor in its roof was open, though the opening was largely covered by a sack. Could anything except a sack be draped so limply? Yes, for it was Steve, his eyes like glass that was forcing their lids wide, his mouth gagged with what appeared to be a torn-off wad of dough—except that the dough had fingers and a thumb.

She was reeling, perhaps over the edge of the shaft. No, she was stumbling back into the foyer, and already less sure what she'd glimpsed. Steve was dead, and she must get out of the building; she could think of nothing else. Thank God, she need not think, for the working lift had arrived. Was there soft movement in the disused shaft, a chorus of sucking like the mouthing of a crowd of babies? Nothing could have made her look. She staggered away, between the opening doors—into total darkness.

For a moment she thought she'd stepped out into an empty well. But there was a floor underfoot; the lift's bulb must have blown. As the door clamped shut behind her, the utter darkness closed in.

She was scrabbling at the metal wall in a frantic bid to locate the buttons— to open the doors, to let in some light—before she controlled herself. Which was worse: a quick descent in the darkness, or to be trapped alone on the sixth floor? In any case, she needn't suffer the dark. Hurriedly she groped in her handbag for her lighter.

She flicked the lighter uselessly once, twice, as the lift reached the fifth floor. The sudden plunge in her guts wasn't only shock; the lift had juddered to a halt. She flicked the lighter desperately. It had just lit when the doors hobbled open.

The fifth floor was unlit. Beyond the lobby she could see the windows of the untenanted office, swarming with rain and specks of light. The bare floor looked like a carpet of dim fog, interrupted by angular patches of greater dimness, blurred rugs of shadow. There was no sign of Mr Tuttle or whomever she'd heard from above. The doors were closing, but she wasn't reassured: if the lift had begun to misbehave, the least it could do would be to stop at every floor.

The doors closed her in with her tiny light. Vague reflections of the flame hung on the walls and tinged the greyish metal yellow; the roof was a hovering blotch. All the lighter had achieved was to remind her how cramped the lift was. She stared at the doors, which were trembling. Was there a movement beyond them other than the outbursts of rain?

When the doors parted, she retreated a step. The fourth floor was a replica of the fifth—bare floors colourless with dimness, windows that looked shattered by rain—but the shuffling was closer. Was the floor of the lobby glistening in patches, as though from moist footsteps? The doors were hesitating, she was brandishing her tiny flame as though it might defend her—then the doors closed reluctantly, the lift faltered downwards.

She'd had no time to sigh with relief, if indeed she had meant to, when she heard the lobby doors open above her. A moment later the lift shook. Something had plumped down on its roof.

At once, with a shock that felt as though it would tear out her guts, she knew what perhaps she had known, deep down, for a while: Steve hadn't been trying to frighten her—he had been trying not to. She hadn't heard Mr Tuttle on the fifth floor, nor any imaginary girlfriend of Steve's. Whatever she had heard was above her now, fumbling softly at the trapdoor.

It couldn't get in. She could hear that it couldn't, not before the lift reached the third—oh God, make the lift be quick! Then she could run for the fire-escape, which wasn't damaged except on the sixth. She was thinking quickly now, almost in a trance that carried her above her fear, aware of nothing except the clarity of her plan—and it was no use.

The doors were only beginning to open as they reached the third when the lift continued downwards without stopping. Either the weight on its roof, or the tampering, was sending it down. As the doors gaped to display the brick wall of the shaft, then closed again, the trapdoor clanged back and something like a hand came reaching down towards her.

It was very large. If it found her, it would engulf her face. It was the colour of ancient dough, and looked puffed up as if by decay; patches of the flesh were torn and ragged, but there seemed to be no blood, only greyness. She clamped her left hand over her mouth, which was twitching uncontrollably, and thrust the lighter at the swollen groping fingers.

They hissed in the flame and recoiled, squirming. Whitish beads had broken out on them. In a way the worst thing was the absence of a cry. The hand retreated through the opening, scraping the edge, and a huge vague face peered down with eyes like blobs of dough. She felt a surge of hysterical mirth at the way the hand had fled—but she choked it back, for she had no reason to feel triumphant. Her skirmish had distracted her from the progress of the lift, which had reached the bottom of the shaft.

Ought she to struggle with the doors, try to prevent them from opening? It was too late. They were creeping back, they were open now, and she could see the subbasement.

At least, she could see darkness which her light couldn't even reach. She had an impression of an enormous doorway, beyond which the darkness, if it was in proportion, might extend for hundreds of yards; she thought of the mouth of a sewer or a mine. The stench of putrid food was overwhelming, parts of the dark looked restless and puffy. But when she heard scuttling, and a dim shape came darting towards her, it proved to be a large rat.

Though that was bad enough, it mustn't distract her from the thing above her, on the lift. It had no chance to do so. The rat was yards away from her, and darting aside from her light, when she heard a spongy rush and the rat was overwhelmed by a whitish flood like a gushing of effluent. She backed away until the wall of the lift arrested her. She could still see too much—but how could she make herself put out the flame, trap herself in the dark?

For the flood was composed of obese bodies which clambered over one another, clutching for the trapped rat. The rat was tearing at the pudgy hands, ripping pieces from the doughy flesh, but that seemed not to affect them at all. Huge toothless mouths gaped in the puffy faces, collapsed inwards like senile lips, sucking loudly, hungrily. Three of the bloated heads fell on the rat, and she heard its squeals above their sucking.

Then the others that were clambering over them, out of the dark, turned towards her. Great moist nostrils were dilating and vanishing in their noseless faces. Could they see her light with their blobs of eyes, or were they smelling her terror? Perhaps they'd had only soft rotten things to eat down here, but they were learning fast. Hunger was their only motive, ruthless, all-consuming.

They came jostling towards the lift. Once, delirious, she'd heard all the sounds around her grow stealthily padded, but this softness was far worse. She was trying both to stand back and to jab the lift-button, quite uselessly; the doors refused to budge. The doughy shapes would pile in like tripe, suffocating her, putting out the flame, gorging themselves on her in the dark. The one that had ridden the lift was slithering down the outside to join them.

Perhaps its movement unburdened the lift, or jarred a connection into place, for all at once the doors were closing. Swollen hands were thumping them, soft fingers like grubs were trying to squeeze between them, but already the lift was sailing upwards. Oh God, suppose it went straight up to the sixth floor! But she'd found the ground-floor button, though it twitched away from her, shaken by the flame, and the lift was slowing. Through the slit between the doors, beyond the glass doors to the street, a streetlamp blazed like the sun.

The lift's doors opened, and the doughy face lurched in, its fat white blind eyes bulging, its avid mouth huge as a fist. It took her a moment prolonged as a nightmare to realise that it had been crushed between lift and shaft—for as the doors struggled open, the face began to tear. Screaming, she dragged the doors open, tearing the body in half. As she ran through it she heard it plump at the foot of the shaft, to be met by a soft eager rush—but she was fleeing blindly into the torrent of rain, towards the steep maze of unlit streets, her father at the fireside, his quiet vulnerable demand to know all that she'd done today.

The Fit

I must have passed the end of the path a hundred times before I saw it.
Walking into Keswick, I always gazed at the distant fells, mossed by fields
and gorse and woods. On cloudy days shadows rode the fells; the figures
tramping the ridges looked as though they could steady themselves with one
hand on the clouds. On clear days I would marvel at the multitude of shades
of green and yellow, a spectrum in themselves, and notice nothing else.

But this was a dull day. The landscape looked dusty, as though from the
lorries that pulverised the roads. I might have stayed in the house, but my
Aunt Naomi was fitting; the sight of people turning like inexperienced models before the full-length mirror made me feel out of place. I'd exhausted
Keswick—games of Crazy Golf, boats on the lake or strolls round it, narrow
streets clogged with cars and people scaffolded with rucksacks—and I didn't
feel like toiling up the fells today, even for the vistas of the lakes.

If I hadn't been watching my feet trudging I would have missed the path.
It led away from the road a mile or so outside Keswick, through a gap in the
hedges and across a field overgrown with grass and wild flowers. Solitude appealed to me, and I squeezed through the gap, which was hardly large enough
for a sheep.

As soon as I stepped on the path I felt the breeze. That raised my spirits;
the lorries had half deafened me, the grubby light and the clouds of dust had
made me feel grimy. Though the grass was waist high I strode forward, determined to follow the path.

Grass blurred its meanderings, but I managed to trace it to the far side of
the field, only to find that it gave out entirely. I peered about, blinded by
smouldering green. Elusive grasshoppers chirred, regular as telephones.
Eventually I made my way to the corner where the field met two others. Here
the path sneaked through the hedge, almost invisibly. Had it been made difficult to follow?

Beyond the hedge it passed close to a pond, whose surface was green as
the fields; I slithered on the brink. A dragonfly, its wings wafers of stained

glass, skimmed the pond. The breeze coaxed me along the path, until I reached what I'd thought was the edge of the field, but which proved to be a trough in the ground, about fifteen feet deep.

It wasn't a valley, though its stony floor sloped towards a dark hole ragged with grass. Its banks were a mass of gorse and herbs; gorse obscured a dark green mound low down on the far bank. Except that the breeze was urging me, I wouldn't have gone close enough to realise that the mound was a cottage.

It was hardly larger than a room. Moss had blurred its outlines, so that it resembled the banks of the trough; it was impossible to tell where the roof ended and the walls began. Now I could see a window, and I was eager to look in. The breeze guided me forward, caressing and soothing, and I saw where the path led down to the cottage.

I had just climbed down below the edge when the breeze turned cold. Was it the damp, striking upwards from the crack in the earth? The crack was narrower than it had looked, which must be why I was all at once much closer to the cottage—close enough to realise that the cottage must be decaying, eaten away by moss; perhaps that was what I could smell. Inside the cottage a light crept towards the window, a light pale as marsh gas, pale as the face that loomed behind it.

Someone was in there, and I was trespassing. When I tried to struggle out of the trough, my feet slipped on the path; the breeze was a huge cushion, a softness that forced me backwards. Clutching at gorse, I dragged myself over the edge. Nobody followed, and by the time I'd fled past the pond I couldn't distinguish the crack in the earth.

I didn't tell my aunt about the incident. Though she insisted I call her Naomi, and let me stay up at night far later than my parents did, I felt she might disapprove. I didn't want her to think that I was still a child. If I hadn't stopped myself brooding about it I might have realised that I felt guiltier than the incident warranted; after all, I had done nothing.

Before long she touched on the subject herself. One night we sat sipping more of the wine we'd had with dinner, something else my parents would have frowned upon if they'd known. Mellowed by wine, I said "That was a nice meal." Without warning, to my dismay which I concealed with a laugh, my voice fell an octave.

"You're growing up." As though that had reminded her, she said "See what you make of this."

From a drawer she produced two small grey dresses, too smartly cut for school. One of her clients had brought them for alteration, her two small daughters clutching each other and giggling at me. Aunt Naomi handed me the dresses. "Look at them closely," she said.

Handling them made me uneasy. As they drooped emptily over my lap they looked unnervingly minute. Strands of a different grey were woven into the material. Somehow I didn't like to touch those strands.

"I know how you feel," my aunt said. "It's the material."

"What about it?"

"The strands of lighter grey—I think they're hair."

I handed back the dresses hastily, pinching them by one corner of the shoulders. "Old Fanny Cave made them," she said as though that explained everything.

"Who's Fanny Cave?"

"Maybe she's just an old woman who isn't quite right in the head. I wouldn't trust some of the tales I've heard about her. Mind you, I'd trust her even less."

I must have looked intrigued, for she said "She's just an unpleasant old woman, Peter. Take my advice and stay away from her."

"I can't stay away from her if I don't know where she lives," I said slyly.

"In a hole in the ground near a pond, so they tell me. You can't even see it from the road, so don't bother trying."

She took my sudden nervousness for assent. "I wish Mrs Gibson hadn't accepted those dresses," she mused. "She couldn't bring herself to refuse, she said, when Fanny Cave had gone to so much trouble. Well, she said the children felt uncomfortable in them. I'm going to tell her the material isn't good for their skin."

I should have liked more chance to decide whether I wanted to confess to having gone near Fanny Cave's. Still, I felt too guilty to revive the subject or even to show too much interest in the old woman. Two days later I had the chance to see her for myself.

I was mooching about the house, trying to keep out of my aunt's way. There was nowhere downstairs I felt comfortable; her sewing machine chattered in the dining-room, by the table spread with cut-out patterns; dress forms stood in the lounge, waiting for clothes or limbs. From my bedroom window I watched the rain stir the fields into mud, dissolve the fells into mounds of mist. I was glad when the doorbell rang; at least it gave me something to do.

As soon as I opened the door the old woman pushed in. I thought she was impatient for shelter; she wore only a grey dress. Parts of it glistened with rain—or were they patterns of a different grey, symbols of some kind? I found myself squinting at them, trying to make them out, before I looked up at her face.

She was over six feet tall. Her grey hair dangled to her waist. Presumably it smelled of earth; certainly she did. Her leathery face was too small for her body. As it stooped, peering through grey strands at me as though I was merchandise, I thought of a rodent peering from its lair.

She strode into the dining-room. "You've been saying things about me. You've been telling them not to wear my clothes."

"I'm sure nobody told you that," my aunt said.

"Nobody had to." Her voice sounded stiff and rusty, as if she wasn't used to talking to people. "I know when anyone meddles in my affairs."

How could she fit into that dwarfish cottage? I stood in the hall, wondering if my aunt needed help and if I would have the courage to provide it. But now the old woman sounded less threatening than peevish. "I'm getting old. I need someone to look after me sometimes. I've no children of my own."

"But giving them clothes won't make them your children."

Through the doorway I saw the old woman glaring as though she had been found out. "Don't you meddle in my affairs or I'll meddle in yours," she said, and stalked away. It must have been the draught of her movements that made the dress patterns fly off the table, some of them into the fire.

For the rest of the day I felt uneasy, almost glad to be going home tomorrow. Clouds oozed down the fells; swaying curtains of rain enclosed the house, beneath the looming sky. The grey had seeped into the house. Together with the lingering smell of earth it made me feel buried alive.

I roamed the house as though it was a cage. Once, as I wandered into the lounge, I thought two figures were waiting in the dimness, arms outstretched to grab me. They were dress forms, and the arms of their dresses hung limp at their sides; I couldn't see how I had made the mistake.

My aunt did most of the chatting at dinner. I kept imagining Fanny Cave in her cottage, her long limbs folded up like a spider's in hiding. The cottage must be larger than it looked, but she certainly lived in a lair in the earth—in the mud, on a day like this.

After dinner we played cards. When I began to nod sleepily my aunt continued playing, though she knew I had a long coach journey in the morning; perhaps she wanted company. By the time I went to bed the rain had stopped; a cheesy moon hung in a rainbow. As I undressed I heard her pegging clothes on the line below my window.

When I'd packed my case I parted the curtains for a last drowsy look at the view. The fells were a moonlit patchwork, black and white. Why was my aunt taking so long to hang out the clothes? I peered down more sharply. There was no sign of her. The clothes were moving by themselves, dancing and swaying in the moonlight, inching along the line towards the house.

When I raised the sash of the window the night seemed perfectly still, no sign of a breeze. Nothing moved on the lawn except the shadows of the clothes, advancing a little and retreating, almost ritualistically. Hovering dresses waved holes where hands should be, nodded the sockets of their necks.

Were they really moving towards the house? Before I could tell, the line gave way, dropping them into the mud of the lawn. When I heard my aunt's vexed cry I slipped the window shut and retreated into bed; somehow I didn't want to admit what I'd seen, whatever it was. Sleep came so quickly that next day I could believe I'd been dreaming.

I didn't tell my parents; I'd learned to suppress details that they might find worrying. They were uneasy with my aunt—she was too careless of propriety, the time she had taken them tramping the fells she'd mocked them for dressing as though they were going out for dinner. I think the only reason they let me stay with her was to get me out of the polluted Birmingham air.

By the time I was due for my next visit I was more than ready. My voice had broken, my body had grown unfamiliar, I felt clumsy, ungainly, neither a man nor myself. My parents didn't help. They'd turned wistful as soon as my voice began to change; my mother treated visitors to photographs of me as a baby. She and my father kept telling me to concentrate on my studies and examining my school books as if pornography might lurk behind the covers. They seemed relieved that I attended a boys' school, until my father started wondering nervously if I was "particularly fond" of any of the boys. After nine months of this sort of thing I was glad to get away at Easter.

As soon as the coach moved off I felt better. In half an hour it left behind the Midlands hills, reefs built of red brick terraces. Lancashire seemed so flat that the glimpses of distant hills might have been mirages. After a couple of hours the fells began, great deceptively gentle monsters that slept at the edges of lakes blue as ice, two sorts of stillness. At least I would be free for a week.

But I was not, for I'd brought my new feelings with me. I knew that as soon as I saw my aunt walking upstairs. She had always seemed much younger than my mother, though there were only two years between them, and I'd been vaguely aware that she often wore tight jeans; now I saw how round her bottom was. I felt breathless with guilt in case she guessed what I was thinking, yet I couldn't look away.

At dinner, whenever she touched me I felt a shock of excitement, too strange and uncontrollable to be pleasant. Her skirts were considerably shorter than my mother's. My feelings crept up on me like the wine, which seemed to be urging them on. Half my conversation seemed fraught with double meanings. At last I found what I thought was a neutral subject. "Have you seen Fanny Cave again?" I said.

"Only once." My aunt seemed reluctant to talk about her. "She'd given away some more dresses, and Mrs Gibson referred the mother to me. They were nastier than the others—I'm sure she would have thrown them away even if I hadn't said anything. But old Fanny came storming up here, just a few weeks ago. When I wouldn't let her in she stood out there in the pouring rain, threatening all sorts of things."

"What sorts of things?"

"Oh, just unpleasant things. In the old days they would have burned her at the stake, if that's what they used to do. Anyway," she said with a frown to close the subject, "she's gone now."

"Dead, you mean?" I was impatient with euphemisms.

"Nobody knows for sure. Most people think she's in the pond. To tell you the truth, I don't think anyone's anxious to look."

Of course I was. I lay in bed and imagined probing the pond that nobody else dared search, a dream that seemed preferable to the thoughts that had been tormenting me recently as I tried to sleep. Next day, as I walked to the path, I peeled myself a fallen branch.

Bypassing the pond, I went first to the cottage. I could hear what sounded like a multitude of flies down in the trough. Was the cottage more over-grown than when I'd last seen it? Was that why it looked shrunken by decay, near to collapse? The single dusty window made me think of a dulling eye, half-engulfed by moss; the facade might have been a dead face that was falling inwards. Surely the flies were attracted by wild flowers—but I didn't want to go down into the crack; I hurried back to the pond.

Flies swarmed there too, bumbling above the scum. As I approached they turned on me. They made the air in front of my face seem dark, oppressive, infected. Nevertheless I poked my stick through the green skin and tried to sound the pond while keeping back from the slippery edge.

The depths felt muddy, soft and clinging. I poked for a while, until I began to imagine what I sought to touch. All at once I was afraid that some-thing might grab the branch, overbalance me, drag me into the opaque depths. Was it a rush of sweat that made my clothes feel heavy and obstruc-tive? As I shoved myself back, a breeze clutched them, hindering my retreat. I fled, skidding on mud, and saw the branch sink lethargically. A moment after it vanished the slime was unbroken.

That night I told Aunt Naomi where I'd been. I didn't think she would mind; after all, Fanny Cave was supposed to be out of the way. But she bent lower over her sewing, as if she didn't want to hear. "Please don't go there again," she said. "Now let's talk about something else."

"Why?" At that age I had no tact at all.

"Oh, for heaven's sake. Because I think she probably died on her way home from coming here. That's the last time anyone saw her. She must have been in such a rage that she slipped at the edge of the pond—I told you it was pouring with rain. Well, how was I to know what had happened?"

Perhaps her resentment concealed a need for reassurance, but I was unable to help, for I was struggling with the idea that she had been partly responsible for someone's death. Was nothing in my life to be trusted? I was so deep in brooding that I was hardly able to look at her when she cried out.

Presumably her needle had slipped on the thimble; she'd driven the point beneath one of her nails. Yet as she hurried out, furiously sucking her finger, I found that my gaze was drawn to the dress she had been sewing. As she'd cried out—of course it must have been then, not before—the dress had seemed to twist in her hands, jerking the needle.

When I went to bed I couldn't sleep. The room smelled faintly of earth; was that something to do with spring? The wardrobe door kept opening, though it had never behaved like that before, and displaying my clothes suspended batlike in the dark. Each time I got up to close the door their shapes looked less familiar, more unpleasant. Eventually I managed to sleep, only to dream that dresses were waddling limblessly through the doorway of my room, towards the bed.

The next day, Sunday, my aunt suggested a walk on the fells. I would have settled for Skiddaw, the easiest of them, but it was already swarming with walkers like fleas. "Let's go somewhere we'll be alone," Aunt Naomi said, which excited me in ways I'd begun to enjoy but preferred not to define, in case that scared the excitement away.

We climbed Grisedale Pike. Most of it was gentle, until just below the summit we reached an almost vertical scramble up a narrow spiky ridge. I clung there with all my limbs, trapped thousands of feet above the countryside, afraid to go up or down. I was almost hysterical with self-disgust; I'd let my half-admitted fantasies lure me up here, when all my aunt had wanted was to enjoy the walk without being crowded by tourists. Eventually I managed to clamber to the summit, my face blazing.

As we descended, it began to rain. By the time we reached home we were soaked. I felt suffocated by the smell of wet earth, the water flooding down my face, the dangling locks of sodden hair that wouldn't go away. I hurried upstairs to change.

I had just about finished—undressing had felt like peeling wallpaper, except that I was the wall—when my aunt called out. Though she was in the next room, her voice sounded muffled. Before I could go to her she called again, nearer to panic. I hurried across the landing, into her room.

The walls were streaming with shadows. The air was dark as mud, in which she was struggling wildly. A shapeless thing was swallowing her head and arms. When I switched on the light I saw it was nothing; she'd become entangled in the jumper she was trying to remove, that was all.

"Help me," she cried. She sounded as if she was choking, yet I didn't like to touch her; apart from her bra, her torso was naked. What was wrong with her, for God's sake? Couldn't she take off her jumper by herself? Eventually I helped her as best I could without touching her. It seemed glued to her, by the rain, I assumed. At last she emerged, red-faced and panting.

Neither of us said much at dinner. I thought her unease was directed at me, at the way I'd let her struggle. Or was she growing aware of my new feelings? That night, as I drifted into sleep, I thought I heard a jangling of hangers in the wardrobe. Perhaps it was just the start of a dream.

The morning was dull. Clouds swallowed the tops of the fells. My aunt lit fires in the downstairs rooms. I loitered about the house for a while, hoping for a glimpse of customers undressing, until the dimness made me claustrophobic. Firelight set the shadows of dress forms dancing spastically on the walls; when I stood with my back to the forms their shadows seemed to raise their arms.

I caught a bus to Keswick, for want of something to do. The bus had passed Fanny Cave's path before I thought of looking. I glanced back sharply, but a bend in the road intervened. Had I glimpsed a scarecrow by the pond, its sleeves fluttering? But it had seemed to rear up: it must have been a bird.

In Keswick I followed leggy girls up the narrow hilly streets, dawdled nervously outside pubs, and wondered if I looked old enough to risk buying a drink. When I found myself in the library, leafing desultorily through broken paperbacks, I went home. There was nothing by the pond that I could see, though closer to Aunt Naomi's house something grey was flapping in the grass—litter, I supposed.

The house seemed more oppressive than ever. Though my aunt tended to use whichever room she was in for sewing, she was generally tidy; now the house was crowded with half-finished clothes, lolling on chairs, their necks yawning. When I tried to chat at dinner my voice sounded muffled by the presence of so much cloth.

My aunt drank more than usual, and seemed not to care if I did too. My drinking made the light seem yellowish, suffocated. Soon I felt very sleepy. "Stay down a little longer," my aunt mumbled, jerking herself awake, when I made to go to bed. I couldn't understand why she didn't go herself. I chatted mechanically, about anything except what might be wrong. Firelight brought clothes nodding forward to listen.

At last she muttered "Let's go to bed." Of course she meant that unambiguously, yet it made me nervous. As I undressed hastily I heard her below me in the kitchen, opening the window a notch for air. A moment later the patch of light from the kitchen went out. I wished it had stayed lit for just another moment, for I'd glimpsed something lying beneath the empty clothesline.

Was it a nightdress? But I'd never seen my aunt hang out a nightdress, nor pyjamas either. It occurred to me that she must sleep naked. That disturbed me so much that I crawled into bed and tried to sleep at once, without thinking.

I dreamed I was buried, unable to breathe, and when I awoke I was. Blankets, which felt heavy as collapsed earth, had settled over my face. I heaved them off me and lay trying to calm myself, so that I would sink back into sleep—but by the time my breathing slowed I realised I was listening.

The room felt padded with silence. Dimness draped the chair and dressing-table, blurring their shapes; perhaps the wardrobe door was ajar, for I thought I saw vague forms hanging ominously still. Now I was struggling to fall asleep before I could realise what was keeping me awake. I drew long slow breaths to lull myself, but it was no use. In the silence between them I heard something sodden creeping upstairs.

I lay determined not to hear. Perhaps it was the wind or the creaking of the house, not the sound of a wet thing slopping stealthily upstairs at all. Perhaps if I didn't move, didn't make a noise, I would hear what it really was—but in any case I was incapable of moving, for I'd heard the wet thing flop on the landing outside my door.

For an interminable pause there was silence, thicker than ever, then I heard my aunt's door open next to mine. I braced myself for her scream. If she screamed I would go to her. I would have to. But the scream never came; there was only the sound of her pulling something sodden off the floor. Soon I heard her padding downstairs barefoot, and the click of a lock.

Everything was all right now. Whatever it had been, she'd dealt with it.

Perhaps wallpaper had fallen on the stairs, and she'd gone down to throw it out. Now I could sleep—so why couldn't I? Several minutes passed before I was conscious of wondering why she hadn't come back upstairs.

I forced myself to move. There was nothing to fear, nothing now outside my door—but I got dressed to delay going out on the landing. The landing proved to be empty, and so did the house. Beyond the open front door the prints of Aunt Naomi's bare feet led over the moist lawn towards the road.

The moon was doused by clouds. Once I reached the road I couldn't see my aunt's tracks, but I knew instinctively which way she'd gone. I ran wildly towards Fanny Cave's path. Hedges, mounds of congealed night, boxed me in. The only sound I could hear was the ringing of my heels on the asphalt.

I had just reached the gap in the hedge when the moon swam free. A woman was following the path towards the pond, but was it my aunt? Even with the field between us I recognised the grey dress she wore. It was Fanny Cave's.

I was terrified to set foot on the path until the figure turned a bend and I saw my aunt's profile. I plunged across the field, tearing my way through the grass. It might have been quicker to follow the path, for by the time I reached the gap into the second field she was nearly at the pond.

In the moonlight the surface of the pond looked milky, fungoid. The scum was broken by a rock, plastered with strands of grass, close to the edge towards which my aunt was walking. I threw myself forward, grass slashing my legs.

When I came abreast of her I saw her eyes, empty except for two shrunken reflections of the moon. I knew not to wake a sleepwalker, and so I caught her gently by the shoulders, though my hands wanted to shake, and tried to turn her away from the pond.

She wouldn't turn. She was pulling towards the scummy water, or Fanny Cave's dress was, for the drowned material seemed to writhe beneath my hands. It was pulling towards the rock whose eyes glared just above the scum, through glistening strands which were not grass but hair.

It seemed there was only one thing to do. I grabbed the neck of the dress and tore it down. The material was rotten, and tore easily. I dragged it from my aunt's body and flung it towards the pond. Did it land near the edge, then slither into the water? All I knew was that when I dared to look the scum was unbroken.

My aunt stood there naked and unaware until I draped my anorak around her. That seemed to rouse her. She stared about for a moment, then down at herself. "It's all right, Naomi," I said awkwardly.

She sobbed only once before she controlled herself, but I could see that the effort was cruel. "Come on, quickly," she said in a voice older and harsher than I'd ever heard her use, and strode home without looking at me.

Next day we didn't refer to the events of the night; in fact, we hardly spoke. No doubt she had lain awake all night as I had, as uncomfortably aware of me as I was of her. After breakfast she said that she wanted to be left alone, and asked me to go home early. I never visited her again; she always found a reason why I couldn't stay. I suspect the reasons served only to prevent my parents from questioning me.

Before I went home I found a long branch and went to the pond. It didn't take much probing for me to find something solid but repulsively soft. I drove the branch into it again and again, until I felt things break. My disgust was so violent it was beyond defining. Perhaps I already knew deep in myself that since the night I undressed my aunt I would never be able to touch a woman.

Hearing Is Believing

Suddenly he wasn't on the bus home after a frustrating day at work, but in Greece, in a taverna by the sea. The sky was a block of solid blue; over the plucking of bouzoukis he heard people smashing their empty glasses. Now sunset was turning the sea into lava, and someone like Anthony Quinn was dancing, arms outstretched, at the edge of the taverna, where waves lapped the stones.

Wells emerged from the daydream several streets nearer home. If he couldn't recall having passed through them, that was hardly surprising; beyond the streaming windows of the bus all the streets looked half-erased by rain, smudges and blotches of dull colour. Around him people coughed and sputtered with February chills. No wonder he preferred to anticipate his trip to Greece, the Greece of a film in which a tycoon married an American president's widow.

He ran home as though he were trying to butt the rain aside. The pavements were quivering mirrors of slate. At the top of the hill, rain scrambled over the ruin of the factory. Last week he'd seen the hundred-foot chimney standing for an instant on an explosion of dust before buckling, keeling over, taking with it two hundred jobs.

His house sounded hollow. Except for his bedroom and the living-room, most of it was uncarpeted. Bare scruffy plaster overlooked the stairs, littered the boards of the spare room. That was the way his father had left the house, which was still preferable to Wells's old flat—more of an investment, for one thing. Soon Wells must get on with decorating.

But not tonight: he'd already done enough work for one day, if not for several. When he'd eaten dinner the living-room fire was blazing; flames snatched at the fur of soot on the back of the chimney. Most of his furniture was crowded into the room, including the Yamaha stereo system, the most expensive item in the house.

He sat with a large Scotch while something by Delius wandered, gentle and vague as the firelight. The coughs of the audience were so far back in the stereo arc that they seemed embedded in the wall. At the end of the music, the applause made the room sound huge and deep. He could almost see the flock of hands fly up clapping.

A soprano began singing German, which Wells neither understood nor found evocative. He imagined the conductor's black-and-white plumage, his gestures at the singer as part of an elaborate mating ritual. Eventually Wells got up and fiddled with the dial. Here was a police call, here was a burst of Chinese, here was a message from a ship out on the Irish Sea. And here was someone whispering beside him, so close that he started back, and the rain came pouring in through the roof.

The voice had a background of rain, that was all. There were two voices, speaking just loudly enough to be heard over the downpour. He couldn't understand what they were saying; even the sound of the language was unfamiliar—not Eastern European, not an Oriental language. Yet he was so impressed by the vividness of the stereo that he sat down to listen.

The two men were in a street, for he could hear the gurgle of roadside drains. It must be dark, for the men were picking their way very hesitantly. Sometimes they slipped—rubble clinked underfoot—and he didn't need to understand the language to know they were cursing.

For a while he listened to the street sounds: the shrill incessant hiss of rain on stone, rain splashing jerkily from broken gutters, dripping on fragments of windows in the houses which loomed close on both sides. It was better than sitting before the fire and listening to a storm outside—or at least it would have been, except that he wished he knew why the men were afraid.

It unnerved him. Had they fled into this area to hide? Surely they would be more conspicuous amid the derelict streets, unless everywhere was like this. Or were they searching for something of which they were afraid? They had lowered their voices; they were certainly afraid that something would hear them, even through the clamour of rain. Wells found himself listening uneasily for some hint that it was near, listening so intently that at first he didn't realise that the men had fallen silent and were listening too.

For a while he could hear only the babble of rain and drains and rubble. The other sound was so similar that at first he couldn't be sure it was there. But yes, there was another sound: in the distance a great deal of rubble was shifting. If something was pushing it out of the way, that something was unhurried and very large. Surely the sound that accompanied it must be a quirk of the storm—surely it couldn't be breathing.

The men had heard it now. He could tell from their voices that they knew what it was—but why was he so much on edge because he couldn't understand? They dodged to the left, gasping as they stumbled over rubble. Now they were struggling with a door that scraped reluctantly back and forth in a heap of fallen masonry. At last rusty hinges gave way, and the door fell.

What use was it to take refuge here, when they'd made so much noise? Perhaps they were hoping to hide as they fled desperately from room to room. Now that they were in the house they sounded closer to him; everything did—the splat, splat of rain on linoleum in one large room, the dull plump of a drip on carpet in another. There must be very little left of the roof.

Now the men were running upstairs, their feet squelching on the stair carpet. They ran the length of a room that sounded enormous; he heard them splashing heedlessly through puddles. Now they were cowering in the corner to his left, where the light of his fire couldn't reach. He would have switched on the overhead light, except that would have been absurd.

In any case, there was no time. Something had hurled the front door aside and squeezed through the doorway into the house. It started upstairs at once, its sides wallowing against the staircase walls; three or four stairs creaked simultaneously. The breathing of the men began to shudder.

When it reached the top of the stairs it halted. Was it peering into the room? Wells could hear its breathing clearly now, thick and slow and composed of more than one sound, as if it came from several mouths. In the corner beyond the firelight the men were straining not to breathe.

A moment later they were screaming. Though nothing had squeezed through the doorway, Wells heard them dragged onto the landing. Their screams went downstairs as the creaking did, and out of the house. Had their captor's arms been able to reach the length of the room?

Wells sat listening reluctantly for something else to happen. Rain shrilled monotonously outside the house, dripped quicker and quicker on linoleum, sodden carpets, bare boards. That was all, but it went on and on, seemingly for half an hour. How much longer, for God's sake? As long as he was fool enough to leave it on, perhaps. He switched off the stereo and went to bed, only to lie there imagining unlit streets where some of the dim heaps weren't rubble. He couldn't switch off the rain outside his house.

Next morning he was glad to reach the office, where he could revive his imagination with the Greek travel poster above his desk, and joke with his colleagues until it was time to let the queue in out of the drizzle. Many of the waiting faces were depressingly familiar. Those who meant to plead more social security out of him were far easier to cope with than the growing number of young people who were sure he could find them a job. He hadn't grown used to seeing hope die in their eyes.

One of them was reading "the novel that proves there is life after death." Perhaps she'd grown so hopeless that she would believe anything that seemed to offer hope. He'd heard his colleagues seriously wondering whether God had been an astronaut, he'd seen them gasping at books "more hideously frightening than *The Exorcist* because everything actually happened." It seemed that any nonsense could find believers these days.

The bus home was full of tobacco smoke, another stale solution. The faces of the riders looked dispirited, apathetic, tired of working to keep up with inflation and taxes. A Jewish shop daubed with a swastika sailed by; the bus was plastered with National Front slogans, no doubt by the same people responsible for the swastika. If that could seem acceptable to some people, what solutions could be found in a worse world?

As soon as he reached home he switched on the tuner. Music would make the house sound more welcoming. He'd left the dial tuned to the station he had listened to last night, and the speakers greeted him with a rush of static. He had begun to alter the tuning when he realised what was wrong. The sound wasn't static, but rain.

There was no mistaking it once he heard its sounds on floorboards and linoleum; he could even hear plaster falling in the derelict house. Who on earth could be broadcasting this? He didn't care if he never found out who or why. He had to turn the knob some way before he lost the station.

That night he listened to records, since static kept seeping into the broadcasts he wanted to hear. Did the music sound thinner than it used to sound at the flat? A dripping tap made the house seem emptier. Perhaps the acoustics would improve once he improved the house. When he went upstairs to bed, remembering the months he'd lived here after his mother had died, during which he'd given up trying to persuade his father to let him redecorate—"Leave that, I like it as it is"—the dripping tap, whichever it had been, had stopped.

In the morning he felt robbed of sleep. Either a dream or the unnatural cold had kept waking him. Perhaps there was a draught that he would have to trace; he wasn't yet familiar with the house. Still, there were places where his life would seem luxurious.

One of his colleagues was reading a novel about an African state where all the workers were zombies. "That's what we need here," he grumbled. "No more strikes, no more unemployment, no more inflation."

"I hope you're joking," Wells said.

"Not at all. It sounds like paradise compared to this country. If someone took charge now I wouldn't care who it was."

Suddenly Wells remembered his dream: he had been here at his desk and everyone around him had been speaking English, yet he couldn't understand a word. He felt uncomfortable, vulnerable, and at lunchtime he went strolling to avoid more of that sort of thing. It didn't matter where he went— anywhere but here. Before long he saw the sky above the Mediterranean, two shades of piercing blue divided by the razor of the horizon. When he returned to the grey streets he found he was late for work; he couldn't recall having wandered so far.

After dinner he found a broadcast of Greek music. A large Scotch and the firelight helped him drift. Soon the lapping of flames, and their warmth, seemed very like Greek sun and sea—though as he began to doze, losing fragments of the music, the wavering of shadows on the walls made them look to be streaming. Perhaps that was why he dreamed he was sitting in a rainstorm. But when he woke, the rain was in the room.

Of course it was just the sound, coming from the speakers. Had the broadcast slipped awry, into static? He thought he could hear water splashing into puddles on linoleum, yet the dial on the waveband was inches away from the broadcast of two nights ago. He had to turn the knob still further before the noise faded.

He slapped the tuner's switch irritably, then stumped upstairs to bed. At least he might get a good night's sleep, if he didn't lie there brooding about the stereo. He'd paid enough for it; the shop could damn well make it right. Tonight his bedroom seemed even colder, and damp. Still, the whisky kept him warm, and drowned his thoughts. Soon he was asleep.

When he woke, the first thing he heard was the shifting of rubble. Something must be up the hill, in the ruined factory—a pack of dogs, perhaps, though it sounded larger. Or were the sounds downstairs, in his house? Certainly the sound of rain was.

He hadn't unplugged the stereo. His drowsy swipe must not have switched it off properly. Impatient to deal with it before he woke fully and couldn't get back to sleep, he swung his legs over the side of the bed. As soon as his bare feet touched the floor he cried out, recoiling.

He writhed on the bed, trying to twist the agony out of his foot. He had cramp, that was all; the floor hadn't really felt like drowned linoleum. When he peered at it, the carpet looked exactly as it should.

He stormed downstairs. The dark, or his inability to wake, made the empty rooms look impossibly large. The plaster above the staircase looked not only bare but glistening. Ignoring all this, he strode into the living-room.

The stereo dial was lit. The room was crowded with sound, a chorus of rain in a derelict house. In the distance there was another sound, a chanting of voices that sounded worshipful, terrified, desperate for mercy. That dismayed him more than anything else he'd heard. He pulled the plug from the wall socket and made himself go straight back to bed, where he lay sleepless for a long time. Somewhere in the house a tap was dripping.

Lack of sleep kept him on edge at work. He could hardly face the youngest of his clients. Though she had failed at interview after interview, she was almost superstitiously convinced that she would find a job. "Why can't I have one of the strikers' jobs?" she demanded, and he couldn't answer. He sent her to another interview, and wished her luck. He couldn't rob her of her faith, which must be all that kept her going.

He was glad he'd reached the weekend. When he arrived home, having visited Greece on the way, he made a leisurely dinner, then sat by the fire and listened to records. Somehow he didn't want to use the radio.

He couldn't relax. Of course it was only the play of firelight and shadow, but the room seemed to tremble on the edge of total darkness. As he drank more whisky in search of calm, he felt that the music was straining to reach him, drifting away. In the quieter passages he was distracted by the irregular dripping of a tap, he couldn't tell which. When he felt he might be able to sleep, he trudged upstairs. Tomorrow he would go walking in the country, or take the tuner back to the shop, or both.

But on Saturday it was raining. Perhaps that was just as well; he'd dreamed he was walking in the country, only to realise that the walk was a daydream that had lured him somewhere different and far worse. He lay in bed watching the sunlight, which was rediscovering the pattern of the ancient wallpaper. Then he flung himself out of bed, for the rain he could hear was not outside the house.

Though the stereo wasn't plugged in, the sounds filled the speakers: a gust of wind splattered rain across sagging wallpaper, waterlogged plaster collapsed, a prolonged juicy noise. He dismantled the stereo, which fell silent as soon as he unplugged the speakers, then he stormed out to find a taxi.

At last he found one, speeding down the terraced slope as if it wasn't worth stopping. It took him back to his house, where the driver stared into space while Wells manhandled the stereo into the taxi. By the time Wells reached the shop he was ready to lose his temper, especially when the engineer returned a few minutes later and told him that nothing was wrong.

Wells controlled himself and insisted on being taken into the repair shop. "This is what's wrong," he said, tuning the stereo to the unidentifiable station. The engineer gazed at him, smugly patient, and Wells could only look away, for Radio Prague came through loud and clear, with no background noise at all.

Wells roamed the shop rather desperately, tuning stereos in an attempt to find the rain. The engineer took pity on him, or determined to get rid of him. "It may be a freak reception. You may only be able to pick it up in the area where you live."

At once Wells felt much better. He'd heard of odder things, of broadcasts that possessed people's hearing-aids, telephones, even refrigerators. To the engineer's disgust, he left the stereo to be overhauled; then he went strolling in the hills, where spring was just beginning. The moist grass was flecked with rainbows, the sun seemed almost as bright as Greece.

That night he was surprised how alone he felt without the stereo. It must be its absence which made the house seem still emptier. At least he could relax with a book, if only he could locate the dripping tap. Perhaps it was in the bathroom, where the light-bulb—years old, no doubt—had failed. The bathroom walls glistened in the dark.

Soon he went to bed, for he was shivering. No doubt the cold and the damp would get worse until he attended to them. In bed his introverted warmth lulled him. A slide show of Greek landscapes played in his head. Starts of sleep interrupted the slides.

When uninterrupted sleep came it was darker, so that he couldn't see his way on the street along which he was creeping. At least the rain had stopped, and there was silence except for the muffled drumming of his heart. When his feet slipped on rubble, the shrill clatter sounded vindictively loud. His panic had made him forget what he mustn't do. There was a car a few yards ahead of him, a vague hump in the darkness; if he crouched behind that he might be safe. But he lost his balance as he reached it, and tried to support himself against its blubbery side. No, it wasn't a car, for something like a head rose out of it at once, panting thickly. The shapes that came scrabbling out of the houses beyond the rubbly gardens on both sides must have been its hands.

He woke and tried to stop shivering. No point in opening his eyes; that would only hold him back from sleep. But why was it so cold in the room? Why were the bedclothes clinging to him like wallpaper? Perhaps his sense that something was wrong was another reason to shiver.

When at last he forced his eyes open he saw the night sky, hardly relieved by a handful of stars, above him where the roof should be.

He couldn't think, because that would paralyse him. He thrust his feet into shoes, which were already soaking. He dragged his sodden jacket and trousers on over his pyjamas, then he fled. Now he could hear the rain, the lingering drops that splashed on linoleum, carpet, bare boards. On the stairs he almost fell headlong, for they were covered with fallen plaster. His sounds echoed in all the derelict rooms.

At last he reached the front door, which appeared still to be his, unlike the house. The street was dark; perhaps vandals had put out the lamp. He reeled out into the darkness, for he couldn't bear to stay in the house. He had still forgotten what he mustn't do; he slammed the front door behind him.

He heard rubble falling. When he grabbed at the door, it was already blocked from within. It lurched when he threw himself against it, but that was all; even though it was off its hinges, it was immovable. He mustn't waste time in struggling with it, but what else could he do? At one end of the unknown street, amid a chorus of unhurried breathing, something was feeling for him along the broken façades.

The Hands

Before long Trent wished he had stayed in the waiting-room, though being stranded for two hours on the teetotal platform had seemed the last straw. He'd expected to be in London just as the pubs were opening, but a derailment somewhere had landed him in a town he'd never heard of and couldn't locate on the map, with only his briefcase full of book jackets for company. Were those the Kentish hills in the distance, smudged by the threat of a storm? He might have asked the ticket collector, except that he'd had to lose his temper before the man would let him out for a walk.

The town wasn't worth the argument. It was nothing but concrete: off-white tunnels like subways crammed with shops, spiralling walkways where ramps would have saved a great deal of trouble, high blank domineering walls where even the graffiti looked like improvements. He'd thought of seeking out the bookshops, in the hope of grabbing a subscription or two for the books he represented, but it was early-closing day; nothing moved in the concrete maze but midget clones in the television rental shops. By the time he found a pub, embedded in a concrete wall with only an extinguished plastic sign to show what it was, it was closing time. Soon he was lost, for here were the clones again, a pink face and an orange and even a black-and-white, or was this another shop? Did they all leave their televisions running? He was wondering whether to go back to the pub to ask for directions, and had just realised irritably that no doubt it would have closed by now, when he saw the church.

At least, the notice-board said that was what it was. It stood in a circle of flagstones within a ring of lawn. Perhaps the concrete flying buttresses were meant to symbolise wings, but the building was all too reminiscent of a long thin iced bun flanked by two wedges of cake, served up on a cracked plate. Still, the church had the first open door he'd seen in the town, and it was starting to rain. He would rather shelter in the church than among the deserted shops.

He was crossing the flagstones, which had broken out in dark splotches, when he realised he hadn't entered a church since he was a child. And he wouldn't have dared go in with jackets like the ones in his briefcase: the long stockinged legs leading up into darkness, the man's head exploding like a melon, the policeman nailing a black girl to a cross. He wouldn't have dared think of a church just as a place to shelter from the rain. What *would* he have dared, for heaven's sake? Thank God he had grown out of being scared. He shoved the door open with his briefcase.

As he stepped into the porch, a nun came out of the church. The porch was dark, and fluttery with notices and pamphlets, so that he hardly glanced at her. Perhaps that was why he had the impression that she was chewing. The Munching Nun, he thought, and couldn't help giggling out loud. He hushed at once, for he'd seen the great luminous figure at the far end of the church.

It was a stained-glass window. As a burst of sunlight reached it, it seemed that the figure was catching the light in its flaming outstretched hands. Was it the angle of the light that made its fingertips glitter? As he stepped into the aisle for a better view, memories came crowding out of the dimness: genu-flecting boys in long white robes, distant priests chanting incomprehensibly. Once, when he'd asked where God was, his father had told him God lived "up there," pointing at the altar. Trent had imagined pulling aside the cur-tains behind the altar to see God, and he'd been terrified in case God heard him thinking.

He was smiling at himself, swinging his briefcase and striding up the aisle between the dim pews, when the figure with the flaming hands went out. All at once the church was very dark, though surely there ought to have been a light on the altar. He'd thought churches meant nothing to him anymore, but no church should feel as cold and empty as this. Certainly he had never been in a church before which smelled of dust.

The fluttering in the porch grew louder, loud as a cave full of bats—come to think of it, hadn't some of the notices looked torn?—and then the outer door slammed. He was near to panic, though he couldn't have said why, when he saw the faint vertical line beyond the darkness to his left. There was a side door.

When he groped into the side aisle, his briefcase hit a pew. The noise was so loud that it made him afraid the door would be locked. But it opened eas-ily, opposite a narrow passage which led back into the shopping precinct. Beyond the passage he saw a signpost for the railway station.

He was into the passage so quickly that he didn't even feel the rain. Nev-ertheless, it was growing worse; at the far end the pavement looked as if it was turning into tar, the signpost dripped like a nose. The signpost pointed down a wide straight road, which suggested that he had plenty of time after all, so that he didn't sidle past when the lady with the clipboard stepped in front of him.

He felt sorry for her at once. Her dark suit was too big, and there was something wrong with her mouth; when she spoke her lips barely parted. "Can you spare . . ." she began, and he deduced that she was asking him for a few minutes. "It's a test of your perceptions. It oughtn't to take long."

She must open her mouth when nobody was looking. Her clipboard pencil was gnawed to the core, and weren't the insides of her lips grey with lead? No doubt he was the first passerby for hours; if he refused she would get nobody. Presumably she was connected with the religious bookshop whose window loomed beside her doorway. Well, this would teach him not to laugh at nuns. "All right," he said.

She led him into the building so swiftly that he would have had no chance to change his mind. He could only follow her down the dull green corridor, into a second and then a third. Once he encountered a glass-fronted bookcase which contained only a few brownish pages, once he had to squeeze past a filing cabinet crumbly with rust; otherwise there was nothing but closed doors, painted the same prison green as the walls. Except for the slam of a door somewhere behind him, there was no sign of life. He was beginning to wish that he hadn't been so agreeable; if he tired of the examination he wouldn't be able simply to leave, he would have to ask the way.

She turned a corner, and there was an open door. Sunlight lay outside it like a welcome mat, though he could hear rain scuttling on a window. He followed her into the stark green room and halted, surprised, for he wasn't alone after all; several clipboard ladies were watching people at schoolroom desks too small for them. Perhaps there was a pub nearby.

His guide had stopped beside the single empty desk, on which a pamphlet lay. Her fingers were interwoven as if she was praying, yet they seemed restless. Eventually he said "Shall we start?"

Perhaps her blank expression was the fault of her impediment, for her face hadn't changed since he'd met her. "You already have," she said.

He'd taken pity on her, and now she had tricked him. He was tempted to demand to be shown the way out, except that he would feel foolish. As he squeezed into the vacant seat, he was hot with resentment. He wished he was dressed as loosely as everyone else in the room seemed to be.

It must be the closeness that was making him nervous: the closeness, and not having had a drink all day, and the morning wasted with a bookseller who'd kept him waiting for an hour beyond their appointment, only to order single copies of two of the books Trent was offering. And of course his nervousness was why he felt that everyone was waiting for him to open the pamphlet on his desk, for why should it be different from those the others at the desks were reading? Irritably he flicked the pamphlet open, at the most appalling image of violence he had ever seen.

The room flooded with darkness so quickly he thought he had passed out from shock. But it was a storm cloud putting out the sun—there was no other light in the room. Perhaps he hadn't really seen the picture. He would rather believe it had been one of the things he saw sometimes when he drank too much, and sometimes when he drank too little.

Why were they taking so long to switch on the lights? When he glanced up, the clipboard lady said "Take it to the window."

He'd heard of needy religious groups, but surely they were overdoing it—though he couldn't say why he still felt they had something to do with religion. Despite his doubts he made for the window, for then he could tell them he couldn't see, and use that excuse to make his escape.

Outside the window he could just distinguish a gloomy yard, its streaming walls so close he couldn't see the sky. Drainpipes black as slugs trailed down the walls, between grubby windows and what seemed to be the back door of the religious bookshop. He could see himself dimly in the window, himself and the others, who'd put their hands together as though it was a prayer meeting. The figures at the desks were rising to their feet, the clipboard ladies were converging on him. As he dropped his briefcase and glanced back nervously, he couldn't tell if they had moved at all.

But the picture in the pamphlet was quite as vile as it had seemed. He turned the page, only to find that the next was worse. They made the covers in his briefcase seem contrived and superficial, just pictures—and why did he feel he should recognise them? Suddenly he knew: yes, the dead baby being forced into the womb was in the Bible; the skewered man came from a painting of hell, and so did the man with an arrow up his rectum. That must be what he was meant to see, what was expected of him. No doubt he was supposed to think that these things were somehow necessary to religion. Perhaps if he said that, he could leave—and in any case he was blocking the meagre light from the window. Why weren't the other subjects impatient to stand where he was standing? Was he the only person in the room who needed light in order to see?

Though the rain on the window was harsh as gravel, the silence behind him seemed louder. He turned clumsily, knocking his briefcase over, and saw why. He was alone in the room.

He controlled his panic at once. So this was the kind of test they'd set for him, was it? The hell with them and their test—he wouldn't have followed the mumbling woman if he hadn't felt guilty, but why should he have felt guilty at all? As he made for the door, the pamphlet crumpled in one hand as a souvenir of his foolishness, he glanced at the pamphlets on the other desks. They were blank.

He had to stop on the threshold and close his eyes. The corridor was darker than the rooms; there had been nothing but sunlight there either. The building must be even more disused than it had seemed. Perhaps the shopping precinct had been built around it. None of this mattered, for now that he opened his eyes he could see dimly, and he'd remembered which way he had to go.

He turned right, then left at once. A corridor led into darkness, in which there would be a left turn. The greenish tinge of the oppressive dimness made him feel as if he was in an aquarium, except for the muffled scurrying of rain and the rumbling of his footsteps on the bare floorboards. He turned the corner at last, into another stretch of dimness, more doors sketched on the lightless walls, doors that changed the sound of his footsteps as he passed, too many doors to count. Here was a turn, and almost at once there should be another—he couldn't recall which way. If he wasn't mistaken, the stretch beyond that was close to the exit. He was walking confidently now, so that when his briefcase collided with the dark he cried out. He had walked into a door.

It wouldn't budge. He might as well have put his shoulder to the wall. His groping fingers found neither a handle nor a hole where one ought to be. He must have taken a wrong turning—somewhere he'd been unable to see that he had a choice. Perhaps he should retrace his steps to the room with the desks.

He groped his way back to the corridor which had seemed full of doors. He wished he could remember how many doors it contained; it seemed longer now. No doubt his annoyance was making it seem so. Eight doors, nine, but why should the hollowness they gave to his footsteps make him feel hollow too? He must be nearly at the corner, and once he turned left the room with the desks would be just beyond the end of the corridor. Yes, here was the turn; he could hear his footsteps flattening as they approached the wall. But there was no way to the left, after all.

He'd stumbled to the right, for that was where the dimness led, before his memory brought him up short. He'd turned right here on his way out, he was sure he had. The corridor couldn't just disappear. No, but it could be closed off—and when he reached out to where he'd thought it was he felt the panels of the door at once, and bruised his shoulder against it before he gave up.

So the test hadn't finished. That must be what was going on, that was why someone was closing doors against him in the dark. He was too angry to panic. He stormed along the right-hand corridor, past more doors and their muffled hollow echoes. His mouth felt coated with dust, and that made him even angrier. By God, he'd make someone show him the way out, however he had to do so.

Then his fists clenched—the handle of his briefcase dug into his palm, the pamphlet crumpled loudly—for there was someone ahead, unlocking a door. A faint greyish light seeped out of the doorway and showed Trent the glimmering collar, stiff as a fetter. No wonder the priest was having trouble opening the door, for he was trying to don a pair of gloves. "Excuse me, Father," Trent called, "can you tell me how I get out of here?"

The priest seemed not to hear him. Just before the door closed, Trent saw he wasn't wearing gloves at all. It must be the dimness which made his hands look flattened and limp. A moment later he had vanished into the room, and Trent heard a key turn in the lock.

Trent knocked on the door rather timidly until he remembered how, as a child, he would have been scared to disturb a priest at all. He knocked as loudly as he could, even when his knuckles were aching. If there was a corridor beyond the door, perhaps the priest was out of earshot. The presence of the priest somewhere made Trent feel both safer and a good deal angrier. Eventually he stormed away, thumping on all the doors.

His anger seemed to have cracked a barrier in his mind, for he could remember a great deal he hadn't thought of for years. He'd been most frightened in his adolescence, when he had begun to suspect it wasn't all true and had fought to suppress his thoughts in case God heard them. God had been watching him everywhere—even in the toilet, like a voyeur. Everywhere he had felt caged. He'd grown resentful eventually, he'd dared God to spy on him while he was in the toilet, and that was where he'd pondered his suspicions, such as—yes, he remembered now—the idea that just as marriage was supposed to sanctify sex, so religion sanctified all manner of torture and inhumanity. Of course, that was the thought the pamphlet had almost recalled. He faltered, for his memories had muffled his senses more than the dimness had. Somewhere ahead of him, voices were singing.

Perhaps it was a hymn. He couldn't tell, for they sounded as if they had their mouths full. It must be the wall that was blurring them. As he advanced through the greenish dimness, he tried to make no noise. Now he thought he could see the glint of the door, glossier than the walls, but he had to reach out and touch the panels before he could be sure. Why on earth was he hesitating?

He pounded on the door, more loudly than he had intended, and the voices fell silent at once.

He waited for someone to come to the door, but there was no sound at all. Were they standing quite still and gazing towards him, or was one of them creeping to the door? Perhaps they were all doing so. Suddenly the dark seemed much larger, and he realised fully that he had no idea where he was. They must know he was alone in the dark. He felt like a child, except that in a situation like this as a child he would have been able to wake up.

By God, they couldn't frighten him, not any longer. Certainly his hands were shaking—he could hear the covers rustling in his briefcase—but with rage, not fear. The people in the room must be waiting for him to go away so that they could continue their hymn, waiting for him to trudge into the outer darkness, the unbeliever, gnashing his teeth. They couldn't get rid of him so easily. Maybe by their standards he was wasting his life, drinking it away—but by God, he was doing less harm than many religious people he'd heard of. He was satisfied with his life, that was the important thing. He'd wanted to write books, but even if he'd found he couldn't, he'd proved to himself that not everything in books was true. At least selling books had given him a disrespect for them, and perhaps that was just what he'd needed.

He laughed uneasily at himself, a thin sound in the dark. Where were all these thoughts coming from? It was like the old story that you saw your whole life at the moment of your death, as if anyone could know. He needed a drink, that was why his thoughts were uncontrollable. He'd had enough of waiting. He grabbed the handle and wrenched at the door, but it was no use; the door wouldn't budge.

He should be searching for the way out, not wasting his time here. That was why he hurried away, not because he was afraid someone would snatch the door open. He yanked at handles as he came abreast of them, though he could barely see the doors. Perhaps the storm was worsening, although he couldn't hear the rain, for he was less able to see now than he had been a few minutes ago. The dark was so soft and hot and dreamlike that he could almost imagine that he was a child again, lying in bed at that moment when the dark of the room merged with the dark of sleep—but it was dangerous to imagine that, though he couldn't think why. In any case, this was clearly not a dream, for the next door he tried slammed deafeningly open against the wall of the room.

It took him a long time to step forward, for he was afraid he'd awakened the figures that were huddled in the furthest corner of the room. When his eyes adjusted to the meagre light that filtered down from a grubby skylight, he saw that the shapes were too tangled and flat to be people. Of course, the huddle was just a heap of old clothes—but then why was it stirring? As he stepped forward involuntarily, a rat darted out, dragging a long brownish object that seemed to be trailing strings. Before the rat vanished under the floorboards Trent was back outside the door and shutting it as quickly as he could.

He stood panting in the dark. Whatever he'd seen, it was nothing to do with him. Perhaps the limbs of the clothes had been bound together, but what did it mean if they were? Once he escaped he could begin to think—he was afraid to do so now. If he began to panic he wouldn't dare to try the doors.

He had to keep trying. One of them might let him escape. He ought to be able to hear which was the outer corridor, if it was still raining. He forced himself to tiptoe onward. He could distinguish the doors only by touch, and he turned the handles timidly, even though it slowed him down. He was by no means ready when one of the doors gave an inch. The way his hand flinched, he wondered if he would be able to open the door at all.

Of course he had to, and at last he did, as stealthily as possible. He wasn't stealthy enough, for as he peered around the door the figures at the table turned towards him. Perhaps they were standing up to eat because the room was so dim, and it must be the dimness that made the large piece of meat on the table appear to struggle, but why were they eating in such meagre light at all? Before his vision had a chance to adjust they left the table all at once and came at him.

He slammed the door and ran blindly down the corridor, grabbing at handles. What exactly had he seen? They had been eating with their bare hands, but somehow the only thought he could hold on to was a kind of sickened gratitude that he had been unable to see their faces. The dimness was virtually darkness now, his running footsteps deafened him to any sound but theirs, the doors seemed further and further apart, locked doors separated by minutes of stumbling through the dark. Three locked doors, four, and the fifth opened so easily that he barely saved himself from falling into the cellar.

If it had been darker, he might have been able to turn away before he saw what was squealing. As he peered down, desperate to close the door but compelled to try to distinguish the source of the thin irregular sound, he made out the dim shapes of four figures, standing wide apart on the cellar floor. They were moving further apart now, without letting go of what they were holding—the elongated figure of a man, which they were pulling in four directions by its limbs. It must be inflatable, it must be a leak that was squealing. But the figure wasn't only squealing, it was sobbing.

Trent fled, for the place was not a cellar at all. It was a vast darkness in whose distance he'd begun to glimpse worse things. He wished he could believe he was dreaming, the way they comforted themselves in books—but not only did he know he wasn't dreaming, he was afraid to think that he was. He'd had nightmares like this when he was young, when he was scared that he'd lost his one chance. He'd rejected the truth, and so now there was only hell to look forward to. Even if he didn't believe, hell would get him, perhaps for not believing. It had taken him a while to convince himself that because he didn't believe in it, hell couldn't touch him. Perhaps he had never really convinced himself at all.

He managed to suppress his thoughts, but they had disoriented him; even when he forced himself to stop and listen he wasn't convinced where he was. He had to touch the cold slick wall before the sounds became present to him: footsteps, the footsteps of several people creeping after him.

He hadn't time to determine what was wrong with the footsteps, for there was another sound, ahead of him—the sound of rain on glass. He began to run, fumbling with door handles as he reached them. The first door was locked, and so was the second. The rain was still in front of him, somewhere in the dark. Or was it behind him now, with his pursuers? He scrabbled at the next handle, and almost fell headlong into the room.

He must keep going, for there was a door on the far side of the room, a door beyond which he could hear the rain. It didn't matter that the room smelled like a butcher's. He didn't have to look at the torn objects that were strewn over the floor, he could dodge among them, even though he was in danger of slipping on the wet boards. He held his breath until he reached the far door, and could already feel how the air would burst out of his mouth when he escaped. But the door was locked, and the doorway to the corridor was full of his pursuers, who came padding leisurely into the room.

He was on the point of withering into himself—in a moment he would have to see the things that lay about the floor—when he noticed that beside the door there was a window, so grubby that he'd taken it for a pale patch on the wall. Though he couldn't see what lay beyond, he smashed the glass with his briefcase and hurled splinters back into the room as he scrambled through.

He landed in a cramped courtyard. High walls scaled by drainpipes closed in on all four sides. Opposite him was a door with a glass panel, beyond which he could see heaps of religious books. It was the back door of the bookshop he had noticed in the passage.

He heard glass gnashing in the window-frame, and didn't dare look behind him. Though the courtyard was only a few feet wide, it seemed he would never reach the door. Rain was already dripping from his brows into his eyes. He was praying, incoherently: yes, he believed, he believed in anything that could save him, anything that could hear. The pamphlet was still crumpled in the hand he raised to try the door. Yes, he thought desperately, he believed in those things too, if they had to exist before he could be saved.

He was pounding on the door with his briefcase as he twisted the handle—but the handle turned easily and let him in. He slammed the door behind him and wished that were enough. Why couldn't there have been a key? Perhaps there was something almost as good—the cartons of books piled high in the corridor that led to the shop.

As soon as he'd struggled past he began to overbalance them. He had toppled three cartons, creating a barrier which looked surprisingly insurmountable, when he stopped, feeling both guilty and limp with relief. Someone was moving about in the shop.

He was out of the corridor, and sneezing away the dust he had raised from the cartons, before he realised that he hadn't the least idea what to say. Could he simply ask for refuge? Perhaps, for the woman in the shop was a nun. She was checking the street door, which was locked, thank God. The dimness made the windows and the contents of the shop look thick with dust. Perhaps he should begin by asking her to switch on the lights.

He was venturing towards her when he touched a shelf of books, and he realised that the grey deposit was dust, after all. He faltered as she turned towards him. It was the nun he had seen in the church, but now her mouth was smeared with crimson lipstick—except that as she advanced on him, he saw that it wasn't lipstick at all. He heard the barricade in the corridor give way just as she pulled off her flesh-coloured gloves by their nails. "You failed," she said.

Again

Before long Bryant tired of the Wirral Way. He'd come to the nature trail because he'd exhausted the Liverpool parks, only to find that nature was too relentless for him. No doubt the trail would mean more to a botanist, but to Bryant it looked exactly like what it was: an overgrown railway divested of its line. Sometimes it led beneath bridges hollow as whistles, and then it seemed to trap him between the banks for miles. When it rose to ground level it was only to show him fields too lush for comfort, hedges, trees, green so unrelieved that its shades blurred into a single oppressive mass.

He wasn't sure what eventually made the miniature valley intolerable. Children went hooting like derailed trains across his path, huge dogs came snuffling out of the undergrowth to leap on him and smear his face, but the worst annoyances were the flies, brought out all at once by the late June day, the first hot day of the year. They blotched his vision like eyestrain, their incessant buzzing seemed to muffle all his senses. When he heard lorries somewhere above him he scrambled up the first break he could find in the brambles, without waiting for the next official exit from the trail.

By the time he realised that the path led nowhere in particular, he had already crossed three fields. It seemed best to go on, even though the sound he'd taken for lorries proved, now that he was in the open, to be distant tractors. He didn't think he could find his way back even if he wanted to. Surely he would reach a road eventually.

Once he'd trudged around several more fields he wasn't so sure. He felt sticky, hemmed in by buzzing and green—a fly in a fly-trap. There was nothing else beneath the unrelenting cloudless sky except a bungalow three fields and a copse away to his left. Perhaps he could get a drink there while asking the way to the road.

The bungalow was difficult to reach. Once he had to retrace his journey around three sides of a field, when he'd approached close enough to see that the garden which surrounded the house looked at least as overgrown as the railway had been.

Nevertheless someone was standing in front of the bungalow, knee-deep in grass—a woman with white shoulders, standing quite still. He hurried round the maze of fences and hedges, looking for his way to her. He'd come quite close before he saw how old and pale she was. She was supporting herself with one hand on a disused bird-table, and for a moment he thought the shoulders of her ankle-length caftan were white with droppings, as the table was. He shook his head vigorously, to clear it of the heat, and saw at once that it was long white hair that trailed raggedly over her shoulders, for it stirred a little as she beckoned to him.

At least, he assumed she was beckoning. When he reached her, after he'd lifted the gate clear of the weedy path, she was still flapping her hands, but now to brush away flies, which seemed even fonder of her than they had been of him. Her eyes looked glazed and empty; for a moment he was tempted to sneak away. Then they gazed at him, and they were so pleading that he had to go to her, to see what was wrong.

She must have been pretty when she was younger. Now her long arms and heart-shaped face were bony, the skin withered tight on them, but she might still be attractive if her complexion weren't so grey. Perhaps the heat was affecting her—she was clutching the bird-table as though she would fall if she relaxed her grip—but then why didn't she go in the house? Then he realised that must be why she needed him, for she was pointing shakily with her free hand at the bungalow. Her nails were very long. "Can you get in?" she said.

Her voice was disconcerting: little more than a breath, hardly there at all. No doubt that was also the fault of the heat. "I'll try," he said, and she made for the house at once, past a tangle of roses and a rockery so overgrown it looked like a distant mountain in a jungle.

She had to stop breathlessly before she reached the bungalow. He carried on, since she was pointing feebly at the open kitchen window. As he passed her he found she was doused in perfume, so heavily that even in the open it was cloying. Surely she was in her seventies? He felt shocked, though he knew that was narrow-minded. Perhaps it was the perfume that attracted the flies to her.

The kitchen window was too high for him to reach unaided. Presumably she felt it was safe to leave open while she was away from the house. He went round the far side of the bungalow to the open garage, where a dusty car was baking amid the stink of hot metal and oil. There he found a toolbox, which he dragged round to the window.

When he stood the rectangular box on end and levered himself up, he wasn't sure he could squeeze through. He unhooked the transom and managed to wriggle his shoulders through the opening. He thrust himself forward, the unhooked bar bumping along his spine, until his hips wedged in the frame. He was stuck in midair, above a greyish kitchen that smelled stale, dangling like the string of plastic onions on the far wall. He was unable to drag himself forward or back.

All at once her hands grabbed his thighs, thrusting up towards his buttocks. She must have clambered on the toolbox. No doubt she was anxious to get him into the house, but her sudden desperate strength made him uneasy, not least because he felt almost assaulted. Nevertheless she'd given him the chance to squirm his hips, and he was through. He lowered himself awkwardly, head first, clinging to the edge of the sink while he swung his feet down before letting himself drop.

He made for the door at once. Though the kitchen was almost bare, it smelled worse than stale. In the sink a couple of plates protruded from water the colour of lard, where several dead flies were floating. Flies crawled over smeary milk-bottles on the windowsill or bumbled at the window, as eager to find the way out as he was. He thought he'd found it, but the door was mortise-locked, with a broken key that was jammed in the hole.

He tried to turn the key, until he was sure it was no use. Not only was its stem snapped close to the lock, the key was wedged in the mechanism. He hurried out of the kitchen to the front door, which was in the wall at right angles to the jammed door. The front door was mortise-locked as well.

As he returned to the kitchen window he bumped into the refrigerator. It mustn't have been quite shut, for it swung wide open—not that it mattered, since the refrigerator was empty except for a torpid fly. She must have gone out to buy provisions—presumably her shopping was somewhere in the undergrowth. "Can you tell me where the key is?" he said patiently.

She was clinging to the outer sill, and seemed to be trying to save her breath. From the movements of her lips he gathered she was saying "Look around."

There was nothing in the kitchen cupboards except a few cans of baked beans and meat, their labels peeling. He went back to the front hall, which was cramped, hot, almost airless. Even here he wasn't free of the buzzing of flies, though he couldn't see them. Opposite the front door was a cupboard hiding mops and brushes senile with dust. He opened the fourth door off the hall, into the living-room.

The long room smelled as if it hadn't been opened for months, and looked like a parody of middle-class taste. Silver-plated cannon challenged each other across the length of the pebble-dashed mantelpiece, on either side of which were portraits of the royal family. Here was a cabinet full of dolls of all nations, here was a bookcase of *Reader's Digest* Condensed Books. A personalised bullfight poster was pinned to one wall, a ten-gallon hat to another. With so much in it, it seemed odd that the room felt disused.

He began to search, trying to ignore the noise of flies—it was somewhere further into the house, and sounded disconcertingly like someone groaning. The key wasn't on the obese purple suite or down the sides of the cushions; it wasn't on the small table piled with copies of *Contact,* which for a moment, giggling, he took to be a sexual contact magazine. The key wasn't under the bright green rug, nor on any of the shelves. The dolls gazed unhelpfully at him.

He was holding his breath, both because the unpleasant smell he'd associated with the kitchen seemed even stronger in here and because every one of his movements stirred up dust. The entire room was pale with it; no wonder the dolls' eyelashes were so thick. She must no longer have the energy to clean the house. Now he had finished searching, and it looked as if he would have to venture deeper into the house, where the flies seemed to be so abundant. He was at the far door when he glanced back. Was that the key beneath the pile of magazines?

He had only begun to tug the metal object free when he saw it was a pen, but the magazines were already toppling. As they spilled over the floor, some of them opened at photographs: people tied up tortuously, a plump woman wearing a suspender belt and flourishing a whip.

He suppressed his outrage before it could take hold of him. So much for first impressions! After all, the old lady must have been young once. Really, that thought was rather patronising too—and then he saw it was more than that. One issue of the magazine was no more than a few months old.

He was shrugging to himself, trying to pretend that it didn't matter to him, when a movement made him glance up at the window. The old lady was staring in at him. He leapt away from the table as if she'd caught him stealing, and hurried to the window, displaying his empty hands. Perhaps she hadn't had time to see him at the magazines—it must have taken her a while to struggle through the undergrowth around the house—for she only pointed at the far door and said "Look in there."

Just now he felt uneasy about visiting the bedrooms, however absurd that was. Perhaps he could open the window outside which she was standing, and lift her up—but the window was locked, and no doubt the key was with the one he was searching for. Suppose he didn't find them? Suppose he couldn't get out of the kitchen window? Then she would have to pass the tools up to him, and he would open the house that way. He made himself go to the far door while he was feeling confident. At least he would be away from her gaze, wouldn't have to wonder what she was thinking about him.

Unlike the rest he had seen of the bungalow, the hall beyond the door was dark. He could see the glimmer of three doors and several framed photographs lined up along the walls. The sound of flies was louder, though they didn't seem to be in the hall itself. Now that he was closer they sounded even more like someone groaning feebly, and the rotten smell was stronger too. He held his breath and hoped that he would have to search only the nearest room.

When he shoved its door open, he was relieved to find it was the bathroom—but the state of it was less of a relief. Bath and washbowl were bleached with dust; spiders had caught flies between the taps. Did she wash herself in the kitchen? But then how long had the stagnant water been there? He was searching among the jars of ointments and lotions on the window ledge, all of which were swollen with a fur of talcum powder; he shuddered when it squeaked beneath his fingers. There was no sign of a key.

He hurried out, but halted in the doorway. Opening the door had lightened the hall, so that he could see the photographs. They were wedding photographs, all seven of them. Though the bridegrooms were different—here an airman with a thin moustache, there a portly man who could have been a tycoon or a chef—the bride was the same in every one. It was the woman who owned the house, growing older as the photographs progressed, until in the most recent, where she was holding on to a man with a large nose and a fierce beard, she looked almost as old as she was now.

Bryant found himself smirking uneasily, as if at a joke he didn't quite see but which he felt he should. He glanced quickly at the two remaining doors. One was heavily bolted on the outside—the one beyond which he could hear the intermittent sound like groaning. He chose the other door at once.

It led to the old lady's bedroom. He felt acutely embarrassed even before he saw the brief transparent nightdress on the double bed. Nevertheless he had to brave the room, for the dressing-table was a tangle of bracelets and necklaces, the perfect place to lose keys; the mirror doubled the confusion. Yet as soon as he saw the photographs that were leaning against the mirror, some instinct made him look elsewhere first.

There wasn't much to delay him. He peered under the bed, lifting both sides of the counterpane to be sure. It wasn't until he saw how grey his fingers had become that he realised the bed was thick with dust. Despite the indentation in the middle of the bed, he could only assume that she slept in the bolted room.

He hurried to the dressing-table and began to sort through the jewellery, but as soon as he saw the photographs his fingers grew shaky and awkward. It wasn't simply that the photographs were so sexually explicit—it was that in all of them she was very little younger, if at all, than she was now. Apparently she and her bearded husband both liked to be tied up, and that was only the mildest of their practices. Where was her husband now? Had his predecessors found her too much for them? Bryant had finished searching through the jewellery by now, but he couldn't look away from the photographs, though he found them appalling. He was still staring morbidly when she peered in at him, through the window that was reflected in the mirror.

This time he was sure she knew what he was looking at. More, he was sure he'd been meant to find the photographs. That must be why she'd hurried round the outside of the house to watch. Was she regaining her strength? Certainly she must have had to struggle through a good deal of undergrowth to reach the window in time.

He made for the door without looking at her, and prayed that the key would be in the one remaining room, so that he could get out of the house. He strode across the hall and tugged at the rusty bolt, trying to open the door before his fears grew worse. His struggle with the bolt set off the sound like groaning within the room, but that was no reason for him to expect a torture chamber. Nevertheless, when the bolt slammed all at once out of the socket and the door swung inwards, he staggered back into the hall.

The room didn't contain much: just a bed and the worst of the smell. It was the only room where the curtains were drawn, so that he had to strain his eyes to see that someone was lying on the bed, covered from head to foot with a blanket. A spoon protruded from an open can of meat beside the bed. Apart from a chair and a fitted wardrobe, there was nothing else to see—except that, as far as Bryant could make out in the dusty dimness, the shape on the bed was moving feebly.

All at once he was no longer sure that the groaning had been the sound of flies. Even so, if the old lady had been watching him he might never have been able to step forward. But she couldn't see him, and he had to know. Though he couldn't help tiptoeing, he forced himself to go to the head of the bed.

He wasn't sure if he could lift the blanket, until he looked in the can of meat. At least it seemed to explain the smell, for the can must have been opened months ago. Rather than think about that—indeed, to give himself no time to think—he snatched the blanket away from the head of the figure at once.

Perhaps the groaning had been the sound of flies after all, for they came swarming out, off the body of the bearded man. He had clearly been dead for at least as long as the meat had been opened. Bryant thought sickly that if the sheet had really been moving, it must have been the flies. But there was something worse than that: the scratches on the shoulders of the corpse, the teeth-marks on its neck—for although there was no way of being sure, he had an appalled suspicion that the marks were quite new.

He was stumbling away from the bed—he felt he was drowning in the air that was thick with dust and flies—when the sound recommenced. For a moment he had the thought, so grotesque he was afraid he might both laugh wildly and be sick, that flies were swarming in the corpse's beard. But the sound was groaning after all, for the bearded head was lolling feebly back and forth on the pillow, the tongue was twitching about the greyish lips, the blind eyes were rolling. As the lower half of the body began to jerk weakly but rhythmically, the long-nailed hands tried to reach for whoever was in the room.

Somehow Bryant was outside the door and shoving the bolt home with both hands. His teeth were grinding from the effort to keep his mouth closed, for he didn't know if he was going to vomit or scream. He reeled along the hall, so dizzy he was almost incapable, into the living-room. He was terrified of seeing her at the window, on her way to cut off his escape. He felt so weak he wasn't sure of reaching the kitchen window before she did.

Although he couldn't focus on the living-room, as if it wasn't really there, it seemed to take him minutes to cross. He'd stumbled at last into the front hall when he realised that he needed something on which to stand to reach the transom. He seized the small table, hurling the last of the *Contact* magazines to the floor, and staggered towards the kitchen with it, almost wedging it in the doorway. As he struggled with it, he was almost paralysed by the fear that she would be waiting at the kitchen window.

She wasn't there. She must still be on her way around the outside of the house. As he dropped the table beneath the window, Bryant saw the broken key in the mortise lock. Had someone else—perhaps the bearded man—broken it while trying to escape? It didn't matter, he mustn't start thinking of escapes that had failed. But it looked as if he would have to, for he could see at once that he couldn't reach the transom.

He tried once, desperately, to be sure. The table was too low, the narrow sill was too high. Though he could wedge one foot on the sill, the angle was wrong for him to squeeze his shoulders through the window. He would certainly be stuck when she came to find him. Perhaps if he dragged a chair through from the living-room—but he had only just stepped down, almost falling to his knees, when he heard her opening the front door with the key she had had all the time.

His fury at being trapped was so intense that it nearly blotted out his panic. She had only wanted to trick him into the house. By God, he'd fight her for the key if he had to, especially now that she was relocking the front door. All at once he was stumbling wildly towards the hall, for he was terrified that she would unbolt the bedroom and let out the thing in the bed. But when he threw open the kitchen door, what confronted him was far worse.

She stood in the living-room doorway, waiting for him. Her caftan lay crumpled on the hall floor. She was naked, and at last he could see how grey and shrivelled she was—just like the bearded man. She was no longer troubling to brush off the flies, a couple of which were crawling in and out of her mouth. At last, too late, he realised that her perfume had not been attracting the flies at all. It had been meant to conceal the smell that was attracting them—the smell of death.

She flung the key behind her, a new move in her game. He would have died rather than try to retrieve it, for then he would have had to touch her. He backed into the kitchen, looking frantically for something he could use to smash the window. Perhaps he was incapable of seeing it, for his mind seemed paralysed by the sight of her. Now she was moving as fast as he was, coming after him with her long arms outstretched, her grey breasts flapping. She was licking her lips as best she could, relishing his terror. Of course, that was why she'd made him go through the entire house. He knew that her energy came from her hunger for him.

It was a fly—the only one in the kitchen that hadn't alighted on her—which drew his gaze to the empty bottles on the windowsill. He'd known all the time they were there, but panic was dulling his mind. He grabbed the nearest bottle, though his sweat and the slime of milk made it almost too slippery to hold. At least it felt reassuringly solid, if anything could be reassuring now. He swung it with all his force at the centre of the window. But it was the bottle which broke.

He could hear himself screaming—he didn't know if it was with rage or terror—as he rushed towards her, brandishing the remains of the bottle to keep her away until he reached the door. Her smile, distorted but gleeful, had robbed him of the last traces of restraint, and there was only the instinct to survive. But her smile widened as she saw the jagged glass—indeed, her smile looked quite capable of collapsing her face. She lurched straight into his path, her arms wide.

He closed his eyes and stabbed. Though her skin was tougher than he'd expected, he felt it puncture drily, again and again. She was thrusting herself onto the glass, panting and squealing like a pig. He was slashing desperately now, for the smell was growing worse.

All at once she fell, rattling on the linoleum. For a moment he was terrified that she would seize his legs and drag him down on her. He fled, kicking out blindly, before he dared open his eyes. The key—where was the key? He hadn't seen where she had thrown it. He was almost weeping as he dodged about the living-room, for he could hear her moving feebly in the kitchen. But there was the key, almost concealed down the side of a chair.

As he reached the front door he had a last terrible thought. Suppose this key broke too? Suppose that was part of her game? He forced himself to insert it carefully, though his fingers were shaking so badly he could hardly keep hold of it at all. It wouldn't turn. It would—he had been trying to turn it the wrong way. One easy turn, and the door swung open. He was so insanely grateful that he almost neglected to lock it behind him.

He flung the key as far as he could and stood in the overgrown garden, retching for breath. He'd forgotten that there were such things as trees, flowers, fields, the open sky. Yet just now the scent of flowers was sickening, and he couldn't bear the sound of flies. He had to get away from the bungalow and then from the countryside—but there wasn't a road in sight, and the only path he knew led back towards the Wirral Way. He wasn't concerned about returning to the nature trail, but the route back would lead him past the kitchen window. It took him a long time to move, and then it was because he was more afraid to linger near the house.

When he reached the window, he tried to run while tiptoeing. If only he dared turn his face away! He was almost past before he heard a scrabbling beyond the window. The remains of her hands appeared on the sill, and then her head lolled into view. Her eyes gleamed brightly as the shards of glass that protruded from her face. She gazed up at him, smiling raggedly and pleading. As he backed away, floundering through the undergrowth, he saw that she was mouthing jerkily. "Again," she said.

Just Waiting

Fifty years later he went back. He'd been through school and university, he'd begun to write a novel at the end of a year spent searching for jobs, and it had been hailed as one of the greatest books ever written about childhood, had never been out of print since. He'd been married and divorced before they had flown him to Hollywood to write the screenplay of his novel, he'd had a stormy affair with an actress whose boyfriend had sent a limousine and two large monosyllabic men in grey suits to see him off home to England when the screenplay had been taken over by two members of the Writers Guild. He'd written two more books which had been respectfully received and had sold moderately well, he'd once spent a night in a Cornish hotel room with twin teenage girls, and increasingly none of this mattered: nothing stayed with him except, more and more vividly, that day in the forest fifty years ago.

There were few cars parked on the forest road today, and none in the parking areas. He parked near the start of the signposted walk, then sat in the car. He had never really looked at a road before, never noticed how much the camber curved; it looked like a huge pipe almost buried in the earth, its surface bare as the trees, not a soul or a vehicle in sight. The wintry air seeped into the car and set him shivering. He made himself get out, the gold weighing down the pockets of his heavy coat, and step onto the sandstone path.

It sloped down at once. A bird flew clattering out of a tree, then the silence closed in. Branches gleamed against the pale-blue cloudless sky, lingering raindrops glittered on the grass that bordered the path. A lorry rumbled by above him, its sound already muffled. When he looked back he could no longer see his car.

The path curved, curved again. The ingots dragged at his pockets, bruised his hips. He hadn't realised gold weighed so much, or, he thought wryly, that it would be so complicated to purchase. He could only trust his instinct that it would help.

His feet and legs were aching. Hollywood and his Cornish night seemed less than words. Sunlight streaked through dazzling branches and broke raindrops into rainbows, shone in the mud of trails that looked like paths between the trees. He would have to follow one of those trails, if he could remember which, but how would he be able to keep his footing in all that mud? He made himself limp onward, searching for landmarks.

Soon he was deep in the forest. If there was traffic on the road, it was beyond his hearing. Everywhere trails led into darkness that was a maze of trees. The sound of wind in the trees felt like sleep. Now he was trudging in search of somewhere to sit down, and so he almost missed the tree that looked like an arch.

It must have looked more like an arch when he was ten years old and could hide in the arched hollow of the trunk. For a moment he felt as if the recognition would be too much for his heart. He stooped and peered in, then he squeezed himself into the hollow, his bones creaking.

It was slippery under his hands, and smelled of moss and moist wood. The ingots swung his pockets and thumped the wooden shell. He couldn't stand upright, couldn't turn. He hadn't turned then, either—he'd stood with his face to the cool woody dimness and listened to his parents passing by. He hadn't been wishing anything, he told himself fiercely; he had simply been pretending he was alone in the forest, just to make the forest into an adventure for a few minutes. Now, as he struggled to stoop out of the hollow, he could hear them calling to him. "Don't lag, Ian," his father shouted, so loud that someone in the forest called "Hello?" and his mother called more gently "We don't want you getting lost."

It was midsummer. The sun stood directly over the path, however much the path curved; he could smell the sandstone baking. The masses of foliage blazed so brightly that, whatever their tree, they seemed to be a single incandescent shade of green. His feet were aching, then and now. "Can't we have our picnic yet?" he pleaded as he ran to his parents, bruising his soles. "Can't I have a drink?"

"We're all thirsty, not just you." His father frowned a warning not to argue; sweat sparkled in his bristly moustache. "I'm not unpacking until we get to the picnic area. Your mother wants to sit down."

Ian's mother flapped a handful of her summer dress, through which he could see the lacy outlines of her underwear, to cool herself. "I don't mind sitting on the grass if you want a rest, Ian," she said.

"Good God, you'd think we'd been walking all day," his father said, which Ian thought they had. "Rest and drink when we get to the tables. I never asked for rest when I was his age, and I know what I'd have got if I had."

"It's the school holidays," she said, that rusty edge to her voice. "You aren't teaching now."

"I'm always teaching, and don't you forget it."

Ian wondered which of them that was meant for, especially when his mother said under her breath "I wish he could just have a normal upbringing, how I wish. . . ." He held hands with both of them and marched along for a few hundred yards. Had he grown bored then, or had he felt their tension passing back and forth through him? He remembered only running ahead until his father called "Hang on, old fellow. Let's find your mother some shade."

Ian turned from the path that seemed to curve away in the wrong direction forever. His father was pointing into the trees. "The tables should be along here," he said.

"Don't get us lost on my account," Ian's mother protested.

His father hitched up his knapsack and nodded curtly at it over his shoulder. "I could do with some shade myself."

"I'll carry something if you like. I did make the picnic, you know."

His father turned his back on that and strode onto the path between the trees, his shorts flapping, the black hairs on his legs glinting as the sunlight caught them a last time at the edge of the shade. As soon as Ian followed his mother under the trees, he realised he had already been hearing the stream.

He could hear it now. The sandstone path that was supposed to lead back to its starting point curved away in the wrong direction ahead, not forever but as far as the eye could see, and there on the left was the path his father had taken. It looked dark and cold and treacherous, shifty with dim shadows. He listened while the wind and the trees grew still. There was no sound at all in the woods, not a bird's or a footstep. He had to take a breath that made his head swim before he could step between the trees.

"We can't get lost so long as we can hear the stream," his father said, as if that should be obvious. His path had followed the stream until the sandstone path was well out of sight and hearing, and then it had turned into a maze of trails, which looked like paths for long enough to be confusing. Ian sensed his mother's nervousness as they strayed away from the stream, among trees that made it seem there were no paths at all. "Isn't that the picnic place?" he said suddenly, and ran ahead, dodging trees and undergrowth. The muffled light beneath the leaves was growing dimmer, so that he was in the glade and almost at the standing shape before he realised it was not a table. "Watch out, Ian!" his mother cried.

He could hear her voice now, in the midst of his laborious breathing. He wasn't sure if this was the glade. Despite the bareness of the trees, it seemed shadowy and chill as he stepped out beneath the patch of blue sky. He was shivering violently, even though the glade looked much like any other: a dip in the ground strewn with fallen leaves and a few scraps of rubble—and then he saw the word that was crudely carved on one of the stones, almost obscured by dripping moss: FEED.

It was enough—too much. The other words must be among the rubble that had been used to stuff up the hole. He fumbled hastily in his pockets and dropped the ingots beside the word, then he squeezed his eyes shut and wished. He kept them closed as long as he dared, until he had to glance at the trees. They looked even thinner than he remembered: how could they conceal anything? He made himself lower his gaze, hoping, almost giving in to the temptation to risk a second wish. The ingots were still there.

He'd done what he could. He shouldn't have expected proof, not yet, perhaps not while he was alive. A branch creaked, or a footfall, one of many, the only one that had made a sound. He glanced round wildly and hurried back the way he'd come, while he still remembered which way that was. He mustn't hesitate now, mustn't think until he was on the sandstone path.

He didn't know what made him look back as he reached the edge of the glade: certainly nothing he'd heard. He blinked, he drew a shuddering breath, he seized a tree twice the width of his hand and peered until his eyes stung. He could see the rubble, the mossy word, and even the droplets of water gleaming in it—but the gold was gone.

He clung to the tree with both hands for support. So it was all true: everything he'd tried for fifty years to dismiss as a nightmare, a childish version of what he'd grown to hope had happened, was true after all. He struggled not to think as he waited to be able to retreat, fought not to wonder what might be under the leaves, down there in the dark.

It was a well. He'd realised that before his mother caught his arm to save him from falling in, as if he would have been so babyish. He read the words chipped out of stones that were part of the crumbling circular rim: FEED ME A WISH. "They must mean 'feed me and wish,' " his mother said, though Ian didn't think there was space for any more letters. "You're supposed to throw some money in."

He leaned over the rim as she held on to his arm. Someone must have made a wish already, for there were several round gleams far down in the dark that smelled of cold and decay, too far for even the sunlight poking through the leaves overhead to reach. She pulled him back and took out her knitted purse. "Here you are," she said, giving him a tarnished penny. "Make a wish."

"I'll reimburse you when we get back to the car," his father told her, join-ing them as Ian craned over the rim. He couldn't see the round gleams now. His mother gripped the back of his trousers as he stretched his arm out and let go of the coin, then closed his eyes at once.

He didn't want anything for himself except for his parents to stop fight-ing, but he didn't know what to wish in order to bring that about. He thought of asking that they should have their deepest wishes, but wouldn't that be at least two? He tried to make up his mind who deserved a wish more or whose wish would be more helpful, then he wondered if he'd already had his wish while he was thinking. He opened his eyes, as if that might help, and thought he saw the coin still falling, within reach if he craned over the rim, still available to be taken back. His mother pulled at him, and the coin had gone. He heard a plop like breath rising to the surface of water or mud.

"Step out now, we must be nearly there," his father said, taking his mother's arm, and frowned back at Ian. "I've told you once about lagging. Don't try my patience, I'm warning you."

Ian ran after them before he'd had time to make sure whether the stones with the words were as loose as they looked, whether they could be placed along the rim in a different order. He wasn't sure now, as he shoved himself away from the glade where the ingots no longer were; he didn't want to be. He was suddenly terrified that he had already lost his way, that he would wander through the winter forest until he strayed onto the path he'd taken that day with his parents, until he ended up where it led, as the short day grew dark. He couldn't shake off his terror even when he stumbled back onto the sandstone path, not until he was in the car, gripping the wheel that his hands were shaking, sitting and praying he would regain control of him-self in time to be able to drive out of the forest before nightfall. He mustn't wonder if the gold had brought his wish. He mightn't know until he died, and perhaps not even then.

His father never looked back, not even when the trail he was following out of the glade forked. He chose the left-hand path, which was wider. It continued to be wider until Ian's mother began to glance about as if she could see something besides trees, or wished she could. "Keep up," she said sharply to Ian, and to his father "I'm cold."

"We must be near the stream, that's all." His father spoke as though he could see the stream among the crowding trees, which were so close now that whenever you moved it seemed that someone was moving with you, from tree to tree. When Ian looked back he couldn't see where the path had been wider. He didn't want his mother to notice that; it would only make her more nervous and start another argument. He struggled through a tangle of undergrowth and ran ahead. "Where do you think you're—" his father demanded. "All right. Stay there."

His change of tone made Ian peer ahead. He'd almost reached another glade, but that was no reason for his father to sound as if he'd meant to come here all along; there was nothing in the glade but several heaps of dead branches. He took a few steps forward to clear his eyes of sunlight, and saw that he must have been mistaken. There were several picnic tables and benches, and no heaps of branches after all.

He cried out, for his father had caught up with him silently and was digging his fingers into Ian's shoulder, bruising it. "I told you to stay where you were."

His mother winced and took Ian's hand to lead him to a table. "I won't let him do that again," she murmured. "He may do it to his pupils at school, but I won't have him doing it to you."

Ian didn't quite believe she would be able to stop his father, especially not when his father dumped the knapsack on the table in front of her and sat down, folding his arms. Ian could feel an argument threatening. He moved away to see what was beyond the glade.

There was another picnic area. He could just see a family at a table in the distance; a boy and a girl and their parents, he thought. Perhaps he could play with the children later. He was wondering why their picnic table looked more like one than his, when his father shouted "Come back here and sit down. You have made enough fuss about wanting a drink."

Ian dawdled towards the table, for the argument was starting: it made the glade seem smaller. "You expect to be waited on, do you?" his mother was saying.

"I did the carrying, didn't I?" his father retorted. Both of them stared at the knapsack, until at last his mother sighed and undid the straps to take out the cups and the bottle of lemonade. She sipped hers as his father emptied his cup in four equal swallows punctuated by deep breaths. Ian gulped his and gasped. "Please may I have some more?"

His mother shared what was left in the bottle between the three cups and reached in the knapsack, then stared in. "I'm afraid that's all we have to drink," she said, as if she couldn't believe it herself.

"You could have fooled me." His father squirmed his shoulders ostentatiously. "What the devil have I been carrying?"

She began to unpack the containers of food, cold chicken and salad and coleslaw. Ian realised what was odd about the table: it was too clean for an outdoor table, it looked like. . . . His mother was peering into the knapsack. "We'll have to eat with our fingers," she said. "I didn't bring the plates and cutlery."

"What do you think we are, savages?" His father glared about at the trees, as if someone might see him eating that way. "How can we eat coleslaw with our fingers? I've never heard such nonsense in my life."

"I'm surprised I packed anything at all," she cried, "you've got me so distracted."

It was like a table in a café, Ian thought, and looked up as someone came into the glade. At least now his parents wouldn't be able to argue; they never did in front of people. For a moment, until he blinked and sat aside out of the sunlight, he had the impression that the eyes of the two figures were perfectly circular.

The two men were heading straight for the table, purposefully. They were dressed from head to foot in black. At first he thought they were some kind of police, coming to tell his parents they weren't supposed to sit here, and then he almost laughed, realising what their black uniform meant. His father had realised too. "I'm afraid we've brought our own food," he said brusquely.

The first waiter shrugged and smiled. His lips in his pale thin face were almost white, and very wide. He made a gesture at the table, and the other waiter went away, returning almost at once with cutlery and plates. He was coming from the direction of the well, where the trees were thickest and the stray beam of sunlight had dazzled Ian. Ian wondered what else he'd failed to notice in passing.

The waiter who'd shrugged opened the containers of food and served it onto the plates. Ian glimpsed a pattern on the china, but the plates were covered before he could make out what it was. "This is more like it," his father said, and his mother pursed her lips.

When Ian reached to pick up a chicken leg, his father slapped his hand down. "You've a knife and fork. Use them."

"Oh, *really*," Ian's mother said.

"Yes?" his father demanded, as if he were speaking to a child at school.

She stared at him until he looked away, at the food he was brandishing on his fork. They couldn't argue in front of the waiters, Ian thought, but feeling them argue silently was worse. He set about carving his chicken leg. The knife passed easily through the meat and scraped the bone. "That's too sharp for him," his mother said. "Have you another knife?"

The waiter shook his head and spread his hands. His palms were very smooth and pale. "Just be careful then, Ian," she said anxiously.

His father tipped his head back to drain the last trickle of lemonade, and the other waiter came over. Ian hadn't realised he had slipped away, let alone where. He was carrying an uncorked wine bottle, from which he filled Ian's father's cup without being asked. "Well, since you've opened it," Ian's father said, sounding ready to argue the price.

The waiter filled Ian's mother's cup and came to him. "Not too much for him," she said.

"Nor for her either," his father said, having rolled a sip around his mouth and frowned, then shrugged approval, "since she's driving."

Ian took a mouthful to distract himself. It was distracting enough: it tasted rusty, and too thick. He couldn't swallow. He turned away from his father and spat the mouthful on the grass, and saw that the waiters were barefoot. "You little savage," his father said in a low hateful voice.

"Leave him alone. He shouldn't have been given any."

To add to Ian's confusion, both waiters were nodding, agreeing with her. Their feet looked thin as bunches of twigs, and appeared to be gripping the earth; he saw grass and soil squeezing up between the long knuckly toes. He didn't want to stay near them or near his parents, whose disagreements felt like thunder. "I want a proper picnic," he complained. "I want to run around like I used to."

"Just don't get lost," his mother said, a moment before his father said "Do as you're told and stay where you are."

His mother turned to the waiters. "You don't mind if he stretches his legs, do you?"

They smiled and spread their hands. Their mouths looked even wider and paler, and Ian could see no lines on the palms of their hands. "Just you move from this table before you're told to," his father said, "and we'll see how you like the belt when you get home."

He *could* get up, his mother had said. He gobbled coleslaw, since he couldn't eat that away from the table, and peered at the fragment of pattern he'd uncovered on the plate. "You won't lay a finger on him," his mother had whispered.

His father took a swallow that made his lips redder and thumped his cup on the table. His bare arm lay beside a knife in the shaft of sunlight, the blade and his wiry hairs gleaming. "You've just earned him a few extra with the belt if he doesn't do as he's told."

"Mummy said I could," Ian said, and grabbed the chicken leg from his plate as he stood up. His father tried to seize him, but the drink must have made him sleepy, for he lolled over the table, shaking his head. "Come here to me," he said in a slurred voice as Ian dodged out of reach, having just glimpsed more of the pattern on the plate. It looked like something large trying to escape as it was chopped up. He didn't want to stay near that, or near his parents, or near the waiters with their silent smiles. Perhaps the waiters didn't speak English. He took a bite of the chicken leg as he ran towards the children, who had left the distant table and were playing with a striped ball.

He looked back once. A waiter stood behind each of his parents: waiting to be paid, or to clear the table? They must be impatient for their toes to have been scratching at the earth like that. His father was propping his chin on his hands as Ian's mother stared at him across the table, which looked oddly ramshackle now, more like a heap of branches.

Ian ran into the clearing where the children were. "Can I play with you?"

The girl gave a small cry of surprise. "Where did you come from?" the boy demanded.

"Just over there." Ian turned and pointed, and found he couldn't see his parents. For a moment he wanted to giggle at how he must have surprised the children, then suddenly he felt lost, abandoned, afraid for his mother, and his father too. He backed away as the children stared at him, then he whirled and ran.

The boy's name was Neville; his sister's was Annette. Their parents were the kindest people he had ever known—but he hadn't wished for them, he told himself fiercely as he started the car now that his hands were under control; he didn't know what he had wished at the well. Surely his mother had just been drunk, she and his father must have got lost and gone back to the car on the road through the forest to get help in finding Ian, only for her to lose control almost as soon as she'd started driving.

If only the car and its contents hadn't burned so thoroughly that nobody could tell how his parents had died! He might not have felt compelled to wish on the gold that what he thought he'd seen couldn't have happened, had never happened: the trees separating ahead of him as he ran, then somehow blotting out that last glimpse of his mother scraping at her plate, more and more quickly, staring at the pattern she'd uncovered and rising to her feet, one hand pressed to her lips as she shook his father with the other, shook his shoulder desperately to rouse him, as the thin figures opened their growing mouths and they and the trees closed in.

Seeing the World

At first Angela thought it was a shadow. The car was through the gates before she wondered how a shadow could surround a house. She craned over the garden wall as Richard parked the car. It was a ditch, no doubt some trick the Hodges had picked up in Italy, something to do with their gardening. "They're back," she murmured when Richard had pulled down the door of the garage.

"Saints preserve us, another dead evening," he said, and she had to hush him, for the Hodges were sitting in their lounge and had grinned out at the clatter of the door.

All the same, the Hodges seemed to have even less regard than usual for other people's feelings. During the night she was wakened by Mozart's Fortieth, to which the conductor had added the rhythm section Mozart had neglected to include. Richard mumbled and thrashed in slow motion as she went to the window. An August dawn glimmered on the Hodges' gnomes, and beyond them in the lounge the Hodges were sitting quite as stonily. She might have shouted but for waking Richard. Stiff with the dawn chill, she limped back to bed.

She listened to the silence between movements and wondered if this time they might give the rest of the symphony a chance. No, here came the first movement again, reminding her of the night the Hodges had come over, when she and Richard had performed a Haydn sonata. "I haven't gone into Haydn," Harry Hodge had declared, wriggling his eyebrows. "Get it? Gone into hidin'." She sighed and turned over and remembered the week she and Richard had just spent on the waterways, fields and grassy banks flowing by like Delius, a landscape they had hardly boarded all week, preferring to let the villages remain untouched images of villages. Before the Mozart had played through a third time she was asleep.

Most of the next day was given over to violin lessons, her pupils making up for the lost week. By the time Richard came home from lecturing, she had dinner almost ready. Afterwards they sat sipping the last of the wine as evening settled on the long gardens. Richard went to the piano and played *La*

Cathédrale Engloutie, and the last tolling of the drowned cathedral was fading when someone knocked slowly at the front door.

It was Harry Hodge. He looked less bronzed by the Mediterranean sun than made-up, rather patchily. "The slides are ready," he said through his fixed smile. "Can you come now?"

"Right now? It really is quite late." Richard wasn't hiding his resentment, whether at Hodge's assumption that he need only call for them to come— not so much an invitation anymore as a summons—or at the way Hodge must have waited outside until he thought the Debussy had gone on long enough. "Oh, very well," Richard said. "Provided there aren't too many."

He must have shared Angela's thought: best to get it over with, the sooner the better. None of their neighbours bothered with the Hodges. Harry Hodge looked stiff, and thinner than when he'd gone away. "Aren't you feeling well?" she asked, concerned.

"Just all that walking and pushing the mother-in-law."

He was wearing stained outdoor clothes. He must have been gardening; he always was. He looked ready to wait for them to join him, until Richard said firmly "We won't be long."

They had another drink first, since the Hodges never offered. "Don't wake me unless I snore," Richard muttered as they ventured up the Hodges' path, past gnomes of several nations, souvenirs of previous holidays. It must be the gathering night that made the ditch appear deeper and wider. The ditch reminded her of the basement where Harry developed his slides. She was glad their house had no basement: she didn't like dark places.

When Harry opened the door, he looked as if he hadn't stopped smiling. "Glad you could come," he said, so tonelessly that at first Angela heard it as a question she was tempted to answer truthfully. If he was exhausted, he shouldn't have been so eager to have them round. They followed him down the dark hall into the lounge.

Only the wall lights were on. Most of the light surrounded souvenirs—a pink Notre Dame with a clock in place of a rose window on the mantelpiece, a plaster bull on top of the gas fire, matches stuck in its back like picadors' lances—and Deirdre Hodge and her mother. The women sat facing the screen on the wall, and Angela faltered in the doorway, wondering what was wrong. Of course, they must have been gardening too; they were still wearing outdoor clothes, and she could smell earth. Deirdre's mother must rather have been supervising, since much of the time she had to be pushed in a wheelchair.

"There you are," Deirdre said in greeting, and after some thought her mother said "Aye, there they are all right." Their smiles looked even more determined than Harry's. Richard and Angela took their places on the settee, smiling; Angela for one felt as if she was expected to smile rather than talk. Eventually Richard said "How was Italy?"

By now that form of question was a private joke, a way of making their visits to the Hodges less burdensome: half the joke consisted of anticipating the answer. Germany had been "like dolls' houses"; Spain was summed up by "good fish and chips"; France had prompted only "They'll eat anything." Now Deirdre smiled and smiled and eventually said "Nice ice creams."

"And how did you like it, Mrs. . . . Mrs. . . . ?" They had never learned the mother's name, and she was too busy smiling and nodding to tell them now. Smiling must be less exhausting than speaking. Perhaps at least that meant the visitors wouldn't be expected to reply to every remark—they always were, everything would stop until they had—but Angela was wondering what else besides exhaustion was wrong with the two women, what else she'd noticed and couldn't now recall, when Harry switched off the lights.

A sound distracted her from trying to recall, in the silence that seemed part of the dark. A crowd or a choir on television, she decided quickly—it sounded unreal enough—and went back to straining her memory. Harry limped behind the women and started the slide projector.

Its humming blotted out the other sound. She didn't think that was on television after all; the nearest houses were too distant for their sets to be heard. Perhaps a whim of the wind was carrying sounds of a football match or a fair, except that there was no wind, but in any case what did it matter? "Here we are in Italy," Harry said.

He pronounced it "Eyetally," lingeringly. They could just about deduce that it was, from one random word of a notice in the airport terminal where the Hodges were posing stiffly, smiling, out of focus, while a porter with a baggage trolley tried to gesticulate them out of the way. Presumably his Italian had failed, since they understood hardly a word of the language. After a few minutes Richard sighed, realising that nothing but a comment would get rid of the slide. "One day we'd like to go. We're very fond of Italian opera."

"You'd like it," Deirdre said, and the visitors steeled themselves for Harry's automatic rejoinder: "It you'd like." "Ooh, he's a one," Deirdre's mother squealed, as she always did, and began to sing "Funiculì, Funiculà." She seemed to know only the title, to which she applied various melodies for several minutes. "You never go anywhere much, do you?" Deirdre said.

"I'd hardly say that," Richard retorted, so sharply that Angela squeezed his hand.

"You couldn't say you've seen the world. Nowhere outside England. It's a good thing you came tonight," Deirdre said.

Angela wouldn't have called the slides seeing the world, nor seeing much of anything. A pale blob which she assumed to be a scoopful of the nice ice cream proved to be St Peter's at night; Venice was light glaring from a canal and blinding the lens. "That's impressionistic," she had to say to move St Peter's and "Was it very sunny?" to shift Venice. She felt as if she were sinking under the weight of so much banality, the Hodges' and now hers. Here were the Hodges posing against a flaking life-size fresco, Deirdre couldn't remember where, and here was the Tower of Pisa, righted at last by the camera angle. Angela thought that joke was intentional until Deirdre said "Oh, it hasn't come out. Get on to the proper ones."

If she called the next slide proper, Angela couldn't see why. It was so dark that at first she thought there was no slide at all. Gradually she made out Deirdre, wheeling her mother down what appeared to be a tunnel. "That's us in the catacombs," Deirdre said with what sounded like pride.

For some reason the darkness emphasised the smell of earth. In the projector's glow, most of which nestled under Harry's chin, Angela could just make out the women in front of the screen. Something about the way they were sitting: that was what she'd noticed subconsciously, but again the sound beneath the projector's hum distracted her, now that it was audible once more. "Now we go down," Deirdre said.

Harry changed the slide at once. At least they were no longer waiting for responses. The next slide was even darker, and both Angela and Richard were leaning forward, trying to distinguish who the figure with the outstretched arms was and whether it was shouting or grimacing, when Harry said "What do you do when the cat starts moulting?"

They sat back, for he'd removed the slide. "I've no idea," Richard said.

"Give the cat a comb."

"Ooh, he's a one, isn't he," Deirdre's mother shrieked, then made a sound to greet the next slide. "This is where we thought we were lost," Deirdre said.

This time Angela could have wished the slide were darker. There was no mistaking the fear in Deirdre's face and her mother's as they turned to stare back beyond Harry and the camera. Was somebody behind him, holding the torch which cast Harry's malformed shadow over them? "Get it?" he said. "Cat a comb."

Angela wondered if there was any experience they wouldn't reduce to banality. At least there weren't many more slides in the magazine. She glanced at the floor to rest her eyes, and thought she knew where the sound of many voices was coming from. "Did you leave a radio on in the basement?"

"No." All the same, Harry seemed suddenly distracted. "Quick," Deirdre said, "or we won't have time."

Time before what? If they were ready for bed, they had only to say. The next slide jerked into view, so shakily that for a moment Angela thought the street beyond the gap in the curtains had jerked. All three Hodges were on this slide, between two ranks of figures. "They're just like us really," Deirdre said, "when you get to know them."

She must mean Italians, Angela thought, not the ranks of leathery figures baring their teeth and their ribs. Their guide must have taken the photograph, of course. "You managed to make yourself understood enough to be shown the way out then," she said.

"Once you go deep enough," Harry said, "it comes out wherever you want it to."

It was the manner—offhand, unimpressed—as much as his words that made her feel she'd misheard him. "When you've been down there long enough," Deirdre corrected him as if that helped.

Before Angela could demand to know what they were talking about, the last slide clicked into place. She sucked in her breath but managed not to cry out, for the figure could scarcely be posing for the camera, reaching out the stumps of its fingers; it could hardly do anything other than grin with what remained of its face. "There he is. We didn't take as long as him," Deirdre said with an embarrassed giggle. "You don't need to. Just long enough to make your exit," she explained, and the slide left the screen a moment before Harry switched off the projector.

In the dark Angela could still see the fixed grin breaking through the face. She knew without being able to see that the Hodges hadn't stopped smiling since Harry had opened the door. At last she realised what she'd seen: Deirdre and her mother, she was certain, were sitting exactly as they had been when their record had wakened her—as they had been when she and Richard had come home. "We thought of you," Harry said. "We knew you couldn't afford to go places. That's why we came back."

She found Richard's hand in the dark and tugged at it, trying to tell him both to leave quickly and to say nothing. "You'll like it," Deirdre said.

"It you'll like," Harry agreed, and as Angela pulled Richard to his feet and put her free hand over his mouth to stifle his protests, Deirdre's mother said "Takes a bit of getting used to, that's all."

For a moment Angela thought, in the midst of her struggle with panic, that Harry had put on another slide, then that the street had jerked. It was neither: of course the street hadn't moved. "I hope you'll excuse us if we go now," Richard said, pulling her hand away from his mouth, but it didn't matter, the Hodges couldn't move fast, she was sure of that much. She'd dragged him as far as the hall when the chanting under the house swelled up triumphantly, and so did the smell of earth from the ditch that was more than a ditch. Without further ado, the house began to sink.

Old Clothes

"Come on, lad, let's be having you," Charlie shouted, and let the back of the van down with a clatter that sent pigeons flying from the cracked roadway. "Anyone'd think it were Fort Knox."

"Don't call me lad," Eric muttered, shoving all his weight against the door of the house. The July sunlight on his shoulders felt like a weight too, but the door didn't budge, not until Charlie stumped along the weedy path and threw his weight against the door. It cracked, then stuttered inwards, crumpling bills and final reminders and circulars and advertising newspapers, which trailed along the greyish hall towards the ragged staircase. "Go on, lad," Charlie urged. "What are you waiting for?"

"Christmas. Christmas, and the fairy to come off the tree and give me a million pounds." Eric was waiting for his eyes to adjust, that was all. Specks of light, dust that had found sunlight, rose above the stairs, but the house seemed darker than it ought to be.

Charlie gave him a push. "Don't be going to sleep, lad. Time enough for a rest when we've cleared the house."

I'm forty years old, Eric snarled inside himself, and I don't like being pushed. "Try finding someone else who'll put up with you," he muttered as Charlie threw open the first door. "We'll start in here," Charlie said.

The room didn't look as if it had been cleaned for months. Plants with grey fur wilted in pots; cobwebs hung beneath the round table, draped the lopsided chairs. Nevertheless, someone had been in the house since the old lady had died, for the drawers of a bureau had been pulled out, spilling letters. Charlie stuffed the letters into the drawers. "Take the chairs," he said over his shoulder. "You can manage them."

Eric resented being made to feel he'd said he couldn't. By the time he'd finished shifting the chairs, he was wearing grey gloves and a wig. Charlie stared at him as if he'd made a stupid joke. "Give us a hand with the table," he growled.

They had to dance back and forth along the hall and up and down the stairs. As they manhandled the table into the sunlight, Eric thought he glimpsed a pattern round the edge, of pairs of hands or the prints of hands. "Get a move on, lad," Charlie panted, glancing at the darkening sky.

The old lady's relatives must have kicked the papers along the hall, Eric decided as he stooped to a wad of letters that had been wedged behind the bureau. They were thank-you letters, one from a woman who lived a few streets away from Eric: thank you for putting me in touch with my father; thank you, said another, for my wife, for my son. . . . "Never mind prying," Charlie said. "I don't care if she's dead, some things are private."

They were starting on the dining-room—spiders fled when Charlie lifted the fat tablecloth—before Eric realised what the letters meant. "What was she, anyway? You never said."

"You never bloody asked, lad. What difference does it make? One of them spiritists, if it's any of your business."

Perhaps it offended him, or maybe he felt that it should, as Eric's father had after Eric's mother died. Eric remembered his father on his knees in church and at bedtime, praying for a sign. They were both dead now, but he'd never felt tempted to contact them, had never been interested in that kind of thing. All the same, he couldn't help peering into each room as he followed Charlie, couldn't help feeling like an intruder as they stripped the beds and unbolted the frames. Venturing into her bedroom, he almost expected to see her or her shape made of dust in the bed. He flinched when something moved, scraping, behind him. It was a raincoat hanging on the door.

The sky was darker when they carried out the bed. By the time they took out the wardrobe, the sky was black. The downpour began as they were about to clear the attic, and so they sat in the cab of the van and ate the sandwiches Charlie's wife had made. She always made half for Eric since she'd taken pity on him, though Charlie gave him less than half. They drank coffee from Charlie's flask, too sweet for Eric's taste, and then Charlie said "Can't wait all day. Back to work."

The grey road looked like a river of tar now, jumping with rain. Charlie shrugged into his plastic raincoat; too bad for Eric if he hadn't brought one. Swallowing the words he would have liked to say, Eric ran out of the cab and into the house. Hall and rooms were squirming with large vague shadows of rain; he thought of the ectoplasm mediums were supposed to ooze, but he grabbed the raincoat from the hook on the bedroom door.

A few shakes and the dust almost blinded him. At least the coat was wearable. He fumbled in the pockets to make sure they were empty. A hint of clamminess in the sleeves made him shiver, but it had gone by the time he'd buttoned the coat on the man's side. Charlie watched him from the bedroom doorway with a kind of dull contempt. "My God, what do you look like."

Eric didn't care, or so he told himself. They cleared the attic. Then he slammed the door of the house. For a moment he thought he heard movement inside; it must be the papers flapping. Charlie was already starting the van, and he had to run.

Charlie left him in the drizzle while he drove along the coast to sell the vanload of furniture and ornaments. Eric strolled around town, reading job advertisements that always asked for people younger or more qualified than he was; then he climbed the streets above the factories that nobody wanted to rent, to his flat.

He reached in the right-hand pocket of the raincoat without thinking. Of course his key wasn't in there, but neither was the pocket empty, though the object was only a flower, easy enough to overlook. Nevertheless, he'd never seen a flower like it, especially one looking so fresh when it must have been in the pocket for weeks. He found an old glass and stood the flower in water.

Later he bought chips in the next street and fried himself an egg; then he tried to watch a film about Hawaii through the snow on the television Charlie had given him from one of the houses. Exhausted by the day's work, he was in bed before it was dark. He saw handprints dancing around a table, heard his parents calling to each other, almost saw a shape with arms that could reach around the world. Once he thought he heard metal jingling further down the room he lived and ate and slept in.

The morning was colder. He waited for Charlie to ring the shaky bell and watched newspapers chasing along the back alleys, birds darting out of the steep slate roofs. He changed the water in the glass on the mantelpiece— the flower was already drooping—then he decided to wait downstairs in case the bell had stopped working. He opened the door of his flat, and metal jingled among the coats on the hook.

He'd hung the borrowed raincoat on top. In the left-hand pocket he found two tarnished coins of a kind he'd never seen before. On an impulse he put one in his mouth and bit timidly. The metal was soft to his teeth.

He was gazing at the bite-mark when Charlie rang the bell. He hid the coins under the glass on the mantelpiece and searched the pockets twice to make sure they were empty; then, abruptly, his mind a tangle of half-formed thoughts—Long John Silver, nothing up my sleeve—he buttoned himself into the raincoat. He didn't want to leave it when he could take it with him.

Charlie looked as if he mightn't even let him in the van. "Slept in it, did you?" he said in disgust. "I'm having my doubts about you."

"I thought it'd keep the dust off."

"No dust where we're going." Nor was there, neither in the house they were clearing nor the one to which the young couple were moving. The wife fussed around them all day, telling them to be careful and not to put that there, and Eric seldom had a chance to feel in the raincoat pockets. There was never anything. Soon he felt more like a stooge than ever, especially when he realised that somehow he'd managed to button the coat on the wrong side, though he remembered buttoning it properly. No wonder the husband avoided looking at him.

Eric half expected the flower and the coins to have vanished: he'd remembered his mother reading him a bedtime story about fairy gold. No, the coins were still there, and the wilting flower. He hung up the coat and tried not to watch it, then made himself go out to the Weights & Scales for a drink. An hour of listening to people decades younger than he complaining about unemployment and immigrants and governments and prophesying the football match up the hill next Saturday, and he went home. The pockets were empty, and so, when he slept, were his dreams.

As soon as he got up, he rummaged in the pockets. Still empty. Much more groping in the old material and he would be finding holes. He put the coat on, out of defiance to Charlie if nothing else, and plunged his hands into the pockets so as to look uncaring as he waited on the doorstep. The right-hand pocket contained a diamond as big as his thumbnail.

He ran upstairs and hid the diamond under his pillow. He ran down, then back up, and hid the coins next to the diamond. The van was just drawing up. Charlie gave him a look that made words superfluous, and took his time in handing over Eric's wages, which were supposed to include Eric's cut from the sale of the contents of the cleared house. The cut seemed smaller than it ought to be. Remembering the diamond, he didn't care. Charlie stared at him when he unbuttoned the raincoat to stow the money in his shirt, but he didn't want to put anything in those pockets in case it might be spirited away.

The diamond made him careless, and so did the old lady whose house they were clearing. "That's not mine," she kept crying as they lifted furniture. "Someone's trying to play a trick on me. Don't bother taking it, I won't have it in my house." They carried on doggedly, hoping her son would arrive soon, and Eric almost dropped a tea-chest full of crockery for reaching in his pocket when he thought he felt it move, and kept on reaching in there for something that would make the day worthwhile.

The son, a middle-aged man with pinched eyes and a woeful mouth, arrived as they started on the bedrooms, and calmed his mother down as best he could while they brought down a wardrobe. "Where have you been? I thought you were never coming," she cried as Eric hurried back to the house, missing a step when something rattled in his pocket. It was a pearl necklace. "That's mine. Look at him," the old lady screeched, "you've brought a thief into my house."

"I don't think that's one of yours, Mummy."

"It is, it is. You all want to rob me."

Before Eric could think what to say, Charlie snatched the necklace. "So that's what you've been up to with your bloody silly coat. I ought to give you your cards right now." He handed the necklace to the old lady. "Of course it's yours, ma'am. Please accept my apologies. I've never had anything like this happen before in thirty-eight years of removals."

"Go on then, give me my cards." Eric was sure there must be plenty more where the necklace had come from. "Don't you be making out I'm a thief. You're a thief."

"Watch your tongue, lad, or I'll knock you down." Charlie nodded fiercely at the son as if to tell him to be angry. "And he will, too."

"Don't call me lad. I'm not a lad, I'm forty, and I'm not a thief—you are. You steal my money you get from selling stuff I carried. And he steals my sandwiches," he told the old lady, thinking that should show her—she was a mother, after all.

"Who said anything about sandwiches? You'll get no sandwiches from me. I wouldn't make you a cup of tea," she screeched, "except to pour it over your head."

Eric had had enough. "See how much you can shift by yourself," he told Charlie. "And when you get tired, Muscles here can help you."

He strode home, feeling as if all he'd said was a burden he'd thrown off, leaving him lighter, almost capable of flying. He didn't need Charlie or his cards, he didn't need anyone. The coat would keep him, however it worked—he didn't need to know how. He restrained himself from searching the pockets until he arrived home, in case it mightn't work in the open. But when he'd closed himself in, he found they were empty.

He hung the coat on the door and went out to the Nosebag Café for a pie and chips. When he returned to find the coat empty, he put it on. For a while he watched television so as not to keep reaching in the pockets; then he switched off the set and kept counting one to a hundred with his arms folded. Eventually he dozed and almost saw the face of the shape with arms or hands that could reach around the world, that were reaching into his pockets or out of them. Once he awoke with his hands in his pockets, and snatched them out in a panic.

In the morning he found a stone the size of the palm of his hand, a smooth stone that glittered and looked precious. As soon as he was dressed, he bought the cheapest newspaper to wrap the coins and jewel and stone individually before placing them in a supermarket bag. That left one sheet of newspaper, which he folded around the dead flower.

He clutched the bag to him in both hands all the way to the museum: there were too many thieves about these days. He wouldn't let the girl behind the desk at the museum see what he had; the fewer people who knew, the better. He waited for the top man and occasionally felt in his pockets.

He refused to open the bag until he was in the curator's office. The first item that came to hand was the flower. He didn't expect it to be worth anything; he just wanted to know what it was, while he anticipated learning how wealthy he was. But the curator frowned at the flower, then at Eric. "Where did you get this?"

"An old lady gave it to me. She didn't know what it was."

"And where did she get it? You can't say? I thought not." The curator picked up the phone on his desk. "She ought to know it's a protected species."

Eric gripped the bag and prepared to flee if the curator was calling the police. Instead he called some doctor to find out if any flowers had been taken from a garden, flowers with a long name that included Himalayas. None had, nor apparently had any other garden been robbed, and he put down the receiver. "What else have you in there?"

"Nothing. I've brought the wrong things." Eric tried not to back away too conspicuously. "I'll have to come back," he lied, and managed not to run until he was out of the museum.

He wandered the thirsty streets. Football fans looking for pubs or mischief elbowed him out of the way. He wasn't sure if he wanted to hide the contents of the bag at home or dump them in the nearest bin. He couldn't take them to be valued until he knew where they'd come from, and how was he to find that out? He was beginning to hate the damned coat; it had made a fool of him, had nearly got him arrested. He'd begun to grow furious, trying to unbutton it and fumbling helplessly, when he remembered the address on the letter he'd seen in the medium's house. At once he made for the hill.

An old lady opened the door of the terraced house and rubbed her eyes as if she had been asleep or weeping. She glanced sharply at his raincoat, then shook her head at herself. "I don't want anything today," she mumbled, starting to close the door.

"I've lost my parents." He couldn't just ask if she knew about the coat. "Someone said you could help me."

"I don't go in for that anymore." Nevertheless, she stood back for him. "You do look lost. Come in if you want to talk."

He didn't, not about his parents: even using them to trick his way in had made him feel guilty. As soon as he was seated in the parlour, which smelled of old furniture and lavender, he said "Why did you give it up?"

She stared, then understood. "The lady who used to put me in touch died herself."

"Was she a good medium? Did they bring her things?"

He thought he'd been too direct, for she stiffened. "That's what killed her, I think."

His hands recoiled from the pockets, where they had been resting. "What, being brought things?"

"Apports, they're called. Them, aye, and growing old." She shivered. "One of her guides was evil, that's what she didn't know."

He gaped at her, out of his depth. "He brought her flowers and treasures until he got to be her favourite," she said. "Then he started bringing other things until she was afraid to hold séances at all, but that didn't stop him. He started putting them in her bed when she was asleep."

Eric was on his feet before he knew it, and struggling to unbutton the coat until he realised that he meant to leave it in her house. She didn't deserve that or the contents of the supermarket bag. "I've got to go now," he stammered, and collided with furniture and doors on his way out of the house.

Football fans came crowding up the hill towards the football ground, singing and shouting and throwing empty beer cans. He went with them, since he didn't know where best to go. He couldn't be sure that the old lady's story had anything to do with the coat, with whatever brought him presents. Nevertheless, when something in the right-hand pocket bumped against him, he found he couldn't swallow.

He wanted desperately to stand still, to prepare himself, if he could, to find out what was there, but the crowd crammed into the narrow streets shoved him onward, wouldn't let him out of its midst. He scarcely had room to reach down to the pocket; he wished he could use that as an excuse not to find out, but he couldn't bear not knowing what was scraping against him with every step. Nor could he simply reach in. His fingers ranged shakily and timidly over the outside of the pocket to trace the shape within.

It felt like a cross. It must be; he could trace the chain it would hang from. He slipped his hand into the pocket and grabbed the chain before he could flinch, managed to raise it to eye level. Yes, it was a cross, a silver cross, and he'd never felt so relieved in his life; the old lady's tale couldn't have anything to do with him. He dangled the cross into the supermarket bag and lifted his hand to his mouth, for a splinter from somewhere had lodged in his finger. As he pulled out the splinter with his teeth, he noticed that his hand smelled of earth.

He had just realised that the cross was very like the one his father had always worn when he realised there was something in the left-hand pocket too.

He closed his eyes and plunged his hand in, to get it over with. His fingertips flinched from touching something cold, touched it again and discovered it was round, somewhat crusted or at least not smooth, a bulge on it smoother, less metallic. A stone in a ring, he thought, and took it out, sighing. It was the ring his mother had worn to her grave.

Something else was rolling about in the pocket—something which, he realised, choking, had slipped out of the ring. He snatched it out and flung it away blindly, crying out with horror and fury and grief. Those nearest him in the crowd glanced at him, warning him not to go berserk while he was next to them; otherwise the crowd took no notice of him as it drove him helplessly uphill.

He tore at the buttons and then at the coat. The material wouldn't tear; the buttons might have been sewn through buttonholes too small for them, they were so immovable. He felt as if he were going mad, as if the whole indifferent crowd were too—this nightmare of a crowd that wasn't slowing even now that it had come in sight of the football ground and the rest of itself. His hands were clenched on the supermarket bag at the level of his chest so as not to stray near his pockets, in which he thought he felt objects crawling. He was pleading, almost sobbing, first silently and then aloud, telling his parents he was sorry, he would never have stolen from them, he would pray for them if they wanted, even though he had never believed. . . . Then he closed his eyes tight as the crowd struggled with itself, squeezed his eyes shut until they ached, for something was struggling in his pocket, feebly and softly. He couldn't bear it without screaming, and if he screamed in the midst of the crowd, he would know he was mad. He looked down.

It was a hand, a man's hand. A man had his hand in Eric's pocket, a scrawny youth who blinked at Eric as though to say the hand was nothing to do with him. He'd been trying to pick Eric's pocket, which had closed around his wrist just as the holes had closed around the buttons. "My God," Eric cried between screaming and laughter, "if you want it that badly, you can have it," and all at once the buttonholes were loose and the coat slipped off his arms, and he was fighting sideways out of the crowd.

He looked back once, then fought free of the crowd and stumbled uphill beyond the streets, towards the heath. Perhaps up there he would know whether to go to Charlie for his cards or his job. At last he realised he was still holding his mother's ring. He slipped it into his safest pocket and forced himself not to look back. Perhaps someone would notice how wild the pickpocket's eyes were growing; perhaps they might help him. In any case, perhaps it had only been the press of the crowd that had been giving him trouble as he struggled with the coat, one hand in the pocket, the other in the sleeve. Perhaps Eric hadn't really seen the sleeve worming, inching. He knew he'd seen the youth struggling to put on the coat, but he couldn't be sure that he'd seen it helping itself on.

Apples

We wanted to be scared on Hallowe'en, but not like that. We never meant anything to happen to Andrew. We only wanted him not to be so useless and show us he could do something he was scared of doing. I know I was scared the night I went to the allotments when Mr Gray was still alive.

We used to watch him from Colin's window in the tenements, me and Andrew and Colin and Colin's little sister Jill. Sometimes he worked in his allotment until midnight, my mum once said. The big lamps on the paths through the estate made his face look like a big white candle with a long nose that was melting. Jill kept shouting "Mr Toad" and shutting the window quick, but he never looked up. Only he must have known it was us and that's why he said we took his apples when kids from the other end of the estate did really.

He took our mums and dads to see how they'd broken his hedge because he'd locked his gate. "If Harry says he didn't do it, then he didn't," my dad went and Colin's, who was a wrestler, went "If I find out who's been up to no good they'll be walking funny for a while." But Andrew's mum only went "I just hope you weren't mixed up in this, Andrew." His dad and mum were like that, they were teachers and tried to make him friends at our school they taught at, boys who didn't like getting dirty and always had combs and handkerchiefs. So then whenever we were cycling round the paths by the allotments and Mr Gray saw us he said things like "There are the children who can't keep their hands off other people's property" to anyone who was passing. So one night Colin pinched four apples off his tree, and then it was my turn.

I had to wait for a night my mum sent me to the shop. The woman isn't supposed to sell kids cigarettes, but she does because she knows my mum. I came back past the allotments, and when I got to Mr Gray's I ducked down behind the hedge. The lamps that were supposed to stop people being mugged turned everything grey in the allotments and made Mr Gray's windows look as if they had metal shutters on. I could hear my heart jumping. I went to where the hedge was low and climbed over.

He'd put broken glass under the hedge. I managed to land on tiptoe in between the bits of glass. I hated him then, and I didn't even bother taking apples from where he mightn't notice, I just pulled some off and threw them over the hedge for the worms to eat. We wouldn't have eaten them, all his apples tasted old and bitter. I gave my mum her cigarettes and went up to Colin's and told Andrew "Your turn next."

He started hugging himself. "I can't. My parents might know."

"They said we were stealing, as good as said it," Jill went. "They probably thought you were. My dad said he'd pull their heads off and stick them you-know-where if he thought that's what they meant about us."

"You've got to go," Colin went. "Harry went and he's not even eleven. Go now if you like, before my mum and dad come back from the pub."

Andrew might have thought Colin meant to make him, because he started shaking and going "No I won't," and then there was a stain on the front of his trousers. "Look at the baby weeing himself," Colin and Jill went.

I felt sorry for him. "Maybe he doesn't feel well. He can go another night."

"I'll go if he won't," Jill went.

"You wouldn't let a girl go, would you?" Colin went to Andrew, but then their mum and dad came back. Andrew ran upstairs and Colin went to Jill "You really would have gone too, wouldn't you?"

"I'm still going." She was so cross she went red. "I'm just as brave as you two, braver." And we couldn't stop her the next night, when her mum was watching Jill's dad at work being the Hooded Gouger.

I thought she'd be safe. There'd been a storm in the night and the wind could have blown down the apples. But I was scared when I saw how small she looked down there on the path under the lamps, and I'd never noticed how long it took to walk to the allotments, all that way she might have to run back. Her shadow kept disappearing as if something was squashing it and then it jumped in front of her. We couldn't see in Mr Gray's windows for the lamps.

When she squatted down behind Mr Gray's hedge, Andrew went "Looks like she's been taken short" to try to sound like us, but Colin just glared at him. She threw her coat on the broken glass, then she got over the hedge and ran to the tree. The branches were too high for her. "Leave it," Colin went, but she couldn't have heard him, because she started climbing. She was halfway up when Mr Gray came out of his house.

He'd got a pair of garden shears. He grinned when he saw Jill, because even all that far away we could see his teeth. He ran round to where the hedge was low. He couldn't really run, it was like a fat old white dog trying, but there wasn't anywhere else for Jill to climb the hedge. Colin ran out, and I was going to open the window and shout at Mr Gray when he climbed over the hedge to get Jill.

He was clicking the shears. I could see the blades flash. Andrew wet himself and ran upstairs, and I couldn't open the window or even move. Jill jumped off the tree and hurt her ankles, and when she tried to get away from him she was nearly as slow as he was. But she ran to the gate and tried to climb it, only it fell over. Mr Gray ran after her waving the shears when she tried to crawl away, and then he grabbed his chest like they do in films when they're shot, and fell into the hedge.

Colin ran to Jill and brought her back, and all that time Mr Gray didn't move. Jill was shaking but she never cried, only shouted through the window at Mr Gray. "That'll teach you," she shouted, even when Colin went "I think he's dead." We were glad until we remembered Jill's coat was down there on the glass.

I went down though my chest was hurting. Mr Gray was leaning over the hedge with his hands hanging down as if he was trying to reach the shears that had fallen standing up in the earth. His eyes were open with the lamps in them and looking straight at Jill's coat. He looked as if he'd gone bad somehow, as if he'd go all out of shape if you poked him. I grabbed Jill's coat, and just then the hedge creaked and he leaned forward as if he was trying to reach me. I ran away and didn't look back, because I was sure that even though he was leaning further his head was up so he could keep watching me.

I didn't sleep much that night and I don't think the others did. I kept getting up to see if he'd moved, because I kept thinking he was creeping up on the tenements. He was always still in the hedge, until I fell asleep, and when I looked again he wasn't there. The ambulance must have taken him away, but I couldn't get to sleep for thinking I could hear him on the stairs.

Next night my mum and dad were talking about how some woman found him dead in the hedge and the police went into his house. My mum said the police found a whole bedroom full of rotten fruit, and some books in his room about kids. Maybe he didn't like kids because he was afraid what he might do to them, she said, but that was all she'd say.

Colin and me dared each other to look in his windows and Jill went too. All we could see was rooms with nothing in them now except sunlight making them look dusty. I could smell rotten fruit, and I kept thinking Mr Gray was going to open one of the doors and show us his face gone bad. We went to see how many apples were left on his tree, only we didn't go in the allotment because when I looked at the house I saw a patch on one of the windows as if someone had wiped it clean to watch us. Jill said it hadn't been there before we'd gone to the hedge. We stayed away after that, and every night when I looked out of my room the patch was like a white face watching from his window.

Then someone else moved into his house and by the time the clocks went back and it got dark an hour earlier, we'd forgotten about Mr Gray, at least Colin and Jill and me had. It was nearly Hallowe'en and then a week to Guy Fawkes Night. Colin was going to get some zombie videos to watch on Hallowe'en because his mum and dad would be at the wrestling, but then Andrew's mum found out. Andrew came and told us he was having a Hallowe'en party instead. "If you don't come there won't be anyone," he went.

"All right, we'll come," Colin went, but Jill went "Andrew's just too scared to watch the zombies. I expect they make him think of Mr Toad. He's scared of Mr Toad even now he's dead."

Andrew got red and stamped his foot. "You wait," he went.

The day before Hallowe'en, I saw him hanging round near Mr Gray's allotment when it was getting dark. He turned away when I saw him, pretending he wasn't there. Later I heard him go upstairs slowly as if he was carrying something, and I nearly ran out to catch him and make him go red.

I watched telly until my mum told me to go to bed three times. Andrew always went to bed as soon as his mum came home from night-school. I went to draw my curtains and I saw someone in Mr Gray's allotment, bending down under the apple tree as if he was looking for something. He was bending down so far I thought he was digging his face in the earth. When he got up his face looked too white under the lamps, except for his mouth that was messy and black. I pulled the curtains and jumped into bed in case he saw me, but I think he was looking at Andrew's window.

Next day at school Andrew bought Colin and Jill and me sweets. He must have been making sure we went to his party. "Where'd you get all that money?" Jill wanted to know.

"Mummy gave it to me to buy apples," Andrew went and started looking round as if he was scared someone could hear him.

He wouldn't walk home past Mr Gray's. He didn't know I wasn't going very near after what I'd seen in the allotment. He went the long way round behind the tenements. I got worried when I didn't hear him come in and I went down in case some big kids had done him. He was hiding under the bonfire we'd all built behind the tenements for Guy Fawkes Night. He wouldn't tell me who he was hiding from. He nearly screamed when I looked in at him in the tunnel he'd made under there.

"Don't go if you don't want to," my mum went because I took so long over my tea. "I better had," I went, but I waited until Andrew came to find out if we were ever going, then we all went up together. It wasn't his party we minded so much as his mum and dad telling us what to do.

The first thing his dad said when we went in was "Wipe your feet," though we hadn't come from outside. It was only him there, because Andrew's mum was going to come back soon so he could go to a meeting. Then he started talking in the kind of voice teachers put on just before the holidays to make you forget they're teachers. "I expect your friends would like a Hallowe'en treat," he went and got some baked potatoes out of the oven, but only Andrew had much. I'd just eaten and besides the smell of apples kept getting into the taste of the potatoes and making me feel funny.

There were apples hanging from a rope across the room and floating in a washing-up bowl full of water on some towels on the floor. "If that's the best your friends can do with my Hallowe'en cuisine I think it's about time for games," Andrew's dad went and took our plates away, grousing like a school dinner lady. When he came back, Andrew went "Please may you tie my hands."

"I don't know about that, son." But Andrew gave him a handkerchief to tie them and looked as if he was going to cry, so his dad went "Hold them out, then."

"No, behind my back."

"I don't think your mother would permit that." Then he must have seen how Andrew wanted to be brave in front of us, so he made a face and tied them. "I hope your friends have handkerchiefs too," he went.

He tied our hands behind our backs, wrinkling his nose at Jill's handkerchief, and we let him for Andrew's sake. "Now the point of the game is to bring down an apple by biting it," he went, as if we couldn't see why the apples were hanging up. Only I wished he wouldn't go on about it because talking about them seemed to make the smell stronger.

Jill couldn't quite reach. When he held her up she kept bumping the apple with her nose and said a bad word when the apple came back and hit her. He put her down then quick and Colin had a go. His mouth was almost as big as one of the apples, and he took a bite first time, then he spat it out on the floor. "What on earth do you think you're doing? Would you do that at home?" Andrew's dad shouted, back to being a teacher again, and went to get a dustpan and a mop.

"Where did you get them apples?" Colin went to Andrew. Andrew looked at him to beg him not to ask in front of his dad, and we all knew. I remembered noticing there weren't any apples on Mr Gray's tree anymore. We could see Andrew was trying to show us he wasn't scared, only he had to wait until his mum or dad was there. When his dad finished clearing up after Colin, Andrew went "Let's have duck-apples now."

He knelt down by the bowl of water and leaned his head in. He kept his face in the water so long I thought he was looking at something and his dad went to him in case he couldn't get up. He pulled his face out spluttering and I went next, though I didn't like how nervous he looked now.

I wished I hadn't. The water smelled stale and tasted worse. Whenever I tried to pick up an apple with just my mouth without biting into it, it sank and then bobbed up, and I couldn't see it properly. I didn't like not being able to see the bottom of the bowl. I had another go at an apple so I could get away, but Andrew's dad or someone must have stood over me, because the water got darker and I thought the apple bobbing up was bigger than my head and looking at me. I felt as if someone was holding my head down in the water and I couldn't breathe. I tried to knock the bowl over and spilled a bit of water on the towels. Andrew's dad hauled me out of the bowl as if I was a dog. "I think we'll dispense with the duck-apples," he went, and then the doorbell rang.

"That must be your mother without her keys again," he told Andrew, sounding relieved. "Just don't touch anything until one of us is here." He went down and we heard the door slam and then someone coming up. It wasn't him, the footsteps were too slow and loud. I kept tasting the appley water and feeling I was going to be sick. The footsteps took so long I thought I wouldn't be able to look when they came in. The door opened and Jill screamed, because there was someone wearing a dirty sheet and a skull for a face. "It's only Mummy," Andrew went, laughing at Jill for being scared. "She said she might dress up."

Just then the doorbell rang again and made us all jump. Andrew's mum closed the door of the flat as if the bell wasn't even ringing. "It must be children," Andrew went, looking proud of himself because he was talking for his mother. Jill was mad at him for laughing at her. "I want to duck for apples," she went, even though the smell was stronger and rottener. "I didn't have a go."

Andrew's mum nodded and went round making sure our hands were tied properly, then she pushed Jill to the bowl without taking her hands from under the sheet. Jill looked at her to tell her she didn't care if she wanted to pretend that much, Jill wasn't scared. The bell rang again for a long time but we all ignored it. Jill bent over the bowl and Andrew's mum leaned over her. The way she was leaning I thought she was going to hold Jill down, except Jill dodged out of the way. "There's something in there," she went.

"There's only apples," Andrew went. "I didn't think *you'd* be scared." Jill looked as if she'd have hit him if she'd been able to get her hands from behind her back. "I want to try the apples hanging up again," she went. "I didn't have a proper go."

She went under the rope and tried to jump high enough to get an apple, and then something tapped on the window. She nearly fell down, and even Colin looked scared. I know I was, because I thought someone had climbed up to the third floor to knock on the window. I thought Mr Gray had. But Andrew grinned at us because his mum was there and went "It's just those children again throwing stones."

His mum picked Jill up and Jill got the apple first time. She bit into it just as more stones hit the window, and then we heard Andrew's dad shouting outside. "It's me, Andrew. Let me in. Some damn fool locked me out when I went down."

Jill made a noise as if she was trying to scream. She'd spat out the apple and goggled at it on the floor. Something was squirming in it. I couldn't move and Colin couldn't either, because Andrew's mum's hands had come out from under the sheet to hold Jill. Only they were white and dirty, and they didn't look like any woman's hands. They didn't look much like hands at all.

Then both the arms came worming out from under the sheet to hold Jill so she couldn't move any more than Colin and me could, and the head started shaking to get the mask off. I'd have done anything rather than see underneath, the arms looked melted enough. All we could hear was the rubber mask creaking and something flopping round inside it, and the drip on the carpet from Andrew wetting himself. But suddenly Andrew squeaked, the best he could do for talking. "You leave her alone. She didn't take your apples, I did. You come and get me."

The mask slipped as if him under the sheet was putting his head on one side, then the arms dropped Jill and reached out for Andrew. Andrew ran to the door and we saw he'd got his hands free. He ran onto the stairs going "Come on, you fat old toad, try and catch me."

Him under the sheet went after him and we heard them running down, Andrew's footsteps and the others that sounded bare and squelchy. Me and Colin ran to Jill when we could move to see if she was all right apart from being sick on the carpet. When I saw she was, I ran down fast so that I wouldn't think about it, to find Andrew.

I heard his dad shouting at him behind the tenements. "Did you do this? What's got into you?" Andrew had got matches from somewhere and set light to the bonfire. His dad didn't see anything else, but I did, a sheet and something jumping about inside it, under all that fire. Andrew must have crawled through the tunnel he'd made but him in the sheet had got stuck. I watched the sheet flopping about when the flames got to it, then it stopped moving when the tunnel caved in on it. "Come upstairs, I want a few words with you," Andrew's dad went, pulling him by the ear. But when we got in the building he let go and just gaped, because Andrew's hair had gone dead white.

The Other Side

When Bowring saw where the fire engines were heading, he thought at first
it was the school. "They've done it, the young swine," he groaned, craning
out of his high window, clutching the cold dewy sill. Then flames burst from
an upper window of the abandoned tenement a mile away across the river,
reddening the low clouds. That would be one less place for them to take their
drugs and do whatever else they got up to when they thought nobody was
watching. "Bow-wow's watching, and don't you forget it," he muttered with a
grin that let the night air twinge his teeth, and then he realised how he could.

A taste of mothballs caught at the back of his throat as he took the binoculars from the wardrobe where they hung among his suits. The lenses pulled
the streets across the river towards him, cut-out terraces bunched together
closely as layers of wallpaper. The tenement reared up, a coaly silhouette flaring red, from the steep bank below them. Figures were converging to watch,
but he could see nobody fleeing. He let the binoculars stray upwards to the
flames, which seemed calming as a fireside, too silent and distant to trouble
him. Then his face stiffened. Above the flames and the jets of water red as
blood, a figure was peering down.

Bowring twisted the focusing-screw in a vain attempt to get rid of the
blur of heat, to clear his mind of what he thought he was seeing. The figure
must be trapped, crying for help and jumping as the floor beneath its feet
grew hotter, yet it appeared to be prancing with delight, waving its hands
gleefully, grinning like a clown. To believe that was to lose control, he told
himself fiercely. A jet of water fought back the flames below the window he
was staring at, and he saw that the window was empty.

Perhaps it always had been. If anyone had been crying for help, the firemen must have responded by now. Among the spectators he saw half a
dozen of his pupils sharing cigarettes. He felt in control again at once. He'd
be having words with them tomorrow.

In the morning he drove ten miles to the bridge, ten miles back along
the far bank. The school was surrounded by disorder, wallpaper flapping

beyond broken windows, houses barricaded with cardboard against casual missiles, cars stranded without wheels and rusting in streets where nothing moved except flocks of litter. Ash from last night's fire settled on his car like an essence of the grubby streets. In the midst of the chaos, the long low ruddy school still looked as it must have a hundred years ago. That felt like a promise of order to him.

He was writing a problem in calculus on the blackboard when those of his class who'd come to school today piled into the classroom, jostling and swearing, accompanied by smells of tobacco and cheap perfume. He swung round, gown whirling, and the noise dwindled sullenly. Two minutes' slamming of folding seats, and then they were sitting at their desks, which were too small for some of them. Bowring hooked his thumbs in the shoulders of his gown. "Which of you were at the fire last night?" he said in a voice that barely reached the back of the room.

Twenty-three faces stared dully at him, twenty-three heads of the monster he had to struggle with every working day. There was nothing to distinguish those he'd seen last night across the river, not a spark of truth. "I know several of you were," he said, letting his gaze linger on the six. "I suggest you tell your friends after class that I may have my eye on you even when you think nobody's watching."

They stared, challenging him to identify them, and waited until dark to answer him with a scrawl of white paint across the ruined tenement. FUCK OFF BOW WOW, the message said. The binoculars shook until he controlled himself. He was damned if he'd let them reach him in his home, his refuge from all they represented. Tomorrow he'd deal with them, on his patch of their territory. He moved the binoculars to see what he'd glimpsed as they veered.

A figure was standing by the tenement, under one of the few surviving streetlamps. The mercury-vapour glare made its face look white as a clown's, though at first he couldn't see the face; the long hands that appeared to be gloved whitely were covering it while the shoulders heaved as if miming rage. Then the figure flung its hands away from its face and began to prance wildly, waving its fists above its spiky hair. It was then that Bowring knew it was the figure he'd seen above the flames.

It must be some lunatic, someone unable to cope with life over there. Suddenly the mercury-vapour stage was bare, and Bowring resisted scanning the dark: whatever the figure was up to had nothing to do with him. He was inclined to ignore the graffiti too, except that next morning, when he turned from the blackboard several of his class began to titter.

He felt his face stiffen, grow pale with rage. That provoked more titters, the nervous kind he'd been told you heard at horror films. "Very well," he murmured, "since you're all aware what I want to hear, we'll have complete silence until the culprit speaks up."

"But sir, I don't know——" Clint began, pulling at his earlobe where he'd been forbidden to wear a ring in school, and Bowring rounded on him. "Complete silence," Bowring hissed in a voice he could barely hear himself.

He strolled up and down the aisles, sat at his desk when he wanted to out-stare them. Their resentment felt like an imminent storm. Just let one of them protest to his face! Bowring wouldn't lay a finger on them—they wouldn't lose him his pension that way—but he'd have them barred from his class. He was tempted to keep them all in after school, except that he'd had enough of the lot of them.

"Wait until you're told to go," he said when the final bell shrilled. He felt unwilling to relinquish his control of them, to let them spill out of his room in search of mischief, sex, drugs, violence, their everyday lives; for moments that seemed disconcertingly prolonged, he felt as if he couldn't let go. "Perhaps on Monday we can get on with some work, if you haven't forgotten what that's like. Now you may go," he said softly, daring them to give tongue to the resentment he saw in all their eyes.

They didn't, not then. He drove across the bridge to be greeted by the scent of pine, of the trees the April sunlight was gilding. Hours later he lay in his reclining chair, lulled by a gin and tonic, by Debussy on the radio. Halfway through the third movement of the quartet, the phone rang. "Yes?" Bowring demanded.

"Mr Bowring?"

"Yes?"

"Mr Bowring the teacher?"

"This is he."

"It's he," the voice said aside, and there was a chorus of sniggers. At once Bowring knew what the voice would say, and so it did: "Fuck off, Bow-wow, you——"

He slammed the phone down before he could hear more, and caught sight of himself in the mirror, white-faced, teeth bared, eyes bulging. "It's all right," he murmured to his mother in the photograph on the mantelpiece below the mirror. But it wasn't: now they'd found him, they could disarray his home life any time they felt like it; he no longer had a refuge. Who had it been on the phone? One of the boys with men's voices, Darren or Gary or Lee. He was trying to decide which when it rang again.

No, they wouldn't get through to him. Over the years he'd seen colleagues on the teaching staff break down, but that wouldn't happen to him. The phone rang five times in the next hour before, presumably, they gave up. Since his mother's death he'd only kept the phone in case the school needed to contact him.

Sunlight woke him in the morning, streaming from behind his house and glaring back from the river. The sight of figures at the charred tenement took him and his binoculars to the window. But they weren't any of his pupils, they were a demolition crew. Soon the tenement puffed like a fungus, hesitated, then collapsed. Only a rumble like distant thunder and a microscopic clink of bricks reached him. The crowd of bystanders dispersed, and even the demolition crew drove away before the dust had finished settling. Bowring alone saw the figure that pranced out of the ruins.

At first he thought its face was white with dust. It sidled about in front of the jagged foundations, pumping its hips and pretending to stick an invisible needle in its arm, and then Bowring saw that the face wasn't covered with dust; it was made up like a clown's. That and the mime looked doubly incongruous because of the plain suit the man was wearing. Perhaps all this was some kind of street theatre, some anarchist nonsense of the kind that tried to make the world a stage for its slogans, yet Bowring had a sudden disconcerting impression that the mime was meant just for him. He blocked the idea from his mind—it felt like a total loss of control—and turned his back on the window.

His morning routine calmed him, his clothes laid out on the sofa as his mother used to place them, his breakfast egg waiting on the moulded ledge in the door of the refrigerator, where he'd moved it last night from the egg box further in. That evening he attended a debate at the Conservative Club on law and order, and on Sunday he drove into the countryside to watch patterns of birds in the sky. By Sunday evening he hadn't given the far side of the river more than a casual glance for over twenty-four hours.

When he glimpsed movement, insectlike under the mercury lamp, he sat down to listen to Elgar. But he resented feeling as if he couldn't look; he'd enjoyed the view across the river ever since he'd moved across, enjoyed knowing it was separate from him. He took as much time as he could over carrying his binoculars to the window.

The clown was capering under the lamp, waving his fists exultantly above his head. His glee made Bowring nervous about discovering its cause. Nervousness swung the binoculars wide, and he saw Darren lying among the fallen bricks, clutching his head and writhing. At once the clown scampered off into the dark.

In the false perspective of the lenses Darren looked unreal, and Bowring felt a hint of guilty triumph. No doubt the boy had been taunting the clown—maybe now he'd had a bit of sense knocked into him. He watched the boy crawl out of the debris and stagger homewards, and was almost certain that it had been Darren's voice on the phone. He was even more convinced on Monday morning, by the way that all Darren's cronies sitting round the empty desk stared accusingly at him.

They needn't try to blame him for Darren's injury, however just it seemed. "If anyone has anything to say about any of your absent colleagues," he murmured, "I'm all ears." Of course they wouldn't speak to him face to face, he realised, not now they had his number. His face stiffened so much he could barely conduct the lesson, which they seemed even less eager to comprehend than usual. No doubt they were anticipating unemployment and the freedom to do mischief all day, every day. Their apathy made him feel he was drowning, fighting his way to a surface which perhaps no longer existed. When he drove home across the bridge, their sullen sunless sky came with him.

As soon as he was home he reached out to take the phone off the hook, until he grabbed his wrist with his other hand. This time he'd be ready for them if they called. Halfway through his dinner of unfrozen cod, they did. He saw them before he heard them, three of them slithering down the steep slope to a phone box, miraculously intact, that stood near a riverside terrace that had escaped demolition. He dragged them towards him with the binoculars as they piled into the box.

They were three of his girls: Debbie, whom he'd seen holding hands with Darren—he didn't like to wonder what they got up to when nobody could see them—and Vanessa and Germaine. He watched Debbie as she dialled, and couldn't help starting as his phone rang. Then he grinned across the river at her. Let her do her worst to reach him.

He watched the girls grimace in the small lit box, shouting threats or insults or obscenities at the phone in Debbie's hand as if that would make him respond. "Shout all you like, you're not in my classroom now," he whispered, and then, without quite knowing why, he swung the binoculars away from them to survey the dark. As his vision swept along the top of the slope he saw movement, larger than he was expecting. A chunk of rubble half as high as a man was poised on the edge above the telephone box. Behind it, grinning stiffly, he saw the glimmering face of the clown.

Bowring snatched up the receiver without thinking. "Look out! Get out!" he cried, so shrilly that his face stiffened with embarrassment. He heard Debbie sputter a shocked insult as the binoculars fastened shakily on the lit box, and then she dropped the receiver as Vanessa and Germaine, who must have seen the danger, fought to be first out of the trap. The box shook with their struggles, and Bowring yelled at them to be orderly, as if his voice might reach them through the dangling receiver. Then Vanessa wrenched herself free, and the others followed, almost falling headlong, as the rubble smashed one side of the box, filling the interior with knives of glass.

Maybe that would give them something to think about, but all the same, it was vandalism. Shouldn't Bowring call the police? Some instinct prevented him, perhaps his sense of wanting to preserve a distance between himself and what he'd seen. After all, the girls might have seen the culprit too, might even have recognised him.

But on Tuesday they were pretending that nothing had happened. Debbie's blank face challenged him to accuse her, to admit he'd been watching. Her whole stance challenged him, her long legs crossed, her linen skirt ending high on her bare thighs. How dare she sit like that in front of a man of his age! She'd come to grief acting like that, but not from him. The day's problems squealed on the blackboard, the chalk snapped.

He drove home, his face stiff with resentment. He wished he hadn't picked up the phone, wished he'd left them at the mercy of the madman who, for all Bowring knew, had gone mad as a result of their kind of misbehaviour. As he swung the car onto the drive below his flat, a raw sunset throbbed in the gap where the tenement had been.

The sun went down. Lamps pricked the dark across the river. Tonight he wouldn't look, he told himself, but he couldn't put the other side out of his mind. He ate lamb chops to the strains of one of Rossini's preadolescent sonatas. Would there ever be prodigies like him again? Children now were nothing like they used to be. Bowring carried the radio to his chair beside the fire and couldn't help glancing across the river. Someone was loitering in front of the gap where the tenement had been.

He sat down, stood up furiously, grabbed the binoculars. It was Debbie, waiting under the mercury lamp. She wore a pale blue skirt now, and stockings. Her lipstick glinted. She reminded Bowring of a streetwalker in some film, that image of a woman standing under a lamp surrounded by darkness.

No doubt she was waiting for Darren. Women waiting under lamps often came to no good, especially if they were up to none. Bowring probed the dark with his binoculars, until his flattened gaze came to rest on a fragment of the tenement, a zigzag of wall as high as a man. Had something pale just dodged behind it?

Debbie was still under the lamp, hugging herself against the cold, glancing nervously over her shoulder, but not at the fragment of wall. Bowring turned the lenses back to the wall, and came face to face with the clown, who seemed to be grinning straight at him from his hiding-place. The sight froze Bowring, who could only cling shakily to the binoculars and watch as the white face dodged back and forth, popping out from opposite edges of the wall. Perhaps only a few seconds passed, but it seemed long as a nightmare before the clown leapt on the girl.

Bowring saw her thrown flat on the scorched ground, saw the clown stuff her mouth with a wad of litter, the grinning white face pressing into hers. When the clown pinned her wrists with one hand and began to tear at her clothes with the other, Bowring grabbed the phone. He called the police station near the school and waited feverishly while the clown shied Debbie's clothes into the dark. "Rape. Taking place now, where the tenement was demolished," he gasped as soon as he heard a voice.

"Where are you speaking from, sir?"

"That doesn't matter. You're wasting time. Unless you catch this person in the act you may not be able to identify him. He's made up like a clown."

"What is your name, please, sir?"

"What the devil has my name to do with it? Just get to the crime, can't you! There, you see," Bowring cried, his voice out of control, "you're too late."

Somehow Debbie had struggled free and was limping naked towards the nearest houses. Bowring saw her look back in terror, then flee painfully across the rubble. But the clown wasn't following, he was merely waving the baggy crotch of his trousers at her. "I need your name before we're able to respond," the voice said brusquely in Bowring's ear, and Bowring dropped the receiver in his haste to break the connection. When he looked across the river again, both Debbie and the clown had gone.

Eventually he saw police cars cruising back and forth past the ruined tenement, policemen tramping from house to house. Bowring had switched off his light in order to watch and for fear that the police might notice him, try to involve him, make an issue of his having refused to name himself. He watched for hours as front door after front door opened to the police. He was growing more nervous, presumably in anticipation of the sight of the clown, prancing through a doorway or being dragged out by the police.

Rain came sweeping along the river, drenching the far bank. The last houses closed behind the police. A police car probed the area around the ruined tenement with its headlights, and then there was only rain and darkness and the few drowning streetlamps. Yet he felt as if he couldn't stop watching. His vision swam jerkily towards the charred gap, and the clown pranced out from behind the jagged wall.

How could the police have overlooked him? But there he was, capering beside the ruin. As Bowring leaned forward, clutching the binoculars, the clown reached behind the wall and produced an object which he brandished gleefully. He dropped it back into hiding just as Bowring saw that it was an axe. Then the clown minced into the lamplight.

For a moment Bowring thought that the clown's face was injured—distorted, certainly—until he realised that the rain was washing the makeup off. Why should that make him even more nervous? He couldn't see the face now, for the clown was putting his fists to his eyes. He seemed to be peering through his improvised binoculars straight at Bowring—and then, with a shock that stiffened his face, Bowring felt sure that he was. The next moment the clown turned his bare face up to the rain that streamed through the icy light.

Makeup began to whiten his lapels like droppings on a statue. The undisguised face gleamed in the rain. Bowring stared at the face that was appearing, then he muttered a denial to himself as he struggled to lower the binoculars, to let go his shivering grip on them, look away. Then the face across the river grinned straight at him, and his convulsion heaved him away from the window with a violence that meant to refute what he'd seen.

It couldn't be true. If it was, anything could be. He was hardly aware of lurching downstairs and into the sharp rain, binoculars thumping his chest. He fumbled his way into the car and sent it slewing towards the road, wipers scything at the rain. As trees crowded into the headlights, the piny smell made his head swim.

The struts of the bridge whirred by, dripping. Dark streets, broken lamps, decrepit streaming houses closed around him. He drove faster through the desertion, though he felt as if he'd given in to a loss of control: surely there would be nothing to see—perhaps there never had been. But when the car skidded across the mud beside the demolished tenement, the clown was waiting barefaced for him.

Bowring wrenched the car to a slithering halt and leapt out into the mud in front of the figure beneath the lamp. It was a mirror, he thought desperately: he was dreaming of a mirror. He felt the rain soak his clothes, slash his cheeks, trickle inside his collar. "What do you mean by this?" he yelled at the lamplit figure, and before he could think of what he was demanding "Who do you think you are?"

The figure lifted its hands towards its face, still whitewashed by the mercury lamp, then spread its hands towards Bowring. That was more than Bowring could bear, both the silence of the miming and what the gesture meant to say. His mind emptied as he lurched past the lamplight to the fragment of tenement wall.

When the figure didn't move to stop him, he thought the axe wouldn't be there. But it was. He snatched it up and turned on the other, who stepped towards him, out of the lamplight. Bowring lifted the axe defensively. Then he saw that the figure was gesturing towards itself, miming an invitation. Bowring's control broke, and he swung the axe towards the unbearable sight of the grinning face.

At the last moment, the figure jerked its head aside. The axe cut deep into its neck. There was no blood, only a bulging of what looked like new pale flesh from the wound. The figure staggered, then mimed the axe towards itself again. None of this could be happening, Bowring told himself wildly: it was too outrageous, it meant that anything could happen, it was the beginning of total chaos. His incredulity let him hack with the axe, again and again, his binoculars bruising his ribs. He hardly felt the blows he was dealing, and when he'd finished there was still no blood, only an enormous sprawl of torn cloth and chopped pink flesh whitened by the lamplight, restless with rain. Somehow the head had survived his onslaught, which had grown desperately haphazard. As Bowring stared appalled at it, the grinning face looked straight at him, and winked. Screaming under his breath, Bowring hacked it in half, then went on chopping, chopping, chopping.

When at last exhaustion stopped him he made to fling the axe into the ruins. Then he clutched it and reeled back to his car, losing his balance in the mud, almost falling into the midst of his butchery. He drove back to the bridge, his eyes bulging at the liquid dark, at the roads overflowing their banks, the fleets of derelict houses sailing by. As he crossed the bridge, he flung the axe into the river.

He twisted the key and groped blindly into his house, felt his way upstairs, peeled off his soaked clothes, lowered himself shakily into a hot bath. He felt exhausted, empty, but was unable to sleep. He couldn't really have crossed the river, he told himself over and over; he couldn't have done what he remembered doing, the memory that filled his mind, brighter than the streetlamp by the ruin. He stumbled naked to the window. Something pale lay beside the streetlamp, but he couldn't make it out; the rain had washed the lenses clean of the coating that would have let him see more in the dark. He sat there shivering until dawn, nodding occasionally, jerking awake with a cry. When the sunlight reached the other side, the binoculars showed him that the ground beside the lamp was bare.

He dragged on crumpled clothes, tried to eat breakfast but spat out the mouthful, fled to his car. He never set out so early, but today he wanted to be in his classroom as soon as he could, where he still had control. Rainbows winked at him from trees as he drove, and then the houses gaped at him. As yet the streets were almost deserted, and so he couldn't resist driving by the tenement before making for the school. He parked at the top of the slope, craned his neck as he stood shivering on the pavement, and then, more and more shakily and reluctantly, he picked his way down the slope. He'd seen movement in the ruin.

They must be young animals, he told himself as he slithered down. Rats, perhaps, or something else newborn—nothing else could be so pink or move so oddly. He slid down to the low jagged gappy wall. As he caught hold of the topmost bricks, which shifted under his hands, all the pink shapes amid the rubble raised their faces, his face, to him.

Some of the lumps of flesh had recognisable limbs, or at least portions of them. Some had none, no features at all except one or more of the grimacing faces, but all of them came swarming towards him as best they could. Bowring reeled, choked, flailed his hands, tried to grab at reality, wherever it was. He fell across the wall, twisting, face up. At once a hand with his face sprouting from its wrist scuttled up his body and closed its fingers, his fingers, about his throat.

Bowring cowered into himself, desperate to hide from the sensation of misshapen crawling all over his body, his faces swarming over him, onto his limbs, between his legs. There was no refuge. A convulsion shuddered through him, jerked his head up wildly. "My face," he shrieked in a choked whisper, and sank his teeth into the wrist of the hand that was choking him.

It had no bones to speak of. Apart from its bloodlessness, it tasted like raw meat. He shoved it into his mouth, stuffed the fingers in and then the head. As it went in it seemed to shrink, grow shapeless, though he felt his teeth close on its eyes. "*My* face," he spluttered, and reached for handfuls of the rest. But while he'd been occupied with chewing, the swarming had left his body. He was lying alone on the charred rubble.

They were still out there somewhere, he knew. He had to get them back inside himself, he mustn't leave them at large on this side of the river. This side was nothing to do with him. He swayed to his feet and saw the school. A grin stiffened his mouth. Of course, that was where they must be, under the faces of his pupils, but not for long. The children couldn't really be as unlike him as they seemed; nothing could be that alien—that was how they'd almost fooled him. He made his way towards the school, grinning, and as he thought of pulling off those masks to find his face, he began to dance.

Where the Heart Is

I've just walked through your house. I lay on your bed and tried to see my wife's face looming over me, the way I used to. I spent longest in your baby's room, because that was where I began to die. Before I do, I want to tell you who I am and why I'm here, and so I'm writing this.

I'm at your dining-table now, but I won't be when you find me. You'll have found me, or you couldn't be reading this. There may not be much of me for you to recognise, so let me introduce myself again. I'm the man whose house you bought. This is my house, and you'll never get rid of me now.

I've nothing against you personally. It wasn't your fault that the two of you nearly destroyed my wife and me—you weren't to know what you were doing. I can't let that stop me, but at least I can tell you my reasons. The truth is, I never should have let you or anyone else into my house.

Maybe you remember coming to view it, in the rain. I was sitting in the front room, hearing the rain shake the windows and knowing it couldn't touch me. I was feeling peaceful and secure at last. As a matter of fact, I was wondering if the rain might be the last thing I ever heard, if I could sink into that peace where my wife must be, when your car drew up outside the house.

By the time you got out of your car and ran up the path, you were drenched. I may as well be honest: I took my time about answering the door-bell. Only I heard you saying you'd seen someone in the front room, and that made me feel discovered. So I took pity on you out there in the storm.

I don't suppose you noticed how I drew back as you came in . As you trod on the step I had the feeling that you meant the house to be yours. Did you realise you hung your wet coats as if it already was? Maybe you were too drenched to wait for me to tell you, but you made me feel redundant, out of place.

That's one reason why I didn't say much as I showed you over the house. I didn't think you would have listened anyway—you were too busy noticing cracks in the plaster and where damp had lifted the wallpaper and how some of the doors weren't quite straight in their frames. I really thought when we came downstairs that you'd decided against the house. Perhaps you saw how relieved I was. I wondered why you asked if you could be alone for a few minutes. I let you go upstairs by yourselves, though I must say I resented hearing you murmuring up there. And all I could do when you came down and said you were interested in the house was make my face go blank, to hide my shock.

You must have thought I was trying to get you to raise your offer, but it wasn't that at all. I was simply feeling less and less sure that I ought to leave the house where my wife and I had spent our marriage. I told you to get in touch with the estate agent, but that was really just a way of saving myself from having to refuse you outright. I should have told you about my wife. You knew I was selling because she'd died, and you'd made sympathetic noises and faces, but I should have told you that she'd died here in the house.

When you'd left I went upstairs and lay on the bed where she'd died. Sometimes when I lay there and closed my eyes to see her face, I could almost hear her speaking to me. I asked her what I ought to do about you, and I thought I heard her telling me not to let my feelings get the better of me, to think more and feel less, as she often used to say. I thought she was saying that I shouldn't let the house trap me, that so long as I took the bed with me we'd still be together. So I accepted your offer and signed the contract to sell you the house, and the moment I'd finished signing I felt as if I'd signed away my soul.

It was too late by then, or at least I thought it was. I'd already agreed to move out so that you could start the repairs and get your mortgage. When the removal van was loaded I walked through the house to make sure I hadn't left anything. The stripped rooms made me feel empty, homeless, as if my wife and I had never been there. Even the removal van felt more like home, and I sat on our couch in there as the van drove to my new flat.

I'd bought it with the insurance my wife had on herself, you remember. We'd always been equally insured. What with our bed and the rest of the furniture we'd chosen together being moved to the flat and her insurance money buying it, she should been been there with me, shouldn't she? I thought so that first night when I turned off the lamp and lay in the bed and waited to feel that she was near me.

But there was nothing, just me and the dark. The heating was on, yet the bed seemed to get colder and colder. All I wanted was to feel that I wasn't totally alone. But nights went buy, and the bed grew colder, until I felt I'd die of the chill in a place I'd let myself be evicted to, that was nothing like home.

You must be wondering why, if I wanted to be with my wife so much, I didn't consult a medium. My wife was a very private person, that's why—I couldn't have asked her to communicate with me in front of a stranger. Besides, I didn't trust that sort of thing much anymore. I hadn't since I'd thought we'd been given a sign that we were going to have a child.

We'd started a child when it was really too late. That was one time my wife let her feelings get the better of her. We'd been trying for years, and then, when she'd given up expecting to be able, she got pregnant. I was afraid for her all those months, but she said I mustn't be: whatever was going to happen would happen, and we'd be prepared for it, whatever it was. She didn't even make the guest-room into a nursery, not that we ever had guests.

She went into hospital a month before we thought she would. The first I knew of it was when the hospital phoned me at the bank. I visited her every evening, but I couldn't see her on weekdays—too many of my colleagues were on their summer holidays. I became afraid I wouldn't be with her at the birth.

Then one evening I saw something that me me think I'd no reason to be anxious for her. I was going upstairs to bed in the dark when I saw that I'd left the light on in the guest-room. I opened the door and switched off the light, and just as I did so I saw that it wasn't a guest-room any longer, it was a nursery with a cot in it and wallpaper printed with teddy bears dancing in a ring. When I switched on the light again it was just a guest-room, but I didn't care—I knew what I'd seen. I didn't know then what I know now.

So when they called me to the hospital urgently from work I felt sure the birth would be a success, and when I learned that the baby had been born dead I felt as if the house had cheated me, or my feelings had. I felt as if I'd killed the baby by taking too much for granted. I almost couldn't go in to see my wife.

She tried to persuade me that it didn't matter. We still had each other, which was pretty well all that we'd had in the way of friendship for years. But she must have thought it was dangerous to leave me on my own, because she came home before she was supposed to, to be with me. That night in bed we held each other more gently than we ever had, and it seemed as if that was all we needed, all we would ever need.

But in the middle of the night I woke and found her in agony, in so much pain she couldn't move or speak. I ran out half-naked to phone for an ambulance, but it was too late. I got back to her just in time to see the blood burst out of her face—I wasn't even there to hold her hand at the end. I just stood there as if I didn't have the right to touch her, because it was my feelings that had killed her, or her concern for them had.

You see now why I didn't tell you where she died. It would have been like admitting I hoped she was still in the house. Sometimes I thought I sensed her near me when I was falling asleep. But once I'd moved to the flat I couldn't sleep, I just lay growing colder as the nights got longer. I thought she might have left me because she'd had enough of me. She still had to be alive somewhere, I knew that much.

By then you'd started work on the house, and I felt as if it didn't belong to me, even though it still did. Sometimes I walked the two miles to it late at night, when I couldn't sleep. I told myself I was making sure nobody had broken in. I remember one night I looked in the front window. The street-lamp showed me you'd torn off the wallpaper and hacked away the plaster. The orange light from outside blackened everything, made it seem even more ruined, made the room look as if it hadn't been lived in for years. It made me feel I hardly existed myself, and I walked away fast, walked all night without knowing where, until the dawn came up like an icy fog and I had to huddle in my flat to keep warm.

After that I tried to stay away from the house. The doctor gave me pills to help me sleep, the old kind that aren't addictive. I didn't like the sleep they brought, though. It came too quickly and took away all my memories, didn't even leave me dreams. Only I knew I had to sleep or I'd be out of a job for making too many mistakes at the bank. So I slept away the nights until you got your mortgage and were able to buy the house.

I expected that to be a relief to me. I shouldn't have felt drawn to the house, since it wasn't mine any longer. But the day I had to hand over my last key I felt worse than I had when I'd signed the contract, and so I made a copy of the key to keep.

I couldn't have said why I did it. Every time I thought of using the key I imagined being caught in the house, taken away by the police, locked up in a cell. Whenever I felt drawn back to the house I tried to lose myself in my work, or if I was in the flat I tried to be content with memories of the time my wife and I had in the house. Only staying in the flat so as not to be tempted to go to the house made me feel as if I'd already been locked up. I went on like that for weeks, telling myself I had to get used to the flat, the house was nothing to do with me now. I took more of the pills before going to bed, and the doctor renewed the prescription. And then one morning I woke up feeling cold and empty, hardly knowing who I was or where, feeling as if part of me had been stolen while I was asleep.

At first I thought the pills were doing that to me. It was snowing as I walked to work, it looked as if the world was flaking away around me, and I felt as if I was. Even when I leaned against the radiator in the bank I couldn't stop shivering. I made myself sit at the counter when it was time for the manager to open the doors, but he saw how I was and insisted I go home, told me to stay there till I got better. He ordered me a taxi, but I sent it away as soon as I was out of sight of the bank. I knew by then I had to come to the house.

You see, I'd realised what was missing. There was part of the house I couldn't remember. I could still recall making love to my wife, and the way we used to prepare alternate courses of a meal, but I couldn't call to mind how we'd spent our evenings at home. I fought my way to the house, the snow scraping my face and trickling under my clothes, and then I saw why. You'd torn down a wall and made two rooms into one.

We must have had a front room and a dining-room. Presumably we moved from one room to the other when we'd finished dinner, but I couldn't recall any of that, not even what the rooms had looked like. Years of my life, of all I had left of my marriage, had been stolen overnight. I stood there with the snow weighing me down until I felt like stone, staring at the wound you'd made in the house, the bricks gaping and the bare floor covered with plaster dust, and I saw that I had to get into the house.

I'd left the key under my pillow. I might have broken in—the street was deserted, and the snow was blinding the houses—if you hadn't already made the house burglar-proof. I struggled back to the flat for the key. I fell a few times on the way, and the last time I almost couldn't get up for shivering. It took me five minutes or more to open the front door of my new building; I kept dropping the key and not being able to pick it up. By the time I reached my flat I felt I would never stop shivering. I was barely able to clench my fist around the key to the house before I crawled into bed.

For days I thought I was dying. When I lay under the covers I felt hot enough to melt, but if I threw them off, the shivering came back. Whenever I awoke, which must have been hundreds of times, I was afraid to find you'd destroyed more of my memories, that I'd be nothing by the time I died. The fever passed, but by then I was so weak that it was all I could do to stumble to the kitchen or the toilet. Sometimes I had to crawl. And I was only just beginning to regain my strength when I felt you change another room.

I thought I knew which one. It didn't gouge my memories the way the other had, but I had to stop you before you did worse. I knew now that if my wife was anywhere on this earth, she must be at the house. I had to protect her from you, and so I put on as many clothes as I could bear and made myself go out. I felt so incomplete that I kept looking behind me, expecting not to see my footprints in the snow.

I was nearly at the house when I met one of my old neighbours. I didn't want to be seen near the house, I felt like a burglar now. I was trying desperately to think what to say to her when I realised that she hadn't recognised me after all—she was staring at me because she wondered what someone who looked like I looked now was doing in her street. I walked straight past and round the corner, and once the street was deserted I came back to the house.

I was sure you were out at work. There was such a confusion of footprints in the snow on the path that I couldn't see whether more led out than in, but I had to trust my feelings. I let myself into the house and closed the door, then I stood there feeling I'd come home.

You hadn't changed the hall. It still had the striped Regency wallpaper, and the dark brown carpet my wife had chosen still looked as if nobody had ever left footprints on it, though you must have trodden marks all over it while you were altering the house. I could almost believe that the hall led to the rooms my wife and I had lived in, that the wall you'd knocked down was still there, except that I could feel my mind gaping where the memories should be. So I held my breath until I could hear that I was alone in the house, then I went up to the guest-room.

Before I reached it I knew what I'd see. I'd already seen it once. I opened the door and there it was, the nursery you'd made for the child you were expecting, the cot and the wallpaper with teddy bears dancing in a ring. My feelings when my wife was in hospital hadn't lied to me after all, I'd just misinterpreted them. As soon as I realised that, I felt as if what was left of my mind had grown clearer, and I was sure I could sense my wife in the house. I was about to search for her when I heard your car draw up outside.

I'd lost track of time while I was ill. I thought you'd be at work, but this was Saturday, and you'd been out shopping. I felt like smashing the cot and tearing off the wallpaper and waiting for you to find me in the nursery, ready to fight for the house. But I ran down as I heard you slam the car doors, and I hid under the stairs, in the cupboard full of mops and brushes.

I heard you come in, talking about how much better the house looked now you'd knocked the wall down and put in sliding doors so that you could have two rooms there or one as the mood took you. I heard you walk along the hall twice, laden with shopping, and then close the kitchen door. I inched the door under the stairs open, and as I did so I noticed what you'd done while you were putting in the central heating. You'd made a trapdoor in the floor of the cupboard so that you could crawl under the house.

I left the cupboard door open and tiptoed along the hall. I was almost blind with anger at being made to feel like an intruder in the house, but I managed to control myself, because I knew I'd be coming back. I closed the front door by turning my key in the lock, and almost fell headlong on the icy path. My legs felt as if they'd half melted, but I held on to garden walls all the way to the flat and lay down on my bed to wait for Monday morning.

On Sunday afternoon I felt the need to go to church, where I hadn't been since I was a child. I wanted to be reassured that my wife was still alive in spirit and to know if I was right in what I meant to do. I struggled to church and hid at the back, behind a pillar, while they were saying mass. The church felt as if it was telling me yes, but I wasn't sure which question it was answering. I have to believe it was both.

So this morning I came back to the house. The only thing I was afraid of was that one of the neighbours might see me, see this man who'd been loitering nearby last week, and call the police. But the thaw had set in and was keeping people off the streets. I had to take off my shoes as soon as I'd let myself in, so as not to leave footprints along the hall. I don't want you to know I'm here as soon as you come home. You'll know soon enough.

You must be coming home now, and I want to finish this. I thought of bolting the front door so that you'd think the lock had stuck and perhaps go for a locksmith, but I don't think I'll need to. I haven't much more to tell you. You'll know I'm here long before you find me and read this.

It's getting dark here now in the dining-room with the glass doors shut so that I can't be seen from the street. It makes me feel the wall you knocked down has come back, and my memories are beginning to. I remember now, my wife grew houseplants in here, and I let them all die after she died. I remember the scents that used to fill the room—I can smell them now. She must be here, waiting for me.

And now I'm going to join her in our house. During the last few minutes I've swallowed all the pills. Perhaps that's why I can smell her flowers. As soon as I've finished this I'm going through the trapdoor in the cupboard. There isn't enough space under the house to stretch your arms above your head when you're lying on your back, but I don't think I'll know I'm there for very long. Soon my wife and I will just be in the house. I hope you won't mind if we make it more like ours again. I can't help thinking that one day you may come into this room and find no sliding doors any longer, just a wall. Try and think of it as our present to you and the house.

Boiled Alive

Each weekday morning Mee was first in the pay-office. He would sip coffee from a dwarfish plastic cup and watch the car park rearrange itself as the factory changed shifts, several thousand random blocks of colour gathering about his green car on the concrete field. He would spend the next four hours at the computer, and three hours after lunch. The chirping cursor leapt to do his bidding, danced characters onto the screen. He had charge of half the payroll, half of the three-letter codes that denoted employees so secretively that he didn't even know if he was in his own batch. Now and then Clare trotted in from the outer office with a handful of changes of tax coding, but Mee was mostly unaware of Till, who computed the other half of the payroll, and Macnamara the supervisor, who was always repeating himself, always repeating himself.

Each day after work Mee listened in his car to wartime crooners rhyming the moon and waited until he had a clear path through the car park. The music rode with him along the motorway to the estate that was mounting the sandstone hills. His street was of sandy bungalows, identical except for curtains or cacti or porcelain in the windows. He parked his car in the garage that took the place of one front room and walked down the drive, round the end of his strip of lawn like a hall carpet, and up the path to his front door.

Each night he prepared the next day's dinner and stored it in the refrigerator. He would eat it facing the view back towards the factory, miles away. Roads and looped junctions left no room for trees, but the earliness of headlights signified the onset of winter. He was digging at his dessert with a fork and watching the swarming of lights, the landscape humming constantly like a dynamo, when the telephone rang.

A darts match at the pub, he guessed, or a message from the Homewatch leader, probably about youngsters using the back alleys to take drugs, as if reality weren't enough for them. Munching, he lifted the receiver, and a voice said "Boiled alive."

"Pardon?" Mee wondered if the man had mistaken him for a restaurant—

but the voice was too lugubriously meaningful. "Boiled alive," it repeated in an explanatory tone that sounded almost peevish, and rang off.

No doubt the caller was on drugs and phoning at random, and Mee wanted to believe the phrase was just as meaningless. He switched on the television and watched manic couples win holidays on a quiz show. A dentist's receptionist was leaping and squealing and popping her eyes at her prize when the phone rang again. "Is this the house of Dr Doncaster?" a voice said.

"I'm afraid not, sorry." Mee waited politely for a response, and was about to break the connection when the voice said "Is this the house of Dr Doncaster?"

"I've already said not. Can't you hear me?" Perhaps deafness was why the man was calling. "You've got a wrong number," Mee said, so loudly that the mouthpiece vibrated.

This time the silence was shorter. "Is this the house of Dr Doncaster?"

"Don't be ridiculous. What do you want?" The doctor, Mee thought, and felt somewhat ridiculous himself. It wasn't the voice that had called earlier; it had an odd quality—a blandness, a lack of accent. "Is this—" it recommenced, and he cut it off.

Had its silences really been exactly the same length? Certainly it had repeated itself with precisely the same intonation. He might have been talking to a robot, he thought, but that seemed to miss the point somehow. He went out to the pub, a longer bungalow, and tried to interest himself in the quiz league's semifinal, questions about places he'd never heard of.

Next day the lassitude he always suffered after a morning at the computer was worse, but the sight of men from the assembly line swapping pirated videos in the windowless canteen wakened him and a memory he'd been trying to gain access to. He stopped at the video library in the wine shop on his way home after work. Horror films had occupied the shelves nearest the window: *Shriek of the Mutilated, Headless Eyes, Nightmares in a Damaged Brain, Boiled Alive.*

The box showed photographs of people reddening and screaming, presumably the actors who were listed, though they sounded like pseudonyms. He would learn no more unless he hired a videorecorder. At home he ate boiled beef and watched the lights until he felt their swarming was preventing him from thinking. He was late for the committee meeting at the church hall, and had to struggle to interest himself in the question of rents to be charged for jumble sales and Boy Scout gatherings. He voted against letting the peace movement use the hall. Life wasn't as precarious as they made it out to be, he thought as he strode home, it had a pattern you could glimpse if you had faith.

The phone was ringing as he reached his path. He slammed the door, dashed to the phone, snatched the receiver. "Is this the house of Dr Doncaster?"

Mee let out a long sigh, which his panting interrupted. "Do I get a prize for the right answer?"

Silence. It really was a total silence, empty even of static. "Is this the house of Dr Doncaster?"

"Where you are, you mean? It may be, for all I know."

Silence. Mee found he was counting the seconds. If the silence was even fractionally longer he would know he'd thrown the caller, as he realised he very much wanted to do. But no: "Is this—"

"Go to the devil where you belong, you lunatic," Mee shouted, and chopped at the cradle with the edge of his palm. He nursed his bruised hand and thought of contacting the police. They would only tell him to keep on receiving the calls so that the caller could be traced, and he wouldn't be able to sleep for waiting tensely. He left the phone off the hook overnight and watched *Boiled Alive,* which varied wildly from dream to dream. Whenever he awoke he felt colder, as if the dreams were draining him.

Next morning he said to Till "You've a videorecorder, haven't you?"

Till blinked at him under his perpetual grey-browed scowl. "Used to have. Can't afford it with the kids at private school. Besides, most of the films weren't fit for them to watch. Puts ideas in people's heads, that sort of thing."

"Something you wanted to watch, Mr Mee?" Macnamara said across the room, his hollow drone resounding. "Was there something you wanted to see?"

"A tape in my local library."

"Bring it round on Sunday. Come for dinner after church, my mother likes the company. You can't get too much use out of a machine, am I right? You can't get too much use out of a machine."

Should Mee let him know the kind of film it was? But he might seem to be rejecting Macnamara's gesture. He busied himself at the screen, wondering afresh whether any of the three-letter codes coincided with the employee's car registration or whether someone had ensured they did not. Certainly none of his highest earners had the same codes as the limousines outside.

That night he hired *Boiled Alive* for the weekend. He'd finished eating dinner and watched the racing lights for some time before he realised the phone hadn't rung. He had a sudden irrational conviction that it wouldn't while he had the videocassette. Such thoughts were dangerous, things didn't work like that. All the same, the only call that weekend was from Macnamara, to make sure Mee was coming.

Macnamara lived in the town beyond the factory, in a house at the top of a flight of railed steps. "Here he is," he announced as he let Mee into the long narrow hall beneath a lampshade like a flower of stained glass. "He's here."

His mother darted out from the furthest doorway. She couldn't really be that small, Mee thought nervously, but when she squeezed alongside her son her head was barely as high as his chest. Otherwise, apart from having all the hair, she looked much like Macnamara: thin oval face, sharp nose, colourless lips. "Didn't you bring the film?" she said in a stage whisper. "Sidney said you were bringing a film."

They made Mee think of the voice on the phone, but neither of them would be capable of that voice. He dug the cassette out of his pocket. "Some kind of comedy, is it?" Macnamara said, raising his eyebrows at the title, and to his mother "Some kind of comedy."

She herded them into the dining-room then—to Mee's acute embarrassment, she pretended to charge at them like a goat, emitting sounds of shooing. Dinner was Greek, and went on for hours. Whenever he thought the end was near she produced another course. "Is it good?" she demanded anxiously before he'd had a mouthful, and as soon as he had "It's good, isn't it?" Her whispering was the result of a throat disease, he realised, but nevertheless she talked constantly, interrogating him about himself long after the details ceased to interest him. Worse, she told him in intimate detail about her problems in bringing up her son after his father had deserted them. "How's my Sidney getting on at work?" she asked Mee, and wouldn't let him mumble vaguely. "Fine, I'm sure," he stammered, yearning for it to be time to watch the film.

Macnamara's reluctance was obvious as he picked up the cassette. "Sounds exciting, *Boiled Alive,*" his mother whispered enthusiastically, and he slipped it into the player with a despairing shrug. "That's funny, isn't it?" she suggested as several thin flat scientists squeezed into sight behind the widescreen credits, then she gasped as they inflated, released from the bonds of the words. Whatever they were doing to measure psychic energy, their experiment was going wrong: laboratory monitors were melting, a man's face was blistering. "How do they do that?" Mrs Macnamara cried in a whisper, and Mee had to restrain himself from hushing her, for one of the scientists had just been called Doncaster.

She talked throughout the film. Mee wondered if she was trying to shut out the sight of people being boiled alive by some vindictive psychic power.

"Is that the kind of car you make at the factory?" she whispered as a scientist's hands fused to a steering wheel. Another man's eyes burst one by one, and she struggled to her feet, croaking "I think I'll go to bed now."

Mee stared open-mouthed at the screen, which was filled with a telephone dial. A detective's finger was dialling Mee's phone number. "My mother wants to go to bed," Macnamara growled, but Mee barely noticed he was speaking as the detective, mouthing, said "Is this the house of Dr Doncaster?"

"I'll see you up, Mother," Macnamara said furiously, and Mee lurched forward to listen to the detective. "Is Dr Doncaster there?" . . . "What do the words 'boiled alive' mean to you?" . . . "We all have hidden powers that only need to be unlocked" . . . "We can't talk now, this may be being traced" . . . "Right, I'll meet you in an hour." But he was boiled en route, leaving only his girlfriend, a reporter, to gun down the culprit in a refrigerator. Suddenly the gun was too hot to hold, and as she dropped it, a silhouette stepped out from behind a side of beef. "I am Dr Doncaster," it said.

"The End." Had something been missed out? The tape began to rewind, and as Mee picked up the remote control he noticed Macnamara, who was watching him from the hall. "That wasn't funny," Macnamara said, even slower than usual. "Not funny at all."

Mee thought of apologising, but wasn't sure what for. Had Dr Doncaster really been the culprit, or only in English? The question formed a barrier in his mind as he followed taillights home. Even the inclusion of his number in the film couldn't quite break through.

In the morning he tried to phone the distributor of *Boiled Alive,* but whenever the number wasn't engaged there was no answer. He had to desist when Macnamara kept glaring at him. Otherwise Macnamara behaved as if Mee's visit had never taken place. Mee crouched over the screen and tried to interest himself in the dance of the symbols, telling himself that they were as real as he was.

He had to make himself return the cassette, for his notion that its presence precluded the calls was even stronger. In the library the proprietor held up a box to the bars of his cage. "Lots of naked women being tortured. By the feller who made the one you just had."

"I've no interest in that kind of thing. I only borrowed this because they used my phone number in it."

"I'd sue them. Or send reporters after them, they'll cough up quick enough."

Mee had meant to consult the factory's lawyers, but the nearest television station was less than half an hour's drive away. His phone call was put through to a bright young woman who wanted him to come in straight away and record an interview for the local news programme. They made up his face, sat him in a puffy leather chair on a metal stalk, shone lights on him while the bright young woman asked him if he thought films like *Boiled Alive* should be banned and how "being haunted by phone" was affecting him. On his way out, his head swimming, he made her promise not to broadcast his number.

Why did the interview persist in troubling him? He spent the evening in trying to think, and flung the phone off the hook when it rang just before midnight. Next day he was so preoccupied that he almost deleted his morning's work on the computer. Working at a screen while waiting to watch himself on another didn't help. He was home well before the six o'clock news. Rising crime and unemployment, nuclear escalation, famines, terrorism . . . The bright young woman appeared at last, and there was Mee, trying to look as if he belonged in the leather chair. How plump and red and blotchy his face was! His voice sounded bland and timid as he said that he believed films should be banned if they did harm, he didn't think much of the film anyway, his privacy had been invaded, at the very least the number should be changed in every copy of the film. . . . They might just as well have broadcast his number, since he'd named the film. His consciousness lurched at that, and then he wondered if he had actually just said "It's Dr Doncaster's number, not mine."

The co-presenter turned from the interview with a look that all but winked. "We tried to contact the film's distributor in Wigan, but we understand they're bankrupt. Serves them right, our friend at the wrong end of the phone might say. Now, if you've ever wondered where flies go to in the wintertime—"

Mee turned him off and waited for the phone to ring. Eventually he realised he'd been waiting for hours, hadn't even eaten his dinner. Of course, he thought, people couldn't phone until they'd seen the film. By midnight he thought they might have, but the phone was a black lump of silence. Even when he closed his eyes and tried to sleep, it stood out from the dark.

At least now Macnamara ought to know why Mee had been interested in the film—but neither he nor Till gave any sign of having seen the interview. Their silence unnerved Mee, made him feel guilty about letting himself be interviewed, but why should he blame himself? In the canteen he sensed that half the people who weren't looking at him had only just looked away. They'd better not offend him. Maybe they hadn't been impressed by his appearance on the screen, but they ought to see themselves, bunches of letters he could treat however he liked.

The calls began that evening. Mee heard smothered laughter and sounds of a party in the background every time a different voice asked for Dr Doncaster. None of them was the bland voice that had plagued him with the exact intonation of the line from the film. To his confusion, he found he almost missed that voice. After the fourth call he went to the pub.

Though he didn't recognise many of the drinkers, he thought they all recognised him. Freddy from the darts team bought him a drink, but his small talk sounded stiffer than the dubbing in the film, and so, when Mee listened, did all the conversations around him. When he began to suspect that some of the drinkers were assuming more than one voice, he stalked home through the floodlit identical streets.

He waited for the voice that knew its lines, but there were no more calls. He slept unexpectedly, woke late, drove hastily to work. He had to park at the far side of the concrete field and trudge between the cooling cars in a drizzle. Several people and some kind of machine paced him beyond two ranks of cars.

"How's your mother now?"

"Getting better, getting better," Macnamara told Till, and they fell silent as Mee came in. If they blamed him for that too, let them say so. Maybe he sounded like three letters on a screen, but they mustn't treat him as if he weren't real. Perhaps the voice that knew its lines hadn't been able to reach him last night because of the hoax calls, he was thinking.

Despite Macnamara's disapproval, Mee switched off his computer in time to beat the homeward rush. But by the time his car started, there was a long queue for the exit. Car, he thought, feeling trapped in three letters. He swung into the course of light at last and edged into the middle lane as soon as he could. He was almost unaware that the car was moving when lights blazed into the vehicle and flung his silhouette onto the windscreen.

He thought of the floodlights at the television interview. But it was a lorry, blaring at him to force him into the outer lane, where lights were racing faster than he was. When he trod on the accelerator the car jerked towards the taillights beyond the half-blinded windscreen, too fast, too close. He swerved into a momentary gap in the outer race, overtook the car in the middle lane, dodged in ahead of it. He was groaning with relief when the entire lorry slewed towards him.

It had jackknifed, swinging across all three lanes. It struck the car behind Mee's, hurling it into the inside lane, where it smashed into another vehicle. The impact jarred a roof light on, and Mee glimpsed the driver's face, lockjawed with terror, in the instant before it went out. As he sped onward he heard traffic crashing into the far side of the lorry and into one another, the tardy screech of brakes, crash upon crash, screams of the injured and dying. When he reached home he could see fires from his window, vehicles blazing hundreds of yards apart. Behind the blaze headlights bunched for miles, a comet's tail.

The local newscast was devoted to the crash. "Some of the drivers were driving as if they had no sense of reality," a police spokesman said. He couldn't mean Mee, since Mee hadn't been involved. Later, at the committee meeting in the church hall, Mee mentioned how he'd been ahead of the crash. How could he have known that the chairman's sister and nephews had been killed in the pile-up? The committee seemed almost to blame Mee for surviving. As he trudged home he recognised screams in an empty street. Someone must be watching the nude women being tortured in one of the neat bright houses.

In the morning there was no sign of the crash. A sprinkling of snow covered any traces it had left on the motorway. Till asked how close to it Mee had been, but Mee denied all knowledge and stood at the window, hardly aware of the plastic tumbler of coffee in his reddening hand. Surely the car park hadn't always looked so short of perspective.

He was restless all day. He felt as if the heat of the fires on the motorway, or of the guilt that everyone was trying to make him accept, were building up in his skull. Even the green screen wasn't soothing. He kept straying near Till's desk, but was never in time to see the letters of his name. If they were there, what would it prove? They couldn't reduce him, nor could Macnamara's inability to get his lines right first time, nor the unnatural silence when the computers were switched off.

There had been no calls while he was at home last night, but tonight the phone greeted him with the young shrill voice of an admirer of *Boiled Alive*, accusing Mee of having put the distributor out of business just because he wasn't able to distinguish between fiction and reality. When it wouldn't listen to his objections, Mee cut it off. On television a streetful of identical houses let out their men to advertise a car, and he saw that one of the men who had the wrong car was himself.

Did they think they could do what they liked with him? Now that he'd appeared before the cameras, was he fair game for however they wanted to edit him? They were trying to undermine his sense of reality, he thought; the police spokesman had as good as said Mee's was above average. That would explain why, when he went shopping at the supermarket, everyone not only pretended not to recognise him but acted like extras around him, most of them using the same voice. When he strode home the only sounds in the glaring streets were his footsteps, as if someone had turned off the other sounds or forgotten to record them.

The idea of living in a film wasn't entirely unappealing. If it had been a better film he might even have been flattered. Being able to repeat favourite moments and speed up the boring parts was certainly tempting, not to mention the ability to say of bad times "it's only a film" or to have a hidden voice explain things when he looked at them. But how much control would he have? About as much as one generally has of one's life, he thought, then felt as if the voice that knew its lines could put him right if he could just work out how to respond.

Next day the snow had melted, but there were no marks of the crash. The view from his car trembled slightly in the frames of the windscreen and windows. It must be the car that was shaking, not the image, for he noticed cameras in several of the vehicles that passed him, filming him. They must have been filming him before the crash—that was how they'd been on the scene so quickly. Why, the camera car might have made the lorry jackknife!

He would have pointed this out to his colleagues, except that they didn't seem real enough to be worth telling, Macnamara and his dogged repetitions, Till and his switched-off silences. The computer screen seemed more real, and took more out of him. But in the canteen at lunchtime, he was unexpectedly upset by the sight of two men smirking at him as they exchanged cassettes, for one of the cassettes was *Boiled Alive*.

They wanted him to see them, did they? Then let them see what he could do. At last he knew why he'd been missing the voice on the phone: he wanted to be told about the hidden powers—but he didn't need it to unlock him. As he stared at the cassette of *Boiled Alive* the fire in his head flared up, yet he didn't feel as if he was focusing it, he felt reality focusing through him, the cassette and the man who held it growing intensely real. "Shit," the man cried, and dropped the cassette deafeningly to clutch the fingers of one hand with the other.

"Hot stuff, eh? Too hot to handle?" Mee suggested, and felt he was cheapening himself. He swung away and hurried through the corridors, past the unstable windowscapes. The shaking of his reality had just been a step in the process of unlocking, then. In an impersonal way, he had never felt nearly so real.

He sat in the pay-office and gazed at his blank monitor. What would happen when they realised what he'd done in the canteen? They already disapproved of him, but now they'd try to use him or stop him, not realising how they would be endangering themselves. It wasn't as if he was sure he could control the power: he felt more like a channel for reality, far harder to close than to open. The inside of his head felt dry and hot and shrunken. He had to think what to do before Till and Macnamara came back.

He prowled the office, staring at the blank walls, at his car in the midst of the random pattern of cars. He even switched on Till's screen and scanned the columns. There were the letters of his name, against a salary several times the size of his. Something about the sight of a version of himself he would have liked to be inspired him. He turned off the computer and slipped down to his car.

Between the factory and home he managed not to pass or be passed by another vehicle. It was a question of balance, he thought. He had to preserve a balance between reality before he'd seen the film and after, between himself and the way the world saw him, between the governments that would want to use him as a weapon. His street was deserted, which was welcome: to be seen at the start of his mission, to have to cope with someone else's perception of him, would only confuse him. It seemed wholly appropriate that he would start by entering so unremarkable a house.

He bolted the front and back doors and secured all the windows. He hadn't prepared tonight's dinner, he saw. That didn't matter; the less he ate, the sooner he would finish. He was surprised how easy it was to take responsibility for the world. He'd expected to feel lonely, but he found he didn't; perhaps there were others like himself. He used the toilet, combed his hair in front of the mirror, straightened his tie, brushed his shoulders, and then sat down by the phone with his back to the window and dialled his own number. When the phone rang he picked it up, knowing that he wouldn't get the intonation quite right and that he'd have to go for retake after retake, especially if he heard any kind of a response. "Is this the house of Dr Doncaster?" he said.

Another World

When Sonny thought his father hadn't stirred for three days he took the old man's spectacles off. His father was sitting in the chair stuffed with pages from the Bible, facing the cracked window that looked towards the church beyond the shattered targets of the maisonnettes, the church that the women came out of. The black lenses rose from his father's ashen face, and sunlight blazed into the grey eyes, ball-bearings set in webs of blood. They didn't blink. Sonny pulled the wrinkled lids over them and fell to his knees on the knobbly carpet to pray that the Kingdom of God would come to him. He hadn't said a tithe of the prayers he knew when the sunlight crept away towards the church.

He had to keep his promise that he'd made on all the Bibles in the chair— proofs of the Bibles they printed where his father used to work until he'd realised that God's word required no proof—but he shouldn't leave his father where the world might see that he was helpless. He slipped one arm beneath his father's shrivelled thighs and the other around his shoulders, which protruded like the beginnings of wings, and lifted him. His father was almost the shape of the chair, and not at all pliable. His dusty boots kicked the air as Sonny carried him up the narrow walled-in staircase and lowered him onto the bed. He flourished his bent legs until Sonny eased him onto his side, where he lay as if he were trying to shrink, legs pressed together, hands clasped to his chest. The sight was far less dismaying than the thought of going out of the house.

He didn't know how many nights he had kept watch by his father, but he was so tired that he wasn't sure if he heard the world scratching at the walls on both sides of him. His father must have suspected that the Kingdom of God wouldn't be here by now, whatever he'd been told the last time he had gone out into the world. Sonny made himself hurry downstairs and take the spectacles from the tiled mantelpiece.

"Eye of the needle, eye of the needle," his father would mutter whenever he put on the spectacles. Sonny had thought they were meant to blind him to the world, the devil's work—that the Almighty had guided his father as he strode to the market beyond the church, striding so fiercely that the world fell back—but now he saw that two holes had been scratched in the thick black paint which coated the lenses. The arms nipped the sides of his skull, and two fists seemed to close around his eyes: the hands of God? The little he could see through the two holes was piercingly clear. He gazed at the room that shared the ground floor with the stony kitchen where his father scrubbed the clothes in disinfectant, gazed at the walls his father had scraped bare for humility to help God repossess the house, the Stations of the Cross that led around them to the poster of the Shroud. Blood appeared to start out of the nailed hands, but he mustn't let that detain him. Surely it was a sign that he could stride through hell, as his father used to.

His father had braved the forbidden world out there on his behalf, and Sonny had grown more and more admiring and grateful, but now he wished his father had taken him out just once, so that he would know what to expect. His father had asked them to come from the Kingdom of God to take care of his body, but would they provide for Sonny? If not, where was his food to come from? You weren't supposed to expect miracles, not in this world. He clasped his hands together until the fingers burned red and white and prayed for guidance, his voice ringing like a stone bell between the scraped walls, and then he made himself grasp the latch on the outer door.

As he inched the door open his mouth filled with the taste of the disinfectant his father used to wash their food. A breeze darted through the gap and touched his face. It felt as if the world had given him a large soft kiss that smelled of dust and smoke and the heat of the summer day. He flinched, almost trapping his fingers as he thrust the door away from him, and reminded himself of his promise. Gripping the key in his pocket as if it were a holy relic, he took his first step into the world.

The smell of the world surged at him, heat and fallen houses and charred rubbish, murmuring with voices and machinery. The sunlight lifted his scalp. Even with the spectacles to protect him, the world felt capable of bursting his senses. He pressed himself against the wall of the house, and felt it shiver. He recoiled from the threat of finding it less solid than he prayed it was, and the pavement that met the house flung him to his knees.

The whole pavement was uneven. The few stones that weren't broken had reared up as though the Day of Judgement were at hand. As he rubbed his bare knees, he saw that every house except his father's was derelict, gaping. Behind him the street ended at a wall higher than the houses, where litter struggled to tear itself loose from coils of barbed wire.

He would never be able to walk on the upheaved pavement unless he could see better. He narrowed his eyes and took off the spectacles, praying breathlessly. The husks of houses surged forward on a wave of sound and smells, but so long as he kept his eyes slitted it seemed he could stave off the world. He strode along the pavement, which flickered like a storm as his eyelids trembled. He had only just passed the last house when he staggered and pressed his hands to his scalp. The world had opened around him, and he felt as if his skull had.

The market stretched across waste land scribbled out by tracks of vehicles. There were so many vans and stalls and open suitcases he was afraid to think of counting them. A crowd that seemed trapped within the boundaries of the market trudged the muddy aisles and picked at merchandise. A man was sprinkling petrol on a heap of sprouts to help them burn. Beyond the shouts of traders and the smouldering piles of rubbish, a few blackened trees poked at a sky like luminous chalk. To his left, past several roofless streets, were concrete stacks of fifty floors or more, where the crowd in the market must live. So this was hell, and only the near edge of hell. Sonny retreated towards the church.

Then he caught hold of his mouth to keep in a cry. It wasn't a church anymore, it was a GIVEAWAY DISCOUNT WAREHOUSE. All women were prostitutes, and he'd thought the women he'd seen leaving the church every night had been confessing their sins—but they'd been using God's house to sell the devil's wares. The realisation felt as if the world had made a grab at him. He fumbled the spectacles onto his face just as three muddy children sidled towards him.

Their faces crowded into the clear area of the lens. "Are you a singer or something, mister?" a boy whose nostrils were stained brown demanded. "Are you on video?"

"He's that horror writer with them glasses," said a girl with a bruised mouth missing several teeth.

"Thought he was a fucking Boy Scout before," said a girl in a mangy fur coat. A fleshy bubble swelled out of her mouth and popped sharply. "That why you're dressed like that, mister, because you like little boys?"

They were only imps, sent to torment him. If they seemed about to touch him he could lash out at them with his heavy boots. "Where can I find the Kingdom of God?" he said.

"Here it is, mister," the bubbling girl sniggered, lifting the hem of her coat.

"He means the church, the real church," the bruised girl said reprovingly. "You mean the real church, don't you, mister? It's past them hoardings."

Beyond the discount warehouse, at the end of the street that bordered the market, stood three large boards propped with timber. Once the stares and titters were behind him, he took the spectacles off. There was so much smoke and dust on the road ahead that the cars speeding nowhere in both directions appeared to be driverless. The road led under hooked lamps past buildings which he knew instinctively were no longer what they had been created for, lengths of plastic low on the black façades announcing that they were VIDEO UNIVERSE WITH HORROR AND SCI-FI AND WAR, THE SMOKE SHOP, THE DRUGSTORE, MAGAZINES TO SUIT ALL TASTES. There was CLEANORAMA, but he thought it came far too late. He peered narrowly to his left, and the hoardings thrust their temptations at him, a long giant sun-tanned woman wearing three scraps of cloth, an enormous car made out of sunset, a cigarette several times as long as he was tall. Past them was the church.

It didn't look much like one. It was a wedge that he supposed you'd call a pyramid, almost featureless except for a few slits full of coloured splinters and, at the tip of the wedge, a concrete cross. Feeling as if he were in a parable, though he'd no notion what it meant or if it was intended to convey anything to him, he stalked past the hoardings and a police station like the sheared-off bottom storey of a tower block, and up the gravel path.

The doors of the church seemed less solid than the doors of his father's house. When he closed them behind him, the noise of traffic seeped in. At least the colours draped over the pine pews were peaceful. Kneeling women glanced and then stared at him as he tiptoed towards the altar. The light through a red splinter caught a sign on a door. FATHER PAUL, it said. Daring to open his eyes fully at last, Sonny stepped through the veils of coloured light he couldn't see until they touched him, and pushed the door wide.

A priest was kneeling on a low velvety shelf, the only furniture in the stark room. His broad red face clenched on a pale O of mouth. "That's not the way, my son. Stay on the other side if you're here to confess."

"I'm looking for the Kingdom of God," Sonny pleaded.

"So should we all, and nothing could be simpler. Everything is God's."

"In here, you mean?"

"And outside too."

He was a false prophet, Sonny realised with a shudder that set bright colours dancing on his arms and legs, and this was the devil's mockery of a church. He stepped out of reach of the hairy hands that looked boiled red and collided with a pew, which spilled black books. The priest was rising like smoke and flames when a voice behind Sonny said "Any trouble, Father?"

He might have been another priest, he was dressed blackly enough. The thought of being locked up before he could have his father taken care of made Sonny reckless. "He's not a priest," he blurted.

"I'd like to know what you think you are, coming to church dressed like that," the policeman said, low and leaden. "It may be legal now, but we can do without your sort flaunting yourselves in church. Just give me the word, Father, and I'll teach him to say his prayers."

Sonny backed away and fled as colours snatched at him. Slitting his eyes, he blundered out of the concrete trap. He ought to take refuge at home before the policeman saw where he lived, and then venture out after dark. But he had only reached the elbow on which the giantess was supporting herself when a car drew up beside him.

He thought he was going to be arrested. He recoiled against the hot giantess, who yielded far too much like flesh, as the driver's square head poked out, a titan's blonde shaving brush. "Are you lost?" the driver said. "Can I help?"

Sonny heaved himself away from the cardboardy flesh and staggered against the car. Not having eaten since before his father had stopped moving was catching up with him. He managed to steady himself as the driver climbed out of the car. "Do you live near here? Can I take you home? Unless you'd like me to find you somewhere else to stay."

He was trying to find out where Sonny lived. "The Kingdom of God," Sonny said deliberately.

"Is that a church organisation? I don't know where it is, but we'll go there if you can tell me."

That took Sonny aback. Surely anyone who meant to tempt him must claim to know where it was. Could this person be as lost and in need of it as Sonny was? "You really look as if you should be with someone," the driver said. "Have you nobody at home?"

Before Sonny could close himself against it, a flood of loss and loneliness passed through him. "Nobody who can help," he croaked.

"Then let's find you where you're looking for. My name's Sam, by the way." Sam held out a hand as if to take Sonny's, but stopped short of doing so. "What's it like, do you know? What kind of building?"

The sensitivity Sam had shown by not touching him won Sonny over. "All I know is it's not far."

"We can still drive if you like."

They would be too close in the car, and Sonny would be giving up too much control. He peered back at the church, where the policeman seemed content to glower from the doorway. "I'll walk," he said.

Past the hoardings, the smell of the market pounced on him. The smoke of charred vegetables scraped inside his head as he hurried by, trying to blink his pinched eyes clear. Ahead of him the road of cars flexed like a serpent, like the leg of a giantess. He dug his knuckles into his eyes and told himself that it was only curving past more old buildings claimed by names, MACHO MILITARIA, CAPTIVATING TOTS, LUSCIOUS LEGS, SEX AIDS. . . . Some of the strips of plastic embraced two buildings. "It is an actual place we're looking for, is it?" Sam said, trotting beside him.

Sonny hesitated, but how could he save a soul unless he spoke the truth? "That's what my father said."

"He sent you out, did he?"

"Into the world, yes." Both question and answer seemed to suggest more than they said, but what did the parable mean? "I had to come," he said in his father's defence. "There's nobody else."

Now that the market and its stench were left behind, the houses appeared to be flourishing. The façades ahead were white or newly painted, their front windows swelled importantly. Gleaming plaques beside their doors named doctors and dentists, false healers one must never turn to. Weren't these houses too puffed up to harbour the Kingdom of God? But the people were the same as the lost souls of the waste land: faces stared at him from cars, murmured about him beyond the lacy curtains of a waiting-room; two young women exhaling smoke sidled past him and hooted with laughter. "He'll get no girls if he goes round dressed like that," one spluttered.

"Maybe he's got better things to do," Sam said icily.

Sonny drew in a breath that tasted of disinfectant, which seemed too clear a sign to doubt. As he strode past the dentist's open door he experienced a rush of trust and hope such as he'd never even felt towards his father. There must be others like himself or potentially like himself in the world, and surely Sam was one. "It's how my father dressed me," he confided.

"Has it anything to do with where we're looking for?"

"Yes, to remind me I'm a child of God," Sonny said, and was reminded more keenly by a twinge from the marks of the birch.

"Does your father dress like that too, then?"

"Of course not," Sonny giggled. "He was, he's my father."

Sam appeared not to notice his indiscretion. "How old are you anyway? You dress like ten years old, but you could be in your early thirties."

"We don't need to know. Years like that don't matter, only the minutes before the fire that consumes the world. If we've spent our time counting our years we'll never be able to prepare ourselves to enter the Kingdom of God.

Not the place we're going now, the place of which that's a symbol. Where we're going now is the first and last church, the one that won't be cast into the fire where all corruption goes. That's because we keep ourselves pure in every way and cast out the women once they've given birth."

Sam's mouth opened, but what it said seemed not to be what it had opened for. "You mean your mother."

Though it hadn't the tone of a question, Sonny thought it best to make things clear. "Questions come from the devil. They're how the world tries to trick the faithful."

"So you have to look after your father all by yourself."

Why should that matter to Sam? Sonny couldn't recall having said his father needed looking after. He tried to let the truth speak through him as he searched the curves ahead, where gleaming houses rested their bellies on mats of grass. Newspapers and boards quoting newspapers hung on the corner of a side street, and he glanced away from the devil's messages, perhaps too hastily: the world seemed to pant hotly at him, the houses swelled with another breath. "Only the pure may touch the pure," he mumbled.

"That's why I mustn't touch you."

Such a surge of trust passed through Sonny that his body felt unfamiliar. "Maybe you'll be able to," he blurted.

"Not if—"

"We can all be saved. We just have to admit we need to be," Sonny reassured Sam, who agreed so readily that Sonny wondered if he'd missed the point somehow. Houses white as virgins breathed their stony breaths and expanded their bellies until every polished name-plaque turned to the sun and shone. For a moment he thought it was God who was filling the virgin bellies, and then he recoiled from himself. How could he let the world think for him? Where had he gone wrong? "Quick," he gasped, and tottered round, almost touching Sam's bare downy arm.

The world twisted and tried to throw him. The fat houses between him and the market began to dance, wobbling their whited bellies. He mustn't think of leaning on Sam, but a distant edge of him wished he could. He held the spectacles to his eyes as he came abreast of the dangling newspapers, but the darkness of the lenses seemed a pit into which he was close to falling. As he stepped off the pavement to cross the side street, he felt as if he were stepping off a cliff.

He faltered in the middle of the side street, though cars snarled beside him. He thought a voice had spoken to him, saying "King God." He snatched off the spectacles so eagerly that one lens shattered between his finger and thumb. Black shards crunched under his feet, the sun went for his eyes, but none of this mattered. He hadn't heard a voice, he'd seen a sign. It hadn't just said King God; only the lens had made it seem to. It said Kingdom of God, and it was in a window.

He ran across the side street, scrambled onto the pavement. How could he have missed the sign before? Surely he needn't blame Sam for distracting him. The Kingdom was here now, that was all that mattered—here beyond the window that blazed like a golden door, like a fire in which only the name of the Kingdom was visible, never to be consumed. He took another pace towards it, and the sunlight drained out of the window, leaving a surface grey with dust and old rain, which he was nevertheless able to see through. Beyond it was ruined emptiness.

He stumbled forward so as not to fall. The sign he'd seen was a faded placard in the window, beside a door whose lock had been gouged out. A rail dragged down by stained curtains leaned diagonally across the window. Several chairs lay on the bare floorboards, their legs broken, their entrails sprung. On a table against the ragged wall, a dead cat glistened restlessly.

Sam pressed his forehead against the window. "This can't be it, can it? Nobody's been here for months."

Sonny's father had been, only days ago: wasn't that what he'd said? He must have meant it as a parable, or meant that he'd met some of the brethren. What could Sonny do now, as the world throbbed with muffled mocking laughter? Go back home in case the Kingdom had come there and if not, stay nearby until they found him? Then Sam said "Don't worry, I'll help you. Shall we see to your father first?"

The window had blackened his forehead as if he'd been branded, and Sonny seemed to perceive him all at once more clearly. "See to him how?"

"Have him taken care of, however he needs to be."

"Who by?"

"I won't know that until I've seen him. I promise I'll do whatever's best for both of you."

Sonny swallowed, though it felt like swallowing chunks of the world. "Who are you?"

"Nobody special, but you might say I help save people too. I'm a social worker."

Sonny felt as if he'd been punched in the stomach, the way his father had punched him sometimes to make him remember. He doubled up, but he had nothing to vomit. People who said they were social were socialists, communists, architects of the devil's kingdom, and he'd let one of them entice him, hadn't even realised he was being led. Perhaps the ruined shop had been set up for him to see, to turn him aside from searching further.

Sam had stepped back. He was afraid Sonny would be sick on him, Sonny realised, and flew at him, retching. When Sam retreated, Sonny turned with the whirlpool of sky and bloated buildings and staggered to the corner of the street, almost toppling into the parade of cars. He jammed the one-eyed spectacles onto his face and fled.

His legs were wavering so much that a kind of dance was the only way he could keep on his feet. The houses joined in, sluggishly flirting their bellies at him, growing blacker as he jigged onward. The giantess lazily raised her uppermost leg, the stench of charred rotten vegetables surged at him down the uneven street. Compared with Sam and the virginal buildings, the smell seemed at least honestly corrupt. It made him feel he was going home.

He was appalled by how familiar the world already seemed to him. The children jeering "Pirate" at him, the pinched faces eager for a bargain, a trader kicking a van that wouldn't start, Sonny thought for a moment which felt like the rim of a bottomless pit that he could have been any one of them. As he stumbled past the discount church and down the disused street he wept to realise that he liked the feel of the open sky more than he expected to like the low dimness of the house. Then he wondered if he might have left his father alone for too long, and fell twice in his haste to get home.

He dug his key into the lock, reeled into the house as the door yielded, shouldered it closed behind him. A smell of disinfectant that seemed holier than incense closed around him. He mustn't let it comfort him until he had taken care of his father. Anyone who'd seen his father sitting in the Bible chair might wonder where he was now, might even try to find him.

His father lay as Sonny had left him, straining to touch his clasped hands with his knees. Sonny gathered him up and wavered downstairs, thumping the staircase wall with his father's shrivelled ankles and once with his uncombed head. Would it look more natural to have his father kneeling in the front room? As soon as he tried, his father keeled over. Sonny sat him on the Bibles and stood back. His father looked at peace now, ready for anything. The sight was making Sonny feel that the Kingdom of God was near when he heard the key turn in the front door.

He'd been so anxious to reach his father that he'd left the key in the lock. He knew instinctively that it wasn't the Kingdom of God at the door. He felt the house stiffen against the world that was reaching in for his father and him. He scrabbled the hall door open. Sam was in the hall.

All Sonny could think of was his father, powerless to defend himself or even to dodge the grasp of the world. "Get out," he screamed, and when his voice only made Sam flinch, he forgot the warning his father had given him, the warning that was so important Sonny's stomach had been bruised for a week. He put his hands on Sam to cast the intruder out of the house.

And then he realised how thoroughly the world had tricked him, for Sam's chest was the memory Sonny had driven so deep in his mind it had been like forgetting: his mother's chest, soft and warm and thrusting. He cried out as loudly and shrilly as Sam did, and flung her backwards onto the broken road. He staggered after her, for he wasn't fit to stay in a house that had been dedicated to God. He hadn't been ready to venture into the world after all, and it had possessed him. In the moment when he'd flung Sam's breasts away from him he'd felt his body reach secretly for her.

He slammed the door and snatched the key and flew at her, driving her towards the waste where the lost souls swarmed under the dead sky. He tore the spectacles off and shied them at her, narrowly missing her face. The lost souls might tear him to pieces when they saw he was routing one of them, but perhaps he could destroy her first—anything to prevent the world from reaching his father ahead of the Kingdom of God. Then he threw up his hands and wailed and gnashed his teeth, for the world had already touched his father. He had been so anxious to take his father to the safety of the Bibles that he'd forgotten to disinfect himself. He'd held his father with hands the world had tainted.

A smell that made him think of disinfectant drifted along the street to mock him. It was of petrol, in a jug that the trader who had kicked the van was carrying. The trader glanced at the spectacle of Sonny lurching at Sam, trying to knock her down as she retreated towards the market with her hands held out to calm him, and then the trader turned away as if he'd seen nothing unusual. He put down the jug in order to unscrew the cap on the side of the van, and at once Sonny knew exactly what to do.

He ran past Sam and grabbed a stick with a peeling red-hot tip from the nearest fire, and darted to the jug of petrol. He had just seized the handle when the trader turned and lunged at him. Sonny would have splashed petrol over him to drive him back, but how could he waste his father's only salvation? He tipped the jug over himself, and the world shrank back from him, unable to stop him. He poured the last inch of petrol into his mouth.

"Don't," Sam cried, and Sonny knew he was doing right at last. The taste like disinfectant stronger than he'd ever drunk confirmed it too. He ran at Sam, and she sprawled backwards, afraid he meant to spew petrol at her or brand her with the stick. Smiling for the first time since he could remember, Sonny strode back to the house.

He was turning the key when Sam and more of the devil's horde came running. Sonny made a red-hot sign of the cross in the air and stepped into the house, and threw the key contemptuously at them. The stick had burned short as he strode, the mouthful of petrol was searing his nostrils, but he had time, he mustn't swallow. The stick scorched his fingers as he took the three strides across the room to his father. Carefully opening his mouth, he anointed his father and the chair, and then he sat on his father's lap for the first time in his life. It was unyielding as iron, yet he had never felt so peaceful. Perhaps this was the Kingdom of God, or was about to be. As he touched the fire to his chest, he knew he had reached the end of the parable. He prayed he was about to learn its meaning.

End of the Line

"*Pook.*"

"Is this Mrs Pook?"

"Who wants to know?"

"My name . . . My name is Roger and I think you may be interested in what I have to offer you."

"That's what you say. You don't know a thing about me."

"Don't you wish you could see what I look like?"

"Why, what have you got on?"

"I mean, don't you wish you could see my face?"

"Not if it looks like you sound. Mum, there's some weird character on the phone."

"Hang on, I thought you said you were Mrs—"

"He's saying would I like to watch him."

"Who's speaking, please? What have you been suggesting to my daughter?"

"My name is Rum, that is, my name's Ralph, and I think you may be interested in what I'm offering."

"I doubt it. Don't I know you?"

"My name's Ralph."

"I don't know anyone called Ralph, but I'm sure I know your voice. What's your game?"

"He said his name was Roger, Mum, not Ralph."

"Did he now. Charlie? Charlie, pick up the extension and listen to this."

"Mrs Pook, if I can just explain—"

"Charlie, will you pick up the extension. There's one of those perverts who like to hide behind a phone. He can't even remember his own name."

"Who the fuck is this? What do you want with my wife?"

"My name's Ralph, Mr Pook, and perhaps I can speak to you. I'm calling on behalf of—"

"Whoever he is, Charlie, his name isn't Ralph."

"My name isn't important, Mr Pook. I should like to off—"

"Don't you tell me what's important, pal, specially not on my fucking phone. What do you want? How did you get this number?"

"Out of the directory. Can I take just a few minutes of your time? We'd like to offer you a way of avoiding misunderstandings like this one."

"It's we now, is it? You and who else?"

"I'm calling on be—"

"Charlie, I think I know who—"

"Tell you what, pal, I don't care how many of you there are. Just you say where I can find you and we'll settle it like men."

"Just put it down. Just put it down."

"What are you mumbling about, pal? Lost your voice?"

"Mrs Pook, are you still there?"

"Never mind talking to my fucking wife. This is between you and me, pal. If you say another word to her—"

"That's enough, Charlie. Yes, I'm here."

"Mrs Pook, would your first name be Lesley?"

"That's it, pal! I'm warning you! If any fucker says another fucking word—"

"Just put it down," Speke told himself again, and this time he succeeded. The long room was full of echoes of his voice in voices other than his own: "I'm speaking on behalf. . . ." "Don't you wish. . . ." During the conversation his surroundings—the white desks staffed by fellow workers whom he scarcely knew, the walls to which the indirect lighting lent the appearance of luminous chalk, the stark black columns of names and addresses and numbers on the page in front of him—had grown so enigmatic they seemed meaningless, and the only way he could think of to escape this meaninglessness was by speaking. He crossed out Pook and keyed the next number. "Mrs Pool?"

"This is she."

"I wonder if I could take just a few minutes of your time."

"Take as much as you like if it's any use to you."

"My name is Roger and I'm calling on behalf of Face to Face Communications. I should have said that to begin with."

"No need to be nervous of me, especially not on the phone."

"I mum, I'm not. I was going to ask don't you wish you could see what I look like."

"Not much chance of that, I'm afraid."

"On the phone, you mean. Well, I'm calling to offer—"

"Or anywhere else."

"I don't rum realum rea*lum* really under—"

"I could have seen you up to a few years ago. Do you look as you sound?"

"I suppum."

"I'm sorry that I'm blind, then."

"No, it's my fault. I mean, that's not my fault, I mean I'm the one who should be sorry, apologising, that's to sum—" He managed to drag the receiver away from his mouth, which was still gabbling, and plant the handset in its cradle. He crossed out her name almost blindly and closed his eyes tight, but had to open them as soon as he heard voices reiterating portions of the formula around him. He focused on the next clear line in the column and, grabbing the receiver, called the number. "Mr Poole?"

"Yes."

"This is *Mr* Poole?"

"Who, you are?"

"No, I'm saying you are, are you?"

"Why, do you know different?"

"Yum, you don't sound—" To Speke it sounded like a woman trying to be gruff—like Lesley, he thought, or even his daughter, if hers had been the voice which had answered the Pooks' phone. "My name is Roger," he said hastily, "and I'm calling on behalf of Face to Face Communications. I wonder if you can spare me a few minutes of your time."

"It'd be hard for me to spare anyone else's."

"Well, qum. Dum. Um, don't you wish you could see my face?"

"What's so special about it?"

"Not just my face, anyone's on the phone. I'd like to offer you a month's free trial of the latest breakthrough in communication, the videphone."

"So that you can see if I'm who I say I am? Who did you think I was?"

"Was when?"

"Before I was who I said I was."

"Forgum. Forgive me, but you sound exactly like—"

"Sounds like you've got a wrong number," the voice said, and cut itself off.

It seemed to have lodged in his head, blotting out the overlapping voices around him. He returned the handset to its housing and made his way up the aisle to the supervisor's desk, feeling as if his feet were trying to outrun each other. The supervisor was comparing entries on forms with names and addresses in her directory. "How's it coming, Roger?" she said, though he hadn't seen her glance at him.

"A bit hit-and-miss this evening, Mrs Shillingsworth," he managed to say without stumbling. "I wonder if I should vary my approach."

"It seems to be working for everyone else," she said, indicating the forms with an expansive gesture. "Have you any customers for me?"

"Not yet tonight. That's what I was saying."

She ticked a box on the form she was examining and raised her wide-eyed placid flawless face to give him a single blink. "So what did you want to suggest?"

"Maybum, jum, just that maybe we could use our own voices a bit more, I mean our own words."

"I'll mention it next time the boss comes on-screen. Have they installed yours yet, by the way?"

"They were supposed to have by now, but we're still waiting."

"It's important to you, isn't it?"

"I didn't think seeing people's faces while I'm talking to them was, but now I know I can. . . ."

"Customers have priority. I'll speak to the engineers anyway. As for your calls, you can play them by ear to a certain extent. Just don't go mad." She looked down quickly, clearing her throat, and pulled the next form towards herself. "Give them another half an hour, and if you haven't had any joy by then I'll let you go."

The conversation had left Speke feeling locked into the formula, which sounded more enigmatic every time he placed a call. "My name is Roger and I'm speaking on behalf of—"

Only half an hour to go . . .

"My name is Roger and I'm speaking—"

Only twenty-eight minutes . . .

"My name is Roger and I—"

Only twenty-six . . .

"My name is Roger—"

Twenty-four minutes, twenty-two, twenty, one thousand and eighty seconds, nine hundred and fifty-seven, eight hundred and forty-one, seven hundred and . . .

"My name is Roger and I'm speaking on behalf of Face to Face Communications."

"Really."

"Yes, I wonder if I can borrow a few minutes of your time. I expect that at this very moment you're wishing you could see my face."

"Really."

"Yes, I know I am. I'd like to offer you a month's free trial of the latest breakthrough in communication, the videphone."

"Really."

"Yes, you must know people who already have one, but perhaps you think it's a luxury you can't afford. I'm here to tell you, Mr Pore, that our technicians have brought the cost down to the level of your pocket, even my pockum. If you'll allow us to install our latest model in your home for a month at no obligation to you, you can see for yourself."

"Really."

"That's what I said."

"Well, go ahead."

"Sorry, you wum— You're asking me to arrange a trial?"

"I thought that was why you were calling, Roger."

"Yes, of course. Just a mum, I'll just gum—" Speke had been growing more and more convinced that Pore was making fun of him. He snatched a form from the pile beside the six-inch screen, on which electrical disturbances continued to flicker as though they were about to take shape. "Let me just take a few details," he said.

Pore responded to his name and address with no more than a grunt at each, and emitted so vague a sound when he was asked what times would be best for him that Speke suggested times which would be convenient for himself, not that it had anything to do with him. When he returned the handset to its nest his half an hour had almost elapsed, but he couldn't call it a day now that he might have made a sale. He pushed the form to the edge of his desk to be collected by the supervisor and found his gaze straying up the column in the directory to Pook, Charles. He crossed out the listing until it resembled a black slit in the page, and then he wished he'd memorised the number.

"My name is Roger and I'm speaking," he repeated as he drove home. Figures were silhouetted against the illuminated windows of shops, or rendered monochrome by streetlights, or spotlighted by headlamps. On the two miles of dual carriageway between the office block and the tower block where he lived he couldn't distinguish a single face, even when he peered in the rearview mirror. Large fierce bare bulbs guarded the car park around the tower block, and the glare of them pulled a bunch of shadows out of him as he left the Mini and walked to the entrance. For a moment numbers other than the combination for the doors suggested themselves to him. He keyed the correct sequence and shouldered his way in.

Although the tower blocks had been gentrified it seemed that a child had been playing in the lift, which stopped at every floor. Someone with long hair was waiting on the seventh, but turned towards the other lift as the door of Speke's opened, so that Speke didn't see his or her face. Until the person moved Speke had the impression that it was a dummy which had been placed near the lifts to lend some contrast to the parade of otherwise identical floors, fifteen of them before he was able to step out of the shaky box and hurry to his door.

Stef was home. The kitchen and the bedroom lights were on, and the narrow hall, which was papered with posters for English-language films which had been dubbed into other languages, smelled of imminent dinner. Speke eased the door shut and tiptoed past the bedroom and the bathroom to the main room, but he had only just switched on the light above the bar when Stef emerged from the bedroom. "Shall I make us drinks, Roger?"

"Rum," Speke said before he managed to say "Right."

"We haven't any rum unless you've bought some. It looks as if we've just about everything else."

"Whatever's quickest," Speke said, sitting down so as not to seem too eager; then he jumped up and kissed her forehead, giving her bare waist a brief squeeze. "Tell you what, I'll make them if you want to see to dinner."

"I'll get dressed first, shall I?"

"I should."

He had a last sight of her glossy black underwear half-concealed by her long blonde hair as she stepped into the hall while he uncorked the vodka. One swig felt sufficient to take the edge off his thoughts. He made two Bloody Marys, with rather more vodka in his, and carried them into the kitchen, where Stef in a kimono was arranging plates on the trolley. "Busy day?" he said.

"We've a class of students all week at the studio. I've been showing them what you can do with sound and vision."

"What can I?"

"Don't start that. What they can. Tomorrow I'll be on the sidelines while they improvise."

"I know how you feel."

Before she responded she ladled coq au vin onto the plates, wheeled the trolley into the main room, switched on the light over the dining-table and set out the plates, and then she said "What's wrong?"

"I'm. . . ."

"Go on, Roger. Whatever it is, it's better out than in."

"I'm sure I spoke to Lesley and Vanessa."

"What makes you say that?"

"You just did."

"Don't tell me if you don't want me to know."

"I dum," Speke said, draining the cocktail and wrenching the cork out of a litre of Argentinean red. "Someone answered the phone and I thought it was Lesley, but it turned out to be the daughter."

"Why are they on your mind again after all this time?"

Speke topped up her wineglass and refilled his own. "Because I spoke to the husband as well. I can't believe Lesley could have got involved with someone like that, let alone married him."

"Well, all of us—" Stef silenced herself with a mouthful of dinner. After more chewing than Speke thought necessary she said "Someone like what?"

"By the sound of him, an ego with a mouth."

"Some partners cope with worse."

"But if she can handle him, why couldn't shum— Besides, what about Vanessa? She must still be at school, she shouldn't be expected tum—"

"Roger, we agreed you'd try and put them out of your head."

"Wum," Speke said, not so much a stutter as a deliberate attempt to shut himself up, and drained his wine in order to refill the glass.

Once he'd opened a bottle of dessert wine to accompany the ice cream it seemed a pity to cork it after only one glass. Stef allowed him to replenish hers when it was half-empty, but placed her hand over it when he tried again. "I have to get up early," she said.

He was washing up the dinner things when it occurred to him that he'd heard a plea in her voice because she wanted them to make love. When he found his way into the bedroom, however, she was asleep. He switched off all the lights and considered watching television, but the prospect of consuming images on a screen—images which were lifelike and yet no longer alive—had lost its appeal. He sat at the dining-table and finished the bottle while gazing out of the window at the neighbouring tower blocks. The window resembled a screen too—perhaps a computer display on which enigmatic patterns of luminous rectangles occasionally shifted at random—but at least he could see no faces on it, not even his own. When he'd emptied the bottle he sat for a time and then took himself to bed.

He awoke with a sense that someone had just spoken to him. If Stef had, it must have been more than an hour ago, when she would have left for work. Sunlight streamed into the room, catching dust in the air. Speke sat up and waited for his equilibrium to align itself with him; then he performed several tasks gingerly—showered, shaved, drank a large glass of orange juice, ate cereal heaped with sugar and swimming in milk, downed several mugfuls of black coffee that shrank the image of his face—before he set about tidying up. He dusted everything except the bottles behind the bar, since they hardly called for dusting. He went once through the rooms with the large vacuum cleaner and then again with its baby. He loaded the washing machine and, when it had finished, the dryer. He rearranged the plates in the kitchen cupboard and the cutlery in the drawers, and lined up tins of food and packets of ingredients in alphabetical order. He found himself hoping that all this activity would keep him there until Stef came home, but the only company he had was the persistent sense of having just heard a voice. Before Stef returned it was time for him to leave for work.

The late afternoon sky, and presumably the sun, was the same colour as the extinguished bulbs above the car park. All the colours around him, such as they were—of cars, of leafless saplings, of curtains in the windows of the chalky tower blocks—appeared to be about to fade to monochrome. If he walked fast he would be at work on time, but if he drove he might feel less exposed. Though he drove slowly he was able to glimpse only a handful of faces, all of which seemed unusually remote from him.

Several of his colleagues were already in the long room, draping their jackets over the backs of their chairs or tipping the contents of polystyrene cups into their faces. As Speke aligned the forms and the directory with the lower edge of the screen on his desk the supervisor beckoned to him, hooking a finger before pointing it first at her mouth and then at her ear. "Yes, Mrs Shillingsworth," he said when he felt close enough to speak.

"Pore."

"Pum."

"Mr Pore. Mr Roger Pore. Does the name convey anything to you?"

"Yes, he booked a month's free trial last night."

"You're standing by that, are you?"

"Yes, I should say sum. He was my only catch."

"And you felt you had to give me one."

"Shouldn't I hum?"

"Only if it stands up. His wife says he never spoke to anyone."

"She must have got it wrong, or the engineers did. They're only engineers, num—"

"It was I who had a word with her, Mr Speke, because there were things on your form I didn't understand. Was it a Scotsman you spoke to?"

"A Scum? No, he sounded more like me."

"Mr Pore is a Scotsman."

"How do you know if you spoke to his wife?"

"They both are. I heard them."

"What, his wife sounds like a Scotsmum? I mean, I'm sorry, I must have, maybe I—"

"I should try harder tonight if I were you, but not that hard," Mrs Shillingsworth said, gazing at him over the form which she had lifted from the desk and crumpling it above her wastebasket before letting it drop.

"You aren't me," Speke mumbled as he headed for his desk. He was sitting down when he realised he had walked too far. About to push back the chair, he grabbed the directory instead and turned quickly to the page corresponding to his assignment. Pontin, Ponting, Pool, Poole . . . He made himself run his gaze down the column more slowly, but there was no entry for Pook.

"Old directory," he told himself, and moved to the desk on his left, where he checked that the directory was up-to-date before heaving it open at the same page. Ponting, Pool. He lowered his face to peer at the names as though the one he was seeking might have fallen through the space between them, then he dodged to the next desk, and the next. Ponting, Pool, Ponting, Pool . . . He didn't know how long Mrs Shillingsworth had been watching him. "There you are," she said briskly, indicating the blank screen on his desk.

He ran at his chair and flung the directory open. "Mrs Pook," he repeated over and over under his breath until he heard himself saying "Mrs Spook." Between Ponting and Pool was an etched line of black ink wide enough, he was almost sure, to conceal a directory entry. He was holding the page close to his face and tilting the book at various angles in an attempt to glimpse what lay beneath the ink when he realised that the supervisor was still watching him. "Jum, jum—" he explained, and fumbling the handset out of its stand, hastily keyed the first unmarked number.

When the screen flickered he thought he'd called a videophone at last, but the flicker subsided. "Poridge?" a voice said.

"Just cornflakes for me."

"Beg p?"

"Um sum, I'm speaking on behalf on behalf of Face to Face Communications and I wonder if, fum. If you can spare me a few minutes."

"Sugar?"

"What?"

"Lots of it for your cereal, sugar."

"How did you know? What are you making out?"

"I think that's enough sweetness," Mr Poridge seemed to respond, and terminated the call.

Speke was grateful to be rid of the voice, whose feminine sound he hadn't cared for. He memorised the next number and turned the directory in an attempt to shed some light on whatever the line of ink concealed as he placed the call. "Pork," a woman told him.

"Y pig."

"What's that? Who's this?"

The screen was flickering so much Speke thought it was about to answer her last question, unless it was his vision that had begun to flicker. When the screen remained blank he said "Miss Pork, my name is Roger and I wonder—"

"Same here."

"You are? You're what?"

"Wondering what I'm being made to listen to."

"I'm not making you. I was jum, just wondering. That is, I'm speaking on behalf of Face to Face Communications."

"That's what you call this, is it?"

"No, that's what I'm saying. I wish we could see each other face to face."

"Do you now?"

Speke's gaze darted from the line of ink to the screen, where the flickering had intensified. "Why?" said the voice.

"Because then I'd see if you lum, if you look, if you don't just sound like—" Speke gabbled before he managed to slam the handset into place.

He kept his head down until he couldn't resist glancing up. Though Mrs Shillingsworth wasn't watching him he was convinced that she had been. He repeated the next number out loud and moved the directory another half an inch, another quarter, another eighth. Something was close to making itself clear: the digits beneath the ink or the restlessness on the screen? He keyed the numbers he was muttering and glanced up, down, up, down. . . . "Porne," a voice said in his ear.

"My name is Roger and I wonder—"

"Porne."

"I wonder what number I've called."

"Ours. Porne."

That was the name in the directory, but Speke suspected that he had inadvertently keyed the numbers which perhaps, for an instant too brief for him to have been conscious of it, had been visible through the line of ink. "Don't I know you?" he said.

"Where from?"

"From in here," Speke said, tapping his forehead and baring his teeth at the screen, where his grin appeared as a whitish line like an exposed bone in the midst of a pale blur. "I expect you wish you could see my face."

"Why, what are you doing with it?"

Speke stuffed the topmost form into the edges of the screen, because each flicker seemed to render his reflection less like his. "Don't you think that your name says a lot?" he said.

"What do you mean by that, young man?"

"You're a woman, aren't you? But not as old as you want me to think."

"How dare you! Let me speak to your supervisor!"

"How did you know I've got one? You gave yourself away there, didn't you? And since when has it been an insult to tell a woman she isn't as old as she seems? Sounds to me as if you've got something to hide, Mrs or Miss."

"Why, you young—"

"Not so young. Not so old either. Same age as you, as a matter of fact, as if you didn't know."

"Who do you imagine you're talking to? Charles, come here and speak to this, this—"

"It's Charles now, is it? Too posh for that ape," Speke said, and fitted the handset into its niche while he read the next number. He fastened his gaze on the digits and touch-typed them on the handset, and lifted the form with which he had covered the screen. His grin was still there amid the restless flickering; the sight made him feel as though a mask had been clipped to his face. He let the page fall, and a voice which felt closer than his ear to him said "Posing."

"Who is?"

"This is Miss Posing speaking."

"Why do you keep answering the phone with just a name? Do you really expect me to believe anyone has names like those?"

"Who is this?"

"You already asked me that two calls ago. Or are you asking if I know who you are? Belum—"

Mrs Shillingsworth was staring at him. He hadn't realised he was speaking loud enough for her to overhear, even if his was the only voice he could hear in the crowded room. The panic which overwhelmed him seemed to flood into his past, so that he was immediately convinced that every voice he'd spoken to on the phone was the same voice, not just tonight but earlier—how much earlier, he would rather not think. "Thanks anyway," he said at the top of his voice, both to assure Mrs Shillingsworth that nothing was wrong and to blot out the chorus around him, which had apparently begun to chant "I'm speaking" in unison. The only voice he wanted to hear, was desperate to hear, was Stef's.

He couldn't remember the number. He stared at the flickering line of black ink while he thumbed through the wad of corners. As soon as he'd glimpsed the number, which now he saw was in the same position as the line of ink, he let the directory fall back to the page from which he was meant to be working. He pulled a form towards him and poised his pen above it as he typed the digits, resisting the urge to grin at Mrs Shillingsworth to persuade her this wasn't a private call. He had barely entered the number when the closest voice so far said "S & V Studios."

"Stef?"

"Hang on." As the voice receded from the earpiece it seemed to retreat into Speke's skull. "Vanessa, is Stefanie still here?"

"Just gone."

"Just gone, apparently. Is there a message?"

"I've already got it," Speke said through his fixed grin.

"I'm sorry?"

"You're forgetting to disguise your voice," Speke said and, dropping the handset into its niche, leaned on it until he felt it was secure. "I'm speaking," said a voice, then another. All the screens around him appeared to be flickering in unison, taking their time from the pulse of the line of black ink on the page in front of him. He shoved himself backwards, his chair colliding with the desk behind him, and was on his feet before Mrs. Shillingsworth looked up. He didn't trust himself to speak; he waggled his fingers at his crotch to indicate that he was heading for the toilet. As soon as the door of the long room closed behind him he dashed out of the building to his car.

He drove home so fast that the figures on the pavements seemed to merge like the frames of a film. He parked as close to the entrance as he could and sprinted the few yards, his shadows sprouting out of him. He wasn't conscious of the number he keyed, but it opened the door. The lift displayed each floor to him, and he wished he'd thought to count them, because when he lurched out of the box it seemed to him that the room numbers in the corridors were too high. He threw himself between the closing doors and jabbed the button for his floor, and the doors shook open; he was on the right level after all. He floundered into the corridor, unlocked his door, and stumbled into the dark which it closed in with him. He was rushing blindly to the bar when the doorbell rang behind him. He raced back and bumped into the door, yelling "Yes?"

"Me."

Speke shoved his eye against the spyhole. Outside was a doll with Stef's face on its swollen head. "Haven't you got your kum?" he shouted.

"Can't you see I've got my hands full? Didn't you see me flashing my lights when you were driving? I've been right behind you for the last I don't know how long."

"I saw some flickering in the mirror," Speke seemed to recall.

"That was me. Well, are you going to open the door or don't you want to see my face?"

"That's a strange way to put it," Speke said and found himself backing away from a fear that he would be letting in the doll with her face on its bulbous outsize head. He wasn't fast enough. His hand reached out and turned the latch, and there was Stef, posing with armfuls of groceries against the blank backdrop of the corridor. He grabbed the bags from her and dumped them in the kitchen, then he fled to the bar. "Drink," he heard his voice say, and fed himself a mouthful from the nearest bottle before switching on the light and calling "Drink?"

She didn't come for it. He traced her to the kitchen by the order in which the lights came on. "Have something to eat if you're going to drink," she said as she accepted the glass. "It's in the microwave."

The sight on the screen of the microwave oven of a plastic container rotating on the turntable like some new kind of record sent him back to the bar. He was still there when Stef switched on the main light in the room and wheeled the trolley in. "Roger, what's—"

He interrupted her so as not to be told that something was wrong. "Who's called Lesley where you work?"

"Leslie's one of the sound men. You've heard me mention him."

"Sound, is he, and that's all?" Speke mused, and raised his voice. "How about Vanessa?"

"Roger . . ."

"Not Roger, Vanessa."

Stef loaded his plate with vegetarian pasta and gazed at him until he took it. "You told me there was no such name before some writer made it up."

"There is now."

"Not where I work."

Speke's voice appeared to have deserted him. He made appreciative noises through mouthfuls of pasta while he tried to think what to say. By the time Stef brought the ice cream he was well into his second bottle of wine, and it no longer seemed important to recall what he'd been attempting to grasp. Indeed, he couldn't understand why she kept looking concerned for him.

He'd taken his expansive contentment to bed when a thought began to flicker in his skull. "Stef?"

"I'm asleep."

"Of course you aren't," he said, rearing up over her to make sure. "You said we agreed. Who? Who are we?"

Without opening her eyes Stef said "What are you talking about, Roger?"

"About us, aren't I, or am I?" He had to turn away. Perhaps it was an effect of the flickering dimness, but her upturned face seemed almost as flat as the pillow which framed it. He closed his eyes, and presumably the flickering subsided when at last he fell asleep.

Was that the phone? He awoke with a shrill memory filling his skull. He was alone in bed, and the daylight already looked stale. When the bell shrilled again he kicked away the sheets which had been drawn flat over him, and blundered along the hall to the intercom by the front door. "Spum," he declared.

"We've brought your videphone, boss."

The flickering recommenced at once. Speke ran into the main room and, wrestling the window along its track, peered down. Fifteen floors below, two tufts of hair with arms and legs were unloading cartons from a van. They vanished into the entranceway, and a moment later the bell rang again. Speke sprinted to the intercom and shouted "I can't see you now. Go away."

"You asked for us now, it says so here," said the distorted voice. "When do you want us?"

"Never. It could all be fake. You can do anything with sound and vision," Speke protested before he fully realised what he was saying. He rushed back to the open window and watched until the walking scalps returned to the van, then he grabbed enough clothes to cover himself and heard rather than felt the door slam behind him.

He couldn't drive for the flickering. The floors of the tower block had seemed like frames of a stuck film, and now the figures he passed on the pavements of the carriageway resembled images in a film advancing slowly, frame by frame. The film of cars on the road was faster. The side of the carriageway on which he was walking forked, leading him into a diminishing perspective of warehouses. On one otherwise blank wall he found a metal plaque which, as he approached, filled with whitish daylight out of which the legend s & v studios took form. He leaned all his weight on the colourless door, which seemed insubstantial by comparison with the thick wall, and staggered into a room composed of four monochrome faces as tall as the indirectly lit brick ceiling. A young woman was sitting at a wide low desk with her back to one actor's flat face. "May I help you?" she said.

"Vanessum?" Speke said, distracted by trying to put names to the faces.

"Yes?" she said as though he'd caught her out. "Who are you?"

"Don't tell me you don't know."

"I only started properly this morning," she said, pushing a visitor's book towards him. "If I can just have your—"

Speke was already running down the corridor beyond her desk. On both sides of him glass displayed images of rooms full of tape decks or screens that were flickering almost as much as his eyes, and here was one crowded with students whose faces looked unformed. Even Stef's did. She was lecturing to them, though Speke couldn't hear her voice until he flung open the heavy door; then she said less than a word, which hadn't time to sound like her voice. "You said we agreed I'd try to put them out of my head," Speke shouted. "Who? Who are we?"

"Not here, Roger. Not now."

Speke closed his eyes to shut out the flickering faces. "Who's speaking? Who do you think you sound like?"

"I'm sorry, everyone. Please excuse us. He's. . . ."

He didn't know what sign Stef was making as her voice trailed off, and he didn't want to see. "Don't lie to me," he shouted. "Don't try to put me off. I've seen Vanessa. I won't leave until you show me Lesley."

Without warning he was shoved backwards, and the door thumped shut in front of him. "Roger," Stef's flattened voice said in his ear. "You have to remember. Lesley and Vanessa are—It wasn't your fault, you mustn't keep blaming yourself, but they're dead."

Her voice seemed to be reaching him from a long way off, beyond the flickering. "Who says so?" he heard himself ask in as distant a voice.

"You did. You told me and you told the doctor. It was nothing to do with you, remember. It happened after you split up."

"I split up?" Speke repeated in a voice that felt dead. "No, not me. You did, maybe. They did."

"Roger, don't—"

He didn't know which voice was trying to imitate Stef's, but it couldn't call him back. It shrank behind him like an image on a monitor that had been switched off, as no doubt her face was shrinking. He fled between the warehouses, which at least seemed too solid to transform unexpectedly, though wasn't everything a ghost, an image which he perceived only after it had existed? Mustn't that also be true of himself? He didn't want to be alone with that notion, especially when the echoes of his footsteps sounded close to turning into a voice, and so he fled towards the shops, the crowds.

That was a mistake. At a distance the faces that converged on him seemed

Campbell, Ramsey,
1946-

Alone with the
horrors.

9/04

$27.95

DATE			

BAKER & TAYLOR